Bantam Books by Alan Ebert with Janice Rotchstein

THE LONG WAY HOME

TRADITIONS

Traditions

Alan Ebert

with
Janice Rotchstein

BANTAM BOOKS
TORONTO • NEW YORK • LONDON • SYDNEY • AUCKLAND

TRADITIONS

*A Bantam Book / published by arrangement with
Crown Publishers Inc.*

PRINTING HISTORY

Crown edition published September 1982

A Book-of-the-Month Club Selection, November 1981

Bantam edition / January 1983

We are grateful for permission to use the following material:

*Portions of the lyric to "The Blue Room" by Rodgers & Hart,
copyright 1926 Warner Bros., Inc. Copyright Renewed. All Rights
Reserved. Used by Permission.*

*Portions of the lyric to "Letters. We Get Letters . . ." Copyright
1955 RONCOM Music Company. Reprinted with permission.*

*Headlines and series of paragraphs from The New York Times
© 1968/73 by The New York Times Company. Reprinted by
permission.*

*An excerpt from I Never Promised You a Rose Garden by Hannah
Green (Joanne Greenberg). Copyright © 1964 by Hannah Green.
Reprinted by permission of Holt, Rinehart and Winston, Publishers,
and the kind permission of the William Morris Agency, Inc., on
behalf of Hannah Green (Joanne Greenberg).*

We gratefully acknowledge
MISS CAROLE SHELLEY
whose initial idea was the inspiration
for this collaboration and book.

Acknowledgments

For sharing their resources and personal experiences, we would like to thank:

The Academy of Motion Picture Arts & Sciences Library; Department of the United States Air Force: active, reserve, and ROTC programs; Book and Magazine Division of the United States Air Force and active duty and retired Air Force officers; Ambassador Hotel, Los Angeles; American Airlines; William Anderson; Archdiocese of Boston Archives; Department of the United States Army Center of Military History and active duty Army officers and enlisted personnel; B. Altman's, New York City; Maureen Bailey, director of sales and marketing, Chateau Marmont Hotel, Los Angeles; Bartow, Florida, Chamber of Commerce; Basuli, Ltd., New York City; Beverly Hilton, Beverly Hills; Virginia Blesso & Associates, Inc., Rancho Santa Fe, California; Bridgeport, Connecticut, Chamber of Commerce; British Information Services, New York City; The Brown Derby, Los Angeles; Brown's, Los Angeles; State of California Governor's Office; California State Division of Substance Abuse Services; California State Division of Veteran Affairs; Canadian Press Office, New York

City; Catholic Charities, New York City and Bridgeport, Connecticut; Helen Chaplin, public relations director, Beverly Wilshire Hotel, Beverly Hills; Chase Manhattan Bank; Chasen's, Los Angeles; Jack Colhoun; Collegiate School, New York City; College Entrance Examination Board, New York City; Columbia University Office of Public Information, New York City; Roderick Cook; Cornell University Office of Public Information, Ithaca, New York; Coward Shoe, New York City; Catherine C. Crane, National Home Fashions League; Cunard Lines, Ltd., New York City; The Dalton School, New York City; Jeremyn Davern; Jack C. Davis; Gerry Day; Alfred DeCicco; Ben Durrance; Eclair Studios, Paris; El Morocco Club, New York City; Ethical Culture School, New York City; Exxon Travel Service, New York City; Mildred Fannon; Irving Fein; Ford Motor Company; The Foundation Center, New York City; French Embassy Cultural Services, New York City; French Tourist Board, New York City; Gainesville, Georgia, Public Library; General Dynamics Convair Aerospace Division, San Diego, California; General Electric Company; George Air Force Base Public Information Office; Carolyn Gilbert; Mo Goldberg, M.D.; Mel Greer, M.D., professor and chairman, Department of Neurology, University of Florida, College of Medicine; Harley-Davidson; George Hern; Christopher Hewitt; Warren W. Hoover, executive director, National Interreligious Service Board for Conscientious Objectors, Washington, D.C.; Hope Enterprises, Los Angeles; Hull, Massachusetts, Historical Commission; Hull Town Hall; Irish Tourist Board, New York City; Italian Lines; John F. Kennedy Presidential Library, Dorchester, Massachusetts; Eleanor Lambert, Inc.; Betty Lanigan, NBC Television; The Leading Hotels of the World, New York City; Jacqueline Leve; Lincoln Center Library for the Performing Arts, New York City; Los Angeles Public Library; Lowell Hotel, New York City; Mary Lyons; Mann's Chinese Theatre, Los Angeles; Massachusetts Institute of Technology Institute Archives and Special Collections, Cambridge, Massachusetts; Maxwell Air Force Base Simpson Research Center; Dan McGoroan; Kevin Meaney; Mexican National Tourist Council, New York City; Michelin Tyre Co., Ltd.; Morgan

uaranty Trust; Richard Moss, M.D.; Motion Picture Studio
Mechanics—Local 52, New York City; Museum of Broadcast-
ng, New York City; The Museum of the City of New York;
ational History Museum, Los Angeles; NBC Television;
ew York City Police Department; New York Public Library;
ew York State Board of Elections; New York State Thru-
vay; Orsini's, New York City; State of Oklahoma Department
f Transportation Office of Public Information; Corrine Pat-
en; Philadelphia Library Theatrical Division; The Plaza Hotel,
New York City; Audrey Pierce; Princess Hotels International,
New York City; Radcliffe College Alumnae, Class of 1956;
Railway Age magazine; Rep. Charles Rangel's office, 19th
Congressional District, New York City; Peter Rossi; Comdr.
Morris Rotchstein, United States Navy, Ret.; Mrs. Morris
Rotchstein; St. Patrick's Cathedral Rectory, New York City;
Santa Fe Railway; Santa Monica Civic Auditorium; Vincent
Sardi, Jr., Sardi's, New York City; Scandinavian Airlines;
Schrafft's, New York City; Selective Service Board, Washing-
ton, D.C.; Susan Shannon; Shreve-Crump-Lowe, Boston;
Shubert Organization Corporation, New York City; Col. Nor-
man Smedes, United States Air Force, Ret.; Mrs. Norman
Smedes; Social Register Association, New York City; Histori-
cal Society of Southern California; Spectrum House, Miami,
Florida; Steuben Glass, New York City; Studios de Boulogne,
France; Robert Renato Talignani, Italian Government Travel
Office, New York City; *Tea & Coffee Trade Journal*; Tiffany
& Company, New York City; Travis Air Force Base Public
Information Office; TWA, Inc.; United Airlines; University
of Miami News Bureau Office of Public Affairs; USO; Veter-
an's Administration Medical Centers and medical center di-
rectors; Wellesley College Media Relations, Massachusetts;
Dr. Harry K. Wexler, New York State Division of Substance
Abuse Services, project director for state program evalua-
tions, and Don DesJarlaid, Ph.D.; Ann Whyte, Pan Ameri-
can World Airways, Inc., Library, Staff Associate, Research/
Analysis/History; Milton Williams; John C. Wolke, Jr.; Richard
E. Wolke, D.V.M., Ph.D.; Wrigley Company, Chicago;

   . . . and to Kathy Robbins, for being there in heart, mind,
and body.

BOOK ONE
1934–1939

1

Thomas Tiernan had only to look at Victoria's eyes to know his wife was angry. Still, she was behaving. No, performing, he corrected, admirably, as a first lady of the theatre should.

She had a right to be angry. Who had invited the press here? How had they known the girls would be boarding The Chief for Hollywood at this hour of the morning? Was this how Hollywood studios acted even from a distance?

Carolyn and Margaret Tiernan posed on the steps of The Chief and, as requested by the photographers, waved to the cameras. As if seeing his daughters with new eyes, Thomas realized "they're lovely." He was surprised, amazed even. His little girls . . . he stopped. They weren't little girls. For a brief moment, Thomas felt panic. Perhaps Victoria had been right. Perhaps the girls were too young to travel alone to California.

No, not too young. That's the problem, he thought. They're too old to be traveling without a chaperone. He looked at Carolyn and looked away in embarrassment. Her breasts were like Victoria's—full, large, and round. They were straining against the white Peter Pan blouse she was wearing over a simple, pleated gray skirt. The baby fat is gone, he realized. But then . . . so is the baby. Carolyn is eighteen, a year older than Tory was when we married.

"Mr. Tiernan, could we have one more shot of you and the missus waving good-bye to the girls as if the train were leaving?" asked one of the photographers, breaking into Thomas's reverie.

"Certainly," he replied as he encircled Victoria's waist with one arm and raised the other in a salutory gesture. Victoria's white-gloved hand arched elegantly toward the girls.

"How did this happen?" she hissed through clenched teeth.

"Damned if I know . . . the studio maybe," whispered Thomas through a perfect and perpetual public-relating smile.

3

"Daddy, your face is going to break if you keep that up."

"That will do quite nicely, Margaret dear," said Victoria i her too-too terribly sweet voice that bespoke of unspeakabl horrors to her younger daughter. As she heard Margare giggle, Victoria thought: That child will never change. Prais God. All the nuns at St. Theresa's couldn't change that mout so why should I try.

That mouth! I'm going to kill her. She's wearing lipstick When did she do that? We parked the car, entered thi inferior imitation of Grand Central Station, and were imme diately met by these barbarians. When could she possibl have sneaked the lipstick? That child is impossible! Tear sprang to Victoria's eyes. *That child* is seventeen. A year o the road had grown her. Well, it's grown us all. This disgust ing Depression. So terrible what it's done to people. To us she thought. We would still be in New York, in our owr home, not separating, if it weren't for the Crash.

"No! I'm sorry but that is not possible," barked Victoria to one of the photographers as he suggested the girls pose sitting on their suitcases with their legs crossed. Glancing up at Victoria Tiernan's face, the photographer knew better than to argue. As he arranged a more respectable pose, Victoria drew back in time again.

The 1933 Broadway season had been a financial disaster. More than five thousand actors were out of work. There were not that many new productions being mounted and even fewer that could afford the combined salaries of the Tiernan family. It was then that Jerome Siegal—never could stand that man but then I've never been able to stand any agent— suggested the year-long tour "of the provinces," as he put it. He's crude and vulgar and Thomas listens to him more than he does to me. Still, Victoria had to admit while other actors struggled and starved over the past years, she and Thomas had not. She had resisted the tour until Thomas said quite simply: "Do you or do you not want to keep the house?" Obviously the question required no answer. So she had acquiesced. On *everything*, she added, castigating herself for her weakness. She never should have allowed the girls to accompany them. College, not the road, is the proper place for young ladies. But Thomas didn't think college was anything but foolhardy for a woman and particularly for a woman who wanted to be an actress. And Lord knows Carolyn and Margaret wanted to be actresses. Still, they should have

4

remained at home, with Augie. Lord knows the girls respected their aunt, but who wouldn't respect such a presence. Then they wouldn't be in Chicago, boarding a train for Hollywood, while their parents were hop-skipping across the country in a car.

"I'm sorry. Would you repeat the question?" asked Victoria when she became aware that the lone woman among the press was speaking to her.

"I had asked, Mrs. Tiernan, how you feel about putting your girls on a train *alone* for fifty-three hours?"

The skin just below Victoria's left eye began twitching. "Is this the first time they've been on their own?" persisted the woman.

"Alone?" echoed Victoria with mock amazement. "How can you call it 'alone' when so many people are on this train? Why, The Chief is like a little town on wheels. Did you know Fred Harvey, the famous restaurateur, does the food? And there's maid service."

"Then you're not worried," stated the reporter as she scribbled on the steno pad.

"Not in the least." Victoria laughed. "What is there possibly to worry about?"

As the reporter drifted away, Victoria began to tremble. Her head felt light and her knees weak as again a premonition took hold of her. She had first felt it when it was first decided the girls would take The Chief to California while she accompanied Thomas on the drive cross-country. Thomas had laughed when she voiced her unidentified fears. But she felt frightened then and she felt frightened now. What was there to worry about indeed! Everything. That's all.

Victoria felt flushed, and had Thomas not been the center of attention as he drew lines on a road map outlining for the press the route he would take as he drove his Ford Tudor sedan, he would have noticed his wife's distress. Her face normally had a reddish glint to it. Only on stage did Victoria use makeup to hide the reddish-brown freckles that seemed to be part and parcel of a redhead's complexion. Now, as beads of sweat collected above her upper lip, Victoria's face was near crimson. To steady herself, she leaned against the green-baked-steel exterior of the train. It felt cool. She wished no reporters were present so she could remove the jacket of her kelly-green linen suit. It had been a cool September morning when they had left the hotel for Dearborn Station

5

and she had dressed appropriately. It would not look right if the cameras caught her wearing just the plain white open-necked blouse she had chosen especially for car travel. And if all this press nonsense had been arranged by the studio, Franklin Killerbrew would not be pleased to see her looking anything but proper. The Tiernans were to be, he maintained, the epitome of the American family. In each of their films they would portray and thus be portrayed as honest, hardworking, upstanding Americans.

A far cry from Shakespeare and Shaw but Thomas had wanted it. When Killerbrew himself had flown to Pittsburgh to sign them to a two-picture deal at more money than they had earned in the past four years combined, Victoria had fought it. Would their talents, honed for theatre, translate to the screen? Thomas was sure they would. We are actors, he said. Actors act no matter what or where the arena. The arena, indeed. From what she heard of Hollywood, they would be the Christians thrown to the lions in the arena of competition and sex. But Thomas literally pooh-poohed her fears, wouldn't take them seriously at all, and the girls were certainly no help. Although not part of Killerbrew's package, they immediately envisioned themselves hobnobbing with the stars.

Jerome Siegal worked out the fine print. He even had the studio pick up the cost of the girls' train tickets and a month at the Chateau Marmont in Hollywood where the family would live until Victoria could find a proper house. "And!" Siegal had announced, as if he had just concluded the most fabulous deal since Manhattan Island was purchased from the Indians for twenty-four dollars, "I've gotten Killerbrew to pay for a governess. She'll stay with the girls till you arrive in Hollywood."

Which was another bone of contention, still not totally resolved. Thomas had been adamant about driving Barrymore—"temperamental but capable of a brilliant performance," said Thomas when explaining his choice of name for his Ford—cross-country. "We will need a car in California. There are no subways and I'm told taxis are impossible and that the buses run as often as Calvin Coolidge." That they could buy a car once settled was unthinkable to Thomas. He had had this one custom-made and there were times Victoria questioned whether Thomas loved her as much as he loved his russet-brown leather upholstery that matched the Ford's winter-leaf-brown

6

ody and molding with cream stripe. Well, thought Victoria, fool and his money may soon be parted, but a man and his motorcar sure aren't.

Thomas had never intended to take Carolyn and Margaret on the cross-country jaunt, which was fine with Victoria. "No daughters of mine will ever be taken by Indians. Besides, they are not of pioneer stock and as far as I am concerned anything west of St. Louis is beyond civilization. If you're so keen on driving, why don't you take Barrymore and I'll take The Chief?" she had said seriously to Thomas.

"Because I want this to be the honeymoon we never had," answered Thomas. "Think of it, Tory. Just you and I alone for the first time in years, sightseeing through this great country of ours. Just us," he had repeated.

She had been touched. After twenty-one years of marriage, her husband still wanted a honeymoon. She looked at Thomas now as he was explaining to the reporters the distances he hoped to travel each day along Route 66. He was the same height and weight as the day they had met at the riding academy. The only difference was that he now had that ridiculous mustache. Yet she had to admit, *it*, and that bandanna scarf he usually wore tied and twisted about his neck, gave him a rakish look. And elegant. But then he always had style. Fashion mattered to him. And they say women are vain, thought Victoria. Who else but her Thomas could wear a knitted short-sleeved navy polo shirt over—not tucked in but over—white duck pants, and look both dashing and masculine?

Which is how he had looked that Sunday morning at the Back Bay Riding Academy, she remembered. Augie had been with her and they both had stopped to stare at the tall, lean young man wearing English breeches with a Harris tweed jacket. He had smiled at Victoria and unlike most "good girls" of her day, instead of casting her eyes demurely on the ground, she looked him full in the face as if daring him to make his move, which he did. He approached, tipped his hat, and asked if he could have the honor of their company on his morning ride. There was only the briefest hesitation on Augie's part and then her older sister, and chaperone, said they'd be delighted.

Actually Augie wasn't delighted. She hated to ride, but sensing Victoria's interest in Thomas Tiernan, she went along for appearances' sake. It was she who extended the invitation

to Thomas for dinner next Sunday at the family home in th
predominantly Irish Catholic section of Dorchester. It w
only later when the girls were cheerily retelling the romant
adventure of the day to each other that they realized the
hadn't the vaguest idea what Thomas Tiernan did for a livin

It was perhaps the second question her mother asked—qui
possibly even the first—of Thomas Tiernan at that wel
remembered dinner. "I'm an actor," he had responded, an
for the next few minutes you could hear the "Saints preserv
us!" as clearly as if the words had been spoken. In Victoria
Irish Catholic, terribly proper Bostonian upbringing, the stag
was the devil's own doing, and an actor the consort of th
archangel himself. But Thomas Tiernan refused to be put o
by the family's prejudice. Shortly after dinner he informe
Victoria that he would marry her, and she had best decid
whether the wedding was to be immediately upon the con
clusion of his run in Boston, or a year later when he was nex
in town to perform with the repertory company in which h
was featured. Having noticed how women reacted to Thom
as's physical presence, Victoria decided not to risk the year
wait but risk her family's outrage, of which there was plenty
Still, when it came time for the wedding, "the baby," a
Victoria was called, was given away by her seemingly stern
father, the Right Honorable Kevin Monahan, who even wept
when "the baby" said her "I dos."

He would have wept even more had he known she intended to join her husband onstage. Ah, the nerve of the
young! Victoria thought. What did I know about acting?
Nothing. What did I know about men? Enough to realize
being onstage with Thomas was better than being off, what
with all those available leading ladies hovering about. That
was such a long time ago, thought Victoria.

Time. What time was it? She looked at the gold Tiffany
watch Thomas had bought for her but a year ago on their
twentieth anniversary. "Thomas, it's eleven. The train leaves
in a quarter of an hour."

Thomas Tiernan checked his own watch, saw it was actually
fifteen minutes shy of eleven, but understood the point his
wife was trying to make. "Fellas," he said to the reporters,
who were still in attendance, "the train leaves shortly and the
wife and I would like some time with our girls." Understanding noises greeted Thomas's words. Pens and pencils disappeared along with writing pads and cameras. As the press

dispersed, so did the crowd of onlookers who had congregated on the platform. Only a handful recognized the Tiernan family. Stage actors, even those who had just played Chicago for eight weeks, didn't have the immediate recognizability of the movie stars who smiled from fan magazine covers in every drugstore in town.

As her husband departed by previous arrangement to grease the palms of those porters aboard The Chief who could ensure or enhance their daughters' safety, Victoria led the way up the steps of the train and down the corridor where compartment 222 proved to be the very last. She was surprised by its compactness. With the girls' luggage neatly stacked by the one couch attached to the painted green wall, there was little space for anything else.

"Each night, the porter, when you summon him, will bring his key to unlock the upper berth bed from the wall. Should you wish to use it during the day, simply buzz for him," Victoria told her daughters. "The people aboard this train are here to serve you. Let them. Like this nasty little toilet in the room—without doors or curtain—is hardly what you're used to. Nor is the sink," she continued, as she pulled down a stainless steel basin from the wall. "I suggest you use the ladies' lounge for your personal needs and privacy. According to the brochure, it has all facilities, including a shower, to assure a lady's comfort. And I'm sure you will both endeavor to remember you are ladies."

"Yes, Mama," Carolyn and Margaret chorused in unison.

"Don't you 'Yes, Mama' me. I'm serious. I know you think you're all grown up but there is still much for you to learn."

"And I'm ready!" Margaret leered.

"You, I'm sending to a nunnery," said Victoria to her younger daughter.

"Make it a monastery and you got a deal," quipped Margaret.

"She's impossible. Absolutely impossible," said Carolyn huffily. "She has a one-track mind."

"If the two of you are quite through, there are certain things I would like to discuss before your father returns," said Victoria. "I think it best if you do not talk to strangers."

"Mother, everyone on this train is a stranger," said Carolyn, making a face. "You're not suggesting we spend two whole days talking to no one but each other."

"Nobody's that cruel," interjected Margaret. "When mother says 'strangers,' she means men."

9

"Exactly. I expect both my daughters to remember their upbringing. When in doubt, pray—particularly ask the good Lord to save us from the barbarians of Hollywood." Looking at her daughters, Victoria knew her words were useless. Within minutes of The Chief's departure, she expected Margaret, followed by Carolyn, to be all over the train.

"I have but one more thing to say," sighed Victoria, "and I'm serious now. Very serious. You're sisters and you are to take care of each other because if you don't, who will?"

A knock on the door announced the arrival of a porter wearing a smile as dazzling as the white of his serving jacket. He was carrying a tray on which sat a sweating, gleaming ice bucket and over its edge, a champagne bottle beckoned.

"But we didn't order . . ." said Victoria.

"Oh yes we did," said Thomas as he entered the compartment carrying four iced champagne glasses. "This is the Tiernan party, isn't it? These are the private quarters of those two young budding stars . . ." Thomas stopped in midsentence, scratched his head in puzzlement, and then said: "What did you say your names were?" The girls laughed. As Thomas struggled to pop the cork from the Dom Perignon, Victoria halfheartedly said: "Thomas, it is but morning." But he was not to be stopped. With a great flourish, he filled each of the glasses to the brim. After he handed them about, Thomas raised his glass. "A toast. To the women in my life and to how much each means to me!"

The girls pretended to sip the champagne, enjoying the occasion far more than the treat itself. Raised among opening nights and the lavish parties that followed, liquor held no fascination for them. Champagne hurt Carolyn's nose, she insisted, and Margaret much preferred a chocolate phosphate.

"I propose we drink to Hollywood, stardom, and lots and lots of money," said Margaret. "For all of us," she added as an afterthought.

"May I remind you, missy," said Victoria, "that it is your father and I who are signed to Killerbrew Studios. Best as I can recall, nowhere in the contract's fine print does it say anything about a Margaret or a Carolyn Tiernan."

"Well, if you want to be selfish about it," sniffed Margaret with fake indignation. "But don't be surprised if we are discovered. Talent will out, you know."

Victoria knew she wouldn't be at all surprised. Her daughters were indeed talented. She had seen that on the nine

10

stages in the nine cities they had toured. Whether it was farce or tragedy, the girls seemed to act instinctively. The usual audience reaction to Carolyn was stunned silence. Hollywood, Victoria was sure, would be quite vocal about her older daughter's beauty. Such perfect skin. Framed by such thick black hair cascading about her shoulders, it looked like a Rembrandt had used his oils to create such an alabaster tone. There was a natural flush to both Carolyn's cheeks and lips. No matter where, no matter the hour of the day, Carolyn always looked as if she had just come rushing in from a romp in winter's cold, fresh air. It was a wonder Margaret didn't hate her. Not that Marg wasn't attractive, thought Victoria. Actually, she wasn't quite baked yet. There was too much leg. Strange how at five feet five, just an inch taller than Carolyn, Marg looked gangly. It was her weight and her small breasts. She had yet to fill out fully. But oh, that face with its impudent green eyes that challenged you from above those spectacular cheekbones! Even the freckles, normally a woman's curse, looked right on Margaret. No, she wasn't pretty yet, but her total effect caught people and held them. It never seemed to matter if Margaret had two lines or twenty in a production, audiences reacted to her.

"This is the first time we will have been separated," said Victoria, giving voice to the words she had been thinking.

Carolyn took her hand. "Mama, we will never be separated. Not really."

"Your future husband—that is, should you ever decide to give us a break and get married—will be thrilled by that bit of news," said Thomas.

"Daddy, don't make fun," persisted Carolyn. "You know what I mean."

The cry of "All aboard!" startled them all.

"Yes, Lynnie, I do indeed know what you mean," said Thomas. "Now say good-bye to your mama and give your old papa a kiss."

"And remember what I told you!" said Victoria.

"You told us something? Gee. I must have forgotten already," teased Margaret.

"Well, don't worry. I haven't," snapped Carolyn.

"Mother, I don't suppose you'd consider taking *her* with you," responded Margaret.

Victoria laughed as she swept her youngest into her arms. Thomas was clutching Carolyn and stuffing still more dollar

11

bills in her hand "just in case." As her eldest glided from her father's arms to her own, Victoria whispered in her ear: "Take good care . . . of both of you." Carolyn, her head buried in her mother's rich red hair, her eyes stinging with unshed tears, nodded her head signaling she would.

And then Victoria and Thomas were on the platform, part of the crowd that was yelling and waving its good-byes. Victoria continued to wave long after the two loved faces pressed against the window glass had faded into the distance. Suddenly, she was again attacked by nausea. Involuntarily she shuddered.

As she felt her husband's hand grasp her under her arm, she heard him say: "If you so much as shed one of those things in your eyes that look suspiciously like tears, I'm going to pinch you so hard you'll really have something to cry about." She looked up at her husband, saw his smile and loved him for it, but even more for the tears that were rolling down his cheeks.

Victoria Tiernan knew her daughters. The Chief was still at a halfhearted chug, barely free of Dearborn Station and the Chicago city limits, when Margaret had removed her saddle shoes and white socks and slipped into her silk stockings and brown pumps normally reserved for nighttime or special-occasion use.

"Okay, I'm ready. Let's go," she announced cheerily.

Carolyn Tiernan did not respond, but continued to search through her luggage until she found what she was looking for.

"You are not going to read a book?" demanded Margaret incredulously.

"I most certainly am," replied Carolyn as she laid the book on her lap.

"Oh c'mon, Lynnie. Don't be an old poop. Let's go see if there are any boys on board."

"Don't you ever think of anything else?"

"Sure I do," answered Margaret. "I think of men. Now hurry up."

"Sit down, Marg. Read one of those magazines you had Daddy buy for you."

"I don't want to read how Mary Pickford and Janet Gaynor are living. I want to do my own living. Now c'mon, Carolyn. Let's at least go to the dining car."

Carolyn reminded her sister that it was not yet twelve. Sit

or one more hour and then we will lunch, she bargained. Margaret, satisfied knowing she could wait sixty minutes for her life to begin, seated herself on the green wool plush-covered couch next to Carolyn. Within two minutes, she was fidgeting. "Damn thing scratches. Isn't it bothering your legs?" she asked Carolyn, who did not answer, pretending as she was to be absorbed in her reading. Margaret peered over her shoulder to see what it was that was so enthralling.

"Would you like this book?" asked Carolyn icily. She hated having anyone read over her shoulder and had told that to Margaret numerous times.

"I do beg your pardon, Your Highness, for having disturbed you. Just wanted to see what you were reading."

"It's *The Merchant of Venice* and you've just given me a terrific idea. Marg, why don't we do scenes to pass the time? There are lots of plays in this book and we can work on characterizations. Look, I'll be Portia and you play Skylark."

"I think you mean Shylock," said Margaret, her head shaking in amazement. *"Pass the time,"* she echoed. "I don't want to pass *any* time. I can't believe you would waste this trip, this golden opportunity, by doing scenes."

"I hardly think perfecting one's craft is wasting one's time," said Carolyn haughtily.

"One can be an awful pain, *one* can be," responded Margaret. *"One* even expects *one* to use the royal *we* shortly the way *one* is going."

"Oh be serious, Marg. We can have a lot of fun trading parts and being different characters."

"You are enough of a character for me," said Margaret. "There's a life out there, Carolyn, and from what I hear it's a lot better than reading scenes."

"Marg, this past year on tour, being onstage for the first time, didn't you feel it?" Carolyn asked seriously. "I mean, didn't you feel alive, *the most* alive you have ever been? And loved! Oh Marg, when all of us were up there onstage, wasn't it just the best!"

Carolyn's obvious sincerity made Margaret consider the question seriously. "Yes . . . no," she corrected. "I mean it was wonderful, but not exactly in the way you mean. How can I explain?" Margaret stood and began to pace as best she could in the small confines of the compartment. "Ah!" she proclaimed as she found her words: "Do you remember how you hated math, particularly geometry and trigonometry?

13

And remember how I loved it?" As Carolyn nodded her head yes to both questions, Margaret plunged on excitedly. "Well acting to me is like an equation to be solved. To make i work, you must identify X, or Y, or both to get Z. In othe words, you must understand the worth of each part to com prehend the whole. It's *that* I love. It's *that* I find terrifically exciting. Like in Toledo, when we did our first real roles in *A Midsummer Night's Dream*. To play Puck and Ariel, we had to understand not only them, but the whole of what Shake speare was saying. Do you understand?"

Carolyn was looking at Margaret quizzically. "I never thought of it that way." The truth is, Carolyn realized, "I never thought of it in *any* way." She had fallen in love with acting the first time her parents had allowed her to watch them from the wings, backstage at the Booth Theatre. She could still hear, and suspected she always would, the utter silence of the audience as they waited for her parents to speak. And when they laughed, reacted to something her mother had said or her father had done, the sound broke across the stage like waves breaking on a beach. And so soon after, there were tears; as sudden and unexpected as a sun-shower in July. All created by the actors. From that day, Carolyn wanted but one thing: to be an actress.

"Will you read with me later?" pleaded Carolyn. "I want to see what you do."

"Scratch my back, kid, and I'll scratch yours," said Marga ret. "Eat with me now in the dining car, and I'll read with you later. And how's this for a deal? Promise we get to visit the club car later, and I'll do the entire works of Shakespeare with you."

"Oh God, isn't this exciting!" whispered Margaret to Carolyn as both waited for the maître d' to seat them. The dining car was only half filled, breakfast for most of the passengers having been but a few hours ago. Although she wouldn't admit it, Carolyn Tiernan was thrilled. Like her sister, she had never been in a dining car before. Looking at the elegant table settings, she was reminded of the service at some of the finer hotels the family had frequented during the tour. But none had been on wheels.

"You could go blind in this joint," said Margaret. "The glare could kill you."

She was referring to the white-on-white. Each table was

14

vered with a stiffly starched and brightly bleached white
ish linen cloth with matching napkins. White-on-white
ina refracted the rays of sunlight that streamed in from
e table-high windows and bounced it about the room. The
aiters too glistened in their bright white shirts and knee-
ngth aprons. The total effect, thought Carolyn, was like
eing in an open field of snow on a bright sunny March
ay.

As the maître d' approached, Margaret again whspered to
arolyn. "Tell him we're expecting two others." When her
ster looked at her blankly, Margaret took the initiative.
We'll be four," she replied when asked how many there
ould be in the party.

"Are you insane?" hissed Carolyn. "You and I make two.
ust two."

"And two does not make a party," answered Margaret. "So
mile pretty and maybe we'll get lucky and be a four shortly.
a fact, don't look now, but those two men back there are
sing us."

"Margaret!" cautioned Carolyn as she seated herself. As she
ok the offered menu from the maître d', she missed the
emure and terribly chaste smile Margaret wafted in the
irection of interest. One of the men smiled as he raised a
ineglass in toast toward Margaret. Not then knowing what
do, she buried her face in the menu.

"Do you know what you're having?" asked Carolyn, herself
ndecided.

"Yes! A fit. My ass itches like crazy!"

"Margaret!" chastised Carolyn through clenched teeth,
raying no one had overheard her sister.

"Well, I can't help it. These damn chairs. There must have
een a closeout on green wool plush."

The waiter stood ready to take the order Carolyn and
Iargaret had written on the check given to them as they sat
own. "And by the way, waiter," asked Margaret, "would
ou know if the club car is also decorated with the same
aterials as the dining car and the compartments?"

"Oh yes, ma'am. The whole train is," the black man re-
lied. "The owners thought green upholstery and sand-colored
arpeting would capture the feel of the desert."

"It certainly has," said Margaret, smiling warmly at the
aiter. "These chairs feel just like I'm sitting on cactus."

As Carolyn groaned, the waiter, confused, but used to the

15

strange mannerisms of white folks, left, replaced almost i
stantly by the two recipients of Margaret's smile.

"A lovely day, isn't it, ladies," said the older of the two,
good-looking man about thirty.

As Margaret was smiling and vigorously nodding in agre
ment, Carolyn, also smiling, said, "Oh, it most certainly i
In fact, my sister and I were just saying how we wish o
parents would hurry. We can't imagine what's keeping the
from joining us and enjoying the day and the view. Not
mention the lunch."

The message received, the men drifted away with a "Pe
haps we'll meet later in the club car."

"What are you doing?" demanded Carolyn as she sa
Margaret scoop up her fork, spoon, and knife onto the pla
with her napkin.

"I'm moving across the aisle to a table for two, since one
us is obviously antisocial."

"Sit down!" said Carolyn, annoyed.

"Don't you use that tone with me," shot back Margare
"You just ruined my lunch. Why did you scare them of
They seemed perfectly lovely. What harm done if they joine
us and we talked?"

"Talk is cheap but we are not," said Carolyn in an exa
imitation of Victoria Tiernan, who had used those very word
many times.

"You make me sick. Sometimes I think you don't like mer
Well, do you?" she badgered as the waiter placed her foo
before her. "I mean if you don't, it's all right with me
Chacun à son goût and all that. But if you don't, tell me."

"What are you talking about?" asked Carolyn, confused an
annoyed at the turn the conversation was taking.

"Do you remember the year Daddy was in the army
overseas at Verdun, and Mother was on Broadway?"

"How could I remember? Were we even born then?"

"What difference. Mama told us . . . well, she told m
anyway . . . about the actress with whom she costarred. Sh
didn't like men either. In fact, that's what ruined her frien
ship with Mama. She was being too, too affectionate."

"You are disgusting!" said Carolyn, outraged and offende(
She pushed her plate away and was about to make a huffy ex
when Margaret reminded her: "You've got the cash. Give
to me. I'll pay the bill and meet you later . . . *after* I've bee
to the club car, of course."

16

Carolyn readjusted herself. She brushed away imagined crumbs from her lap as she brushed her very real anger to the side. "I like men just fine. Not that it is any of your business," she added, her voice near breaking.

"I have always believed anything that affected either of us was both our business," said Margaret, upset that she had hurt her sister even though it was unintentional.

"It's not that I don't like men," explained Carolyn, responding to Margaret's sincerity. "It's just that I have certain principles. I don't think a woman should be easy or loose."

"How about available?" asked Margaret. "Why is it wrong to be available . . . to want to talk with a man?"

"Because men are not just interested in talk."

"Lynnie, haven't you ever been interested in more than talk? Now stop looking so shocked. I'm asking 'cause I need to know. We're sisters—same parents, same blood. I can't be the only one having these feelings."

"What kind of feelings?" asked Carolyn, despite her knowing exactly what Margaret meant.

"About men. About 'It' and what 'It' would be like."

"You should not be having those thoughts or feelings until you're married," said Carolyn. "Where were you when the nuns were talking about the sanctity of marriage and a union between husband and wife that had God's blessing?"

"Not listening, I assure you. I never thought those 'things' in black ever knew what they were talking about."

"Margaret!" cautioned Carolyn.

"Stop Margaret-ing me. Let's get down to brass tacks. When you went out with the theatre owner's son in Pittsburgh, didn't anything happen?"

"Nothing!" said Carolyn, indignant Margaret would even ask a question so ridiculous.

"That's too bad. He was cute and a terrific kisser."

The effect of Margaret's words was immediate. "Oh, c'mon, Lynnie. Close your mouth or you'll catch flies."

"And just when did you go out with him?" demanded Carolyn, her face flushed and her voice tight.

"I didn't exactly 'go out' with him. How could I with Mother's 'not-until-you're-eighteen-unless-your-sister's-along.'"

"Well, you obviously managed," said Carolyn sarcastically.

"Yes, but I let my conscience be my guide instead of a chaperone. Besides, there's not much you can do on a five-minute rehearsal break."

17

For a while, the only sound was the tinkling of ice in th crystal water goblets that were kept filled on each of th tables, occupied or vacant. Carolyn sat unnaturally still. Sh was thinking of all the cities and all the boys who had mad obvious their interest in her. She was that most desired ages, eighteen, old enough to do what she wanted. He mother had encouraged her to accept the many proposals f dinner or the movies. What better way to learn about wh you want in a man and in a marriage, she had reasoned. A she had learned, thought Carolyn, is that most men want kiss you good-night and some . . . She involuntarily shud dered as she remembered the "some"—those who dared t reach for her breast as they took the kiss they often seeme to think was theirs by right.

"Did you like it?" asked Carolyn as her eyes remaine fixed on the landscape flying by the train window.

"Did I like what?" replied Margaret, confused by Carolyn' question coming as it did from nowhere.

"Being kissed."

"Of course," said Margaret. "Didn't you?"

Carolyn's eyes drifted from what she wasn't really seeing t her own reflection in the double glass doors that separate the diners from the kitchen.

"I hope your silence is by choice and not because a mar has yet to kiss you," bantered Margaret, trying to break he sister's mood. " 'Cause Lord knows if a man hasn't kissed you by now, the family has wasted a fortune on your braces." When Carolyn still didn't answer, Margaret reached across the table and took her hand.

"Doesn't it scare you?" asked Carolyn, her tiny voice a statement.

Although the "It" could have referred to many things, Margaret knew exactly what her sister meant.

"No, it doesn't," she answered, "not since Mama . . ."

"Mama talked to you about this?" said Carolyn, amazed.

"Yes, a year or so ago when I asked her. She said when you're in love and married, it's a lovely way for two people to share what they feel for each other."

"She *told* you!" repeated Carolyn, registering stupefaction.

"Well, not specifics. She never mentioned THE word. In fact, the way she went on and on about love, marriage, love and marriage, communication and respect, gentleness and caring, she made it all seem rather dull. Yet, she did say . . ."

18

"Don't repeat it!" interrupted Carolyn, shuddering at the prospect of hearing intimacies about her parents. "Some things simply shouldn't be talked about."

"They should just be done!" agreed Margaret and then threw a napkin at her sister's mouth, which had opened in shock. "You don't fool me for a minute, Carolyn Tiernan," said Margaret, evil in her grin. "I know you're just dying to find out what 'It's' like."

"I can wait," said Carolyn, regaining her composure and a posture she identified with the dignified and elegant.

"I'm sure you will," countered Margaret.

"As if you won't," challenged Carolyn.

"Lynnie, my dear, quaint, old-fashioned girl of a sister, let me assure you if when we get to Hollywood Clark Gable and Gary Cooper are dying to have their way with me, I don't think I'll protest. Well . . . maybe I'd protest but that's about all."

"Well, that's *you* but it's not me," said Carolyn as she pushed away from the table and rose to leave the now nearly empty dining car.

"You know what really puzzles me?" asked Margaret. As Carolyn wore a God-only-knows look on her upturned face, Margaret said: "Why my ass itches from this damn wool plush and yours doesn't."

The sun was setting when Margaret stood, stretched, and announced, "That's it! Enough is enough." She had been good to her word and after spending the afternoon reading scenes with Carolyn felt "the wanderlust. So c'mon, Carolyn, let's go wander-and-lust in the club car."

"I'm not leaving here until I fix my face," said Carolyn as she pulled the washbasin down from the wall.

"Fix your face!" exclaimed Margaret. "We only have two days. Couldn't you settle for minor repairs? By the way, can I borrow your Torrid Tangerine lipstick? I'm sick of Cheery Cherry. If you want to know the truth I'm sick of *being* a cheery cherry."

"Margaret! Straight to hell you're going to go with that kind of talk," protested Carolyn.

"Could we first go straight to the club car?" pleaded Margaret. "What's one detour before the real thing?"

At full steam, The Chief was rocking vigorously, making the wearing of high heels hazardous for girls still more accus-

19

tomed to flats. After carefully negotiating the narrow san
carpeted corridors, they entered the club car and saw the tv
men from lunch engrossed in a card game at one of the ma
tables set up for that purpose.

"Shall we join them if they ask?"

Before Carolyn could respond, one of the men recognize
the sisters and immediately turned his back to them. "I c
believe our *parents* have dampened the gentlemen's enthus
asm for our company," said Carolyn in a tone that said "Se
What I told you about men-and-conversation was correct."

There were but two women in the club car, Margar
noticed, both "brassy types" as her mother would say. The
sat with legs crossed in overstuffed chairs near the bar wi
highballs in hand, laughing too loud at what Margaret wa
sure were off-color jokes. Although no words were addresse
to the sisters, the many eyes that roamed their bodies an
faces, looking for signs of availability, said enough. "This i
not for us," said Margaret angrily. "Let's try the observatio
car."

Carolyn followed her wordlessly. Once the door to the clu
car had shut behind her, she staggered and would have falle
had not Margaret been there to steady her.

"Your face is as green as the wall," said her sister, con
cerned. "Did the smoke in there get to you?"

"No, the men did," answered Carolyn as she took deep
breaths. "We've been on dozens of stages, Marg, but never
have we been stared at quite like that."

"They weren't looking at us, Lynnie. Not any more than
audiences really look at us. Not the real us. It's all about
illusion and fantasy," said Margaret. "People see what they
want to see. Those men didn't want us to be as we are, but as
they would like us to be. As the man said, kid: 'All the world's
a stage,' and we were just players in Dante's *Inferno*."

Carolyn looked at Margaret with surprise. "How did you
get so smart?" she asked.

"It's not about smart, Lynnie. It's about intuition, or again
to quote a play, it's *What Every Woman Knows*."

The observation car felt comfortable to the girls. As many
women as men were there, some laughing among themselves,
still others enjoying the company of men. The laughter that
punctuated the many conversations had a pleasant rather
than ribald ring. Friendliness was as much a part of the car's

atmosphere and decor as its couches and the globe ceiling lights that bathed everyone in a mellow glow.

Carolyn found two empty couches facing one another. She motioned for Margaret to sit opposite her, which Margaret did, but only after she had spread a borrowed sheet over the upholstery. She then watched in open-mouthed amazement as Carolyn switched on the recessed light on the wall atop the window and took her knitting from her bag.

"You're not!" she said.

"But I most certainly am," said Carolyn, and did as Margaret's eyes began making the rounds.

"Well, I'm going to mingle," said Margaret, and before Carolyn could advise or protest, she was gone. For the first few minutes, Carolyn's eyes were watching Margaret as closely as the slipover sweater she was knitting for her father. But soon, as Margaret settled into a mixed group that seemed to be having a virulent discussion about Roosevelt and the New Deal, she relaxed. Within minutes, she was approached by several women who wished to exchange knitting secrets with her. The group attracted men, of course, and without being quite aware of when or how it started, Carolyn found herself in the midst of a sing-along.

It was Margaret, not Carolyn, who grew conscious of the hour, who announced if they wanted dinner, they had better remove themselves to the dining car before it closed. Carolyn was actually reluctant to leave. She had had fun being a part of people. Previously, she had enjoyed performing for them. Performing *with* them was a totally different experience. For those brief hours, she had felt close to strangers, and closeness was something she had only shared with Margaret and to a lesser extent with her mother. Carolyn had never thought it unusual that Margaret was her best friend. She assumed that must be true for all sisters.

"Carolyn, you ole former fogy, I'm proud of you," said Margaret as they headed toward the dining car. "You actually showed signs in there of being human. There's hope for you yet. Now I know why they say travel is broadening."

"Don't you just wish Mom and Dad were with us. Aunt Augie, too," said Carolyn, her face flushed with excitement.

"I do believe you are getting the spirit of adventure," said Margaret. "Next you'll be saying such mad impetuous things as . . . I can't wait to get to California."

"I can't!" admitted Carolyn, laughing. "I just wish we could

21

have packed up our entire house in Murray Hill and taken i
with us. That way, the whole family would be along."

"Aunt Augie in California? I can't quite see it." Margare
laughed. "Not unless there's a Schrafft's serving tea sandwiches every three blocks."

Augusta Monahan had walked home slowly, savoring the
autumn afternoon with all her senses. There would not be
many more days like this, she thought, as she turned off
Lexington and onto Thirty-sixth Street, where the afternoon
sun was coloring the brownstones on the north side of the
street in orange and red hues. A gorgeous day—truly
gorgeous—she repeated to herself. It was always a gorgeous
day for Augusta Monahan when none of the babies on the
ward died.

Although she had worked both as a volunteer and on staff in
the children's ward at Bellevue Hospital for eleven years,
Augusta Monahan had never learned how to defend against
an infant's death. Whereas others around her quickly grew
hardened to hospital reality, she suffered each time a child
did. This past year, Augie had suffered more than usual. No
longer could she leave Bellevue's sick and dying to find
sustenance and life in her home in Murray Hill. There was no
life there; not since Tory, Thomas, and the girls had gone on
the road. Just empty rooms that contributed to Augie's sense
of her own empty life. This past year, she had seen just how
dependent she had become on her sister and her sister's
family. She determined as soon as Tory returned to New
York, she would change that; she would make a life of her
own, take an apartment crosstown, separate and apart. It was
time, she had decided.

She had spoken to the family just last night and felt Tory
was strained. She worries too much about the girls, thought
Augusta as she opened the wrought-iron gate that separated
the Tiernans' property from the street. The short walkway to
the steps, up to the mahogany paneled door with its brass
lion-head knocker, was covered with leaves from the elm tree
in the garden. It's too soon, thought Augie. I'm not ready.
Wait awhile, she silently asked of the tree as she surveyed
the rest of the garden she herself, and not a gardener, tended. There is something sad about roses blooming in late
September, she thought. Like a remission period before death.

t's so falsely reassuring. She shivered and then chastised herself for such morbid thinking.

When Augie opened the door and stood in the marble-walled and -floored vestibule, she was surprised by the lack of smell. Rose always had a hot lunch waiting for her at this time of day. Unless the old woman was sick again. Poor old Rose. If it wasn't her rheumatism it was her lumbago.

"Rose?" called Augusta as she removed her small-brimmed navy hat, and carefully placed it next to others on the top shelf in the hall closet. When there was no response, Augusta impatiently called the housekeeper's name again as she draped her lightweight matching coat over a cloth hanger.

It was the moan Augusta heard first. She wheeled in its direction. From down the hallway, the kitchen door swung open and Rose Wheaton, disheveled and disoriented, staggered and stumbled against the wood-paneled walls as she groped her way toward her.

Carolyn Tiernan's eyes fluttered open and the strange face she saw frightened her. Panic seized her stomach, and it didn't relax its grip until Carolyn shook free of sleep and remembered where she was.

"Feeling better, dearie?" asked the face that was now smiling at her.

"Oh yes, much," said Carolyn.

"Well, my shoulder doesn't," groused Margaret. "You have very heavy head. Do you know you've been sleeping for almost two hours?"

Carolyn Tiernan had awakened that morning feeling exhausted. Unlike the first night, when the train's rhythmic rocking had lulled her to sleep, last evening it had stimulated her. She was now comprehending that with every passing minute they were moving closer toward a new life. And she felt ready. She was glad they would be arriving in Los Angeles at three that afternoon.

The smiling face had a name she remembered—Mrs. McCord. The girls had met her the previous night in the observation car. Actually, everyone in the car had met Mrs. M, as she preferred to be called. Somewhere during the early evening's jocularity she had put aside her knitting and her "bit-of-the-brew," as she called it, and greeted "the folks" with her own rather unique rendition of "Brother, Can You Spare a Dime?" Two hundred pounds of woman was flutter-

23

ing and floundering about as she put her considerable all into a rather incongruous shimmy as she sang the Depression ditty. When the assembled group cheered and applauded with good-natured enthusiasm, Mrs. M admitted, "I've always wanted to be on the stage." Later, when she learned Carolyn and Margaret were not only actresses, but Irish, she adopted them. "Like the daughter of my own I'm off to visit in San Bernardino," she explained. It was "Mother M," as Margaret dubbed her, who looked at Carolyn's drooping face and announced: "It's off to bed with you for your beauty sleep."

The girls had indeed been exhausted. So much had flown by their windows that first full day aboard The Chief—so much that they had never seen in books or films—that their senses and minds were overloaded. At breakfast, the dry and dusty prairies of Kansas had flown by the dining car windows. By midmorning, they watched The Chief add yet another engine at Raton Pass to take them up and over the towering Rockies, which seemed an impossible task. Yet they soon were at what seemed to be the top of the world. To the east were mounds of gray sandstone—mesas, the porter had called them. To the south stretched miles and miles of plains that seemed to end where the mountains on the horizon began, mountains whose peaks were lost somewhere in the clouds. As the train thundered through New Mexico and land so parched it was cracked like lips that had been overexposed to wind and sand, it seemed as if civilization had been left behind forever. Not even the occasional roads that ran parallel to the train's tracks showed signs of life, and the gas stations that infrequently dotted the roadside seemed painted on the landscape rather than real. By early afternoon, the soufflés and salads of luncheon were forgotten as more mesas, salmon-streaked stumps that turned fiery red when caught in the blaze of the afternoon sun, appeared. Toward six that evening, as Carolyn prepared to nap, the compartment door burst open and Margaret, who had been "hobnobbing," screamed: "Indians!" When Carolyn stared at her uncomprehendingly, Margaret excitedly explained: "Albuquerque, dummy. We're in Albuquerque, and there are Indians on the platform. So hold on to your scalp and hurry."

Indeed Indians, in their full native costume, were all along the red brick platform with their handmade wares on display. "You barter with them," whispered Margaret as Carolyn fingered a string of turquoise beads. "I'll offer them your virgin ity for the beads, a handmade hatchet, and a wigwam."

Ignoring her sister, Carolyn chose a necklace of multicolored stones for her mother and a buffalo-skin wallet for her father. Had there not been the "All aboard!" signaling the end of the twenty-minute stop, Margaret would have bought a full Indian headdress that caught her fancy.

"And just whatever for?" had asked Carolyn.

"The Easter Parade, Miss Know-It-All. What else?" Margaret had answered.

Carolyn, as she remembered how Margaret had looked in the headdress and how she had chastised herself all evening long for not having purchased it, started to laugh.

"What's funny?" asked Margaret as she continued to massage the shoulder where Carolyn's head had rested.

"You!" said Carolyn as she sat up to tuck in the blouse that had come free from her skirt as she slept. "Has anyone an idea of the time?" she asked.

"Well, we left Barstow about a half hour or so ago, so it must be moving up on noon," answered Mrs. McCord. "I guess I should think about picking up this big ole body of mine and taking it back to my compartment. San Bernardino's coming up in an hour." Mrs. M stuffed her knitting in her cylindrical knitting bag and hoisted herself up. "Well, dears, have an absolutely lovely life. I'd give you both a big kiss, but it would mean bending over and that would risk my falling on top of you, and you wouldn't want that." She laughed. "Oh, what the hell. You only live once." Steadying herself by placing one hand on the back of the couch where the girls were sitting, Mrs. M bent and kissed first Carolyn and then Margaret warmly but wetly on the cheek. "And for God's sake eat something," she said to Margaret. "You're much too thin."

The car felt empty after Mrs. M left, despite the presence of several other passengers. Feeling the void, the girls grew impatient. "I'm sick of watching sand and cactus," said Margaret. "Let's go back to our compartment and try on outfits."

"What do you mean *outfits*? We only have the three or four with us. The rest are in our suitcases in the baggage car," said Carolyn.

"*Were* in the baggage car," corrected Margaret with a mischievous smile. "Oh, stop looking like such a worrywart, Lynnie. I gave the porter fifty cents to retrieve *a* suitcase."

"Yours, of course," said Carolyn wryly.

"Of course. With your looks, Lynnie-girl, you could walk off this train wearing this rotten green wool plush and everyone would fall dead at your feet. I need something dramatic to capture attention. Like my red cape. That would dazzle the press."

"Margaret, there will be no press. Must I remind you the reporters in Chicago were there to see our parents, *the* stars, and not us. In Hollywood, we are nobodies. Children of stars are a dime a dozen here."

"All the more reason to wear my red cape," said Margaret. "But what with it? Something simple. Something stark and simple."

"What a pity you didn't buy that Indian headdress. That would look smart with your red cape," said Carolyn, dripping sarcasm. Still, she followed Margaret, who had her pumps in hand and was running toward their car and their compartment.

Margaret was in the midst of "out-of-town tryouts," as she termed her wardrobe changes, when the train pulled into San Bernardino. From the window, she watched Mrs. McCord scoop a woman almost her size, but half her age, into her arms. A man the girls presumed to be her son-in-law collected her baggage and walked the women off the platform and toward his waiting horse-drawn wagon. The San Bernardino Mountains were more interesting than the desert, particularly as they became more green and lush. Soon, they were more foothills than mountains and the first of the citrus groves and vineyards appeared, just as Margaret finally decided on a plain gray dress—a long, narrow silhouette that ended at midcalf—which she accented with a wide black belt. "A great effect, don't you think?" she asked Carolyn, who was pretending to ignore her. "A red cape and a gray dress. Passion and yet good taste all in one package."

"Marg, come quick!" said Carolyn in an urgent whisper.

Los Angeles was making its debut on the horizon. It was framed by mountains and blue skies. The foreground was the stucco and wooden bungalows painted in the pink, red, and purple colors of the fuchsias that were planted everywhere. The background was of solitary skyscrapers, sparkling white towers set apart from one another basking proudly in the afternoon sun. A palm tree—the first the girls had ever seen—waved its branches as if in greeting as the train moved into the city proper. Dominating the downtown area was a huge building whose buttressed tower was capped with a pyramid dome. Even by the New York standards by which the girls judged, City Hall was imposing.

As the train lumbered over a ridge, their destination rose up like an Arabian fantasy to greet them. La Grande Station, terra-cotta and domed, looked more a mosque than a terminal. As the train inched into the station, the girls spotted their first Californians and saw from their attire that the end of summer didn't mean in Los Angeles what it meant in New York—a sea of white, pink, and baby-blue shirts and skirts caressed their eyes. And the women were hat- and gloveless! Unheard of in New York.

When the train screeched to a halt, Margaret asked, "What's the name of the warden who's to meet us?"

"Not a warden, Margaret. Miss Bennington is a housekeeper."

"And just how are we to recognize her? By her broom and dustcloth?" asked Margaret.

"In that red cape, you're hardly traveling incognito so you needn't worry," said Carolyn just as there was a knock on the door.

"Yes?" she asked of the tall, gray-haired man in the dark plaid suit, carrying his felt hat, who stood in the doorway.

"Miss Tiernan, I'm Louis Gardner, vice-president of publicity at Killerbrew Studios, and this," he said as he brought into the compartment a younger man in a blue blazer, "is my assistant, John Ollson."

"I'm Carolyn Tiernan and this is my sister, Margaret. We were expecting a Miss Bennington. Is anything wrong?"

"Miss Bennington is waiting in the limousine. We must hurry," said Gardner as he began gently removing the girls from their compartment.

"But our luggage!" said Margaret, confused.

"It is being cared for, I assure you," said Gardner. "Now shall we hurry?"

"But why?" asked Margaret.

"Miss Tiernan, there is a crush of photographers and reporters waiting. Very typical for Hollywood. We wish to sneak you out the back way to avoid them."

"Avoid them?" said Margaret incredulously. "After I've done all this for them?" she asked as she swung open her cape to give the men its full effect.

"There is no time to explain," said Gardner. "John, help me escort the ladies to the rear of the train. We'll disembark there and make a run for the limousine."

27

Each man took one of the girls firmly by the arm, and led her down the corridors past the people who were still struggling to remove themselves and their luggage from the train. At the last car, Gardner turned to his group and said: "From the moment we walk down those steps, we turn our heads neither left nor right, but move quickly ahead toward the entrance and the car that awaits."

It was the cry "That's them!" Margaret heard first, and then the sound of footsteps ricocheting off the domed roof of the terminal as a score of men ran toward them. Suddenly they were engulfed. Louis Gardner stepped in front and John Ollson in back of the girls. They tried to shepherd them toward the door, but the crowding made it impossible. The reporters had descended like locusts. Questions rained down on the girls in a jumble. Carolyn tried to hear what was being said, but she could hear nothing, and she understood less. And then she heard the scream, a scream that ended in a wail that filled the terminal. It was coming from Margaret's direction. It was coming from Margaret. My Margaret. My Margaret is being hurt.

Carolyn Tiernan flailed at Louis Gardner, who was holding her fast, trying to shield her from the whirlwind of events. Hysterical, screaming, she bit Gardner on his hand, broke free, and kicked and punched her way through the mass of men toward Margaret.

"Marg!" she screamed. *"Margaret!"* she cried out as she clawed her way through the men surrounding her sister. "Don't you hurt her!" she screamed as her fists pounded on the backs of strangers.

"Mamaaaa!" screamed Margaret. "Maaaaa!"

"Margaret, I'm coming. I'm here," sobbed Carolyn as she broke through the crowd of men at the very moment Margaret collapsed and fell to the ground. As the photographers rushed to photograph the prostrate girl, Carolyn Tiernan threw her own body over her sister's and screamed: "Go away. Go away." It took the strength of several men to pull her off the unconscious girl she was protecting.

"Miss Tiernan . . . Carolyn . . . please . . . listen to me," said John Ollson as he lifted and held the trembling girl to him. "Your parents . . . yesterday . . . they were killed in a car crash."

Long ago, Augusta Monahan had stopped fearing death. Having been its reluctant companion at the hospital for so many years, she accepted it as an unwelcome reality of life. But as the TWA twin-engine plane pitched about the blackened skies, she was terrified. Augusta had never flown before, and had destiny not dictated, she would not be in a plane now. She had not had time to experience anxiety prior to boarding the Douglas aircraft. From the moment Rose Wheaton had collapsed in her arms crying, "They're dead. Our precious Tory and Thomas are gone," there had been no time for feeling.

At first, Augusta would not believe the old woman. But even under careful cross-examination, Rose Wheaton's story remained fixed. The Illinois police had called. The Ford sedan's license had been traced to Thomas, as had the car's serial number. Further proof was the gold watch that had been found on one of the charred bodies. The inscription read: "Tory, my love. Thomas." Augusta Monahan had sat heavily on the highly polished wood steps of the stairway leading to the second-floor bedrooms and had absentmindedly stroked the hair of the woman who sobbed as Augusta held her. The girls! she suddenly thought. Oh my God, Carolyn and Margaret. She ran to the den and to her rolltop desk. In one of the drawers, she found what she was looking for: The Chief's itinerary. There was still time, she saw. Still time to reach Los Angeles and be the one to break the news to the girls.

The Keane Travel Agency that handled the Tiernans' tours had been quick to respond. Within twenty minutes, Augusta was assured her seat on the TWA flight leaving Newark at five and arriving in Los Angeles at seven the following morning, a full eight hours before The Chief. A limousine would take her from Pennsylvania Station, she was informed, to the airport.

Next, Augusta had phoned Jerome Siegal. The agent had been shocked, but was not allowed by Augusta to give in to or to express his grief. "I want you to call Killerbrew Studios. I want you to insist they keep this from the press until I arrive. I am certain they can use their connections with the Illinois police to do this." Jerome Siegal assured the woman he had heard about but never met that he would comply with her wishes and was certain Franklin Killerbrew would do likewise. After that, she packed—a simple procedure as her summer wardrobe had not yet been stored for the New York winter. Her last task before leaving for the station was to call Rose Wheaton's sister and arrange for the care of the old woman, who had been in the family's service from the time Tory and Augusta were babies in the house in Dorchester.

The trip had begun routinely enough. Dinner had been served "somewhere over Pittsburgh," as the copilot informed them. Trouble began on their approach to Chicago. A thunderstorm delayed their arrival by twenty minutes. It was another two hours before the weather permitted the plane to take off again. Now the plane seemed helpless to right itself as it was pummeled by winds and rain. Through the rain-streaked window, she could see huge, intermittent streaks of lightning slicing through the sky. The other woman besides herself among the fourteen passengers was mouthing the rosary as she clutched her baby to her. When the plane again shook from the force of the winds and suddenly plummeted, several people cried out. Not Augusta. Over and over she was repeating to herself: "I will not die now. I will *not*."

She was unaware the plane had touched down until a bolt of lightning illuminated the one-story brick building toward which the plane taxied. When stairs were brought to the plane for the passengers to disembark, the ground personnel met them with umbrellas and rushed them into the terminal.

Kansas City was to have been but a twenty-minute stop. Now, said the copilot, because of the storms throughout the Midwest, he had no idea when they would be off the ground again.

Augusta could hear her heels click-clacking on the marble floors as she sought the ladies' room. The uniformed employee manning the high wooden TWA desk pointed her to the left and down the bare-walled hallway. When she entered the white-tiled facility, she found the woman who had sat behind her on the plane leaning against the wall, holding her baby as sweat poured from her face.

"Would you like me to hold her for a bit?" asked Augusta. When the woman nodded that she would, Augusta took the infant and cradled her against her shoulder. The woman instantly began to cry. She kept both hands over her mouth so that her guttural sounds would not upset the child. The episode was violent, but brief. When she had collected herself, the woman washed her face, thanked Augusta, and left with her baby still asleep as it nestled in her arms. Alone, Augusta went into one of the booths, closed the door, raised the toilet seat, and threw up.

*   *   *

Franklin Killerbrew smiled at the newspaper headlines and remembered how he was not smiling at the news two days ago. The "bulletin" had disturbed a meeting. Franklin Killerbrew did not like to be disturbed in meetings. Interruptions broke not only his concentration, but the spell he knew his presence had on a roomful of peers and underlings. His was an emphatic and insistent voice. It could be as imposing and intimidating as his size. But the buzz of his intercom refused to be ignored. If Dorothea Wolfe was challenging his orders, Killerbrew knew it was an emergency.

"Yes?" he had demanded of his secretary. He had scowled as he listened. "Okay, put him on," he had replied. Killerbrew felt the eyes of his employees upon him. Turning his back, he had picked up the phone from its stand by the side of the solid oak conference table and carried it to where he was the most distant from the stares aimed at his back.

"What's the problem, Siegal?" were Killerbrew's first words. "I understand," he had said after listening briefly. "Assure Miss Monahan her wishes will be complied with. What? Yes . . . a terrible tragedy," Killerbrew had said as he hung up abruptly.

"Gentlemen, the meeting is adjourned." Although what had been under discussion was inconclusive, the men, knowing better than to question Killerbrew's judgment, had gathered up their scripts, budgets, and designs. When the last exited, Killerbrew had pushed a button on the paneled rear wall and waited for the fully stocked bar to rotate into service. He then poured a tumblerful of Wild Turkey. Killerbrew always found bourbon best in times of stress. It hit the mark faster than other hard liquors. "Son of a bitch!" he had said aloud. "Son of a fucking bitch!"

Angrily, he had dropped his six-foot-two frame into the massive oak chair at the head of the conference table and put his feet up on the much smaller chair nearest him. Bringing Victoria and Thomas Tiernan to Hollywood had been his brainchild. Talkies had changed the face of the film industry. Every studio owner in town was taking a hard look at New York actors—people whose voices didn't sound like chalk screeching on a blackboard. The problem was, most were ugly. But not the Tiernans. They had both sounded and looked good, even though she was getting a little long in the tooth. Still, she was a beauty. Audiences would love her as the all-American mother.

31

The daughters? Who the hell knew they'd be valuable. No one uses teenagers in movies—not with the Hayes Office and that goddamn Legion of Decency. But shit. I should have signed them anyway. In family pictures, you need kids. Even teenage kids. Well, screw it. I didn't think of it, and that fat-assed agent of theirs didn't suggest it.

Two days ago, Franklin Killerbrew had asked himself as he drained his glass of bourbon, What have I got? His answer was: Two dead Tiernans, and two live ones—who don't know about the dead ones—arriving on The Chief. Some aunt flying in to meet the train and an agent, who upon the aunt's request, wants to keep this gripping story from the press. Then, as now, Franklin Killerbrew knew nothing in Hollywood stays quiet for long. Then and particularly now, as he gazed at the newspaper and the story chronicling the latest development in the Tiernan sister saga, Franklin Killerbrew realized that can be a very good thing. The realization broadened the contented smile that was already on his face.

The black crepe dresses had been provided by the studio. The limousine had been provided by the studio. The funeral arrangements—from the white camellias to the velour-lined caskets—had been provided by the studio. Everything, but everything, had been provided by the studio, thought Augusta—ever since she arrived in Los Angeles less than an hour after the girls. How thoughtful! How very thoughtful indeed, she thought, without the slightest feeling of appreciation.

Sitting in the back of the limousine between Carolyn and Margaret, Augusta was serving as a single bookend of support. No one was talking, but at least now, all could. A difference from when Augusta first arrived at the Chateau Marmont. With the help of a studio chauffeur who had met her plane at Mines Field airport, she had fought her way through the crowd of reporters that had congregated in the hotel's baroque lobby and into the Tiernan suite. Margaret was sitting in a straight-backed Louis Philippe chair. Sitting, that's all the child was doing. There was a bruise on her forehead the size of an orange—the result of the fall she had taken at La Grande, Augusta was later to learn—and her eyes had the look of the blind. They saw nothing and her ears obviously heard nothing as Carolyn kept up a steady stream of childish babble. She was cooing, talking gibberish, desperately trying to make Margaret respond to her.

32

There was no hello or other greeting spoken by Augusta Monahan. "Have you called the doctor?" she demanded of a woman she presumed to be Miss Bennington.

"We've been unable to reach Mr. Killerbrew," said a distinguished-looking gentleman in a dark plaid suit. "We thought it best to get his opinion before proceeding."

Augusta Monahan took a deep breath before speaking. "I don't give two pins for your Mr. Killerbrew. This child is in shock and the other needs sedation. I want a doctor and an ambulance called *now*. And if you don't move, I will."

Louis Gardner immediately did as told. It was a scene his associate, John Ollson, would never forget. From the moment all hell had broken loose at the station, he had been fighting his own emotions. He had wanted to help the girls, but he had no words to comfort Carolyn, and no skills with which to snap Margaret out of her shocked state. Now, here, in the space of a minute, this woman, hardly bigger than either of her nieces, had taken total control of the situation. And she hadn't yet stopped. She was demanding the hallways be cleared of press, so that Margaret would not have to face any further strain should a stretcher be required to take her to the hospital. She was also demanding to know how the press had learned of the tragedy.

"We don't know," answered Louis Gardner. "We thought it had been kept quiet until we reached the station and found them waiting. I guess this kind of news travels fast."

How very fast! thought Augusta as the limousine rounded a corner and pulled up before a church that looked from its white-painted wood exterior more like a farmhouse. Margaret had barely been registered in the hospital when newspapers were publishing her picture as she lay crumpled on the station's concrete floor. And when they exhausted that, they used the one of Carolyn, protecting her sister's body with her own. Awful, awful, awful, thought Augusta. And even worse was the circus at the hospital. Reporters camped there for the three days of Margaret's treatment. They bribed nurses and doctors for information, and when none was forthcoming, they concocted their own and reported their fiction as fact. So vulgar, thought Augusta. Imagine calling her girls "Orphans in a Storm" and "Waifs in the World" when she, Augusta Monahan, was there.

Often Augusta had the feeling the circus was being choreographed and orchestrated by invisible forces that knew the

33

family's every move. When she left the Chateau to visit Margaret, the press was there. When Carolyn, assisted by John Ollson, who had been assigned by the studio to tend to the family's needs, tried to visit her sister, the press was there. The press was always there. Even now, thought Augusta as she saw the reporters at curbside, their cameras trying to invade even the sanctity of the limousine.

"Mother would have hated this," said Margaret venomously as she looked out the window at the mass of people waiting outside St. Victor's. "She would have hated the very idea of being buried in California."

Indeed she would have, thought Augusta, again wondering how it had happened. The studio, of course, she remembered. Caught as she had been between Margaret's needs at the hospital and Carolyn's at the hotel, Augusta could not think with the usual clarity of her businesslike mind. So Franklin Killerbrew did her thinking for her. It was he who had had Tory's and Thomas's remains shipped from Illinois to Los Angeles. Had I been clear of head, thought Augusta, I would have told the studio to turn those remains around, and send them back to New York where they belong. But Margaret was in no condition to travel. None of them was, and so she had somehow allowed the funeral to take place this noon at St. Victor's with Father Parsons to conduct the high requiem mass. Interment would then take place at Holy Cross cemetery.

It took a cordon of men, including Louis Gardner and John Ollson, to push the women through the screaming mass of strangers, who had assembled to witness real life drama, and into the church. Almost instantly, they were confronted by the matching coffins. As Margaret stared at them, her head was shaking in disbelief.

"It's not them, Margaret," said Carolyn as she stepped next to her sister. "You must remember that is only their worldly remains. Their souls are with Him, in heaven. Our loss is His gain."

The color that had drained from Margaret's face returned with a flush. "If you believe that lunacy, you're a fool," she spat at her sister. "A decent, kind, and loving God would not kill our parents for His own gain."

Carolyn reacted as if slapped. Shock gave way to tears and tears to sobs. Before Augusta could react, Margaret, herself crying, roughly grabbed Carolyn and pulled her into her

34

arms. "Oh, Lynnie, Lynnie. Believe what you want. If it helps you, fine. I don't want to take anything more away from you. You've lost enough. We both have. Only I have nothing to replace my loss."

"You have Him!" pleaded Carolyn.

Margaret shook her head. "No, I don't. I truly don't."

Father Parsons led the camellia-covered coffins down the center aisle of the church. The women, their arms linked, followed. The church was filled with people standing in the side aisles that led to the final stations of the cross near the altar. Again Augusta wondered who these people were. Had she been aware of Hollywood's political machinations, she would have known that attending the Tiernan funeral was for many, particularly those under contract to Killerbrew Studios and those who hoped to be, a command performance. For still others, the funeral was a means to an end, a way for their names and faces to appear in the newspapers.

At the front of the church, Father Parsons slowly climbed the three steps leading up to the altar where he would conduct the mass. The twin coffins were side by side at the railing before him, the bereaved but a few feet away. As he began the service, his tongue savoring each of the Latin words he spoke, Augusta Monahan, gazing at the small stained-glass windows above, smiled. She had traveled in time to yet another church, and some other mass, so many years ago. She could hear Mary-Margaret Monahan whispering she had better behave or she'd have the devil to pay later. But Tory was making her laugh. Tory was doing her own Latin, as the priest did his, only hers was thinly disguised gutter talk. Wherever did she learn such words, Augusta had often wondered. And if Mary-Margaret Monahan had ever heard them, then there'd *really* have been the devil to pay!

They had had the most wonderful time as kids, remembered Augusta. Kevin Monahan was one of Boston's first Irish-American lawyers, and although the Brahmin group on Beacon Hill, who ruled Boston's social set, never accepted him, the Dorchester community where they lived thought he was the cat's pajamas. We Monahan girls had a reputation before we ever set foot in Sacred Heart. And we certainly added to it. Or Tory did. The nerve that child had! She was the only teenager at the convent school who wasn't afraid of mice, and who thought recess meant giving the mice she collected a chance to stretch their little legs. What pandemonium that caused!

35

Augusta could still see, as if the remembrance was yesterday's, Sister Thomasina, her black skirts clutched in he
hands, standing on a chair and screeching. She could also se
Tory rising to confess to the heinous crime. Tory alway
confessed as she had a very practical view of Catholicism.

"You can do anything you want in life, Augie. Anything,"
she had stressed. "All you gotta do to square yourself i
confess."

Victoria Monahan spent a great deal of time at confession
Augusta smiled as she remembered the Toys-for-Tots Christmas drive when Tory stood before the lectern and addressec
the entire convent class in a Jewish accent.

How old was I then . . . fourteen? No, I was fifteen and
Tory was fourteen because it happened the year—just after my
birthday—when Mama had unexpected company that Sunday
afternoon. Oh my, when I think of it! Mama would ask Tory
repeatedly if she thought maids were created in heaven solely
to pick up after her. Tory was never one for neatness. Whatever came off her back was on the floor, or at the bottom of
the closet. And then that Sunday. Mama was showing off the
house and Tory, hearing her coming, picked up everything—
oh God, what a bundle of sweaters and blouses and under-
things—ran down the hall to my room, opened the door, and
threw it all on the floor, and ran back again. The look on
Mother's face when she entered my room! The look on my
face! What could I say?

And speaking of looks. What about when Mama found that
book Tory wrote for me when I was going off to Wellesley.
What was it called? *The Irish-Catholic Girl's Guide to Being
Good*. Lord only knows where Tory found those pictures.
Mother cried—called us "fallen women." But we weren't.
But God knows Tory could have been.

Augusta recalled vividly and still with some jealousy how
the boys buzzed about Tory. Particularly at the annual Spring
Ball at the Somerset Hotel. Tory had worn a white chiffon
gown trimmed with pink ribbons and embroidered forget-
me-nots about the neckline. She was flushed with success but
she was also pouting, as one of the boys she particularly liked
had been monopolized by Rose Fitzgerald, who certainly had
her own way with the boys.

And Mother, so hopeful her daughters would meet their
proper—Oh God, they *had* to be proper!—"matches made in
heaven." Was she ever dismayed when she learned I wanted

to attend college, recalled Augie. She thought it unnecessary for a girl. "Too expensive. We can't afford it!" she had grumbled. Which of course was ridiculous as Daddy did very well although I'm sure every penny he made went into that house. The cost alone of the walnut paneling that stretched up the walls of the library, den, and dining room could have paid for a year's tuition for ten girls at Wellesley. And all that velvet upholstery. Not to mention that outrageous Turkish divan. Wine colored it was, and with matching tasseled draperies that were so heavy, it took two maids to hang them. And hadn't Tory insisted on having both the divan and the draperies when Mama passed on! The divan was sitting there now in the upstairs bedroom in Murray Hill. "It makes me feel like Theda Bara," Tory had once said. "I think one day I shall lie on it nude and munch grapes."

Tory had adored Dan Dunahey and he, her. They were kindred souls—both full of the blarney. Oh, that look on Dan's face when Tory came up to him one day, put her finger to his shirt, and pushed and prodded. "And just what are you doing?" he had asked. "Checking for stuffing," Tory had replied. "You can't be a Harvard man as you profess without being a stuffed shirt."

And Tory had known Dan was in love with me long before he ever said it. "And just what are you going to do about it?" she had asked. Talk about looks on faces. Oh, the look on hers when I said, "You know, Tory, they do teach more than book-biology at Wellesley."

Then came the drowning. Augusta had not thought of that particular year or the one immediately following it for a very long time. But now, there she was, a young girl running down the stairs from her bedroom in the Dorchester house to answer the doorbell.

"Why, Mrs. Dunahey, what brings you here?" she had asked, and almost instantly regretted that she had. Her mother-in-law-to-be had come to tell her Dan had drowned in a swimming accident at Revere Beach. "Impossible!" Augusta had instantly replied. "He could not possibly have as the wedding invitations are in the mail. In fact, some who received them early have already replied. And Mother and I just yesterday settled on the menu for the buffet. So, as you can see, you've made a terrible mistake."

She had then fainted and later she learned she had remained "in some other place," as they delicately put it, for many days. Her only recollection, and it was faint, was of her mother praying over her. Then, too, she thought she could see the Judge sitting and reading the newspaper to her nightly. Tory . . . she couldn't remember what Tory did. Tory, like most things, was a blur. Until that morning when Tory had torn into her room, thrown open the heavy velvet draperies that closed out reality, and pulled the patchwork quilt off the bed.

"Now get up, dammit! C'mon, Augie, get up!" Tory had screamed. "You've been mean and miserable long enough. No more." And before Augie could think about it, Tory had pulled her from the bed.

As soon as her feet touched the worn Persian rug, Augie had spoken her first full sentence in a year. "But he's dead, Tory. Dan Dumahey is dead," Augie had replied in a voice that said, Why bother?

"Yes, he's dead," said Tory firmly. "But you're not and you're stuck with that fact. And since you have obviously chosen not to die, you had better learn how to live."

And Tory had made her live, dragging Augie with her wherever she went. Augie smiled as she remembered the day they met Thomas Tiernan. He had never had a chance. His fate was sealed from the time Tory saw him. And the Right Honorable Kevin Monahan and Mary-Margaret had proved to be no match for Tory. If she wanted to marry an actor, then marry an actor she would. And did. If she wanted to be an actress, then an actress she would be. And was. And such a good one. Thomas claimed she had learned it all in but a few weeks; that Tory had instantly grasped how acting is child's play.

"You make believe you are the character," he would say. "You make believe you know what he wears, where he lives, what he likes to eat, who he knows, and where he has been. You make believe an entire life that he has enjoyed or hated or both before your audience ever meets him. You make believe a whole person and you then make believe you are that person for three hours every night. There is nothing more and nothing less to it."

Thomas used to credit make-believe with saving his life. While other boys his age in the orphanage often were sickly or even died for the lack of care or the overwork, he survived because he had another life. At night, he lulled himself to sleep making believe he was someone else, a someone with a big farm or a big castle but always with people who loved him.

Thomas was always vague about how he became part of the acting troupe. Tory suspected that he had become the leading lady's lover when he was only fourteen. How else could he have become a prop master and then a supporting player? Certainly, even long after his marriage, Thomas stayed in touch with the woman and when she was on her deathbed, he had left Tory for a week, closed down the play in which they had been starring, to be at the woman's side. That was typical of Thomas, thought Augusta. He was a man with a very strong sense of family loyalty probably because he had never had a family of his own.

Augie had never been treated like a sister-in-law but more like a sister and dear friend by Thomas, and she would never have left Boston if he hadn't been every bit as insistent as Tory. "You are rotting away up there!" Tory had screamed. Of course she was right. After Dan's death, Augie found college pointless, as was the typing and filing she did in her father's office. Her parents had been vehemently opposed to her leaving but Tory had fought them off as she packed Augie up.

"I need her to run the house while Thomas and I do our business," she had stated.

What Augie had thought to be a ruse, a ploy, had turned out to be true. Tory had indeed needed her to run the house as Tory's talents did not include figures. Bills were paid only when she had nothing better to do. The budget never balanced, and the kitchen was either overstocked, resulting in wasteful spoilage, or devoid of the barest necessities.

Thomas had called Augie "the Admiral," as he insisted he never saw anyone put chaos into such shipshape order quite so quickly.

But it was second nature to me, thought Augie. So much so that soon I had too much time on my hands. And again, there was Tory with her suggestions. "You should volunteer at the hospital. Who knows, you might even meet a doctor," she had said with a leer.

And I did—Arthur—but like all the other doctors I met, he was married and did not need the total me the way the babies on the ward did. No, they wanted me in parts—my personals—but not me. Not the real me. But the babies, they needed each and every part of me and whatever I could give them. Babies always need so much. Babies, thought Augusta, and the thought jolted her back into the present. Babies, she

thought again as she felt her nieces' bodies on either side o
her. They will need so much now, so very much, she thought
and Tory, my dear, dearest Tory, help me to give them al
they need. Oh, Tory, we will miss you so.

Both Carolyn and Margaret reached to collect and enfol
their aunt as she finally gave way to the emotions she ha
stored away ever since learning of her sister's and brother-in-
law's deaths. Augusta's sobs were uncontrollable and the
punctuated the high requiem mass that was near completion.
Carolyn and Margaret continued to hold their aunt firmly a
they left the church for the drive to the cemetery. But a
Holy Cross, where the bodies of Tory and Thomas Tiernan
were lowered into the ground, it was Augusta Monahan who
held each girl just above her elbow, making her stand upright, which is how Tory and Thomas had made them all face
the world.

2

The Pierce-Arrow turned slowly onto Gower. In the distance, beyond the hot-dog and tamale stands, rose Killerbrew Studios. Each of the women was lost in her own thoughts as the chauffeur-driven car sent by the studio brought them closer to their first face-to-face encounter with its owner.

More than three weeks had passed since the funeral, and as Augusta Monahan rested her head on the gray felt upholstery, she thought how the three weeks seemed more like three years. So much had changed in all their lives. In so many ways, the girls weren't girls anymore. Sudden death, tragedy, had robbed them of something that could never be retrieved. Still, they were so young, so vulnerable, and so uncertain. Neither knew whether it was a career in Hollywood or a life on the stage that mattered most. While they were trying to decide, Franklin Killerbrew had been quietly persuasive. In all their time at the Chateau Marmont they had not seen a bill. Nor would they. And it must cost a pretty penny, thought Augusta, for the private two-bedroom bungalow near, but not too near, the swimming pool to which they had moved. And the Pierce-Arrow had been constantly at their service. As was John Ollson, although Augusta was not certain whether he was provided by the studio or by his own very obvious desire for Carolyn. I wonder if the child is aware of the young man's interest, thought Augusta. There I go on . . . the *child*. Carolyn will be nineteen in December. Hardly a child, Augusta told herself, and yet . . . so barely a woman.

Carolyn Tiernan was hiding her face by pretending to be absorbed in the parade of film extras strolling on Gower with their cups of coffee and breakfast rolls in hand. To be made up and costumed before eight in the morning was unusual to Carolyn. Theatre people were only half through their night's sleep at that hour. All different, she thought, and that brought

41

a rush of new tears. Do *not* cry! she was ordering. Despite her admonitions, the tears fell. It was a "bad morning," she told herself. I'm feeling sorry for myself . . . selfish. Father Parsons had told her that time heals all wounds. She believed him just as she believed it was not hers to question the wisdom of the Lord. "He giveth and taketh, and ours is not to question why," the priest had said. "They are at peace Carolyn. So you must be." But she wasn't. She missed her parents and wished it were Tory and Thomas Tiernan—not Carolyn and Margaret—who were discussing a film career with the head of Killerbrew Studios at breakfast this morning. If only John were with us, I'd feel better, thought Carolyn. But at eight, John Ollson was due at his desk in the publicity department, which is where he now sat, wondering what Killerbrew would say, and what the sisters would decide.

Irony was sitting as close to Margaret Tiernan as her aunt and sister. In fact, she felt crushed by its proximity. So there she was after all en route to stardom and money. We should be careful what we ask for, she thought, as she remembered her toast aboard The Chief and her mother's words. "May I remind you, missy, it is your father and I who are signed to Killerbrew Studios. Nowhere in the fine print does it say anything about a Margaret or a Carolyn Tiernan." Now it might, and the possibility aroused and yet confused Margaret. She had seen enough of Los Angeles in the three weeks of accompanying Carolyn as John squired her about to know she could enjoy living here. Actually, the idea of leaving the powder-blue French provincialism of the Chateau Marmont, its calculated elegance, to return to what was once home, but now could never be again, made her queasy. There would be a finality she did not want to face should she enter the Murray Hill brownstone at this time. Besides, films intrigued her much as they had her father. But why us? she had wondered when Jerome Siegal called from New York to tell them of Killerbrew's interest. Why did Franklin Killerbrew want them now and not before?

Through his partially opened louvers, Franklin Killerbrew watched from his office on the second floor of the main building that housed his administrative staff as the Pierce Arrow approached the studio's gates. Now he would see if his manipulations had been successful. You put the Christians in the den. After that, it's up to the lions, he thought as he saw

he usual throng at the wrought-iron gate that separated the
eal world from the one created on the nine sound stages of
Killerbrew Studios. These were the people who assembled
each morning long before breakfast hour; the people who fed
on glamour rather than cornflakes. As it was calculated to do,
he white Pierce-Arrow drew their attention. Like flies to
butter, they were drawn to see who was in the car. Their
screams and roars made Franklin Killerbrew smile triumphantly. The girls had not only been recognized but were
adored in that peculiar way that guarantees the sale of tickets.

As the car passed through security and began its drive onto
the lot, a contented Killerbrew dropped himself into his
oversized leather swivel chair and propped his feet on the
massive desk, whose golden oak wood was a perfect match to
the louvers and the paneling that covered his office walls.
Since there was no one he could ask to congratulate him,
Killerbrew did the honors himself. He had pulled it off; the
crowd's reaction to the sisters assured him of that. Only God
can make a tree, but Franklin Killerbrew can make a star, he
thought.

It had been no accident that the press was at La Grande
Station when the sisters arrived; no accident that the Tiernans'
funeral at St. Victor's played to a standing-room-only crowd;
no accident that photos and stories about the Tiernan sisters
continued to appear in newspapers across the country. Franklin Killerbrew had paid good money to obtain all that. He had
hired sub rosa a private press agent to do the honors. Yes,
thought Killerbrew, news travels fast in this town but only
when someone gives it a swift kick in the ass.

From the moment the senior Tiernans had been killed,
Killerbrew's energies were expended on ways to turn losses
into gains. The sisters were a potential gain—provided a deal
could be made. A deal would *have* to be made. Thanks to the
national publicity, they were celebrities now. Filmgoers all
over America would rush to see them in a picture, *any*
picture, because most people fed off the lives of others when
their own were so drab.

Franklin Killerbrew was not a mean or cruel man, although
no one ever accused him of being the soul of sensitivity or
kindness either. Killerbrew was about "bottom line." He
dealt in hard facts, cold cash, profit and not loss. Reality.
"You want kindness and sensitivity—synonyms for pure
fantasy—go to Disney," he would say. Filmmaking was

43

strictly a business to Killerbrew, and actors and actresses were like office machinery. You bought the best, kept them well oiled and serviced, and then dumped them when newer, better model became available.

Yet, in his own way, Franklin Killerbrew was ethical. Some see life in terms of black and white, but Killerbrew saw only black and red, and no one in Hollywood ever wanted to see red unless he didn't mind losing control of his studio. Right now, Killerbrew had lots of red showing on the page marked "Tiernan" in his ledgers, but he knew the sisters could change the color with one picture.

That he might be wrong about the Tiernan sisters never entered Killerbrew's mind. It was his instinct for success as much as his intelligence that saw him named vice-president of Blanchard Pictures at twenty-one. He had come to Los Angeles from Chicago shortly after his father's death. Although he had few liquid assets, he had something better in the days of studio block-booking—124 movie houses sprinkled throughout the Midwest. If a film company could control that number of theatres, it could block-book or force-feed into them the good and the bad product they produced. Blanchard Pictures made good product, so good that the studio was nearly bankrupt when Killerbrew came to its apparent rescue. Bernard Blanchard took great pride in his films, many of which won awards, but lost money, and he saw Killerbrew as a bright young man who could strong-arm his theatres into taking Blanchard product whether they liked it or not. Killerbrew went one better. In three years' time he strong-armed and took Blanchard Pictures for his own. He had traded his 124 movie houses for one third of the company's stock. He then traded his single status by making Nancy Quentin Blanchard Mrs. Franklin Killerbrew, and thus acquired still another 25 percent of Blanchard Pictures' stock.

Nancy Blanchard Killerbrew, her mother an institutionalized alcoholic these past twelve years, thought it sad her father chose *her* study in *her* home to shoot himself. It so totally disrupted the household she had so artfully assembled during the first two years of marriage, and his brains had ruined the Oriental rug. Blood simply didn't wash out. Still, the sixteen-room Spanish-tiled and terrazzo-floored hacienda in Laurel Canyon was the most talked about residence in the house-conscious industry of Hollywood. People fought to attend Nancy Killerbrew's Christmas party, given each year in n elegant living room where palms and plants sipped the California sun through a glass-domed skylight roof that opened nd closed with the press of a button.

Franklin Killerbrew had not married Nancy Blanchard to ain control of her father's studio—that would have happened ooner or later regardless—but to gain control of her. Their arriage was never about love. For Killerbrew, love belonged n the big screen and bore as much relation to real life as ost of the films Hollywood made. Nancy Blanchard was a ood-looking woman, handsome but not beautiful. She had yle, however. More important, she had an attitude that allenged a certain kind of man. She would fix her steel-blue yes on a man and appraise him as one could a stud horse for ire. Her every gesture and facial mannerism said: "You can arry me, you can fuck me in every orifice known to man— ut you'll never have me." *That* is what had been Nancy uentin Blanchard's appeal for Franklin Killerbrew. That was ill what appealed to him after eight years of marriage, though he had learned with the passage of time that he, deed, never could "have" her. No one "had" Nancy illerbrew. Even those times when their mutual contempt d hatred for each other drove them clawing and punching to bed and she would straddle and ride him, urging and emanding he service her as she wished, it was *she* who imaxed when *she* was ready. He had never fucked her, as er *self*-satisfied smile told him. Still, they maintained the çade of marriage, mainly because it was convenient and ecessary. Nancy Killerbrew was a brilliant hostess, the per- ct wife to help consummate the perfect deal. She gave him he little woman" assistance a studio head needed, and her percent stock, all in exchange for social status and respect- ility; something she most assuredly could not have achieved ith any of the endless women she entertained in her private ed-à-terre in the Valley.

ranklin Killerbrew stood as Dorothea Wolfe ushered in "the ernan party." He saw Augusta Monahan take in every last tail of his office as she took his hand in greeting. When her ves rested for the briefest of moments on the seascape above e built-into-the-wall bar, he saw the flicker of recognition. es, Miss Monahan, he wanted to say, it is indeed a Winslow omer. Although his own eyes seemed to be focused on all a group, Killerbrew was actually sizing up Carolyn Tiernan.

45

Silently, he was thanking God for her breasts. Even in tha piece of green gabardine garbage you can see the girl's looker, he thought. As he beckoned the women to the twi tufted leather couches and the coffee table between them, o which breakfast was being served by Dorothea Wolfe Killerbrew was appraising Margaret, or "the horsey one" a he had already categorized her. Too lean. Too angular, an what the hell was she doing in that red cape . . . auditionin for the remake of *Zorro*?

"How do you think you'll like working in films, Mis Tiernan?" Killerbrew asked, coming to the point, as he per sonally poured coffee from the steaming sterling pot int Augusta Monahan's china cup.

"I don't know that I would," said Carolyn, "and I don know that I wouldn't. It is totally beyond my experience."

As Killerbrew launched into his standard talk on film, th exposure it guaranteed an actor, the millions to be reache on screen versus the thousands on stage, Margaret was sittin quietly, her legs crossed despite the silent reprimand i Augusta Monahan's eyes. She was fascinated by Killerbrew Lord knows he didn't look like a Goldwyn or a Mayer. No even a Thalberg. How old was he? Thirty-five . . . forty? H had been standing when they entered, and he had *loome* before them. Margaret instantly decided she liked men wh "loomed." She also liked a man who was so obviously prou of his body that he chose to display it in a short-sleeved whit tennis shirt and well-fitting gray flannels. She had been ex pecting standard serge—blue, of course—and a white starche shirt with a *discerning* tie. She certainly had not been expect ing a man whose skin was as brown from the sun as his eye and hair were by birth.

Either it is very warm in here, thought Margaret, or I hav just discovered the meaning of the word *sexy*.

Franklin Killerbrew was adroit at social amenities. He ha trained himself to speak on anyone's level. In her "smart navy dress with its white piqué collar and cuffs, August Monahan was asking "smart" questions—not about mone but about directors and script approval. "All those things m late sister and brother-in-law took for granted, but which suppose we can't." Killerbrew had caught her drift and pa ried it charmingly as well as skillfully.

"Why don't we have this as a creative meeting," he su

gested, "and leave the business to be discussed at a more propitious time with Jerome Siegal."

"Have you a property in mind for us?" asked Carolyn.

"No," lied Killerbrew as he thought of the screen treatment he himself had written, although his name would never appear as the writer should a film come of it.

"What kind of film do you envision for the girls?" persisted Augusta.

"A family picture, of course," said Killerbrew. "We certainly wouldn't want to offend the Legion of Decency," he added lightly.

"Or the Tiernan tradition," said Augusta, not at all lightly.

Even as he mentally applauded Augusta Monahan's spirit, Killerbrew was aware of Margaret Tiernan. At first he thought it was her silence that was making him perspire, but when he realized the sweat was only in his groin, he thought: I'm being fucked from across the coffee table and by a goddamn kid at that. A skinny, flat-chested, no-assed kid!

"And how old are you *exactly*, Miss Tiernan?" asked Killerbrew, a question that seemed a total non sequitur to everyone but Margaret, who understood.

"Old enough to know better and young enough to learn," he said without missing a beat.

"Margaret! I don't know what kind of a response you consider that to be, but I do think you might answer Mr. Killerbrew's question a little more appropriately," said Augusta Monahan.

"I will be eighteen in November," said Margaret, smiling ever so sweetly. "And Lynnie will be nineteen in December, and Aunt Augie, forty in . . ."

"Margaret!" interrupted Augusta furiously. "Honestly, I don't know what possesses her sometimes," she said to Killerbrew, aware she was sounding like *the* maiden aunt. Augusta was going to suggest Margaret apologize when she saw Killerbrew was laughing. Well, she thought, there's no harm done after all. He obviously enjoyed Margaret's response.

Augusta Monahan was partially right. It was not the response Killerbrew had enjoyed so much as the respondent. There just might come a day, he thought, when I might take the horsey there for a ride.

As John's Ford Phaeton rounded a curve that brought the Pacific Ocean into view, Margaret said, "I think it's time John

47

arranged a blind date for me." When Carolyn gasped and wa[s] about to protest, Margaret added: "Unless neither of you care that never once in your lives will you be alone."

"Ugh! What a horrible thought," said Carolyn, her body faking a shudder. "It's like having a rash that won't go away."

"You know, Lynnie, you are mean. Basically you lack human kindness," said Margaret as John laughed. "Go ahead. Make light of it, John Ollson, but you should worry, not laugh. She is cold and cruel. God has given her this cross to bear to keep her humble, only His plan doesn't seem to be working. Bu[t] the worm will turn. One day, Lynnie, you will be a little ol[d] lady selling apples on a street corner. You'll ask me fo[r] pennies and what will I do? I'll give them to you, because I'[m] not the one who is mean. Just dateless."

They were all laughing. Carolyn, sandwiched between Mar[-]garet and John in the front seat of the car, felt safe an[d] happy. She prayed Margaret was feeling the same. She wa[s] so worried about her sister and the nightmares that plague[d] her. Margaret would awaken sobbing and wet with perspira[-]tion. She never told Carolyn exactly what the nature of he[r] dreams was, but Carolyn knew they were about her parents. "Oh, Lynnie, they are gone," she had once cried, and Caro[-]lyn had no words with which to comfort her sister. What wa[s] consoling to Carolyn was now confusing to Margaret. Th[e] sisters, so close in all other ways, were far apart in thei[r] religious beliefs. They had reacted and continued to react t[o] their lives differently. Margaret had lost her naïveté. Whe[n] John took them about Los Angeles, whether to the studio or [a] restaurant or Grauman's Chinese Theatre, she watched peo[-]ple as they walked and talked to one another. She could tel[l] now whether a man saw her as a child or as a woman. She could also see when certain men looked at one another in th[e] way she would have preferred they look at her. This did no[t] shock her any more than learning that Franklin Killerbrew, although married, was a legendary lover to many. Since he[r] parents' death, what others did with their lives no longe[r] mattered to Margaret. Since life, she had learned, could b[e] short, she was interested in but one thing: getting on wit[h] her own.

The sisters had discussed John Ollson, who had slippe[d] into their lives naturally and comfortably. "I think I like hi[m] very much," Carolyn had confided one day, and Margaret, moved by the simplicity of her sister's admission, knew bet[-] er than to make light of it. "Not that I have much basis for comparison, but I feel he is very special," added Carolyn, wearing a new expression that Margaret found most affecting.

"Well, he *is* gorgeous but not my type," said Margaret. "He's too much of a gentleman. I want a man I can call a brute or a big lug and that's not John."

"Praise God and hallelujah!" said Carolyn, and then added, "Do you really think he's gorgeous?"

They are both gorgeous, thought Margaret as she caught their faces in profile seemingly mesmerized by the California coastline. The waves were flirting with the shore, first darting in and about, before running away to the sea. And the sun was glancing off the whitecaps of the water in such a way that Nature seemed to be laughing as she played.

"She often smiles to herself or at nothing at all," Carolyn was saying to John. "It's a family secret we've tried to hush up but . . . the truth will out."

"Speaking of 'out,' are we going to sit in this car all day or are we getting out to feel this beauty?" asked Margaret.

"Out!" answered John.

The three walked from the parking area onto the beach. Margaret, noticing the Santa Monica pier was but a few hundred feet away, turned and said, "Look, you guys, I'm going to commune with nature for a while. It's good for the soul, they say. So why don't you take a hike?"

As Carolyn looked anxiously at the pier, Margaret added, "Lynnie, there are hundreds of people up there. Nothing can happen. So go on. Git! Live!"

John took Carolyn's hand, grateful to Margaret for the time they could now spend alone. The air was October crisp and as they wordlessly strolled up the beach, John felt the beauty of California.

"It is so beautiful," said Carolyn as if reading his mind.

"Yes," said John seriously. "On the surface, everything in California is beautiful."

Had Carolyn's life not been sheltered and filtered through the rose-colored glasses of family and church, had she not been trained to listen more to cues than for the meaning of words, she might have realized there was something more to this tall, straw-blond, blue-eyed young man, something more than just good looks, manners, and charm. She let his statement go unchallenged, and if John minded, she was unaware of it.

John Ollson was accustomed to his physical appearanc
working both for and against him. Although it attracted peo
ple, it put off teachers and employers, who classified him a
"just another pretty face," as he had once quipped to Carolyn
Few at first saw the inquisitive and acquisitive mind that wo
him scholarships to Northwestern and Yale as well as th
athletic scholarship to Notre Dame. His own preference woul
have been the Ivy League college for its proximity to Ne
York and its possibilities for fun as well as education. Hi
stoically Swedish parents, unacquainted with fun, chose Notr
Dame.

John didn't berate his parents for their nonjoyous nature
but understood that the hardships they had endured from th
time they came to America had changed them. What h
could not understand was the bleakness with which the
lived. Yes, the influenza epidemic had robbed them of tw
children, and yes, they had struggled for their own surviva
but they had made it. Their one grocery store had grown to
chain. They were successful and rich and yet they lived
small, stingy life.

"By the time I was born, my mother was forty-one and m
father, forty-four," John had once told Carolyn. "They wer
old, much older than their years. They did not know how t
enjoy a child. Also, I sometimes think because they had los
two, they withheld a part of themselves from loving me, i
case I, too, should be taken from them. My parents gave m
everything a child could ask for. They just didn't know how t
give of themselves."

When John had confided this to her, Carolyn felt the tear
begin a slow trek down her cheeks. Her own parents ha
loved her so very much that she hurt for John's loss—for hi
not ever having known such family—as well as for her own
She also didn't understand why his parents felt it was foolis
of him to begin anew in California when they had worked s
hard to ensure his future in Rochester, Minnesota, where h
was born. Her own parents had been so different. "See th
stars up there, Lynnie?" her mother had said when she wa
still a child. "There's more than one way to reach them." Sh
had never forgotten that and had remained aware that option
other than acting existed in life.

"I would write if I had something to write about," John ha
once told Carolyn. When he arrived in California directl
from graduation and Notre Dame, he thought Hollywoo

50

ould be his "open book." Two things happened to close that
ook. First, his startling, midwestern, Swedish good looks
orked against him. Hollywood could only see a man as a
riter if he wore glasses, had messy brown hair, and yellow
icotine stains on his fingers. Blonds were actors. Second, "I
ced a typewriter daily until I had to face I had nothing to
ay. Which is why I work at Killerbrew Studios. People like
ou and Margaret give me what to write about. It's safe and
's comfortable. It's taught me a lot."

If John Ollson had thought it proper to discuss such things
ith a lady, he could have told Carolyn of all life at Killerbrew
tudios had taught him. He was twenty when Louis Gardner
red him as a junior publicist, fully aware, although John
as not, that his looks would sell as many stories to the press
s his abilities—if he had any—to write. Gardner, himself
ill a very handsome man at fifty, knew how advantageous
ood looks were to a publicist in manipulating the studio's
lent.

John was a virgin when he arrived in Hollywood, not
nusual for a graduate of the morally chaste and very Catholic
otre Dame. Within his first weeks at Killerbrew Studios, he
iscovered sex was a commodity and that it came in assorted
zes, shapes, and colors. He learned "the lay of the land"
om a nineteen-year-old actress when he accompanied her to
hat was a first interview for both. Afterward, she told him,
You continue to do for me and I'll do you." He was uncer-
in of her meaning until he found her hand in his crotch as
e talked about "cute little items in the trade papers and
nny little stories in the mags." Shocked by her aggressive-
ess, he pulled back from her. Instead of taking offense, the
rl laughed. "Sorry, John. I didn't realize you were one of
e boys."

He hadn't known what she meant, and since he almost
nmediately overcame his shyness and shock, she never both-
red to explain. For a month or more, John did for her and
e . . . did him. By the time she moved up to "bigger
ckings," she had introduced him to several of her girl
iends who found John just about the best castoff in all of
ollywood.

At first, John, yet to graduate from emotional adolescence,
ll in love with each girl who wooed and won him. It took
im nearly a year to understand that sex and love were on
ifferent shelves and on separate shopping lists in Hollywood

51

supermarkets. He learned not to punch Sonny Stevens, tł studio's leading cowboy star, known in the press as a tw fisted, hard-drinking womanizer, when he would become over comradely in the lot's steam room. John soon understood I was a commodity that attracted people without his working it. Many wanted his body, and after the initial reserve ar moral compunctions with women were broken, he gave willingly. Women were the unspoken fringe benefits Killerbrew Studios. Yet, when John became emotionally i volved with Carolyn, he had no desire for other women. Sl was his fantasy; an incredibly beautiful girl who was also lady. From the moment she had thrown her body prote tively over Margaret's, John felt he had found what he w unaware he had been ready for: A girl. A steady. A fiancé His feelings for her increased when he saw she wasn't abo to ask for "favors" or give any.

"John, what do you want from life?" Carolyn sudden asked as she sat down on the warm sand to watch the wav playing tag with the beach.

"What do *you* want?" responded John, borrowing time.

"To be an actress, a wife . . . a mother. To be as happy my mother was. She had it all you know . . . fame . . . love Carolyn had begun to sculpt the sand as she talked. "Sl seemed so certain about things. Nothing about life seemed frighten her."

"Are you frightened, Carolyn?" asked John.

Before Carolyn could respond to John's question, or r member that he had never answered hers, Margaret can striding up the beach.

"All right, you two. You've had enough time together. I' lonely. What are you sculpting, Lynnie?"

"I guess from the shape it's taking, a man," Carolyn ar swered. "In fact, why don't you help us and we'll preten he's Franklin Killerbrew."

"If you think I'm going to sit here with my complexion this afternoon sun and sculpt a six-foot-two replica of Killerbrev you're crazy," said Margaret. "Unless I get to make th private parts."

Carolyn screamed as she threw sand at Margaret.

John simply said, "Well, you can't, Marg. Not unless yo want to be here the rest of the day and halfway into th night."

* * *

As Augusta Monahan poured a steamy bland brew into his teacup, Jerome Siegal pulled a crumpled white handkerchief from his back pocket and mopped his bald head and brow. The agent always perspired when he was nervous.

Augusta resented the man sitting before her. If this is how he was presenting himself to them—in crumpled suit, stained tie, and dirty handkerchief—she assumed this was how he was presenting himself to others. And not just presenting but *representing* HER girls. Augusta Monahan was not pleased by her thoughts about first impressions.

"Lemon?" she asked Siegal, venting her venom in the single sentence of seemingly offered hospitality.

Carolyn and Margaret were seated on the pale blue velvet couch, unmindful and unaware of Siegal's sloppiness. The man had been their father's trusted agent and that was reason enough not to question his abilities. Siegal was uncomfortable in the straight-backed Louis Philippe chair, the velvet sticking to his winter-wool pants. Yesterday's meeting with Franklin Killerbrew was still with him, as his ulcer bore witness. Siegal was used to New York ways where producers and agents *hondled* over chicken soup and chopped liver. But Killerbrew didn't *hondle;* he handled. From behind that oak desk—"the stage at the Little Theatre should be so big" he had joked to either deaf ears or a face that wouldn't or couldn't crack a smile—the *momzer* dictated what he wanted. It was not good. Not good at all. Siegal sighed.

"A petit four, Mr. Siegal?" asked Augusta.

The agent's stomach rose rebelliously at the mere possibility. It was having enough trouble with the *goyish* tea. Shamrock, it was called. Better the Irish should stick to whiskey and leave the tea to the Jews, thought Siegal. Still, not wishing to offend, the agent took one of the cookies and rested it on his saucer. Again, the agent reached into his pocket, produced his handkerchief, and mopped his forehead.

"Are you quite well?" asked Augusta Monahan, somewhat concerned by the agent's obvious distress.

"Frankly, I could be better," said Siegal. "It's true Mr. Killerbrew wants to do business . . . with the *Tiernan Sisters*." Siegal paused and waited for an objection. None was offered. "Killerbrew feels a film starring the Tiernan Sisters would have great appeal at this time." There, he had said it again! Still, there was no reaction. A part of Jerome Siegal, who had known the girls from birth and who had liked

53

Thomas Tiernan as much as he disliked Victoria, wanted to say: "He's buying a sisters' act, not actresses." There were many reasons Siegal did not. The selfish ones were about Norman's college tuition and Ruthie's wedding next spring—both to cost a fortune. And 10 percent of what Killerbrew was offering to capitalize on "The Sisters" was a fortune—far more than what Siegal would have made on the senior Tiernans. One thing you could say in the *momzer*'s favor, though, Siegal, he pays top prices to whore around. And that's what it was about . . . whoring. Killerbrew was offering a one-picture deal with an option for a second to be made within the contract's same calendar year. If the studio exercised its option, the sisters would be paid double what they had received for the first. A fortune!

"And what option do the girls have?" Siegal had asked Killerbrew, already knowing the answer.

"None. I'm paying premium dollar—twice what you'd get down the street at Metro or Warner's—to hold all the cards."

That was true. No novice to *hondling*, Siegal had already put out feelers to the other majors and although several were interested, none were at the figures Killerbrew was offering.

"And just remember, I'm the one taking the gamble," said Killerbrew. "I'm trusting *waifs* are big box office this year. If I'm wrong, I lose a bundle."

"Supposing my clients go for this . . . *deal*," replied Siegal, using the slightest edge of sarcasm that the situation allowed, "and find after the first picture that they do not like working for you. What then?"

"I'd say *you* would have a problem," answered Killerbrew as he swiveled his chair to face the open louvered windows, thus effectively turning his back on Siegal. The gesture was not lost on the man.

"Siegal, take the money and run," said Killerbrew.

"Not so fast," said Siegal to the back of the chair. "I have a few demands."

"Demands!" boomed Killerbrew as he swung around to face Siegal. "Demands?" he repeated threateningly.

Siegal stood his ground. He had thought of a way to sweeten the pot and do some sort of service for his clients. "The girls' aunt, Augusta Monahan, is to be employed by the studio as business manager and secretary. The girls must have a trusted someone to run their home, and your staff will need a liaison to arrange interviews and such. We want two hundred a week."

"One and a quarter and don't even think about it but grab t," said Killerbrew.

"What about script approval . . . choice of director?" asked Siegal.

"Why are you wasting my time?" was Killerbrew's response.

"But what protects my clients' professional reputation?" pleaded Siegal.

Killerbrew rose slowly from his chair and walked from behind his desk to the front where Siegal was sitting. Looking down at the agent he said: "*What* professional reputation? They have none. They're nobodies. Their parents had reputations but they have nothing other than press clippings which *I* arranged, and national sympathy which they lose when a more gory story captures America's fancy. So I repeat: don't think, Siegal. Grab!"

"I gotta tell you," said Siegal to the women as he took another sip of the Shamrock tea to ease his parched throat, "it's not such a hotsy-totsy deal. Another studio would give you—*maybe*—more control. But at much less money."

"Suppose we don't like the script. What then?" asked Carolyn.

"We can ask for changes," said Siegal, knowing they could ask but they wouldn't get.

"But we would have to make the film like it or not," summarized Margaret.

"Essentially, that's correct," said Siegal, wishing the questions or his ulcer would cease pounding at him.

"Mr. Siegal, if the girls returned home, what are their prospects for starring on Broadway?" asked Augusta.

"Unless you know something I don't, not good. My phone hasn't been ringing off the hook asking for them," said Siegal.

"Odd, isn't it?" said Augusta.

"Odd? What's so odd?" said Siegal honestly. "Does the world know if the girls have talent? Who knows anything in this crazy business? Who knows anything in this crazy world anymore? A market crashes and people fly off buildings or in tin toy planes. Don't look for sense, Miss Monahan, when there are only oddities."

"What my aunt meant," said Margaret, "is you would think the same business sense that exists in Hollywood would exist in New York. A freak show is after all a freak show and if money is the question, then Carolyn and I can get up a tour. Play the Palace for beginners. 'See the Waifs, folks.' We'll do a two-a-day and if that's successful, we'll tour the Kenmore circuit. We can do a medley of our tragedies. What can Killerbrew offer us that's better?"

"A shot," said Siegal honestly. "That's the heart of it—shot. If the film works, you'll be names, and not just freaks. That might just make you bankable on Broadway. Who knows. Then, too, let's not forget money," added the agent as he reached into his peeling leather briefcase and withdrew some papers. "As you suggested, Miss Monahan, I talked with your lawyers. These papers tell us what's what. Altogether, the situation is far from too terrible. Worse, I've seen. The house in Murray Hill is willed to the girls, as are all the furnishings. It's free and clear except for taxes and upkeep. You could sell and take a little apartment, but why? Better you should hold on to it for investment purposes, and besides, whatever you'd pay for some little place wouldn't be too much less than your upkeep. There are, however, a few outstanding debts. Nothing serious. In fact, the insurance money will cover that and a little more."

"Just how much more?" asked Augusta, concerned.

"About ten thousand dollars would be left, which means although you're hardly 'waifs,' you're not exactly heiresses either. Not unless there are other monies I don't know about."

"Just the cottage on Nantasket," said Augusta.

"But that's yours, Aunt Augie," protested Carolyn.

"Ours!" corrected Augusta. "I have no idea of its worth but it's a lovely little house and so near the ocean."

"That would bring a nice piece of change," said Siegal.

"But I have no wish to sell," said Augusta, upset at the thought. "It's all I have to leave to the girls."

"Then rent, perhaps?" suggested Siegal.

"Strangers in our home? Oh, no. That's quite impossible. Quite!" Augusta repeated lest Siegal doubt her.

"Which means we now have two houses with two upkeeps and only *one* minor inheritance," said Siegal. "It would seem you will need to work. Therefore, considering everything, I suggest you work at top dollar."

"I could get a full-time job," said Augusta. "I'm sure the hospital would be delighted . . ."

"Miss Monahan," interrupted Siegal, "you already have a job. A very good one, I might add. Providing the girls *do* sign with Killerbrew, I've arranged for you to be employed by the studio in a fairly broad capacity. Nothing very strenuous or demanding but . . . necessary."

As Siegal spelled out specifics, Augusta was reacting. *Earning money* was not something she had been raised to do. Her work for Thomas and Tory, managing their lives, she had never viewed as work per se. Her time at the hospital was also not viewed as work but as dues one paid, and paid happily, for being healthy and privileged. That anyone would deem her services worth one hundred twenty-five dollars a week staggered her. And, she thought, I would be earning it, as the girls do need the very services Mr. Siegal has outlined.

"Thank you, Mr. Siegal," said Augusta, rising to indicate the meeting was over. "We will discuss this among ourselves and let you know within a day of our decision."

"There is nothing to discuss, Aunt Augie," said Carolyn. "We know it, Mr. Siegal knows it, and it would appear Mr. Killerbrew knows it."

"Carolyn, please. Let's not be hasty," urged Augusta.

"She's right, Aunt Augie," said Margaret. "Mr. Siegal, tell 'Killer' he's just been named temporary guardian of two orphans."

Siegal sighed with relief and tried to offer a congratulatory smile. As he raised his teacup to symbolize a toast, he silently asked the big *Macher* upstairs to please make the sisters' first picture as nice an affair as the one he planned now to throw for Ruthie's wedding.

Sidney Barasch received the *order* that Franklin Killerbrew wanted the script done *fast* on November 10, the very day hundreds of press attended the lavish contract-signing party for the Tiernan Sisters at Hollywood's posh Brown Derby restaurant. But Barasch, a recent Brooklyn College graduate who had several "lower Broadway" repertory company successes to his credit, wasn't about to be rushed on his first screenplay for the studio, particularly when he felt the screen treatment was an abomination of clichés. Only meaningful exchanges of dialogue or a miracle can bring this "thing" to life, thought Barasch as he set himself to the task.

Perfectionists did not win points with Franklin Killerbrew, certainly not when time was of the essence—or of the money, thought Barasch when he read Killerbrew's terse memo that chastised him for missing his deadline of December 1. But Barasch had considered the "three-weeks-*tops*" initial order for product unrealistic and had refused to take it seriously. But the tone of this particular memo from Killerbrew made it obvious that if Barasch planned to stay in Hollywood, let alone at Killerbrew Studios, he had best have a final draft on the studio head's desk immediately. Still, Killerbrew did not have a completed script delivered to him until the fifteenth of December, the original start-date posted for the production. It wasn't until a new date of January 2 had been announced to the press that Barasch learned that no further rewrites were expected, a development that distressed him. He had hoped Killerbrew would demand some changes—*anything* that would have borrowed more time for the writer and allowed him to do "further fixing."

Barasch met the Tiernan sisters briefly when the studio celebrated Margaret's eighteenth birthday on the twenty-first of November. In the commissary, Margaret, with the help of every major star on Killerbrew's roster, blew out eighteen candles on a cake of eighteen tiny layers, all covered with roses and whipped cream, as the press photographed the event for publicity and not posterity. Barasch had been surprised that neither of the girls knew who he was. He didn't press the issue or inform them that he was writing their script.

Margaret had hated the "party" Killerbrew had magnanimously given for her. A celebration of any kind was not what she had had in mind this year. But Killerbrew, announcing to the press, "We are her family now," refused to let "the rite of passage into womanhood" go unheralded. So the "small" and "circumspect" party was arranged as was the smile pasted on Margaret's face throughout the afternoon's festivities. But her anger collapsed that evening along with Augusta's cake, which refused to rise to the occasion. The would-be birthday cake leaned more than the Tower of Pisa. Margaret tried to keep a straight face as Augusta, never known for her domesticity, carried it from the kitchen to the living room where the girls and John had just finished dinner. As Margaret fought for her composure, Augusta said, "It's all right Margaret, you can laugh. Lord knows I did." The dam burst. The tension of the afternoon vanished amid roars of laughter. The inside of the cake was no better. It was either half baked or overcooked.

"As the engagement ring I once wore proved, happily, there is indeed a way to reach a man other than through his stomach," quipped Augusta. It was the first time either of the girls had heard Augusta joke about the tragedy, or make any comment that could have been called off-color.

Augusta's birthday party for Margaret set the tone for the holidays. She carried the family through Thanksgiving, during which the absence of Victoria and Thomas was deeply felt, and into Christmas. December was always a happy time for Augusta. Dan Dunahey had proposed and she had accepted on Christmas Eve. Through New Year's, the couple had lived in a whirl of well-wishers and parties. Despite her subsequent loss, Augusta came alive at the season as it brought back joyous, not sad, remembrances. This Christmas Eve, there was yet another sense of Dan Dunahey and that time so long ago. There was another gentleman caller, so to speak, and they all looked at John as if he were already a member of the family. They were awaiting him now as they put the finishing touches on the huge tree they had put up in the far corner of the living room by the window. It was late but John had warned he would probably be detained, as on the eve of the holiday the entire publicity department was expected personally to take gifts from the studio to all the important press who lived in the Hollywood area. A mammoth job.

So accustomed was the front desk at the Marmont to seeing John come and go that they no longer bothered to announce him, and so no one was surprised when he was suddenly there, offering to affix the angel to the top of the tree.

"Not with your shoes on, John," had screamed Augusta. "Not on a Louis Philippe. Better to stand on the girls' shoulders than on a Louis Philippe!"

John had laughed but he had stepped off the chair and removed his shoes before standing on it again to top the tree with its ornament. As he strategically placed the tinsel about the treetop, he said, "I left a goody for you on the table."

"Another present?" asked Carolyn, whose birthday was celebrated on Christmas Eve, a day after the actual event.

"You might say that, but not from me," replied John.

"Well then, from whom?" asked Margaret.

"From your lord and master," said John.

"It's the script!" screamed Carolyn as she dashed to where John had left the three copies he had brought with him. "And there's a memo with it. My God! It says we begin filming January second. It's not possible. What about costume fittings . . . rehearsals . . . meetings with the director?"

Margaret, already sprawled on the floor reading the script,

59

titled *Dust Bowl*, answered, "I don't think you need worry about fittings, Lynnie. As best as I can read, we are dirt-poor farm girls without a pot to pee in."

"Margaret!" boomed Augusta angrily.

"Sorry," said Margaret, faking a contrite look to match her voice. "What I meant was . . . we haven't an indoor toilet in which to pee. Okay? Better? Now how about some quiet so I can read."

Carolyn was still reading *Dust Bowl* when Margaret closed her script and groaned, "Oh, my God!"

"How many times have I asked you not to speak the Lord's name in vain?" snapped Carolyn.

"When you finish reading this, Lynnie-love, you'll be speaking His, Shakespeare's, O'Neill's, and Noel Coward's—*all* in vain."

Minutes later, Carolyn, furious, sat with the script open in her lap, waiting for Augusta and John to finish the one they shared. When they did, she heard Augusta rattle through the desk in the living room. She watched silently as her aunt raced through the Killerbrew contract.

"We have no choice," is all Augusta said as she put down the papers.

"Oh, yes we do!" snapped Carolyn. "We'll go to jail first."

"Speak for yourself," said Margaret, " 'cause I intend to make the most of this garbage."

"As Mother once said: You can't make a silk purse out of a sow's ear," protested Carolyn.

"Our mother would not have known a sow if she stumbled on one. Look, Lynnie, despite this script being personally insulting and offensive, we are actresses and we can pull it off. The fact that the story is tasteless is exactly why Killerbrew had it written. He would say: Of course the heroines of *Dust Bowl* bear an uncanny resemblance to the Tiernan sisters. So? Haven't you ever heard of literary license? It's often a synonym for money in the bank."

Carolyn slumped onto the couch, and as John sat next to her, she reopened the script and once again read the synopsis.

DUST BOWL
Property of Killerbrew Studios
Copyright 1934

Written by
Sidney Barasch

Fred and Elsie Appleton are dirt farmers in Oklahoma. They are poor, but proud and honest people. Although their lives are hard, they do not complain, but are grateful that over the years the poor land they own has given them enough to feed themselves and their daughters, Sara-Jane (Margaret Tiernan) and Sally-Sue (Carolyn Tiernan). Together, the little family has fought famine, flood, and dust storms.

The Depression has ravaged the country and the Appletons work the farm, not for the small profit they had once hoped for, but for the bare necessities of survival. At the start of the film, hunger is shown as Cora, Sally-Sue's cow, dies from starvation. The loss of her friend devastates the young girl. She will miss the cow, and the family, its milk. Soon the chickens begin dropping with their droppings. It's a cold, hard winter in a cold, hard world.

Papa Appleton is old beyond his years. He is bent, but not broken. Elsie Appleton is a frail bag of bones held together by grit and determination. In rain or snow, the couple work the meager land. Often, stragglers, hungry and weak from the Depression, pass through their land. They are never denied the last crust of bread. Until there is nothing more to share . . . not even a turnip.

One afternoon, a darkness settles over the small farm. Papa Appleton goes out to shut the barn door, to protect what's left of the chickens. Suddenly, a windstorm gathers. Dust swirls. He stumbles. The wind and the dust increase. Papa Appleton is knocked senseless by a flying piece of wood. Even as her daughters try to prevent her from doing so, Elsie Appleton gathers a shawl about her and runs into the storm and to her husband. The dust storm gathers in its intensity. From the window of their shacklike house, the girls watch their mother battle the dust and wind until she, too, is lost in the swirl. But then she reappears, holding up her husband. As they make their way back to safety, there is an even greater wind. A huge noise is heard. The barn is collapsing . . . right where the Appletons seem to be.

Sally-Sue tries to rush out the door to help her parents, but she is stopped by Sara-Jane. Sally-Sue is hysterical, crying for her parents. Sara-Jane, too, is crying. She knows her parents are dead as they go out in the storm.

When the storm lifts, a funeral is taking place on the hill. Only a handful have gathered to pay final respects to the Appletons. Sally-Sue holds Sara-Jane in her arms as the baby sister weeps.

The girls return to farm the land. Bills are due, bills they cannot pay. Sara-Jane determines that somehow they will survive; that they will not be humiliated and forced to go to the poorhouse. "God will see us through, Sally-Sue. You'll see," says Sara-Jane.

The girls work long days and many hours on the farm. Their once pitiful smocks are now rags; their once clean hair, matted. A prowler comes to the house and Sara-Jane, although terrified, fires the shotgun and scares him off. Winter is very difficult. The girls huddle by the fire. Sally-Sue catches cold. For days, she languishes by the fire looking wan and sneezing.

Winter rages on. Sara-Jane works the farm herself as Sally-Sue recuperates. Sally-Sue, watching her sister's bent back, leaves her bed before she should. She wanders into the fields to help. The wind exhausts her. She faints. When Sara-Jane finds her, Sally-Sue is nearly frozen, yet burning up with fever.

Sally-Sue has pneumonia. She is at death's door, her lovely little light a mere flicker. Sara-Jane is the strength. She does all the household chores as she also tends to the farm. When they come to foreclose the mortgage, Sara-Jane begs for an additional week's time. Reluctantly, the landowners give it to her.

Sara-Jane scours the countryside looking for any kind of work—washing, mending, cleaning—but there is nothing. Everyone is destitute. Each night she rushes home to Sally-Sue who is fading . . . fading . . . fading. When the mortgage holders return to claim what is legally theirs, Sara-Jane falls to her knees and begs them not to throw them out in the cold. As she begs, beseeches, a halo surrounds the bed. Sally-Sue begins speaking to her mother and father. The delirious girl sees them in heaven. She tells Sara-Jane not to worry about her or the farm, because she is going to the Big Farm in the Sky. Why, she says, she even sees Cora, her cow! Sara-Jane, at her bedside, is sobbing, "Don't leave me, Sally-Sue." But Sally-Sue now sees bacon and eggs—scrambled and sunnyside—and corn pone and grits. "Oh, Sara-Jane, it is so lovely and warm in my new farmhouse," says Sally-Sue, just before she dies in her sister's arms.

The men, devastated, conscience-ridden, look at the devastated land, the meager house, the ravaged Sara-Jane, and give her the mortgage. Sara-Jane, bent, old like her mother was much before her time, goes to the window. A lovely light shines about her. It is the spirit of Sally-Sue. Sara-Jane knows she is not alone; that she will never be alone; that each in her way has survived the storm. Sara-Jane will live as Sally-Sue lives (she can see her now as the bells ring) in heaven.

END

"It's crass and cheap," said Carolyn disgustedly.

"It's Hollywood and you better get that straight," replied John with a vehemence that surprised them all. "I can well understand your being outraged, but I can also understand Killerbrew's thinking. This is a four-handkerchief movie. And the more tears an audience sheds, the more money the next one will spend to have the same crying good time. And I'll tell you something else, the film's got possibilities. If you could divorce yourself from the resemblance to real life, you'd see two corking good roles. Both of you have strong characters with which to chew up the scenery. And if the dialogue still needs work, make it up or call the writer. It happens to be his first screenplay, and I hear he's pretty anxious about it. So I think instead of grousing, you should make it work for you."

Carolyn looked admiringly at John. "Well, Sara-Jane, what do you think?" she asked Margaret.

"That the wrong sister has the right man," replied Margaret.

Carolyn laughed, and then, abruptly, her expression grew serious. "Margaret, I know your feelings, but would you and Aunt Augie attend mass with John and me tonight? It would mean so much. All of us to be together . . . really together on Christmas."

Margaret picked herself up from the floor where she had been half-lying and half-sitting and said simply, "Just give me a minute to get ready." Only Augusta saw the tears in her younger niece's eyes.

"Oh, Marg, I'm never going to say another mean word about you!" said Carolyn as she jumped up to hug her sister.

"In that case, forget it!" said Margaret. "I'm not going to live with someone who's bucking for sainthood and who also has a cow named Cora for a friend."

Sound Stage 7 was the largest on the Killerbrew lot and set designers had turned 35,000 square feet of it into Oklahoma farmland. Dirt, hardened and weathered by heat and drought, lay fallow. The farmhouse, a gray, slanting building of rotted wood, stood near the even more gray and more rotting barn. In the middle was a well, its wooden bucket chipped and hanging precariously from a frayed hemp rope. Chickens, also gray and dusty, cackled about the barnyard. Trees, planted by the studio nursery, used their branches to supplicate water from the heavens.

The interior of the farmhouse was another set of three walls of still more weathered wood. A partition suggested a bedroom while a big brass bed in the "living room" suggested poverty. No sofa or couch here. Just two rocking chairs, the bed, a kitchen table, and some roughhewn shelves. Had the set been on a stage, it would have been home to Carolyn, but surrounded as she was by equipment and men—many standing just feet from her at the camera's side—it was never that. Just another problem. Whereas an audience never distracted Carolyn, the grips, the electricians, the cameramen did. Often, in the middle of her lines, Carolyn would lose her concentration because of the distractions she could not eliminate from her sight.

The first week of filming on *Dust Bowl* was discouraging for Carolyn. Without prior film experience and without rehearsal, she was left to her own devices, many of which would have been perfect for the stage, but were wrong for film. Used to projecting to the back rows of theatres, she was constantly reminded to "cut it in half," "make smaller gestures," and "don't yell!" On her first day of filming, Carolyn decided the ugliest and unkindest words in Hollywood's dictionary were: "Cut!" and "Let's do it again."

Margaret, too, had difficulty on Day One. Hers occurred at 6 A.M., in Makeup, when she found her hair being sheared without her permission. When she protested, she was told

Killerbrew had ordered it—that he wanted her character to have a totally different look from "Sally-Sue." When Margaret looked at the results of the shearing in the mirror, she wailed: "I'm not pretty." To which the makeup man replied, "Listen, sweetie. You're playing Fanny Farm Girl, remember? You're not supposed to be Polly Pretty. No one in Oklahoma is. Pretty is for Hollywood. When it's time for you to be pretty, I'll make you gorgeous."

Unlike Carolyn, Margaret found it easy to pull the scene in—to make everything smaller than you would on a stage. She found herself, without thinking, playing to the camera. She saw no one beside, in back of, or atop it. To her own surprise, she found she liked the short-scene approach to filmmaking. She could focus immediately on who she was and what was happening, and could just as easily forget it when the director called "Cut!" Yes, she agreed with Carolyn, the waits between takes were interminable, but they were also profitable if you used them properly. Which Margaret did. Within a few days, she knew the name and the function of every job on the set. She also learned the names of the men in those jobs. Because she took an interest in them, they took an interest in her. They showed her just how to hold her head, which lighting favored her best side, and how to "look without looking" at the camera during a closeup. Almost immediately Margaret realized that in filmmaking what you presented to the public could be manipulated far more than it could be onstage. All it took was know-how.

Because Franklin Killerbrew did not want the press to see the Tiernan sisters learn by error, *Dust Bowl* was a closed set. All interviews were either at lunch in the studio commissary, or "drinks" after work and before dinner. When requests were greater than the time the girls could spare for interviews, the Killerbrew publicity department supplied the answers, often as if they were Carolyn and Margaret Tiernan. The girls had been taught from childhood to accept the press much the way one would accept the eccentricities of a slightly addlepated relative. Which they did until articles appeared in national magazines and newspapers that put Carolyn's voice to her religious beliefs. So shocked was she by this invasion into her privacy that she personally called Jerome Siegal in New York and told him to make sure the stories stopped.

"I don't want to see one more article that makes it seem I talk to God as often as most actors talk to their agents," she fumed.

When Siegal hesitantly called Killerbrew to voice his client' wishes, the studio head replied: "My money is invested in this film, and good publicity—and any talk about God is good publicity—protects that investment. If Miss Tiernan is upset tell her to pray on it."

The concocted stories continued, but Carolyn's ability to reach Jerome Siegal on the phone did not. The agent was "Out!" said the secretary each time she called and "Yes!" she would have him return her call, which he never did. Thus, to his considerable surprise, Franklin Killerbrew found himself discussing the matter with John Ollson in his office one morning.

"I understand Miss Tiernan's concern, but you and I both know it's a business I run here," said Killerbrew, carefully watching John's face for a reaction.

"Miss Tiernan understands the value of publicity and is willing to do all that's necessary to promote the product, but she insists the articles about her religious beliefs be stopped immediately," said John, his voice as firm as his manner.

"Insists?" said Killerbrew with sarcastic surprise in his voice. "Miss Tiernan *insists*? And by the way, are you speaking for Miss Tiernan or is this a joint statement? As a matter of fact, what the hell are you doing here? Last I looked you were in *my* employ. Don't bother to respond. Just listen. I've got some advice. It's like medicine, Ollson. Take it if you know what's good for your health. Forget Carolyn Tiernan. I don't want my star linked with a publicity hack." Sensing John was about to respond, Killerbrew rolled on. "I'm not asking, but telling you, Ollson. Unless you want a job picking oranges, stay off my property. Yes, the double entendre was intended. The public thinks of Carolyn Tiernan as a luscious young fruit, just ripening and waiting to be plucked. I want every man and boy in America to continue to think he's the one who can pluck her. Got that, Ollson? Pluck her. In case your college education didn't cover that, it's a euphemism.

"Now, you can tell Miss Tiernan since she finds those stories so deeply distressing, I'll have them stopped. But also tell her, if I hear so much as a whisper about what studio hack and future star were seen putting their bare asses in cement at Grauman's Chinese, you're through out here. Now beat it."

When John stood his ground, his eyes fixed on his

Killerbrew knew he did not have all the facts and thus was not holding all the aces.

"You got hearing problems? I said get out," barked Killerbrew. When John didn't move, he sighed with resignation. "Okay, Ollson, it seems you're going to make some kind of grandstand play, undoubtedly a costly one, so get on with it."

"I'm no longer in your employ—I resigned this morning," John began. "But we still have to do business with one another."

"I don't have to do business with you," interrupted Killerbrew. "You're just some little shit off the farm."

"I'm also the Tiernan sisters' manager and all major decisions regarding their careers have been turned over to me. And that includes publicity and publicity tours. I strongly urge—I don't give advice, Killerbrew—that you do business with me, if you want the girls to do any publicity whatsoever. If you'll check the contract *you* imposed on them, nowhere is there a clause that states the girls must do anything but make your movies."

"What do you want?" said Killerbrew, who did not remember the specifics of the contract, but who knew from John's attitude that he had the facts straight.

"You're going to hire me at the same salary I was earning to arrange important, key interviews for the girls," said John, still staring directly at his former boss.

"I have a staff for that," said Killerbrew, meeting his new adversary's eyes.

"The girls will no longer listen to your staff," replied John evenly. "Let me add that I fully intend to work for the money you pay me—for the girls' sake and not yours. Let's be clear about that. I will consider every request your publicity department submits to me. I will not arbitrarily turn down anything that seems reasonable. I will also personally try to secure magazine breaks to coincide with the opening of the film."

"Goddamn, Ollson, but you must be a pretty good lay to have arranged all this for yourself!" said Killerbrew sarcastically.

"Get two things straight," said John in the same even tone with which he had been speaking. "I did not arrange this for myself, and . . . if ever you make such a reference to Carolyn Tiernan again, I'll kick your teeth down your throat or die in the attempt."

"Good God, it's love!" said Killerbrew, not at all threatened. "Only love could make a man behave like such an asshole. Listen, kid," said Killerbrew, accenting the "kid," "as they say in films, I like your style. You ever get tired of your new job, give me a call. I think we can do business."

John smiled. As he prepared to leave, Killerbrew said, "Hey, John, a favor for an old studio owner's sake. Keep away from Miss Tiernan when the press is around. You've been in this business long enough to know it really isn't good for the picture right now. You understand?"

John nodded that he did and left, leaving Killerbrew smiling in appreciation at a style he had seen only once before. About ten years ago. And in this very office. It resulted in an old man's eventually shooting himself in his left temple and his becoming head of Blanchard Pictures. But that was the end of the comparison.

Carolyn Tiernan would have preferred to lunch in the relaxed comfort of the dressing room the studio had designed to her specifications, but Margaret wouldn't hear of it.

"What's the matter? Don't you like costume drama?" asked Margaret, referring to the cowboys, Indians, dance hall girls, mobsters, and Vikings that shared the tables with them at the commissary. Like it or not, Carolyn accompanied her sister, and like other actresses on the lot, wore her makeup and film attire into the huge dining room, filled with the rattle of plates and the aromas of tuna and chicken salad.

It was not the costumes but the drama that bothered Carolyn. As soon as she and Margaret set foot into the commissary, the men acted as if they had come center stage. "Why do men carry on so?" she whispered one particular attention-getting day to Margaret.

"Worry only when they don't," was Margaret's response.

It was Carolyn's beauty and disinterest that interested the producers, directors, writers, and actors who traipsed by their table, each with an opening line that sounded different, but whose meaning was the same. They came to call on Carolyn, but they stayed to make merry with Margaret, who was not shy, or hesitant to express herself. Nor was she cheap. Margaret just *was*, which made her most uncommon in Hollywood.

Carolyn envied her sister's ease with men. But not Augusta Monahan, who frowned on "such shenanigans." Augusta had yet to accept her girls were women and she tended to act the maiden aunt more often than it pleased her. Still, she had to laugh when she broke up Margaret's and one young man's ardor by turning to her niece and saying rather loudly, "Drink your milk, dear. We do want you growing up with strong and healthy bones, don't we."

As the actor slinked off, Margaret hissed, "Do you know who you just chased away? Do you? Do you?"

"I do believe the young man said his name was Leon Errol," replied Augusta.

"No!" Margaret fumed. "It was *Flynn*. Errol Flynn. Just the most attractive man in all of Hollywood, that's all."

"Pity," said Augusta. "But maybe he'll wait until you grow up."

Augusta Monahan may have been the only one who didn't realize Margaret Tiernan *was* "grown up." Certainly the men on the Killerbrew lot knew it and had word not come down from above to "lay off and not lay" the sisters, Margaret would have been besieged with offers. But no one questioned the word from On High unless he was dumb or deaf. Donald Malloy was neither. He just wasn't a good listener. From the time the big, burly Irishman had seen Margaret on the set, his interests were aroused. Margaret would finish a scene and look up to find the electrician watching her. She liked that. The way his eyes took in her body made her feel fuller, as if her breasts were larger and her figure more round than it was. She was, therefore, not at all surprised when Malloy worked his way into her dressing room one evening on the pretext of checking its ventilation system. But she was surprised when Malloy came right to the point.

"Are you going to go out with me or not?" he asked abruptly, his hands on his hips, a gesture that seemed to defy her to say no.

"Are you asking me for a date?" asked Margaret cordially.

"A date!" repeated Malloy dumbfounded. "You mean one of those *things* where you go bowling?"

"Or to a movie," said Margaret, unaware she was being mocked.

"Gee! A movie," sneered Malloy. "Wouldn't that be neat. But tell me, little girl, why would a man who works in the movies want to go see one, particularly when he thinks they're pretty dumb stuff to begin with. And at twenty-six, I'm just a little old to sit and hold hands in the balcony."

"I don't hold hands on a first date," said Margaret, now giving back in kind what she had been receiving. "And I certainly don't sit in the balcony. Heights give me nosebleeds."

"And my skin burns badly in the sun, so don't suggest a beach party or a picnic either," said Malloy.

"My only suggestion is that you leave. It seems I've made a terrible mistake for which I do apologize," said Margaret as grandly as what was left of her dignity would allow.

Had it been at all like the recent movies Margaret had seen, the redheaded pug-nosed Irishman would have taken two giant steps, swept her into his muscular arms, and crushed his lips to hers. Instead, he opened her dressing room door and was halfway out when he turned to say: "We both made a mistake. See you 'round, *kid.*"

"Damn!" spat Margaret as Malloy closed the door behind him. "He gets the exit line and I get the egg on the face. Who the hell wrote this scene?" Embarrassed and angry, she muttered: "I'm going to break him!" Hearing herself, Margaret laughed. "I *must* stop seeing those Bette Davis movies. They're doing terrible things to my head."

"You're never satisfied. I would have thought you'd be *thrilled,*" chirped Augusta Monahan, although she was well aware her niece was not. "All those months of complaining and now you finally have a date and you're still not happy. Truly, Margaret, you confuse me."

Margaret glowered at her aunt and refused to answer.

"She's just nervous," offered Carolyn as she brushed Margaret's hair. "It's not every day a girl gets to go out with one of America's most adored men. . . ."

"Boy!" corrected Margaret. "He's eighteen. A *boy.*"

"Why, most girls in this country would give their right arm to be out with that cute Bucky Denton. Aunt Augie's right," said Carolyn somberly. "You are a most confusing girl."

"If the two of you are *quite* through with your little jokes, you may stay. If not—git! I've enough to contend with without listening to you being mean," said Margaret.

"Nervous, dear?" said Augusta sweetly.

"Oh, no. Me? Nervous? Don't be ridiculous. Just because this is my first premiere, and my date is some child I've never met before, and there will be hundreds of celebrities, and hundreds more of press, why should I be nervous?"

It had been Franklin Killerbrew's idea that Margaret be

70

seen on the arm of Bucky Denton, the studio's gift to the mothers and daughters of America. That they would be photographed together was exactly what Killerbrew had in mind. He could see their young, eager faces smiling from fan magazine covers for months to come. Great preopening publicity for *Dust Bowl*. Wardrobe, under very specific orders from Above, selected a gown befitting the occasion and "a vestal virgin," complained Margaret as she tried it on.

The white formal had a gathered waist, little puff sleeves, and a pink velvet sash that tied into an enormous bow around Margaret's middle and then fell to the floor. "Perfect!" declared John, whose consent for Margaret's appearance had to be obtained before the studio could arrange the "date." When Margaret groaned, he had added, "It was you who asked me about a blind date, wasn't it?"

Carolyn was taking a consoling tone. "You look gorgeous. I'd be jealous if I didn't have this silly prejudice against boys with oily skin and acne."

"Carolyn," said Margaret, turning from the full-length mirror to face her sister. "Remember how I promised to buy one of your rotten apples when you're a broken, little old lady? Well, forget it! You can starve for all I care."

The doorbell ended further conversation. From the hallway, Augusta was calling. Carolyn accompanied Margaret to the door.

"Oh, I forgot one thing," said Margaret as she turned back toward the bedroom. She returned a minute later, a triumphant grin on her face.

"Margaret Tiernan, you cannot wear that red cape!" screamed Carolyn.

"You wanna bet?" responded Margaret as she flew out the door.

The limousine was waiting. As the chauffeur assisted her into the studio's Duesenberg, Margaret extended her gloved hand to Bucky Denton, who grasped it as he helped her into the back seat of the car. It wasn't until she was settled that Margaret realized there was another person seated next to Denton. "Why, Mr. Gardner. What a surprise," she said to the publicity head.

"Miss Tiernan . . . a pleasure," replied Gardner. "Mr. Killerbrew thought it best I be along to help manage you through the press and crowds," he gratuitously explained.

Bucky Denton was fidgeting. Sweat lined his upper lip and

his hands were shaking. Margaret thought it endearing that America's biggest young star still was nervous at premieres.

"My mother used to say six deep inhalations and six total exhalations help," she whispered to Denton who looked at her as though she were mad. "Really. Breathe!" she urged. When Denton neither breathed nor replied but stared straight ahead, Margaret turned her attention from the rude boy to Hollywood Boulevard. As the limousine passed one movie theatre after another, Bucky Denton's shakes became audible as well as visible.

"Come on, Mr. Gardner. Let me have some now," he said in an almost pleading manner.

Gardner checked the car's position and noted the Pantages Theatre, with its klieg lights and commotion, was just ahead. Reaching into the breast pocket of his satin-trimmed tuxedo, he withdrew a silver flask which Denton grabbed for upon sight. Calmly, Gardner slapped the boy's hands away. He then unscrewed the metal top, tilted it toward Denton's lips, and watched as the boy drank. When Gardner barked "Enough," Denton, tears running down his cheeks, settled himself into the cushioned interior of the car, and said to an openmouthed Margaret, "Now how many did your mother say to do?"

"Six in and six out," she responded trancelike as the car came curbside.

Suddenly the door to the Duesenberg was flung open. As a gloved hand reached in, Denton edged back farther into his seat.

"Go, Bucky," said Gardner calmly.

The hand lifted Denton to the street where his appearance was greeted with screams. As he waved to the crowd piled into bleacher seats, Denton flashed his most winsome and heart-grabbing smile—duly noted, of course, by the press. He then reached into the limousine for Margaret, whose appearance caused the "Oohs!" of delight rather than the "Ahs!" of desire that had greeted Denton. As the couple walked to the front of the theatre where the premiere was being broadcast to America, the crowd applauded. A microphone was thrust in Denton's face. After he had said a few words, the interviewer turned to Margaret.

"And Miss Tiernan, isn't this your first premiere?"

Before she could answer, the host replied to his own question. "Hollywood is very exciting for a young star, isn't it?"

"More than you can imagine," replied Margaret, thinking of what had just taken place in the car.

"Well, you two kids, the picture is about to start, so why not go in, and have a wonderful time," said the interviewer as he thrust his microphone into the face of the next star who was dutifully making an appearance.

The film was a typical "confessional": the nice-girl-gone-wrong-who-must-pay-for-her-sins story. Margaret would have been bored into a nap had she not been busy fighting off the below-the-waist grabs of America's boy next door.

"Would you stop that!" she whispered loudly in his ear.

Stunned, the boy asked plaintively, "Do you really mean that?"

"I most certainly do!" Margaret responded angrily.

"Thank God!" sighed Denton, and promptly relaxed in his seat where, within minutes, he was fast asleep.

Carolyn tried, but eventually she couldn't suppress a giggle.

"You wouldn't think it funny had it been you," said Margaret testily. "And to add insult to injury, just guess what those damn seats in the theatre were covered with. Right! Green wool plush."

That did it. Carolyn collapsed on the bed and rolled about on its quilted coverlet, screaming with laughter. It was just after midnight and she had waited up despite an early morning call on the set to hear about Margaret's evening. "Please," pleaded Carolyn, "you're making my stomach hurt." When she had finally regained her composure, Carolyn offered: "Well, at least you weren't bored."

"It is rather difficult to be bored when a man is trying to get his hand up your dress," said Margaret caustically.

"Not a man but a boy. And a boy with a drinking problem," said Carolyn softly. "It's really sort of sad. It sounds as if he also has a problem with sex."

"Carolyn, you said the word!" said Margaret, feigning shock as she jumped up on the bed. "Oh, my heart!" she said as she let herself topple down in dead-man fashion onto the mattress. "I have lived to see Saint Carolyn the Pure admit there is such a thing as sex."

"Yes, the mighty have fallen," said Carolyn with a faint smile.

"Oh, yeah?" said Margaret, now wide awake. "Just how far?"

As Carolyn pulled down the quilted coverlet and edged into the bed, separated from Margaret's by a nightstand, she said softly, "Not very. Just far enough to see how close heaven is to hell."

"Now what's that supposed to mean?" asked Margaret, truly curious.

Carolyn's response was to turn off the nightlight, throwing the room and her sister into the dark.

Margaret was not surprised to find Malloy sprawled over the three steps leading up to her trailerlike dressing room. Although neither had acknowledged the other's presence on the set in the two weeks that had passed since their first encounter, they were aware of each other. Margaret would often find her eyes searching for him in the darkness just beyond the cameras. Just as often, she would find him staring at her.

The lopsided grin he wore disproved that anything unpleasant had occurred between them. "Hey, kid, can I buy you an ice cream cone? I got my allowance today," he asked.

"Give me ten minutes and I'll take chocolate," replied Margaret. A doff of Malloy's cap said he would wait. But why, he wondered. What the hell was he doing with a part-prissy, part-prim, but *all* virgin?

Malloy was not a man who thrived on *the* hunt or *the* challenge. Quite the opposite. He wanted his women to be eager bedmates. Since he had turned sixteen, they were. Sex to Malloy was like a good steak and brew: there to be enjoyed. If a woman preferred cottage cheese and skim milk, count him out!

Margaret's hands would not be still. Even as she ran a brush through her cropped hair, they shook. Applying fresh makeup required using one hand to steady the other. Finally dressed in the brown skirt and pink silk blouse she had worn to the studio that morning, she decided it was much too everyday. Desperate, she knocked on the door that connected hers and Carolyn's dressing rooms.

"Loan me a dress," said Margaret when Carolyn appeared in the doorway.

"What are you talking about? I only have the dress I'm wearing," said Carolyn.

"It'll do fine. Come in here and give it to me," said Margaret as she pulled her sister into the room and began to

74

undo the hooks at the back of her dress. "And your stockings. And oh my God, your shoes. Mine are low heels."

"Margaret, you know you can't wear my shoes. They're too small for you. Now will you stop this and tell me what's going on?" demanded Carolyn.

"No time. Just hurry."

"May I keep my underwear?" said Carolyn testily as she stood in a pile of paraphernalia.

"Yes, you may. I do not believe things will go *that* far on a first date," teased Margaret as she slipped into her sister's marine-blue jersey dress. The cream pumps were a problem. "I think I'll die," complained Margaret.

"Wear your own then," snapped Caroline as she stepped into Margaret's skirt.

"I'd rather die," said Margaret. She turned and pirouetted in the full-length mirror by her makeup table. "Ooo, I'm kind of cute, don'tcha think?"

"Margaret, I insist on knowing where you're going and with who," said Carolyn vehemently as she buttoned up Margaret's blouse.

"It's with a who*m* and who*m* is none of your business, but if you must know, it's with Donald Malloy . . . the electrician. Now you hold it right there, Carolyn. You just put those words right back where they came from and close your mouth," cautioned Margaret. "He is buying me an ice cream cone. That's all. Now be a good little girl and go back to your room. And Carolyn," added Margaret as she eased her sister out of her dressing room and back into her own, "you really must do something about your clothes. That skirt and blouse you're wearing are so . . . well, plain, dear. Really plain."

Margaret closed the door between the two rooms and then quickly opened it again. "Don't forget to tell Aunt Augie I'll be a little late," she hollered at Carolyn's back. The door closed again. Margaret took a last look at her reflection in the glass and spoke to it lovingly. "Be calm, Miss Margaret. Just be calm."

Margaret was more than just surprised when Malloy's beaten-up '31 Plymouth roadster pulled up before C. C. Brown's on Hollywood Boulevard. So he had really meant ice cream cones! Disappointed, she waited for Malloy to walk around the car and open the door for her. After a very long time he finally did. "Do that again and you'll find yourself sitting on your ass for the evening," he grumbled.

"You are no gentleman," she replied.

"Then we're even 'cause you ain't quite a lady yet either," he countered.

Although she briefly waited, it soon became apparent that Malloy was not about to open the door to Brown's for her either. "That's all horseshit," he explained as a waiter showed them to one of the many highly polished wooden booths. "What's wrong with your arms that you can't open doors for yourself?"

She was considering this when the waiter handed her a menu that featured so many flavors served in such a variety of ways that Margaret was embarrassed to order a plain chocolate soda with chocolate ice cream. She was delighted when Malloy ordered something more exotic—a "black-and-white" was what she heard—but was disappointed to see when it arrived that it was merely vanilla ice cream in a chocolate syrup base.

"You look nice," was all he said to her as they ate in otherwise silence.

"So do you," she replied, even though he had not changed from his workman's overalls and the matching gray jacket he wore on the set.

That killed further conversation. The two sat staring at their ice cream, treating it as though it were the most fascinating object on earth, and doing everything, but failing, to avoid one another's eyes. When Malloy drove her back to the Chateau Marmont it was Margaret who broke the silence with: "Aren't you going to kiss me good-night?"

"You did it again, dammit," fumed Malloy. "Took the goddamn initiative. Look, girlie, when I want to kiss you, I'll tell you. Girls don't ask, they wait."

"Why, you hypocrite! You . . . you . . . phony baloney," she sputtered. "The hell I'll wait! If I can open my own goddamn door then I can ask for my own goddamn kiss!"

Malloy's anger dissolved into laughter. "Well, I guess you can at that," he said as he reached across the door and pulled Margaret into his arms. His mouth pressed to hers.

"Shit! Didn't anyone ever teach you how to kiss?" he said disgustedly.

"Matter of fact, no," said Margaret thoughtfully.

"Well," said Malloy with a grin. "Come here, gorgeous. Class is starting and teacher here is going to teach you all he knows."

Their second date found conversation flowing easily from the moment Margaret met Malloy in the studio parking lot, and slid into the front seat of the Plymouth. "How was your day?" he asked.

"You should know; you were there. How did it look to you?" she answered.

"You interested at all in how electrical currents work?" he responded. When Margaret shook her head that she wasn't, Malloy said, "That's how I feel about acting. To me, there's nothing dumber than a bunch of grown-ups acting like children. Now don't take it personally; it's just how I feel. So why am I working in pictures, you want to know. Right? Money. That's why. When I got to California, I had been bumming around the country for two years. I had left Philadelphia at sixteen knowing a little about a lot. I was always good with my hands. I got that from my old man. He built things for people. Just like a carpenter only he didn't know shit about slide rules or levels. He worked by instinct. Same as me. Me, when I got here, didn't have a dime. But I was always good at sniffing out odd jobs—never had to stay at no flophouses either—and one odd job led to one oddball after another, all of whom worked in pictures. And one of them guys introduced me to some big shot at Killerbrew Studios and the rest I did for myself. Went to electrician's school, got a state license, and here I am."

"And where is that?" said Margaret.

"Living the good life. I have a nice little house that I've fixed up on Hilldale—nothin' grand, mind you, just someone's converted garage—but it's all mine. I live alone now and like it."

"What do you mean *now*?" asked Margaret.

"You got good ears, little girl," said Malloy. "I mean I had a wife, but I don't anymore. Which only proves there is a God."

Twenty-six *and* divorced. The family would really be thrilled, thought Margaret.

"How old are you?" asked Malloy suddenly. "I mean . . . how old are you *really*? I know what the studio says you are but . . . I mean . . ."

"I'm eighteen and three months," said Margaret.

"Oh, Christ!" groaned Malloy. "It's true? You're that young? Jesus Fucking H. Christ!"

77

"My, but you do have a way with words, don't you?" she chided as the car parked before the Pacific Dining Car, Malloy's favorite steakhouse. "I dare say you could sweet-talk a girl into most anything."

They had come directly from the studio. She had not seen the Hollywood Bowl before and since it was March and the air still quite cold, particularly for California, they were the only people there at the twilight hour. Happily, Malloy had thought to take a blanket. He had wrapped it around them both and as they sat huddled together under its woolen warmth, they watched the sun set beyond the chaparral-covered hills that surrounded the sixty-acre amphitheatre. Had anyone observed them, they could not have seen Malloy's hand under Margaret's sweater massaging her breast. Her nipple was hard, she realized, as hard in its small way as his penis was in its large way. Her hand was resting comfortably atop his lap and she could feel the heat of his groin through the thickness of his dungarees. It was such a beautiful night, thought Margaret; and Malloy was such a beautiful man. Together, she and he did such beautiful things. For the first time since that day in September, Margaret was happy.

It was not Augusta Monahan's way to "drop in" unannounced and uninvited. That kind of informality she deemed rude more than she did improper. Thus, when Margaret answered the knock on her dressing room door and unexpectedly found her aunt standing there, grim-faced, she instantly understood this was no I-happened-to-be-in-the-neighborhood visit. Reluctantly, she stepped aside and let Augusta in.

Augusta was nervous more than she was angry. It went against her Bostonian background to intrude on anyone's privacy. Margaret was, after all, eighteen. Still, Augusta had reasoned, I have accepted a responsibility and it doesn't end with a chronological number. Margaret is away more than she is at home and always with the most unlikely excuses. Time to end the subterfuge. If there was a boy involved, Augusta wanted to know it.

"It will be a relief to have this out in the open," said Margaret, pretending an assurance she was not feeling.

"For you, perhaps," said Augusta. "I'm not so certain there isn't a grain of truth to the proverbial ignorance is bliss."

"If you believed that, you wouldn't be here," countered Margaret.

"True enough," admitted Augusta. "So then, formalities concluded, you're hardly ever home and you say it's because you're doing interviews which I discover don't exist; so . . . who is he?"

"Aunt Augie, I'm not a child. I'm eighteen . . . a woman," said Margaret, her defiant face, thought Augusta, a mirror of her mother's at her age.

"Margaret, age does not a woman make," she replied, suddenly aware both were still standing but feet away from the door.

"I'm involved," said Margaret, choosing her words carefully. When Augusta did not respond, she added, "I am being *intimate*. With a man, not a boy."

"Ah, that it should be intimacy. Is it, Margaret?" asked her aunt.

"We're *fucking* if that's what you mean," replied Margaret, purposely using the word to elicit a particular response which didn't come. Augusta neither shook nor seemed faint.

"Margaret, my dear," began Augusta sweetly. "If you really think 'fucking,' as you so quaintly put it, is intimacy or that it makes you a woman, then, my dear, you are, in a word, 'fucked.' The lowest form of animal life knows how to . . . shall we say 'fornicate,' now that we've mutually impressed one another with our sophistication? It's how one does it I think that makes one a woman."

Margaret was upset. She sat down heavily on the blood-red upholstered couch and clutched her Raggedy Ann doll to her breast. The picture made Augusta want to laugh and cry. The baby, *her* baby now, insisting she was a woman, a woman clutching a doll in a dressing room she had demanded to decorate herself. Blood red were the furnishings—"for passion," Margaret had explained—and black—"for the aura of mystery"—were the walls. Dramatic, it was, Augusta granted. But comfortable? Only if you were viewing it from the tenth row of the orchestra in some theatre.

"If you've come here to make me feel guilty, let me tell you Carolyn has already tried and failed," began Margaret. "I don't believe in good girls and bad girls. But I do believe, because I know, that being with a man makes me feel good. About *me*. Together, *we* make me feel good. About me. Can you understand that?"

79

Augusta could, and did. "I do hope he loves you," she said after a brief silence. "It is so much better that way, but then you'll discover that for yourself one day if he doesn't. Margaret, I didn't come here to lecture on your moral virtues or lack of same. Well, maybe I did, now that I think about it. I do not like lies. Deception, between those who love each other, is unnecessary. I am not going to pretend I am thrilled you are engaging in adult activities. Forgive me that. It's a quirk of us adults. We continue to see our children as children and pay little mind to chronological age. But why pretend? Why should either of us lie to the other? That is what makes for ugliness."

"I didn't think you'd understand. He's divorced, which seems to have posed grave problems for Carolyn although it poses none for me. And . . . he's twenty-six. I was certain you'd object to the fact that he is so old," said Margaret.

"I know you'll find this hard to believe, Margaret, but twenty-six is not old," replied Augusta. "Actually, as I remember—and we senile folks of forty do have such trouble remembering—twenty-six is quite young. So, I want you to bring him home. I want him to pick you up at *your* house and return you from whence you came. I will not have you sneaking about. Shame is such an uneasy partner to live with. And now that that's settled I want to know what precautions you're taking."

"Precautions?" echoed Margaret vaguely, her pose of confidence now a thing past.

"Oh, good Lord! Margaret, you do know how to prevent pregnancy, don't you?" asked Augusta.

"I think Donald is taking care of everything," replied Margaret, but not certain that he was.

Augie wanted to clutch her child/woman/niece to her breast. "Margaret, dear, I think we'd best visit a doctor and have you talk to him about birth control. A woman, Margaret, a *grown* woman, never lets a man take care of everything."

Margaret nodded her head in understanding. As she did, tears splashed onto her face. Augusta, feeling somewhat teary herself, sat next to her niece and put an arm around her shoulder. Margaret took her aunt's hand. "You know, Aunt Augie, I love you. I always have." Augie nodded that she knew. "You really are such a peach!" High praise, indeed, thought Augusta. "But tell me," said Margaret as she looked up and into her aunt's eyes. " 'Shame is such an uneasy

80

partner to live with.' Where the hell did you ever get a line like that?"

"I do believe it was 'Ma Perkins,' " said Augusta seriously. "But then again, it could have been Mae West."

One hour later, Augusta Monahan found herself in the front seat of a beat-up 1931 Plymouth Roadster watching Sunset Boulevard fly by as they drove home to the Chateau Marmont.

Father Parsons rose from the stately stiff-backed chair behind his cluttered mahogany desk and greeted Carolyn. As he took her hand, he felt it cold in his. There were distress lines about her eyes, and her cheeks seemed more drawn than they had been at other meetings. There was, he decided, a lackluster look that he had never associated with this child.

"Do you wish to confess, my child?" he asked when Carolyn had removed her light cotton coat.

"No, Father. I mean, yes, but not immediately. Could we talk first? I called, because I must have someone to talk to. May I sit down?"

"Of course, my child," answered Father Parsons, indicating with a wave of his hand that she seat herself in the wing chair near his desk.

"My sister is having relations with a man . . . a divorced man" (*"You must pray for her soul."*) "and I find I am judging her." (*"Judge not lest ye be judged."*) "Yet I envy her" (*"Envy can be a mortal sin."*) "because she is not troubled."

Whereas I am, thought Carolyn as she dimly heard the priest intone: "Forgive her, Lord, for she knowest not what she does." Not true, thought Carolyn. Margaret indeed "knowest" what she does and what's more she is happy. Why her and not me? It wasn't the prospect of marriage to John that was frightening or disturbing. It was the interim, the now. Often what began as a casual kiss between two people became something quite different with very different people. Who was that man who would push his face in her breasts, moan as he turned his head from side to side, biting and nibbling at her nipple through the cloth of her dress? And who was that girl who would grow breathless and *wet!* At first, she had been frightened by John's erection. How could something so big possibly enter her? But now, her fear had turned to curiosity and she found often that without wanting

81

to, she was thinking of *it* and John and those two different people.

John never pushed her or pleaded for further explorations. But God help her, sometimes she wished he would. At a certain point in their kissing, he would reach into his pocket, extract a handkerchief, and place it over his erection. Carolyn, her eyes closed as she kissed John, would sense from his breathing and the rhythmic rocking of his body that something was happening. She wanted to look but was afraid.

"Miss Tiernan, was there something else?" said Father Parsons interrupting Carolyn's chain of thought.

"What I mean is . . . I think I am judging Margaret because she is doing what I would like to do." (*"Say ten Hail Marys and ask for God's forgiveness."*) "His forgiveness for what? That's my confusion. Shouldn't my passions be aroused by the man I love, the man I intend to marry?" (*"My child, perhaps you would feel more comfortable in the confessional?"*) "But there is nothing to confess. I want to make love with John. I have these feelings. . . ." (*"You must pray. You must ask God to take these impure thoughts from your heart."*) "But why are these thoughts not impure once you are married?" (*"You must ask the Lord to give you strength."*)

Carolyn looked at the priest whose eyes were shut. His hands were folded on his chest and his lips were moving, mouthing words at her. He went on preaching as she gathered her things, slipped on her coat, and walked to the door. Had it not been for the tiny sound of the latch clicking into place as the door closed, he would not have known Carolyn Tiernan had left.

"Marg, I've got to talk to you."

Margaret was about to say no, that she would listen to no more lectures about Donald Malloy, when she caught a glimpse of Carolyn's tear-streaked face. "Lynnie, what is it?" she asked, running toward her sister, in the process dropping the book she had been reading.

"I'm frightened," cried Carolyn. "I'm so frightened." It was as if a plug had been pulled. Carolyn collapsed sobbing in Margaret's arms, the tears drowning out the words she was trying to speak in explanation. In the bathroom, Margaret dampened a washcloth and cooled Carolyn's face with it.

When her sister was finally composed, bedded down for the night in her Chinese silk pajamas, Margaret sat on the edge of her bed and said, "If all this is because you just saw a rough-cut of *Dust Bowl* and we stink in it, we should both be packing instead of you lying and me sitting here."

Carolyn giggled. "No, it's nothing as important as that. It's about sex. At least I think it's about sex. Marg," said Carolyn, her voice beginning to waver again, "does anything happen to you . . *down there* when you and Donald are . . . I mean . I'm not sure but something might be wrong with me. I get sticky . . . wet . . . when John touches me. Do you know? I mean could I have an infection and . "

"Lynnie, that happens to *all* women. It's supposed to. It helps," said Margaret.

"Helps?" said Carolyn, confused.

"You're going to make me explain this whole thing, aren't you? The Birds and the Bees by Margaret Tiernan. Boy, what a spot to be in!" complained Margaret good-naturedly. "Oh well, maybe it's fair. You did teach me to roller-skate and ride a bike.

"Now listen carefully 'cause I think I can only get through this once. For sex to be comfortable, nature has provided a woman with a natural lubricant. Hey, how's that for a classy choice of words? Anyway, this lubricant makes it easier to accommodate the man when he enters her."

"Does it hurt?" asked Carolyn as her fingers played with the edges of the quilted comforter.

"Only at first and then, no," answered Margaret. "You know, Lynnie, the best way to learn about life is to live it."

"Oh, I couldn't!" said Carolyn. "That's the problem, too. I can't. I just can't. It goes against everything I was taught."

"But Lynnie, this is 1935! Nobody believes anymore in the old saving-it-for-the-wedding-night."

"I think I do. Maybe it's hypocritical—I mean if you want to do it but don't, maybe it's the same thing. Maybe the thought or the desire is as sinful as the act."

"It isn't sinful, Lynnie. It's natural," said Margaret. "Like what happens to your body is natural. It was designed to do that. Do you think your body knows whether it is married or not? It just behaves *naturally* as nature intended."

"Ah, that it was so simple," said Carolyn.

"But it is," insisted Margaret. "It is every bit that simple."

"Marg, don't you ever think what you're doing may be a sin against God?" asked Carolyn.

"Not anymore," said Margaret thoughtfully. "If there is a

God, I can't believe He would think lovemaking is sinful."

"Life would be so much easier if only I could share your belief," said Carolyn, her eyes misting again. "All week long what with so much time on our hands now that we're waiting for the Great Man to decide about our futures, I've read, I've read, I even went to see Father Parsons. But even though I can at least *hear* you now, what I hear even more are all the words I was taught ever since I was a child by the nuns, by Mama. I can't change, Marg, and I really don't know if I want to, or that I should. Unlike you, I really do believe, and if it is His will that we do not make love before marriage, then that's what I must do. The conflict is between what I want and what He wants for me."

"And only you can solve that conflict. No one else has the right," said Margaret as she removed her bathrobe and prepared for bed.

"Marg, I've asked you once before, now I'm asking you again, how'd you get so smart?"

"It's like this, Lynnie. This God of yours gave you beauty, so He had to give me something, right? I mean fair is fair," said Margaret as she tucked her sister into bed.

"Marg," said Carolyn, reaching for her hand, "come sleep with me tonight. We'll cuddle like we used to when we were kids. Remember how you used to crawl into bed with me when the thunder would frighten you?" Margaret remembered. She picked up the coverlet and slipped in beside Carolyn. She rested her head on her sister's shoulder and could almost hear the thunder again.

"You know, Marg, you have two things wrong," said Carolyn thoughtfully. "First—and I know you won't believe this now, but someday you will—He is *your* God, too. Second. About your not being beautiful. Marg? Are you listening? Or are you asleep?"

"Listening," mumbled Margaret.

"Then imagine a mirror. Go ahead, imagine a mirror. Now look in it. Take a good look and tell me what you really see."

"A skinny, flat-chested girl whose hair is finally growing back in," mumbled Margaret sleepily.

"Right! But just remember looks aren't everything," said Carolyn, giggling until Margaret's index finger poked her rudely in the ribs.

*   *   *

Franklin Killerbrew, slouched low in his easy chair, his legs propped up on an ottoman, was still staring at a screen that had faded to black minutes ago. Damn but it was good! thought Killerbrew as he hoisted himself out of the cushioned comfort that was specifically nameplated as his. Only the New York critics would hate it, but they hated everything. Then again, the Tiernan name might make them go soft. What the hell, it didn't matter. The film was a winner— provided nothing, and nobody, interfered with its success.

As Killerbrew walked down the deserted hallways of the administration building, he was still marveling at what had taken place on screen. It didn't happen often, but when it did, everyone in town recognized it. Funny how you could never tell who had it and who didn't until he or she got into bed with the camera. Carolyn Tiernan was a beauty. No taking that away from her. A good actress, too. But it was the horsey one who had the magic, who would be a star unless she fucks herself in the process of fucking. Well, fuck her! She's not going to fuck with *my* film. None of her shit is going to hit my studio's fan.

Killerbrew slammed the door to his office. Dorothea Wolfe had left for the day but that didn't disturb him. He could dictate into the Dictaphone what he wanted done. After pouring himself a tumblerful of bourbon, Killerbrew settled into his swivel chair. There were several issues to be considered here, he realized: the immediate potential of *Dust Bowl*, and any other film the studio might make with the sisters if they chose to exercise their option; and the long-range potential of the star for that very same studio if the situation was manipulated properly.

The immediate problem was the possibility of scandal; great for newspapers, but lousy for movies. I don't need the Legion of Decency camped on my doorstep. "Miss Wolfe, it is eight P.M. Wednesday evening. I want the following memo attached to the synopsis of *A Prince Awaits*, to be on all department heads' desks Friday morning."

Killerbrew clicked off the machine and picked up the bound copy of the script on his desk. Originally he had hoped to borrow Bette Davis from Warner's and team her with Bruna Hass, the studio's hope for another Dietrich or Garbo, but Hass, in her first product for Killerbrew, proved what was "big" in Germany was called "fat" in America. Her bust— figuratively and literally, thought Killerbrew, smiling—hardly mattered as Davis after reading *A Prince Awaits* had a few choice words for it—none of them good.

Davis was unreasonable, Killerbrew thought then and now. *Prince* wasn't meant to be good. Just commercial. A field day for the actresses and their audiences. America loved costume dramas as did every studio in town who could redress old sets and touch up even older costumes with some feathers, ribbons, and gauze. Everything could be made to look like new. Except the script.

Killerbrew fingered through the pages of his daily diary. If *Prince* started in three weeks, it could be done in four, maybe five, tops. Six weeks at the most. At a cost of peanuts. It would be product to cash in on the success of *Dust Bowl*, a quickie that could turn a helluva profit. But it all depended on avoiding scandal and moving fast.

Killerbrew clicked on the Dictaphone. "Sorry for the interruption, Miss Wolfe. The memo is to read: '*A Prince Awaits* is the next film to star the Tiernan Sisters. Production is to begin on or about May first with Carolyn Tiernan as the peasant girl and Margaret Tiernan as the princess. You may tell your contacts that a search is on to find our prince and that we are talking to Gable, Cooper, and Flynn, among others. Please keep the story line vague and under no circumstances release this synopsis, except in part.'

"Miss Wolfe, make this next part of the memo an addendum. 'Note: The title of *Dust Bowl* has been changed. Effective immediately, the new title is . . . *Waifs in the Wind*.'

"Finally, Miss Wolfe, tomorrow morning, please call John Ollson and arrange to have Margaret Tiernan in my office sometime on Monday. Alone. If Ollson insists on accompanying her, stress that I will not be pleased. If he persists, acquiesce. Also, make sure on Friday that a hand-delivered copy of my memo to department heads, and the synopsis of *Prince*, is on Ollson's desk at the Tiernans' apartment at the Chateau Marmont. Last, Miss Wolfe, the following letter is to accompany Donald Malloy's paycheck on Friday afternoon. If you are ready. 'Dear Mr. Malloy . . .'"

Before he opened the envelope the Killerbrew errand boy had delivered, John Ollson knew what was inside. He had been preparing Carolyn for what he felt was inevitable: Killerbrew exercising his option to make another film with the sisters. Carolyn refused to consider the possibility. She wanted to go home to New York, back to the life she knew on and off stage.

Ollson knew *A Prince Awaits* had been kicking around Killerbrew Studios for several years and that Bette Davis had once turned it down as had Joan Crawford when she was later offered it. Since the publicity department was rarely given scripts to read prior to production, he was unacquainted with it. Well, best not to keep the prince awaiting too long, thought John as he settled himself into a lounge chair by the Marmont poolside and began reading.

A PRINCE AWAITS

A Killerbrew Studios Film
Copyright 1933
Story by
Penelope Cranstan

On the same day of the same year in a kingdom in Europe, during the seventeenth century, two girls are born—one to the queen; the other to a peasant woman. Despite their growing up in the same township, the two girls' lives are totally different. One lives in luxury; the other, poverty. The peasant girl (Carolyn Tiernan) is beautiful . . . a dreamer . . . a good and kind person. The princess (Margaret Tiernan) is spoiled and scheming . . . a willful woman who wants what she wants when she wants it. And gets it. When a passerby accidentally causes mud to spatter on her royal robes, she has him executed. He is hanged as the other girl—the little princess of the fields—ministers to wounded rabbits and a sick mother.

A prince comes to the town to marry the princess. He is tall, dark, and handsome. When he meets the princess, who knows how to be pleasing, he finds her attractive. Although not in love with her, his duty to his country makes his marriage to her a must. His is an impoverished little land while hers is rich in produce.

One day while hunting in the fields, the prince sees and watches a young peasant girl tending to a baby deer. He loses his heart. When he makes his presence known, she, frightened, runs away. He loses her in the forest. Thus begins a continuous search that the prince conducts between royal doings at the palace until he finds the peasant girl in a little run-down church where she is praying for the soul of her recently departed mother. They speak. They fall in love. The prince is torn. Shall it be love or duty to his country?

Back at the palace, the princess is suspicious. She has the prince followed and when her henchman tells her about the peasant girl, the princess is furious. She has the girl's meager little home destroyed by fire and the girl placed in irons. She herself conducts the evil interrogation of the girl.

When the prince learns of his love's fate, he tells the princess he will marry her immediately, if she frees the peasant girl. The princess agrees. The prince, true to his word, tells his true love of what he must do. The couple bid one another good-bye with tenderness . . . with love . . . with passion.

At the castle, the wedding is taking place. But as the princess makes her entrance at the top of a long staircase, her bridal train gets caught under the feet of one of her henchmen and the princess topples. She falls the length of the staircase and lands at the foot of her groom. Her neck broken, she dies in the arms of the prince, begging his forgiveness.

The peasant girl, leaving a town that holds nothing more for her, is interrupted by the prince as she pores over the scattered ashes that were once her home. He tells her all and offers to share his poor, but happy kingdom with her. When she agrees, he lifts her into his arms and onto a waiting horse and together they ride off into happiness.

END

"It's shit! Shit! Do you hear me?"

Franklin Killerbrew continued to file his nails as Margaret Tiernan vented her anger. "When you're through, do sit down, Miss Tiernan," he said when Margaret paused for breath.

"Don't you *dare* 'do-sit-down' me," said Margaret, leaning over Killerbrew's desk, her face no more than inches from his. "You cannot patronize me—not now or ever. Make no mistake, Mr. Killerbrew. You are *this* close to having your face smashed to smithereens."

Franklin Killerbrew looked up. Not even in Nancy Blanchard Killerbrew's eyes had he seen such hatred. "May I offer you some coffee, or milk perhaps, Miss Tiernan?" said Killerbrew as though he were participating in some other conversation. "It's lovely in California this time of year, don't you think?"

"You son of a bitch!" fumed Margaret.

"Sit down, Miss Tiernan. I'm a busy man and you're being very boring," said Killerbrew. "I called you here today . . ."

"I assume to apologize," said Margaret, standing her ground.

She's a damn good opponent, thought Killerbrew as he mentally congratulated Margaret for standing up to him. "You certainly have become the poised young woman, Miss Tiernan. Quite a change, I must say."

"Yes, the loss of one's parents, one's trust, and one's virginity does make for changes," said Margaret sarcastically.

"It does indeed," said Killerbrew. "In fact that's why I asked you here today . . . to discuss your lost virginity."

"Why? Was it turned in to the Lost and Found?" said Margaret.

"Miss Tiernan, I asked you here . . ."

"I don't give a damn *why* you asked me here," stormed Margaret. "I'm here to demand an explanation, to demand that you rehire Donald Malloy, that you cancel *A Prince Awaits*, and that you correct your disgusting change of title on my sister's and my film."

"I've had enough, Miss Tiernan," said Killerbrew, rising to his full six feet two. "Now sit down and shut up! It is not your film, but mine. Do you hear me? Mine. I own it."

"*It* but not us," said Margaret, still standing.

"You're wrong again, Miss Tiernan. *You*, too. You and everyone else in my employ. You're my possessions. I hire and fire and account to nobody, least of all some hot-pants child who doesn't know shit from Shinola. Sit down, Miss Tiernan. Game time is over."

Margaret sat in the armchair at the side of Killerbrew's desk.

"Number one. Never again after today—did you catch that—*never*—wear slacks to this studio for as long as you are in my employ," began Killerbrew. "Whether you are one or not, you will dress like a lady. That's just for openers. You see this?" asked Killerbrew as he rattled some bound papers in Margaret's direction. "It's your contract. Have you read it? Specifically, have you read the morals clause? It gives me the

89

right to sue your ass off if your ass is being slung around town. We write our contracts to protect us from being fucked by those who fuck indiscriminately. Number two is coming up, Miss Tiernan, so listen good. There is to be no more fucking around until your second film is finished and you're off the lot. I will not have you jeopardizing my investment just because you've discovered dick. Now just in case you didn't understand me or in the unlikely event your hearing is not as good as your cunt, let me repeat: I can sue you, Miss Tiernan, and win. Your house in New York and whatever else you think you may own."

"Mr. Killerbrew, if I may," began Margaret in soft, seemingly conciliatory tones, "let *me* make something clear. You can take that contract and shove it up your ass. No! *You* do sit down, *Mr.* Killerbrew, and *you* listen. First, you can, but you won't sue me. You wouldn't dare. How would it look in the newspapers: 'Multimillionaire studio head sues *Waif* for her home. Takes away everything she owns.' Won't the public just love that? And another thing *Mr.* Killerbrew, when we get to this imagined court of law you propose, think of the reaction of that very same public when they learn you knew all along about the *immoral* behavior of Margaret Tiernan, but chose to ignore it to save your investment. What's the expression? Oh, yes. You'll never work again in this town, *Mr.* Killerbrew."

"Nor would you, Miss Tiernan," said Killerbrew, aroused and impressed by Margaret's spunk.

"True," said Margaret. "But I could take it and I don't think you could. I don't thrive on power and manipulation."

"You're an actress, aren't you?" asked Killerbrew. When Margaret nodded, he added, "Then don't kid yourself, kid. You're no different. Your whole life is about power and manipulation. What do you think you're doing up there on the screen and usually off."

"I want you to rehire Donald Malloy," said Margaret, abruptly coming to another sore point. "It isn't fair that he should lose his job."

"He disobeyed orders," said Killerbrew flatly.

"He never heard them, and that's the truth," said Margaret, without adding that he would not have obeyed them if he had. "I don't see why he should be punished for my mistake. Hire him back, and you have my promise I will not be seen with him publicly."

"Miss Tiernan," said Killerbrew, "a good fuck is easy to find. A good job isn't."

"How quaint. I'll have a sampler made of it. Why, I might even have it crocheted on a throw pillow," said Margaret.

"Goddamnit, Margaret! You're good. Really good. You've got star potential. Don't throw it away on the first fuck you meet."

That he had used her given name did not go unnoticed by Margaret. "If you really think I'm good, why are you doing this to me?"

"I'm not doing a goddamn thing anyone who knows his business wouldn't do," answered Killerbrew, looking directly into Margaret's eyes. "You find the new title offensive? From your point of view, it is. From mine, it's a money-maker. It capitalizes on the months of publicity that has been designed from the moment you stepped off that train to make you a commodity and me a profit. I run a business, Miss Tiernan, and not a little theatre group supported by a government grant. *A Prince Awaits* is again about turning a profit and again at your expense. Except, Miss Tiernan, a lot of folks out there are going to see you in our little pageant who will not have seen you in *Waifs*, because realism and apple pie don't always go together. So take an old money changer's advice, Miss Tiernan, when the camera rolls, act the hell out of your princess."

"I want Malloy rehired," said Margaret evenly as she put on Malloy's lightweight cotton jacket, watching Killerbrew for his reaction, and headed toward the door. "I will not have you *or* me messing up his life."

"Very honorable, Miss Tiernan. Tell your Mr. Malloy he can return to work tomorrow. Also tell him if he should so much as look at you where others can see, the only job he'll get in this town is picking lettuce. Have I made myself clear, Miss Tiernan?"

"So you really think I have star potential," mocked Margaret as she stood by Killerbrew's door, her hand on her hip and a baseball cap, also borrowed from Malloy, perched arrogantly on the side of her head.

Killerbrew's eyes took in the total effect. As he felt a familiar ache in his groin he replied, "Yes, I do, Miss Tiernan. Very definitely star potential."

As Margaret met Killerbrew's unrelenting stare, she heard words that did not match those in his eyes. "I have block-booked *Waifs* for a Fourth of July opening throughout the country. The official premiere is in Tulsa and we are expecting the First Lady, the Vice-President, the governor, the Army Marching Band, Jessica Dragonette, Orphan Annie, and Rin-Tin-Tin to pay homage to the film that pays homage to the grit and guts of America. Wouldn't it seem, Miss Tiernan, that anyone foolish enough to mess with that parlay would just about mess up the rest of her life?"

Carolyn was clutching Margaret's hand, squeezing it reassuringly every few seconds. Even as the photographers—many the same to have photographed their arrival in Los Angeles—asked them to wave to imagined well-wishers, Carolyn could sense Margaret searching the entranceways to La Grande Station with anxious eyes. The cold wetness of Margaret's hand spoke of her distress.

Augusta Monahan, standing off to the side, could feel Margaret's pain. Checking the plain but functional Bulova watch, the one she usually wore only at the hospital, she noted it was but fifteen minutes to departure time. If Donald Malloy was to say his good-byes, it had best be soon. Very soon, she thought, as she reluctantly followed the redcap with their luggage up the steps of the train and down the hallway to the two compartments the studio had purchased for their trip to Tulsa and then on to New York. And via Chicago first, mused Augusta. She wondered what effect, if any, this trip in reverse would have on the girls. Well, at least they would be comfortable, she decided as she checked out the compartments which were twins to the one Carolyn and Margaret had shared on their trip west last September. Poor John. He would have to do with a sleeper. Killerbrew had refused to do better. Actually, John felt he had won a great battle. That Killerbrew was paying any portion of his fare to the East was a victory. Augusta didn't bother to understand that one. Let the men do business; she had her own to do. As soon as she knew the family's arrival date in New York, she had written to Rose Wheaton. The house, thank God, would therefore be ready. She had also phoned Arthur and he had arranged for John to sublet his studio in Gramercy Park. The doctor had been so kind, so eager to assist. But hadn't he always. "Of course, of course, stay as long as needed," he had said. He would be with "the wife" at Long Beach. "The wife" was always at Long Beach. Summer and winter. Well, that was past history. It's current events that are troublesome now, thought Augusta. Why is this Malloy man doing this to Margaret? He seemed like such a nice chap. Distracted, Augusta tipped the porter a dollar, far more than she had intended and he had expected.

Also distracted, Margaret answered by rote the predictable questions asked by the reporters. Yes, she would miss Los Angeles. Yes, she hoped to return. No, she hadn't any immediate plans, not beyond Tulsa. Her future? Well, that's really up to all America, isn't it, she bantered with a lightness she wasn't feeling. Malloy, where are you? Where the hell are you? she thought and asked and thought and asked, but only of herself.

Donald Malloy was sitting on a barstool in a seedy saloon on Melrose. It was twenty minutes to midnight and Malloy was on his sixth beer en route to oblivion—he *hoped*. The Chief would be gone in five minutes, he realized as he drained his glass and immediately signaled the bartender for another. That fucking son of a bitch! That bastard, thought Malloy. Why the fuck did he wait? Why not yesterday . . . this morning? But the call had come through just as he was leaving his home that evening for the station. If you want your job tomorrow morning, make your face scarce tonight. No fond farewells in public. None.

Once again Malloy cursed Agnes Hoffstetter, alias Alicia Allison, the cunt-turned-actress he had married and divorced but who continued to hold his balls in her hand. If his alimony payments were but three days late, her lawyer was threatening jail. And she didn't need the money; the bitch got extra work almost every goddamn day of the week. If he didn't need Killerbrew's fucking job so fucking bad he would be at the station right this second. The kid deserved that. Shit! The only promise he had ever made to her he had failed to keep. As his eyes found the Balboa Beer clock on the wall, Malloy raised his glass to Margaret and the train that was leaving La Grande Station.

THE TULSA RECORD
July 5, 1935

WAIFS IN THE WIND

A brilliant socioeconomic film about the heartland of America opened yesterday at the Jewel Theatre. *Waifs in the*

Wind stars the Tiernan Sisters as two Oklahoma farm girls who fight and overcome—each in her own way—the elements of nature and environment. The film is a statement of universal courage, a tribute to each of us who has faced and fought adversity and despair. The Tiernan Sisters portray their roles with vivid understanding and heart. *Waifs* is a triumph for all concerned.

Lavinia Tarkington

THE CHICAGO HERALD AMERICAN
July 5, 1935

WAIFS IN THE WIND

An American opus of sweeping magnitude swept across the screen yesterday at the Strand Theatre. Starring Carolyn and Margaret Tiernan, the latter breathtaking in her screen debut, *Waifs* is about the plight of two sisters who suddenly find they must survive in a hostile world without the protection of family. The drama is a thinly disguised parable of current American life. It asks: Should the system be responsible for the individual or should the individual rise above the system and hold himself responsible for his own fate. . . . A most significant film for these times.

Barkley Stimson

HOLLYWOOD CITIZEN RECORD
July 5, 1935

WAIFS IN THE WIND

. . . A BOFFO FILM, guaranteed to play to SRO houses. *Waifs* will blow up a box office storm. Carolyn Tiernan is a real looker! Margaret Tiernan lights up the screen. A winner from Killerbrew.

Norman Fullerton

NEW YORK WORLD HERALD AMERICAN
July 5, 1935

Waifs in the Wind, which opened at the Capitol Theatre yesterday, stars Carolyn and Margaret Tiernan, the daughters

94

of the late and much missed Thomas and Victoria Tiernan. It is to be hoped the Tiernans are still resting comfortably this morning but it is feared they are turning over in their graves. *Waifs* is cheap, exploitative melodrama, capitalizing on the personal tragedy of its stars. The studio in its publicity maintains the film is a commentary on the American way of life. Agreed, *if* you believe that at the root of this country's Depression was, and is, greed and exploitation.

Happily, the film serves to introduce Margaret Tiernan, who has a decided way with the camera. Carolyn Tiernan, although a great beauty, seems strained when using mannerisms more familiar to the stage, yet is oddly compelling. Also to the film's credit are the sets and special effects. The re-creation of the dust storm is harrowing, although not as harrowing as the witless plot.

If you haven't been already depressed by the Depression, see *Waifs*. If you're not crying for a New Deal after this one, you never will.

Francis Lawson-Crenna

3

Carolyn had often maintained there was nothing like a Broadway opening night. With five minutes to curtain time, as John Ollson stood in front of the Booth Theatre, the strong October winds buffeting him as rudely as the latecomers who fought to find their way into the theatre and their seats, he knew she was right. Three months of work, of fears and anxieties, hopes, dreams, doubts, and distress, had preceded this night. Now, there was nothing left for him to do, as he had done it all. The theatre was filled. The evening was a social event. For weeks, the talk along the Main Stem had been about this particular opening. Not even the dismal reviews of *A Prince Awaits* could dampen the excitement surrounding the Tiernan Sisters' debut on Broadway. Even the mayor was in attendance, sitting next to the Lunts, of all people. Kit Cornell was three rows up and Helen Hayes one back. An event indeed!—particularly with the never-seen-before-and-probably-never-to-be-seen-again pairing of Louis B. Mayer with Harry Cohn, both wifeless this evening, "batching" it and sitting side by side in row F, seats 101 and 103. Even Franklin Killerbrew had "skyed"—that's what *Variety* called it—from Los Angeles, bringing Nancy Killerbrew with him. How did "Killer" ever get her to leave her home on the society pages of the Los Angeles newspapers, John wondered.

John Ollson's plan for Broadway had been formulated before the family had boarded the train for New York via Tulsa. It had emerged from a conversation held at the dining table of their Chateau Marmont bungalow. Carolyn had voiced her relief at leaving Los Angeles; Margaret her distress at doing so. Carolyn spoke of her yearnings for the stage; Margaret, her dread of it. Margaret wanted a film career while Carolyn wanted theatre. How best to serve two mistresses: that was the problem to be solved.

As John had explained, at that moment no studio was

camped on their doorstep offering a contract to either or both of the sisters. Similarly, no Broadway producer had put out a call for their services. John expected *Waifs* to create a certain amount of interest in the girls. Having seen a rough-cut of *Prince*, he expected that interest to wane somewhat after its release. The solution therefore was to capitalize on *Waifs'* sure-to-come success. Find a stage vehicle that would show the individual acting talents of both girls. Mount it before *Prince* could do damage. If the play was a success, he, John, could negotiate a film contract for Margaret and a play for Carolyn.

The play's *the* thing, John quickly learned when the girls agreed with his career planning. Established playwrights refused to talk to John, a newcomer, and even the new breed of writers weren't creating vehicles in which two women could star. Only Shakespeare did that, John realized. And so the idea was born.

John looked up at the marquee and laughed. *Much Ado about Nothing*. What a misnomer! If the last three months and this very night were nothing then I'd hate to be around for the wear and tear of *something*, he thought. No one had greeted his idea with open arms. In fact, groans from the New York intelligentsia were all John heard when he sought financing for his production. Didn't Ollson know the Bard habitually went broke at the box office? But the groans turned to grudging grunts of admiration when John announced a Broadway first: Carolyn and Margaret Tiernan would alternate in the roles of Hero and Beatrice on alternate nights. Now that was news! That was inventive! That was courageous! That still took money and John was an untested and unknown producer searching for funds in a city that had only heard Jerome Siegal's side of his dismissal as the Tiernan Sisters' agent. Still, John had persisted. He was surprised but not overly so when Killerbrew's New York representative phoned to say the studio head was interested in backing Ollson's production. John knew Killerbrew's thinking; knew the man expected heavy grosses on both *Waifs* and *Prince*, even though the latter would take a critical drubbing. "No one will like it but the public," said Killerbrew. And he was proven right. Killerbrew was also aware that Hollywood was investing in Broadway. M-G-M had backed *Jubilee* and rumor had a major studio behind George Abbott's *Boy Meets Girl* a few streets up at the Cort.

Killerbrew made it clear he believed Margaret Tiernan could be a major Hollywood star. He had his representative tell John he was willing to put his money where his mouth was on *one* condition: that if M-G-M or RKO or any major studio offered her a contract, he, Killerbrew, had "topping privileges." That meant, explained John to the sisters, if Universal offered her X dollars for X years, then before Margaret could accept the offer, Killerbrew had the right to make a better offer. That didn't mean, however, Margaret had to accept it. Just consider it.

John thought it was an excellent deal, one without risk. Carolyn wasn't certain. She worried whether Margaret was being made the sacrificial lamb, but Margaret had no such fears. "If that bastard is willing to invest in *our* play, because he wants *me*—not a movie but *me*—then damn, it means that money-grabbing S.O.B. sees *me* as an investment. And knowing how he loves money, he's going to do everything to protect his investment so I say grab it, John."

Which John had done. To date, Killerbrew had been good to his word. He had stayed clear of the production, allowing John with Augusta Monahan's help to hire "theatre people," many of whom had worked with the senior Tiernans on their stage successes. Augusta proved to be quite competent with budgets and union demands, which left John free to handle what he knew best: promotion and publicity. It was not mere chance that had made the Tiernan Sisters' debut the event of the social season. Not at all, thought John as he entered the theatre, noting mentally where each of the columnists and reviewers he had painstakingly cultivated were sitting. The houselights dimmed just as he took his seat next to Augusta Monahan. There's nothing to worry about now, he decided. Nothing at all—unless one gives a damn about the future of all concerned.

The three-month limited engagement of *Much Ado* was extended to six and could have been extended six more, such was the demand for tickets, had not Margaret's contract with Killerbrew Studios called for a June 15 start date. That she was returning to Hollywood was alarming to everyone but Margaret. She would resume residence at the Chateau Marmont and was not, she insisted, as a woman soon to be twenty, in need of a chaperone. Augusta Monahan was not convinced, and Carolyn, with concerns she was not sharing, efused to consider the separation. Carolyn was a great success now. Her performance had been lavishly lauded by all he critics. It was strange how she naturally dominated a tage while Margaret just as naturally captured the cameras. Margaret's reviews had also been excellent, although her Beatrice, critics maintained, was far more effective than her Hero. Hollywood must have agreed, as most of the studios hat did, indeed, as hoped and predicted, bid for Margaret's services talked of featuring her as the "best friend," the wisecracking, always-good-for-a-laugh, heart-of-gold kid. She had already been referred to as a "young Katharine Hepburn," which Margaret found hilarious as Hepburn, one of her particular idols, was but seven years older. Franklin Killerbrew cinched his deal with the family when he said the magic words: "Leading Lady." He offered a seven-year exclusive contract beginning at fifteen hundred dollars per week; to be raised after two years to two thousand *if* the studio renewed, and then to thirty-five hundred for the final two years of the contract *if*, again, the studio exercised its option. Typically, Margaret had no options. She was guaranteed a minimum of two films per year, nothing more, nothing less. Creative control remained in the hands of the studio. This worried her as it did John. It was true Killerbrew had the best won-and-lost record in Hollywood but it was also true, just as he boasted, "Killerbrew makes pictures, not stars." He had no talent for that, said the industry. Killerbrew would not have agreed. He left the hand-holding to the M-G-Ms and Paramounts and then "borrowed"—a ridiculous term considering what it cost to "borrow" a star—the Harlows and Gables to do his films. Not that there weren't several top name actors on he Killerbrew lot. Besides Sonny Stevens, Connie Carstairs and Daniel Wells were household names. John actually felt it boded well for Margaret to be Killerbrew's "Leading Lady." Explained John: "He plans to make you his class act."

"Which is like P. T. Barnum telling the Fat Lady he's going to make her big in the business," said Margaret sourly. "What does it mean? What does Franklin Killerbrew know about a class act? Would he even know class if he fell over it?"

"He wants you, doesn't he?" John said simply, which put a cap on further conversation and any remaining doubts.

Strangely, the major film offer was made by M-G-M but not to Margaret. They wanted Carolyn, promising to make her another Garbo, a Shearer . . . a Star! Each time the response was "not interested," the studio raised its offer. Finally, when Carolyn refused a contract that would have made her independently wealthy, they realized she was not interested, that she was one of those "strange" *New York* actresses who chose art over money. Known in Hollywood as . . . a real *meshuggeneh*.

When Broadway learned—and John made sure it did—that Carolyn had rejected Hollywood's offers, she found herself inundated with scripts. Before reading any, she and John decided that after the cotton-dress dreariness of *Waifs*, the peasant-poor rags of *Prince*, and the costumes of *Much Ado*, she should next do a contemporary play—preferably of high style—where her own "leading lady" attributes could be shown to their best advantage. Again, once the word was sounded, scripts of that nature arrived by messenger, through the mail, and in envelopes left on doorsteps. All Carolyn needed was time to read and make her decision, and she welcomed the closing of *Much Ado* for that reason. However, she did not have the time she thought she would have to herself. Suddenly it was gone, lost in a whirlwind of activity that centered around her. It had all happened so quickly—only it hadn't, she realized, not really.

John had gone to California to iron out last-minute contractual difficulties with Killerbrew and returned with a contract of his own. Killerbrew had taken John to lunch at the Players, presumably to discuss Margaret. John described how, as they sat on the restaurant's terrace, a flight above Sunset Boulevard, Killerbrew had suddenly turned expansive, complimenting John on the production values of *Much Ado* and the way he, John, had "merchandized"—that was the word Killerbrew had used—Carolyn and Margaret. Killerbrew was looking for a man to take over the New York office, always the weakest link in the studio; a man who would scour the New York scene for talent, be it in the form of persons or scripts. He felt John was that man. John had told Carolyn he was so shocked by the offer that he spilled his wine on the red-checkered tablecloth. Killerbrew had laughed and offered to have the umbrella over their table opened if the afternoon sun was making John feel faint.

"Killerbrew laughed?" Carolyn had responded in surprise. Of all the capabilities she knew Killerbrew to have, she had not imagined laughing as one.

"He laughed until he grew serious again," John had explained. The job was his on one condition—always a condition—that John not produce any more plays for Carolyn. There could be no cries of nepotism aimed at the studio. If Carolyn was to work on Broadway, and obviously she would, it would have to be under someone else's aegis. And that, said Killerbrew, should be no problem. Hadn't he heard the Shuberts were making overtures to star Carolyn this fall in a light comedy? There are no secrets in this business, Killerbrew explained as he saw the surprised look on John's face.

When John phoned Carolyn that night from his room in the Beverly Wilshire Hotel, he informed her she was talking to a new vice-president of Killerbrew Studios, effective as of August 1. She was surprised by John's excitement, and distressed by her sense of loss. She had assumed he would remain at her side, guiding her always.

"And I will," said John, "but as your husband and not your producer." Which is how Carolyn suddenly found herself at the center of a whirlwind, becoming a June bride with all the pomp and pageantry associated with a wedding at St. Patrick's Cathedral.

For what must have been the tenth time that morning, Augusta Monahan checked her appearance in the hall mirror. Again she chastised herself for having selected the "terribly proper" Dresden-blue taffeta suit instead of the mauve satin cocktail dress which Altman's featured with a matching sequined bolero. If you can't do it up at a wedding, thought Augusta as she pushed the few gray streaks in her hair under her Dresden-blue hat, when can you? But the saleslady had insisted one ensemble was proper for before-noon wear while the other was strictly "after six." Had it been a shiny June day such as this I'd have bought the damn cocktail dress and to hell with propriety. One should never shop in April. Dreary weather makes for dreary choices.

From the foot of the stairs, Augusta looked up. Seeing and hearing nothing, she yelled, "Carolyn, the car is waiting. Do hurry!"

Honestly, that girl is going to be late for her own wedding! thought Augusta as she grumbled her way into the living room where so much of her recent adult life had been spent. Seeing the silver-framed picture of her parents smiling from atop the marble mantel of the fireplace calmed her. "So they'll wait. They'll *all* wait. It's *our* wedding. *We* are paying for it. And besides, if a girl can't be late for her own wedding, when can she be?"

As Augusta leaned against the baby grand piano near the windows overlooking Thirty-sixth Street, she absentmindedly played with the fringe on the paisley throw that all but covered the Steinway. She imagined it was the wedding, another rite of passage, that was bringing the past into the present. Two years it would be this fall since the accident. Two years. A lifetime ago and yet . . . exciting. Everyone's life had changed and moved forward. Everyone's but hers, she thought ruefully as her fingers now moved to the tassels on the wine velvet draperies. Long postponed had been her resolve to move into her own apartment. Now, when it seemed the appropriate time, Carolyn wouldn't hear of it. Losing Margaret was enough, the child had said, and to lose Augie, too, would be much too much for her to bear.

If I'm to continue living with anyone, it should be Margaret, thought Augusta. Imagine that girl alone in California and working for that dreadful man! Still, she reasoned, that *dreadful* man had turned benefactor. The terms of Margaret's contract were hardly those of a Simon Legree. But alone in California? *My* Margaret? And sending Rose Wheaton with her was like buying a snowsuit in July. A fat lot of use you could make of it. Rose could cook and clean but she was no match for Margaret's headstrong whims.

As if conjured up by Augusta's thinking about her, Rose Wheaton stood at the entrance to the living room.

"Rose, how lovely you look!" said Augusta, thinking how perfectly awful the big woman looked in that huge floral-print dress. She looked like a walking botanical garden.

"Why don't you wait in the limousine, Rose. The girls should be down in a minute." As Rose did her bidding, Augusta thought how difficult it would be for the old woman to leave this house after so many years. It would be hard for her, too, she realized. But John had been right to sell it, to want a fresh start in a new home without ghosts or memories. She would have wanted that for herself and Dan Dunahey, too.

Everything in the house had gone along with the sale, except for a few pieces Augusta wanted for her bed-sitting room in the newlyweds' apartment on Central Park West. They were her physical ties to Dorchester and to her early days in New York. They had little or nothing to do with Tory and Thomas, who lived in her heart and not in meaningless objects or furnishings.

"Carolyn?" she called again from the bottom of the stairway. "Your public awaits. Carolyn?" yelled Augusta, growing impatient with her niece's lateness. Suddenly Margaret was standing at the top of the stairs. Although Augusta had known Margaret would be wearing the very same Empire dress she herself had worn as maid of honor at Tory's wedding, she was unprepared for the beauty in the flowing pink chiffon and the crimson Juliet cap that crowned her niece's sumptuous auburn hair. "Oh my dear God," she said in reaction. "My *dear* God. Margaret . . . you are so beautiful. So very beautiful," Augie repeated as tears momentarily blinded her vision.

"Don't let it fool you, Aunt Augie. It's all done with mirrors and trick photography. And what nature has forgotten, I've amply stuffed with cotton."

But Augusta was not fooled by Margaret's self-deprecating humor. The gangling girl was gone, replaced by an assured and elegantly beautiful young woman. "Would you please find your sister. We're going to be late." As her niece vanished from sight, Augusta felt a pang of guilt. Well, I cannot go with her. Any more than I will stay all that long with Carolyn. I must make my life just as they have made theirs. I will not be denied.

When Margaret did not find Carolyn in her bedroom, she intuitively knew she would be in their parents' room, a floor above. There, Carolyn sat on the Turkish divan Victoria Tiernan had so loved. "A penny for your thoughts," said Margaret softly as she sat down next to her sister.

"Just reminiscing," said Carolyn, "remembering Sunday mornings in this room. Do you remember how as kids we would wait until we heard them stirring and then rush upstairs to climb into bed with them?"

"It's a good thing they were only *stirring*," said Margaret straight-faced.

"You don't remember, do you," said Carolyn, disappointed

"Of course I do, Lynnie. Daddy would read the papers to us. . . ."

"And Mama would have Rose serve us all breakfast in bed and no one cared about the crumbs and the mess. It was such a lovely time, except then you would tickle my toes and make me spill my milk."

"Well, soon enough it will be your kids climbing all over you and John in bed," said Margaret as she stroked Carolyn's casually combed hair.

"But it won't be the same, Marg. Nothing will ever be the same," said Carolyn, biting her lip.

No, nothing will, thought Margaret. The thought and the sadness that accompanied it had been with her all morning as she dressed for the wedding. It was a new day of a new life, for Carolyn and for her. Neither would ever see this house again. Neither would ever share another bedroom. Carolyn had a husband and a new home and she, a career. Yes it was sad but it was also exciting. Margaret yearned to be back in Hollywood. Somehow, despite the many dates she had had in New York, she felt strange, disoriented, in her own city. It wasn't Malloy she missed although she did think of him periodically. There had been an exchange of letters, even a phone call at Christmas, but Margaret knew this was no great love affair for either. She had not pined for Malloy and she knew better than to think he had kept a candle burning in his window for her return. It was possible, she realized, that that part of her life, like the one she was leaving this day, also belonged to the past.

"Marg, I asked them to come to the wedding," said Carolyn. Margaret didn't have to ask, she knew exactly whom her sister meant. "I want Daddy to give me away. I want him beside me as I walk down the aisle. I want my mama . . . I want my mama to tell me what to do. Marg, I don't *know* what to do. No one ever told me how to be married."

"They'll be there, Lynnie," said Margaret as she continued to smooth her sister's hair. "And Lynnie, no one knows how to be married—not at first, any more than one knows how to be a mother. I suppose it's like riding a bicycle. You do it until you learn not to fall off. And if you do fall . . . well, you get up and try all over again."

"Marg, aren't you ever afraid?"

Margaret considered the question. "Lynnie, I guess I'm a leaper first and then a looker. So far I've landed on my feet. Now enough of this true confessions. Stand up. I want to see how you look in Mama's wedding dress."

Like an obedient child, Carolyn stood before Margaret and then pirouetted. Wearing no makeup, her skin a near perfect

104

match to the ivory satin gown that was nipped at her waist and then flowed to a train of five feet, Carolyn was an ethereal and perfect beauty. The tiniest of seed pearls embroidered on the gown's bell sleeves and scooped neckline created an old-fashioned-girl effect. For a moment, Margaret was startled. Carolyn could have been their mother incarnate.

"Something old," mused Margaret as she looked at the wedding gown, "and something new," she continued as she placed the matching, but recently purchased, veil on Carolyn's head. "What's borrowed? Oh, yes. Aunt Augie's pearl earrings. Perfect. Now, what have we that's blue?"

Carolyn looked panic-stricken. "Don't fret, Lynnie, I've got it. Did you hear the one about the farmer's daughter and the toothless old man?"

"Margaret!" boomed Carolyn.

"Well, that's about as blue as you can get," explained Margaret. Carolyn was laughing and at that moment she took Margaret's words away.

"You are the world's most beautiful bride," Margaret said finally.

"Oh, Marg," whispered Carolyn as the sisters embraced, holding one another as though they never would again. "We're leaving it all behind."

"No, dear heart. We're not. Not ever. It's all coming with us. This house, our parents, you and I, all of it will live for as long as we do," answered Margaret as she used her gloved finger to dry the tears from Carolyn's face.

"Marg, we've never been separated before. Promise me if you need me or if I need you—I mean, you *know* what I mean."

"Lynnie, we'll never be separated. We're stuck with each other, kid. I mean *someone's* got to keep you from getting up on that high horse of yours and someone's got to keep me from getting trampled by mine. Now come on, you big silly, let's go get married."

As the girls reached the second-floor landing, Margaret said, "Give me a second."

"For what?" asked Carolyn as Margaret disappeared into her bedroom.

"For this!" said Margaret as she brandished her red cape. "Finally, for once in my life, what with all this pink fluff I'm done up in, I can wear this thing and be stylish."

As the girls walked arm in arm down the remaining flight

of stairs where Augusta stood waiting at the bottom, Margaret said, "Lynnie, you really should have insisted I buy that Indian headdress in Albuquerque. It certainly would have lent character to this wedding."

"To steal a line from someone near and dear to me, Margaret, you are about *all* the character this wedding can take unless one is very big on farce. And, my love, do me a favor," added Carolyn as though butter wouldn't melt in her mouth. "Take off that dumb red cape. You're Margaret Tiernan, dear, not Superman."

Watching the sun rise was something Carolyn had begun doing toward the end of the second week of her honeymoon. It reminded her of years gone by when she was a child and her father would wake her to watch the dawning of a new day. Now, the early morning was her time alone, her time to sort out the changes in her life.

Carolyn was bundled in her quilted bathrobe, its collar turned up against the chill wind that blew in from the ocean. As she lazed in the wicker rocking chair, her hands wrapped about a steamy hot coffee mug for warmth, she watched and waited. Suddenly, it peeked just over the ocean, shy and hesitant. Bit by bit it braved the dark until finally, there it rose, more orange than red, but more yellow than orange. It would be a beautiful day, another in what had been a long string of perfect summer weather.

As she sat on the porch of the summer house on Strawberry Hill overlooking Nantasket Beach, Carolyn felt just the slightest sadness. Tomorrow they would return to New York so that John could begin his work at Killerbrew Studios. She was not ready to leave, not ready to leave behind *their* summer.

They had been like children at play. They lived in a wooden, two-story white Victorian dollhouse filled with white wicker furniture, Martha Washington bedspreads, and yards and yards of white Irish lace. Their playground had been Paragon Park where she and John would ride the roller coaster and the merry-go-round. They played in the cold water of Nantasket and amused themselves in the House-of-Fun and the shooting gallery at the amusement park. She would never part with the cheap painted porcelain pig she had won for knocking three tin cans off their perch with a baseball.

They had hiked and biked the three-mile length of the

predominantly Irish resort area and, on one bleak day, journeyed to Boston as tourists. For two months they had lived a sequestered life, interrupted only casually by frequent letters to and from Margaret and the twice-weekly phone calls from Augusta, who surprisingly refused to join them for so much as a week. I am happy, thought Carolyn as she sipped the still hot coffee. As she wrote in her last letter to Margaret, "I like being married." She was the girl who had everything—a husband asleep in the bedroom just above the porch where she was sitting, a home that according to Augusta was shaping up just as she and John had designed, and . . . a new play that would begin rehearsals just after Labor Day.

As the sun grew stronger, more regal, and took its rightful place in the sky above the ocean, Carolyn debated between rereading the script and writing her remaining thank-you notes for wedding presents that continued to arrive. Augusta had sent proofs of the wedding pictures just that week and she and John were still choosing the ones they wanted for their album. She had found it strange looking at pictures of a wedding she could hardly remember despite its having been her own. For a moment she relived that second in time when she realized her father was not at her side as she walked down the very long center aisle of St. Patrick's. Had Margaret not perceived her distress from where she stood at the altar, had she not come to escort her, she might still be standing there, thought Carolyn. So it had been Margaret who gave her away. At least she had that. John had had nothing. She still could not understand his parents' pleading age and illness and sending a check, with their love, for five thousand dollars instead of attending. Nothing would have prevented her parents from attending, not even death, she had hoped. But if his parents' absence had mattered, John hadn't spoken of it.

As Carolyn watched the gulls diving into the choppy waters of the ocean, her memories rolled in with the waves. She did not like remembering her wedding night. It had not been pleasant. From the moment she entered the bridal suite at the Plaza Hotel, saw the turned-down covers on the double bed, the champagne in the ice bucket, the long-stemmed roses, she felt as if she were an actress in an old and tired play in which there were no new scenes. Everyone knew what was supposed to happen, *should* happen. They were there to do one thing. *That,* and the champagne, made her sick to her stomach. She borrowed time by lounging and lingering in a hot bath. Try as she did, she could not recall the feelings John had aroused in her during the months of premarital foreplay. Finally, fearing John would grow angry, she talked herself into doing her "wifely duties." She put on the pink billowy negligée—a present from Margaret, who else?—brushed her somewhat damp hair till it had some kind of shine, and presented herself to her husband.

Despite John's gentleness, it had been painful. Then, when it was not, it was boring. All of that effort and for what? She felt nothing but tired and fell asleep sick at heart, which was worse, she decided, than being sick to her stomach. But it had gotten better. Much better. Once on Nantasket, she became with each passing day more comfortable sleeping next to a man, and a naked one at that. It took her a week before she could look at John's body without embarrassment. It was lean and compact and it was first to excite her; then John. He was a skillful and—although she did not know it—a passionate lover. He took time with his pleasure, believing she found hers just as he found his. She never told him otherwise.

From the beginning, Carolyn and John fought about practicing birth control. For Carolyn, only one method, rhythm, was acceptable. Only it wasn't to John, who refused to be denied. Most often, he would solve the problem of conception by pulling out of her and depositing his semen on her belly. She hated that; hated that it was sinful—in effect, a "spilling of the seed"—and hated the feel of it. But she said nothing. She would wait until John was asleep and then slip into the bathroom where she would sponge herself clean. What Carolyn liked best about sex was the feeling of closeness. She loved the warmth of two people meshing into one. It made her feel complete. It made her feel protected. It made her feel loved. She did not know there was much more she could have felt.

"Aunt Augie? I'm leaving now," Carolyn called to the closed door at the end of the long hallway.

"Be right out," was her aunt's reply. Within seconds, Augusta Monahan strode toward her niece wearing a pale pink blouse and gray slacks.

"I don't believe it!" said Carolyn with mock astonishment. "You? In slacks?"

"Really, Carolyn. You needn't look so shocked," said Augusta stiffly. "I may not be a Dietrich but I'm not exactly a Dame May Whitty either. Frankly," said Augusta as she turned front and back to examine herself in the floor-to-ceiling hallway mirror, "I think I look rather chic."

"I do declare, Aunt Augie, this move to the West Side has changed you," continued Carolyn mockingly. "Next you'll actually leave the house without wearing a hat. Goodness, gracious!"

Augusta Monahan laughed. She had not worn a hat since Carolyn's wedding and now that her hair was longer and rinsed a stylish blue, she was not about to cover it except when the elements dictated. "What time do you expect to be back?" she asked her niece.

"We're rehearsing eleven to six this week so figure six-thirty to seven, the latest. By the way, you want to visit this afternoon? Guests are not allowed but managers and agents are."

"I'm just the bookkeeper, part of the hired help, remember?" said Augusta dryly. Then noting the disappointed look on Carolyn's face she added: "You don't really need me, you know. Your mother . . ."

"My mother had my father," snapped Carolyn. "I have no one."

"You have an agent, that nice Mr. Lowell at William Morris, and you have yourself. That's quite enough," said Augusta with surprising severity.

"When Mother was upset with the director or another actor, all she had to do was mention it to Daddy," complained Carolyn.

"You should have been there when your father went off to war and your poor, sweet, little, shy, retiring mother had no one to fend for her when she costarred with *that* woman in that silly play. That mouth could have destroyed all of Germany singlehandedly. Ah, had the War Department but known of her!"

"Mother? *My* mother?" said Carolyn aghast.

"None other. She only deferred to your father because she thought that was what a woman should do," said Augusta. "She wasn't called 'Tiger Tiernan' by her fellow thespians for nothing, you know."

"Mother? *My* mother?"

"Carolyn, you've said that already. Yes, *your* mother. Lessons over for the day, what say we all get to work. Dinner will be waiting at seven. I'll cook tonight so have a big lunch."

"Don't forget Sloane's is delivering the living room rug today," said Carolyn as she draped her yellow cardigan around her shoulders.

"Since it was *I* who told *you*, I hardly need to be reminded," snapped Augusta.

"You're becoming quite the feisty old lady," said Carolyn as she blew a kiss in her aunt's direction and then beelined for the door before Augusta could throttle her with a response.

Augusta was laughing as Carolyn made her hasty exit. Feisty? Perhaps. Old? Not yet. Not when she felt younger than she had in years. It had been a wonderful summer, the best since she was a girl being courted by Dan Dunahey. What a difference a man makes!

When Carolyn had left with John for Nantasket and Margaret for Hollywood, Augusta had found herself alone as she had been for the year the Tiernans had toured. And not just alone but in unfamiliar surroundings. No comforts from the past were in the unfurnished and unfinished apartment when she initially took up residence and supervised the construction. At first, when she wasn't distracted by the architects and workers who were dismantling and dismembering the pantry, laundry, and maid's room to make one large space that would serve as Augusta's "apartment"—complete with its own entrance from what was previously the servants' and delivery door—she felt frightened. Being alone after forty was something women feared. What to do about it was the question she asked herself. Keep busy was one answer. Since she had undertaken the family's bookkeeping, there were certain hours in the day when she was occupied. All of Margaret's bills were paid from New York. Thus, Augusta maintained one set of books for her and others for Carolyn, the actress, and Carolyn and John, the married couple/private citizens. Additionally, having assumed responsibility for overseeing the apartment renovations, she "officiated" until the painters mixed the exact Wedgwood blue Carolyn wanted for the living room and made the appropriate "threats" when Schumacher delivered flocked floral wallpaper for the dining room instead of the Wedgwood blue-and-white stripe that had been ordered. And her phone battles with Sloane's were invigorating, if not satisfying. Amazing how the words "imnediate delivery" can mean different things to people. The Open Field Kirman Oriental rug, "in the overall blue, not ivory or red please," was ordered in June. It was *immediately* delivered in late July—in green. Now, God willing, it was arriving again today, a week before autumn. The lined white Belgian linen draperies were due "on the next boat" provided it didn't sink or go via the Cape of Good Hope. Honestly, but tradesmen were impossible these days!

Augusta continually congratulated herself for refusing to part with her past . . . in part. Although her room was the last to be built it was the first to be completed as she had furnished it with many of the things she had lived with, first in Dorchester, and then in Murray Hill. The wine velvet, tasseled draperies now hung from a new but matching valance that went wall to wall above the windows that overlooked the courtyard. Hers was the sole room in the apartment to have the afternoon sun. It made the Persian rug on which she had first learned to crawl and then walk look even more wonderful than it had, once it was cleaned and "spot fixed." Its deep reds looked lovely contrasted with the warm gray of the walls. With her huge brass bed and Tory's Turkish divan, Augusta felt "positively Continental."

Her wardrobe reflected this feeling. As she now stood in her walk-in closet, shuffling through the recently purchased silks and chiffons, looking for something "appropriate," but not too, for lunch, she recalled the exact moment her wardrobe changed. The day the cleaners returned the "proper" suit she had worn to Carolyn's wedding, Augusta decided it and a life-style had to go. It went to Catholic Charities along with several other "mature" outfits. Actually, as she remembered, her "old self" was last seen entering Altman's to buy—if they still had it—that mauve satin cocktail dress with its matching sequined bolero. Well, Lord knows, thought Augusta, that isn't quite the thing for lunch at the Colony. What then? The black shantung. Smart . . . sophisticated and not exactly unsexy either.

Had Augusta not met Stephen Cartwright, she might not have become—as Carolyn put it—"West Side" quite so quickly, if at all. Actually, it wasn't all that quick. Cartwright had been in her life for six months before she became aware of him as someone other than a lawyer in the firm that handled legal matters for John's *Much Ado* production. Although they talked on the phone frequently, and had even met several

111

times at the theatre during rehearsals, Augusta had paid no mind to the man, as men seldom paid mind to her. Except for the good doctor, of course; but that was different. She was surprised and more than just pleased when Cartwright, shortly before the production closed on Broadway, invited her for drinks at the Astor bar. Then it was lunch at the Algonquin followed by "dinner" a week later at a hot-dog stand in Yankee Stadium where she saw her first ball game.

She had kept Cartwright her own little secret mainly because she wasn't sure what there was to tell or whom to tell it to. Augusta was well aware her nieces thought her "above" or beyond all that, as had she. Then, too, Augusta was uncertain of her feelings. She knew she liked Cartwright, but she could not ascertain if she liked the man himself as much as she liked the idea of a man like Cartwright liking her. That he was divorced, the father of a married daughter and a boy at Yale, did not matter to her. Nor did it that he was Protestant. That he was fun, that they had fun together, this was the "matter" and the miracle to Augusta.

It was shortly after Augusta took up what could have been her lonely residence on the West Side that Cartwright began to phone regularly. Since it was summer, there were no operas or ballets to attend. When Cartwright kept looking for "cultural events" to amuse her, Augusta confided: "I know I have the look, and the sound, of a woman born to the arts, but I'm afraid operas and museums bore me." Cartwright had not only understood, but had said she was a woman after his own heart. She was not at all certain of that.

Several times Augusta found herself dancing at the Biltmore's roof garden to Paul Whiteman's band or to Tommy Dorsey at the Manhattan Room of the Pennsylvania Hotel. Best of all were the Saturday and Sunday drives to either the Jersey or Long Island shore. It was on one of those gorgeous summer weekend days that Augusta realized: I'm being courted.

Today's lunch was to celebrate Cartwright's fifty-third birthday for which she had bought him a simple sterling cigarette case, which if he chose he could later have initialed. As she prepared her bath, sprinkling the scalding water liberally with scented salts, she removed her clothes. In the medicine chest mirror which was quickly clouding over with steam, she noted with pleasure that her self-imposed diet and exercise plan had slimmed her. It may not be the body of a Harlow, she accepted, but nor was it any longer a human advertisement of Jell-0. If it ever came to "that," she would not be embarrassed to be with a man. The question was, thought Augusta, as she lowered herself into the bubbling bath, would it come to "that" and if so, when?

ADELPHIA HOTEL

October 26, 1936

Dear Marg,

I'm still sick that we missed each other's phone calls Sunday but we're now rehearsing day and night—*every* day and night. It seems like every time I learn my lines, they throw new pages in my face. Ugh! I still can't believe I played the first act of last Saturday's matinee with Thursday's script. No wonder the audience didn't know what I was talking about. You'd think someone on stage would have given me a clue.

Why didn't anyone tell me it was going to be this hard?????

Give me ole Will Shakespeare any time. Nobody rewrites him in hotel rooms at eleven P.M. each night.

And Marg, we open in a week! We'll never make it. John tells me the advance word in New York is gloomy and the box office reflects this. New Haven killed us. Such shabby reviews. Except for me.

Incandescent . . . radiant . . . do you believe it? Me . . . incandescent!!!

Since New Haven, we've improved a lot. The Philadelphia critics have been much kinder. Again, the reviews for me were just terrific. I wish the play's reviews had been as good. Funny, when John and I first read *Weekend*, we laughed and laughed. Maybe it's one of those scripts that reads better than it plays. Still, I'm getting laughs which is a whole new feeling. I was about to write . . . no one ever found me funny before, but I just know what you'd do with that opening. Anyway, I treasure each and every laugh I get. They've been hard won. The director, Daryl Tristan, should not be directing this play. An Englishman doing an American comedy is wrong, wrong, wrong! And the leading man—do you remember Robert Clairborne from *Shepherd's Staff*—we saw it together just before we went on tour with Mom and Dad—well, he thinks he's playing Chekhov. Impossible! But you'd be proud of me. The first couple weeks I kept my dainty mouth

113

closed but . . . well, I'm now known as "Tiger II." I still can'
believe Mother was actually called Tiger Tiernan.

By the way, my wardrobe is absolutely gorgeous. Very
stylish and there is one peignoir that I'm going to steal when
the production closes, which is liable to be one night after we
open. Perish the thought.

John pops down each weekend. He is more hopeful about
the play than I am. But I think, next to what's coming in this
season—*You Can't Take It with You, The Women, Room
Service*—we're going to come in a very poor second. Second?
Tenth. Twentieth. Oh, well. *C'est la vie*.

Almost forgot. John also said you are absolutely wonderful
in *Street Urchin*. Really! He says Killerbrew was right and
you were dead wrong. Do you think he's becoming a company man? And guess what? Killerbrew being Killerbrew,
he's opening it one week after *Weekend*. At the Strand. He
thinks you following me (sorry about that, dear) will be good
publicity. Boy, could he get his comeuppance if we're a
disaster.

I know this is a dumb thing to say *but* . . . I wish you could
be here for opening night. To hold my hand and crack those
awful jokes. Oops, speaking of awful jokes, I keep reading
about your torrid romance with Sonny Stevens. That's almost
as funny as you starring in a horse opera. I hate to say this
but . . . *John says* (for a man who is basically taciturn, he
certainly says a lot, doesn't he?) that *Raton Pass* may be a
crummy movie but a moneymaker. He thinks you need to be
seen in a Western, that it broadens your appeal to audiences.
And the publicity—about you and Sonny being "that way"
about one another—can only do you, and the movie, of
course (see? I think he really *is* becoming a company man), a
lot of good.

Do you know yet whether you can get home for Christmas?
Your room is finished. It's gorgeous. It's alternately known as
Margaret's and the guest room, although what guests we'll
ever have other than you is beyond me. Anyway, I'm not
going to tell you a thing about it other than it is *très, trés*
terrific! Mainly a lot of midnight blues, which you must admit
is very romantic.

Speaking of romance, is there any?

Speaking of romance, part II. I'm getting the strangest
feeling about Aunt Augie. I swear if I didn't know better, I
would say our aunt is having a fling. I had to all but get down

114

n my knees and beg her to accompany me on these out-of-own tryouts. John didn't want me going off alone and I certainly wasn't looking forward to it either. You should have heard Aunt Augie's excuses! What do you think? Is it possible?

Did I tell you in my last letter that the living room is finally done? Well, it is. You know about the rolled-arm sofa, the one done in the impractical white cotton twill—well, the two chairs John and I found months ago in one of the antique stores on Third Avenue—they're called "fauteuils" but don't ask me to either translate or pronounce because I can't—arrived yesterday. We had to have them upholstered. Luckily, before I left for New Haven, I found the loveliest blue and white print, with flecks of green, at Schumacher (where else?)—a tiny floral, it is—and it took the upholsterer all this time to do them. Anyway, we now have what's known as a conversational grouping—the sofa, flanked on either side by the two chairs facing one another—so you must come soon so we can all make conversation.

Does my going on about the apartment bother you? Say so and I'll stop. But I'm having such a good time doing it. By the way, are you still thinking of moving from the Marmont into a house?

Oh, Marg, why can't you be making movies here?

I miss you, miss you, miss you.

Do write soon and we'll talk this Sunday.

Love,
Lynnie

P.S. Just realized we can't talk Sunday. It's our last day of rehearsal before opening Monday in New York. The very mention of "opening" gives me the shivers. Keep your fingers crossed that both me and *Weekend* make it through . . . the weekend.

XXXXXX
Lynnie

Margaret carefully folded Carolyn's letter and placed it with her others in the top bureau drawer. She had just returned from her first day of filming on *The Back Bay Way* and was still reentering what had become her harsh reality. As she cold-creamed her face, she was surprised to find it wet. Of late, it seemed tears came and went at will; theirs, not hers.

What to do? Lynnie, I miss you, too. Oh God, how I miss you now!

Margaret's body was arched convulsively over the bathroom sink as she sobbed. The whole of her ached from a lack of sleep and a pain she couldn't localize. It was everywhere, flitting about her body and soul at will. Once more, as she dried her face, she reached for the telephone. Once again, she placed the receiver back in its cradle before she could dial. It would not be fair to call now. Best to wait till after Carolyn's opening. Besides, it was just a hunch. Wait for the reports. Wait. Wait.

Oh God, I've *been* waiting and nothing's been happening, she thought. That's the problem. New sobs brought new convulsions. Exhausted, Margaret collapsed on her bed. The knock on her door was unexpected and so twice as upsetting.

"Margaret, dear. Are you all right? I thought I heard someone crying."

It was Rose Wheaton.

"Everything's fine, Rose. It must have been the radio," lied Margaret. "One of the soap operas."

One of the soap operas indeed! That's what her life now resembled. From the moment she returned to Hollywood there had been little of its renowned gaiety and glamour but much trauma that now bordered on the tragic. She had been in town but two days when rehearsals—if you can call two days of readings rehearsals—began on *Street Urchin*. When she found the script awaiting her arrival at the Marmont, she was naïve enough to think she was the "urchin" of the title. She was not. She was but a featured player in a *Shirley Temple*—a vehicle for Killerbrew's child star. She was on screen maybe fifteen minutes at best. Only Margaret thought it was at *worst*. She played Tessie, a streetwalker, the girl who befriends the urchin, the child she finds wandering about the streets of Chicago after her mother dies in a hospital ward. Rather than go to a state orphanage, the urchin has run away. When she is at her most cold and hungry, she meets Tessie, the tough-talking but good-as-gold streetwalker who takes her into her humble-but-clean apartment. There, the child is sheltered and comforted as Tessie plies her trade. She gives everything to the urchin—including her health, which suffers when she forgoes her own medication so that Tessie can have a dress to wear to school. When the urchin is finally found by distant relatives and taken off to live in a big house, Tessie is left alone . . . sick and lonely but richer for the experience.

116

Margaret's first thought was: How many goddamn ways are there to play Stella Dallas? She hated the script. She hated even worse the blond wig and the garish makeup that would serve to introduce her to the public as Killerbrew's new "leading lady." Margaret's initial reaction was to march herself into Killerbrew's office and do battle. John persuaded her otherwise. So she compromised. If the role of Tessie was outrageous—which indeed it was—she would be outrageous playing it. She had her wig bleached even blonder than it was, her lipstick and rouge deepened, and her bras broadened. Her "invention" lasted for her two weeks of filming during which time she was announced as Sonny Stevens's costar in *Raton Pass*. This time after reading the script, Margaret did march to Killerbrew's office.

She had not seen her employer since her return to Hollywood. She had thought flowers would be waiting at her hotel. They were not. She had thought there would be some sort of luncheon arranged. There was not. A phone call. A note. Nothing.

"Margaret, what brings you here?" Killerbrew had said in greeting as she strode into his office.

"If the mountain won't come to Mohammed, than Mohammed will go to the mountain," she responded airily.

"Oh, are we expecting someone else? You have a brother named Mohammed, perhaps?" he replied mockingly.

"Since you insist, I *will* sit down," said Margaret as she plopped herself into the wing chair by his desk. "First I *must* thank you for all your kindness since I arrived. I know the only reason you didn't send flowers or candy was to save me from writing thank-you notes. You are the kindest man."

Killerbrew leaned back in his chair. As he twirled his sterling pencil, he grinned. He also said nothing, which infuriated Margaret. The staring match ended when he leaned across his desk and into a conversation with "I see you haven't changed a bit, Margaret."

"I liked it better when you called me Miss Tiernan."

"That was before I owned you," said Killerbrew evenly.

"You don't *own* me," protested Margaret.

"I've got a contract that says I do—for seven years, *Margaret*. Seven of them."

"I'll make you a deal. Having just read *Raton Pass*, let me work off my contract in some way other than as your . . . *leading lady*," said Margaret with all the sarcasm she could muster. "Why don't I cook and clean, do the laundry, the

117

gardening even, around your home—be a real little helper for Mrs. K—and after a year, we'll call it quits. We'll be even."

"Fifteen hundred dollars a week for a cook, laundress, and gardener? I don't know. It seems to me you'd have to throw in other *services*," said Killerbrew, leaning heavily on the word to make clear his meaning, "and frankly, I don't think those *services* are worth fifteen hundred a week. Do you know how much *service* that would be at two bucks per *serve*?"

"Why must everything you say be an innuendo?" asked Margaret angrily.

The response surprised Killerbrew. "A good question. I'll think about it. But I have a feeling, Margaret, it's you who cause it. Anyway, let's get to the point," said Killerbrew as he rose from his chair, walked around his desk, and sat on its edge facing Margaret. "*Raton Pass* goes before the cameras next month. With you in it! Now hold on," continued Killerbrew, raising his hand to silence Margaret's protests. "It's garbage, right? That's what you want to tell me, right? Well then, let's move on. We agree. But—and now listen carefully, Margaret—it's not just that this kind of Western makes money, it also makes stars. Sonny Stevens is the number five box office draw in this country. People flock to see him and a horse. Now I'm giving him a real woman—I mean *you*—to play with. It'll do him good and it is going to expose you to an audience who might not know you . . . yet." Again Killerbrew held up his hand for silence. "Margaret, by now you should trust me. I didn't sign you for seven years—at damn good money by the way—to exploit you. Not yet, anyway. The goal for you at this studio is stardom. I know how to get you there. All you have to do is follow my directions."

As Margaret silently considered this, Killerbrew continued, the excitement growing more and more evident in his voice. "Margaret," he said almost cajolingly as he moved back to his desk and reached into a drawer, "*this* is going to do it for you." Margaret looked up and saw a script in Killerbrew's hands. She reached to take it but he snapped it back out of her reach. "No! It's not finished. But it's good, damn good." She looked from the script to his face. Reading it, she saw he was sincere. "It's yours after *Raton Pass*," Killerbrew continued. "You and you alone star. With three supporting male leads. Think of it, Margaret. *You, dominating the movie from start to finish."*

With rapid movements, Margaret collected herself. She picked up her shoulder bag from the floor by her chair, tucked her white satin blouse into the matching flannel slacks and was at the door without a word.

"Nothing to say?" said Killerbrew grinning.

"What's to say? The mountain *is* coming to Mohammed or it's making it a helluva lot easier to climb."

"See ya, Margaret," said Killerbrew.

"Westward Ho!" she responded as she closed the door behind her.

Killerbrew had laughed. She thought she heard him laughing throughout her first reading of *The Back Bay Way.* What a joke! On her. Priscilla Parkington, a Beacon Hill/Boston beauty, is in danger of losing her home and social position now that "Daddy" had died, his last will and testament proving he was a ne'er-do-well and fraud. Priscilla uses her beauty to marry "well" and often. She destroys the marriages of others to have the men she needs. After a third disastrous marriage, Priscilla Parkington becomes "infirm": nerves. Her illness causes a premature graying of her hair. She suffers. She is rejected by all who once knew her and loathe her still. She is reduced to living in Back Bay. But . . . as God is her witness, she vows the Back Bay Way is not her way and she will return to the splendor of Beacon Hill again.

On her second and then third reading, Margaret saw *The Back Bay Way* for what it was—an up North *Gone With the Wind.* It was also a class A starring vehicle. Priscilla Parkington was a bitch with dimension. She used her emotions as she used her men—to get what she needed. Yes, Priscilla Parkington has everything, Margaret thought. Except likability. The actress would have to create that. If the character was to work, an audience had to care about Priscilla. That would be the challenge. Excited about the possibilities, Margaret sent a thank-you note to Killerbrew. He did not respond. Thought Margaret then, why should he when no one else had?

By "no one else," Margaret meant men. At the few parties her shooting schedules allowed her to attend, she was approached only by those young like herself, actors in search of stardom. They were interested in success and sex—in that order—and to them, she was part of the recreational pleasures for which Hollywood was known. The more established male stars played within their own social stratum. In public, that is. In motels along Santa Monica, under an assumed name, they played with those willing to play the game. She was not. Which was why she resumed with Donald Malloy. She had phoned Malloy shortly after her arrival in Hollywood. He had been friendly but definitely not amorous.

"Have you a girl?" she demanded outright.

"Sorta. Nothing serious. We've been seeing each other on and off for about six months," said Malloy. "But if it don't bother you, it don't bother me."

But it did bother her. She had thanked Malloy "for your truly gracious offer" and hung up.

Friday nights were always the worst for Margaret. Faced with the weekend, with two whole days alone, without cast and crew to be her family, to comfort and care for her, she would crawl into bed at ten and huddle until sleep came. Two months after her first call to Malloy, there was a Friday night when sleep was impossible. She not only felt lonely, but bereft, as though she were losing some vital part of herself. She needed something. No, she corrected, she needed some*one*. Which is why she called Malloy. He would not come to her hotel—"too risky. If Killerbrew found out he'd have a shit fit"—so she taxied to his place on Hilldale. When the weekend ended, so had she, finally and conclusively, with Malloy. In their year's separation, things had changed. Although Malloy had much he could give her, among them were not comfort and caring. And what had once seemed so exciting, so necessary to her very being, now felt forced and mechanical. So why continue? For what? she reasoned.

The weeks between *Raton Pass* and *The Back Bay Way* were difficult. There were just so many hours Margaret could fill preparing for a role. It came as a relief to be nervous, excited, and apprehensive about the sneak of her first film. When Margaret threw up the first morning, she simply attributed it to nerves: the Riverside preview was that night. The following day, when she again threw up, Margaret again attributed it to nerves. After all, it was quite a jolt seeing a stranger on screen who the credits insisted was you. She was still reacting, still feeling queasy, when a messenger arrived at the hotel with a sampling of the preview cards from the night before. The first made her laugh. "Tessie's got my two bucks anytime." The second she read was brief but emphatic. "Margaret Tiernan is great. <u>Period!</u>"

It was the word "Period," underlined, that smacked her. Period . . . when had hers last been? Period . . . when had she last been with Malloy? Period . . . had she remembered to wear her diaphragm? Period . . . think, dammit, Margaret. Think! Period . . . when, damn, when was it? Period . . . had he taken precautions? Margaret . . . go back. You dialed, phoned for a taxi. What next? Did you insert the damn device? Margaret, damn you, remember!

The following day she went to the doctor who had first fitted her for a diaphragm. He took a urine sample and told her he would call. When he did it was to say the laboratory had somehow lost her sample. She gave him another. The weekend passed. Her first day of shooting had passed. "The doctor was detained in Santa Barbara, Miss Tiernan. He'll be back tomorrow," his receptionist said when she called. Another day to wait. Another night to get through. Margaret switched on the lamp by her bed. It was after eleven, much too late now to call Carolyn. Much too late in all ways.

Carolyn was upset. The switchboard at the Marmont said Miss Tiernan had left a "Do not disturb" on her telephone at eleven and they were sorry but they could not ring her room. Reluctantly, Carolyn hung up the receiver.

"John, something is wrong," she said as she turned so John could unzip her dark blue velvet gown. "I know she sent flowers but she didn't call. That's not Margaret."

"Carolyn, you're making something out of nothing," said John with an assurance he was not feeling. "How could Margaret have possibly called you? And where could she have called you? At the theatre? Impossible on opening night. At the Shuberts' party afterward? Come to bed. Margaret will call tomorrow."

"If she doesn't, I will. I know my sister. Unless something was wrong she would have reached me—even if it meant renting the news bulletin sign at the Times Building on Forty-second Street. Oh John, I do hope she's all right."

As Carolyn sat on the edge of the double bed, the events of the day were suddenly upon her. "John, it's over. It's actually over," she said of her opening night.

"It's just beginning, Lynnie," answered John as he massaged her shoulders. "Did I tell you how wonderful you were?"

"About a hundred times, but tell me again. I like hearing it," Carolyn said as she relaxed against her husband's chest.

"You were wonderful. You *are* wonderful," said John as he slipped his hand over her breast and pulled her down atop him on the bed.

"Now let me see if I've got it right," said Margaret. "There were . . . three 'incandescents,' three 'luminouses'—or is that lumini?—two 'radiants,' two 'very beautifuls,' one 'the very lovely,' and . . . a partridge in a pear tree. Is that right, John? Oh, so sorry," said Margaret as John corrected her. "That was *three* 'very beautifuls.' "

"Do you want to speak to herself?" asked John.

"Do I dare after such reviews? A better question is . . . does madame deign to speak with me?"

"She deigns," said John. "She's been deigning for two days."

"Yes, we've been missing each other," lied Margaret, who had been avoiding Carolyn's calls until she felt composed and certain about everything. Which is why she had waited until Wednesday. She knew it was shortly before noon in New York and that Carolyn could not speak for long on the phone as she would be preparing for her matinee.

"Well, here she comes, Margaret," said John. "The next voice you hear will be that of the incandescent, luminous, radiant, and . . ."

"Oh, shut up and give me that phone," Margaret could hear Carolyn say merrily. "Marg, is that finally you?"

"Hi, Lynnie-love. Congratulations! My gawd, but those are some reviews!"

"Oh, Marg, how I wish you had been here. It was the most exciting night of my life."

"As one who loves you, Carolyn, I would have hoped it was the second most exciting night of your life."

"I am not going to dignify that remark with a response. I refuse to stoop to your level," responded Carolyn with mock severity.

"Which is why your opening was the most exciting night of your life," replied Margaret. "You'll regret it someday."

"Do be serious, would you. I want to know if you're all right."

"Me? It's you we're talking about. John tells me there are lines at the box office each day."

"Yes, it's incredible because the reviews for the play were not that good."

"It must be your luminous incandescence that's selling tickets."

"Would you stop! You know I'm none of those things . . . except maybe radiant . . . and very lovely."

"But were you good?" said Margaret, suppressing giggles.

A suddenly very sober Carolyn responded: "That's the best of it. Yes, I think I was. The first few minutes were rough but then I lost me and became her. And she's so wonderful to be. Sophisticated . . . witty."

"How smart of the producers to go against type," bantered Margaret.

"Go ahead, make fun. But . . . are you sitting down? . . . *But* . . . the talk in the papers is . . . I will be tested for Scarlett in *Gone With the Wind*. Put that in your pipe and smoke it!"

"To think you owe it all to me and those two dreary days you put me through, teaching you to act."

"When did you ever teach me anything about acting?" demanded Carolyn.

"On The Chief, when you *forced* me into sharing the secrets of the stars with you. And I want to tell you now, if you get the Scarlett O'Hara role, I will strangle you with your rosary beads."

"That's no way to talk to the 'New Star on the Broadway Horizon.' That's what the *World-Telegram* called me and you know if they said it, it's so. What? Oh. Marg, hold on a second. John's leaving."

Margaret, three thousand miles away, could hear the sound of the kiss. Carolyn's happiness brought her own distress to the surface.

"Marg? Sorry. John had to leave. Killerbrew's been terrific about the time off John took this week—the opening and all. He's really been the ideal boss."

"He does seem to know what he's doing," agreed Margaret thoughtfully.

"Marg, that's another reason I was dying to talk to you," said Carolyn excitedly. "Oh, I've got so much to tell you! Marg, John sneaked me into a press showing of *Street Urchin* yesterday afternoon. Marg, you're so awful, you're good!"

"You saw what I was trying to do then," said Margaret, again momentarily distracted from her immediate distress.

"It took a lot of courage. You make it work by a hair. John thinks you're going to get a nomination. He says Killerbrew is going to spend a fortune to publicize you."

"A nomination?" said Margaret, dumbfounded.

"Yes, dopey. Supporting actress. Why not? It's a terrific performance, Marg. Tessie's big. She's right there. You can't forget her."

"Boy, is the mother of the brat who plays ole Urchin going to hate me! What an awful woman. Thank God, our mother was never like that."

"We have a lot to thank God for," was Carolyn's reply.

In the ensuing silence, as Margaret's distress lumped itself in her throat, Carolyn contentedly looked about her peach and gray bedroom with its damask wallpaper and canopy bed. Last evening's party dress lay draped carefully over the pale peach moiré chaise longue on which one could sit and look out the windows at Central Park. It was a lovely room. It was a lovely life. It was lovely to be . . .

"Marg, I'm pregnant," blurted out Carolyn. "I'm going to have a baby. Marg, a baby! Me."

Carolyn heard her sister crying. "I know, I know. I cried too, when the doctor first told me. It's so wonderful. I'm due in June. Imagine. A June bride and a June mother. John says it's all worked out perfectly. The producers really don't think the play will last through the spring. Marg, you've got to promise me, if it's at all possible, you'll come East when I'm due."

The crying on the other end of the line was soft but persistent. As if first hearing it, Carolyn's ebullient mood vanished in a pang of anxiety. "Margaret, what is it?" she demanded urgently.

That her sister was finally there, tuned in to her, caused Margaret to break down totally. When her sobs made it impossible for her to speak, Carolyn hysterically demanded to know: "Margaret, *please*. Talk to me. Are you sick?" When there was still no response, Carolyn, her world now focused on a telephone, cried, "Marg, you're scaring me to death. Are you in trouble? Please . . . what is it?"

Franklin Killerbrew pressed on the intercom button. "Yes, Miss Wolfe, what is it?"

"Margaret Tiernan on the line, sir. Shall I put her through?" asked the secretary in her usual starched manner.

"Put her on," said Killerbrew, wondering what could be Margaret's complaint. There were no sounds of discontent emanating from *The Back Bay Way* set that he had heard.

"How are you, Margaret," he said crisply, the question meant to reach the immediate point of her phone call.

"I have a problem," said Margaret tersely, which made its urgency seem all that more evident to Killerbrew. After quickly checking his appointments, he said, "Be here when you break. I'll cancel my lunch." When he hung up the phone, Killerbrew heaved himself up from his swivel chair and lumbered to his bar. So what if it's only nine-fifteen? My gut doesn't know that. Nor does Margaret Tiernan's problem— whatever it is. As he poured a tumblerful of bourbon, he wondered: What problem could Margaret Tiernan have? His head shook emphatically rejecting his first thought. Impossible! Not Margaret.

Shortly after noon, Margaret, wearing that morning's costume, a white organza gown etched in petunia-pink feathers, flounced into Killerbrew's office. Killerbrew greeted her with: "Had I known, I'd have dressed for lunch. Somehow, tuna fish salad doesn't seem to suit you right now." He waited for a smile, anything that would lighten the moment. There was nothing. Margaret, taking pains not to crease her dress, sat in the wing chair by Killerbrew's desk.

"We broke in the middle of Priscilla's coming-out party. The scene wasn't working and Cukor wanted to rethink it. He should rethink this damn dress, too. It's wrong, all wrong. I keep telling him Priscilla is not about frills or feathers. But will he listen? No."

For a moment, Killerbrew had hopes that *this* was Margaret's problem. For a moment.

"I'm pregnant," she said suddenly, not waiting for a natural break in the conversation to segue from one topic to the next. "Eight weeks and four days pregnant."

"By such a precise 'nose count,' I assume you know who the father is," said Killerbrew, his voice reflecting none of the emotion he felt.

"This will come no doubt as a great shock to you, considering how *concerned* you were with my misspent youth, but . . . there has only been one man since I returned to California. One man and one weekend. Both were a mistake."

"What does he intend to do about your mistake?" asked Killerbrew.

125

"Nothing, because he knows nothing about it and I intend to keep it that way," said Margaret. "He would not want to marry and I, frankly, would not want to marry him."

"Okay, I'll take care of it," said Killerbrew. "I'll get you off early Friday from shooting. We'll have it done Friday night and you can have the weekend to rest up."

"We'll have *what* done?" said Margaret angrily. "Do you think I came here to have you arrange an abortion? I am having this child!"

Her words shocked Killerbrew. Used to actresses throwing themselves at his feet, begging his forgiveness for their stupidities, promising him a forever of abstinence if only this once he would save them by arranging a "little surgery," he was unprepared for what Margaret was suggesting.

"You want to have this baby?" he said, sounding stupid even to himself. When she nodded, he said evenly, "Are you aware this will kill your career? Not injure or maim, but kill You'll be through . . . finished." Again, Margaret nodded her understanding. "But why?" asked Killerbrew, amazed. "Oh, God, it's that Catholicism shit, isn't it?" he moaned as he answered his own question.

"No. It has nothing to do with religion," said Margaret thinking of Carolyn's reaction. Her sister had been horrified, not by the "mistake"—about that she hadn't said a word—but at the mere contemplation of abortion. "It's Antichrist . . . a mortal sin," she had fussed. They had fought when Margaret bitterly said: "Your God certainly does strange things with His powers. He gives me a life I do not want or need and He gave me death—two deaths to be precise—that I also did not want or need. Your God certainly does work in mysterious ways."

"That's blasphemy. Stop it!" Carolyn had demanded

"Preach at me and I'll hang up," threatened Margaret.

"You come home, you hear me? You come to me and John," Carolyn had said, near tears. "I do not want you going through this alone. My house is yours. We will take the baby. No one need ever know it isn't ours. We'll say I had twins."

"Don't you think, Lynnie dear, that someone, maybe a doctor, a nurse or two at the hospital, might notice you are delivered of one, just one baby?"

Still, when Margaret hung up the phone, she felt relieved. She was at the very least assured she had a place to go. She had sought Killerbrew because she felt her employer had a right to know of her decisions. That he would fire her, exercise the morals clause in her contract, and that no one would blame him for doing so, she expected.

"If it has nothing to do with religious beliefs, what then?" demanded Killerbrew. "What is prompting you to ruin your life? You haven't gone mental on me, have you?"

"If you mean have I taken leave of my senses, who knows?" answered Margaret. "I just know I cannot kill . . . cannot take a life."

"Then it *is* religious," said Killerbrew, grasping at some straw of understanding.

"No, it isn't. I do not believe for a second in sin or divine retribution. It is the fact that something is there inside me . . . growing. Is it or isn't it entitled to its growth? Would I be committing murder by having an abortion?"

"You talk as if it were alive . . . conscious, a living person," said Killerbrew.

"Are you so certain it isn't?" Margaret answered.

Killerbrew shook his head in disbelief. "You never fail to amaze me. So you're going to throw away a career rather than do what a few hundred women in this town do yearly."

"What others do has never interested me, and doesn't now," snapped Margaret. "And if you think this is easy for me, some whim of a madwoman, guess again. I don't want a baby—not this one or any one. I hate the whole idea of being a mother . . . now. I'm an actress. A damn good one. I want to prove it. You've heard this before so it shouldn't knock your socks off: I want to be a star but, unlike these women you mention, I won't kill for it."

"Then tell the guy and make him marry you," said Killerbrew sullenly.

"Let me ask you something, *boss*. How would my publicity read married to Donald Malloy?"

"Oh, shit!" said Killerbrew as he slapped his forehead with his hand. "Oh, shit!" he repeated. "I'll have the fucker fired."

"No! That's not fair. I was the instigator."

When Killerbrew's face registered surprise, Margaret continued. "This is a strange town you co-own, Mr. Killerbrew. A girl who does not play by its rules can get very lonely. We make mistakes when we're lonely. We settle for crumbs when we're starving."

"Aren't you the least bit frightened?" Killerbrew asked as Margaret looked at him defiantly.

"Terrified," she said, her expression not changing.

Killerbrew swung his swivel chair around until he was facing the windows.

"Don't turn your back on me!" yelled Margaret.

"For once in your life shut up. I'm not turning my back on you or your problems. I'm thinking. Eat your tuna fish. Chew gum. Do anything but talk."

In the next five minutes, Killerbrew spoke once. "You're on a six-week shooting schedule, right?" When she verified what he already knew, he said, "You shouldn't be showing at less than four months." Then, not a word. Finally, he swiveled back to face her.

"Okay, I've got it all solved. It'll work. It'll save your ass and his and my picture."

"Would it be too much to ask what you're talking about? I hate to pry but it is my life we're still discussing, I assume."

"Your life and the part of it I own," Killerbrew said as he pressed down on his intercom's buzzer.

"Yes, Mr. Killerbrew," came Dorothea Wolfe's voice from the machine.

"Find Sonny Stevens. He's either on Sound Stage Six or on the back lot. If he's shooting, tell the director to knock it off until Stevens gets back. I want him up here and fast."

Killerbrew clicked off the intercom without waiting for a reply. Then, as if Margaret were not there, he began leafing through the interoffice memos that had accumulated in his in-box, making notes on some and returning others to a box marked "file." As Margaret watched, she was both furious and fascinated.

"What kind of a man are you? The very least you could do is tell me what's going on," she said angrily.

"I'm organizing things—like people's lives," said Killerbrew, his face still among the pages. "I'm killing two birds with one stone—saving Stevens's ass and yours. Remember that when you want to open that mouth of yours and make what will surely prove to be dumb noises."

"I don't have to take this," said Margaret as she stood, her body quivering with rage.

"Sit down, Margaret," said Killerbrew without raising his voice. "I'm about to let you have your baby and your career."

Margaret sat.

"Mr. Stevens is here," announced Dorothea Wolfe via the intercom. When the door opened, Sonny Stevens, in cowboy

128

hat, chaps, neckerchief, spurs, and boots, stood hesitantly in the doorway, a sheepish grin on his face. "Hi there Mr Killerbrew," he said in that lazy, near Southern drawl for which he was famous.

"Kill the Southern shit and sit down, Sonny ⸱⸱⸱ got some news for you."

The Western star did as Killerbrew said, acknowledging Margaret with a doff of his hat as he did. Margaret forced a smile in reply. "I've just been checking shooting schedules," began Killerbrew, "and you two lucky kids both get to have this Friday off. A three-day weekend. How about that, kids?"

"Hey now, Mr. Killerbrew, that's really neat," said Stevens, grinning like a kid who has been rewarded with ice cream for being good. "How about that, Margaret. Ain't that swell of Mr. Killerbrew?"

"Swell," said Margaret sourly, her eyes fixed on the studio chief, awaiting his next move.

"By the way, Sonny, I want to be the first to congratulate you," said Killerbrew.

"Well yeah, thanks. Sure. But . . . what for?" said Stevens, his grin now covering confusion rather than delight.

"On your marriage," said Killerbrew.

The grin was gone. So was all trace of the drawl when Stevens spoke. "What are you talking about? I'm not getting married."

"Oh, yes you are, Stevens. This weekend. In Yuma. Friday night. And to Miss Tiernan here. Now doesn't that make you the lucky man?"

"I'm not getting married to no one," said Stevens dully.

"I say you are, Stevens," said Killerbrew. "Actually, you've been planning this for months but Margaret here has been too busy making films to fly away with you for a long weekend."

"I'm not getting married," said Stevens, his eyes fixed on the Winslow Homer on the far wall.

Killerbrew shot up out of his chair and was around his desk and positioned in front of Stevens in less than a second. "You're not, eh? Okay, Stevens, then we'll let the son of a bitch who has the negatives—you know which ones I mean, Stevens, the ones showing you with a dick in your mouth while another is up your butt—share those goodies with the press. And speaking of 'goodies,' in the future, when you're getting yours off the Santa Monica pier or cruising along Hollywood Boulevard, I don't pay off the police for keeping it

129

quiet when you've been arrested by the vice squad for lewd and indecent behavior."

"Stop it!" screamed Margaret, horrified not by the facts but by Killerbrew's methods of intimidation.

Killerbrew turned on her with a fury she had not expected. "I told you, keep your mouth shut! You made *a* mistake; he's made many. One *too* many. Tell Margaret," said Killerbrew to Stevens, whose hands now covered his face as he stood, his body bent in submission, "where we found you this weekend. Since she is so concerned, shouldn't she know about you and the two kids—I believe the law calls them minors—that you were found with in Griffith Park in, shall we say, a 'compromising position.' "

"Don't do this to him. Please, I beg you," said Margaret, her tears falling out of control.

"Miss Tiernan, I'm not doing anything to him in comparison to what would have been done if I were not Franklin Killerbrew. He'd be in jail, the key thrown away for about thirty years. He would be out on his ass, without a job, penniless. No house on the beach; no Bentley to drive. Isn't that right, Stevens?"

The actor nodded his head that it was.

"And Miss Tiernan, something else you should know. This studio, like all major studios, provides 'special services'—if you get my drift—for men like Mr. Stevens who have 'special' sexual tastes. We make it easy and safe. But does Mr. Stevens avail himself of these services or does Mr. Stevens make a fucking fool of himself and endanger not only his career but his life. Don't look so shocked, Miss Tiernan, we aim to please here. If you were interested in a little physical activity that some would call bizarre—you know how small-minded some people out there in the heartland can be about certain things—we would provide it. We do everything to make life comfortable for our stars. Including marriage.

"I'm doing you a favor, Stevens," said Killerbrew, again turning his attention to the man now sitting on one of the leather couches weeping. "I'm giving your career and your reputation a much needed shot in the arm. I'm killing the talk about your being a fag. I'm giving you a wife who in about seven months is going to give you a baby. You're going to be a father, Stevens. Hey, how 'bout *that*! And you won't have to do a thing to be one. The photographers will take pretty pictures of you and baby, and all that talk will be

130

forgotten. Everyone knows fairies don't make babies. And your wife here, she gets to keep her good name and her career. And her baby, too, whether she wants it or not."

"How long?" asked Stevens, his voice husky but once again strong.

"That's up to you and Miss Tiernan. But I would say a year would do nicely. Then she can file for divorce on the grounds of mental cruelty. You live together till then. And you toe the line, Stevens. Any extracurricular activity, you come to us—you use the service."

"How much?" said Stevens.

"He means how much is this going to cost him," Killerbrew explained to Margaret. "Not one thin dime, Stevens. You're getting in for free. And out, too. No alimony and no child support. The lady here will decline both at the divorce trial. She'll be a regular suffragette. Isn't that right, Margaret?"

But Margaret was not responding to Killerbrew. She had risen and crossed the room to sit next to Stevens, who was trembling, his face ashen. She stroked his light blond hair and pushed it off his forehead. When his eyes still wouldn't meet hers, she lifted his chin, put her hand to his cheek and then, when he finally looked at her, she kissed him lightly on the lips. She then put both arms around him. As she hugged Stevens, he began to cry. Margaret continued to hold the man until he became calm and composed. Then he adjusted his hat, rose from the leather couch, and said from the doorway in his drawl: "Thanks, boss. I'll never forget you for this." What struck Margaret most was: Stevens meant his every word. As she stood, watching the door close behind the man who had been ordered to be her husband, she became dimly aware of Killerbrew behind her. As he very gently put his hand on her shoulder he said, "In dealing with children, you have to be firm. Spare the rod and you spoil the child."

Margaret turned to face him. "I think you're sick," she said contemptuously, "and your sickness contaminates everything and everybody."

"All you have to do then is see another doctor," said Killerbrew as he walked back to his desk. "But you won't. None of you ever do."

By seven Friday morning, they were driving to Yuma. Behind the wheel of his Bentley, Stevens had his peaked cap pulled low over his forehead to keep the rising sun's rays out of his eyes. It was the first time Margaret had ever seen the actor without his cowboy gear. The morning had been difficult for Margaret. The fact that this was her wedding day was inescapable. For a moment, she saw the humor in her situation as she searched through the closet for something appropriate to wear. Not many brides suffered with the what-should-I-wears. She chose a pale blue linen suit for the drive and the wedding, and packed a simple cotton print dress, a pair of beige slacks, and two brightly colored blouses for changes. But no pink negligée or purple-passion peignoir, she realized as she folded a pair of cotton pj's into her suitcase and a black silk robe she felt was more functional than sexy.

When Margaret Tiernan had fantasized as a girl about her wedding day, she had envisioned something small and elegant, perhaps at home in the family garden or in the well-appointed den of a noted judge. She saw herself in a white tailored suit or dress, depending on the hour of day, about to be married to the catch of the century. Well, thought Margaret, that I'm getting if one is to believe the fan magazines.

To the last, Carolyn had insisted: "You don't *have* to do this. We'll manage." But Margaret had to do "this" and it was John who was both understanding and supportive. When Carolyn's concern unintentionally became emotionally abusive, it was John who pried her off the phone and gave Margaret back her composure. Carolyn could not accept "It is not forever, just for now. For now and the baby. We'll be divorced before you know it." The last Margaret discovered was not comforting to Carolyn, who remained disconsolate. "At least come to New York and let me make the wedding," she pleaded. But there was no time. Both Margaret and Sonny had only a weekend before resuming work on their current films.

"Don't worry, Lynnie," Margaret had said. "Next time up you can do the honors. Then it will matter; now it doesn't."

But it did matter, Margaret had realized that morning as she dressed. Call it what you would—a marriage of convenience, a shotgun wedding, even—it *was* a wedding, and to Margaret's dismay, she had her feelings about it. None of them good. How strange it suddenly felt about to be married to a man she hardly knew. When they had been filming *Raton Pass*, Sonny had always been respectful and friendly but remote. He never sought her company at lunch or during breaks. But she had liked him because he was a generous actor. He never fought over "best sides" and when in doubt, gave the advantage to Margaret without being asked to do so. He was a thoroughly professional if limited actor. Even when he was hung over, which was frequent, he was on time and prepared, his lines memorized. What she had seen of Sonny Stevens, she liked. What she had heard about his off-screen behavior, she paid little mind to. Now that she was marrying him, she hoped that behavior would modify.

What most couples do when they're courting, Margaret and Sonny did on their drive to get married: "got acquainted." He had been born in St. Louis but had moved to a small town in Iowa where a farm kept the bare essentials on the table for his two brothers, three sisters, and him. His real name was Stanley Stinkowski and he went through his youth nicknamed "Stinky," which gave him ample practice for the fake fights he would later make famous in film. He had left home at sixteen and had not seen his family in the eleven years since. At Christmas, they sent a card; he, a check for a hundred dollars.

Stevens's life story, as it were, depressed Margaret all the more. Suddenly she was crying and Stevens, concerned, abruptly pulled the Bentley off to the side of the road. "Aw, Margaret, it won't be that bad," he said consolingly. "It's only for a year or so and I promise I'll try real hard to be nice and all. I mean . . . I like you, Margaret. I really do. You're a nice gal. I know we ain't exactly Romeo and Juliet but we won't hurt each other, which is more than a lot of folks can say. And that's gotta count for something."

Through her tears, Margaret saw her "lover."

"You know, Sonny," she said as she took a handkerchief from her handbag to blow her nose, "you're right. We're going to have a good time. As a matter of fact, we should shoot for the Best Twelve-Month Marriage ever recorded in Hollywood."

"Now hey, that's what I like to hear," said Sonny as he revved up the motor. "Say, Margaret, you know how to play Monopoly? Or poker? Yeah, poker. I'm real good at both but I'm extra good at poker. I can teach you. I also like the movies a lot. We can go a couple times a week, get hamburgers and stuff. I'm telling you, Margaret, we're going to have a lot of fun."

Margaret looked at Sonny, who was smiling as he hit the

car's top speed on the highway. "Sure, Sonny," she said. "I'd love to go to the movies with you."

The marriage ceremony in Yuma was brief. The judge was thrilled to be marrying *the* Sonny Stevens but not as thrilled as his wife, a kewpie-doll woman who giggled when she said to Margaret: "I don't mind standing up for you, honey, but I'd rather lay down for him." The judge, instead of being mortified, shook with laughter as he clapped Sonny on the back: "Ain't that just like a young hot-to-trot filly! Just can't stop kicking up her heels." An hour later, Margaret realized she was really married, truly Mrs. Sonny Stevens, when the local radio station announced their "nuptials." Later that day, the evening papers wrote: "Cowboy Star Corrals His Leading Lady." The "cowboy star," Margaret noted, was taking full advantage of the new Beautyrest mattress in the Bridal Suite at the Yuma City Hotel. Despite their "arrangement," Margaret could not help being physically aware of the man sleeping next to her in just his shorts. Unlike Malloy, Stevens was smooth-skinned, his blondness burnished gold by the sun. Margaret had not known it was possible for a man to have such beautiful skin. She found herself wanting to touch its smoothness. She also found herself wanting to trace the lines of his pectoral muscles that ended where his stomach became washboard flat. She found herself *wanting* and that frustrated her. Sonny Stevens was after all "a big lug" and he was lying next to her on their wedding night. Yet, for all he cared, she could be one of the boys, she thought, and then she laughed. Ah, that I should be so lucky!

134

4

She dominates the screen, thought John as he took another
bite of his egg salad sandwich. She's like a Lombard or a
Davis . . . mesmerizing. If the Academy doesn't nominate
her for *Urchin*, she's got it locked up next year. John was
rerunning in his mind the rough-cut he had seen that morning of *The Back Bay Way* as he waited for the prearranged
telephone call from Franklin Killerbrew. Soon, thought John
as he checked his watch, we will know. In a matter of
minutes the Oscar nominations for 1936 would be announced
in Hollywood. John knew Killerbrew had hopes for Margaret
in *Urchin*. He wondered if Margaret cared as much as
Killerbrew seemed to about a nomination. She had sounded
so listless the last time they had spoken as if even simple conversation was an effort. It had worried John to hear Margaret
without her usual banter. Well, he thought, she will certainly
perk up once Killerbrew shows her *Back Bay*.

Incredible about that man, mused John. His instincts were
infallible. Particularly about holding *Back Bay* for fall release.
"No one goes to the movies in the summer to be depressed.
And a film about some dame who winds up in the nuthouse is
depressing no matter how you slice it. Hold the film till late
fall or winter when people suffer better," he had decreed. Of
course Killerbrew was right. In the seven months that John
had been working for the man, he had discovered the studio
head was invariably right—about his product and his industry. He was also being proven right about Margaret. Still . . .
a laugh spontaneously burst free of John, causing him to spit
up egg salad as he recalled Franklin Killerbrew's terse cri-
tique of Margaret's performance in *Raton Pass*. "She sits on a
horse as though it was cactus. Thank God the only thing she
rides in *The Back Bay Way* is a train."

The sudden blast of wind that rattled the windows of his
twenty-sixth-floor office overlooking Broadway startled John

back into the present. He hoped Carolyn would be home from WEAF and WJZ before the predicted snowstorm began, although if Carolyn ran true to her recent form, she'd be out in the park building a snowman before leaving for the theatre. His wife continued to amaze him. Five months pregnant and showing no signs of slowing down. She had added soap operas to her daily schedule as she found it "boring" sitting at home, waiting for either John to return or the end of the day when she was due at the theatre. When her agent suggested acting on soaps, Carolyn acted with a vengeance. Within weeks, she was doubling and tripling, changing voices and characterizations on the late morning and early afternoon fifteen-minute serials. That *Weekend* was still running was a tribute to word of mouth about her performance. The producers had hoped after the reviews for a three- to four-month run at best. Now, it looked as if the play could go six to eight if Carolyn could. The costumes had been altered as much as possible to keep the illusion of glamour. Lots of Empire and free-flowing chiffon hid Carolyn's bulging belly, but the way she was recently expanding, she would soon need a tent.

His wife was blooming, the picture of happiness. So happy had she been about motherhood, she had taken to wearing maternity clothes in her third month when she was showing nothing. Already completed was the nursery, decorated in an "all-purpose" pink *and* blue. Carolyn, John saw, was preparing for motherhood with the same excitement and diligence with which she prepared for a play. According to all the published reports, not only was she Broadway's brightest new star, and he a bright young executive, but they were The Perfect Couple starring in The Perfect Marriage. And John agreed. He was the man who had everything *except* a sex life, but that would resume, he was certain, as soon as Carolyn delivered.

When the phone rang, John was deeply immersed in a fantasy of lovemaking as it would be with his beautiful wife. His erection, trapped by his jockey shorts, made it difficult for him to sit comfortably as Killerbrew started to read off the list of pictures, stars, directors, and writers nominated for Academy Awards.

The past five months had trickled by for Margaret. Sonny's Malibu Beach house was a lovely retreat if one felt the need to get away from it all. Margaret, who wanted *in*, not out or away, hated it. The sun was her enemy, and lethargy prevented her from enjoying the ocean. The highlight of her day had been driving the Bentley to the studio to pick up Sonny, who had taught her to drive. Louella found this nightly ritual "sweet" and "loving" and said so often to her readers. Actually, it was sanity-saving but Louella could not have known that any more than she could have known that the drive to and from the studio gave meaning and movement to Margaret's day.

Unlike other expectant mothers, Margaret did not have that special glow associated with pregnant women. Nor did her hair or her eyes shine with an extra luster. But she did have hemorrhoids. And doubts. And fears. All itched constantly. The hemorrhoids should go away but her motherhood would not and that disturbed her greatly. By her fifth month, Margaret was listless and in a chronic state of mild depression. The movies three and four times a week with Sonny became a chore. As did the Monopoly games. Soon, Sonny sought new playmates. He began to "work late" at the studio. She knew what that meant, having "worked late" herself when she had met Donald Malloy. She did not begrudge Sonny his "work" but she did hope he was taking care. Common sense was not his strongest suit, she knew. Alone much of the day and many an evening, she read newspapers, magazines, and books. She listened to the discussions and news broadcasts on radio. She answered the letters of those who wrote her after they viewed *Waifs* and *Urchin*. She cursed her "rotten luck," which seemed to turn when Dorothea Wolfe called shortly after ten one February morning to announce Margaret had been nominated for an Academy Award in the new Best Supporting Actress category for her performance in *Urchin*. That lent excitement to her life. The month prior to the awards, she lived in constant excitement, her mind dwelling on what she would say if she won. When Dorothea Wolfe called again in March to say Mr. Killerbrew did not wish her to attend the awards ceremony, Margaret was furious. Who the hell was he to decree: Pregnant women should be heard but not seen. Her rage was company until Oscar night. Then, when she heard Gale Sondegaard win in her category, she was glad for Killerbrew's mandate and glad she had not attended.

In her seventh month, Margaret's funk was interrupted when a special courier arrived from the studio. At first she

137

thought the script he delivered was for Sonny. Then she saw her name on it. Her hands trembled as she opened it. An hour later, as she sat on the awninged deck overlooking the ocean, her hands trembled as she closed it. Not daring to trust her first impression, Margaret hoisted her cumbersome body from the deck chair and waddled to what was once Sonny's den but was now her bedroom, where she lay down to read the script again. When she finally finished it, she was in tears. *How Does Your Garden Grow?* was brilliantly written and the role of Dominique Klaussen was rich in its many facets. She was a convent-bred French girl married to a doctor, a German Jew who refuses to see his immediate world in Berlin with the same clarity of vision as his wife does. Dominique Klaussen was real, a flesh-and-blood woman—no princess, waif, or semicrazed social climber—determined to save her husband and her marriage from a world she saw was rotting and thus collapsing. It was his refusal to believe that the worst was about to happen, and her insistence that the worst *had* happened, that gave the drama its impetus. The film's tragic ending brought the issues of the day into focus and, if one accepted the writer's vision, was a foretelling of the future.

Prior to her pregnancy, Margaret would not have felt the full impact or the implications of the script. Then, she was not reading the political analysts or listening to such soothsayers as Lowell Thomas and Gabriel Heatter, who warned of Hitler and the dual rise of Nazism in Germany and fascism in Italy. In the past six months Margaret had discovered there was a world apart from filmmaking, a world that often did not have a happy ending. When she tried to discuss Hitler and the Nazis with sweet, considerate Sonny, he was not interested. If she had persisted and mentioned the Rhineland, she was sure he would have offered to trade Park Place or Boardwalk for it and then plotted to build houses. Which is why after consuming the script a third time, she applauded Franklin Killerbrew for his foresight and courage. *How Does Your Garden Grow?* was a great departure from the usual Killerbrew film. That he was giving Dominique Klaussen to her was hard to believe. Twice that morning, she looked at the envelope to assure herself that indeed the script had been meant for her. When she finally accepted the fact, she wrote—as she had once before—a thank-you note to Killerbrew and he, as before, once again did not respond.

Just as Carolyn, from her letters, seemed obsessed with having a baby, Margaret was obsessed with having her film. *Garden* was the silver lining in her currently clouded sky. It was her tranquilizer and motivator. It lifted her doldrums and it increased her impatience to "have this baby and be done with it." That she thought and worried more about Dominique Klaussen than she did about her baby was bothersome only when she allowed herself to think about it.

There was never any question about where Margaret would be when Carolyn's and her own baby were born. Thus, in the beginning of her eighth month, Margaret took The Chief to Chicago and the Twentieth Century from there to New York where the family gathered at Grand Central Station to greet her. Sonny would follow when Margaret's "time" grew closer. Killerbrew would see to that as he would to the photographers who would be alerted to photograph the new "range-rider" when he made his appearance.

Despite "Margaret's Room" being the name affixed to the guest room, Margaret felt both guest and stranger in what was Carolyn and John's home no matter how often they said it was also hers. Had that been true, the dark and the drearies of the midnight blues Carolyn so loved would have gone within twenty-four hours of Margaret's arrival. Only Augusta's room had the comfort of the past while existing in the present.

Her aunt had changed, Margaret noticed. She was much more attractive, womanly, but didn't seem very happy about it. Margaret was surprised when she learned Augie had resumed her volunteer work at the hospital two afternoons a week. She would have thought her aunt's duties as the family's bookkeeper had been exhausting enough.

A few weeks after her arrival, Margaret found herself taking tea with her aunt as they went over her financial situation.

"Some would say you're a very wealthy young lady," said Augusta. "Besides your share of the monies from the sale of the Murray Hill house, you also have whatever you've saved since *Much Ado*, and whatever criticism might be leveled at you, Margaret, extravagance is not one."

"Oh?" said Margaret, her eyebrow arching much the way her mother's would when she was being sarcastic. "Is criticism being leveled at me? You wouldn't be the critic, would you, Aunt Augie?"

Augusta removed her reading glasses and put them down

139

on the ledger marked "Margaret Tiernan." "Just what provisions have you made for your baby when you return to Hollywood?"

"There's a layette in my room. I've bought a crib and Carolyn has purchased enough diapers to change all the children in Beverly Hills, Pasadena, and Orange County."

"But who is going to take care of your child?" persisted Augusta.

"What do you mean, 'who'? For beginners, there's me."

"I do believe you said *Garden* begins filming the first Monday in September and will last longer than most—about eight weeks. Is that not right? Well then," continued Augusta when Margaret nodded her head that the information was correct, "who will be staying with the baby?"

"I'm taking Rose back with me," said Margaret.

"Rose Wheaton is an old woman. She cannot raise your child."

"Sonny will help. You have no idea how excited he is about the baby," argued Margaret.

"From what you have told me, Sonny Stevens is a baby himself. His interest will last until a new toy comes along. Instead of playing Monopoly, he's found a new game called Daddy. How long do you think that will last?"

"Why are you being so obnoxious?" asked Margaret angrily. "The last thing I need in my life right now is further complications."

"I would agree," answered Augusta stiffly, "and that's what I'm trying to avoid. Whether you like it or not, you have 'complications'—a baby, it's called. And you owe it something."

"Thank you for reminding me of my obligations," said Margaret. "It's sweet of you and I'll never forget it."

"I hope not," snapped Augusta. "Margaret, listen to me. I recognize you will live your life as you see fit. And frankly, that's how it should be. I have no quarrel with that. You pick and you choose. But Margaret, babies cannot pick and do not have choices. Their mothers, whether they like them or not, are their mothers. They are victims and I see scores of these little victims at the hospital. Don't let your child become one of them."

"What are you talking about?" screamed Margaret. "My baby isn't even born and you already have it sickly, in the hospital, abandoned and abused."

"Because I see you have already abandoned your child and that is an abuse!"

Augusta's vehemence lashed at Margaret. She not only heard her aunt's words but felt their truth. "I guess I'm not what one would call a 'born mother,'" she admitted feebly. "I don't know what I'll do when the baby is born. I wish I could say I'll love it to pieces but I don't know that, and why lie? So you'll continue to love me?"

"That's not even at question here, Margaret," said Augusta. "My loving you has absolutely nothing to do with my liking your every action. It never has. You have always felt more like my daughter than my niece. How often I've heard how some mothers try to live through their daughters. I could almost have done that. I respect what others would call your selfishness but which I see as strength. I doubt if you'll have many regrets in your lifetime, Margaret."

"Oh, I don't know," said Margaret with an uneasy laugh. "I think I'll always have one," she said as she pointed to her nearly nine months of pregnancy.

"Your regret should not become your child's cross to bear. That's all I'm saying," said Augusta,

"Of course you're right," answered Margaret. "Aunt Augie . . . come back with me to California. I need you."

"No, dear. I cannot do that. You must learn to live your life just as I am learning to live mine."

"Do you want to talk about it?" asked Margaret softly as she refilled her aunt's teacup with the still hot Shamrock tea.

"About what?" asked Augusta, confused.

"About whoever he is or was and what he has to do, if anything, with your being back at the hospital," said Margaret as she stirred the two sugars and cream into Augusta's cup.

"There is nothing to talk about. Really, Margaret," said Augusta when she saw her niece was about to protest. "I'm not hiding anything or maintaining a privacy I don't need with you. I knew a man—a lawyer—Stephen Cartwright, and he knew me. We knew each other, and then we found we didn't know each other at all. Or what we did know didn't seem as attractive as it initially did. What more is there to add? Think back, Margaret, did you have anything to say when you knew it was finished between you and Donald?"

Margaret thought for a moment. "Nada. Niente. Not a damn thing. Sooo, Aunt Augie, tell me. What else is new?

Read any good books lately and how would you like a blind date with the milkman?"

Augusta laughed as did Margaret. In the middle of their girlish giggles, they looked at one another and simultaneously started to cry.

"For an 'arranged' marriage, Sonny certainly calls a lot," said Carolyn as she poked about the Woolworth's on upper Broadway. "Are you sure this is a platonic relationship?"

"Very sure," replied Margaret. "We're just friends, very good friends, and that's so strange since we hardly knew each other when we got married. He's a nice, nice man, Lynnie."

"Ugh!" shuddered Carolyn. "But he does those awful things."

"The 'things' may be awful to you, maybe even to me—I don't know—but he is not. Besides, did it ever dawn on you that maybe he thinks what you do with John is awful?"

"He may be right," said Carolyn, laughing her way to the counter where the diaper pins were on display.

"Carolyn, put down those pins and look at me. No jokes. Do you think what you do with John is awful?" asked Margaret, aghast at the thought.

"Margaret," whispered Carolyn. "The five-and-dime is hardly the place to discuss my sex life!"

"Are you having one?" demanded Margaret.

"During my pregnancy? Don't be ridiculous," answered Carolyn. "I wouldn't think of it."

"But John might. He might be thinking about it right now . . with someone else."

"Think about it? Maybe. But do it? Not John. He's not that kind of man," said Carolyn as she moved toward the sundries counter and added baby powder and baby oil to her purchases.

"Carolyn, listen to me," said Margaret urgently. "You will lose him with that attitude. All men are 'that kind' of man. Do you plan to regain and retain your virginity throughout the next fifty years of your marriage?"

"Margaret, you pay far too much attention to sex," was Carolyn's response.

"And you, not enough!" replied Margaret, concerned. "Lynnie, a man is different from a woman. He . . ."

"Please, Margaret!" interrupted Lynnie. "People can hear you. Besides, what are you getting so upset about? It's not like I'm planning total abstinence."

Margaret momentarily froze. Then she whirled her sister about until they were facing one another. "What's *that* supposed to mean?"

"Just that it will be the rhythm method from here on," said Carolyn as she added Vaseline to her purchases. "Time now to devote myself to other things."

"You mean raising your child," said Margaret, feeling a pang of guilt.

"Oh, no. That won't be a problem. Not with adequate help. No, what I mean is: I don't need more babies but I do need a good play. A *vehicle* as the expression goes, one with *legs*."

"With what?" echoed Margaret dumbly.

"Legs! Something that will run," answered Carolyn. "Do you realize nothing I've been in has lasted more than six months? I need a *smash*, some kind of vehicle I can take to London."

"Keep talking in terms like 'legs' and 'smash,' and the only vehicle you'll take is the one that goes daily to Reno," cautioned Margaret.

"Don't be stupid," said Carolyn angrily "You're being a worrywart over nothing. John will adjust. He loves me and he knows I love him. Really, Margaret, sex isn't that important in a marriage. Not when two people love each other."

"You're in for a big surprise one day, kiddo," said Margaret as she signed an autograph for two women who had recognized her. "You amaze me. You not only look like the *Hindenburg* but given your attitudes on sex, I fully expect your marriage to go down the way it did."

"Thank you for your vote of confidence," said Carolyn. "As I've always said, it takes a blimp to know one. Now what say we pay for all this stuff and go home. I'm having gas pains. It must be the tuna fish we had earlier. Tuna fish always gives me gas."

"Are you sure you're not just having an allergic reaction to the mere mention of the word *sex*?" bantered Margaret as she took the package from the salesgirl behind the cash register.

Carolyn laughed. In mid-giggle, she gasped and then doubled over.

"Lynnie, what is it?" demanded Margaret, terrified.

"Oh my God, I'm in labor," said Carolyn, her face contorted. "Marg, I'm having the baby."

"Not here you're not. No relative of mine is going to be born in the five-and-dime. Come. You sit here," said Margaret as she took Carolyn by the arm and sat her down at the store's lunch counter, "and I'll call a cab to take us home."

"Marg, I don't think so," said Carolyn, biting her lip. "I think we'd better go straight to Doctors Hospital."

"Lynnie. I'll call John. Just stay right here."

"Margaret, where would I possibly go?"

"Knowing you? To a manger or to three wise men—whichever was closer."

Within the half hour, John, Dr. Randolph Garber, and Margaret were grouped around Carolyn's bed in her pale aqua room in the hospital. Thirty minutes later, Augusta arrived, having detoured from Bellevue up to the Central Park West apartment to gather Carolyn's things. The assemblage made awkward conversation as they watched Carolyn for signs of progress.

"Why don't you sit down, Mrs. Stevens," suggested Dr. Garber.

"On that couch?" replied Margaret, pointing to the overstuffed sofa covered in turquoise chintz. "I'd never get up. It would take a derrick. I'm fine here," she said as she moved a light cane-back chair to the side of Carolyn's bed.

"On second thought, perhaps it might be best if we all left and let Mrs. Ollson get some rest," said Dr. Garber as he noticed the sweat on Carolyn's forehead and the pain in her eyes.

"I'll stay here," said Margaret, reaching for Carolyn's hand.

"I don't think it's advisable," said the doctor, "not in your condition."

"I'm not moving," said Margaret, her voice firm and forbidding, "not unless Carolyn wants me to."

When Carolyn signaled she did not, the doctor withdrew. Augusta was first to kiss her niece and squeeze her hand in support. "Well, it looks like it's true after all. You're going to make me a great-aunt," she said, smiling down at Carolyn.

"You're already a great aunt," said Carolyn. "You're just going to be a little greater."

John sat by his wife's side, toweling her forehead as his free hand covered hers. As he did, Carolyn touched his cheek. "You better go if you want me to get on with making you a father." John touched his lips to hers and then whispered in her ear.

"I love you, too," Carolyn replied softly. "I love you, too."

"Good evening, Mr. and Mrs. North America and all the ships at sea. Let's go to press. Flash! From the two-for-the-price-of-one department. That gorgeous Broadway baby Carolyn Tiernan had not one but two bouncing babies of her own this week. The lady's leading man is Killerbrew pix New York studio chief John Ollson. The Perfect Couple is calling their brand-new productions Thomas and Martha. Top billing goes to Master Thomas as he was first to take the stage at Doctors Hospital June twelfth, while Miss Martha made her debut a few minutes later on June thirteenth. . . . Flash! Robert Taylor and Barbara Stanwyck . . ."

In the back seat of the chauffeur-driven Packard, Margaret, her shoes off and her feet up on the collapsed seat in front of her, watched as the sun became a memory of the day gone by. She had never even glimpsed it, she realized. The car had called for her at five-thirty that morning and by six-fifteen, just as the sky was turning pink, setting the stage for the sun's arrival, she was driving through the gates of Killerbrew Studios. By six-thirty, her hair was being washed and set. At noon, she took lunch in her dressing room, too weary to attempt the stroll to the commissary. They were in the last week of shooting on *How Does Your Garden Grow?* It had been chaotic from the beginning. Killerbrew, after viewing the first week's rushes, had the director replaced. That, plus endless retakes, had the picture over budget and running well beyond its initially anticipated finish date. Despite the false starts and setbacks, throughout the studio there was an air of expectancy about *Garden*. Word was out it was an "important" film.

Hollywood, noted Margaret, respected "importance," particularly if dollar signs were attached to it. Now that the reviews for *The Back Bay Way* had established her as a star, she found she had the peer respect that previously had been denied her. Now, she was propositioned by the best and not just the mediocre or the would-bes. There were other "simple" pleasures awarded with "importance" and stardom. The studio-driven car was one, particularly appreciated this Friday when every bone ached after a twelve-hour day. And her dressing room had more new appliances and conveniences than most new houses. She could iron, curl, wash, dry, and whirlpool herself into pampered ecstasy if she chose. She didn't. For her professional life, Margaret preferred the simple, uncluttered look; her dressing room remained sleek and spare.

Margaret's personal life had much the same look. Except for Vinnie, it was uncluttered and uncomplicated. Physically, the baby took up little room; emotionally, he dominated her homelife. Sonny, on the other hand, was there when she wanted him to be. In typical Sonny fashion, he generously gave her and the baby the upstairs bedroom, actually a suite of connecting rooms that spanned the length of the house, as he settled into what was once his den and later, Margaret's bedroom. The arrangement provided a certain amount of privacy for both. When Margaret chose to—which was seldom—she could open the front door and go directly to her quarters without ever seeing Sonny. Of course, if she wanted kitchen privileges or to see Rose Wheaton, whose room was off the cooking area, she had to go through the communal living room and pass the den. It was a comfortable living arrangement. Both had agreed from the beginning of their marriage that they would not bring home their "dates." Both had complied with that agreement, a feat much easier for Margaret who had had none.

Which is probably part of the reason gossip in this town has me a lesbian, thought Margaret as the Packard sped along the Pacific Highway, drawing nearer to the Malibu colony. That plus my marriage to Sonny. Why else would I marry him if I weren't like him in my sexual tastes. To Margaret's amusement, these rumors never took into account her motherhood. Was Vinnie an immaculate conception? And wouldn't Carolyn laugh at that one. Eventually I will make changes, thought Margaret, too tired to give much thought to what was not really a problem in her life. When *Garden* is finished, when I'm rested, I'll look for a place for Vinnie and myself.

The thought of Vinnie made her smile. He was adventuresome like his mother, at five months wanting to walk before he could crawl. He was a good child although demanding. He loved an audience, someone to play before or with. A rattle, two fingers, a bracelet, or a key chain were all props to be used in his self-centered world. Everything fascinated him; he had been born that way. This was a baby who couldn't wait to see the world. It still struck Margaret as terribly funny, in an ironic sense, that Carolyn, who so much had

146

wanted to be a mother, took fourteen hours to deliver, while Margaret, who had no such desire, took one hour and twenty-two minutes.

Vincent—named for her mother, of course—was born ten days after his cousins Martha and Thomas—with a full head of rich black hair making him look even more ugly than Margaret thought he was. Unlike Carolyn, who was cuddling and cooing to two as she nursed them between her stretch and stomach exercises . . . and running a household . . . and learning the lines to the new play she had settled on . . . and baking a pie, an angel food cake, a soufflé (she is so easily hateable, that sister of mine), Margaret was an uneasy mother. She had difficulty holding Vinnie comfortably. Whereas the babies' crying merely distracted Carolyn, it irritated Margaret. While Carolyn remained calm throughout the day and night feedings, Margaret lost weight and was exhausted. "And I'm not even breast-feeding my child!" complained Margaret about her tiredness. "I just have to warm a bottle while you have to warm your entire self."

Carolyn's "entire self" had grown during and after her pregnancy while Margaret remained just short of skinny. Within ten days, Margaret's stomach was nearly flat. Carolyn had not only gained twelve pounds in nine months—"six per breast," Margaret had needled—but had lost much of her muscle tone. It took Carolyn two months of strenuous daily exercise to regain her former shape. Again Margaret laughed at the irony. There she was, basically slothful, her body hating the abuse of any kind of exercise, but reacting to it instantly, while Carolyn, who enjoyed skating and tennis, even those sadistic calisthenics she did each morning, had a body like an errant and mischievous child. It wandered and roamed unless kept on a tight rein.

As the car drove onto Malibu Road, Margaret could see the beach house in the distance. Sonny's Bentley was in the driveway. He was making steaks and salad for dinner tonight, she remembered. Dear Sonny, she thought, how come I love you and yet resent that my baby has your last name? I guess because you had nothing to do with him, at least the makings of him, although Lord knows you've been about as attentive and loving as any father could be. Without Sonny, without his conveniently having been between films, she would never have had the peace of mind so necessary to bring Dominique Klaussen to life. Killerbrew had been right about the mar-

147

riage. She had her career, her baby, and her *good name*. I just wish Vinnie shared that good name with me, she thought as the car came to a stop at her front door.

As she turned the key in the lock and opened the massive structure of wood and wrought iron that served as both door and gate, she heard Vinnie crying. Not unusual, she thought, the way he likes his attention. And Sonny, Lord love him, did exactly what the books say you shouldn't: pick baby up and rock him. Rose Wheaton was no better. All that woman knew was hugs and kisses and nips and bites.

It took Margaret a few seconds before she distinctly felt all was not right in the house. It wasn't the sound of Vinnie's crying that disturbed her so much as the absence of cooing and other sounds of appeasement. And why was the down-stairs in darkness? Where was Sonny?

"Rose?" she called urgently. When there was no response, Margaret ran up the stairs, her heart pounding in fear even as she told herself there was nothing to fear. That *was* Vinnie crying, so how wrong could anything be? In the nursery, sprawled on the daybed, lay Rose Wheaton, her snores assuring Margaret the woman was alive. Vinnie was in his crib, screaming as his feet kicked angrily at the air. She rushed to pick him up. He was wet but otherwise seemed all right.

Where the hell is Sonny, she thought.

"Rose! Rose, wake up!" she yelled as she pushed the woman awake with her one free hand. "Didn't you hear the baby crying?" Margaret asked as the not-quite-awake face looked at her uncomprehendingly. "Rose, where is Mr. Stevens?"

"He was here when I came upstairs at four. . . ."

"Four! Rose, it's after seven now. Have you been asleep—has the baby been alone all this time?"

"He's not alone, Miss Margaret. I've been here," said Rose in injured tones, unaware of how deep her sleep had been and how long Vinnie had been crying. "And Mr. Stevens said he'd feed the baby at six."

"Did he?"

Abruptly, Rose Wheaton began to cry. She did not know whether or not the child had been fed. "It's all right, Rose," said Margaret comfortingly. "It's not your fault." And it wasn't, thought Margaret. It was hers. Where was Sonny? It didn't make sense for him to pick up and go. Not without calling. Not without leaving a note. He would never leave Vinnie unattended. Except Vinnie wasn't unattended, was he? Rose was here. It's probably nothing . . . an urgent phone call from his agent or possibly the studio. Any number of things could have taken him away unexpectedly. And I was due home after six. But, she suddenly remembered, his car is in the driveway. That doesn't mean a thing either. He could have been picked up, driven, chauffeured. In this town, that's an everyday courtesy. There is nothing to worry about.

By midnight, when Sonny had not arrived or telephoned, Margaret was upset. Although he had seldom told her where he was going or with whom, Sonny had been good about saying when he would return. They had both given one another that consideration. As Margaret lay on one of the two corduroy-covered couches that flanked the fireplace, enjoying the warmth of the flames that did much to dissipate the dampness and chill of the November night, she thought just before she dozed off: This cannot happen again. Rose . . . Sonny . . . me. I must make changes.

That same night, her voice firm, Carolyn stood before the assembled cast onstage at the Forty-sixth Street Theatre and said: "This *must not* and *will not* happen again!" Still dressed in her third act costume, Carolyn, her face flushed with anger, was insisting: "No one in this production is going to phone in his or her performance. No one is ever going to take one of *my* audiences for granted. No one is ever going to be anything less than professional. I will not have it. Do you understand?"

Shining Hour had opened that Tuesday to the season's best reviews. Not only had Carolyn been lauded, virtually assured of winning every major award at the end of the current season, but the play was touted as a possible Pulitzer Prize winner. That the company was letting down now that the notices were in was something Carolyn would not abide. As soon as the final curtain came down that Friday night, she told the stage manager to assemble the cast onstage.

It was not the first time Carolyn had taken cast and crew to task. The out-of-town tryouts had begun peaceably enough; the New Haven reviews were excellent considering the play was still not quite ready. In Boston, when the director couldn't direct, Carolyn could. She began telling the actors how to speak their lines, at least when they were in scenes with her. Of course her actions were resented. One supporting actress quit in protest; another was fired at Carolyn's instigation.

That she was the object of talk, none of it complimentary, seemingly did not bother Carolyn. She had her job to do and if others couldn't bring to the play the same dedication and professionalism that she did, then she would not be the one to suffer. Similarly, she was not about to let a basically unimaginative director ruin what she felt could be her own shining hour. Eventually, Carolyn's performance, the one offstage rather than on, made its way to New York.

"They say the tiger in Tiernan, that's Carolyn and not Margaret, is giving a mighty roar backstage in Boston and that her attacks have left claw marks on several cast members," wrote Louella Parsons in her syndicated column.

Carolyn battled on, juggling the gossip, the resentment, the rehearsals, the babies who, with their nurse, had traveled with her, *and* John, until her next-to-last week in Boston. And that was all John's doing, she had rationalized. Hadn't she told him not to come up—that last-minute rewrites made things chaotic? Had he listened? No! She had warned him that the twins were impossible, keeping awake the entire Touraine Hotel with their objection to the bottle rather than the breast now that they were being weaned. Was it her fault he decided to come anyway? Was it her fault she came to bed exhausted that night? Who wouldn't have been after a strenuous performance and then an hour's worth of notes from the writer and the producers? If he hadn't awakened when she came in they never would have argued. But he had reached for her and . . . well, she was just too tired for any of *that*. And hadn't she told him in advance Saturday would be an impossible day? A matinee followed by an evening performance with little time to do anything other than play with the babies, who were brought at her insistence to the Wilbur Theatre whenever her schedule prevented her from spending time with them in her suite. Was it any wonder then that she was tired again that night?

Sunday had started out well. They had enjoyed a late breakfast and a noontime stroll in the Commons wheeling their babies in their pram. Then, while the infants napped, they made love in their room, only John said he did but she didn't, accusing her of being unresponsive throughout.

"But John, what can you expect? I have a play that opens in New York in less than two weeks. I can't just switch that off to please you."

His response was angry. "To please *me*? I had hoped it would also be pleasing to you."

"You simply do not understand," she said, ending the conversation, and he hadn't, as his hurried departure from Boston late that afternoon proved. Alone, she had cried most of the evening. Why couldn't he understand, she kept asking. Why couldn't he be patient? At midnight, when she was certain he would be at home, she telephoned. She was sorry, she said. So was he. I love you, she declared. He loved her, too. Things will be better, she promised, once she was in New York and the play had opened. And they were, until opening night. And what an opening night it was! For a full five minutes after the curtain had come down, the audience cheered. They were demanding she take another bow and when she did, what pleased her most was the cast and crew in the wings who stayed to applaud her triumph also. The party was grand. The producers had taken over El Morocco for the evening and spared no expense. Nor had Carolyn. Her gown was a loosely cut crimson crepe that gravitated toward and then clung to the curves in her body. Her black hair, brushed till it shone, was loose about her shoulders. Tiny ruby earrings matched the ruby pendant that hung to where her ample cleavage began. She was the belle at her own ball, dancing with her producers, the writer, her leading man, even the director, well-wishers, and eventually, John. All was well until John learned from Walter Lowell, Carolyn's agent at William Morris, that they were preparing a weekly dramatic anthology for radio. If one of the networks bought it, Carolyn would serve as hostess and star. Each week, she would bring theatre to American homes by presenting classics and current plays in an hour's framework.

"Why didn't you tell me about this?" John asked when the car was taking them home.

"Because nothing will come of it," said Carolyn offhandedly. "I'll probably be back on the soaps in a month or so," she continued, fully aware that the position she had now attained in theatre would prevent her from ever being just a voice again.

"And suppose it sells?" asked John as the car was driven through Central Park en route to their West Side apartment. "What demands will that make on your time?"

"Oh, John, why talk about something that has yet to happen and probably won't? This has been the most wonderful

151

evening. Let's not argue, particularly since there is nothing to argue about."

They found something almost immediately. In bed, when he reached for her, she pulled away. "According to the calendar, it isn't safe yet. I could still get pregnant." John groaned in frustration. He then took her hand and moved it down to his erection. He guided it up and down, finding the rhythm he best enjoyed.

"John, stop!" she said. "Certainly you can wait another three days."

"Carolyn, it's been so long," he urged, his voice choked with frustration and passion.

"Three days, John. Certainly you can exert that much self-control."

John's erection immediately disappeared. Carolyn's control and his lack of it always affected him. According to her, he was intemperate and inconsiderate. And his soul was in constant mortal danger. He had never questioned her right to deny him because of her religious beliefs as she was convinced it was not denial but necessary moral abstinence. This night, he felt denied. This night she could not make him feel guilty. Just angry and irritable. He rolled away to his side of the bed and did not answer when she said, "Good night, John."

As Carolyn stood onstage at the Forty-sixth Street Theatre, berating her cast and crew for their unprofessionalism, she seemed poised, sure of herself, and totally in command. She displayed none of the effects of the scene she had had with John earlier that evening. He had arrived from the office early. By five, after two martinis, he had grabbed at her. When she had shied away, he became gruff, pawing at her as he had never done before. She had fled to the bedroom where he followed. "What's the matter *now*, Carolyn? It's been three days, hasn't it? Or has it been three months! I forget. Let's *fuck*, Carolyn. Let's *fuck* now!"

Frightened by this side of John she had never seen, she had locked herself in the bathroom where she stayed until she heard the front door slam. Then, she had quickly dressed and come to the theatre. Their confrontation had been forgotten the moment she began her concentration on her character one hour before curtain time. Now, as she chastised those who had not given their full selves to their work, the early events of the evening were slowly wending their way into Carolyn's consciousness. Panic stabbed at her. For the first time in her life that she could remember, Carolyn was frightened.

Fear stabbed at Margaret the moment her eyes opened and she realized she was in the living room. The house was still; the only sounds reverberating through the quiet were the gulls on the beach and the birds at their predawn rites. Margaret looked at the clock on the fireplace. Almost six. She looked toward Sonny's room. No light appeared under his door. He could have come in during the night and not wanting to disturb her, gone right to bed, she rationalized. She tried to walk slowly, confidently, to his room. Let him be there, she pleaded with some unknown entity. He wasn't. Without hesitation, Margaret went to the phone and dialed Killerbrew Studios.

"This is Margaret Tiernan," she announced to the switchboard operator. "Would you please ring Mr. Killerbrew at home . . . Yes, I know what time it is, operator, and that it is Saturday, but this is an emergency."

In less than a minute, she heard the operator say: "He'll call you immediately, Miss Tiernan."

When the phone rang, she found she could barely speak.

"What's wrong?" asked Killerbrew, knowing hellos and similar salutations were superfluous if Margaret was calling at this hour.

"Sonny is missing," she said in a whisper.

"Start from the beginning. Take your time but tell me everything," said Killerbrew. When she had finished he asked if Sonny had been drinking or they had been fighting. When she replied no to both, he prodded:

"Think! Is anything missing from the house?" Nothing was except Sonny. "And his car is in the driveway?" It was. "Okay. I'll call my man at the police. Do nothing till I get there. I'm on my way."

In the time before Killerbrew arrived, Margaret washed her face, brushed her hair, and changed into a fresh pair of wool slacks and a bulky knit sweater. Still she felt chilled. She awakened Rose Wheaton and asked her to tend to Vinnie. She then prepared a pot of coffee and as she waited for it to perk, seated herself on a stool by the kitchen counter. She was still cold, trembling at intervals, when the doorbell rang. The sight of Franklin Killerbrew filling her doorway brought

153

the tears. Placing an arm around Margaret's shoulders, Killerbrew steered her toward the living room.

"Get hold of yourself, Margaret. We don't really know if something is wrong. Sonny has quite a history of disappearances. Sometimes it's a bender; other times a . . . *something* that also lasts a few days. He's like a kid who runs away just for the hell of it. So stay calm. When Lieutenant Foster arrives, answer truthfully whatever he asks. He knows the story and can be trusted."

But when Bill Foster of the Los Angeles Police Department arrived, there was nothing more she could tell him than what she had already told Killerbrew. No, there had not been "men" or "boys" about, around, or in the house, she said testily. Killerbrew calmed her. "Margaret, he *must* ask these questions. He must know every detail if—and I said *if*—something is wrong and we're to find Sonny."

Margaret explained she was not protecting Sonny Stevens. The truth was that in the year they had been married, he had never stayed away overnight and had never entertained guests of either sex after ten in their house. And when he did entertain, she was always invited if not always present.

Foster was courteous and as kindly as any investigating officer could be. After a search through Sonny's room and closet, he told Killerbrew he would begin checking with the neighbors to see if any had seen Sonny yesterday afternoon. He then left. Killerbrew followed soon after. "I'll call if there is any news at all," he promised. "Have you someone to stay with you?"

She nodded that she did—meaning Rose Wheaton—but felt she did not. She thought of that afternoon in New York and the moment when she had said: "Aunt Augie, come back with me to California. I need you." Margaret wished with all her heart her aunt was with her now.

Augusta Monahan had awakened that Saturday morning with the same sinking feeling with which she had fallen asleep. It had been an awful night. First coming home from the hospital just as John was storming out. He had not even acknowledged her as he slammed the door. And his face! The man was beet red. Although she had thought to knock on Carolyn's door, she did not, deciding it was best to let the young folks work through their own problems. Best to mind one's own business. Which is exactly what she told Mrs. Worthington when the nurse came from the nursery to see about the ruckus. "Married people *do* fight," she had muttered to the startled woman. My God do they fight! she thought, remembering the histrionics that often accompanied the emotional turbulence of Tory and Thomas's marriage. But her concern had grown when she heard John come in shortly after Carolyn's departure for the theatre and then leave again shortly before her niece was due home. As she lay in her bed, she heard Carolyn come in before midnight. She never did hear John. When she awoke during the night, restless and uncertain, she put on her robe, opened her bedroom door, and peered into the hallway. The light was still on, which meant John was still out. Although she knew it was wrong, she walked to Carolyn's bedroom and listened at her door not knowing what she hoped, or feared, she would hear. No matter. She heard nothing. Now, as she lay awake, she wondered what she should do for Carolyn. Should she broach the subject, and if she did, could she help? If it's about men and marriage, she doubted it. I don't seem to help myself very well these days so how can I help her, thought Augusta as she tied her flannel robe around her, thinking how good coffee would taste once she made it.

When she pushed open the kitchen's swinging doors, Augusta was surprised to find Carolyn sitting at the round wooden kitchen table, drinking coffee and looking tired. Without a greeting, Augusta, after pouring herself a mugful of steaming coffee, said as she seated herself opposite Carolyn, "Do you want to talk?" With a shrug, Carolyn indicated she did not.

"He'll be back, Carolyn," assured Augusta. "Men have a way of taking walks when they're upset or angry. Your father once walked from Murray Hill to Coney Island after a rather bad tiff with your mother."

Still Carolyn said nothing, remaining mute and immobile until both women simultaneously heard the sound of the front door opening and closing.

"John?" Carolyn called as she rose from her chair. "John?" she was screaming as she ran from the table, through the kitchen doors and into the hallway. "John" was the last word Augusta heard. Then, only the sounds of crying.

The front door opening startled Margaret, who had been sitting on the deck, looking at the gray clouds hovering over the wind-whipped ocean.

"Sonny?" she called excitedly as she ran from the deck toward the doorway. She stopped short when she saw Franklin Killerbrew.

"I thought you might have been resting so I let myself in," he explained, as he removed the scarf that served as his only protection against the weather.

"But how did you get in?" asked Margaret.

"A key. Many of my employees leave me access to their homes. In case of an emergency."

"Have the courtesy to knock from now on. This is *my* home and I do not like people bursting . . ." Margaret stopped in mid-sentence. "I'm sorry. I shouldn't have snapped at you. But at first, I thought you were Sonny. It's not that I mind your having Sonny's key. It's just . . . well, I would never give mine to anyone unless they were family."

"You might if you were prone to blackouts, benders, and blackmail," Killerbrew replied quietly.

"You still don't understand that Sonny isn't like that anymore," she said angrily. When Killerbrew began to speak, she waved off his response with a terse: "Forget it. Is there any news?" she asked as she seated herself in the rocking chair facing the fireplace.

"Foster called an hour ago. He said to meet him here around three," said Killerbrew as he sat on the sofa facing her.

It was a little after four when the phone rang, startling Margaret from her mindless rocking. "It's Foster," she said, handing the phone to Killerbrew.

"Yes, Bill." As Killerbrew listened, his face remained impassive. Hard as she tried, Margaret could not read any meaning into it. After Killerbrew laid the receiver in its cradle, he took Margaret by the arm and seated her again in the rocking chair. "Sonny was seen by several neighbors with a youngish man. The last to see him thought there were three men in the party but that one was hanging back, as if searching the shore for shells. But he wasn't really certain they were all together. Anyway, Lieutenant Foster wants me to meet with him. I'll be back as soon as possible. Sit tight till I get back."

Killerbrew's heart was racing as fast as the motor on his Rolls roadster as he sped toward that part of the beach where the private sector ended and the public area began. What he had not told Margaret had made his stomach turn in panic. It

156

was still turning. Two police cars with their doors open were parked at the end of the dead-end street which separated pavement from sand. He parked alongside and then walked quickly down to where the rocks were piled up along the beach, thus effectively blocking the view of any who might want to see what was taking place below them. The area was a favorite trysting place for the young, for those who hadn't apartments of their own, or those who enjoyed their passion under the stars. Climbing over the rocks, he saw Foster waiting. With him were three uniformed policemen.

"Whoever the guy is, he's a mess," said Foster. "The face is gone. Frank, the guy is well over six feet, well built, and blond. It could be him. Are you sure you want to look?"

The last thing Franklin Killerbrew wanted was to look but if he didn't, the person he least wanted to—Margaret—might. He didn't want that. He signaled Foster to remove the green tarpaulin from the body, and then looked until he could not look anymore.

"A brick, we think," said Foster. "Smashed him with it. Bashed in his head and his face."

But Killerbrew was no longer listening. He had turned from the pulp of dried blood and was walking toward the ocean. Tears were streaming down his face while screams were stifled in his throat. "It's not Sonny," he kept repeating to himself. "It's not him. Not Sonny."

"Frank," called Foster. "Can you positively identify the body? 'Cause if you can't, we have to call Mrs. Stevens and ask her to come down."

"The hell you do!" yelled Killerbrew as he strode back toward the lieutenant. "Not on your life. I don't care how you manage it, Bill. Check his fingerprints, his dental x-rays, blood samples, but do not bring Margaret Tiernan here or to the morgue. You got that?"

Bill Foster nodded that he did. "Okay, what have you got?" asked Killerbrew.

"Just guesses. Probably he was lured here and robbed. But we can't be certain. We don't know if he was wearing a watch or carrying a wallet so we don't know if they were taken. We don't know anything. It could be he put the make on two guys who couldn't just say no."

"It was robbery. Remember that," said Killerbrew. "And if you find the guys and they say otherwise, they're lying. Everybody knows Mr. Stevens was a happily married man and a devoted father. That's the story, Bill," concluded Killerbrew as he wondered what he could tell Margaret that she would buy.

Margaret was sitting on the deck watching the rain collect in swirling black clouds over the ocean when Killerbrew returned to her beach house. She was tightly wrapped in layers of sweaters, her face drawn and pale.

"You found him, didn't you," she said before he could speak.

"We're not sure," said Killerbrew as he drew a chair up next to hers.

"He's dead, isn't he?" asked Margaret.

"Yes, we think so," said Killerbrew cautiously. "Margaret, he was murdered." When her face remained impassive, Killerbrew added: "Brutally murdered."

Margaret uttered a one-word command: "How?"

Killerbrew looked at the set of Margaret's face in profile and decided it was best to tell her all. When through, he waited for her response. Several minutes passed before it came. "I found his wallet by the toaster. He must have left it there while he was making his lunch."

Killerbrew, realizing Margaret understood it was not robbery that had brought about Sonny's death, reached for her hand. If she felt his touch, Margaret gave no sign and made no movement. It was then Killerbrew phoned the studio doctor and advised him to attend to Margaret immediately. He then rang John Ollson in New York and broke the news to him. "I want you on the next plane out. She's going to need somebody," Killerbrew said. In the background, the studio chief heard a hysterical Carolyn Tiernan demanding to speak to her sister. Killerbrew refused. "She'll only upset Margaret even more. Can she come with you?" John replied he didn't think that possible; that the producers of *Shining Hour* would not release their star and box office draw for a week. Even as John spoke, Killerbrew heard Augusta Monahan three thousand miles away, stating, not asking, that she was going with John.

When the doctor arrived, Killerbrew made one other phone call—to Dorothea Wolfe. He told his secretary to gather "The Five," as they were known at the studio, that he wanted to meet with them before the day was through. Dorothea Wolfe said it would be arranged. Within the hour she called back.

The meeting was set for Killerbrew's office at eight that evening; the studio guard was alerted to admit the unusual Saturday traffic. The Five would, Killerbrew knew, write the story as he dictated. They were those key members of the press who were beholden to Killerbrew Studios for "services rendered"—all tax-free—during the course of the year. They would see to it that Sonny Stevens's death was attributed to robbery and that he had died as he lived: bravely . . . valiantly even.

Before leaving for his office, Killerbrew sat with Margaret, who was beginning to feel the effects of the sedation the doctor had administered. "I know no one ever said life is fair," she said groggily, "so why is it we all think it should be?" With tears streaming down her face, Margaret turned to Killerbrew. "You're the big, wise man. Tell me. *Why?*"

A week afterward people were still talking about Sonny Stevens's funeral, which even by Hollywood standards was an extravaganza. Sonny's coffin had lain atop a stagecoach drawn by the four horses Sonny had ridden in his films. But no one talked about—because no one but Margaret was surprised—Sonny's will, which left his house and its contents to "the very best friend I ever had," Margaret Tiernan, and half his estate—roughly twenty thousand dollars—to Vincent Tiernan Stevens. The other half was left to the family in Iowa he hadn't seen in more than twelve years. Sonny's gesture, unexpected but typical, deepened Margaret's depression. She had suspected that she was all Sonny had despite his fame. Having her suspicion verified immobilized her. For several days, she remained in bed, refusing to dress and doing nothing more than reading her mail and listening to the newscasts. She was alone in the house, having sent John and Augusta home with Vinnie and Rose, promising to join them as soon as *Garden* was completed, which would be long before the approaching Christmas holidays.

Killerbrew had closed down the *Garden* set for the week after Sonny's funeral. But when he saw his star languishing, making no effort to help herself, in fact sliding deeper into her depression, he arrived at her home one morning unannounced and raging.

"I want you at work tomorrow. This is costing me money," he stormed.

"I'm not well," she pleaded.

159

"Then get well unless you want *Garden* canned," he threatened. "Besides, this town has already seen two productions of *A Star Is Born* so yours is not only late but boring. You want to play Mrs. Norman Maine, do it on the set. But get your ass in gear and get it at the studio tomorrow morning or you're suspended."

It was the possibility that Killerbrew might be serious and that she would lose Dominique Klaussen that had Margaret putting one foot on the bedroom floor as soon as she heard the door close behind her employer. Life might be shit, she thought, but Dominique isn't.

The next day, Margaret Tiernan had to suppress the laugh that welled up inside her when the entire crew of *Garden* chose to greet her return with a standing ovation. Only her better judgment prevented her from saying: "Ladies and gentlemen, this is Mrs. Sonny Stevens."

5

Vinnie was cradled in the crook of Augusta's arm and against her shoulder as she bottle-fed him with her free hand. Above the noises of the ceaseless traffic on Central Park West, she heard Carolyn cooing as she helped Mrs. Worthington feed the twins. It was a house geared to children and if Carolyn was at all fazed by having Vinnie with her, she didn't show it. If anything, Augusta decided, she doted on her nephew. And certainly John was giving as much attention to Vinnie as he was to the twins. It is, Augusta kept repeating to her inner self, an amazing situation. But then, Margaret certainly is her own amazing woman.

More than a tinge of sarcasm coated "amazing" when Augie thought of it in terms of Margaret. Perhaps I'm just old-fashioned, or of the "old school," as Mother used to say, but I believe a child should be with his mother, no matter how excellent the mother's excuses are. And Margaret's excuses are excellent and valid and have been ever since that day shortly after the funeral when she suggested John take Vinnie back to New York so that she and Carolyn could care for him. It made sense. First, Augie reminded herself, Margaret was barely able to take care of herself after Sonny's death. She needed time. Then, too, as Margaret said, she would be in New York for the Christmas holidays and that was but a week or two away. That was fine, reasoned Augusta. It's always and all fine. Margaret had arrived, spent the holidays with the family, and then taken off. Without Vinnie, but with good—there you are again—*good* reasons. The house was being remodeled. Totally and completely and the noise of the drills and the hammers would be very disturbing to a child. Then, too, with Rose Wheaton no longer able to care for an infant, proper help had to be found and Lord knows that was no easy trick to accomplish. It all made sense. Margaret always had a way of making the nonsensical or the unthinkable into sense, thought Augie, surprised by her bitterness. Why was it she was the only one in the family who thought it unusual for a mother to part with her own baby no matter how excellent or valid the excuse?

And such a baby! thought Augusta as she looked down at what she called her "Irish imp." Such black eyes and black ringlets. There is some Margaret but there is much more Malloy to this child's looks, thought Augusta. Suddenly, Vinnie spit up and with the napkin she held in her hand, Augusta dabbed at his mouth and chin where some of the spittle had dribbled. That done, she put Vinnie over her shoulder, patting his back as she did. At the window, she watched the March wind tear through the park, whipping up debris and dust and then dropping it carelessly without thought or plan. Through the window, Augusta could feel the cold of the day in contrast with the warmth she felt from the little body pressed to hers. She wondered how she would feel when Margaret arrived next month, after completing both the film and the house. She would miss Vinnie when Margaret took him back with her. *If* she took him back with her. Augusta found she no longer trusted Margaret to do that. Lord knows what other excellent excuse might arise to prevent it. Still, thought Augusta, the little tyke doesn't seem to mind so maybe I'm just being old-fashioned and stuffy. As she patted Vinnie's back lightly, she listened for what she thought was one of the world's loveliest sounds—the burp of a baby.

April 19, 1938

Dear Lynnie,

A brief note: *Cuckoo Cupid* wraps Friday night. I'll let you know which flight I'll take Saturday. Would you ask John if he can arrange tickets for me for *Our Town*? Has he seen it? If not maybe he and/or Aunt Augie would like to go. My treat!

You wouldn't consider closing down *Shining Hour* for a week so you and I could go play? I didn't think so. By the way, I think it's awful that Warners is buying *Shining* for Davis. You'd think after what RKO did with your *Weekend*, they'd know better. No one should ever be allowed to do your roles.

Speaking of roles, I heard your first show last week. Lynnie, it was wonderful! I was so impressed. It must be hard as hell

162

making a three-hour play work in less than an hour. But you did it. When do the ratings come in? Is Sunday at six considered a good time period? I know nothing about radio so you'll have to bear with me. But I must tell you . . . when I tuned in and heard: "Welcome to 'Front Row Center' starring Carolyn Tiernan," I damn near bust my buttons. Oh Lynnie, isn't it wonderful the way our lives are going? Although I must admit it would be a lot more wonderful had I won the Oscar for *The Back Bay Way*. I was disappointed. If only everyone hadn't been so sure I would win. Frankly, I do think it piggish of Luise Rainer to have won again. Of course Killerbrew is assuring me I've got the award locked up for next year with *Garden*. Meantime, Jack Warner is giving Davis the same line. Swell!

People out here will tell you anything *they* think you want to hear. Except the truth. Everyone except Killerbrew of course. Damn that man! Have I told you he called me on the carpet in February for giving my house-under-construction party? He thinks I should be publicly observing a longer mourning period. The hell with that! I'm twenty-one and I've had enough mourning of one kind or another to last me a lifetime. Now I want to be counted among the living.

This town is filled with hypocrisy. It doesn't matter what you're doing or with whom as long as you don't flaunt it. Sneaking around is considered quite the art here. But let people go public—like, say, a Gable and a Lombard—and they become pariahs. Killerbrew claims he doesn't give a damn who I go out with, how often, and where, so long as I'm not seen. Try being inconspicuous with an Errol Flynn or a Tyrone Power. It's damned impossible.

The beast—that's Killerbrew—is also unhappy with my performance in *Cuckoo Cupid*—says I'm not very funny. I told him, you want funny, get Crawford. Whether she knows it or not, she's a million laughs. Speaking of La C., guess who is writing her latest picture? Bucky Denton. Yes, my first studio-arranged date. The Secret Grabber. Only now it is Robert Denton if you please. He has given up acting (not that what he did could be called "acting" by any stretch of the imagination) and is churning out some pretty decent scripts. He's also given up drinking, you'll be happy to know, but not trying to get his hands up a girl's dress. We're motoring to take a look at this Palm Springs place this afternoon. It seems everyone in this town is buying up property there.

I've had enough of "property" to last me a lifetime. The house was finally finished this week. I was promised it would take six weeks and it took twelve. Horrible. However, it looks quite respectable now. Don't ask me about the decor as I'm not very good about that. My decorator says it's "Mediterranean/Spanish." Me? I only know I love the hammock that swings from wall to wall in my bedroom. I can lie in it, watch the sky, the ocean, and rock away my everythings. The room really suits me. It's all done in beiges and browns. The living room is painted sand with lots of wood paneling throughout. It's all very "earthy," Spanish-style, and without a trace of green wool plush anywhere! What was Sonny's den and my bedroom is now a separate apartment with its own entrance. So come visit. We'll put the kids in a hotel. Let them order their pablum from room service.

Speaking of kids, *that picture of Vinnie!* The resemblance to his father is staggering. He is so gorgeous that it's hard to believe he is mine. The snapshot of the twins is also spooky. If you didn't know better, you would think they were unrelated, what with him having that gorgeous blond hair, and her looking so much more like her cousin. I'm dying to see them all. Speaking of that, how do you manage? The theatre six nights a week, the radio show Sundays, and rehearsals—there *are* rehearsals for radio, aren't there?—when do you have time to do it all? I *will* get to see you, won't I?

Love,
Margaret

It is ironic that I should find this particular letter from Margaret, thought Carolyn as she continued to pack for the family's annual summer vacation. What was it doing in her dresser drawer rather than in the sachet-lined wicker basket with the others?

How do I manage, indeed! According to my husband, not at all that well. *When do I have time to do it all?* According to that very same husband, I don't.

I will not be depressed, decided Carolyn as she found what she was searching for in her bottom bureau drawer. She lifted the billowy pink peignoir and shook it free of imagined dust. There, it looks like new, thought Carolyn. Well, it should. I haven't worn it since the honeymoon. "*I do have* time and I will manage," she said fiercely as she placed the peignoir carefully atop the rest of her lingerie in the suitcase.

164

It's a rotten time to take a vacation, she thought as she began to pack her toiletries in an overnight bag. How can I relax when we return to the air two weeks after I get back? Stop that! she cautioned. You have time. You can manage. A week at Nantasket will do you good. It will do you *and* John good. You'll talk to him. You will get him to change his mind about the job. He's just being unreasonable.

It seemed to Carolyn they had been fighting over "time" for months. John claimed she never had any for him. If she wasn't at the theatre, she was at the radio station. When she was home, she was with the children. Well, shouldn't she be? she had yelled at him during one of their more recent fights. "But what about me?" he had demanded to know. "You sound like a child," she had responded. But even as he stormed out of the room, Carolyn knew he was right. They were not spending enough time together. It was the radio show. Everything had gotten out of hand with its success. Suddenly there were at-home layouts for the press, luncheon interviews, photo sessions. One successful radio show had done for her what a movie and several plays had not: made her a star. "And I like it!" she had said almost fiercely to Margaret when she had visited.

And that, too, caused dissension. "When Margaret came to New York in April, you dropped everything. You made time," complained John. "Why for her and not for me?"

"Because you're here and she isn't!" Carolyn replied angrily. "I see you daily but I see Margaret only a couple of times a year."

"In case you haven't noticed, Lynnie," said John sarcastically, "you see more of Margaret in those 'couple of times' than you do of me all year long."

Margaret had sensed the difficulty and the day she took Vinnie back with her to Hollywood to spend an early summer on the beach, she had told Carolyn: "You can't have it all. Something has got to go. It shouldn't be John." That was back in June. It wasn't until last night that she was able to part with *Shining Hour*. Although the play would continue with another actress in the role she had created—a fact she preferred to ignore—she had closed out a ten-month run so that she and John could have a week on Nantasket before the summer's end. They would be alone. Mrs. Worthington was on her week's holiday and Augusta had elected to "enjoy having the apartment to myself."

165

The first time Carolyn had suggested John leave his job with Killerbrew Studios to produce her radio show and whatever theatre she might do in the future, he had exploded. "I am not going to be an appendage of my wife the actress. I will not be known as Mr. John Tiernan."

"It is the only way we can spend more time together," she had argued. "And I need you. It's that selfish and simple. What was the highest rated of the thirteen shows I did last spring? The one you suggested—the two-parter with Margaret. Why hadn't anyone else thought for us to do *Much Ado*? But you did! You always do. If we worked together, we would see more of one another. And no one ever referred to you as Mr. Tiernan when you produced for me before."

But John had remained stubborn. What time they did spend together that summer was strained. It was in July, she remembered, that he stopped waiting up for her. She would rush home from the theatre only to find him asleep by eleven-thirty. "What do you expect?" he had challenged. "I'm due at my desk at nine." As a result, one worry was removed from her mind. Given the state of their marriage, there was thankfully no chance of an unwanted pregnancy.

He had been pleased when she announced she would leave the play Labor Day weekend, thus allowing them the summer's end on Nantasket. She had thought he'd be displeased that Mrs. Worthington was taking her vacation at the same time. But on the contrary, he had been delighted. "We will be alone . . . like a regular family." He had a lot to learn, her husband did, she thought with a fond smile. Regular families and regular fathers change diapers, wipe up drool, and go running in the middle of the night when baby starts to cry.

He had come to the theatre for her final performance last evening and afterward had surprised her with a supper party at the Stork Club. The professional good sense with which he had always guided her career was never more evident than it was last night, she thought as she closed the latches on the last of the suitcases. Not only had John invited the producers, director, and others connected with her *Shining Hour* success, but had rightfully included the staff of "Front Row Center" and those key executives at the radio network who could make or break a show and its star. That Ed Sullivan and Winchell were there was hardly accidental. That Dorothy Kilgallen wasn't was not, as she had written a particularly harsh feature on Carolyn prior to the play's opening.

166

It had been a very special evening, thought Carolyn, warmed by the memory. John had even thought to have Margaret call. And what brilliant words of wisdom had her sister for her? "Lynnie, do you remember the pink peignoir I gave you for your honeymoon? Pack it unless you want to pack in your marriage."

For John, nothing had changed, except his father was dead. The house was still overheated by its coal-burning furnace yet cold in its austerity. None of the furnishings had been altered or replaced. Even the starched white doilies that covered arm- and headrests on the sofa and chairs seemed the same. The carpet was frayed and worn to its threads on the steps leading up to the bedrooms. His mother, too, was unchanged. Although she seemed smaller than he had remembered, her shoulders more rounded and stooped, she was still unsmiling and stoic. The cotton housedress she wore could have been the same one she purchased from Sears, Roebuck years ago. She remained stingy, with herself and others, but did not know it. Despite her wealth, meals remained meager, as did her affections. She did not seem surprised that Carolyn had not come with him for the funeral and she expressed neither concern nor disappointment. Nor did she display any of the usual grandparent's pride when he showed her pictures of Thomas and Martha.

When he extended Carolyn's invitation, his mother had stared at him uncomprehendingly. "Why on earth would I want to come to New York? What would I do there?" He didn't know. His mother was not the kind to take in a matinee or do the shops and museums. Her life was the church and the people in Rochester. It was a small life for a small person. She could not imagine there was another way to live. Her one question to him proved that. "You thinking of moving back now that your father is dead? I could use some help here." When he told her no, she simply shrugged as if to say: No accounting for some people, and dismissed the subject and him.

John had planned to stay with his mother four or five days but when he realized she did not need him, he took the train to Chicago to catch the Twentieth Century into New York the day after the funeral. When he left Rochester under sixteen inches of a late March snow, it was with the knowledge he would never see it, and probably not his mother, again. He

167

felt no remorse. She was his mother but she was not his family. They are but hours away, he thought, as the train swept through snow-covered Pennsylvania and into New Jersey. He and Carolyn might have their problems but she and the kids were still the best thing that had ever happened to him.

They had grown closer since last summer's week in Nantasket. Away from "Carolyn Tiernan," she was the near perfect Mrs. Ollson, wife and mother. Her ease with the twins had actually surprised him. She was not flustered when both cried. She was firm yet loving. As young as they were, the babies minded, although it was already apparent that Martha had a mind of her own and if allowed would have seen the world, at fifteen months, crawling about on her hands and knees. He had wondered then why he had thought Mrs. Worthington was raising his children. Had she been, would Carolyn have been humming and whistling as she changed and laundered diapers? Would she so easily have bathed both babies in the bathinette at the same time? With all, she cooked and cleaned and when a baby-sitter could be arranged in the afternoon, went clamming with him on the far end of the beach. Most women would have complained about such a "working vacation," but Carolyn had enjoyed it. They both had enjoyed it. They did things together—from feeding the twins to making love. Five days in a row they had made love. And then she had resisted. It was no longer safe. She could conceive. So they had talked about having another baby but she was adamant—later, yes, but now, she wanted her career.

Her withdrawal in bed was frustrating as she was not just his wife but quite possibly the most beautiful woman he had ever met. He slept next to but not with her. He could look but not touch and she would do neither. There could be no kind of sexual release other than what the church allowed, she decreed. He forced her into discussing her decision.

As John sipped his brandy, remaining oblivious of the smoke and noise of the club car, he remembered his argument. "Carolyn, there is an inconsistency here that I do not understand. Why is it comfortable for you to make love on those days when you know you cannot conceive? Isn't this, as you would say, 'spilling the seed,' when you know conception is not possible? What difference then if 'the seed is spilt' in some other way? Love is love and I do not understand why an

xpression of it always has to produce, or be an attempt to
roduce, children. I do not want my enjoyment of you, of *us*,
be restricted to when He or they decide it's all right."

She had tried. From the very beginning, with that silly
ink peignoir, he saw that. But something within her could
ot tolerate his ejaculating on her stomach or between her
aighs. Nor could she comfortably masturbate him; her atti-
de was as unbending as her hand. So they compromised to
make him comfortable," as Carolyn so delicately put it. He
ould masturbate himself while she allowed him to kiss and
ndle her. It wasn't ideal for either of them. Although he
ould peak, he would still feel strangely unsatisfied after-
ard, and she suffered, although silently, with her guilt.
till, as he continually reminded himself, she had tried.

It was her trying that had convinced him he must too. If
arolyn felt it would not only help their marriage but make
er feel more secure if he produced "Front Row Center" and
hatever else she might do, why not? Radio was big and
ould be every bit as enjoyable as working for Killerbrew
tudios. Then, too, he would be involved with film and
heatre, as Carolyn wished to pursue both. Killerbrew had
ot welcomed his decision but neither had he fought it. They
arted amicably, which was better than the current "parting"
etween Killerbrew and Margaret—but that was her prob-
m. And Killerbrew's, John realized.

When a yawn surprised him, John checked his watch. It
as late but he still had his reading to do. Now that "Front
ow Center" was firmly ensconced among the top ten in the
looper ratings, Carolyn was searching for other outlets. A
lm had been offered and its shooting schedule was perfect.

would be shot at the Astoria Studios in New York and
ould require but five weeks of her time, beginning in June,
e same week the radio show began its summer hiatus. The
lm would therefore not conflict with their annual vacation
n Nantasket. It would be John's decision as to whether the
ript was strong enough for Carolyn's talents. It had better
e, he thought, as his wife had her heart set on making a film
efore 1939 and the decade ended, and this was the only one
ffered to date.

In his compartment, after he had removed his flannel
orts coat and his blue-striped tie, John stretched out on the
ouch and opened *Deep Purple*. A major part of him hoped
e script was bad. He feared Carolyn working day and night

again, feared her plans to do both the radio show and another play this fall; feared that what had happened once would happen again. And, thought John, I never want to hurt anyone ever again the way I am hurting Sandra. She want more than I can give. It isn't fair. When does someone give to me?

"I don't give a flying fuck what you want! That's why I'm on suspension, remember?" screamed Margaret across the desk to the impassive face of Franklin Killerbrew. "It's what *I* want that you have to deal with and what I want is no more *Cuckoo Cupids* or *Desert Devils*."

"They can't all be Oscar winners," said Killerbrew as he calmly lit a Pall Mall and deliberately puffed the smoke in Margaret's direction.

"Find one that is!" snarled Margaret, displaying how fresh still were her wounds from having lost the Academy Award for *Garden* to Bette Davis in *Jezebel*.

"*Desert Devil* is going to double the rentals of *Garden*," said Killerbrew as he leaned back in his swivel chair, his feet now arrogantly atop his desk.

"I'm not interested in money," said Margaret.

"The rich never are and if I hadn't made you so damn rich I wonder just how high and mighty you'd be acting right now."

"But I'd be *acting*, which is a helluva lot better than what your friggin' films are requiring of me," she stormed.

"Come on, Margaret. Be reasonable. Three Oscar nominations in as many years is pretty good acting," placated Killerbrew.

"If you're going to take a bow for my talents, take it. But don't expect me to applaud," said Margaret.

"I want you to make *Cajun Woman*," said Killerbrew as if everything Margaret had already stated about the film had been obliterated from his memory.

"You're crazy, you know that?" Margaret said, shaking her head in disbelief. "I walked out on you a month ago and I'll walk out again. There will be no *Cajun Woman*. There will be no Margaret Tiernan on this lot unless some good scripts by name writers come her way."

When Killerbrew said nothing but simply stared at her as he continued to puff on his cigarette as though it were a choice cigar, Margaret fixed the white wool beret on her head

nd rose from the chair where she had been sitting. "I can
e I'm wasting my time. I thought you had called me here to
iscuss our professional differences but I was wrong. The
ext time, don't call me; call my agent."

She was halfway to the door when Killerbrew spun out of
is chair and was upon her in a few giant strides. He grabbed
er roughly by the shoulder and whirled her about. "You're
oing to make *Cajun Woman*. No 'ifs' or 'buts' or you'll be
tting out your life. Make no mistake about that," he added,
is face a study in fury. "I own you. Lock, stock, and barrel.
ou want to do theatre? You can't. Your contract forbids it
ithout my approval. You want to do radio? No way, not
ithout my approval. How about home movies? Forget even
aat. All you can do on your own is go to the bathroom.
here's nothing about you for hire. The one thing you could
ave sold I hear you're giving away, *piece by piece*."

Margaret raised her hand to strike him. Killerbrew caught
er arm in midair before it came near his face. "You need me
nd don't forget it. I made you and I can break you."

Margaret laughed in his face. "Where the hell did you get
aat line? *Cajun Woman* . . . *Cuckoo Cupid* . . . or both? I
on't need you, Mr. Big Shot. Not you," said Margaret as she
ed the belt of her white polo coat firmly about her waist.

"Bullshit!" snarled Killerbrew. "You need to work. Not for
ae money. Not even for the fame. But for *work's sake*, which
how you phrased it the last time you were in here acting
ke a Duse or a Bernhardt in search of a Shakespeare. Well,
weetheart, art is costly in Hollywood. We don't even have a
auseum among the orange groves. But I've created some
orks of art for you and there'll be more if you don't forget
ho's patron and boss around here—whose *Cajun Woman*s
ay for the real treasures."

"But it's mainly about who is boss, isn't it?" demanded
Margaret. "You wouldn't want the industry to think big,
old, bad Franklin 'the Killer' Killerbrew was bested by an
ctress, would you?"

"That's right," said Killerbrew as he returned to his desk.
I win at all costs. Even if it means killing off my number one
ear attraction."

"You won't have to. *Cajun Woman* will do it for you if
Desert Devil hasn't already. I can't afford another bad picture."

"In this town," said Killerbrew calmly as he once again
ased himself into a languorous position in his swivel chair, "a

171

bad picture is one that loses money. None of yours ever has."

"You and I define *bad* differently," said Margaret. "Look this is getting us nowhere. Work it out with my agent."

"I talk to *you*. No one *but* you," said Killerbrew as Margaret stood by the door. "Get that straight and this, too," he added as he flung a script at her. Instinctively, Margaret raised her arm to ward off the unexpected object flying toward her. It caught her on the elbow, causing her to cry out in pain. As she rubbed the sore spot, Killerbrew said softly "Pick it up, Margaret. Pick it up, read it, and then see if you still won't talk to me."

Margaret's coat and hat were where she had dropped them next to her shoes under the hammock where she rocked. As she watched the ocean, she wished she were as calm as it was that day. "That bastard," she muttered. "That rotten scheming bastard." The script lay in her lap, dropped there after reading it a second time. *Little One* had intelligence and wit qualities the character she would play did not. Just extreme vulnerability and an emotional life to replace the intellectual one she could never have as a retarded person. It was again an "important" film as it spoke about the need for human compassion and justice for all even when one of the "all" is in some way not equal to others.

Margaret knew without asking what the "conditions of sale" were. *Little One* was hers the moment she acquiesced on *Cajun Woman*. "That bastard," she muttered.

"Damn that man," she said aloud as she dialed the phone "Damn, damn, damn!" she repeated until Dorothea Wolf answered the private number that rang in her office and Franklin Killerbrew's.

"Taxi, Mrs. Ollson?" asked the uniformed doorman.

"Yes, Joseph, please," replied Carolyn as she removed one white glove to search the bottom of her purse for tip money Finding a quarter, she gave it to the doorman as he held open the door to a Checker cab.

As the car crossed Central Park en route to the East Side Carolyn felt butterflies again sounding their alarm in her stomach. She focused on the park, hoping to distract herself It was a gray day and it would probably snow. And wouldn't that at least be nice, she thought. A white Christmas. Th

172

ildren would love that. Again she opened her purse. This
ime she withdrew the letter from Margaret.

She would be arriving with Vinnie Christmas morning.
Thank God, thought Carolyn. Someone to talk to—and that
dear, darling child. How I've missed that baby! Some baby.
She laughed. He's done more traveling in his two and a half
years than I have in my lifetime. And to think some people
believe children don't travel well. They are wrong if Vinnie is
any indication.

Carolyn thought about Vinnie frequently. The boy had a
decided way about him. Or with me, she mused. She thought
about the past summer at Nantasket and how wonderful it
had been having him there with the other children while
Margaret came and went as Margaret was given to do. But it
was easy for Margaret to do that, thought Carolyn; easy
because Vinnie so obviously adores me. We're a mutual
admiration society, and I think of him almost in the same way
that I think of Thomas and Marti. Marti, indeed. She belonged solely to her cousin. He had even named her. The
last of the three children to talk, Vinnie somehow could not
say 'tha' so Mar*tha* became Mar*ti*. And everyone liked it.
Everyone used it. He was much like his mother, that child
was, thought Carolyn as the taxi pulled up at the Fifth
Avenue and Eighty-third Street address she had given. Fear-
less. The only baby she had ever seen who threw himself at
the waves unmindful that some were bigger than he. Of
course Marti had to follow suit. Such a tomboy. Well, there is
something to be said for that, too. No one steals her yellow
pail. Not for long anyway.

Carolyn had asked to see Dr. Garber after his normal
visiting hours and he had accommodated her. If she was
pregnant, no need to have the news broadcast by a Winchell
or a Kilgallen who seemed to have spies in every noted
obstetrician's office in New York. But I'm *not* pregnant, Carolyn reminded herself as she removed her Persian lamb coat
and lifted the veil off her face and onto the top of the navy
fedora she wore on her head. Looking around, she was glad
the doctor had not altered or redecorated his office. Today,
there was something comforting in its sameness. She needed
the familiarity. Early American is very reassuring, she decided
as she settled into a chair by a magazine stand.

Lacking the patience to read, Carolyn's thoughts drifted to
when she had first come to this office. Then she had been so

excited about possibly being pregnant. Not this time. N
now when there was so little time. The radio show, of cours
was no real problem. She could do that from the delive
room if she had to. But the play required a nymph, a wraithli
creature. Hard to play that with bulging belly and swoll
breasts. And there were no costumes that could hide a pre
nancy this time. Not when there was just a leotard and a l
of gauze.

This was not a good time to be pregnant, she decided aga
as she unbuttoned the jacket of her navy suit and stuck
finger in the neck of her frilly blouse that suddenly seemed
be strangling her. *What a Nymph Knows* had opened but
month ago and was running on the strength of her name a
certainly not the reviews. If it closed, it would be the fi
time any of the productions in which she had starred h
been unprofitable. It would be worse for John. He had p
the backers together. Act of God or not, they would not l
pleased.

Why hadn't she told John she might be pregnant, sl
wondered as she waited for Dr. Garber's office door to ope
John was busy, she told herself. She didn't want to ups
him. He was so occupied with "Front Row Center" and t
upcoming release of *Deep Purple*. He had seen a rough-c
just the other day and she knew simply from his insisten
that the film could not be judged without the music add
and further editing, that he had not been thrilled with it. B
then, why should he be when she wasn't when making it r
cannot do scenes out of sequence, she explained to herself
if someone were insisting that she should. Suddenly, she f
very glad she was but one of four stars in the film. John h
been wise to insist that the full weight of success and failu
not rest yet on her shoulders. John was always wise. She kne
about everything. Well, almost everything. He did not know
and if he did, then he did not understand—about fait
Often, of late, he accused her of hypocrisy. He thought
ridiculous that she let so much of church dogma go unque
tioned. It worried her that he feared so little for his immor
soul. It worried him, he said, that she worried so much abo
her own.

How had she become pregnant, she again asked herse
Not at Nantasket. Too long ago and besides, John had on
come up for but one of the four weeks—he was that bu
with preproduction on *Nymph*. Was it after or before openi

174

night? Certainly she should remember, particularly since John's lustfulness was now under his control.

"Mrs. Ollson," said Dr. Garber from his doorway. "Sorry for the delay. Won't you come in?"

Aglow, Killerbrew Castle, as it was known to Hollywood cynics, was a beacon to all below the mountain on which it perched. As Margaret gazed at it from the back seat of the limousine proceeding up the hills of Laurel Canyon in its direction she thought: All it needs is a torch and a sign reading: Give Us Your Gorgeous, Your Greedy.

At the Killerbrew driveway, as the car waited in a long, winding line of limousines, sports cars, and other status symbols on wheels, Margaret checked her makeup in her compact's mirror. The Nancy and Franklin Killerbrew Christmas party was an annual event of the holiday season and Nancy Quentin Blanchard's sole concession to being the wife of a Hollywood studio head. Once a year, she not only let in the riffraff but also mingled with them. The party was an industry brouhaha with everybody who was anybody invited and everybody who was nobody hoping to be. An invitation to the Killerbrew Christmas *Klatsch* was considered as hard to get as an invitation to join the DAR and the New York Athletic Club.

Margaret had heard much about the legendary "castle" and was curious to meet the dragon rumored to guard over it. She couldn't believe *La Dragonessa* was more fearsome than the man who paid the bills. Nancy Killerbrew's reputation had to be a gross exaggeration, Margaret had decided. Just more Hollywood talk.

In other years, Margaret, although invited, had missed the gala as she was traditionally in New York in mid-December to spend the holidays with her family. But this year, *Little One*'s two additional days of shooting would keep her in Hollywood until the twenty-fourth. Although Margaret had made it a rule never to party when due on a film set at seven the following morning, she could not deny her curiosity. The plain truth was she wanted to meet the famed and infamous Nancy Killerbrew. She also wanted to see Killerbrew in a nonbusiness setting. Rumor actually maintained he was as charming a host as he was a bastard of an employer. Margaret had had very little communication with Killerbrew since the day she had nearly struck him and he did strike her, albeit accidentally. After *Cajun Woman*, Margaret had flown East with Vinnie to spend a month—which was now called Vinnie's month—with Carolyn on Nantasket. During their stay, she visited the institutions in the New England area that housed and trained the retarded. The research for *Little One* was disquieting. Although an excellent observer, Margaret could not participate with the residents. Their differences upset and frightened her. She thanked God or Someone or Something daily for Vinnie's good health.

Carolyn should be the actress making *Little One*, Margaret had thought then. Carolyn was a Pied Piper. Children flocked to her. She had infinite patience and affection to give. It was on Nantasket that Margaret realized Vinnie adored his aunt. Not a particularly demanding or affectionate child with her, Vinnie, with Carolyn, became a child rather than the little person she knew who could amuse himself or be amusing when he chose. It was obvious that he was happier with his cousins than alone at home. He and Thomas and Marti would play with their pails and puddles at the beach for hours. Unlike most children, they never fought among themselves.

By the time Margaret returned with Vinnie to Hollywood in the fall, despite her own misgivings, she was the character in *Little One*. To her own amazement, when she saw the rushes she saw a fourteen-year-old retarded girl rather than herself. Now that the film was in its final days of shooting, Margaret was physically and emotionally exhausted. In the film she had aged seven years but in real life, Margaret felt it had been a hundred. Suddenly nothing in her life felt right anymore. She was glad of the month she would soon be spending with the family. Perhaps there she could sort out her feelings about work and play.

"Good evening, Miss Tiernan," said the servant in livery as he helped her from the back seat of the car that had finally come to a stop in front of the sprawling Spanish hacienda. From the marble-walled and terrazzo-floored vestibule, Margaret could see down into the living room that fanned out like a rainbow. With one glance she saw that her recent past was present. Too many of the men had been her "dates." Once.

As she navigated the five-step drop into the living room, a well-known voice said: "Margaret, you look ravishing. Like a vanilla ice cream cone."

"Errol, you sweet-talking man. Merry Christmas."

176

"You know Howard Hughes, don't you?" he asked Margaret of the handsome man by his side.

"Of course," said Margaret as she flashed Hughes her obligatory party smile which he did not return. The bruise on her arm from their first meeting had healed but obviously the bruise on his ego had not. A nasty man, thought Margaret as she "pleasantried" her way from Flynn toward the middle of the room where she was startled to realize she was the center of attention. Why me? she wondered when there were far more beautiful women. Like Ginger over there with the Rathbones. And Joan Fontaine. In another life, I want to come back looking like her. But not in that dress. As she accepted champagne from a passing waiter's tray, Margaret waved to Lana who had not one, not two, but three eligible men surrounding her. Still, Margaret felt the stares upon her body.

It was Adrian, she decided. She had worn his white strapless satin sheath that undulated when she did. Over her shoulders, a short matching cape shimmered. Her white pearl-studded evening bag was Adrian's also. The auburn hair, however, swept up and held in place by a white orchid, was hers.

"My dear, you look positively virginal. What a memory you must have!"

"Joan, how nice to see you without your shoulder pads. A pity you didn't leave your mouth home with them," said Margaret as she moved away from the actress she most disliked in Hollywood. Margaret had honed a technique she employed at industry parties where her presence was required rather than wanted. She would float about the room making what she called "wee talk—even less meaningful than small"—being totally charming and very noticeable so that when she left, usually within an hour of her arrival, everyone knew she had been there and her presence could be duly noted in the columns

A brief chat with the Gary Coopers was followed by hugs and chitchat with Claudette and Jean Arthur who always looked pained at these events. Ronald Colman was his usual charming self but again did not pick up the cues she put down that she was interested. Hedda wanted to know who was the new man in her life and Margaret replied that after her most recent rumored romances, she thought Goofy would do just fine. Hedda thought that hilarious and made Margaret promise not to "give that" to Louella.

After thirty minutes of greeting the "hired hands," Margaret began searching the room in earnest for her hosts. No departures could be made without that act of protocol being observed. Margaret had already formed an impression of Nancy Killerbrew just by taking stock of the woman's living room. The walls were painted a soft cream-yellow. The paintings that adorned them had a similar softness. Monets, Manets, a Rousseau, and Matisse were mere background in a room that was subtly seducing. There was nothing that commanded your attention. No knockout punch—except the skylight roof. Otherwise, everything blended into one harmonious unit. The long L-shaped couch, upholstered in raw tussah silk of light yellow, was inviting in its luxurious lushness. Before it stood the Mies van der Rohe chrome and glass square-topped coffee table, to its side, Mies's Barcelona chairs done in brown leather. The grouping was tied together by a light brown and beige geometric print rug. The room was a total success if, Margaret thought, you like good taste. Whoever did it had imagination and guts, mused Margaret as her eye surveyed the combination of French provincial and chinoiserie furnishings in cream and pale blue fabrics that decorated the other half of the room.

"Margaret, I don't believe you've met my wife. Margaret Tiernan, Nancy Killerbrew."

"Mrs. Killerbrew, I was just admiring your home," said Margaret as she shook hands with the woman who stood before her.

"How nice of you to notice. It is fun, isn't it?" said Nancy Killerbrew.

Fun? thought Margaret. Is Buckingham Palace *fun?*

"By the way, Miss Tiernan, let me return the compliment. Your work is also so very tasteful," said Nancy Killerbrew as she smiled and swept away toward her other guests.

Margaret watched as Nancy Killerbrew bestowed her presence on others. There was something mesmerizing about the woman but not pleasantly so. The green tulle evening dress was elegant. It was by Worth. No doubt of that. But the emerald dress clip and matching earrings and necklace were, thought Margaret snidely, by Great Profits and Inherited Wealth Unlimited. The steely blue eyes, perfect white teeth, and flawless complexion had to be Born to the Station. She

178

was not at all the kind of woman she would have thought Franklin Killerbrew to have married. Too perfect. Too clean. Looking at the Killerbrews together as they mingled, Margaret thought: What is wrong with this picture? When she could not find the answer she decided: the hell with it. I've seen stranger couples, although other than Leopold and Loeb, I can't think of who.

The party was noisy—Jolson and Jeanette had made a combat zone of the piano—when Margaret excused herself from the first intelligent conversation of the evening—a discussion with Ronald Reagan and Dashiell Hammett about the possibilities of America joining England in its war against Germany—to take some air. She found of late, starved as she was for this kind of communication, that it depressed her when it took place. There was so little of it in her life. Hollywood was not part of the United States. The war in Europe existed only on screen, and then only if it was box office. Otherwise . . . who cared? It was an unreal world and Margaret had begun to feel unreal in it.

Although the December night was chilling, Margaret, her short cape wrapped about her, strolled the grounds. The lawn was magnificently manicured, perfect for the croquet games she heard Nancy Killerbrew so loved to play. To its sides rose lemon and wisteria trees. The short bushes she assumed to be azaleas and fuchsias. Spring must be an incredible sight here, she thought as she walked past the gazebo—silly useless thing—toward the tennis courts. As she stood at the top of the steps leading down to the play and swimming area, Margaret looked back toward the house where the music of Xavier Cugat could be heard. It was at least three hundred feet away.

The swimming pool was Olympic-sized and as seen by the light of a nearly full moon, aquamarine in color. Several "Grecian" urns and lounges were on its four sides. There was also a shuffleboard court. Margaret could not imagine Nancy Killerbrew using the pool. A Nancy Killerbrew type never gets wet. Never. She probably sends herself to be dry-cleaned at Elizabeth Arden's once a week, thought Margaret.

Beyond was the pool house, a round, white stucco adobe. The palest of light shone through its windows. Margaret's curiosity pushed her past the unlocked door. The smell of lightly scented mineral salts invaded her consciousness before

179

she became aware of the gushing water as it sped around the whirlpool in the center of the room.

Peering into it, Margaret saw its bottom was a mosaic of tiny pieces of blue, green, gold, and white tiles. On both of its sides, on raised brass platforms, were the same Grecian lounges that were by the pool. The adobe's walls were one long wraparound mural of the Aegean Sea, interrupted only by two doors—one marked *Gods*, the other *Goddesses*. Under the latter, a flicker of light appeared. The handle on the door, a brass lion's head, was cold to the touch but turned noiselessly.

At first, the candlelight made Margaret think it was another mural she was staring at. A blue velvet chaise was filled with green tulle atop black crepe. The green tulle sat up, the top of her dress pulled down, exposing small breasts with hardened nipples. The black crepe stirred languorously, much the way she did on screen, and sat up on an elbow. Her long chestnut hair fell to her shoulders and over one of her round breasts, red from the tiny bites it had been enjoying.

In a calm but heavy voice Nancy Killerbrew said, "Either join us or close the door behind you on your way out."

Margaret backed up in the doorway and screamed as her body collided with another. Running, she fled from the pool house and careened up the manicured lawn, aware someone was running behind her. Terrified and confused by shock, she ran into the heavy wooded area that separated Killerbrew property from forest. A low branch scratched her face. Twisted vines wrapped themselves about her feet. She was falling when a hand grabbed her arm and roughly held her upright.

The sight of Franklin Killerbrew standing before her released her frenzy.

"Liar!" she screamed as she punched at his chest. "Liar!" she screamed as his hands held her helplessly by the wrists.

"Margaret, listen to me," pleaded Killerbrew.

"You freak. You lying freak. She's got your balls!" cried Margaret as she kicked at his shins. The pain caused Killerbrew to release her. In a second, her evening bag came up and hit him above the eye. She was scratching, clawing at his face when his hand reached up and grabbed her hair. The orchid came free and with it, the upsweep she had labored over.

"You fucking faggot!" Margaret screamed hysterically.

With one hand Killerbrew slapped Margaret across the face. With the other, he ripped her gown from bodice to waist. Her fists flew at him again. Crashing through the

180

woods, they tripped to the ground, his weight pinning her beneath him.

"I hate you," she was screaming. "I hate you!" His leg had pushed hers open and as one hand yanked her head to the ground, the other pulled up her dress. Realizing what he was about to do, Margaret dug her nails into his face. He yelled in pain. Blood dripped from his cheek onto her neck. She stared at him and he, at her. He then dropped the full force of his weight over her. His mouth covered hers as he entered her. Breathing in hard, short gasps, he filled her mouth with his exhalations and spittle. She felt him pulsating within her, his tongue probing one orifice while his penis, like a jack-hammer, probed the other. She was wet, wildly, uncontrollably wet, from passion and tears. He was sucking her tongue, biting her lips. She used her body to arch him deeper into her. Together, as they rolled in the dried leaves and underbrush damp with dew, they clung to one another, fighting to merge further when no further merging was possible.

Neither had spoken since he had carried her from the woods to the garage. If the car was noticed as it came around the house and sped down the driveway toward the highway it would take to Malibu, in the darkness of night the identity of its occupants remained secret. Now, as Killerbrew raced the roadster to its maximum speed, he roughly grabbed Margaret's hand and massaged his crotch with it. Then, he raised it to his lips. After he kissed her palm, he took each finger, one at a time, into his mouth and sucked on it painstakingly.

When they reached her house, she removed her mud-spattered cape and threw it into the fireplace. He looked at her standing there with her dress ripped to the waist and with one hand tore the rest of it from her. He knelt before her and pulled off her shoes as he kissed her calf, her ankle, her thighs. She pulled him up by his hair and guided him toward the downstairs bedroom so that they would be undisturbed by the rest of the household. As they kissed, she unzipped his trousers, moving him toward the bathroom all the while. Without leaving him, she managed to turn on the faucets that would fill the bathtub. He was removing his white formal shirt, dropping it to the floor. His face was purple where the evening bag had struck it. Dried blood, where her fingernails had torn him, laced his cheeks. In the tub, she gently sponged his wounds. The water was soon darkened by mud and blood. She freshened it and as the water ran from the spigot, he took her feet, washed one at a time, and then nibbled at her toes. When they were both still wet, he lifted her to the bed where he propped pillows under her hips, raising her pelvis high in the air. And then he probed her, slowly, steadily, first with his lips and then with his mouth. His hardened tongue entered and left her and then entered and left over and over again, leaving her writhing and moaning. His mouth moved from the inside of her thighs to the back of her buttocks and down her legs, then up again until his lips were covering her nipples.

Margaret's head was shaking convulsively from side to side when the pillows were yanked from under her and Franklin Killerbrew thrust himself into her. He rolled her over, atop, then under him; reversed the positions again, never letting her go, never withdrawing or releasing her from his steady contact. She felt the bed slide out from under her and disappear with time and place. A train was rushing through her, speeding recklessly down the tracks, out of control, toward its final destination. She screamed as he clutched her to him. She screamed again as she felt the power surge from him and into her. She screamed and this time her own was matched by his . . . long, deep, and guttural.

She fell asleep in his arms, not caring that in just three hours a car from his studio would arrive to take her to a full day's filming.

Margaret didn't know what to expect. Between scenes, her mind would trace the events of the previous evening. Hardly a word had passed between them that morning as they dressed. At the door, when he left, he held her with a tenderness not experienced the night before. And then he was gone. When she returned to the house that evening, it was with misgivings. It seemed empty of everything but the memory of the previous night. Absentmindedly, she played with Vinnie. At eight, as she put him in his crib for the night, she heard a car in the driveway. She didn't have to look to know who it was. When she opened the door, he entered with a bag of groceries from the A & P. All he said to her was: "I like mine medium-rare."

Augusta Monahan cast an approving eye on her handiwork. The table looked beautiful. The holly and red cranberries

182

intertwined about the blue Steuben candlesticks made a stunning centerpiece. And wasn't it lovely that they still had Tory's treasured Royal Crown Derby china for special occasions. That luscious Gregory rose in the center of the plate made one feel so privileged, thought Augusta. The tablecloth was of white Belgian linen and the napkins were green and red paper. Festive and functional, particularly with three babies in highchairs. And wasn't that Vinnie something! He came off that plane and into her arms as if he had seen her only yesterday. His mother sure had a cat-that-swallowed-the-canary look about her, didn't she.

In the kitchen as she took the fruit compote from the refrigerator, the smell of the turkey cooling on the counter reminded Augusta that she hadn't eaten since breakfast. No lunch was served today as Carolyn had been in church when John went to pick up Margaret and Vinnie at the airport.

"Well, I think we're ready," announced Augusta to no one other than herself. "Margaret? John? Get Carolyn and the children, we're set for dinner," she called down the hallway, hoping her voice would carry to the various bedrooms.

"The kids are in the living room with me, Augie. We'll be right in," yelled John. He had proven Carolyn wrong. The children were not too young to enjoy a train set. They were still sitting quietly watching the locomotive pull its cars around the Christmas tree. That Marti and Vinnie were sitting still so long was beyond unusual, thought John. Thomas, of course, was something else.

"How go, Da-da?" he kept asking. "How go?" His son was bound to be an engineer. He was not the kind of child to enjoy his toys at face value. "How go?" was a question Thomas was forever asking.

"Let's have our Christmas dinner, kids," he said as he hoisted a squealing Marti onto his shoulders. Thomas immediately took his hand and Vinnie, in monkey-see-monkey-do fashion, took his other. This, thought John as he took his children to Christmas dinner, is what it's all about. At that moment, it made all else very unimportant.

"I must say," said John as he bumped into Margaret in the hallway, "no one would ever know you've been up all night on a plane."

"I will take that as a compliment, sir," said Margaret, whose glow matched the rose silk dress she was wearing. "And I was not up all night. I actually slept like a baby. It's baby, here," she said, signifying Vinnie with a pat on his head, "who was up all night playing airplane pilot. I'm sure there will be a sign posted at airports all over the country banning this kid of mine from travel."

"Where's Carolyn?" asked Augusta. "Everything is ready and on the table."

Where's Carolyn indeed, thought Margaret, as she volunteered to see what was keeping her. She is certainly acting strange. Think of how she'd act if she knew about Killerbrew and me! I wonder if she's annoyed with me about something. She seems so distant.

The door to Carolyn and John's bedroom was closed. When there was no answer to her knocking, Margaret opened the door and walked into the room. The light was on in the bathroom.

"Miss Tiernan, you're wanted onstage," called Margaret gaily toward the bathroom. "Miss Tiernan, your public awaits," she bantered when Carolyn did not respond.

"Now listen, Lynnie. What the hell is keeping you?" Margaret exploded angrily as she walked into the bathroom. What she saw as she entered made her scream. Carolyn, her eyes glazed, was standing silently in a pool of blood.

"Her system has suffered an enormous shock. It is not unusual for a woman who has miscarried to be withdrawn and depressed. But she is young and strong and I'm sure she'll snap out of it in a matter of days."

So Dr. Garber had insisted to John, Margaret, and Augusta as they clustered anxiously in the waiting room at Doctors Hospital that Christmas Day. But that was four days ago and Carolyn was still laconic and mute. Garber's advice was: "Take her home. Her children will be the best medicine."

But they weren't. Carolyn showed no more interest in them than she did in anything else. Not understanding, the children became irritable, their anxiety resulting in nightmares. As New Year's approached, Carolyn, when not lying in her bed, sat bundled in bedclothes, staring at but not seeing the snow-white beauty of Central Park. Augusta wondered as she tended to Carolyn's breakfasts and lunches what would unlock whatever was keeping Carolyn's mind and feelings so firmly shut.

On his most recent house call, Dr. Garber suggested a psychiatrist be consulted.

"My wife is not crazy," said John hostilely.

"No one is suggesting she is, Mr. Ollson," soothed the doctor. "Psychiatry is more for the troubled or traumatized than it is for the insane and your wife seems to be having grave emotional difficulties."

"My wife has lost a child. As you yourself have said, many women go through difficult times after a miscarriage."

Garber knew when to withdraw. "Very well. What I suggest then is patience and caring. Include her in as many family activities as she will permit. Talk to her as if she were *there*, listening and responding. Do not coddle but be gentle with her."

John Ollson spent many hours being gentle with Carolyn. He had been shocked by her miscarriage and hurt that she had not confided in him. He told Augusta and Margaret what he himself did not believe: that Carolyn had wanted to surprise them all at Christmas dinner with the news of her pregnancy. No one contradicted him. As John sat by Carolyn's side, holding her unresponsive hand, he told her: "It's going to be all right, Lynnie. All of it. We've made our mistakes but from here on, it's going to change." As he thought of the life he had been living apart from Carolyn, John said, "I love you, Lynnie. It begins and it ends with that. What we have to find is a middle we can live with."

Margaret was having difficulty following John.

"She can't work, Margaret. Even when she snaps out of this, she'll need a week or so before she could possibly resume the radio show and the play. But she will need to do both. She'll need the activity. It will take her mind off her loss. The understudy cannot carry *Nymph*. People won't pay six-fifty to see an unknown, but they'll pay that and more to see you. And Marg, it's only until Lynnie is well enough to return."

"But when will that be, John?" asked Margaret, her concern bringing her near tears.

John put his hands on his troubled sister-in-law's shoulders. "God only knows, Marg," he replied.

"Do you believe in God, John?" asked Margaret as she composed herself.

"Yes, I do. But not in the way Carolyn does."

"I don't know what I believe in," sighed Margaret.

John put his arms around Margaret and held her as she

185

trembled. "She's going to be all right, Marg. I promise you. We've had a rough time the past few months but that's all going to change. Marg, if you'll step in for Carolyn, do 'Front Row Center' and *Nymph*, I'm going to take her away for a month. We'll spend January in Palm Beach. She'll like that. It'll be a fresh start in a new year."

"I'll do it, John," said Margaret. "For all of us. It'll be fun. Shit!" she added as she remembered her contract. "I can't do it unless Killerbrew gives his okay."

"He already has," said John with a smile that spoke of how pleased he was with himself

"You spoke to him?" asked Margaret, suppressing her desire to add: Did he ask about me?

"Franklin said if it is okay with you, it's okay with him. He said he has nothing in mind for you just now anyway."

Nothing in mind for me, Margaret repeated silently. She thought of all Killerbrew had had in mind for her during the three nights they had spent together. She hadn't known it was possible for a man to have so much in mind and so often. She had relived those nights every day since, recalling each detail and particularly how nothing had been said between them. In bed or out. No declarations or promises. He had not phoned to say good-bye the day she left and he had not called to say hello since she had arrived in New York. It was obviously true. He had nothing in mind for her, so why not stay on in New York.

Margaret was sprawled on the carpet at Carolyn's feet in the living room studying the script for *What a Nymph Knows*. "It's madness, Lynnie, do you hear me? Madness! Me, trying to learn two-and-a-half hours of dialogue in three days, is committing professional suicide. You're the quick study. Not me. Damn, Lynnie, if you had any compassion whatsoever, you'd be helping me."

Carolyn was sitting quietly in the chair whose name she had never learned to pronounce. Whether or not she was listening to Margaret was impossible to tell. A cup of tea was by her side on the drum table and occasionally she would sip from it. A small victory, thought Margaret. At least now she is feeding herself.

"Madness!" repeated Margaret. "You're the one born to the thea*tah* . . . the ham of the family. Also, Lynnie-love, when the cat gives you back your tongue, you must tell me

186

why you ever decided to do this play. Who cares what a nymph knows?"

"Mama, come-park. Play," said Vinnie as he barged into the living room wearing his red snowsuit.

"Darling, Mrs. Worthington is taking you. Mama can't right now 'cause she's learning her lines. Why don't you ask Aunt Carolyn to go with you?"

"Aunt Carolynnie, play-park?" beseeched Vinnie as he pulled at his aunt's hand. Carolyn looked down at the curly-haired child and touched his face. "Why, yes, dear. That would be nice. Let me get my coat and galoshes."

Carolyn was halfway to the hallway closet when Margaret found her voice. "Lynnie, where are you going?"

"The children want to go out and I thought I'd give Mrs. Worthington a hand with them. You know how the kids get in the snow."

Margaret had walked toward Carolyn, trying to measure her sister's state from the expression on her face. "Do you feel strong enough?"

"Why shouldn't I? Honestly, Margaret, sometimes you talk as silly as John. Always treating me like a child, thinking I'm doing too much. Don't you know by now I'm strong as a horse?"

"Vinnie, go with Mrs. Worthington," commanded Margaret. "Aunt Carolyn and I will catch up in a bit."

Wordlessly, Margaret helped Carolyn into her winter gear. They were in the elevator, the operator having greeted Carolyn profusely as he inquired after her health, when the car stopped on the third floor and a young woman wheeled in her baby carriage. She positioned it so that the baby, bundled in blankets, its pink-cheeked face peering out from under its white wool hat, was facing Carolyn and Margaret. When the elevator doors swung open, Carolyn remained rooted at the back of the car.

"Did you forget something, Mrs. Ollson?" asked the elevator operator, thinking Carolyn meant to go back upstairs.

"Yes . . . my baby," she said as tears trickled down her face. "I forgot my baby."

Back in the apartment, Margaret crooned as she rocked Carolyn, sobbing against her breast.

"I lost my baby," Carolyn kept repeating as if to explain something Margaret didn't already know.

"Yes, dear. But it is all going to be all right."

"Margaret, you don't understand. I was being punished," sobbed Carolyn.

"Punished? For what?"

"For being bad, Margaret."

"Lynnie, you're the goodest person I know. So stop such foolishness."

"I didn't want a baby," said Carolyn, her voice flat.

"Lots of women don't," said Margaret, remembering clearly how she had felt. "But they adjust."

"I mean I didn't want *this* baby," cried Carolyn, exasperated that her sister did not understand. "*I* wanted what *I* wanted when *I* wanted it."

"Lynnie, make sense. I don't understand you."

"I was living my plan for my life rather than His. It was His will that I be pregnant and I was resentful of it. I kept wishing it away. And so He took it from me. He punished me."

"Lynnie, we've had this discussion in a hundred different ways," said Margaret patiently. "You know what I believe. If there is a God, He created life so man, whom He also created, could live it. As man sees fit."

"Oh, Marg, no. That's where you're wrong. Can you imagine what this world would be like if people lived as they saw fit? There would be no law, no order. Just chaos."

"Lynnie, I'm not the one to help you. I see no conflict or evil in the things that disturb you. You must learn to distinguish between what you were taught and what you yourself believe. The responsibility for your marriage rests firmly on your shoulders."

"Oh, no," repeated Carolyn calmly. "That I know isn't true. It rests with both John and me. I know you believe sex is as much a part of a couple's repartee as conversation. In fact you think it is conversation—a form of communication of some kind. Perhaps. I no longer know. I am not totally stupid, Margaret. I do question much of what I've been taught, although I don't question Him. I don't know about sex but I do know John and I have to come to some kind of understanding we both can live with. And I'm going to try!"

They were standing at the living room window, looking out over Manhattan, Carolyn's head resting on Margaret's shoulder as Margaret's arm encircled her waist, when the clock struck twelve. As the street below exploded with the sound of cars honking their horns, John and Augusta bustled out of the kitchen carrying a tray filled with sandwiches and champagne.

"Happy New Year, my darlings," said Augusta as she hugged both her nieces at the same time. Observing the three women entwined, John raised his glass and said· "To the three most wonderful women a man could have in his life."

Carolyn and Margaret looked at each other, both remembering another time not so long ago when their father had made a similar toast.

"And," continued John, "to a new year, a new decade, and . . . new beginnings!"

Yes, new beginnings, thought Augusta as she sipped from her champagne glass. Old morals and old values belong to an old decade. If you love the man, do something about it, she told herself.

"Out with the old and in with the new!" she toasted the assemblage.

"To family!" said Carolyn as she raised her glass. "To my family and to the tradition of family everywhere."

The telephone ringing in the hallway interrupted Margaret's thoughts.

"I'll get it," offered Augusta, as she rushed off. "I can't imagine who'd be calling at this hour," she added over her shoulder. Seconds later, she returned, her face set in a perplexed expression.

"It's for you, Margaret. It's Franklin Killerbrew."

BOOK TWO
1943–1948

1

Kerry Jones was sitting on the fake grass in the middle of a circle composed of Thomas, Vinnie, and Marti. "Now remember, when I say 'Action!' all you have to do is exactly what we did before. Marti, you're going to grab a cupcake from the baker's tray while Tommy and Vinnie are talking to him. When the baker sees what you've done, you're going to run toward me and the camera. As the baker gets closer and closer to you, you take another bite of the cupcake. Now, Tommy, when the baker gets close to Marti, you whistle through your teeth, get his attention, and then run, with Vinnie, with the rest of the cupcakes. Has everybody got that?" When the children nodded their heads that they did, Jones called out: "Let's do it!"

"Quiet on the set, please!" called one of the men near the camera. "*Tiernan Tots Triple Trouble*. Take one. Scene sixteen. Roll 'em."

From behind the camera where she was sitting in a canvas-backed chair, Carolyn was watching "the Tiernan Tots," as they were now billed, make their first motion picture. As she knitted, a yawn verified what she already knew: that filmmaking was a bore, particularly when it involved children. Even her own. Yet, she knew Killerbrew was right. America would have a love affair with the Tots. Marti was an adorable pixie whose eyes spoke of mischief but in whose mouth butter wouldn't melt. Vinnie? The devil disguised in black curls and black eyes. And finally Thomas, the Kellogg's Corn Flakes kid—blond, blue-eyed, and All-American handsome. John all over again, thought Carolyn. Another yawn, this one stifled, made her stretch and yearn for her bedroom. How I miss my Mondays, she thought, my one day of do-nothingness. But now, Monday meant Brooklyn. Flatbush to be precise. Only Franklin Killerbrew would choose an ugly barn of a studio in the middle of nowhere.

"Cut!" yelled Jones impatiently. "What are you doing?" he asked Marti and Vinnie as they rolled around on fake grass, laughing as they groped and scratched at one another.

"She's had two bites of the cupcake and won't give me one," protested Vinnie.

"It's mine," screamed Marti as she attempted to stuff what was left of the disputed object in her mouth.

"Dumb kids," sneered Thomas. "It's made of paper, you jerks!"

"Oh yeah, Mr. Smartypants?" said Vinnie, giggling. "Well I happen to like paper. It's great with ketchup."

"Can we do this again?" asked the director.

"You're the boss," said Marti, throwing up her hands.

The crew laughed, as did Carolyn. The precocity of that child! Six years old and never at a loss for words. Takes after her aunt. The thought of Margaret reminded Carolyn of the letter she had intended to write this day. Reaching into her briefcase, she pulled out the blue stationery with *Carolyn Tiernan* engraved in script across the top, and began writing as the call for "Lights! Camera! Action!" again reverberated throughout the huge sound stage. It was only when she wrote the date at the top of the page that Carolyn decided it was not Margaret she would write that morning.

February 15, 1943

Dear John,

Happy day after Valentine's Day, darling!

It's Monday, m'love. My turn to baby-sit with the kids at Vitagraph—although why I bother is beyond me. Mrs. Worthington manages quite nicely when she's here and she gets all the help she needs from the tutor the studio provides. Still, I feel it's terribly important I be here for two reasons. I want the children to feel I'm close at hand . . . I want the film crew to know these children have a family to protect them. Augusta now comes on Thursday, the one day she manages to keep free. My aunt must be the busiest woman in New York.

In case you've worried, your children (and I include Vinnie) have taken to the limelight as if born to it. Which I suppose they were. So far—repeat: so far—they seem to be having great fun and have not become brats. Believe me, the minute I see that happening it's off to parochial school with them for

194

a little humbling. Actually, I think because they've seen Margaret and me work all their young lives, have seen strangers approach us often, they find nothing very unusual or head-turning about what they're doing. Good! Let's hope that continues. If it doesn't, you'll have the devil (me!) to pay as it's all your doing. It was, if you'll remember, your idea that I read Dickens's *Christmas Carol* on "Front Row Center" last Christmas. And it was *you*, dear heart, who suggested I take the kids to the studio with me and just have them "react," as you put it, as they sat with me. Well, they reacted all right, as did all America and Killerbrew Studios.

Carolyn put down her pencil and paper and remembered the radio show that had created the Tiernan Tots. The children had acted no differently from when she read them their nightly bedtime story. They were inquisitive and spontaneous. At first, when she was asked to host the Saturday morning children's radio show, she balked, but by mid-January, "Storytime," starring Carolyn Tiernan and the Tiernan Tots, was on the air and on its way toward the top of the daytime Hooper ratings. Killerbrew had instantly seen the possibilities for an *Our Gang* success with the Tiernan Tots so . . . here they were, completing the first of what was to be a series of twenty-minute features. In Brooklyn! In Flatbush!

Carolyn picked up the pencil and began writing again.

By the way, I didn't tell you that Vinnie is listed in the credits as Vinnie Tiernan. Killerbrew thought that best—that the Tiernan Tots should all be Tiernans for billing purposes. Frankly, I see no harm in it as Thomas and Marti are after all Ollsons and not Tiernans and as ole Shakespeare once said: What's in a name? And ole Margaret is thinking about having Vinnie's name changed legally anyway. Again, to be frank, I understand how she feels. How do *you* feel about all this? I really want to know and would value your opinion.

By the by, your son Thomas seems the least excited about the "make-believe," as the director calls the work, but he sure does love the limousine ride to Brooklyn. I still don't know how in this day and age the studio is able to finagle gas, what with rationing and the scarcity of it. But they do and I for one—even if it is unpatriotic of me—am glad, as I would not allow the children to ride the subway every day. Anyway, Thomas thinks the Statue of Liberty and the Brooklyn Bridge are the greatest inventions ever. He asked me how a bridge is put in water. I told him to ask his father, which I'm sure he will do when you return. Marti's dream is to ride the ferry I'm not sure if the one we see each morning goes to Weehawken, Hoboken, or Staten Island but it does look like it would be fun. In the spring! And certainly not now in February. Brrr. Anyway, it appears as if Marti will be either an explorer or a sailor when she grows up. Frankly, I feel like an explorer when I come out to Brooklyn. I am constantly amazed at how pretty certain parts of this borough are. Like the country. Really. Vitagraph is in the middle of what must have been farmland not so long ago. Avenue M is a small main-street type of thoroughfare. It even has a movie house. The Elm, it's called. And in and around the studio—like along Bedford Avenue—you see homes with frontage that resemble Beverly Hills. It must be very pretty in the spring.

Sometimes I can't quite believe where everyone is. Marg, of course, is in Hollywood. Augusta is . . . Lord only knows where. The children are making movies in Brooklyn no less! And you, my love, are somewhere in Africa . . . I think, fighting a war while I continue to make people laugh, or cry, on radio and onstage. It's all so strange.

I do hope you don't disapprove of "the Tiernan Tots." Marg and I discussed it from every vantage point. We couldn't see how it could do the children any harm. But we worry. We want the kids to have normal lives, or as normal as their lives can be considering who their mothers are (that's a joke, son!). Although to be honest, John, how anyone can have a normal life—particularly a child—in these times is beyond me. Like last Thursday night. We had a blackout. The air raid sirens terrify the children. Marti and Vinnie hide under their beds. I must admit that Mama, here, finds them scary, too. We have blackout curtains, as do most people, and after they're drawn, we sit in total darkness. Thursday, I peeked out the window and looked at the skyline. Without a moon, it wasn't there. I mean . . . with no lights and no moon, the city wasn't there! I can't tell you how strange that made me feel. And if it makes me feel strange, what does it do to the children? Just the other day Marti wanted to know if Germans lived in the Bronx. She had heard something about the Bronx Bomber (is that baseball talk?) and thought "he" or "they" were Germans from the Bronx who were going to bomb us.

The children ask about you constantly. I tell them you're away, working (I never say *fighting*) to make us all safe, and that you'll be home as soon as your work is done. Of course they then want me to define "soon." Try doing that for six-year-olds. Yet, the wonderful thing about kids is that . . . they're kids. I don't know how else to say it. They know "there's a war on" but it's not real to them (thank God). They still play their games; listen each night to Jack Armstrong and Hop Harrigan (he's "America's Ace of the Airways"), and come to the radio show each Saturday without thinking it, or they, is (are) very unusual. However, I'm a wreck. Before every broadcast, I die a little. Do they know or care? No. Are they nervous? No. They simply sit at my feet, unaware that as soon as the director gives the signal, every word we say goes out all over America on . . . the Blue Network.

By the way, we are now the second most popular ("Let's Pretend" is still number one) Saturday morning children's show. It wasn't bad enough that the radio publicists wanted to make our kids the nation's number one family but Killerbrew, too, now has his entire sales *force* (and believe me, most publicity is *forced*) making them household words. Both Margaret and I are taking every possible precaution against having the children exploited. We've already turned down clothing and breakfast food endorsements.

Margaret calls as often as she can get through. Yes, even long-distance phone service is limited. But (with Killerbrew's help, I imagine) she manages to get through at least twice a week. I wish it were more. Vinnie is acting strangely. I hope it's just a stage but sometimes when Marg calls, Vinnie pretends indifference. He says, "Tell her I'm busy" when Marg asks to speak to him. I don't think he understands why he is here and Marg is there. Or if he does understand, he doesn't like it. Marg thinks he's punishing her when he refuses to talk with her. But guess what happens? Marti grabs the phone and pretends she's Vinnie. She has this long talk with Margaret and tells her everything that they've all been doing. This, of course, tickles Marti but infuriates Vinnie. You should see those two together! Mutt and Jeff. Forever fighting and forever kissing and making up. Thomas looks at both of them with all the "wisdom" and disdain of the eldest.

Speaking of wisdom and the eldest, I know it's not wise to live in the future but Margaret returns around Easter and I can hardly wait. She is coming by train as plane travel is almost impossible. Not that obtaining train reservations is easy either but . . . Killerbrew can pull the necessary strings. I'm glad she's coming. With you gone, Augusta off at the hospital, Rose Wheaton so recently departed (may she rest in peace), I get lonely. No, I'm not feeling sorry for myself. That selfish I'm not. There you are—somewhere—and here I am surrounded by children and familiar objects. But, there is a void without you. Margaret eases the ache. Besides, she's so much better at managing the ration books than I. If it were left to me, I'd use up all the meat coupons the first week. Margaret does the menus for the month. We not only have meatless Fridays, of course, but meatless Tuesdays . . . and meatless Thursdays and Saturdays as well. Which in our house is no problem. Our children would be very happy indeed to live on macaroni and cheese.

We're told to write only cheery things to our loved ones overseas but I miss you so that it's hard not to whine and complain. I'm sorry. But not knowing exactly where you are and how you are is very hard. I am trying to be you to the children and it's an impossible task. I'm trying to be you to me and that's even more of an impossible task. I feel like I'm missing an arm or a leg which is just another way of saying . . . I need you . . . I love you.

Carolyn

After she addressed the envelope and folded the letter into it, Carolyn became aware of the stillness on the set. Looking up, she was surprised to see the klieg lights off and the set empty.

"Where is everybody?" she asked a passing workman.

"At lunch I guess, Miss Tiernan."

Collecting her things, Carolyn walked to the trailer just off the set occupied by the children. From outside she could hear the screams and laughter. When she opened the door, the first sight she saw was jam oozing down the wall behind Vinnie. The second was Marti, her hand held high as it was about to fling a fistful of Welch's grape jelly at her cousin. Thomas, wearing a bemused expression, was sitting on a hobbyhorse scraping peanut butter from the bottom of a Skippy jar.

"All right, missy. Just hold it right there," stormed Carolyn from the doorway. Looking from Marti's jelly-stained overalls to Vinnie's "Who, me?" face, Carolyn was hard pressed to suppress a laugh. "There will be no wasting of food in this household. In case you haven't heard . . ."

"We know," interrupted Marti.

"There's a war on," she chorused with Vinnie and Thomas.

Margaret turned the two-door Plymouth right on Sunset and onto Cahuenga Boulevard. As she approached the redwood-planked building that looked exactly like what it once had been—a stable—she saw a parking place directly across from her destination. Once parked, she checked her makeup and hair in the car's rearview mirror. Perfect. Ready for action, she decided as she swung open the car door.

It was six o'clock, an hour before the Hollywood Canteen opened, yet there must have been two hundred soldiers and sailors waiting to get in. She waved as she strode briskly by, enjoying the wolf whistles and the calls of "hubba hubba" as she made her way to the rear entrance. Normally she wore slacks but this was Saturday night and so she had chosen a cool but clinging jersey print dress. It was festive and decently suggestive.

Margaret had been a member of the Hollywood Canteen from its inception in October of '42. Bette Davis had asked her cooperation and Margaret had gladly given it. The idea of the Canteen appealed to her even if its decor did not. She had fought for a sound stage type of feeling. Instead, Hollywood designers had built a barn within a barn, using to full advantage the huge beams that trellised the ceiling. It wasn't the wagon wheel chandeliers Margaret objected to. Actually, with the kerosene lamps dangling from them they were kind of fun. But those Gay '90s murals! she had complained. No one had agreed and certainly the servicemen didn't care. They came for fun and food, dance and not decor. They came and they came and they came—about twenty-five hundred a night—"and," Margaret had complained to Betty Grable one evening, "my feet feel as if I've danced with every one of them."

Margaret usually attended the Canteen Saturday nights as she had little else to do on what could be her loneliest night of the week. Killerbrew could not get free on weekends. Saturday night was when he and that dear Mrs. Killerbrew socialized, as the society columns so dutifully reported in detail on Monday morning. And Sundays were the tennis matches. Very high-falutin stuff. So the Saturday nights at the

Canteen were, Margaret told herself, a blessing. Only her feet dared to disagree.

The Canteen was still pleasantly cool, the heat of the July day not yet permeating its interior. Give it a few hundred men and some jitterbugging and that would change, thought Margaret. Kay Kyser, setting up with his men on the bandstand, waved to her and as she walked into the kitchen she waved back. "You on sandwiches tonight, Margaret?" asked Walter Pidgeon as he hurried by, struggling under the weight of a huge coffee urn.

"Rita and me. Hedy, too, I think," said Margaret as she took one of the three thousand sandwiches being prepared for the evening. After pouring herself a mugful of coffee, she sat on a folding chair gobbling the ham and cheese on rye. "It's been a helluva day!" she exclaimed as she reached for a doughnut.

Stop that! she admonished herself. No need to stuff your face just because you're upset.

Margaret sighed. And to think it had started out to be just a Saturday—no different from any of the past year. Shortly after eight that morning, Franklin had slipped out of bed, into his clothes, and out of her house. Standard Saturday morning procedure. She would undoubtedly not see him again until Monday if Los Angeles's social calendar ran true to form. Maybe not even until Tuesday if business demanded. For more than two years now they had lived in this semidomestic fashion if not bliss. No, never bliss. Except in bed. At first the arrangement was pleasing enough. Margaret had her work and her man. But recently Margaret's feelings had changed. She had her work . . . period. Her man was not hers at all. Nothing was hers except her house and her career. Her own son seemed determined to disown her.

Margaret's seven-year contract with Killerbrew Studios had expired last month and Killerbrew was annoyed and confused by her hesitancy to sign another. But the expiration of the contract had triggered off emotions she hadn't known she was feeling until the lawyers called and asked her to sign for another five years.

"What have I to show for my seven years?" Margaret had asked Killerbrew.

"You gotta be crazy. Show for it? Twenty-four films, five Oscar nominations, and one win for *Little One*. Not to mention enough dough to fix you financially for life. Now I'm offering you still more money and you're asking me what you've got to show for it. Come on, Margaret, be sensible."

Without thinking, Margaret reached for another doughnut. She kicked off her pumps and put her legs up on a nearby chair. As she nibbled the chocolate off the doughnut, she thought about the conversation they had had in bed the previous night.

"I don't want to stay in Hollywood," she said. "But I don't want to leave either."

"Then what the hell do you want?" Killerbrew asked angrily.

She had been turned from him, on her side. Now she rolled over. "You!" she said evenly as she faced him.

She saw the cloud that passed over his eyes. "You have that already," he said in what was for him a soft voice.

"No, I don't, Frank. I really don't," she said again as her hand reached out to cover his.

He had pulled her to him, held her, kissed her hair. "You have more of me than any woman can, could, or ever will. You know that."

That was the pain of it, thought Margaret. Through all their fighting about scripts, Hollywood mores and values, even the world at large, they loved each other. More than loved. He cared about her welfare and did whatever he could to ensure that her working and living conditions were everything money and power could buy. For two years they had successfully fended off the Gossip. They were never seen together publicly and only a few neighbors at Malibu were aware that Killerbrew was a frequent visitor. Those few would frequently see him playing on the beach with Vinnie.

At first, their "illicit affair," as Margaret dubbed it, was exciting to her. She felt as if she were the heroine in her own movie. God knows, she thought, there was mucho melodrama in her life.

As she sipped her coffee, Margaret relived her "meeting" with Nancy Quentin Blanchard Killerbrew a year or so ago. It had damn near ruined the first blush of spring, she thought.

She and Franklin had "stolen hours" almost every day of the week. They couldn't get enough of each other. Little by little, trust had been born. She came to understand that from the day she had arrived in Hollywood, in his own often strange and even ugly fashion, he had looked after her. They had been walking the windswept beach on a particularly blustery March day when almost as a non sequitur he said,

"Do you remember when you screamed at me: 'She's got your balls'?" When Margaret nodded that she did indeed remember, Killerbrew said, "You were right. She does. Nancy was willed twenty-five percent of Blanchard Pictures. If I leave her, which I've wanted to do, she sells it to Louis B. or Harry Cohn. That's what she's threatened and knowing Nancy, that's what she would do. Margaret, it would kill me to lose control of my studio. The Duke of Windsor gave up his throne for the woman he loved. I can't. Love is not enough for me to live on. I took that studio when it was crumbling and made it what it is today. You once accused me of loving power. Mea culpa. I also love making films. I don't think I could live without my studio."

"But you could live without me," she added. "Isn't that what you're saying?"

He hadn't answered.

"Wonderful. We have here, folks: one marriage. In name only of course. One woman—the socially prominent Mrs. Nancy Quentin Blanchard Killerbrew—who gets to have what she wants in life. One man—that's you, Franklin—who also gets—with a small exception perhaps—what he wants from life. And then there's me—a part-time 'wife,' a part-time mother, and a full-time actress with an Oscar to prove it."

She had cried bitterly that day on the beach. He had held her, not caring who might be watching. In his arms, she buried her fears and hurts.

"There was a part of me that believed it would work out," Margaret heard herself saying as she finished her coffee. Embarrassed, she looked about to see if anyone had heard her talking to herself. Well, I did, she thought. I was so used to playing happy endings in my films that I confused my life with celluloid. Even *that* crazy day didn't seem real.

Margaret's mind drifted to an afternoon in the summer that followed that "first blush of spring." Her doorbell had rung and upon answering it, she was face to face with Nancy Killerbrew.

"What a *pleasant* surprise," said Margaret with all the disdain she could inflect into one sentence. "If you're selling Girl Scout cookies, I'll take two boxes."

"Just take two minutes instead," said Nancy.

"I'll give you one," said Margaret, making it clear from the way she positioned herself in the doorway that Nancy would not be invited into the house.

"Your contract with Killerbrew Studios does not include my husband. You are not the first *actress* he's taken up with and I'm sure you won't be the last of your kind. But he is spending more time on your *career* than he has on others in the past. That must stop. People in this town do talk and I have a position to maintain. Unless you want your name dragged through the mud, I suggest you ply your trade elsewhere."

Before Margaret could recover and respond, Nancy Killerbrew was speeding off in her Chrysler convertible toward the main highway.

"That bitch!" screamed Margaret as she began running toward her car, not thinking of what she was doing. "That bitch!" she screamed again as her Plymouth barreled down the road in pursuit of Nancy Killerbrew. At the entrance to the highway, Margaret accelerated on the gas pedal. Her speed brought her alongside Nancy. She beckoned her to pull over. When Nancy refused, Margaret pumped still harder on the gas. Her Plymouth surged ahead of Nancy's Chrysler. It was then Margaret veered the steering wheel to the right and cut off Nancy sharply. She heard the crunch of metal on metal but was out of the Plymouth before the contact could register on her. She yanked open Nancy's car door and screamed at the shaken woman.

"Now *you* listen to me and *you* listen good. I'll see as much of your husband as I like. You got that? I don't give a shit what you want. It's what I want, lady, so get that straight. And what are you going to do about it? Divorce him? Not on your life. Right? Without being Mrs. Killerbrew, you'd be just a cloutless cunt, a diesel dyke without a husband to hide behind. No protective cover to cover up your little pool house plays. If anyone's name gets dragged through the mud, it's yours. And you know what that means, sweetie? I'll draw you a picture. Cancellation of your membership in every exclusive club in town. You may think you've got your husband by the balls but guess who's got yours! Finally, if I ever see you near my property again, I'll kick your ass clear out to Pasadena!"

Nancy Killerbrew simply sat with her head cocked looking up at Margaret as if she were listening to the weather report.

"Well done, dear," she said as she patted Margaret's hand that was resting on the car door. "No wonder Franklin is enamored of you." As she turned the key in the ignition, trying to start up the damaged car, she added: "Did anyone ever tell you you're beautiful when you're angry?"

Seconds later, as Nancy Killerbrew sped away in her somewhat dented Chrysler, she left an amused Margaret Tiernan. *The woman's a cunt but a classy one,* thought Margaret as she stood in Nancy's dust.

There had been nothing amusing or classy about Nancy or him in this morning's confrontation with Killerbrew, she remembered as she put on her shoes. That woman was standing between her and marriage. "Only she isn't," Margaret had screamed at Killerbrew. "What stands between me and marriage to Franklin Killerbrew is *you,* Franklin Killerbrew. You and your goddamn movie studio."

He had been furious. "I never said otherwise," was all he said as he left for the weekend. The five-year contract he had brought with him the previous evening remained unsigned. She had torn it up. There was no way she was going to lose another year of her life, let alone five. An Oscar was not a Franklin in bed. Time to get out. "Time to get out," she repeated as she heard the jukebox blare "Shoo, Shoo Baby" from the main room where the servicemen were now entering.

"Dance? I'd love to dance, soldier," Margaret said to the young boy who had snatched the cap from his head when he had seen her enter through the kitchen doors.

Tears were slipping down John's face and still he sang.

"Sleep in heavenly pea-eace. Slee-eep in hea-venly peace."

Sleep. There hadn't been any in days. Perhaps weeks. Maybe even months. Who could remember? Hard as a rock, people used to say about bad beds. Now they slept in rocks, on rocks, happy for the mountains that shielded them from enemy fire. Rocks and dreams. Gunfire and memories. Richard Crimmings, Barney Stoneham, Phillip Kessler, George Davenport, Paul Secor, Donnie Goldstein, Stewart . . . What was Stewart's name?

Dead. All dead. Buried in sand. Buried in mud. Buried in rock. Buried and underfoot. His men. Dead and gone. Except in his mind where he kept them alive by repeating their names night after night, day upon day. If you can remember them, then they are not dead.

"Shepherds quake at the sight."

He quaked, too, at the sight. He quaked and quaked and worried that he wouldn't stop quaking each time he saw a man drop from a bullet, from a bomb, a shell, each time he saw a leg or an arm or a face blown away. Like so much sand in the limitless desert where they had fought. Did they win or lose? Was it then or now?

What was time anyway? They sang of Christmas so it must be that. Peace on earth. Goodwill toward . . . toward whom? John wondered. But if it was Christmas, what had happened to September . . . to Halloween? And the year? What year was it? The year of our Lord, right? But which year? Think back. It was 1942 when I enlisted. April one. Guess who was the April fool? He giggled. The induction center at Governors Island. And the physical. And he couldn't piss. Too nervous. The oath of allegiance. To the flag of the United States of America. Then what? Yes, Fort Dix. Basic training. What was basic about it? Basic survival. Basic ways to kill. Officers training in . . . Fort Benning. In Georgia. Sweet Georgia Brown. Bob Brown got his balls blown off just the other day in Sicily. His ass went with them. They didn't tell us about that one at Camp Pickett! Taught us to prepare for the Northwest African campaign but not how to get through life without your ass and your balls.

"It came upon a midnight clear, that glorious song of old."

It wasn't a midnight clear when they put me and my men on a troopship in November. Second Lieutenant John Ollson, Third Infantry Division reporting for duty. Me and my men are in the front line of battle. Very brave. Very honorable. We came upon a midnight clear at Fedala—that was it, near Casablanca. Lost Kessler there. On to Tunis. We're on the road to Tunisia! Nice desert. Hot sands. A little too hot. Actually, stinking hot. Sand in hair . . . eyes. In mouth and ears. K rations. Nice place to visit but I wouldn't want to live there. Crimmings and Secor live there now. Or pieces of them do. Stoneham's and Goldstein's guts—no, not Goldstein. He died in the mountains. He and his guts. He fell into goat shit. Guts and goat shit. Only Stoneham shit in sand. You shit when you die. They don't teach you that at Benning or Pickett either

"God rest ye merry, gentlemen, let nothing you dismay."

It's funny. Yesterday, Rafferty was alive. Today he's dead. Tomorrow I and my troupe will be off somewhere else playing the European theatre. All the world's a stage, Carolyn. Just as you said. Only it wasn't you who said it, was it? It sure wasn't the Sicilians. I remember that. We seized the port of

Syracuse in July and lost Davenport in Palermo, or was it near Reggio? Naples? Hospital zone. Quiet! Sssh. Do you think they listened? Men dying all over the place and still they made noise. The howitzer guns and the bombs . . the howitzer bombs and the . . . no, it's howitzer *guns*. Deaf, death, and diarrhea. And on to Rome. That's it. See, John boy, you know where you are. Outside Rome, dug into the rocky ground for protection. Christmas in Rome. Dear Carolyn. How are you? I am fine. Are the children well? What are you doing for Christmas? I'm spending mine at the Vatican. With the Pope. Sorry to hear the children are frightened by the blackouts and the air raid sirens. Tell them there is nothing to fear but fear itself. Roosevelt says so but then Roosevelt was never in sand and shit and goats and gunfire. Tell our children Roosevelt's full of shit and that there is everything to fear . . everything! . . . and the sooner they learn that, the quicker they will live. Love, Second Lieutenant John Ollson. Fa la, la, la, la, la la, la, aaagghh!

I've never held a man before, thought Augusta as she clasped the sleeping Arthur Abel to her breast. I've been held; I've been loved, but I've never been the one to give rather than receive. Wouldn't the nurses, and the doctors, too, at Bellevue who thought Arthur so insensitive in his strength be surprised to know the doctor also has hurts and fears. He, too, cries.

He had fallen asleep, which meant she would have to gently extricate herself so as not to awaken him. Stupid convention. Silly woman, she chastised herself. That's right. Get up, Augusta. Leave this warm bed and this man you love so you can sleep in your own apartment. No one must know; no one must talk. Perish the thought! But if it were your own apartment, he and you could stay like this all night. Well, as soon as John returns, I will have my own apartment.

She managed to slip from the bed without waking him. Standing at the bay window looking out over Gramercy Park, Augusta saw by the lamplight the April buds on the maple trees that promised an early spring.

"Augusta, are you leaving?" came Abel's voice from the bed.

"I must," said Augusta as she put on her panties. Abel threw aside the blankets and in one quick movement was off the bed and beside her

"I can't get dressed if you continue to do that."

"Yes, I know," said Abel as he took her in his arms, nibbled at the tip of her nose, and then gently kissed the corners of her mouth. "I love you," he murmured into her hair.

"I feel that," she said softly. "Yes, I can definitely feel that," she added saucily as his hardness grew against her body. Was this the man who but an hour ago was weeping, hurting from a pain all his skills as a doctor could not cure?

"Augusta, I love you," he repeated. She understood it was all Arthur Abel could say, all he had ever been able to say and perhaps all he would ever be able to say. She accepted that . . . now.

He had married Rose Abel thirty-two years ago. "Such a long time back," he had explained. "I had just finished my residency at Columbia Medical Center I was considered quite the catch. I was twenty-nine . . a professional man. Rose was twenty-four, an independent beauty. So independent her family had stamped old maid on her. No one was good enough for Rose. Then she met me; I met her; and the rest is, as they say, history."

They had had a "good marriage." She was a "good" woman who had made a "good home" for him for many years. She was a "loving and kind" wife and mother. She allowed him his work; he allowed her her life. She had been independent to the end. She went to the opera, the ballet, the museums, alone, aware he disliked such cultural events. She was an unusual woman. She deserved better, he had wept.

Thirteen years ago, just before Augusta met Abel, his wife became . . . different. No one could diagnose that difference until some years later. You see, Abel had explained, thirteen years ago, Rose was only forty-four. Much too young for arteriosclerosis. That only occurs in old people. The young's arteries don't harden—don't cut off the flow of oxygen to the brain. But they did in Rose's case. Slowly, almost imperceptibly at first, she began to deteriorate. First it was forgetfulness; then it was speech. It became slurred and incorrect verbs or nouns were used. Then the condition accelerated. Her movements became clumsy, like a baby's. Soon, she could not feed or dress herself or make herself understood. It was like watching your own horror movie in your very own home. He had taken the studio apartment off Gramercy Park to get away. He only used it once or twice a week at first. He needed his rest, his peace of mind, and he did have a live-in companion for Rose who saw to her every need.

Augusta had learned about Rose Abel shortly after her first lunch date with Arthur. At first, knowing he was married, she had resisted the attraction that was obviously strong between them. A simple lunch would be nothing more than that, she told herself. Several simple lunches later, things were complicated. First, he was married and second, he was Jewish. Third, she could be in love with him as he professed to be with her. No, she had decided then. Not for her. But as the years went by, she began thinking . . . who is for me? The men she met lacked the comfort she found just in talking to, being with, Abel. That was his charm: his comfort. Not that he wasn't attractive. For a man his age then, and now, he cut quite a figure. The nurses always talked about him. He was the one doctor who didn't *suggest* or insinuate or bluntly ask for favors beyond the realm of nursing.

There had been something about that New Year's Eve that changed everything for Augusta. It was the passing of one decade into another and the realization that she was hardly a young woman; that her chances were indeed limited and that the one thing she wanted in life she was rejecting for perhaps the wrong reasons. So he was married. She wasn't. So he was Jewish. She wasn't. What's that about opposites, they say? They attract. So be it! she had decided. It wasn't as if he would not marry her if he could. It wasn't that age-old story.

That night when they had come to the apartment from dinner, she had sensed his upset. In bed, he could not even feign interest in sex. Without a beginning he simply said: "It's Rose. She no longer recognizes me." He had not discussed Rose with her for a very long time. They had both decided to keep that aspect of his life free from the one they shared together. If she and this studio apartment were to be his refuge, let it be filled just with them. But this night there was no refuge.

"She's a vegetable, Augie. My sweet Rose is an incoherent vegetable. It's so sad to see a woman who was so independent now be so totally dependent for every little thing." He had wept and as she held him, she was surprised by her own lack of resentment. There is no refuge from life, she thought. There is only what we share at any given moment.

"Augie, she could go on for years like this." Abel had cried more for Rose than for himself or Augusta.

That would have bothered her years ago. Now she knew that although she might never legally be Mrs. Arthur Abel, in what they now were to each other, she was already that. Tuesdays and Thursdays were their days and nights together. They went directly from their jobs at Bellevue to their volunteer work at St. Albans Hospital on the outreaches of Queens. Here, like the children's ward at Bellevue, the babies cried, needed comfort, assurance, and love. Except here the babies were eighteen, nineteen, and twenty years old. Soldiers but babies. Veterans yet infants. Burned and scarred. Scared and scarred. Hopeful and hopeless. She did what she could for them, which was not much as she was scarcely trained to be of use. Had it not been for Abel's intervention and insistence, she would not have been allowed on the wards at all but relegated to rolling bandages just as Carolyn did as a volunteer several times a week. Augusta did what Carolyn could not: she talked to the boys. For her, each man was not John, as he would be for her niece.

From the hospital, Abel would take her to his favorite Chinese restaurant for spare ribs and egg foo yung. Then, it was back to the apartment. Often she would not leave and return to Carolyn's until well after midnight. Only once had Carolyn confronted her, asking of her whereabouts and her reasons for coming home so late. Only once. Augusta had been quite firm and to the point about that not happening again.

"Gussie, could you stay?" Abel whispered in her ear. "Just this once, Gussie, stay." He was trembling as he held her. Could she stay? Of course she could, she decided. She walked toward the bed where the telephone rested on a night table. This would be easier if it were Margaret, thought Augusta as she dialed.

"Carolyn? I know it's late, dear, but I phoned to let you know I will not be home tonight. No need to worry. Everything is fine and I'll see you in the morning." Augusta hung up before her niece could say a word. Yes, she could not have phoned. But Augusta knew Carolyn often waited up—waited and worried as if Augusta were a little girl rather than a very grown woman.

Better to do what I did, thought Augusta. Lord knows if it were the reverse I would want her to call and tell me. Besides, a voice within her added somewhat fiercely, you have nothing to be ashamed of.

*   *   *

"Aunt Augie? Turn off the lights," called Margaret from the kitchen. Augusta rose from the dining table, slapping Vinnie's hand away from the ice cream as she did, and flipped the switch for the overhead crystal chandelier.

"Vinnie Tiernan, you keep your hands off the ice cream!" yelled Thomas.

"Snitcher! Nobody likes a big tattletale," yelled Vinnie.

"Happy birthday to you. Happy birthday to you. Happy birthday dear Marti, Thomas, and Vinnie. Happy birthday to you."

Margaret and Carolyn were singing as they came through the kitchen doors, each holding a side of the plate that held a huge chocolate-frosted cake, aglow with three clusters of seven candles each.

"Now group around the cake, you three," directed Carolyn.

"Everyone gets to blow out his candles," said Margaret.

"Ma, where's the one for good measure?" asked Thomas.

"Oh, Marg, he's right. We forgot," groaned Carolyn.

"They screwed up," said Marti solemnly.

"*What* did you say, young lady?" said an amazed Carolyn. "Any more talk like that and birthday or no birthday you'll go straight to your room." Noticing Margaret trying to hide a smile, Carolyn said, "There's no mistaking with that mouth who *she* takes after."

"Don't forget to make a wish," urged Augusta.

"I'll wish for Daddy to come home," said Thomas.

"Don't tell, stupid," sneered Marti. "It won't come true if you tell."

"Stupid yourself!" replied Thomas.

"Children, please. Just blow out your candles," said Carolyn wearily.

Thomas, Marti, and Vinnie took a deep breath and blew hard at the cake. All but a few candles went out.

"Yugh! Your breath stinks!" Marti said to Vinnie "Let me blow out the rest."

"How'd you like your brains blown out," muttered Vinnie.

"If you do not stop all this," cautioned Augusta as she cut into the cake. "there will be no ice cream. no cake, and no presents."

"Can I give my presents now?" asked Vinnie plaintively.

"After your cake," replied Carolyn.

"No, now. Please, Aunt Carolynnie."

210

Unable to deny her nephew anything, Carolyn agreed. Suddenly the table emptied as the children scurried for the presents they had been hiding from one another for days. Their gifts from Carolyn and Margaret—two-wheeled bicycles—had been discovered in their rooms that morning upon awakening, and broken in at the park before lunch.

Vinnie was the last to return to the table. He was carrying two boxes. One was three feet by three feet. Margaret couldn't begin to imagine what was in it.

"It's for Marti," Vinnie said conspiratorially to Augusta, who was eyeing both the box and the boy suspiciously. That was an awfully big present for a child who was only given a dollar a week allowance despite the huge monies he earned working for Killerbrew Studios.

Thomas was happy with his presents. Marti gave him ten Classic Comics and Vinnie came through with the Captain America cape and shirt—with the bolt of lightning across it—he had been hinting about. Vinnie received a translucent belt that glowed green in the dark from Marti—"I sent four boxtops from Kix and thirty-five cents for it. All the way to Battle Creek, Michigan," she proudly revealed—and another of the *Boy Commandos* books from Thomas. "Neat," he proclaimed about both gifts.

Marti had saved Vinnie's large present until last. What she had desired she now had as all eyes were upon her as she unwrapped the pretty pink paper from the box. With gleaming eyes, she opened the lid "just a bit" on the box and peeked in. Her scream shattered the anticipatory silence in the room. As she jumped away from the table, jumping after her was a hamster. Jumping after the hamster but in opposite directions were Carolyn and Margaret.

"Vinnie Tiernan, you get that thing back into the box and out of here if you know what's good for you," demanded Augusta as she stood on a chair feeling ridiculous.

"You hear your aunt? Out!" yelled Margaret from behind the kitchen door which her hands kept firmly shut. "And be quick about it!" added Carolyn from the hall closet.

Vinnie Tiernan was still seated at the dining room table, calmly spooning his and everyone else's ice cream and cake into his mouth. Thomas was sitting beside him, watching and waiting to see what would happen next.

"Can I come out yet?" Marti's pleading voice asked from her bedroom. When no one answered, she decided it was best not to. Shaking his head at the commotion, what had caused it and the effect it had had, Thomas eased himself off his chair and began looking for the rodent that was hiding somewhere in the apartment.

Just another typically quiet day in the typically quiet lives of the Tiernan household, mused Augusta as she stepped down from the chair, making sure first there was nothing underfoot.

"I've got it!" yelled Thomas as he entered with the hamster in his hands.

"Well, get rid of it," Carolyn yelled back.

"Where?" yelled Thomas impatiently.

"Anywhere but in this house," said his mother.

"Give him to me," said Vinnie as he calmly took the hamster from Thomas and put it back in its box. "Marti?" he called. "Do you or do you not want Zorro?"

"Zorro?" yelled Marti.

"The hamster!" explained Vinnie.

"No!" said Marti emphatically, her voice muffled by the door she kept open only a crack.

"Okay for you," yelled Vinnie as he carried the box toward his room.

"Young man. Where are you going with that?" asked Augusta in a voice she could only hope was intimidating.

"Well, if she doesn't want Zorro, I do," explained Vinnie.

"You don't fool me for a second, Vinnie Tiernan," said Augusta. "You knew your cousin wouldn't want a hamster. Spending all that money and for what?"

"For this!" said Vinnie gleefully. "Don't you think all this excitement was worth it at any price?"

"You better put Zorro in his cage before they put you in one," advised Augusta. When Vinnie had disappeared into his room, Augusta yelled out: "You can come out now. The all-clear has been sounded."

When they had all reassembled at the table, Carolyn, looking at her watch, said, "It's after eight. I want all of you ready for bed in ten minutes."

"Aw, come on, Ma. It's our birthdays and besides, it's still light out," complained Thomas.

"And you're still seven years old," Carolyn replied. "Now go on. Git! Into your pajamas."

"It was a terrific party, Mama, until stinko here had to go ruin it," said Marti as she gave her cousin a murderous look.

Vinnie stuck out his tongue at Marti. "Good cake," he said to his aunt, as he gave her a hug. "Really good cake," he repeated as he walked to his room.

"Hey, what about me?" asked Margaret. "Doesn't your old mother get any credit for having frosted it? That should count for something."

Vinnie returned to the dining room table. He threw his arms around Margaret and said, "Yup. That counts for something but not a lot." Before Margaret could respond, he was gone.

"He's been that way ever since I came home," said Margaret broodingly to her sister and aunt.

"Maybe you should talk to him," ventured Augusta. "I think he misses you."

"If he does, he has a very peculiar way of showing it," said Margaret.

"He's a child, Marg. He doesn't understand why he has a mother in Hollywood and no father at all," said Carolyn.

"He's told you that?" asked Margaret.

"Not in so many words but . . . I think he's angry. I have to all but sit on him to make him write you a letter," said Carolyn.

"*Make* him write! Oh, God! He won't write; he won't talk on the phone. That damn well decides it!" said Margaret.

"Decides what?" asked Augusta. "Please, Margaret, none of your talking in riddles."

"I'm coming back. There is no reason to stay in Hollywood. I'm not happy there and my son isn't happy here."

"He's happy," interrupted Carolyn as she scraped cake from one plate onto another. "Make no mistake about that. Vinnie is a happy little boy. I just think he's confused about things."

"He's not the only one," said Margaret as she sliced another piece of cake. "What am I doing?" she asked aloud. "I'm not the least bit hungry. I've already had a piece of cake. . . ."

"Two," corrected Augusta.

"Two," continued Margaret, "and I'm working on a third. And all because I'm not happy."

Augusta drew her chair closer to Margaret. "What can we do?"

"It's not what anyone can do but me," explained Margaret, her tone of voice drawing Carolyn to a seat at the dining room table. "My life is—how did Marti put it?—screwed up.

213

That woman will never divorce him. Not ever. He asked her. Oh, yes. I didn't tell you but Franklin finally asked her for a divorce and she said no. And that, in effect, says no to me. Still I hang on. To what? Franklin wants me to sign a one-year extension on my contract. I refuse. What does he do? He dangles a carrot . . . a script. And not just *a* script but one of the best I've read. Now here's the awful part . . . about me! I'm tempted. It would seem I'd sell my soul and my son for a great script."

Carolyn slung her arm around Margaret's shoulders. "You know that isn't true. Vinnie lives here for many reasons."

"But one is purely selfish," said Margaret. "We all know it so let's not kid ourselves or one another."

"But the other reasons are realistic. Vinnie has a constant home here, companions, and the films are made here," reasoned Carolyn.

"Maybe the films shouldn't be made at all," said Margaret. "It's an abnormal life."

"Marg, they love it," said Carolyn, surprised by her sister's attitude. "Why, they've already earned their tuition for college and they're getting a wonderful education from the best tutors money can buy."

"They should be with children their own age. They should be among normal people, learning about the world—the real world—by working and playing among real people. The only life they know is the one we've set up for them and, Carolyn, it's not enough."

"I think you've touched on something very important," said Augusta. "I don't want to interfere . . . they're your children after all."

"Augusta Monahan, I am not in the mood for that kind of bullshit. If you have something to say, say it. Spare me the polite and proper," demanded Margaret.

"Very well. What you said is very true," said Augusta. "I think you should decide and tell Mr. Killerbrew the children are going to a public school and will not be able to make films during the school year."

"The contract has another year to run," Carolyn reminded everyone.

"So another year then," said Augusta. "They'll still be quite young, only eight; still time enough to catch up with their peers."

"Catch up?" said Carolyn in amazement. "These children read and write and do sums. They're little geniuses."

"They need to catch up in other ways," said Augusta, "ways that have more to do with socialization than education."

"You really think this is true?" Carolyn asked Margaret.

"Yes, I really do."

Carolyn sighed. "All right. I'll begin investigating Catholic schools in the neighborhood immediately."

"Not for my child you won't!" said Margaret vehemently, "and if you understood a word of what Aunt Augie was saying, not for yours either. We are talking about the *real world*, Carolyn, and that's not to be found in a parochial school."

"I want my children to have a formal religious education," Carolyn insisted.

"Then give it to them at home or in church on Sundays," said Margaret. "What the kids need is a professional children's school, a place where they can use what they know while they learn what they don't—which is that the world is bigger than they are—that other people besides them live in it."

"Margaret's right," said Augusta. "The children are precocious—as we all just witnessed."

"Carolyn Tiernan Ollson, look at me!" said Margaret. "You weren't by any chance hoping my niece would become a nun, were you?"

"A fat chance with you around," replied Carolyn. "Okay, I see what you're saying. When the kids' contracts are up, it's professional school for them. That settles that. Now, how can we settle you?" asked Carolyn as she turned toward Margaret.

"I'm going to make the film. It's too good not to," said Margaret. "So I'm a whore, what can I tell you? Afterward, I'm coming home."

"And what would you do?" asked Carolyn.

"Do? What do you mean by 'do'? I'd be a mother, for one thing, a person for another," said Margaret. "I think I'd like to live in the Village for a while. Off Fifth Avenue."

"But what would you *do*? Your *work*!" said Carolyn.

"My work? It's ruled me. It still rules me. I'll have no life if I don't learn to do something else . . . be someone else. I could do theatre or . . . I could do nothing. Haven't you ever yearned to just do nothing?"

"No," said Carolyn flatly. "Particularly now. The more I

can do, the less time there is to think. When I'm onstage, I can forget there's a war going on. Radio is another kind of magic. Have you ever thought of the millions—millions, Marg!—who are listening? One broadcast reaches more people than a year's worth of Broadway performances."

"We're both impossible. You know that?" said Margaret. "We are both selfish and narcissistic, although very obviously accomplished, articulate, and attractive women."

"Don't forget incandescent and luminous," said Carolyn. "I've been called that many times."

"You've been called other things many times, too, but I don't hear you bragging about them," replied Margaret.

The sound of the doorbell surprised the three women. Who would call unannounced at this hour? Annoyed by the interruption, Carolyn pushed away from the table. "I'll see to it," she said as she stood. "Not that either of you were rushing to see if it's Prince Charming."

Seconds later, the apartment reverberated with Carolyn's scream. "No! No!" she repeated, terrified.

Augusta and Margaret ran for the hallway. There, by the door, Carolyn stood facing the Western Union delivery boy, refusing to take the telegram from his outstretched hand.

As Margaret reached for the telegram, Augusta reached for Carolyn. Closing the door behind her, forgetting in her consternation to tip the frightened boy, Margaret ripped open the envelope. She read the printed message once and then again. When she turned to Carolyn, tears were running down her cheeks. "He's missing in action, Lynnie. John is missing," she said again as if she, too, couldn't believe her own words.

Before the telegram's news could fully register, Carolyn was encircled in the arms of her sister and her aunt. When she let go, they did not.

It was late September before production on *Homeward Bound* began at Killerbrew Studios, Margaret's refusal to leave Carolyn having necessitated a change in the original start-date of the film by three months. Franklin Killerbrew had understood and sympathized, as had the press and public. Letters by the hundreds arrived at Carolyn's apartment weekly. Since it was summer and both radio shows were on hiatus, Carolyn, with little to do other than *Broadway* each evening at the Longacre Theatre, read and answered most of the well-wishing and supportive messages. Work to Carolyn was, as Augusta properly if unimaginatively, said: "a blessing."

John's mother had been impassive, or as John would have said, "stoic," when Carolyn told her the news. Greta Ollson simply said, "Please call if you learn anything further." It was only after Carolyn had hung up that she realized her mother-in-law had not asked after her grandchildren or her. It was surprising and yet, it wasn't, Carolyn thought.

Franklin Killerbrew had called and had the first conversation with Carolyn since the one in his office ten years ago. Wanting to help but not knowing how, he had offered her a role in one of his upcoming films. Although touched by his gesture, Carolyn declined.

In August, when the Tiernan Tots went before the cameras for an additional ten twenty-minute features to be made over the next ten months, Carolyn once again accompanied them to Vitagraph in Brooklyn. On those days when the filming ran late, not leaving enough time for a family dinner at the apartment, Carolyn took sandwiches and the children to her dressing room backstage at the Longacre before sending them home to Mrs. Worthington or Augusta. Although she told Augie she did this for the kids, it was in fact to anchor herself. Without knowing where John was, Carolyn felt adrift and uncertain, frightened at being alone.

She was not alone or unoccupied often. Margaret initially saw to that. She introduced Carolyn to the Stage Door Canteen in the basement of the Forty-fourth Street Theatre. Although Carolyn was not much of a dancer, she proved, despite her own worries, to be a good listener and many of the young boys, away from home for the first time and about to be shipped overseas, found hers a comfortable shoulder to lean on and ear to bend. Also, Margaret instigated a War Bonds drive that saw the sisters tour the five boroughs. Their week-long effort raised more than a quarter of a million dollars. After her initial shock and the outpouring of fear and grief that came with it, Carolyn never mentioned the telegram or John to Margaret again. Her fears she gave to God each night in her prayers. But that, too, caused an anxiety. For the first time in her life, Carolyn could no longer say, "Thy will be done." She wanted *her* will done—wanted *her* John returned, the same man he had been before the war.

For the children, Carolyn presented a strong exterior.

"Is Daddy dead?" Thomas had asked, coming straight to the point after Carolyn had read them the telegram.

"Not that we know of," Carolyn had answered truthfully.

"Well, what is he then?" Marti had asked. "Tell me again what he is?"

"Just like the telegram says . . . Daddy's missing," Carolyn had replied.

"Like my scarf."

"Yes, Marti. Like your scarf."

"But, Mama, that's around here somewhere. We just don't know where," Marti had said. "Is that the same with Daddy? He's somewhere but we don't know where?"

"Yes, dear," Carolyn had said.

"Well then, he'll turn up. You always say that about my scarf, so why not Daddy?" With that, Marti had dismissed the subject.

Thomas had asked nothing more; Vinnie, nothing at all. Carolyn had thought her explanation had gone rather well until she came upon Vinnie later that day rummaging about in the hall closet, pulling out coats, hats, umbrellas, and galoshes.

"Vinnie, what are you doing?" she had asked.

Without looking up from the bottom of the closet where telephone books and Christmas ornaments were stored, Vinnie had said, "Looking for Marti's scarf."

Margaret resolved to stop crying the moment she heard his car pull into the driveway but for now, why not cry? she asked herself. You bleed if you cut your finger, scream if you stub your toe. So why not cry if you hurt your heart. Oh, stop being so damned melodramatic, Margaret, she said to herself impatiently. Your heart's been shoved around and mugged a little but it will heal. In fact, she thought as she looked at the wall clock hanging over the kitchen counter, in twelve hours' time, when the train takes you East, you'll be well on your way to recovery.

The realization that four years of her life with Franklin Killerbrew would end in twelve hours caused Margaret to cry anew. And I haven't told him! she chastised herself. Quite a Christmas present I'm giving him. Hello. Merry Christmas. I love you. Good-bye forever. Why haven't I told him? Don't I owe him that?

Margaret was sitting on the sofa wrapped protectively in

218

her full-length sable coat. She had bought it for special occasions, she had told Carolyn. Like this one, she now thought. She felt safe snuggled in the fur. She luxuriated in its warmth. "Nothing seems very bad when I'm inside looking out," she had said of the coat to Killerbrew. She had worn it that day two months ago when she left the set of *Homeward Bound* in hysterics. The film was difficult. It taxed her partly because of what she had left behind in New York. Her character, Carol Lawson, has just learned her husband is being returned to the States after having sustained physical and emotional torture behind enemy lines in Europe. Not having known the past months whether her husband was alive or dead, neither has Carol Lawson known how to live her life or whether to live at all. Now, although joyous that her husband has been found, she fears the future. What will he be like? What will she be like? What will they be like together?

Carolyn's experience gave Margaret some insight into Carol Lawson's character and dilemma, but mainly she drew from her own with Killerbrew. She, too, did not understand their future and whether they had one or not. There were days when Margaret could not distinguish where she ended and Carol Lawson began. If Carol complained of not sleeping, Margaret didn't sleep. If Carol was anxious, Margaret was beelike, buzzing about, unable to settle down in one place. Which is what made her totally unprepared and vulnerable to the news that just wafted in her direction one morning on Sound Stage Four. It was during a break, and she was taking her coffee with the men on the set, when she heard one say, ". . . shame about Malloy."

"Malloy?" she asked. "Donald Malloy?"

"Yes, you knew him, didn't you, Miss Tiernan? Big Irish bloke. He worked some of your pictures. He was killed in the Pacific—Guadalcanal, I hear."

The coffee splattered all over her dress. Her hands could not stop shaking and her heart pushed against her breast as if trying to break out. Breathing was impossible. She gestured with her hands that she was choking and one of the men slapped her back forcefully. The physical pain released the emotional. She started screaming. The doctor was called. He sent her home for the day. She cried all that night as Killerbrew held her, his hands massaging her through the pelts of sable. It was then she decided to make a total break.

And that's why I didn't tell him, she remembered. That

219

moment—his hands, his comfort—that moment should have lasted a lifetime. But it couldn't. Not all the lovemaking in the world could change that fact. There was no *lifetime* in their future. Just todays. Not enough. No more. He would not have agreed. There is *only* today, he would have argued. It's all any of us has, he would have said. Fine for those who have it all, thought Margaret. They have their cake and eat it this day and every day.

She heard him brake—always abruptly, always the screech of the tires as he defied gravity, determined to park in her garage in one motion of the steering wheel. She rose from the couch to fix him his bourbon and soda. She heard the car door slam, the key turning in the front door lock and him call "Hi!" as she added ice to the already well-chilled soda. Predictably, she heard the thud of his briefcase as he sort of flung it onto the kitchen counter. A light thud meant one script to read that night; a heavy . . . several.

"I see you're all packed," he said in greeting. "Chrissake, Margaret, you've got enough bags there to last you the duration."

"At least," she said softly as she handed him his drink.

He grasped it as he kissed her on the cheek, his hand automatically reaching for her breast. "I brought you home a present—besides this one," he said as he moved her hand down to his erection.

Four years, thought Margaret. Four years and the man still brings me home the same "present." Who says passion cools?

"It's a damn good script," Killerbrew was saying when she began listening. "It needs some work but I wanted you to see it in rough. That Denton is too fucking much. He said he wrote it expressly for you. It's probably what he also is telling Stanwyck and Wyman."

Killerbrew was fighting the fireplace, trying to light it with his usual impatience. When Margaret took the matches from him, he didn't resist. As she put kindling and paper together, he kicked off his penny loafers and collapsed on the couch.

"Funny thing about Denton, he's one of the few writers in town who is changing with the changes. You'll see what I mean when you read the script, Margaret. Denton sees the new day coming. We're all done with the June Allyson/Van Johnson film in this town. I don't think we're ever going to see the boy-meets-girl, boy-loses-girl, boy-gets-girl film again. Denton sees there are issues that need answers. He's writing to this. The age of innocence is over, Margaret. Over and done with. I don't know if that's good or bad. I was innocent once. Betcha didn't know that, did you?"

When Margaret didn't answer, Killerbrew patted a place beside him on the couch, beckoning her to sit. When she did he said, "Okay. Let's have it. Your face is full of dialogue."

She hadn't expected him to take the lead. All day she had worried how she would begin. She had plotted her opening line. Now her tears were not just a line but a speech.

"That bad, eh?" said Killerbrew, his tone of voice trying to make light of a heavy moment.

"Frank, the house is up for sale—the house and everything in it. The reason there are so many suitcases stacked up in the hallway is that I am not coming back here. What's left behind I've donated to War Relief. I'm sure some homeless refugees will look terribly smart in my Mainbochers and Schiaparellis."

"Margaret, what the fuck are you saying? Is this a joke of some kind?"

"That's it, Franklin. A joke. And I'm it, I hear. In fact, I'm told I'm one of the biggest jokes in Hollywood. Franklin Killerbrew's very own Marion Davies. Only I'm not her and I refuse to be her. I want more. I need more. It's not that you won't give it to me—you would if you could but you can't."

Margaret's tears had stopped. Facing Killerbrew she said, "There was a time I understood about you and your goddamn precious movie studio. I really did understand what it meant to you because of what my movie career meant to me. But Franklin, here's what's funny. I'd give up my career for you. But you wouldn't give up your studio for me. Not that you should. You'd hate me if you did. So where does that leave me? A twenty-eight-year-old 'star.' Unmarried, unavailable, and unhappy. Franklin, we've had a wonderful four years together. Oh, God, they were wonderful! But they were not a life."

"We had a life. We *have* a life," said Killerbrew quietly.

"It's not enough, Frank. I think I need something more permanent. For me. For Vinnie. I can't find that here, Franklin, which is why I'm leaving."

"You'd leave your career just to get away from me? Margaret, use your head. You're a free agent. Go to M-G-M or Paramount, but don't throw it all away."

"You know what's funny, Frank? I don't feel I'm throwing

221

anything away. Not anymore. You once said that actresses, *all* actresses, thrive on power; that we have insufferable and insatiable egos. We do, Frank. We do. I love the glory, the fanfare. But you know what? My ego doesn't. It feels defeated out here. Moving to another studio wouldn't change a thing. You'd still be here. I would still be thought of as Franklin Killerbrew's girl. How long would it take me to convince people I wasn't? How long before a man would believe I had done more than just change studios?

"Franklin, I want to change my life," continued Margaret. "I can live without making movies. I can live without glory and fanfare. I really can, Franklin. I'm leaving because I don't know if I can live without you. And I must!"

Franklin Killerbrew pleaded with himself not to beg. Instead, he roughly grabbed Margaret and pulled her to him.

"I love you!" he said fiercely, his eyes locked with hers.

"I know, Frank," said Margaret as she began once again to cry. "If you didn't, it wouldn't hurt and . . . if you didn't, then I could stay."

2

From their windows overlooking Central Park, the Tiernan/ Ollson family watched as New York reacted to the news that victory in Europe had been achieved. Up and down the street, an impromptu parade of people passed. Some were one-man bands of drums or pots upon which they clanged with metal spoons. Others were dance groups who needed no music other than their joy. Mothers and daughters made sons and fathers of the servicemen they did not know. There were tears and laughter for the May Day celebration America would never forget. The boys were one step closer to coming home.

Thomas's question had been typically Thomas: "Will Daddy be found now?"

Carolyn had answered the only way possible. "I don't know. I can only hope so, dear."

In the past few days, with the newspapers and radio buzzing about the approaching end of the war in Europe, Carolyn's hopes and fears had surfaced. Was John alive? Was he a prisoner behind enemy lines? If so, when would he be freed? And if no word came, was he therefore dead? Did life go on? And if so, when? Long after the children had gone to bed the previous night, Carolyn was sitting by the radio, knitting as she listened to the same news reported in different words by different newscasters. When Margaret finally switched off the Stromberg-Carlson, the women sat in silence for several minutes. When Carolyn spoke, she asked if Margaret would pray with her.

"I wouldn't know what to say."

"You don't have to say anything if you don't want to, Marg," encouraged Carolyn as she reached for Margaret's hand.

Margaret bowed her head. If He existed, prayer might help and if He didn't, it couldn't hurt. She could not find an opening, a salutation to the "person," the "entity" Carolyn so believed in. Yet she was surprised by the lump that gathered and quickened in her throat. Her entire being suddenly ached with the pain she had refused herself since leaving her home and Franklin Killerbrew that December morning. To blot out the past, Margaret focused on John. She concentrated on his face, from the sharp chinline to the soft blond hair that frequently fell at will over his forehead. You are alive! she insisted silently. You are alive.

Margaret knew it was only a remote possibility. More probably John Ollson was dead. Killerbrew had told her that. At her request, he had used his extensive Washington connections to obtain whatever information he could about the last days of John Ollson. He had given Margaret as full a report as he had received.

> John Ollson, having been promoted to first lieutenant, led his battalion in the assault on Anzio. Some twenty miles from Rome, Ollson's unit encountered strong resistance by the German forces positioned in the Alban Hills. The battalion was under constant heavy bombardment and gunfire. As part of the advance line of attack, Ollson and his men—it is now believed—became separated from Allied Forces. Many casualties were reported. Due to severe burnings, identification in some cases was not possible. Several of Ollson's men have been reported by German officials to be prisoners in their war camps.

Carolyn had surprised Margaret. Upon reading Killerbrew's report from Washington so many months ago, she had remained impassive. No outpouring of grief or prayer. But this past week, with the news of impending victory, Carolyn's calm and composure were gone. She had little patience with the children and even at their prayers last night, there seemed to Margaret to be more tears than solace.

I don't know what to do for her, thought Margaret as she walked into Central Park with the children who had wanted to join the carnival atmosphere of the city. She hadn't known since her return. Actually, it was Carolyn who had done for her. The winter in New York had been bleak and Margaret's mood matched it. Vinnie didn't help matters when he told Margaret he would rather not live with her if it meant leaving

Marti, Thomas, and Aunt Carolynnie. "I do not want to move!" he had stated emphatically. When it came down to it, neither did Margaret. With the door so recently closed on one part of her life, she needed the other held wide open. Which Carolyn and Augusta did.

It was Carolyn who insisted she join her on "Storytime" and it was Carolyn who said after she had done several of the shows, "Why are you only playing princesses and witches? Why can't you just be Aunt Margaret or Mama on the broadcast?"

To which Margaret had replied, "Because I'm not all that certain who Aunt Margaret or Mama is right now."

That was the truth of it then, thought Margaret as she chose a bench sheltered from the strong spring sun by a spreading elm tree. As the children went to play on the swings that dominated the small playground area, she took her book from her shoulder bag. She remembered the look on Killerbrew's face when she had told him the morning she left that he could buy the damn book but he better damn well realize, she would read it but not star in the film made from it. She wondered if he thought she regretted her decision now that *The Egg and I* was a best seller. Well, I don't. Not in the least. Carolyn's teeth may ache, as she puts it, to act, but mine don't. The problem was, as Margaret perceived it, she ached for nothing except the relationship she no longer had.

If only I were more like the children, Margaret thought as she watched Vinnie push Marti higher and higher on the swing. When they get hurt, they cry. Seconds later, they've forgotten the pain and they are laughing again. She had not forgotten and she wasn't laughing. Yet! she added to herself.

Marti's shrieks of fake fear drew her attention. Flying high above her immediate world, Marti was afraid but loving it. Margaret remembered the feeling. She watched as "America's sweetheart"—her nickname for Thomas—gauged the height of Marti's swing and then called out something to Vinnie. She saw her son shrug and then immediately move back from the swing. Gradually, the height of Marti's swing lessened.

The boys got along well despite Thomas's very Ollson-like trait of taking charge. Thomas was smart, the most reasonable of the three, and the least impulsive or volatile. Marti and Vinnie were more alike, although Vinnie never cried when he was hurt and Marti cried as easily as she laughed. Actually, thought Margaret, whatever Marti felt, she expressed; whatever she wanted, she asked for. Margaret didn't have that feeling about Vinnie Although he was outspoken, she felt there was much more he could say if he wished to. Margaret often felt herself at a loss with Vinnie. "Loving him doesn't necessarily mean I know what to do for him," she had recently confided to Carolyn.

"Be careful with that pocketknife!" Margaret yelled toward the children as they engaged in a game they called Territories but which she knew as mumblety-peg. "I'm watching, Aunt Margaret," said Thomas, his voice disdainful of his aunt's concern.

He *is* a strange child, thought Margaret. Smart, efficient . . . a cold fish. Real straight up. Not conniving like Vinnie, who would question her authority and try to put Carolyn in the middle between them. And when that failed, he would then try to draw his Aunt Augie into his web. But his Aunt Augie was too busy weaving webs of her own to get involved with Vinnie's.

Margaret laughed to herself as she moved several feet down on the bench to avoid the sun that was blazing through a gap in the tree's branches. That party! An impromptu little get-together, indeed. It was a setup. "So what of it?" her aunt had confessed indignantly. "It will do you good to get out of that house," Augusta had maintained. "What point is there in staying home night after night when Carolyn's at the theatre?"

What malarkey! But it had worked. She had gone to the get-together and had been introduced to—what was his name?—that young pediatrician. Very young. Too young. And that pompous Chief of Staff. What a pill! The Head of Forensic Medicine was attractive but talked as if he were weaned on *Gray's Anatomy*. The best of the bunch, she had told Augusta as they shared a taxi back to the apartment, was Arthur Abel.

"Yes," Augusta had said quickly. "He's married, you know," she had added. "He's married to a very sick woman who is not going to get any better . . . or worse . . . soon."

It was Augusta's afterthought that made Margaret stare at her aunt. "She has absolutely nothing to do with me or his feelings for me," Augusta explained as she faced out the window, looking without seeing Eighth Avenue. "Nothing!" she added fiercely as though Margaret might disagree. But

Margaret said nothing. She was too surprised—and yet I'm not at all surprised, she thought—that her aunt was having an affair and obviously, from the tone of her voice, a very important affair at that.

"Of course you understand why I have not discussed this in detail with Carolyn," Augusta continued. "There are a great many obstacles to her understanding."

Although she had said nothing, Margaret was not certain she agreed. She remembered Christmas night and how Carolyn had been with her when she finally opened the sole remaining present under the tree. It was from Killerbrew and Margaret had avoided it, determined to let nothing interfere with Christmas, the children, and her. The box was white and tied simply with a big red ribbon. A child could have opened it easily but Margaret's hands were shaking so that Carolyn had to help her slide off the ribbon and open the lid. The sable hat that matched her coat made her gasp. The card simply read: *"Warmly . . . Franklin."* Carolyn had held her, crooning "I know, I know," neither preaching nor mouthing platitudes. She had comforted and loved, as Margaret had cried.

The sounds of the children's arguing interrupted Margaret's daydreaming.

"When I can't remember, I look at the picture of him Mommy keeps in the bedroom," she heard Marti saying.

"Don't be dumb, Marti," said Thomas angrily. "What do you mean you can't remember Daddy?"

"Sometimes if I shut my eyes real hard, I can make his face appear. But sometimes I can't," said Marti.

"Well, I remember my Uncle Franklin even though I don't see him no more," said Vinnie.

"But that's not the same," insisted Marti. "He's not your daddy. My daddy is your daddy."

"No he isn't," snapped Thomas. "His daddy is dead. Our daddy belongs to us and don't you forget it, Marti Ollson!"

Seeing the expression on Vinnie's face, Marti screamed, "You stink, Thomas Ollson. You know that? You stink!"

"All right, kids, let's not have another war just as one is ending," said Margaret as she rose from the bench.

"Aunt Margaret, tell Marti my father is not Vinnie's father," demanded Thomas.

Margaret quickly considered her choices. There was only one. "Thomas is right," she said, trying to keep her voice free

227

of any emotion. "Vinnie has his own father. He's dead. But your father," she added, looking directly at Marti, "has been like a father to Vinnie so in that respect you're right."

"Well, I still think you stink, Thomas Ollson," said Marti as she hooked her arm through Vinnie's. Thomas looked at his sister and cousin and turned away.

"I'm going home now, Aunt Margaret. I want to finish my model airplane," said Thomas as he headed toward the entrance. "Would you cross me at the corner, please?"

As Carolyn measured her appearance in the hallway mirror, Augusta Monahan was shaking her head as she recalled a day gone by.

"It *is* amazing what changes time brings," she said to her niece.

"And just what is that to mean?" asked Carolyn as she adjusted the scarf that would protect her hair from the wind.

"The first time you went to meet with Franklin Killerbrew you were shaking from head to toe."

"And wearing that awful gabardine suit!" cried Carolyn as she remembered.

"Then, you were all too happy that your old aunt was accompanying you," said Augusta, acting the discard. "Now that you're all grown up, your poor old aunt is put out to aunt-pasture. Ah, the outrageous arrows of slings and fortunes!"

"I don't think you have that *bon mot* quite right," said Carolyn. "And since you ask, you're more than welcome to leave your pasture and join me at lunch. I'm sure Franklin would be delighted to see you again."

"What do you think is on his mind? . . . Margaret?" asked Augusta.

"No. I don't think he would ever discuss *that* with me. More likely a film," said Carolyn as she used her pinkie to remove the lipstick that had crept off the edge of her lips. "Besides, if it were about Margaret, he wouldn't have asked that she join us."

"Is she going to?" asked Augusta.

"Last night, it was 'Absolutely not!' This morning, it was a definite maybe. The limousine is at her disposal. If she chooses, she can let the children wreck Vitagraph while she wrecks my nerves at lunch. Well," said Carolyn as she whirled from the mirror to face her aunt, "how do I look?"

"How do you always look?" replied Augusta as she surveyed her niece in the blue-on-white dotted-Swiss dress. "Gorgeous, although I would prefer blue shoes to the white."

"They're my lucky shoes. I wore them on my wedding day," said Carolyn as she kissed her aunt on the cheek. "By the by, what's on your agenda for the day?"

"I'll be at St. Albans late this afternoon," said Augusta.

"And tonight?" asked Carolyn casually, as if she were not prying, which both she and Augusta knew she was.

"Let's just say I have hopes," said Augusta through her sweetest and most insincere smile.

"I'll pray for you," said Carolyn with mock solemnity.

"Please do. I'd be so grateful," said Augusta, adopting Carolyn's tone. "Between your prayers and my wiles, who knows, those hopes just might become a reality."

Carolyn laughed and gave Augusta a robust hug. "See you, my fallen angel," she said as she closed the door behind her.

Although it was lunchtime, the streets were relatively quiet. To her delight, for the first time in many such trips, Carolyn did not have to share her taxi with a stranger and was able to sprawl out in the back seat. Soon, she thought, there would be no more war and no more gas shortage necessitating the sharing of cabs. Life would return to normal. Suddenly, she was upset. She opened her white purse and fingered the rosary that was always with her. As the cab turned toward Ninth Avenue, she said her silent prayers. It had been a year since the telegram had interrupted her already interrupted life, a year of uncertainty and of unspoken terrors. She could not imagine life without John but she also could not imagine life with him when and *if* he did return. Would he have changed? Would he find her different? Would her bed be as safe and as warm with him in it as it was now? The last thought was pushed aside instantly. The taxi was on Forty-fourth Street and Carolyn wondered if Margaret would join them for lunch. She and Franklin had not been in touch, except through agents, since her return. Whenever his representatives had asked if Margaret was ready to make another picture, her representatives had said no. It amazed Carolyn how Margaret seemed so little interested in her career. It was even more amazing, considering her past, how even less interest was shown in dating. There had only been dinner with Sidney Barasch when he passed through New York en route to Europe and with the doctor she had met through

Augusta. That sneaky old woman. I just wish I knew what she was up to, thought Carolyn for the hundredth time.

The taxi screeched to a halt before the entrance to Sardi's. The usual motley mob of autograph seekers was camped at the door. Carry your head high and keep walking as you sign the first three papers shoved at you, Carolyn reminded herself. Smile. Say thank you. And keep walking. Which is exactly what she did until greeted inside the restaurant by Vincent Sardi himself. Heads turned as he led her to Franklin Killerbrew's table in the center of the room. As he saw her approaching, Killerbrew rose. He was still as commanding a presence as he had been the morning in Hollywood when they had first met.

"It's good to see you, Carolyn," said Killerbrew as he took her hand.

She laughed. "I must say, I never thought the day would come when I would say the same to you. But . . . it *is* good to see you, too."

As she seated herself Killerbrew whispered, "I still maintain *Waifs in the Wind* was the right title for that movie. And I've the box office receipts to back me up."

"I refuse to argue, particularly if you're paying for lunch. You *are* paying for lunch, aren't you, Franklin?"

"Are you cutting down on expenses now that you're retiring the children?" asked Killerbrew.

"You're not mad about that, are you?" asked Carolyn, concerned. "I mean . . . we did give you plenty of notice and we never heard anything from your people to suggest you might be annoyed."

"Nothing like that," said Franklin Killerbrew. "I not only understand your point of view, I agree with it. The kids should be in school. From a businessman's point of view, the reason I didn't do my usual squawking when you handed in the kids' notice is . . . I think the day of that kind of escapist fare is over."

The gasps and cries that rose over the normal din of dishes and silverware clanging in unharmonious meeting heralded the arrival of Someone Special. From the look on Killerbrew's face, Carolyn didn't have to turn toward the doorway to see who that someone was. When she did, she saw Margaret in a white silk sheath, white pumps, and a white straw hat with a red ribbon flowing from it. It was the single red rose Margaret carried in her hand that made Carolyn laugh.

"It could have been worse. It could have been a red cape," she muttered.

"Beg your pardon?" said Killerbrew distractedly.

"Nothing," said Carolyn. "Talking to myself," she added as Margaret, after greeting a chosen few at the more importantly placed tables, reached theirs. "Just a simple entrance by a simple girl," jested Carolyn. But Killerbrew wasn't listening and if Margaret heard, she made no mention or motion. She stood staring at Killerbrew and he, at her. Killerbrew had risen and was still holding her hand as neither spoke.

"Would you both please sit down," pleaded Carolyn. "You're embarrassing me."

Margaret sat.

"Are you drinking?" asked Killerbrew as the maitre d' hovered anxiously over their table. Margaret shook her head no.

"No one asked me if I was," said Carolyn, pretending to be hurt.

"Shut up, Lynnie. If you want some Bosco or Ovaltine, just say so and we'll get it," snapped Margaret. Then, without missing a beat, she turned to Killerbrew and said, "Sooo, Franklin . . . tell me. What's new?"

Killerbrew laughed loudly, causing groups at several tables to focus attention on them. When his laughter subsided, he sat silently staring at Margaret, who smiled as she looked back at him. Her hand reached out to pat his. He took it, and in a single slow yet swift motion, kissed her fingers and then returned the hand to the table where it rested.

Carolyn didn't know whether to turn away, pretend nonchalance, or watch, which is what she wanted to do. Killerbrew was just smiling at Margaret and her sister was smiling back even though a tear was running down her cheek. Effective as hell! thought Carolyn.

"Listen, you two, I refuse to be a supporting player during one of your big scenes. I came here to have lunch, not chaperone or officiate," said Carolyn pretending annoyance. "Are the kids all right?"

"As all right as anyone can be in Brooklyn," said Margaret. "We do have a slight problem, however. Your forever curious son wants to ride the subway home. He has heard it's an even better ride than the limo."

"Well, I think he should do it," said Carolyn. "What do you say, Mr. Killerbrew? I know it's not in the contract but do you think you can supply two bodyguards to take three

231

kids on the BMT? It's not too much of a star demand, is it?"

"I think we can arrange it," said Killerbrew. "Things have been tough at the studio ever since our star here deserted ship but we can still afford the subway. We're expecting big returns on our Missing Person's last film. Which reminds me, you do know *Homeward Bound* opens in August at the Victoria Theatre?" Killerbrew asked Margaret.

"Is it good?" asked Carolyn ingenuously.

"It's one of your sister's two or three best performances," said Killerbrew, the quiet but intense tone of his voice alerting Margaret to his contained anger. "The picture could be better, however."

"He says that about every picture," said Margaret dryly.

"Except the one of you on the wall there, Carolyn," said Killerbrew. "Who's the guy next to you?"

"The 'guy,' as you put it, is Alfred Lunt and if his Lynn overheard you, you'd be sporting a shiner right now," replied Carolyn.

"Listen, if you two are through playing footsie, why don't we let Franklin get to the point of this little reunion," snapped Margaret.

"It's not about a film," said Killerbrew softly.

Why don't I ever learn? Margaret asked herself. Why did I come this day? There were no medals for this kind of valor, no morphine administered on the battlefields of Sardi's to ease her pain. "Franklin, what is it you want?" she asked wearily.

In the minutes that followed, Franklin Killerbrew, to a spellbound audience of two, spelled out his plan. He wanted to produce the Tiernan Sisters in a Tenth Anniversary Broadway revival and celebration of *Much Ado about Nothing*. The studio would fully finance the production and they could choose the director and male stars. He was offering them the chance to play Lady Macbeth and Gertrude or Ophelia or both in *Hamlet*.

"Why?" was Margaret's comment.

"Who cares why?" said Carolyn. "The miracle is he wants to do it and it won't interfere with 'Front Row Center.' Marg, think of it! Lady Macbeth, Ophelia . . ."

"That's it, Lynnie, play hard to get," said Margaret, annoyed by her sister's blatant enthusiasm.

"There are no strings, Margaret," said Killerbrew. "Not a one."

"Don't be stupid, Franklin," snapped Margaret. "Of course there are strings. A cord, to be precise. All the way from California, it ties me to you. It undoes everything I've been trying to do these past months."

Margaret's upset was more in her face than in her voice. Carolyn, seeing it, wanted to embrace her. Instead she said, "Franklin, we thank you. But it's just not possible."

"Oh, stop being dumb, Lynnie," sighed Margaret. "Of course we'll do it. You as Lady Macbeth is something I gotta see. What are you going to do, oh holy one, when you get to her famous line—say 'Out, *darned* spot'?"

"It's going to make a pile of dough," said Killerbrew.

"So are we. This time we don't come cheap," Margaret warned Killerbrew.

"You never did," he said simply as he drained his bourbon and soda.

The maître d' was standing by their table, waiting for a pause in the conversation. "Miss Tiernan," he addressed Carolyn, "there's a phone call for you."

Alarmed, Carolyn quickly took the napkin from her lap and placed it on the table. "It must be the children," she said. Margaret instantly rose to go with her. She waited by the maître d's stand as Carolyn listened to the words coming over the receiver. When she hung up, Carolyn stood motionless. When she turned toward Margaret, there were equal parts of tears and disbelief in her eyes.

"He's alive, Marg. John is alive," Carolyn said again as if the repetition might help her to believe what she had just heard

The waiting room was cold. A single battleship-gray radiator had whistled the arrival of steam some minutes earlier but it was either a false alarm or an abortive effort. Outside, a waning October sun looked as weak as Carolyn felt. It had taken over an hour to drive to the Northport V.A. Medical Center—a long time not to think. Still, the question knotted her stomach and parched her mouth. How much of the man who had been her husband was alive and how much was dead? She had lived with the question ever since the phone call that had taken her so unaware and unprepared at Sardi's.

Through Franklin Killerbrew's offices, Carolyn had learned that the troopship carrying John Ollson and a thousand others like him was docking in New York September 1—as it turned out, the day before Japan surrendered. Despite the family's

233

disapproval, Carolyn was at the West Side pier to watch and wonder which of the men being carried by stretcher from ship to shore, and a waiting ambulance, was John. Since that day, all Carolyn could do was wonder. And wait. What information she did glean about John came through Arthur Abel, who used his considerable reputation to learn through sources at the Long Island medical facility that John was neither responsive nor responsible. He did not speak or react to his environment or the people in it. As tactfully as he could, Abel told Carolyn of the electroshock treatments that were being used to jar John into the present.

Initially, the doctors at Northport thought it best that Carolyn not visit. Experience had taught them that the shock of seeing a loved one in a catatonic state was more than many could handle. Some women even required treatment themselves afterward. When the doctors had phoned to ask if Carolyn felt ready to see her husband, she had replied that she was. The doctors then prepared her for the worst, rather than the best. Yes, there had been considerable improvement but John was still not speaking. But they were encouraged. He was now tending to his personal needs as well as feeding and dressing himself. Perhaps even more significant was his attentiveness to the psychiatrist who interviewed him regularly.

"Your husband does not respond but we are certain he does hear," Carolyn was told. "We are hopeful your visit at this time might—and I stress might—elicit some further response from him."

Carolyn trembled. For a moment, she felt as if she were going to throw up. She had been forewarned that John had lost weight. But how much? Would he be like those horrible pictures of other concentration camp victims? Would his eyes be holes, black bottomless pits of despair and fear?

"Margaret, I can't go in there," she whispered. "I can't. Margaret, I've got to go home."

Margaret's urge was to take her sister in her arms, comfort and protect her, and then bundle her into the car for the drive home. Instead, angrily, she replied, "Yes, you can, Lynnie. You *can* go in there. What's more, you will!"

"You don't understand. I can't. I'm too afraid," whispered Carolyn, her voice sounding much as it had when she was eight or nine.

Hoping her words would verbally slap sense into Carolyn's

head, Margaret said, "You are an actress, Carolyn Tiernan. For the first time in your life you have a chance to give a performance that really matters. Give it, damn it. Give it!"

Carolyn Tiernan had always responded well to good direction. When the doctor finally appeared, announcing they were ready for her to see John, she stood, pulled her shoulders back as she tilted her chin and head up, and followed the doctor out to the wards in strong, swift strides

John was lying on his bed, its wool blanket scratching at his sensitive skin where his clean, stiffly starched pajamas did not. His hands were behind his head, clutching the iron pipes that served as head- and footboard. His feet were sweating inside his slippers although he was not. As he shifted his weight to face the door—they said company was coming, didn't they?—the bedsprings squeaked. He hated the sound. At night, he was afraid to turn in his bed because of the noise. Ugly bed. Ugly room. Shit-brown walls. He hated it. Much better outdoors. Big, grassy lawn. The building looked nice from the outside, too. Always did like reddish brick. Like a fancy hotel. Only the guests here were all nuts. Or burned. Or burned and nuts. At least he didn't have to share a ward with fifteen others anymore. Moving up in the world. Or out. Just me and the dummy over there. It doesn't bother him that we don't have blinds or shades or draperies. No privacy. None. Anyone could walk in at any time. Still, it was better than . . . better than what? He couldn't remember and lately, he'd tried. But when he did, it was like turning the dial on a radio and leaving it between stations. All there was was static

There was always static. All day long. Static and questions. Why were there always questions? Why had people always thought he had the answers. Well, even if he did, he wasn't going to give them anymore. Let them find their own answers. I'm not giving any, he decided. Besides, sometimes things are best left not only unanswered but forgotten

"Your husband has actually responded quite well to treatment," Dr. Fielding was explaining to Carolyn as he walked her down the institutional-green corridors. "Certainly his physical improvement is near miraculous. When Lieutenant Ollson arrived here, he weighed one hundred and twenty-one pounds. Now, in just six weeks, he's up to one forty. He

235

has quite a ways to go yet but on that score we're not worried."

Noting how Carolyn was nervously biting her lip, Fielding decided she need not know, now or ever, of her husband's former physical condition. Best she should be spared such knowledge, thought the doctor. Besides, he reasoned, the fungus was all but gone and the insect—or were they rat?—bites had healed. As had the rectal bleeding. From dysentery or some form of sadistic torture? They were not certain. Only the scars remained. The ones that were physical would disappear. The others? Who can really say? thought Fielding.

"Mrs. Ollson, we cannot know how or if your husband will respond to you," said Fielding gently. "Do not take it personally, as many do, if he seems not to know you. So many women feel rejected, even betrayed, when this happens. I do not mean to be condescending but the best advice I can give is to remind you that this is not a Hollywood movie. Do not expect your husband to burst into speech and glorious emotional well-being upon seeing you. Our hope is that in some way, seeing you will free him just a bit more from his self-imposed exile. Well, Mrs. Ollson, we are here," Fielding said as he stopped before the first door in a short corridor that ended at the elevators. "This is where your husband lives. Are you ready to visit him?"

Carolyn pulled Margaret's sable coat more tightly about her for the protection and warmth her sister had promised it offered. "Yes, doctor, I'm ready." Drawing her shoulders back as she raised her head, Carolyn reiterated, "I most certainly am ready."

The children had been a problem. "If Daddy's back, why can't we see him?" Thomas had asked when they were told John was staying at the Northport medical facility. The explanation that Daddy-was-sick-and-needed-rest satisfied them momentarily. But when Carolyn came back after her first visit, there was no curtailing their impatience.

"Doesn't Daddy want to see us?" Marti asked.

"It is not that he doesn't, it's that he can't," Carolyn replied.

"Is Uncle John blind?" asked Vinnie.

"No, dear," and Carolyn, deciding it was best to tell the children the truth and let them live with it as best they could.

236

"He's forgotten us," Thomas said, injured.

"Not you, Thomas. Everything. Everybody But he'll remember soon," Carolyn replied.

"Promise?" Marti asked, fighting the tears that would earn her taunts of "crybaby" if she shed them.

"I promise," Carolyn said, not knowing what else to do. John had not spoken when she entered the room. Nor did he speak during her ten-minute stay. But his eyes did follow her as she nervously crossed and uncrossed her legs and walked to the window to stare at a view other than the one that was once her husband. But when she left . . . for a moment . . . when her hand touched his, his fingers fluttered about hers until they rested on her knuckles. How could she explain to the children what hope that little gesture had given her? When she left John's room, she told the doctor: "He will be all right." It had absolutely nothing to do with medical science, yet Dr. Fielding somehow felt there was truth in Carolyn Tiernan Ollson's words.

On November 1, John Ollson remembered. As he was being walked by an orderly to yet another in his series of electroshock treatments, a patient came running down the corridor toward John screaming for help. The look of terror on the man's face made John recall another man and his terror. It was Santis. Private Sylvester Santis. It was he who was screaming at John for help. And John responded. He rushed to his man, grabbed him by the shoulders only to feel him go limp as warm, wet liquid ran from his head and neck onto John's hands. Santis was staring at John. His eyes and mouth were open. When John let go, the man fell at his feet, a mess of blood-covered khaki.

John's screams rang throughout the ward's corridors. He broke free from the grasp of the orderly attending him and started to run, looking for a place to hide—anyplace he could find cover . . . escape. As he groveled under a bench he felt the warm wetness run down his leg. Just like then. As arms reached to extricate him, he pushed farther and farther into the corner. Just like then.

On November 2, after an afternoon and evening of drug-induced sleep, John awoke. At first, he could not remember who or where he was. Then he could. He was First Lieutenant John Ollson and he was a prisoner at Stalag 9B, Wegscheide, near Orb, Germany. He was one of sixty-five hun-

237

dred prisoners rotting in a compound of eighteen rotting wood shacks. Filled with rotting flesh. A pile of prisoners. A pile of bodies—some living, some dead, some not knowing which they were. Still better than the cages. They had been the worst. Looking around his antiseptic room, John thought: It's the hospital again. The experiments . . again. Trust no one; say nothing, he told himself.

On November 11, Armistice Day, ironically, John Ollson knew who he was, where and how he had gotten there. Although his doctors were deliriously happy, John was not. He just lay on his bed and cried. On November 12 and 13. John Ollson was still crying

Margaret was seized by the sadness she had been trying to avoid. It often swept over her now, unexpected and unexplained. Lunch was a bore. Accomplished, witty women, no matter how chicly casual they appear, are horribly depressing when they are unrelentingly clever. Margaret shuddered as she remembered the scene she had left at the Algonquin dining room fifteen minutes ago. Women of letters. Women of taste. And me, the token actress, but a coup for the camp because I've denounced Hollywood. I have seen the light and come to New York to be saved. What bullshit! This may have been the only luncheon in history where four women sat for two hours and never once mentioned a man. Not as a man/man anyway. Those ladies protesteth too much, thought Margaret. To eliminate men, as men, is not only unusual but unhealthy.

'Tis the season to be jolly, Margaret chastised herself as she watched the shoppers crush themselves, their fellowmen, and their packages as they scurried into Saks. Fifteen minutes in this taxi and we're no farther along than Rockefeller Center! She looked at the tree before the skating rink and thought of the tree-trimming party she had attended the night before. She wondered what Christmas meant, if anything, to Tallulah, Rubirosa, and Elsa Maxwell. In this circle of Noels and Coles, what meaning did anything have? Were they aware that this Christmas would be like none other in their lifetime—that the war was over and so many families would be sitting down together at Christmas dinner tomorrow for the first time in years? Like her own, Margaret thought, and immediately felt the anxiety creep over her again. Let tomorrow take care of itself, she urged her inner fears. Stick to what's happening now.

As the taxi inched its way past St. Patrick's Cathedral, Margaret vowed there would be no more lunches with "the girls"; no more of their terribly clever, snide little asides. Nor would there be any more parties in penthouses with the Wise and the Witty. Hollywood was easier to take. There, the only standard was Pretty. But in New York, one had to be urbane, sophisticated, and deliciously decadent. Don't forget erudite. Why, here a well-turned phrase was far more important to a girl than a well-turned ankle. The effort it took to keep up with such cleverness! And who the hell were they all kidding with their contempt of Hollywood. There wasn't one among the lot who wouldn't have killed to be a Pretty rather than a Wise and Witty. Better to vegetate, Margaret decided. I should never have allowed Sidney Barasch to drag me out of my inertia. "Portia Faces Life" and "The Romance of Helen Trent" were all the stimulation I needed. Of course if *Much Ado* hadn't been postponed until Carolyn could give it her full attention, there would have been that to occupy my time. So what the hell. So I've drifted from day to week into month. It could've been worse. I could have drifted from man to man. It's not that I'm switched off, thought Margaret, as she remembered the men who had asked and whom she had refused. It's that no one has switched me on. A whole year, dammit, and not a feeling or a flash. Just dry and uninterested. What a difference a year makes. Was there a night when Franklin and I didn't go at each other like starving vultures?

Again the sadness crept through the warmth of the mouton coat she was wearing. I will not think about that, she decided as she turned her attention to the fountains before the Plaza Hotel. Franklin Killerbrew was part of my life. He is not anymore. It is not even *him* that I miss, she argued with an unconvinced inner self. It's the comfort of the relationship.

The cab had turned west on Fifty-ninth Street. On the corner of Sixth Avenue, Margaret found herself suddenly staring at two people who were indeed her aunt and Arthur Abel. They were walking arm in arm and it was quite obvious to Margaret even from a distance that it was not just holiday cheer giving their faces their glow. It's a pity the doctor isn't coming to dinner tomorrow, mused Margaret, and then thought . . . perhaps not. There is enough tension with John coming home on a pass for the first time.

Margaret recalled her visit to John at Northport some

239

weeks back. It had been an unnerving experience. John looked fine, was, but wasn't. He had put his arms around her in greeting and had then sat for fifteen minutes, her hand lightly held in his, without speaking. When she left, as she hugged him, she could feel him trembling. She held him to her for a very long moment. Afterward, he spoke his only words: "Thank you, Marg." For what? she had wanted to ask. Sitting in the taxi now, she still wasn't certain.

No, there never had been before and quite possibly never would be a Christmas quite like this one, she thought to herself again. Our own little production of *The Man Who Came to Dinner*. Lord only knows how it will play. Shit! I've had enough drama this week, she thought, upset again by the meeting she had had with Vinnie's fourth grade teacher the day school broke for Christmas recess.

"He is a wonderful student. So quick and bright," Miss Pennington had gushed. "Even though he's so much younger than most, he's the best reader in class."

"It's the acting he's done—learning lines, reading scripts," offered Margaret, happily embarrassed.

"Perhaps. Lord knows his little cousins are also advanced although we don't have the same discipline problems with them."

She had slipped it in that easily. "Problems?" Margaret had asked, realizing she had just risen to a compliment that had been used as bait.

"I'm afraid Vinnie is a very disruptive influence," said the teacher, looking directly at Margaret as she spoke. "He talks in class when he shouldn't and creates little disturbances. And punishing him seems not to faze him. In fact, it is better to ignore him. That, he hates. Your son, Miss Tiernan, would take all my time, and the class's too, if I permitted it."

The meeting had greatly disturbed Margaret. At home, Vinnie was hardly quiet but neither was he as vocal as Marti or as authoritative as Thomas, who seemed to decide what games, if any, the children would play. Carolyn, of course, promptly decided it was all nonsense. But then, with Vinnie's Aunt Carolynnie, anything that was troubling about her nephew was nonsense. "He is just used to attention, to people fussing and fawning over him. Suddenly, all that's been taken away. No radio show. No films. Just the normal life you wanted for him—only he isn't, nor are any of the children, what one would call normal. We weren't either if you remember."

240

All true enough, agreed Margaret, but wasn't it possible Vinnie was demanding attention today because she hadn't been attentive enough yesterday? She had asked Vinnie if he wanted to go to Radio City or the Children's Museum with her during his Christmas vacation. Not without Marti and Thomas, he had said. So she promised to take them all and by doing so had stubbed her toe on a recent past event. How had Vinnie felt a few weeks back when Carolyn took Marti and Thomas to see John but hadn't included Vinnie? She had recounted the conversation for Carolyn. Vinnie had come into her room after school and came right to the point.

"Ma, Marti and Thomas went to see Uncle John yesterday 'cause he's their father, right?"

She had replied that was correct.

"Who was my father, Ma? Tell me again."

"Sonny Stevens."

"And he was a cowboy star."

"More than that. Much more. He was a kind and sweet man. He cared a great deal about both of us."

"He died."

"Yes, he did."

"How?"

That was the new question. She wondered what, if anything, he had heard. A part of her wanted to scream: "Your father was not Sonny Stevens but a man named Donald Malloy who is also dead. He never knew about you, which might have been a mistake on my part. But I didn't love him and he didn't love me, although at one time, in some way, I think I did and he did. And then we didn't."

"Your father died in an accident," she heard herself say. "At the beach where we used to live."

"Ma, if my father's name was Stevens, why isn't mine?"

"As I once told you, Vinnie, Uncle Franklin thought it would be best for billing—that's about business—if you and Thomas and Marti were all called the Tiernan Tots because the name Tiernan is famous. I later changed your name legally because it seemed simpler. And I guess to be selfish. You were mine and I didn't want to share your name with anyone."

"Is Uncle Franklin really my uncle?"

Where is this leading? thought Margaret. What is he trying to ask?

"Not like Uncle John is really your uncle. We call him

241

Uncle Franklin because he has been like an uncle to you. Vinnie, what's bothering you? No, don't shrug like you usually do and walk away. Please, tell me what's wrong."

Vinnie turned at the doorway. "There's nothing wrong, Ma. I'm just trying to figure out who belongs to who."

"Oh, my God, doesn't he know?" Margaret had cried to Carolyn. "Has he been so much with you that he is that confused and hurt?"

"It's all my fault," said Carolyn, upset. "I should have taken him with us. Where was my head? What could I have been thinking of? I guess I was so frightened how the children would react, how John would react, that I never thought about Vinnie. I'm so ashamed, Margaret. And afterward, it didn't dawn on me because . . . well . . . John was still so strange then. Not like he is now. But that day he just stared at the children and they at him. They were strangers to one another. And I was left to chatter on for both. Oh, why am I telling you something you've already heard a million times. Look. It's all going to be all right," Carolyn said, totally assured of what she was thinking. "Vinnie is really only asking where he belongs once John comes home. I think he's worried whether he'll still have a place here. It must seem to Vinnie, with all the excitement Marti and Thomas feel about John coming home Christmas Day, that he's being left out. But he won't be, Margaret. I assure you. He *won't* be. John will make everything all right. You know how he was with the children. He never showed any partiality It's going to be fine, Margaret. All it needs is time."

But I have no more time to spare or to waste, thought Margaret. Too much time has passed already. I'm almost thirty years old. There is nothing in my past but memories and I'm much too young to live in them. I need new memories and more time with my child. I must make changes. First: it's back to work. With or without Carolyn; with or without *Much Ado*.

The taxi had pulled up in front of the apartment house on Central Park West. As Margaret reached from the back seat to give the driver his money, she noticed the crumpled *New York Times* by his side. "May I have the real estate section if you're done with it?" she asked.

"Sure thing, miss. You thinking of buying the Brooklyn Bridge for Christmas?"

"Only if it's got a two-bedroom apartment to go with it,"

said Margaret as she hopped out of the cab, energized by new resolve and new hope.

Except for an involuntary sob, Marti's crying had all but stopped. She sat, thumb in mouth, on her aunt's lap, lulled by Margaret's continuous rocking. Carolyn was not as lucky. Vinnie had locked himself in the bathroom and Thomas was negotiating his release by demanding to know exact days when overnight visits would be permitted. In the hallway, Augusta was supervising the move itself, which consisted of several steamer trunks and numerous suitcases, and two men who were seemingly intent on banging the paint off the halls with their carelessness.

Hearing the unresolved commotion from the boys' bedroom, Augusta Monahan, now that the demolition experts were safely out of the house, marched past Carolyn and with her face pressed to the bathroom door said loudly: "I will give you ten seconds to come out of there, Vincent Tiernan, or I'll come in and give you what-for."

The door opened a crack. Vinnie peered out as Augusta peered in. "Yes, I mean it!" snapped Augusta in nonconciliatory tones. As the door opened a bit wider, she said more softly, "I know how you feel. Changes are never easy for anyone. Even when they are for the best. Part of growing up, young man, is realizing that if you don't stay the same, why should anything else?"

Standing in the doorway, Vinnie, his lower lip trembling, asked, "Are you going to visit me?"

Augusta sank to her knees before Vinnie. She placed her hands on his shoulders and said, "Of course I am. We all will. We're family."

Carolyn, with her arm around Thomas's shoulder, was watching as Vinnie lost his fears in Augusta's arms. She wished she could hide there too. All morning she had been on the verge of tears. It wasn't separating from Margaret that was difficult but the separation from Vinnie. He was as much her child as Thomas. True enough, he was only moving across the way. In fact, from the living room windows you could see the Savoy Plaza. As Margaret said: if she hung her old red cape out the window, Carolyn would know she was in flagrante delicto. Still, Carolyn felt an enormous loss. The house would be a little empty without Vinnie. As if suddenly feeling just how empty it would be, Carolyn began to cry.

243

"Oh, do be still, Carolyn!" admonished Augusta. "If Marti hears you, we're all in for it again."

Although she gave no outward sign, Augusta was deeply troubled. The left side of her, as she put it, thought Margaret had done the absolutely right thing. Margaret and Vinnie *should* make their own home, Augusta had reasoned with herself. And Margaret had been quite wise to take a furnished suite of rooms at the Savoy. Let her see how she likes New York apartment living first before she settles into one of her own. And the benefits of the Savoy are enormous. Maid and concierge service, excellent security, babysitters, too, if needed. Not to mention those crystal chandeliers in the lobby. And the French gilt. As Arthur Abel had said, You need *gelt* for such gilt.

But the right side of Augusta was "meanly upset," as she had told Abel. It's Margaret again, making the move, and not me. Margaret, my niece, my junior, is showing the way once again. Come summer, when Carolyn has only *Much Ado* to do and not "Front Row Center," when her life is organized, I am leaving, too. That's how it should be. John and Carolyn will make their lives, Margaret hers, and me, mine.

The insistent buzzing of the intercom in the hallway demanded attention. Thomas, taking charge, answered it. "The car is here for Aunt Margaret and Vinnie," he said. From the first, Thomas had seen no reason to be upset by his cousin's move downtown. Quite the contrary Thomas was pleased he would now have his own room. No more of Vinnie's sloppiness, his comic books and clothes thrown haphazardly over dressers and chairs. And since he would see Vinnie every day during and after school, still have Saturday afternoons at the movies with him, overnight visits on weekends, what was really changing?

Marti felt her entire world was. Margaret smoothed the child's hair as Marti melted through her lap and into her very being. I would have been so much better with a daughter, Margaret thought as she silently rocked her niece.

"Aunt Marge, you won't forget me, will you?" whispered Marti.

"What a question! How could I forget you?" Margaret said earnestly.

"Daddy did."

The simple response startled Margaret but it revealed the nature of Marti's inner fears. "That was different. Marti You

244

must try to understand your daddy didn't forget you, he just couldn't remember for a while. And there *is* a difference. Your daddy was sick. His sickness made him not remember. But as he got better, he stopped forgetting. Remember Christmas Day and how he held you on his lap? He knew you then. And Marti," continued Margaret as she gently pushed her niece off her lap and turned the child so she could face her, "I've known you all your life. I've known your father a good part of my life. He's the kind of man who would never forget anyone—least of all his pretty little girl—unless he was sick. As for me, I'm just across the park. Someday soon, when you're older and bigger, you'll wave out your window; I'll wave out mine, and then we'll walk toward one another and meet halfway—probably in the Sheep Meadow. Besides that, you and I can have a special day. For girl things. On Saturday, we can go . . . Well, we can go *anywhere*. Where would you like to go, Marti?"

"To the movies with Thomas and Vinnie," said Marti.

"From the mouths of babes." Margaret laughed. "Well, we'll just have to find some other day to go get our hair done and shop."

"How 'bout Monday or Tuesday?" Marti asked brightly.

"Oh, you'd like that, wouldn't you. I'm on to your tricks, Miss Hookey-Player of 1946."

Marti giggled. "You once said I'm no dope."

Margaret laughed again. "You most assuredly are not. Now let's get a move on. I think your cousin needs a big, big send-off."

Hand in hand, aunt and niece walked from Margaret's room to the hallway where Augusta had marshaled Carolyn and the boys. Marti smiled shyly at Vinnie. "Don't take any wooden nickels," she advised in parting.

Vinnie stared at Marti. Assuming a pose he thought properly imitative, he replied: "Here's looking at you, kid."

Carolyn began sniffling. As Margaret showed signs of following suit, Augusta said, "That does it. Everyone get their coats. The children will ride in the limousine; we'll follow in a taxi. And I suggest if we are ever to get this move done we had better leave now. Perhaps together, we can assure one another that the Savoy Plaza is not at the other end of the world."

Fielding was thumbing through the memoranda on his clipboard. "Medically, there is no reason to keep you in this hospital. Except for your reluctance to leave it. Why is that, Lieutenant Ollson?"

John turned his attention from the doctor to the rain mixed with snow that was falling insistently. A terrible day to move, he thought. I hope Margaret doesn't think it a portent of things to come.

"Lieutenant, are we going to discuss this?" asked Fielding insistent but not angry.

"How many times have I asked you to call me John?"

"How many times have I asked why my calling you Lieutenant disturbs you?" countered Fielding.

"You're the doctor. You tell me," said John hostilely.

"I'd rather you heard it straight from the horse's mouth, as they say. You know, it might give you some insight as to why you are reluctant to return to your home when the consensus of medical opinion agrees there is no reason to support you here any longer."

"So kick me out," said John as he pushed his chair away from the desk where Fielding was sitting. Ugly desk. No lines. Just big and clumsy. Chipped and cheap. Scratched and battered. Like everything and everyone else around here. Just give it a coat of shellac and it'll be like new. Rising, John paced the green and gray linoleum floor, aware that Fielding was observing him. Fielding always observed him during their "interviews." As John stared out the window at the hospital golf course, frozen over by February frost, he heard Fielding say from behind his desk: "I'm not the enemy, John."

John threw himself full-length onto the couch on the wall farthest from Fielding. Its musty leather was cold and, where torn, its sharp edges cut into John's body. He lay there, silent, wishing Fielding and his own memories would disappear. He remembered when he could do that—make a man, a memory, a year disappear. No more. John covered his face with his hands.

"I'm still here, John." said Fielding "As is Carolyn; as are you."

"I hated being a lieutenant." John blurted. "Hated it! Hated being asked questions and never being able to answer the one they all wanted to know. Could I save them? Could I, Lieutenant John Ollson, their leader, bring them safely through the war?

"I remember and God knows how I tried to forget. Santis

246

coming at me, his face contorted by pain. The goddamn guy was dead on his feet but he was still asking me to help him. He was literally crying his guts out—they spilled on my pants—and I couldn't save him. Not him or any of the others."

"And you felt you should," offered Fielding.

"It was my job. Those men entrusted their lives to me. I was their Lieutenant, do you hear me? Lieutenant: a synonym for savior. Some fucking savior. Do you know how many of my men survived?"

"How does that make you feel?" asked Fielding.

"Don't give me that psychological shit, for chrissake. You've asked me that a hundred times. Guilty, dammit. I live; they died."

"Why are you so angry, John?"

"Why the fuck shouldn't I be? Why should I have been responsible for the others? And why should those guys have gone through hell for nothing? And it was for nothing. It's one thing to walk through shit if you can come up to the roses. Those guys will never come up to anything again. They went to their final reward screaming and crying their guts out. They'd be dead but I'd hear them screaming. And then I stopped hearing them, shut them out."

Fielding pulled the chair John had been sitting in to the side of the couch to be near his patient. "John, tell me about Anzio, the capture."

Although his eyes remained closed, John's lids began fluttering as did the twitch under his left eye that had been dormant for some weeks. His fists clenched and his body tensed as if ready to attack. When he remained silent, Fielding said, "Let me begin for you. Your battalion is in the advance line of fire. There is heavy bombardment all around you. Suddenly, you realize you're surrounded, completely cut off from safety."

"They don't teach you what to do in that situation; don't teach you how to sit and wait."

"Wait for what?"

"Judgment Day or help, whichever comes first. Neither did. I remember the morning they captured us. There was this small sun rising. Never saw a sun so small, so almost white that it matched the snow. Even the air seemed white. They put us in cages. Like chickens. Wire coops. No place to sit. No place to get out of the wind. No food. Just fear."

"Were you afraid, John?"

247

A bitter laugh answered the question.

"You bet your fucking A I was, but don't tell anybody."

"Why's that, John?"

"Didn't your mama ever tell you big boys don't cry?"

"Did you cry, John?"

"No. Never!" snapped John. "They almost got to me with that kid Miller. Big wide face, always a smile. Nice kid. Seventeen at the most. He was in the birdcage with me when they came to move us out. I remember walking through the white to the trucks, hearing the motors running but seeing no guards. I smelled a trap but before I could say anything, this Miller kid makes a run for one of the trucks and about a dozen bullets blast him to pieces. The guards came out of their hiding places, laughing and congratulating one another. Did you know, doctor, that it's legal to shoot a prisoner if he is trying to escape? Bet you didn't know we actually have rules telling us when and how it's okay to kill people. Anyway, the day wasn't white anymore. Not with all the red."

"Miller's blood," said Fielding.

"Give that man a cigar," John sneered.

"So you were taken to Stalag 9B and imprisoned."

John's silence was deafening.

"There were sixty-five hundred of you, about half Americans, shut up in a four-hundred-square-foot barbed-wire compound. All of you lived in shacks. About twenty. Is that right, John?"

Fielding looked at his silent patient and watched helplessly as the tears streamed down John's face. It was the advantage he had been waiting for. "Do you remember, John?" he pressed, his voice harsh.

"It wasn't a shack," said the whisper. "It was a hole. A hole with no chairs, no beds, no nothing but men. One lousy fucking spigot from which maybe, if you were lucky, you could get a few drops of rusty water. No soap, no paper. Not even to wipe your ass. You know how we slept? Standing up or we took turns lying down because there wasn't enough room on that freezing fucking floor for all of us to lie down at the same time. So after a while you learned to sleep against a wall or piled up against a man. But after a while, after they had starved us with that shit-green grass soup, the man was all bones and they'd jut into yours when you tried to sleep on him. You didn't mind his stink but you minded his bones.

"Since you seem to know so much about Stalag 9B,

248

Wegscheide, did they tell you about our toilet facilities?" asked John bitterly. "We had a hole in the floor. Sometimes you made it there; other times you went where you had to. And you didn't care. Nobody else did either. After a while, when you're treated like shit and you live in shit, you feel like shit. Sometimes I think shit is treated better than we were. It's just flushed away. But the Germans, no. Every morning they'd come into our hole and when another man couldn't or wouldn't get off the floor, they would shovel the one that couldn't into a hole, and club the one who wouldn't. Did you know even a dying man, too weak to walk, screams? Always the screams. To God. To Mama. Neither ever came to the rescue. But oh, God, what it sounds like when a grown man calls out for his mama! In the beginning, just about all the men prayed. Oh, God, did they pray! They would be praying as their eyes bugged out, as they shit blood, as the lice crawled up our assholes and into our hair and crotch. Then they stopped praying."

"What did you do, John?"

"I died. I gave up and died. And being dead was better than being alive because you didn't feel a thing and nobody wanted anything from you."

"How long were you dead?"

"Till a minute ago, okay? You happy now? I remember, goddammit. I remember every last detail. Worse, Dr. Fielding, the smell. Did you know death smells, *doctor*? Did you know when you get too close to a man who has had it you can smell death on him? Fear and death. They smell worse than any stench from one shithole for hundreds of men in something you call a 'shack' but wasn't even that. I can still smell my own fear. Did I tell you when I realized in that white morning that the Germans were coming to take us that I shit in my pants from fear? And you want me to pack up and go home. And do what? Take care of my wife and family? My *responsibilities*. I can barely take care of me so why do I always have to take care of everyone else?"

"Is that how you feel?" asked Fielding, a statement implicit in his question.

John bolted upright and faced the doctor. "Stop the shit. Stop the analytic approach. Talk to *me*, dammit. I'm here now. It's not just how I feel, it's how it was, always, and how it would be again. When I was a kid, it was be good, be strong, be responsible, be anything but a burden to your

249

parents. When I was six, they would leave me alone because they had to work. I was afraid of the dark, of wind, of thunder. And I was always told I shouldn't be, so after a while, I wasn't. Except inside I was. No one knew. No one is ever supposed to know you're afraid. Who would have believed me anyway? Big, strong John. The biggest and the best, in school and out. Captain of his team in real life; a lieutenant in war."

"Didn't you want to be a leader?" asked Fielding.

"I didn't know I didn't *have* to be," cried John, anguished. "I always had to do the taking care of."

"Your parents clothed and fed you."

"Yes, they even loved me in their own very limited way. You can't give what you haven't got."

"John, do you stay here to be taken care of? Is that it?" asked Fielding.

"Why not?" asked John as he started crying again. "Why can't it finally be my turn to get something?"

"Didn't your wife give you 'something'?"

"I always did the holding."

"Did you ever ask her to hold you?"

"I couldn't; it so goes against my grain," said John with a new understanding. "And before, well, I liked to do the holding. That really *is* me. But when I was home Christmas, I saw that the kids need so much. They need more than a father, just as Carolyn needs more than a husband. And I feel I need more of me than they do. I'm alive. For what reason? Certainly not to produce Carolyn's plays. I've got to produce me."

"Do you think you're doing that here?"

"No," said John seriously, "and I won't, will I?"

"John, have you the resources with which to see you through until you can, as you say, 'produce' yourself?"

"Money is no problem. I have my own and Carolyn is well fixed. Between what she's going to earn on Broadway and her radio show, we are very comfortable."

"Then be comfortable. With yourself. Take time and *take love* to take *you* where *you* want to go."

3

The light knock on the dressing room door was unmistakably Carolyn's. "*Entrez!*" called Margaret as she sat before her dressing table cold-creaming her face.

"Just wanted to say good-night," Carolyn said as she entered wearing a summer dress of the palest pink. "Good audience tonight, don't you think?"

"How do you get dressed so quickly?" asked Margaret, ignoring the question. "Don't you realize at your age it should now be taking you twice as long to look half that good?"

Carolyn laughed. "You and John do wonders for my ego. He still thinks I'm the world's most beautiful girl."

"The last remains of his illness, I'm sure," said Margaret as she wiped the last of the Pond's from her face. "And yes, it was a good audience tonight, although I'm already sick of *Much Ado*. Thank God for Gertrude and Lady MacB. or I'd go nuts. By the way, I won't see you until Monday, will I? My Lady M. is the matinee and yours is the evening. And Sunday, we're off. Wheee!"

"You are coming to dinner Sunday, aren't you?" asked Carolyn as she seated herself on the cerise chaise Margaret had ordered for her dressing room.

"Oh, damn, Lynnie, I'm sorry. I meant to tell you but I forgot. After the show tomorrow, I'm driving up to the mountains—Swan Lake, I believe it is—for the weekend. With a friend."

"Vinnie, too?"

Margaret's gaiety turned abruptly sour. As she slipped out of her Chinese silk kimono she replied, "I don't think so. He has what he calls a 'weekend pass' to your house. You'd think I was his jailer."

Margaret's tone touched Carolyn, who knew the effort her sister had been making to break through Vinnie's detach-

251

ment. "Sometimes I think it might be better if we canceled all leaves for a while," she said.

"I doubt it, Lynnie. At least Vinnie is happy at your house. He has you, the children, and John is just wonderful with him. Why deprive him of that? I'm coming to the conclusion that hotel living, although it has its advantages, is not a home. Gold leaf leafs me cold. Vinnie, too, it would seem."

"Are you thinking of moving or just removing their furnishings and putting in your own?"

"Right on both counts, although I can't seem to make a firm decision. Would a house help? Or is it true, as Polly Adler says, that a house is not a home? Why is it I feel so much better and Vinnie doesn't? The past six months, working, celebrating our success, getting out again—if you catch my meaning, kiddo—have been wonderful. But I haven't neglected him. I've tried to reach him but my son seems to be permanently angry at me. And you know what?" Margaret said as she spun on her mules to face her sister. "It's beginning to piss me off. I know he's my son, and just a little kid, and you wonder . . . how can you be mad at a child. Let me tell you. Very easily. He's impossible. Well, I've had enough. When he's ready, I'm here for him. Till then, no more sacrifices."

"Who's the 'friend'?" asked Carolyn as she absentmindedly took a tissue and dusted the black enameled coffee table before the chaise.

Margaret, applying her makeup in her dressing table mirror, said through lips tightened and drawn for the lipstick she was smoothing onto them, " 'Friend' is a euphemism. It's a date and not a Mickey-and-Judy-type date either. Nothing platonic. Just your nice, average, meaningless relationship based solely on him, Tarzan, and me, Jane. You get my meaning?"

"Margaret, subtlety was never one of your strengths. Even in Cleveland they would get your meaning. Hussy!"

Laughing, Margaret, as she rose from her chair and walked to her closet, said, "He is twenty-six, immature, and insincere, but very relaxing. He also thinks he is in love with me—he's not. He also thinks I'm very nice—I am. The truth is: he is, too. You know him. By sight anyway. He's the—oh God, I hate to admit this!—the ingenue lead in *New Directions* across the street."

"Well, as long as he's toilet-trained," said Carolyn, rising to leave.

When Margaret's laughter had subsided, she said seriously, "It ain't exactly a match made in heaven, kiddo, but it's okay. It's all I can handle for now. At least I feel alive again." As she slipped into a light cotton dress that buttoned down the front, Margaret faced her sister. "Lynnie, it may be wrong to ask this but . . . if Vinnie should ever talk to you about me, about what's bothering him, if you think you can, would you please tell me?"

"He'll outgrow it, Marg. It's just a phase," replied Carolyn reassuringly. "Look at Marti. She's angry at me because whenever the kids play, she has to be Dale Evans instead of Roy Rogers. She thinks it was very unfair of me to have made her a girl instead of a boy."

"How that reminds me of all the times I had to be Valentino to your Vilma Banky or Theda Bara or whoever was gorgeous and about to be ravished for her charms."

"Gorgeous? Yes. But ravished never entered into it," said Carolyn, amused at the remembrance. "How could it? I didn't know what ravished was. In fact, for years I thought ravish and radish were one and the same."

"I do hope you know better now." Margaret laughed until she caught the strange expression on her sister's face. "Is John still carrying on like the Sheik of Araby?"

"As I said, he still thinks I'm the world's most beautiful girl," said Carolyn, her voice devoid of emotion.

"Most women would kill to be in your place," said Margaret lightly.

"I don't believe that's what most women want, Margaret, but I won't argue the point because I'm not most women and neither one of us has ever exactly mingled with the masses. It's just difficult right now because of the time it's taking for John to find himself. He's been through a terrible ordeal. He seems to need more of me than he ever has. If he had more of himself, it would be different. But he is adamant about not producing 'Front Row Center' this fall. In fact, he's adamant about never producing again. I think he's being foolish. Better to do something than nothing, although he maintains that taking long walks, reading, thinking, is not doing nothing."

"Lynnie, John is doing something that perhaps only he understands. I know because I've recently been there. As you just said, he's been through an ordeal. That ordeal is over but the experience lives on. Like an aftershock of an earthquake. You feel it long after the actual danger is past."

"You really loved that man, didn't you?" said Carolyn.

There was no need for Margaret to ask which man as both women knew whom Carolyn was referring to. "Listen," said Carolyn when she saw Margaret's face cloud over, "if your plans should change on Sunday, don't even bother to call, just come up for dinner. And if you want, bring Baby Leroy with you. We can always set another place at the children's table."

As Augusta lay still damp from late afternoon lovemaking, Arthur Abel, one arm about her waist as he lay on his side, was resting. In the distance, Augusta could hear the recreational sounds of Nantasket. The roar of the roller coaster competed with the strains of the merry-go-round and although it was noisy at this hour of the day, it was peaceful in the bedroom. As she lay drifting between consciousness and sleep, Augusta thought about John and the children. How they had loved their stay! She had seen that just from the way John had sat in the wicker rocking chair on the porch and . . . rocked. That was it, he sat and he rocked. He was content to just be, whether it was by himself or with the children. She was glad she had taken the week to help him. With Carolyn and Margaret on Broadway, John needed someone other than Mrs. Worthington; he needed family, to help with the children. And they were a handful! That Vinnie. Standing instead of sitting on the merry-go-round horse. He could have broken his neck. And Marti thinking it was just wonderful. Glad to have them; glad to see them go, thought Augusta as Arthur stirred.

"I need a Bromo," the doctor explained as he slipped out of bed and walked into the bathroom. "Too much good food at lunch."

"Good food? Oh, you old sweet-talker, you. Tell me more when you come out," said Augusta as Arthur's nakedness disappeared into the bathroom and the door closed.

John had not pressed for an explanation when she had insisted on remaining alone through the Labor Day weekend. Nor had he reacted when Thomas said, "I betcha it's causa Dr. Abel." The child's remark made Augusta realize the doctor must be the topic of considerable conversation at home. The doctor or me, she corrected herself. A little laugh bubbled from Augusta's joy as she thought of their lovemaking but minutes ago. They had been "bathing" in what

254

Arthur romantically called "the afterglow" when he asked if she had ever considered oral sex.

"I should say not!" she answered, shocked and somewhat indignant.

"Stop sounding like an old prude, Gussie," he chided.

"Well, that's what I am, so how else should I sound?"

He laughed and pinched her bottom in appreciation.

"Stop that!" she said, pretending to be outraged.

"You can't fool me, you know," he whispered in her ear. "I know you for the wild woman you are. So don't kid around with old Abel here. Admit it. Haven't you ever wondered what it would feel like?"

"How *what* would feel like?" she asked, borrowing time.

"A tongue, all wet and moist," he said, still whispering in her ear. "A mouth nibbling, devouring you as if you were—which you are—the most delectable morsel."

Augusta refused to answer although she was aware that between the image his words presented and the way his breath was hot in her ear as he whispered them, she was getting moist again.

"What does it feel like?" she asked when she no longer found it difficult to speak.

"Ah, Gussie, my love, that I should only know!" was Abel's soulful response. "But I'm willing to find out if you are."

"I'll think about it," Augusta replied.

"Gussie, this is not something you think about but something you do!"

She was smiling as she thought about it. About Arthur. Where was he? What was keeping him? "Arthur?" she called to the closed bathroom door. "Are you all right in there?" The only sounds were of birds cawing on the beach where children still played in the water. "Arthur?" she called as she edged out of bed. Later, when Augusta was able to think about it, she remembered her hesitation at the bathroom door. Something within her knew that once she opened it, the life she had known would be inextricably changed.

"Hello? Yes. Franklin. Yes. It's me. Listen, I'm terribly sorry to bother you at home on a Saturday. . . . What? No. I'm all right, Franklin, it's not me. It's Augusta. She called minutes ago from a hospital on Nantasket. Franklin . . . Arthur Abel . . . the doctor she has been seeing . . . has had a heart attack.

Yes, in her house. I don't know how serious but it looks bad. Anyway, she is alone up there and I'm frantic. It's just a small town hospital.

"Franklin, please. Don't tell me again to calm down. I can't. Listen, when I wanted to do research on Little One in Boston, you knew every top specialist in town. Do you know anyone there in cardiology? Yes? Oh, Franklin, could you get him to Nantasket? . . . On Labor Day weekend?

"What? Yes, I'm leaving right now. Carolyn has the evening performance anyway. Yes, I've chartered a plane, how else? Franklin, please. Can you keep this out of the newspapers? He's married . . . to an invalid. Children? Yes, I have the son's number right here. Klondike 5-1968. Yes, I promise. As soon as I land I'll call."

Carolyn was surprised but not at all displeased to find John waiting in her dressing room after her performance. It was the cap to a splendid day and a splendid audience whose applause for her performance could still be heard as she closed the door on one world and entered another.

"Lady Macbeth is a killer. In all senses of the word," she said, happy and exhausted. "Is Mrs. Worthington with the children?" she asked as she slipped out of her fifth-act costume. "Oh, good!" she gushed when John nodded. "That means we can go out and celebrate. You didn't know we're celebrating, did you?" asked Carolyn, standing before John, her wig removed, her feet shoeless. "So since you didn't know, and since you're not clairvoyant, to what do I owe this honor?"

Without moving from the daybed which Carolyn used for between-shows napping and for after-the-show seating for guests, John told her about his call from Franklin Killerbrew and the current state of Arthur Abel's health. A coronary . . . too soon to know how bad but bad enough. The immediate family had been notified and had seemingly handled well, if not the news itself, then the circumstances surrounding it. Margaret, John explained, after depositing Vinnie with him, had taken a charter flight from Teterboro Airport to Nantasket.

"Augusta . . . did you speak to her?" asked Carolyn as she sat down slowly next to John.

"No. She's at the hospital. She's staying there till he's out of danger. Carolyn, I brought the car. I even packed a few things if you want to drive up. We can be there by morning

256

and since the theatre's dark tomorrow, you won't have to fly back until Tuesday."

Carolyn was quietly weeping. "We had better not, John," she said unhappily. "The doctor suggests I don't exert myself for a while." When John looked at her uncomprehendingly, Carolyn shrugged. "That's why I wanted us to celebrate tonight. Garber's office called me today. The laboratory tests confirmed his diagnosis. John, we're going to have a baby."

Although it would undoubtedly take an hour with New York traffic being what it was at five o'clock, Augusta Monahan had decided to take the Eighth Avenue bus to Central Park West. She could use the time to think and relax, if the first would allow the second. Major changes always create anxiety, she assured herself, and this was a major change.

Augusta had walked from Fifth Avenue through Greenwich Village to the bus stop at Abingdon Square. She found the strong autumn wind chilling but refreshing. She had been flushed, heated by nerves and nausea when she left the apartment on Ninth Street. Now, as she sat in the middle of the bus, watching the ugliness of Eighth Avenue grow as the vehicle inched up the thoroughfare, she began to tremble. Now that the worst was over, this happened to her frequently. As did the crying jags which came without reason.

Doctors had been reassuring. Just nerves . . . a letting go after a holding on, they had concurred. And certainly she had held on. She was proud of that. Never once had she lost control. From the moment she had opened that bathroom door and found Arthur lying face down on the tile floor, she had negated any and all emotions in order to do what was necessary. She remembered how no precious time was lost by her taking his pulse or checking for other vital life signs. No. She had gone directly to the phone and instructed the operator to send a rescue squad and an ambulance. Her presence of mind enabled her to be fully dressed when the sirens announced that help had arrived.

When Franklin Killerbrew called, although most of her was in intensive care with Arthur, she heard the studio chief's short but precise statements informing her of the heart specialist en route and what she should do, and not do, should Arthur fail to respond. She understood. She continued to understand through the first tense days that his children would arrive and that she must not take anything they said or

257

did personally. Their attitude made it clear that they understood the situation without understanding at all. They took over and made the arrangements to have Arthur, once out of danger, moved to a Boston hospital by ambulance. They were most courteous to her and appreciative of her efforts as they thanked and dismissed her. She knew better than to wait for Arthur in Boston. He would be nestled in the bosom of family and she would be the outsider. So she waited in his Gramercy Park apartment until his daughter, Edna, walked in one day "to check on things" and made it clear she was not pleased to find Augusta there. It was then, for a moment, but just for a moment, that Augusta nearly lost her control. "You have no right," the girl had said. The words still echoed in her ear at night.

Then he had called. From Boston. A blustering October evening. "Gussie, where are you? Why haven't you visited?" She told him *exactly* why. He said he would rectify it. He did.

The next day, Edna Abel Sternberg called and apologized. "You must understand it is hard for me to accept you because my mother is still alive, but I will. My father has explained to me about your relationship. I want you to know that a part of me is very grateful he has had someone to make him happy all these years." Harold Abel, much more accepting from the first, called later to ask if there was anything he could do for her. Nothing, she said as she thanked him. I will do for myself, she had thought. Henceforth and forever more I will do for myself.

That had been her vow, her credo, her oxygen and plasma. It was what propelled her once Arthur came home to the one-bedroom apartment off Fifth Avenue. With woodburning fireplace and brick wall in the living room. A pullman kitchen but sufficient, as Betty Crocker she was not. A three-year lease at ninety-eight dollars a month. My own. *Our* own, if he chooses. Which he did. But the lease was in *her* name so that no one, ever again, could question *her* right to be in *their* home.

As the bus reached Columbus Circle, Augusta fingered the keys to her apartment. That very day she had supervised the painters as they spread a second coat of golden beige on the walls. Tomorrow, she and Arthur would shop for all new furniture. Tomorrow. Tonight, she would tell the family her happy news.

"People will talk!" Carolyn said angrily.

"Your mother always said: talk is cheap but we are not. *I'm* not!" replied Augusta as she stormed from Carolyn's bedroom. "And who gives a damn what people say," she continued from the hallway. "They don't pay my rent."

"But who does will matter to them very much," persisted Carolyn as she followed Augusta down the hallway and into her bedroom. "No matter where you turn, you will feel their judgment."

"Theirs or yours?" challenged Augusta. "Don't bother to answer. It makes no difference. I don't understand you, Carolyn. I tell you that I am finally making a home of my own with Arthur, a life together, and you preach at me. And I thought you'd be happy for me," Augusta said, her voice rising in proportion to her anger.

"Now you listen to me, Augusta Monahan," said Carolyn, annoyed and upset at being misunderstood. "Of course I want you to be happy. Oh, God, Aunt Augie, as He is my witness I swear I want nothing but the best for you. But is this the best?"

"I am a grown woman," Augusta said impatiently. "Let me be the judge."

Both women grew silent, each nursing her bruises. Augusta had arrived at the apartment a half hour ago just as John and the children were leaving "to throw a football around" before dark covered Central Park. In her excitement, Augusta burst into Carolyn's bedroom where her niece was taking the "rest" prescribed by Dr. Garber. Already, there was a revealing roundness to her body that would soon turn to protruding proportions. When Augusta told Carolyn of the apartment and of sharing it with Arthur Abel, to her surprise, Carolyn had reacted first with shock and then, seemingly, with displeasure.

"I just don't want to see you get hurt," said Carolyn unhappily as she sat on the Turkish divan that had once been her mother's.

"Then stop hurting me," said Augusta bitterly.

"I'm trying to protect, not hurt you. Protect all of us for that matter," Carolyn said. "There are certain aspects to all this you might not have thought of. First, whose name will be on the mailbox? Will you use his name as if you were Mrs. Doctor? Or will both your names be on the door—like roommates? How do you think your neighbors will react, and don't tell me you don't care because you will when they snub you. Not to mention the whispers behind your back which you will feel if not hear. Also, tell me, what will the cleaning lady and the milkman call you—Miss Monahan or Mrs. Abel? No matter. Think what they will call you when you're not in earshot. And what about Arthur's colleagues or, for that matter, the hospital itself? Do you think they'll allow you to continue on there when they learn you and Arthur are cohabiting? Use your head, Aunt Augie, the world lives by rules whether you like it or not."

"Have you finished?" asked Augusta dryly. "No! Scratch the question. You *are* finished. I will not hear another word. I am moving to West Ninth Street. I will live with Arthur Abel and to hell with what anyone thinks! And to hell with rules; theirs *and* yours, Carolyn. Arthur nearly died. Had he died, a part of me would have gone with him. Well, my dear, he has been spared. The doctors can't say for how long— maybe a year, maybe twenty. They don't know. We don't know. We know nothing other than I am fifty-two and he is sixty-three. Oh, yes. We also know we love each other and that we intend to spend together whatever time we have left. I promised myself that on Nantasket. I vowed if Arthur lived, I would live . . . with him if he would have it. Remember this, Carolyn: nothing and no one matters in comparison."

"Whether you like it or not you have a responsibility. Yes, you do!" said Carolyn emphatically as her aunt began to protest. "Not to me. But to my children. To Margaret's. You can say you love Arthur and want to live with him. Fine. I understand. Look at me, Aunt Augie. I said I understand. It's not lip service; I mean it. But because I understand doesn't mean the children will. What kind of example are you setting for them? They learn one thing in Sunday school and at home and see you do another. What am I to tell them?"

"That Arthur and I love each other but due to circumstances which neither of us has any control over, we cannot marry. Oh to God, Carolyn, that we could'" cried Augusta. "Oh to God that I could be Mrs. Arthur Abel. But I can't. So I will take the only other choice available."

Augusta was crying, sobbing as she had only twice before: when Dan Dunahey and Tory had died. Instantly, Carolyn was off the divan and by her side. Augusta's tears brought her own to the surface. As she held her aunt, she gave in to the emotions she had been holding back for several months. Her tears turned to sobs. In a choked voice she said, "I don't know how to do all this anymore."

Augusta felt Carolyn's pain knife through her. "Do all what?" she asked as she composed herself.

"Be a mother, a friend, a woman, a wife. With rules. Without rules. A Catholic. I don't understand anymore," said Carolyn, sobbing anew. "Everything keeps changing, only I don't. I don't understand what's right and what's wrong anymore. I can't do it all. I can't. I don't know how."

"Carolyn, I want you to lie down this instant," said Augusta as she steered her niece back toward the divan.

"How can a man not want his own baby?" cried Carolyn. "Tell me, Aunt Augie? Tell me."

It did not seem to Augusta that this was the right time to remind Carolyn that not so long ago, she had had feelings quite similar to those of her husband.

On Thanksgiving Day, Arthur Abel took Augusta Monahan to formally "meet" Mrs. Arthur Abel—Rose—at the Ocean View Nursing Home in Long Beach. Had she not understood Arthur as well as she did, Augusta would have refused his request. But Arthur was a man who did things, well . . . properly. He wanted Rose, as best she might, to "know" Augusta. "Everything is to be aboveboard," he explained. "There is to be no shame."

Foolish? Not the conduct one would expect from a man who had dealt with life-and-death situations for nearly forty years? Perhaps. But it was Arthur Abel, and this part of him was particularly dear to Augusta. She also understood that he wanted her to meet the woman who felt like her enemy but who Augusta understood in reality was not.

He was withdrawn when they left Rose after their visit. Also understandable. The pathetic creature sat in her wheelchair and stared at nothing and comprehended nothing. Augusta did not know the woman and still she felt upset that anyone could end life as such a shell.

The following day, Augusta and Arthur moved into their apartment on West Ninth Street. Carolyn and John brought champagne; Margaret, sandwiches from the Stage Delicatessen. The children were not present, a decision Carolyn made after considerable introspection. As John uncorked the champagne, Edna Sternberg arrived, spouting apologies for the lateness of her train from Long Island. She was an incongruous sight in her ranch mink coat carrying an A & P shopping bag.

"I'm not upstaging anyone here. Honest," she said as she put the shopping bag on the fireplace mantel. "Besides, in this crowd, how could a Hunter girl with a bachelor's in English upstage such talent. But before the toast, please, some tradition. An old Jewish tradition." Edna Sternberg reached into her shopping bag and withdrew a five-pound bag of sugar. As she handed it to her father, she said, "So there will always be sweetness in your life. And spice, too," she added as she gave a box of salt to Augusta. "And in this house, in addition to the love that nourishes, let there also be the nourishment necessary for body, mind, and soul." With that, a loaf of bread was handed to the astonished Augusta. "Last," said Edna as she turned again to her father, who made no attempt to hide his tears, "light!" From the bag, Edna produced wax candles. "Forever light!" she said to Augusta. "For the rest of your lives, light in your life and lightness in your heart."

The ensuing silence was broken only by the popping cork on the champagne. John poured and the group drank silently.

"After that," said Margaret, still moved, "pastrami and pickles fall somewhat short of the mark."

"Not in our home," said Arthur as he reached for one of the sandwiches wrapped in wax paper.

A home, thought Margaret. That's exactly what it is. Looking about the living room, whose aroma of fresh paint competed with the aromas of freshcut flowers and fresh pastrami, she felt the room's comfort. A single couch served as both a room divider and the room's center. Behind it was the pullman kitchen. Before it, ten feet away, was the fireplace set into the brick wall. Before the eight-foot sofa, which was covered in a soft-colored silk, was a glass-topped coffee table, beneath which was a brown wool carpet that totally covered the floor. Facing the couch were three cane-back chairs and a few steps beyond them, just under the windows, was a baby grand piano. "Arthur plays, you know," Augusta had explained. "Quite sweetly," she added proudly.

The bedroom was through a doorway from which the door had been removed. It was also in browns, but its specifics were lost on Margaret. She had seen the double bed with its highly polished brass head- and footboard and suddenly realized her Aunt Augie was sleeping there with a man. It was the strangest revelation. Of course, she rationalized, she had already known that Augusta and Arthur were sleeping together. But to know and then to see proof positive of it had jarred Margaret, much to her surprise. Despite that one discomfort, Margaret felt this was a happy apartment. It made her feel happy. Yet, it also saddened her. Why? she wondered, until she realized that she was envious of her aunt; envious of her home, of her relationship with Arthur Abel, and of the life she was about to begin.

John Ollson was also envious. He thought how he and Carolyn had missed out on living in such simplicity. Too soon their lives had been complicated and overwhelmed by family, career, and position. As he looked at the box of candles he wished that they could go back. Repeat. Perhaps then, there would now be lightness in their hearts. Not that it would be any different, he thought. Carolyn would never separate herself from her family any more than she could separate from her religion and the traditional values with which she was raised—even if they had long since become outmoded. Carolyn was exactly what he had fallen in love with and married: an old-fashioned girl. He still loved her for that, for her naïveté and even her trust in God. For all her stardom and stature, she was a simple girl, thought John, who just happened to be incredibly complicated.

Was he ever like her? he wondered. He must have been. He married her, didn't he? Still, his own mother, when last they spoke, had accused him of being a stranger. And certainly his response had been that of a stranger, even to him. He had laughed. He had laughed at his own mother. Derisively. And just what had she been to him all his life? And what was she to her grandchildren and daughter-in-law? "You don't understand," she had said in explanation. He agreed with her; he didn't. There was very little he understood, John decided as he watched from Augusta's second-floor-windows two men, dressed exactly alike, walk down Ninth Street toward Sixth Avenue.

Carolyn's advice these many months of his nonunderstanding had been to keep busy. With what and why? he had asked until recently. It was then her turn to not understand. Her work and her life were in order. If some things got out of place, she was certain she could right them with prayer and patience. He didn't think so. Not of his life.

You are born. You live. You die. Three facts. Nothing new about any of them. Birth. Life. Death. Only over one do you have any control whatsoever. Sometimes. When you're in the military, you have no control at all. Afterward, you are still at the mercy of the life around you unless you take a stand. Most people didn't, John realized. But then most people mistook existing for living. They "got through" each day until days piled into months and years. All gone. All "gotten through." For what? Why did people persist in existing? How come they didn't question, as he did, life . . . living?

Carolyn had no answers mainly because she didn't have the questions. But then Carolyn hadn't been in Africa or in Anzio or in Stalag 9B. Carolyn hadn't recovered from an "illness" —as everyone genteelly referred to it now. Only he had been sick. Despite what the doctors said, he was still sick . . . of them and all others who settled for existing and called it living. They opted for the former and didn't suffer as he did with depression and doubt. "An occasional depression is normal for a man who has been through the war," they had con- curred. Only his wasn't occasional. It just was. Ever present. You can forget the details of a painting but not its content. Particularly a still life when it is viewed by one whose life is very still indeed. What had the war meant? he was constantly asking himself. There had to be a meaning in the camps. In surviving. Otherwise, what had the deaths, the mutilations meant?

The answer was gnawingly apparent, only he wasn't ready to accept it. For if he did, it would mean opting for existence rather than living. The painting was coming to life again. Daily. Germany was divided and conquered. The war to end all wars was giving birth to yet another. They called it *Cold*. Other wars were fought daily. The enemy however didn't have foreign names but was called Smith and Brown and Green and Jones and unless you paid them money under the table, you couldn't find an apartment to rent unless you had connections and money like Augusta. Like Carolyn. Like him. The black market was not just a condition of race in Harlem. The war went on everywhere. Jews who had sur- vived concentration camps in Europe were being killed in more sophisticated ways by the English in Palestine. Negroes who had fought for the American Way in the war found the American Way had not changed for them. They still went to their jobs as porters via the back of the bus.

And into this world a baby. Why? For what? To be mutilated in the next war? This world needs no more babies. It needs adults who will care for the children who exist rather than live because this world doesn't encourage or foster living for its people.

Carolyn's sole response had been: "You need help, John. You must see a doctor. It's not normal to feel as you do."

Which was precisely what he had been trying to tell her. Not that he needed help but that it was abnormal rather than normal to feel as he did. "People should not just be without being at all, Carolyn," he said, hoping she would comprehend. "All God's children do not have wings." The confused look on her face told him what he already knew: she did not understand. That he did is what finally gave impetus to his life.

The note read: "Thought you might be interested in seeing this March issue of *Esquire*." At first, Franklin Killerbrew thought it was Louis Gardner taking bows for some particularly good publicity break he had achieved on a Killerbrew picture. On close inspection Killerbrew saw it was not. "Letters to My Unborn Child" was the outpouring of one man's rage against war, a world wasteful of its human resources, and a political system designed to protect the powerful interests of a very few. It was written by John Ollson.

Killerbrew buzzed Gardner on the intercom. When the publicity chief answered, Killerbrew asked without a greeting: "Do you think he has a film in him?"

The response was immediate. "I sure do. Don't you?"

Which is why Killerbrew valued Gardner. He was one of few in Hollywood who would commit himself before asking what the other thought.

"It's possible. Put out some feelers. See if he'd be interested in talking."

"I already did. I spoke to his wife yesterday. Ollson is on assignment in Europe. The magazine sent him over a few weeks ago. He's doing some sort of report on postwar sickness and recovery in Berlin, Paris, and London."

Now Killerbrew was certain Ollson had a film in him. That was one helluvan assignment. And once the article was published, all thoughts, feelings, and reactions belonged to the writer. We could nurse them to the screen, thought Killerbrew. In fact . . . Killerbrew began scribbling notes furiously: *a film*

*that traces the return of the soldier to three families—one in
London, the other Paris, and the last . . . Berlin. Terrific.
Three different points of view and the first film to examine
the life of an enemy soldier returning to his occupied country.* It's terrific stuff, decided Killerbrew. It's another *Best
Years of Our Lives* but from a different vantage point. Great
roles. Even *she'll* do it. Damn her!

Beneath *Esquire* was weekly *Variety*. Killerbrew flipped
through the pages till he came to the one devoted to Broadway.
The grosses on *Macbeth* and *Hamlet*, in their final weeks and
without Carolyn, had held up. Still a sellout. Not surprising.
Not when the mailroom still received scores of letters for
Margaret Tiernan even though the lady vanished from Hollywood more than three years ago. No question that the
public loved her even if her own industry didn't. Hollywood
was quirky on some things. It hates being rejected. It'll never
forgive Garbo for her disappearing act, thought Killerbrew,
and it still doesn't know what to make of Kate Hepburn
coming and going as she pleases, calling her own shots.

Killerbrew remembered how the immediate wrath of Hollywood toward Margaret was evident from the moment the
Oscar nominations were announced in '45. Although *Homeward Bound* had received six, none was for its star. A calculated
oversight, an I'll-show-you petulance. It's all bullshit, thought
Killerbrew. The moment she mends her ways and returns to
the fold, all will be forgiven. Only her agent insists she is not
returning, not to the stage or to film. Her only commitment,
he had said, was to Carolyn: to finish out "Front Row Center"
while her sister has her baby.

What the hell was John doing in Europe anyway so late in
Carolyn's pregnancy, thought Killerbrew suddenly. What the
hell business is it of yours? he answered himself. If they've
got troubles, who hasn't? He thought of his own marriage.
He measured whether he was most contemptuous of it, his
wife, or himself. Let's look at reality, he told himself. Nancy
is a very smart lady. If she weren't you could have been long
divorced by now. But Nancy Blanchard wanted it all and she
got it. Now we come to you who also wanted it all but only
has it in part. As they say, you've got to spend money to
make money. But you're not willing to do that. You're not
willing to give up a thing to get what you want. Not yet.
Because there has to be another way. And there is, dammit.
There is!

Killerbrew pressed again on his intercom buzzer. "Miss Wolfe, locate John Ollson for me in London. His wife should know his whereabouts. Then get me Margaret Tiernan at the Savoy Plaza. Also, check with my wife and if we have nothing on the agenda the week after next, book me on the first afternoon flight into New York a week from Sunday."

As soon as he released his intercom button, it rang. "Where do you wish to stay, Mr. Killerbrew?" asked Dorothea Wolfe.

"Make it the Plaza," Killerbrew replied as he thought that where he wished to stay, and where he would, were two separate places. Soon, he decided. Soon, he reassured himself as his mind played with the plan that was beginning to take shape.

As the Pan Am Constellation nosed its way up and above the murky air that seemed to perpetually cover London, John Ollson's mind felt as fogged in as the airport had been prior to their delayed departure. He felt both sorry and relieved to be leaving London, which was exactly how he felt about returning home. He hoped the fourteen hours he was about to spend in flight would give him time to sort things out.

Think later; work now, he decided as he reached under his seat and into his briefcase for his notebook. If he outlined his article for *Esquire* between London and New York, he could write and finish it within days, particularly since he had hunks of it already completed. That would then give him extra time to work on the screen treatment before Killerbrew arrived a week from today.

It was not Killerbrew's phone call that had surprised him so much as the man's general idea. A film that would trace the lives of three men, returning to three families in three different countries after the war, could make a powerful statement. From what John had seen in his month abroad, he knew that many marriages—and, thus, the family unit—would not survive. Still to be decided was which three countries to focus on. John felt it was important to examine the enemy. He had been overwhelmed with sadness in Berlin. What was the old expression? A house divided against itself crumbles or falls? Berlin . . . divided . . . crumbling. Schizophrenic in its division. Old hurts and new allegiances. Families separated. Guilts not yet purged but covered by a new and deserved rage. John had no sympathy for the Germans as a nation but he felt empathy for the soldier, like himself, who went to war

267

a child and returned a man without a country, a home, and an identity. That had to be in the film.

England, and London in particular, had been astounding. Whole areas had been bombed out, destroyed, obliterated. But the people, if they knew it, refused to recognize the fact. Their pride was unlike anything John had ever seen or imagined possible, and quite unlike the pride of the French. He thought of Paris, intact, its monuments and landmarks untouched because the Parisians had surrendered their city without a fight. Save history; lose face. Was it worth it? Only time would tell, John realized. But what he could feel was the guilt. The Arch of Triumph stood, but where was the triumph for the people? The prideful Parisians were without honor, much like a virgin who has lost her hymen but insists on her virtue. He had spoken with several men who had fought in the French Army. Having suffered such great losses on the battlefield, they initially insisted they were glad not to have lost their city. But as they unwound, as John took them deeper into their feelings, there was a hidden resentment that a city had been preserved while lives had not.

Paris looked today much as it must have looked before the war, John thought. The Opéra had reopened, as had the Metro. Buses and taxis were available. Stylish shops, featuring couturier clothes, lined the fashionable boulevards. They seemed incongruous in an atmosphere of strike talk caused by a high inflationary spiral and low wages.

John had been obsessed with Killerbrew's proposed film almost from the moment it was presented to him. An article in *Esquire* was one forum for one's ideas but a motion picture cut through social, sexual, economic, and racial boundaries. If it were artfully written, it could sway the thinking of a populace and thus possibly alter the course of world events. As soon as he chastised himself for "such elaborate, lofty, and idealistic" thinking, John would encourage himself to promote change by promoting thought. He had realized during his incarceration in Stalag 9B that often the best way to change a man's thinking is to grab and then twist his guts. Evelyn had understood this. As a former producer of West End plays, and now one of very few women to be employed in the hierarchy of the BBC, she read daily the works of the young who didn't just think, but believed the burden for social change rested upon their typewriters. She was not at all certain they were not right. If John Ollson could put to paper both what he had seen and what he felt, it could produce a wondrous work of art. And even if he couldn't, as far as Evelyn Randolph was concerned, the man himself was quite enough of a work of art anyway.

The Pan Am Constellation was two hours out of London when the rains came, hitting upon the plane with a vehemence the passengers could see but not hear or feel. The plane was pushed and pulled by raging winds which luckily exhausted themselves as rapidly as they did the airborne. Soon, the plane was between the blue of the sky and the ocean again. As he looked on the endless waters, John thought how he no longer feared death. If the winds had blown the plane apart, so be it. If he died, and if there was an afterlife, he would complain like hell to whoever was in charge, however, that this was no time for him to die. It wasn't that he feared death. He just would resent its intrusion now that there was every reason to live.

With his *Esquire* article fully outlined, John allowed his mind to drift, attempting to outline his own life. He was entering its middle, having passed through its beginning. The present seemed clear, or as clear as a second act or a good middle should be, but the ending, his future, was inconclusive, as up in the air as he was at this very minute. That there were women like Evelyn Randolph had surprised John. In Hollywood, he knew actresses who were "loose" or "fast." He understood their wants and needs and how they bartered to fulfill them. And then there was Sandra; women who entered into a relationship in the hope that eventually it would lead to some kind of lasting commitment. He understood that kind of woman, too. But Evelyn did not barter or seek commitment. Her first concern was not home and hearth but herself and what she herself wanted. She was not shy about sex nor was she a hoyden—just available and agreeable when the situation warranted. She did not love him, or him, her, and she did not expect that they should. That they liked and enjoyed each other was quite enough. Although he was his most relaxed with Evelyn, her ease also made him nervous.

That he was "straying" and being "unfaithful" were words no longer revelant in John's expanding lexicon. He remembered how guilt-ridden he had been during his affair with Sandra. Not so now. Not with the girls whose names he no longer remembered, and not with Evelyn. What he shared with them all belonged to that time and space. In John's

269

mind, it had nothing to do with his marriage. Carolyn was his wife. She lived her life as she saw fit or as those she placed above saw fit for her, and he did likewise, only now there was nothing and no one he placed above himself and his freedom.

He had spoken to Carolyn as often as he could get calls through. When he phoned from London, she was even more distant than the three thousand miles between them. Despite his having arranged the trip to be home well before her due date, she was upset when he had first told her of the assignment. Not that she said anything but her face did, and that was quite enough. Amazing how Carolyn, great actress that she was, could mask her emotions onstage but not off. He tried to explain what the assignment from *Esquire* meant to him. He was still queasy about the worth of "Letters to My Unborn Child" when they offered him this plum. And by doing so, they bestowed literary acceptance on him. "Carolyn," he pleaded, "it means I must be good if they are willing to send me to Europe for a month." He could understand her feelings of desertion; her need to have him there by her side after so many years when he had not been. But what of his need? A life he had always wanted but couldn't move toward was now moving toward him after he had taken the first tentative steps.

She said she understood but she didn't. Had she, she would have been at La Guardia when he took off for Berlin on American Overseas Airways. Pregnancy or no pregnancy. The pang in his stomach was one of the few guilts John felt. Pregnancy meant baby and try as he did, John couldn't *feel* himself the father of the child that would soon be his. Worse, he had difficulty feeling a father to the children that were his. They were as much strangers to him as he was to them. He had been enraged two nights ago when Carolyn told him of Thomas's difficulties at school. But not in defense of Thomas. No. His rage had been against the parents—brutes of society, the perpetually and proudly ignorant who foisted their stupidity and brutality on their children and others. How could they think his article had been anti-American? And how dare they throw their misguided shit at his son.

"Tell me exactly what happened," he told Carolyn.

Thomas had been taunted for days by his classmates; Marti, too, but she said sticks-and-stones-will-break-my-bones-but-names-will-never-harm-me. But Thomas hated the idea of anyone associated with him—and those were his exact words, at not quite ten years old!—being called a commie or a rotten Red. So there had been a fight and Thomas, although he received a bloody nose, according to school authorities, had blackened several eyes and several bullies' egos and reputations with his fists. He was now both hero and villain at school, but not happy in either role. And he was estranged for the first time from Vinnie, who had watched the fight from the sidelines because it was not *his* father, as Thomas often reminded him, who was being insulted.

"Put Thomas on the phone, please," he said to Carolyn.

"But John, it's one in the morning here. You forget the time difference."

"I forget nothing. Put him on," John ordered.

Carolyn didn't reply. The next voice John heard as he lazily stirred his morning coffee was that of his son.

"Listen, kiddo," John said as soon as the hellos and how are yous had been exchanged, "I want you to know I am not, never was, and never will be a communist. You can tell your little friends that after what I've seen in Berlin I can't understand how anyone could be a Red."

"But the kids say you are," said Thomas, sleepiness still evident in his voice.

"People years ago said the world was flat. I'm sure there are some who still believe it is. You should pay as much mind to them as to those who say I'm a commie. Okay? You understand?"

"I do but they won't," said Thomas.

"I don't much care about them, although I realize you do because they're in your life. You'll have to live with it and fight it but not with your fists. Thomas, maybe one day you'll understand this but I think all of us adults are about to learn that battles—fights—wars don't solve a damn thing. Now go back to bed and tell your mother good-night for me and that I'll see her Sunday in the early evening."

When he had told the story to Evelyn, she advised he become accustomed to people calling him names. "We are living in very new and strange times, John. People are sensitive to what they and the world have just gone through and they do not understand these new traumas and the labels they bring. They weren't told about Iron Curtains and Cold Wars but were promised a war to end all wars and a lasting peace. Somewhere, they're beginning to realize they've been

271

had and the results of their disillusionment will be felt for years and years to come."

A good and wise woman, and a good lay to boot, he told her. She laughed and then remembered she had a favor to ask him. Would he bring Margaret a play ironically titled *A Lasting Peace*. It was written by a British veteran with his one remaining hand and he and the producers felt Margaret would be perfect as the American wife torn between her war-torn husband, war-torn London, and an easier life in America. Yes, John promised he would give the script to his sister-in-law, although he doubted if she would leave the country for any length of time at this point in her life. Not now when she seemed so settled, enjoying herself rather than her stature as an actress or her stardom as a film personality.

With the draperies drawn the length of her bedroom window, Margaret could not tell the hour of the day. As she lay twisted among the damp bedsheets and blanket, she judged it must be near dawn as she could hear the traffic begin its activity up and down Central Park South. Her bed looked like a battlefield torn about by mortar shells. Two pillows lay like the wounded or the dead on the floor near a bedspread that had also been kicked free in her night of unrest. As she lay on her stomach, Margaret reached down to retrieve a pillow. Punching it into some form of soft comfort, she wrapped her arms about it as she pressed her head to its coolness.

There was not a part of her that didn't hurt; that hadn't hurt through the longest night she could remember since leaving Hollywood and Franklin Killerbrew. This could not be happening to her again. She would not allow it to, she vowed. As she lay totally still, hoping her immobility would stabilize her breathing, she heard the March winds whip past her windows as they raced toward the Hudson River. Involuntarily she shivered as if chilled by the cold outside when in fact her body was wet with perspiration. The clock on the nightstand caught her eye. Almost six. The night was nearly over, thank God. She unraveled the sheets from the blanket and wrapped them about her.

No one to blame but herself. Totally her fault. She should have said no when he called. But he had been so damned clever. The dinner invitation wasn't to her but to *them*. All of them. And at the Café des Artistes, so that Carolyn only had to walk around the corner. She should have called a halt

272

to it then. Franklin Killerbrew was a steak and salad man. He used French restaurants as if they were weapons. He had once told her that; outlined for her his philosophy of dining. Use a *very* French restaurant to impress and intimidate. And who and what can be more impressive and more intimidating than a maître d' and an indecipherable menu! How often do the intimidated pretend indifference by saying: You order for me. Which he could and did with aplomb. And why? Because he would have a secretary call in advance to determine the *plats du jour*—to translate the entire menu into English for him. His dining guests were put at an immediate disadvantage through his culinary acumen. The bastard!

Again, the contractions in her stomach demanded attention. She refused to adhere to their blackmail. They had controlled her throughout the night. No more. She would rise above them just as she would rise above Franklin Killerbrew.

When she arrived with Carolyn and John, he was waiting, looking very New Yorkly elegant in his single-breasted gray suit. Only his hair looked different after two years. It was graying. But against the bronze of his perpetually suntanned face, it was somehow "youthening" rather than aging. He hadn't changed. Not really. He still stared at her with that arrogance that made her want to bite him. That, and his damned attitude of male superiority and dominance hadn't changed. But hadn't he been all charm and graciousness. "You look so beautiful," he had said oh so sincerely to Carolyn. She looked like a walking pink tent for chrissake! A blow fish at its bursting point. Not to mention her distress etched on her face along with her Elizabeth Arden eyebrows and lashes.

It was Carolyn who was killing her. That's right! she decided as she rolled onto her back and stared into the room's semidarkness. When Killerbrew had talked about the film— talked of the two of them costarring in it—her face! Such hope. At first, it seemed like happiness but it wasn't. It was hope—that if she appeared in a film that John wrote, would *rewrite* even as they worked together on location, their marriage might solidify. They would be together for at least two months. He would be at her and the children's side. Oh, yes. That, too! Killerbrew hadn't forgotten a damn thing. How Carolyn had squealed with such pure delight when the son of a bitch had sneaked that one in! The children, too, would be in the movie. Why not? he asked. It can be made this summer, during their vacation. How could he have known of Carolyn's concern for the children? He wasn't there when Marti came to Carolyn last week and asked if Daddy didn't like her and was it because of her that Daddy was away so much of the time?

How do children think up such things? What goes through their little minds when adults are acting in nonprescribed ways? Her own son was such a mystery to her. Not speaking to Thomas for almost two weeks now. And poor Marti, caught in the middle. Thomas called her a traitor if she played with Vinnie, and Vinnie . . . he said nothing, which proved to be the greater pull. Combine them all, Carolyn, John, Vinnie, Marti, and Thomas and you have . . .

What Franklin Killerbrew wants. John, too. How transformed he is! Back from the dead. And writing. Not just words but images and dialogue that bear repeating and repeating. No doubt he could write a brilliant film. He would bring to it all the honest emotion, the ugly part of a person's soul—all that was still missing from A *Lasting Peace* even after the rewrite that she had asked for and received.

Goddamn that man. Goddamn the web he has woven. He, the spider; she, the fly. Such a web. Carolyn, aglow with the possibilities and promises of a family togetherness. John aglow with the possibilities and promises of a vehicle that would bring to life *his* life, the external and the inner. And the children were part of the Promised Land Killerbrew offered. Why, if they had a dog, he would cast it in the film as well. To avoid the trap meant hurting others, others she didn't want to hurt. It wasn't fair. Damn! Damn! Damn! It wasn't fair. I've worked so hard, been through so much, not to be drawn back. Now he does this. A film, he said. A, one, single film. In Hollywood. On *his* lot. What happens to me then? What then? He knows what happens. He has the script already written.

"I could kill him!" Margaret screamed aloud, the sound splitting the room's silence and frightening her. She wondered if it had awakened Vinnie. As she began to cry, the house phone rang. A mistake. It had to be. At this hour, no one calls me. It'll stop in a moment. It didn't. This will really wake Vinnie, she thought as she dragged herself from her bed to the house phone in the hallway.

"Miss Tiernan," began an agitated voice. "Terribly sorry to

disturb you, mum, but there is a gentleman here who insists . . ."

"Margaret, I'm coming up!" interrupted a voice.

"You can't!" said Margaret, panic again in her stomach. The phone had gone dead. She ran to bolt the already bolted door. The house phone startled her as it rang again.

"Miss Tiernan. We are so sorry. We tried to detain him but he insisted. Shall we call the police?"

She hung up without answering. She unbolted the door and stood before it in the hallway. When he turned the corner, he saw her standing there in her pink nightgown, its dampness causing it to cling to her body. "You cannot come in. Do you understand?" she screamed at him. "I will call the police. I promise you. You *cannot* come in."

He didn't say a word but stood before her, disheveled and with an air of defeat about him she had not seen before. His face was blotchy, a beard beginning to show its telltale signs, and his red eyes reflected a sadness she had only seen once before. They stood staring at each other until his arms opened. There was no hesitation as she came to him. She trembled as his arms encircled her. As her defenses collapsed, so did she. He lifted and carried her through the doorway and toward the open door he presumed to be her bedroom. As her head rested against his shoulder, he covered her face with kisses. Murmuring words . . . sounds, neither saw the little boy peering out from behind his door, unable to see in the darkened hallway the man who was carrying his mother into her bedroom.

From the time Carolyn had begun "Front Row Center" in 1938, rehearsals for each week's new production began at noon on Thursday, Friday, and Sunday and at two on Tuesday when only a reading of the new material took place. Margaret, ever since replacing Carolyn in the final weeks of her pregnancy, had Vinnie meet her Tuesday nights at the studio for a six o'clock supper at a restaurant of his choice, invariably Reuben's, where he could order the *Carolyn Tiernan,* a concoction of turkey, pastrami, chopped liver, and Bermuda onion on three layers of rye bread. Dr. Brown's celery tonic was the predictable beverage and chocolate ice cream with chocolate syrup, the dessert.

Margaret's evenings with Vinnie had produced some progress between them. If nothing else, Vinnie talked about "the kids" at school, throwing out their names as if she knew "the gang" involved. From week to week, he tested her and if she couldn't distinguish Bobbie from Robbie and Betsy from Benny he would grow sullen. But still, Tuesday nights were theirs.

She was only somewhat concerned when Vinnie was not at the studio at six-ten. Punctuality was not one of her son's strengths. By six-twenty, she thought perhaps the late afternoon snowfall had hindered the doorman at the Savoy in obtaining a taxi to take Vinnie to the studio. By six-thirty, she was angry. Only once before had he been this late and then she had not been at all shy in telling him how she felt about it. She would not be shy now either. A perfect capper for a perfect day, she thought sarcastically. Her head throbbed from the lack of sleep and the abundance of Killerbrew, unmistakably *there*, a factor in her life. He had wanted to return that evening but she had said no—that Tuesdays belonged to Vinnie. Only there was no Vinnie. As it neared seven, Margaret, still angry but now concerned, phoned the hotel. When there was no answer in her room, she asked the desk clerk if he had seen her son. No, he had not. No one recalled seeing him that entire day. Alarmed, Margaret immediately called Carolyn.

"Of course he's here. Where else should he be?" said Carolyn, confused. "What? But he told me you said for him to come here for dinner. In fact, he asked if it would be all right for him to stay over since you would be out late at a meeting. Which reminds me, what kind of meeting takes place at night? Have you a date?"

Quickly Margaret explained to Carolyn that Vinnie's story was a total fabrication. But why, Carolyn wanted to know. Margaret had no answer but was sure Vinnie did. She told Carolyn to put him on the phone. Seconds later, Margaret could hear the argument taking place in Carolyn's apartment.

"I don't care what you want, young man, you go talk to your mother right now! Do you hear me? March!"

"What do you want?" were the hostilely spoken words Margaret heard first.

"What I *want* is an explanation and then an apology. Where have you been? And why are you at Aunt Carolyn's when you were supposed to meet me?"

"None of your business!" said Vinnie angrily.

"All right, Vincent Tiernan. You just wait until I get there and then we'll see whether it is my business or not. Now put

276

your aunt on the phone. . . . Carolyn? I'll be there in ten minutes. Don't let that child out of your sight. Do you hear?"

Again Carolyn asked if Margaret knew why Vinnie was acting in such a fashion.

"With him, who knows? Whoever knows?" she said and then hung up.

In the taxi, Margaret's mind raced through the possibilities of what could be bothering Vinnie. She could think of nothing but was certain something had triggered his behavior. When she had paid the driver, she rushed through the lobby and into the elevator. When she rang the bell, she could hear noise coming from within the apartment, but no one came to the door. She rang the doorbell again and finally Marti, with tears running down her face, stood in the doorway.

"Marti, darling, what is it?" asked Margaret as she dropped to her knees before the child.

"It's Mama," sobbed Marti. "She's sick in her bedroom. She's got pain in her stomach and Daddy's not home."

Instantly, Margaret was on her feet, striding toward Carolyn's bedroom where she found her sister, sweat on her forehead, breathing heavily, as she lay on the bed.

"It's either your time," said Margaret, "or you're brushing up on your Stanislavski and pretending to be a beached whale."

Carolyn managed a weak smile. "It's my time. But don't worry. I've called the doctor. He's meeting me at the hospital. I've left word with John's service to have him meet me there too. I'm just catching my breath for a few minutes. Those first few pains were lulus."

Noticing the three children watching from the doorway, their faces a triple reflection of fear, Margaret turned toward them and said, "It's nothing to be worried about. We are all having another baby—only your mother, and your aunt," she added, addressing Vinnie, "is doing the work. And it's hard work . . . very difficult, which is why she yells out from time to time. Now," said Margaret, turning her attention to Carolyn. "Is your suitcase ready?" Carolyn replied it was standing packed to go in her closet. "And you've called the hospital and Augusta?" Carolyn nodded that she had. "Yes, right, you said that," Margaret reminded herself. "Well then, my dear, in typical Carolyn Tiernan Ollson fashion you have done everything."

"Except locate John," said Carolyn, trying to smile at her

277

weak joke but grimacing instead from the sudden stab of pain that said in no uncertain terms that they had better be going.

"Carolyn, do me a favor," said Margaret as she helped her sister into her coat. "Try to tighten the scene, would you. No more seventeen hours just to get to the punch line."

Arthur Abel knew the hospital administrator so the rules of No Children Allowed were broken. As they stood behind the glass window, Thomas, Marti, and Vinnie were looking at the baby born three days earlier.

"God, is he ugly!" said Thomas seriously.

"Thomas Ollson, you just take that back," said Marti furiously.

"Aw, c'mon, Marti. Look at it. He's all shriveled up like a pink prune," complained Thomas.

"Jerk! All babies look like that," said Marti.

"Listen to Miss Know-It-All," teased Thomas. "Hey, Marti, just how many babies have you had?"

"If you had any brains at all—which you obviously do not—you'd know women know about these things instinctively," said Marti disdainfully.

"Marti, you gotta admit, it does look kind of weird. It's bald. And blotchy," said Vinnie.

"It's not an *it*. It is a *he*," replied Marti impatiently. "And I think you're both awful. *He's* gorgeous."

"And you're nuts!" said Thomas.

"No wonder they don't allow children in here," said Marti, looking at her brother meaningfully.

"Get ready for her 'You're-so-immature speech,' Vinnie. I can smell it coming," said Thomas.

"Well, you are, and when Uncle Arthur comes back from visiting mother, I'm going to suggest he give you your bottle and take you to potty."

"How many times have I told you he is not our uncle?" snapped Thomas. "To be someone's uncle, you gotta be their mother's or their father's brother or the husband of an aunt."

"Thomas, you give me a headache," said Marti, hoping her tone matched that of her mother's when she was "up to here" with one of the children's peculiarities.

"You talk like that to me and I'm going to knock your tits off," threatened Thomas angrily.

"Oh, yeah! Well, I ain't got any," said Marti, standing nose to nose with her brother. "You want to make something of it?"

"What are they calling it? Do you know?" asked Vinnie, acting as peacemaker.

"Not IT, *him*," screamed Marti. "John Junior. That's what Mother wants but Daddy hates the idea."

"How do you know?" challenged Thomas.

"I heard them fighting about it a day or so before Mother came here. She said she wants the baby to feel like Daddy's and to be like him. I don't know why that made him so mad."

"I like that name," said Vinnie. "Like John Wayne and John Payne. There's no movie stars named Vinnie."

"And the only Thomas that's a star in movies is Thomas Mitchell and he's an old man," said Marti triumphantly, knowing that information would bother her brother. "And before you get smart," she added, turning to her brother, "let me remind you my real name is Martha and Martha Scott is a perfectly lovely actress."

"Marti, I wish you'd talk normal. All this 'perfectly lovely' is crap," said Thomas sourly.

"If Mother heard you, she'd wash your mouth out with soap," warned Marti.

Vinnie was staring at the baby, its fingers curled tightly into a ball. He had asked Thomas the night his Aunt Carolynnie had gone to the hospital if he knew how babies were born. Thomas said he wasn't sure but he had found this book in Aunt Augusta's room, a kind of encyclopedia, and he was pretty certain that the man did something to the woman and she then had the baby. Only Thomas wasn't sure how the baby got in there and how it got out.

Vinnie then asked if the pains came because of the baby fighting to get out. Thomas thought that was probably right. Vinnie hoped it was. Since that Tuesday night, he had worried that perhaps he had been the cause of his Aunt Carolynnie's pain. One minute she had been yelling at him; the next second, she was screaming with pain. He had wanted to ask his mother but he wasn't talking to her, although in the excitement of Aunt Carolyn's having a baby, she seemed to have forgotten about Tuesday night. But he hadn't. And not about Tuesday morning either.

"Someday I'm going to have lots of babies of my own," Marti said as she slipped her hand into Vinnie's. "You want to help me?"

279

"Marti, you're so dumb!" Thomas said disgustedly. "You don't even know what you're saying."

"Oh yeah, Thomas Ollson! Oh yeah? Well, let me tell you, big brother, *I*, at least, know how a baby gets *in there* and how it gets out."

"Vinnie, she was listening!" said Thomas, horrified. "That snoop was eavesdripping."

"Dropping, not dripping, you drip," said Marti. "And next time you want to know something, why don't you ask Mother. She was the one having the baby so she had to know as good as any book."

When he called, Margaret used Carolyn and the new baby as an excuse to avoid seeing him. She should have been but wasn't surprised when she found him visiting Carolyn in her flower-laden room the next day. He always found a way to have his way. She hadn't been seated more than ten minutes when he asked her to show him John Jr. As they stood before the glass separating them from the nursery, it was she who looked lovingly at the baby while he looked at her. He was returning to Los Angeles the next day. He would prepare for a July start-date on John's still untitled film. Her role, that of the Englishwoman who must leave her lover to resume her marriage with her husband, thought to have been killed in the war, would befit an actress of her magnitude. And he was certain he could persuade David Niven to play her husband. He was very much looking forward to her return and if she liked, he would rent a little house for her at the top of Bel Air. It was a hideaway where she would not be disturbed. There was a kidney-shaped pool . . . for Vinnie. All she had to do was say the word and he would arrange its rental. He would also provide the car, the chauffeur, and a cook.

Everything, thought Margaret. Everything she had once had could be hers again. But she couldn't have *that*, she said silently as she looked at Carolyn's baby. She couldn't even have what Augusta had. She heard him ask if she would have dinner with him that night. She heard herself say . . . "Just dinner." He said . . . "That's all I asked for." She told him she could not leave Vinnie now, and that he would have to accompany them. He did not ask for an explanation, but agreed.

Dinner was not pleasant. Vinnie refused to speak to either of them, and he also refused to eat. As soon as the check was paid, they took him home. Nothing, but nothing was said, and nothing was accomplished. Nothing, thought Margaret, has changed.

He went up in the elevator with them. When he took the key from her to open the door, Vinnie entered the apartment first and sat down in the living room. She looked at him strangely. Usually, he couldn't wait to reach his own room and the radio that endlessly supplied him with company and entertainment. What was he thinking? What is making him behave in such a fashion, she wondered. What am *I* thinking? What is it I understand about Franklin Killerbrew that is making *me* act in such a fashion?

He remained in the hallway. She stepped out, closing the door behind her. She did not resist when he gently took her into his arms. She responded when he kissed her, not caring who might come out of the elevator or the nearby apartments. She felt him kissing her deeply, probing, as if by tongue and mouth he could discover where her emotions lay. Her kiss said one thing; her tears, another. He left confused. Confused, she closed the door. She felt as if a hand had gripped her throat. She didn't think about that. Instead, she thought of Vinnie who was no longer just sitting in the living room. The light under the door and the unmistakable voice of Fanny Brice as Baby Snooks told her he was in his room and the world he did not allow her to enter.

4

With John Jr. cradled in her arms, his fingers still touching her breast even as he slept, Carolyn felt safe and warm as the rocking chair lulled her farther into her daydreams. The breeze that filtered through the freshly painted green bedroom smelled of June and Central Park below that was bursting with color. Midmorning was Carolyn's favorite time of day. The house was still. But it was a nice stillness, she thought, not at all lonely like other stillnesses she had known. The children were in school and would return at three. John was in Hollywood and would return . . . she didn't exactly know. But he *would* return and that was different from the time not long ago when she didn't know that for a fact. A whole week had gone by. It seemed impossible. When had he called—last night? The day before? He had seen the sets and the costumes—what little there was of them—and was pleased. *Distant Relations* was in its final blue pages of revision.

She had not read a word of John's script although she had certainly read about it. From the first, she had thought it strange that the newspapers and the trades had announced that she and Margaret would be starring in *Distant Relations*. She understood studios often announced stars for pictures before contracts were signed, but still, this was strange. Neither she nor Margaret was used to having her name bandied about for future properties. It was embarrassing, particularly when the "deal" didn't materialize, as it didn't this time. Killerbrew had gotten the news from the newspapers, and had been furious. But not John. It was his ideology, not the casting, that interested him, he said.

Soon she would read the script, she thought, as she lazily rocked herself and Baby John, as she had taken to calling her youngest. The script had arrived in the morning mail, along with the letter with the stamps covering nearly all of the envelope's face. John had been good to his word. He had

282

promised that as soon as there was a final draft, or as final as any script that would soon go before the cameras could be, she could read it. Well, she mused, if I've waited this long, I can wait a little while longer. Nothing took her away from this special time with Baby John. She wouldn't allow it. He was her miracle. He was also, she hoped, the glue that would hold John's and her marriage together. Not that John could be held. When Killerbrew suggested he come to Hollywood for last-minute revisions, John, without consulting her, had booked his flight and left. Was she wrong to have felt hurt? Was Margaret right when she said so many weeks ago that John would never be the picture of a dutiful husband again; that he had changed—and in his mind for the better. He was obviously much happier.

Happier? That Carolyn couldn't understand. Was her memory that faulty? She had never thought of John as anything but happy until he returned from the war. Margaret insisted it didn't matter what had changed John, only that something had and that Carolyn had better make some changes right along with him.

Margaret had been so sure, so certain then. And just a few weeks later, she was lost in her own confusion. Carolyn thought of the letter waiting atop the dresser next to John's script. Its very definite handwriting immediately identified the writer. Nothing tentative or weak about those strokes. Who would ever think she was the same person who could barely function but weeks ago.

Carolyn tried to brush away the memory of that April day but it persisted in clinging to her thoughts. She remembered the morning and the incessant rain it had brought. At first, she wasn't sure the doorbell had rung, so loud was the thunder. But the knock, more like a pounding on the door, was not to be denied. John was not home and it was with considerable trepidation that Carolyn walked to the door. When she looked through the peephole, she recognized Margaret and felt relieved. But that relief turned to panic when she opened the door and Margaret, disheveled and distraught, flung herself into the room, dripping water as she did.

"Carolyn, don't be mad," she kept repeating. "I would do it for you if I could. But I can't." And then the tears came followed by sobs. Carolyn held Margaret, uncertain what her distress was.

"Please, you must explain to John it's not his script. Please, Carolyn. Don't let John be mad at me."

She tried to make Margaret sit but couldn't. Agitated, Margaret kept moving about the room as she talked incoherently. "I just can't do it, Lynnie. I can't. I can't go back to that life—to that half life. Please, Lynnie. Understand. I can't be like Augie. I must have all or none of Franklin Killerbrew."

No further words were needed to explain how Margaret felt. Carolyn knew. She could feel her sister's panic as she held her.

Very consciously, Carolyn decided she was not going to relive any more of that morning. Easing herself ever so gently from the rocking chair, she placed John Jr. in his crib, taking pains to cover him with a thin cotton blanket despite the warmth of the June day. She then took both letter and script from the bureau, curious now as to what both loved ones in her life had to say. Margaret, first, since hers was the shorter. With her fingernail, Carolyn slit open the envelope and pulled out the pages that had resulted in such exorbitant postage.

SAVOY HOTEL
LONDON, ENGLAND

June 2, 1947

Dearest Lynnie,

I am fine. I thought I would say that at the top because (1) I know you worry and . . . (2) It is true. Finally, I am fine. No longer a nutty person. I've crossed the bridge, which is far better than wanting to jump from it. And in this town, sister mine, there's a bridge to jump from every few feet. They cross the Thames, you know. From my balcony—did you get that? *My* balcony. Very Romeo and Juliet—I can see London Bridge. Like yours truly, it is no longer falling down. I can also see Big Ben, the Houses of Parliament, and the Tower of London.

Now, where was I? Oh, yes. Feeling much better. So much better that I no longer feel I have to apologize to anybody. Quite the opposite. I'm pissed. Pissed as hell. I feel now as though I was pushed, silently coerced into a film I never wanted to make. Whether that's true or not, I feel it. Part of that is my fault. I was keeping quiet because of you—hoping our all being together—note the underlining, please—would help you and John. But it wasn't helping me and I'm angry with you for not realizing that. You should have been the first to say Stop! You know how I felt about that man. Anyway, if I'm wrong, I'm sorry. Oops. See? I still can't stop apologizing. What's the difference. I love you and miss you and when they sing "God Save the Queen" over here, I keep looking around for you.

Speaking of you, I think back to our conversations and, Lynnie, forget everything I said. Who am I to advise you on marriage? What do I know? Me, who has made such a mess of things. Dumb me. Not smart enough to have just slept with the man. Oh, no. I had to fall in love with him, too. But I did try. Got to give myself that. I mean . . . there were several men—mind you, Lynnie, I said several and not many—after Franklin but none had for me what he does. Strike that. What he *did*. Past tense. Which means I'm some sort of masochist. Often I ask myself how you can love a man that you often don't like. Someone should write and ask Dorothea Dix that one! Need I remind you, oh "waif," what an S.O.B. that man can be?

Hold on! A knock at the door.

Back again. Gawd, but everything in this hotel is such a Cecil B. De Mille production. Three men in tie and tails delivered El Snacko (brunch to be exact). One wheeled in the serving cart and bowed. Another moved me to the table where I now sit and write as I "dine" (we dine here, not eat). And the last poured the wine and served the food. I'm sure in a half hour someone will arrive to wipe my mouth. Regarding the Savoy: to paraphrase Miss Davis: What a dump! It reminds me of The Chief. It's a city unto itself. Would you believe it generates its own electricity and has its own housekeeper, valet, chambermaids, waiters, and little invisible people who shine your shoes, pop fresh towels in your room, and turn down your bed? This place caters to your every need. Well . . . almost. I can think of a need or two I'm beginning to have again that it doesn't cater to. Although it might. Who knows since I haven't asked?

Now where was I? Somewhere between the kippers and the eggs I know, but I mean in thought. I'm going to apologize again. I can feel it. A real affliction. This one is for being so vague in my first few letters. I just didn't feel like going into anything. I wanted to leave it all behind. Thank God for the rehearsals. As you know, work relieves one of all responsibility to oneself and others. Selfish but nice . . . at times.

And I thank you for not having pried in your letters. Which reminds me: no, I don't feel bad about the reviews. Not that I'm happy about them either. But I never thought *A Lasting Peace* was a good play. It could've been with changes. But I didn't do it for its merit. You know that. It was *there*, a lifeline, an exit. I took it. My own personal reviews were so mixed I don't know what to think. Half thought I was the greatest American export since the hot dog and the other half hardly represented what is called "British reserve." Still, it amazes me. People wait for me outside the hotel and outside the theatre. Interviewers call daily. My films must have had some impact here. Lord knows this play hasn't. A good thing Evelyn Randolph couldn't get the Savoy Theatre. *Life with Father* is doing splendidly there and I doubt if we could have filled more than half of its eleven hundred seats. We're much better off at the Ambassadors. I doubt however if we'll last past the summer.

Summer? What summer? London is cold and foggy even in June. Not at all my cup of tea (a little play on expressions there. I hope you got it). No one seems to mind however. Very stiff upper lip here. I mentioned Evelyn Randolph before. Imagine a *lady* producer, who is not only tough and bright, but attractive. And noncompetitive. She has introduced me to some interesting people here, some in theatre, just as many not. It is largely due to her that I am getting out again and feeling like a human being. She has never asked but I think she knows I've had some kind of a trauma. She also seems to know another trauma would be easily induced if I got swept into London "society"—all of whom seem to hang out right here at the Savoy Grill. There's Gertie and Noel and Chaplin and his Oona—the Très Chic and Très Gai crowd, if you get my meaning—although it was lovely to run into Danny Kaye and John Wayne (not together, you ninny, just here for a visit). Anyhoo, Evelyn has held quite a few soirées in my honor and it's been rejuvenating. I'm really not much for being tragic for too long a time.

Carolyn, this will surprise you—it does me. It's kind of frightening—but I have no recollection of how I got to your house that day or why I went out in the rain without an umbrella or raincoat. It had just been such a succession of awful weeks. I couldn't sleep and I just couldn't relax. If it wasn't Vinnie, it was Franklin. Every other day someone else would call. "Miss Tiernan, we have found another house for you—this one is a lovely chateau in the Canyon." And "Miss Tiernan, this is Ritz Employment. We have found a couple who might be suitable for your needs. Shall we send you their résumés?" And "Miss Tiernan, this is Cadillac Motors. Would you like a four- or a two-door convertible for your stay here?" And then it was Dorothea Wolfe wanting to know if I wished to come by land or by air. Not that he ever called. Oh, no. It was I'm sure much like the campaign that won us the war in Europe. It was unrelenting. I felt I couldn't breathe. And Lynnie, if I went to Hollywood with you all, I just know I'd be there forever.

Speaking of Hollywood: if Vinnie decides, as he seems to have already, to join you all there instead of flying to be with me in London, don't force the issue. I've thought about this a great deal and maybe it's best that I not fight him, not force myself on him at this time. But on one thing I remain adamant. I do not want him in the film. If when he gets older he chooses to be an actor, so be it. Now, to whatever extent it is possible, I want him to have a normal life. I can hear the experts laughing at that one!!!

Oh God, Carolyn, I'm so crazed where that child is concerned. I shouldn't have left him and I should have taken him with me are thoughts forever in my head. But how could I have taken him? I could barely function, could hardly take care of myself then, so how could I have taken care of him? And as you know, I could not stay there. I had to get away. He had school. But he needed me. Strike that! He needs something—needs it desperately—but I don't know what. And although I would dearly love to be the one to give it to him, I seem to be the person he wants it from the least. Thank God he has his Aunt Carolynnie. Thank God I have his Aunt Carolynnie. Is he all right? I have a feeling you stand over him with a switch to make him write. He says nothing but at least he does write.

Well, my darling, it is time to don my mink and take my daily exercise. I trot about the lobbies of the Savoy. Not very elegant (me, not the lobbies) but it is better than croquet and rugby. Such marble floors I've never seen before and probably never will again. And pillars. Big on pillars. I keep expecting Fred and Ginger to dance around them. There is—strike that!—there *are* (plural) roaring fireplaces throughout. Yes, even in June, which tells you a lot about London in the summer. There are also roaring fireplaces in my suite.

They are the only things that roar in my suite, which tells you a lot about my sex life.

I love you,
Margaret

P.S. Tell me where I should write to you in California.

When Carolyn put down the letter, she found even as she was smiling, she was brushing away tears she had not realized were there. She carefully folded the many pages of the letter and placed it back in the envelope. She would reread and think about it later. Now, she opened the red binder on *Distant Relations*. The note signed with just a large *J*. read: "You are Madge."

A little over an hour later, Carolyn Tiernan Ollson put down the script. There was no smile on her face now but there were tears; too many for the one handkerchief she had clutched in her hands. "You are Madge" he had written. His intent was all too clear. Madge was the wife, the good woman, who kept the home fires burning during the war. She remained constant and true. Which proved to be her problem; *the* problem in her marriage when her soldier husband returned from the war. He had changed, matured, and hardened. He had grown to some place she neither understood nor wanted to be. Although each tried to bring the other to where they were in time, they could not. The marriage failed.

"You are Madge," he had written.

"Well, I refuse to be!" said Carolyn as she all but leaped out of the rocking chair and went to the telephone.

It was only when the wire services carried pictures of Carolyn and the children watching the changing of the guard at Buckingham Palace that John, and the rest of America, learned Carolyn Tiernan was in London. At first, it was thought she was visiting and vacationing with her sister before recrossing the Atlantic and the continent to begin *Distant Relations* in Hollywood toward the end of July. That thinking abruptly changed when it became known that the role of Madge Carter was being offered to such actresses as Olivia de Havilland, Jane Wyman, and Claudette Colbert. Hedda Hopper was the first to suggest that the Ollsons had come to a parting of the ways. Then, Dorothy Kilgallen wrote: "More than an ocean separates Carolyn Tiernan and hubby, John

Ollson." When Carolyn was cornered at the Savoy by a group of reporters, her response to the speculation was brief: "Of course we are separated—by five thousand miles." In Hollywood, John, per Killerbrew's advice, released an unsatisfying "No comment."

It was Franklin Killerbrew who was first to have Carolyn's "vacation" in London explained. Without offers or apology or recompense, her New York agent called and simply "excused" her from the film. Killerbrew was not as angered by Carolyn's withdrawal as he was by this new "tone" of the agent. How different it was from the days of Jerome Siegal. But it was all part and parcel, he realized, of the changes Hollywood was undergoing. Whether he or Jack Warner or Harry Cohn liked it, the industry's power was being equalized.

When Killerbrew strode into John's office hoping to receive some sort of explanation for Carolyn's unexpected behavior, he was surprised to see from the look on John's face that it was, as he said, all news to him. Were his own wounds not still tender, Killerbrew would have offered John some kind of support, but just as Margaret had remained an undiscussed topic between them, so did Carolyn.

John continued to work on *Relations* as though there was nothing untoward in his life. Carolyn's bizarre behavior could not interfere with his rewrites. That had to come first. After eight, when he would leave the studio, he would find an anger snaking its way up through his body. What was she doing? And why? After a week of her silence, John called the Savoy.

"What is the meaning of this?" were his first words.

"The *meaning* is in your script. Let me tell you here and now I am *not* Madge Carter. I will not play villain to your hero. Nor will I keep the home fires burning while you seek your *warmth* elsewhere."

"Then you've left me," said John, trying to define the exact state of Carolyn's mind.

"No, John. The truth is: *you* left me. Some time ago to be exact, only it has taken me a while to realize and accept it."

"You're talking foolishness," said John. "I'll discuss this with you when the film is completed and you are back in New York."

"*We* will discuss this should you come to London," Carolyn corrected and hung up.

In the next nine weeks, the time it took to make *Relations*,

289

John called London weekly. He spoke to his children at whatever length they would permit. Marti was effusive; Thomas, distant. His conversations with Carolyn were confined to weather reports and the state of each person's health. Carolyn's tone said the weather in London was chilly going on cold. John's very controlled voice said a storm was brewing in Hollywood that would rival any that the winds blew in from Santa Ana.

Despite their estrangement, Carolyn acted as if nothing of any great consequence were happening in her life. Margaret could not recall ever seeing Carolyn quite the way she was and worried about her guardedness. When she tried to draw her out, Carolyn all but snapped a response that was a polite mind your own business but said in friendlier words. None of what was happening made sense to Margaret. From the time Carolyn had called from New York to say she would be arriving on the next crossing by the *Queen Elizabeth*, Margaret had been confused and worried. But not panicked. Carolyn's determination was comforting even as it was disconcerting.

Even Augusta could not shed further light on Carolyn's behavior. When Margaret called, Augie was at wits' end with that girl. She had asked "perfectly logical questions and she nearly bit my head off," Augusta complained. "As if I weren't family. I simply said perhaps it wasn't advisable to take a three-month-old baby on an ocean liner. And she said, *your* sister: 'It's only not advisable if the ship has the bad taste to sink.' Now Margaret, stop laughing. I don't find that at all funny. I even said to her: 'Carolyn, running away is never the answer.' To which *your* sister replied: 'I do not define what I am doing as running away but running toward.' You make something of that. I can't. So I leave that girl to you and your good sense, which undoubtedly means you'll both run off and join the circus."

Carolyn's determination to "run toward" found her securing reservations on the *Elizabeth* and passports within days; time enough to close up the apartment and pack several trunks of clothes with Mrs. Worthington's help. The woman was positively thrilled to be making the trip since, as she explained, her only boat travel had been on the Staten Island ferry. Ah, that the children had reacted as well, thought Carolyn. Marti had been upset. She had counted on "summering with Daddy," making it seem like a Margaret O'Brien movie in which she would star. Thomas was annoyed because

290

John had promised him a meeting with Roy Rogers and Gene Autry, with some sort of chuck-wagon spread at Gabby Hayes' ranch on Hollywood and Vine. To Carolyn's relief, both Marti's and Thomas's unhappiness with the change of plans turned to great excitement when they saw pictures of the *Elizabeth*, its swimming pools and dining rooms. A faint promise that he could also visit the engine room totally won over her son. There was no such good fortune with Vinnie. He did not care about seeing a London bobby or Big Ben. He preferred to stay with his Uncle John and, if John didn't want him, then with Augusta.

Patiently Carolyn explained that of course Uncle John wanted him, but was unable to take care of him since he was at the studio all day. And Augusta and Uncle Arthur were spending two weeks at Long Beach with his daughter and her family. Besides, said Carolyn, she couldn't leave him behind; she would miss him too much.

"Is my mother there with anyone?" Vinnie asked suddenly.

"What do you mean 'anyone'? I'm sure she's made some friends by now."

"Men friends?" asked Vinnie.

Carolyn looked at her nephew quizzically. "Vincent, your mother went to London alone and as best I know is still alone. Anything further you wish to ask, ask her! I will say only one thing: your mother loves you, Vinnie. You should have heard how excited she was when she heard we were coming. Now that is the last word on the subject. Do you understand?"

"No," said Vinnie simply and walked away.

That was not the end of Carolyn's problems with the children. During the crossing, while Marti and Vinnie played Esther Williams and Fernando Lamas in the swimming pool, Thomas without preface or fanfare asked: "Are we divorcing?" When she had stared at her son in disbelief, he added: "You and Dad," thinking from her stunned look she had not known what he meant. "Walter Winchell said 'Splitsville.' Are you?"

"No!" Carolyn said angrily.

"Well, it wouldn't matter to me," said Thomas as he swung his yo-yo into the round-the-world spin he had perfected. "He's not much of a father if you ask me."

"I didn't ask you, Thomas Tiernan Ollson, and unless you are looking to be punished, do not speak badly of your

291

father," said Carolyn, furious yet frightened by her son's words and the calm with which they were spoken.

"Aw, c'mon, Ma. Face it. First you make us pray all those years for Daddy to come home to us and then when he does, he can't wait to get away again."

"Thomas, it's your father's work that takes him away."

"Tell it to the marines," said Thomas as he worked the yo-yo into a complicated cat's cradle maneuver.

"Thomas, you are wrong," said Carolyn, upset by a conversation she felt was being controlled by a child rather than herself. "Your father loves you very much. He calls every week just to speak to you."

Thomas shrugged but said nothing more, as for him, there was nothing more to say. It was Carolyn who couldn't let go of the conversation. "Does your sister feel the way you do?"

"Nah. She loves Daddy. She just wishes he loved her."

But he does, Carolyn wanted to scream. But to whom? And would it be true? Carolyn no longer knew.

When the *Elizabeth* docked at Southampton, it was Marti who sighted Margaret. There she was, waving a British flag in one hand and an American in the other. Even from the first-class deck Carolyn could see that the girl who had looked so ravaged in her apartment in April was quite the stunning woman in June. She was a vision of propriety in beige and black, colors Carolyn had never seen Margaret wear before.

When the family passed through customs, Margaret's first words as they came through the gate were for Vinnie. "Blimey and blow me down if the bloody bloke hasn't grown a bloomin' bunch! What a sight for sore eyes you are, me ducks." When Margaret held out the British flag to Vinnie, he took it, but when she knelt before him and said: "I've missed you," he looked at her eyes but said nothing. Still, when Margaret spontaneously clasped him to her, he did not resist. Soon he was engulfed in hugs and all the "sloppy stuff" as Carolyn and Marti surrounded both him and Margaret with affection. Only Thomas held back. He extended his arm for a handshake, thereby making it clear he did not wish to be embraced. With a what's-this-all-about-look at Carolyn, Margaret took Thomas's hand and formally greeted him.

Within a day, Carolyn had brought Margaret up to date on each of the children. She replayed for Margaret the disturbing conversation she had had with Vinnie and suggested Margaret talk with him. The following day, Margaret took

Vinnie on what she billed as "a jolly jaunt through London town." It began with a stroll along the Victoria Embankment. Vinnie looked at the Thames but not at Margaret. He began talking at the zoo in Regent's Park and chattering when both climbed to the top of the Tower of London. Late in the afternoon, they had tea in Hyde Park. The sun had come out, quickly drying the grass that had been damp from the nearly daily drizzle.

"You shouldn't sit in the sun," said Vinnie.

Surprised that he remembered, and pleased, Margaret suggested they pack up their sandwiches and move toward the Serpentine just a little farther on. There, from under an umbrella, they could watch the bathers, if there were any, as they talked.

"You'll be recognized," Vinnie warned.

"Perhaps," said Margaret, unconcerned. "It's different here. People don't make quite the same fuss over actresses. Or else they have better manners. We won't be disturbed."

The area about the serpent-shaped lake in the park was nearly empty. Just as they had seated themselves and had unwrapped the tea sandwiches and cakes, heavy dark clouds again threatened the afternoon. Margaret was looking at Vinnie sitting on the straight-backed chair next to her own. Realizing for the first time that his legs no longer dangled but reached the ground made her want to cry.

"You've grown up," she said aloud, verbalizing what she had been thinking. "So I guess it's time we had a grown-up talk." When he didn't respond but fixed his black eyes on her face, Margaret knew Vinnie was listening.

"When I left New York—do you remember?—the day we moved out of the Savoy and I brought you to Aunt Carolynnie's, I told you I was going to England to do a play. And I said I thought since it was a strange country, it would be best if I went alone and then sent for you during the summer when school was done. Do you remember?"

Again there was no response but the expression on his face told Margaret he remembered. "I lied to you and I'm sorry. On two counts. First, I always told you it's wrong to lie and it is. But sometimes we adults do it because we think it's easier or kinder to children. The truth is, Vinnie, I left New York because I was sort of sick. Not sick the way you sometimes get with fever and a cough or a stuffed-up nose, but sick in a way older people sometimes get. And that made me unable to think clearly. You remember how you felt when you had the flu a winter or so ago? Do you remember how you just wanted to lie there and die? Well, that's sort of how I felt. Weak and tired. I could barely take care of myself and I felt then I couldn't take care of you. Not like a mother should. Not like I wanted to. So I figured I had to go away to get well again. I thought working would be the best medicine. You've always loved your Aunt Carolynnie, and she has always loved you, so I thought you would be just fine with her. And you were. But I think you've been angry with me and I want you to know you've every right to be and I'm sorry. Sometimes when you're sick you do things that are wrong 'cause you just don't know any better."

Vinnie's response startled Margaret. "Did that man make you sick?" As he sat staring at her with his penetrating eyes, her mind raced back to the weeks and then months before she came to London. "What man?" she finally asked, confused. She could see from the expression on his face he did not accept her question. He got up from his chair and said as he looked at the sky, "It's going to rain. We better go."

Again Margaret went over the months before her departure for England. Never, not once, had any man she dated stayed over at the Savoy apartment. Except for that morning with Franklin. But that was the morning and Vinnie was in his room.

"I made myself sick," she said to Vinnie as he stood looking at the Serpentine rather than at her. "There was a man, a friend, but as it turned out, he was no one special. Had he been, you would have known."

Vinnie turned and looked at Margaret curiously. He was about to speak when pouring rain drove away further conversation as they raced for shelter under the trees.

In the following weeks, Margaret continued her efforts to draw closer to Vinnie. Quickly she saw he was too restless for the National Gallery and to a lesser extent, even the British Museum. He liked the noise of Piccadilly Circus and the crowds that frequented the West End and Soho. He went with Margaret to the theatre one night and was at first embarrassed and then acted "as if born to it" when his mother tugged him onstage with her for her final bow. Although he was never consistently communicative, Margaret noticed he was at his worst, withdrawn and hostile, the mornings after she had made it visibly clear from the pains she took with her wardrobe the night before that she had a late-night date.

"It's emotional blackmail," she complained to Carolyn, "and I'll be damned if I'll pay it," she added angrily.

"Look at it this way," said Carolyn placatingly. "Ten years from now when he brings home a girl, you can be awful to her. That will pay him back in kind."

"I give up," said Margaret, plopping herself down on the blue-and-white-striped silk-covered couch next to the fireplace. "With him *and* with you. All of a sudden I'm getting Eve Arden or Maisie lines from you. And when you're not talking fast, you're moving even faster. You've taken off after London as if another blitz were imminent. Is there a part of the city you haven't toured?"

"It's very instructional," said Carolyn.

"Would you get off it?" said Margaret impatiently. "Instructional to you is *Variety* or *The Knitting Monthly*."

"Not anymore," Carolyn said. "It is one thing to have seen the war in the pages of *Life*, it's quite another to walk the streets and see the bombed-out blocks, the broken pavements, the holes in the middle of nowhere where once an apartment house stood, the cracked building walls."

"Speaking of cracks, how about the one in your head?" snapped Margaret. "What is with you anyway? You've been here a month and you've done everything but talk. Would you finally stop playing Mrs. Miniver and sit down and talk to me?"

"You don't want to talk, Margaret Tiernan, and you know it," said Carolyn evenly. "You want to pry. To pry and to analyze. That's quite the thing today. To analyze. Everyone walks around thinking he's a Ziegfeld Floyd."

"I do believe, *Mrs*. Ollson, you mean Sigmund Freud, and you're wrong. Now, if you will just lie down over here on this couch and open your psyche and say *oy*, we can begin."

"There is nothing to begin," said Carolyn angrily. "Actually, who are you kidding? You know the beginning. And the middle. It's the end you don't know. Well, nor do I. But let me tell you this. John has written a very good script. The role he wrote for me is that of Madge Carter. She's very good. Oh, my, is she good. I do hope Claudette Colbert plays her. It's perfect for her kind of goodness. And, I repeat, oh, is that woman good!"

"Madge or Claudette?" asked Margaret, confused.

"Margaret, now you listen to me," demanded Carolyn. "John's film, especially the American segment, has a very particular point of view. Its message, subtle but clear, is: provincialism and Catholicism can stunt one's growth, not to mention one's marriage, when new sensibilities and dogma clash. And guess who is the winner and who the loser? Guess who is the villain and which, the hero? Well, sister mine, I refuse to have my marriage held up for public scrutiny. John's vision of 'the good little woman' is just that: good and little; one of the trusted many who also served as she stood and waited. Or some such rot. Well, Miss Floyd or Freud, I'm not standing and I'm not waiting or serving another second longer. Case closed."

"What do you intend to do then?" Margaret asked.

"When I know exactly, you'll be the first to know," answered Carolyn. "Till then, as they say here in merrie ole England, tally-ho!"

"Now what's that supposed to mean?" asked Margaret, annoyed.

"As I just said, when I know exactly, you'll be the first to know."

It was such a small thing to have happened but it cut to the core of what he was feeling. When the taxi stopped outside the building, as John strode into the lobby, the doorman stopped him with a courteous but quizzical "Yes, sir?"

"What do you mean, 'Yes, sir'? I live here," John said, annoyed.

"Sorry, sir, but I must ask for some identification," insisted the doorman politely.

The man was new and just doing what he was paid to do: protect him and others who lived in the building, yet John wanted to strike him. This was no time to be questioned about his identity. There had been enough of that.

The apartment, too, had not been welcoming. It was dark, the draperies having been drawn across the living room windows. Instead of the usual homelike smells of Maxwell House and Bon Ami, the odors were musty and stale. A gloom covered the house as completely as the sheets covered the furniture. There was no life in this house. No identifying marks that could be washed from the walls with sudsy water.

Even as the taxi had brought him in from La Guardia, John had wondered whether he would be more comfortable at the

Waldorf. But he wanted to be "home" . . . somewhere, even if the house was under wraps as this one was. In this bedroom, John laid his suitcases on the stripped bed. He then drew open the green floral-print draperies and opened the windows to the crispness of the late October day. When he went to hang his jacket in the closet, he saw his clothes in a garment bag. The smell of camphor was a reminder of Carolyn's housewifery. She seemed always to be waging a never-ending war against moths and cockroaches. In his dresser drawer he found his spare shirts and underwear under protective layers of cellophane. He smiled as he unwrapped it. This was the home the Waldorf could not provide and this, now, was what he needed.

But the house was quiet, so quiet that it assailed his ears. Running the water in the tub helped. Watching a silverfish slide down the drain, John wondered, given how he felt, if he, too, would slide away that easily. Ah, that his pain would! And his loneliness. Carolyn's bubble bath sat on the edge of the tub. Without thinking why, he sprinkled the lavender scent into the water. His clothes piled atop the hamper, John stepped into the bubbling water, hoping its warmth would ease away the terrible coldness he felt inside.

As his head rested on the edge of the tub, John thought about the series of events that had brought him "home." He had lunched with Killerbrew that day and the studio head had offered him a three-picture deal. It was a gesture and John knew it, a "hope" to ease another kind of coldness he was feeling, which Killerbrew called the postpartums. *Relations* had finished filming and was now being processed in the lab before it was edited and scored. John felt bereft. There was nothing to occupy his day and his thoughts. Killerbrew, excited about a new venture he was planning to enter, drove John to NBC's studios where John watched actors on a sound stage, no more than ten feet away from where he stood, appear on a screen mere inches away from him and Killerbrew.

"It's going to change the habits of this country," Killerbrew said. "In ten years' time, men like you will be able, through television, to reach millions with their ideas."

Sandra had laughed when he told her. Change the world? That's what they said about the telephone and airplane and as far as she could see, the world was still a sewer for the poor and a treehouse for the rich.

She hadn't been cynical or sardonic when they had first

met nearly ten years ago. If he had known how much she had changed, he would never have accepted her invitation—and it was *her* invitation—for coffee when he accidentally bumped into her at the May Company while shopping for birthday presents for the children. Yes, his fantasy but her invitation. After all these years . . . Sandra. Only she wasn't the Sandra he remembered. Not only was she older but also wiser in ways he did not like. Gone was the skirt and blouse. Now she was "the little black dress and a rope of pearls." This Sandra no longer allowed her hair to fly every which way. No. She was coiffed and couturiered; a Beverly Hills matron who could not possibly ever have lived in two rooms—one painted orange with black molding and woodwork—in Greenwich Village. She had married a young director who had graduated from army training films to Paramount, where he did well but his marriage did not. She was not bitter. But she wasn't Sandra. He knew she would no longer have a cat named Der Bingle but who also answered to Crosby. This Sandra had a nice, well-appointed house on North Canon Drive, a nice, well-appointed daughter named Marissa, and a nice, well-appointed life that permitted sex when Marissa was at school. It was nice sex but not what he remembered; not the clutching and crying of clashing orgasms that had left drenched sheets and drenched participants on Morton Street. More postpartum depression. One completed film and one finished fantasy. All gone. His bubbles burst like the ones with him in the bathtub.

He had just come from Sandra's and was sitting at the pool at Sunset Towers West where he had rented a bungalow when the call from Rochester came *collect* telling him of his mother's death. A quick but efficient coronary, the attorney had said before asking him to come to the town to "close out the books." Yes, that's what he had said . . . close out the books. He wondered then whether he should call Carolyn. There was no reason to, really. Greta Ollson had never acknowledged Carolyn's presence so why should Carolyn acknowledge her death, particularly since Carolyn was barely acknowledging him? Their phone calls remained infrequent and unsatisfying. Much of what he knew of her he learned through the newspapers. It hadn't just surprised but it astounded him when he learned Carolyn had rented a house on Rutland Street near Hyde Park and had enrolled the children in a very advanced secondary school. She had even taken on the network and, despite their objections, was recording "Front Row Center" in London, with British actors, for American listening. From all that he read, Carolyn seemed hardly to be the woman who had wrapped her apartment in sheets and cellophane before leaving it.

He could sense her with him in the bathtub now, the scent of her lavender bath salts bringing her near. But he never could get her to take a bath with him, to make love under the warm water . . . under the bubbles. She had thought it improper and became angry when he had persisted in suggesting it. She had been so much like his mother that way. It had to be prescribed or it wasn't done.

He could not imagine his mother in bed. Not with his father or anyone. He remembered her flannel pajamas and the wool bathrobe in which she would wrap herself before climbing into the four-poster and disappearing under its down comforter. That had been there, he now remembered, the crazy-quilt down comforter, frayed and stained by coffee that had lapped over her chipped white cup.

He should never have walked through the front door of that house. She was gone and it with her. Willed to the church—her soul and her house. Well, the house had never been his. He should have left the disposal of "things" to the attorney. What made him think there might be some*thing*, any*thing*, in that house he might have wanted? There was nothing, no reminder or memento, that he wished to take. The ones he had were enough and they were hardly comforting. More losses. Not gains.

Except money. Clearly he heard the lawyer who stood by his side say his mother's estate was valued at better than a half million dollars—all willed to him and the children. A half million. How fitting! A wealthy woman who wore Sears housedresses and Red Cross shoes. And how fitting that a woman who had given him nothing throughout her life gave him her all upon her death. And it wasn't enough. It would never be enough, he suddenly realized as his rage rose. He asked the attorney to leave, telling him he would phone soon. The man left, thinking John wanted to be alone with his thoughts for a last time. As soon as he departed, John began screaming as he ripped doilies, yellow with age, from the backs of chairs and their arms. Had she been there, he would have struck his mother. Of that he was certain. But she wasn't. She never had been. He had not spoken with her in

299

months. Actually, they had never spoken, he realized in his fury. He had remained a stranger to his mother although she wasn't a stranger to him. He looked about the house. It resembled her life: drab. She had repainted it a dreary, depressing brown. Not a "golden wheat" or a "harvest beige" but brown. John could hear his mother: "But it won't show fingermarks." But Mother, there are no more fingers in your life to make marks, and Mother, wouldn't it be nice if there were? She would not have understood. Not her. Not a stupid, brown-walled woman who could leave money but not a memory of her as a mother.

John lay totally still in the tub, hoping to still the memories that assailed him. A ripple on the water rippled the memory of that moment, in his mother's house, and that ridiculous, but not ridiculous thought, that punched him as though it were a person's fist to his stomach. "I am an orphan," he said aloud. The thought was funny, as who thought of thirty-five-year-old men as orphans. But John didn't laugh. Instead, he cried. Because that is how he felt and that is what he was. More postpartums. Another fantasy gone. And this one he hadn't known he had. What person ever realizes he still treasures the hope that a woman—a brown woman with a gray life—will one day be the longed-for mother who loves her son. Such a false fantasy, particularly when he knew she could never be to him what he so much wanted and needed.

It made him think of Carolyn. She, too, couldn't give him what he needed but it wasn't her fault. He saw that now. Carolyn couldn't make up for all he had missed. She gave what she could, which was different from not giving at all. But she could not replace what should have been given to him years ago as a child. And she couldn't make right a world that had gone wrong. She was part of that world and all that was wrong with it. She trusted the dogma just as she had trusted him. Is it stupid to trust or is it something rather special and wonderful?

And she gives, he realized. And she loves as best she can. She was not in any way like his mother. Carolyn Tiernan Ollson could never live a brown life because she was a pink and blue and red and green and yellow woman.

The water in the bathtub had turned cold but John didn't move. For the first time in days, he felt warm. Content, he lay back in the tub as he turned on the hot water tap. Soon he would get up, dry himself, eat a lovely dinner, have a lovely sleep, and then get on with what could be a lovely life.

When John arrived unannounced and unexpected in London in mid-November, he had thought Carolyn would be thrilled. If she was, she disguised it well by refusing to put out the welcome mat for him. He could not, as he had thought, stay at the Rutland Street house, "but when you're settled, John, you are most welcome to visit."

Visit? Visit my own wife and children?

"Visit!" she had repeated, and despite his insistence that her position was ridiculous, Carolyn remained intractable. Since the children now knew and accepted in some fashion that they were separated—and that had been a very difficult adjustment in itself—she was not about to jeopardize their well-being by giving them false hope about a possible reconciliation.

"What false hope?" John said angrily. "We might be."

"We have problems . . . differences, John, and until they are resolved, you cannot have access to my home because here, my home is my life. If you enter one, you enter both. I'll be happy to see you when you're settled."

Margaret had been of some help but not much. Not that she didn't try. Even with her considerable pull, the Savoy was sold out. Not a room available for days.

"You certainly picked a helluva time to pop in," she said. "John, didn't you realize half the world is attending, or trying to, Princess Elizabeth's wedding? There's not a vacancy from here to Budapest. I'd give you the couch in the living room but I do think Carolyn might not appreciate that. But listen. I have a thought. Remember Evelyn Randolph? She knows everyone and everything in this town. I'll call her. You might wind up sleeping on a cot in Prince Albert Hall, but what the hell. Give me a call back in ten."

Yes, Margaret, he thought, I remember Evelyn Randolph— just as he was sure she remembered him. Kindly, he hoped, and discreetly. But how could he have forgotten the wedding? It was one of the assignments *Esquire* had offered him—how the rich squander and the poor love it. He had turned it down in favor of the study offered by the *New York Times*. In the next few months, John would tour London, Paris, Rome, Vienna, and Madrid to measure how the entertainment presented in each country reflected the mood or the politics of the people.

When Margaret answered the phone on the first ring, John said, "Is it a park bench or has Evelyn worked her magic?"

"Evelyn is calling a friend in Paris. He is arriving tomorrow for the wedding and she is sure he won't mind sharing his suite at the Carlton House with you. Seems he recently divorced and is not about to be running girls through his flat."

"What do I do until tomorrow?" asked John.

"We risk Carolyn's wrath and you move in with Vinnie for the night or you sack out on the living room sofa and keep me up till all hours with the juicy gossip from America."

"He never mentions you. It's like you never existed. If someone speaks your name, he pretends he didn't hear and changes the subject. Of course throughout the studio, it's like a goddamn museum to Margaret Tiernan. Pictures everywhere. For a while, I expected to find them draped in black. He has a new girl. She is blonde, has blue eyes, and probably could say more than hello and my-but-doesn't-California-have-lovely-oranges if her brain was as big as her tits. That *is* what you wanted to know, isn't it, Margaret?"

"When did you become such a prick, John?" Margaret asked, a sudden weariness sounding in her voice.

"Don't confuse honesty with hostility, Margaret. Not you, of all people. I told you what you really wanted to know. Now that it's out of the way, I'd like to grab a taxi . . . and then grab my favorite sister-in-law for a big hug. Besides, I have a present for you from Augusta. Apple strudel. She baked it herself."

"Apple strudel? Aunt Augie?"

"It's delicious. She packed a piece for me for the trip."

"Apple strudel? Aunt Augie?"

"Margaret, repetition is not the thing that becomes you most. Yes, apple strudel, baked by the very hands of Augie Crocker Pillsbury."

"Apple strudel?"

"Good-bye, Margaret. See you in a bit."

When James Philip Carrington opened his door to admit John and Margaret, who was helping with the luggage, he certainly didn't seem like the kind of man who would, upon a moment's phone call, share his rather elaborate surroundings—

and the Carlton was elaborate—with a stranger. Margaret credited Evelyn Randolph that he was. Men not only found her irresistible, but did not resist, no matter how imposing her request. Carrington swung open the door and managed a pleasant but hardly effusive smile. Had he not agreed to house her brother-in-law, Margaret would have found Carrington not to her liking. Men who answered their door at ten in the morning wearing three-piece suits were sure to be terribly proper even in their improprieties.

"I'm going to run," she announced as soon as she placed John's attaché case on a chair.

"But why didn't you let the bellman carry that?" asked Carrington.

"Let a stranger carry John's novel? That would be like God allowing Beelzebub instead of Moses to carry the Ten Comandments. I'm flattered he let me," said Margaret.

Carrington looked at her the way she imagined he looked at a bill to see if it were counterfeit. "That's rather amusing," he said, a faint smile fighting to make its way on his face.

"Yes, I can see you could die laughing from it," said Margaret as she extended her hand. "I'm sure we'll see each other later at Evelyn's party. Nice meeting you, Mr. Carrington."

"And you, Miss . . . I'm sorry. But I don't believe I got your name," said Carrington apologetically.

Margaret could feel John laughing as he watched the scene. What most annoyed Margaret was her own reaction. How dare he not know her!

"Allyson. June Allyson," she said, smiling sweetly as she closed the door behind her.

"Charming woman," said Carrington as he turned his attention to John. "A friend of your wife?"

"Her sister," said John.

"Sister," echoed Carrington. "Tiernan is your wife's name, is it not? Carolyn Tiernan. My wife and I went to see her in *Shining Hour* on one of our anniversary trips to New York. Splendid evening. A very talented woman your wife is. She's appearing in London now, is she not?"

John explained it was Margaret Tiernan, and not Carolyn, who was closing this very week in a production.

"Well, I must see her then, mustn't I?" said Carrington.

"You just did," replied John and then, watching the dots connect on Carrington's face, added: "Don't take it personal-

303

ly. My sister-in-law has a rather bizarre sense of humor."

"Yes, it borders on rude," agreed Carrington, "but it is also rather delightful."

Had Margaret stayed that morning, she would have discovered that beneath the gray flannel and discreet red-and-blue-striped tie, there was a man John warmed to almost instantly. Although Carrington had been in the suite only an hour, he had already divided closet and medicine chest space to make his guest comfortable. He had also ordered a late breakfast, taking pains to have both coffee and tea delivered, not knowing which John preferred. When John commented on this rather distinct and hospitable—"not to mention downright charitable"—behavior, Carrington explained: "It's the banker in me. The only reason one bank succeeds while another fails is service. I'm a vice-president at the Morgan Bank because I'm an expert provider, also known as pimp to my nonsupporters. What most people do not know is that banking is a highly personal business. Clients must be treated with special care. The bank even hires couples for the clients. You do know what couples are, yes? Ah, I see from your face you do not. They're servants, husband and wife, who will run a home or an estate. You would be surprised how many of our clients, heads of General Motors, Ford, Singer, NCR, come to Europe for a stay and need that kind of service. Banking is far more than investments, borrowing and lending and foreclosing mortgages on poor widows who have no place to go."

The glint in Carrington's eye was unmistakable. "I should think that the best part of the job," said John seriously.

"Only when there are children involved," Carrington replied just as seriously.

"What you describe sounds as much like public relations as it does high finance," said John, more as a question than a statement.

"Exactly. People like to say today that appearances are no longer important. That may be true everywhere but in banking, where the appearance of solidarity, of strength and sureness, is your best public relations tool. It is a role that comes easily to me as I am your basically stuffy and humorless Englishman."

Again the glint was in Carrington's eye. "Does your wife by any chance go by the name of Jane Powell or is she just plain Carolyn Tiernan?"

"I'm afraid I'm missing something," said John, "and I have the feeling it's meant to be very funny."

"Has she another identity, one that seems to be as far-fetched as June Allyson is to Margaret Tiernan?"

"As a matter of fact, yes. She is Carolyn Ollson and at the moment that seems to be very farfetched to her. We are sort of separated," said John. "Not considering divorce but not yet working toward a reconciliation, although I think we will once I see her. Which should be later at Evelyn Randolph's."

"I have found it very difficult to be separated," said Carrington, "although we no longer are. We're divorced, which they say is different. But is it? I fail to see how. I'm still separated from my wife, only now it is legal and forever."

"I'm sorry," said John as he heard the despair in Carrington's voice.

"Six months now. And still difficult. Which most people find hard to understand. A single man in Paris . . . successful, not exactly still a stallion but not a stud put to pasture either. People expected I would not be alone for a moment. And if left to the matchmakers among us all—and there are matchmakers about everywhere, so be careful what you say and to whom, as loose lips sink bachelordom—I'd be the gentleman on the right at dinner eight days a week. But I've shunned that. I'm not yet interested in other women. And you?"

Carrington's question was asked not for salacious reasons, but to gather information for his own adjustment, which is why John answered.

"I have seen other women," he said slowly, "which seems to have helped me see my own wife much more clearly. She's a good woman."

"My wife is somewhere here in London, probably helping Elizabeth to dress for her wedding at this very moment. She became quite class-conscious in her old age. Although forty-four is not old, is it? Not to her. She has a rather young man in attendance. Not so young as to be indecent, mind you, but young enough to make me look foolish. Deirdre was born in a castle in Kent. I'm afraid she never really left it. Our daughter is carrying on in the old tradition but in America. She is Park Avenue's most perpetual partygiver and an all-around Palm Beach poop. A thoroughly unlikable girl who made a most 'significant' marriage to a man of means—integrity and humor not being among them. They send me ties from Sulka each birthday and Christmas."

"You're finding it difficult going it alone, aren't you?" asked John.

"Mr. Ollson, sir. I realize that for strangers we are talking very personally indeed, which is rather unusual for us British. We are known for our reserve, you know. My sojourn in America ruined me, I'm afraid. Twenty-one in Harvard's class of nineteen-twenty-one. Father wanted Oxford but I was rather insistent. Loved America. Still do. But the bank beckoned—we do have a Morgan here, you know—and Father had connections and quite frankly, I regret none of it. My wife enjoyed her role. She was the perfect hostess. No one could hold a fish fork quite like she did. I rather admired her. Liked her, too. Yes, we were friends. Good ones, actually. I had thought by forty, the fact that passion and mystery were missing from our marriage was a relief. Obviously, she didn't share my thoughts. So be it. And it *will* be. I'm adjusting. Paris has wonderful diversions. The Opéra and the Comédie Française and this very year we had André Gide's translation of *Hamlet* and Jean Genêt's *Les Bonnes*." Noting the surprised look on John's face, Carrington added, "We bankers do more than just read the *Wall Street Journal* and sit in stuffy men's clubs and steam rooms. We even read remarkable articles in *Esquire* written by rather remarkable, sensitive men who write letters to their unborn children."

"You understood what I was saying, then," said John, pleased.

"Yes," said Carrington, his face clouding, "I lost my son, Laurence, in the war. He was a good boy, although he worried his mother endlessly. He simply saw no hurry to settle down. At *anything*. A delightful child. I miss him greatly. And you? Any children?"

"Two," said John as he put the last of his things away in the closet. "Twins. A boy, Thomas, and a girl Martha, whom everybody calls Marti. They're ten now."

"I envy you," said Carrington. "I'd love to have children again."

John didn't answer as he was too busy asking himself how he could have forgotten John Jr.

"I think if I had children now, I wouldn't make the same mistakes," said Carrington.

"We always make mistakes," said John. "It's a condition of parenthood."

"Well, I must be off for the bank. This is not all holiday for me," explained Carrington.

"Or me," said John as he explained the research he needed to do throughout the key cities of Europe for his *Times* article.

"But then you must stay with me when you're in Paris," Carrington said. "If you choose, of course. I'm most conveniently located on the Ile Saint-Louis. It's a big, sprawling apartment, very French, which suited Deirdre but which I'll give up as soon as I'm ready to give up the past. It has several bedrooms with their own baths. Really, you're most welcome unless you prefer the Ritz, which is just down from my office in the Place Vendôme. We keep a room there for visiting dignitaries. And," added Carrington as he gave John a mock appraisal, "you could pass for a dignitary."

"You realize you just offered your home to someone you hardly know," said John, surprised and pleased.

"Sir," said Carrington seriously. "We are sleeping together and we hardly know each other—although I gather with this postwar morality that's hardly anything to raise an eyebrow anymore—so why not offer you what's there and unused? Besides, a recommendation from Evelyn Randolph is all the credentials one needs. She has wonderful judgment. Except when it comes to women. Best you reconcile, John. Believe me. You can't imagine how barbaric it is to be on the open market, particularly when you haven't been for many years. Do you know, would you *believe*, they . . . *women* . . even get on top these days!"

John looked at James Philip Carrington's straight face and decided just before the glint and the faintest of smiles interrupted it, that he liked the man and his face very much indeed.

5

"What am I doing here? Would you tell me that? Please. Would someone—anyone—explain whatever possessed me to do this fool thing?" asked Carolyn as she paced back and forth from her dressing table on one side of the room to Margaret's on the other. "If you hadn't agreed, if you hadn't said: 'Oh, yes, it's a wonderful idea!' to that woman, none of this would be happening. And you do realize what's about to happen, don't you?"

"Yes, I most certainly do," Margaret said as she rose from her chair and walked to the window which overlooked the heart of the West End theatre district. "I'm about to scream!" Which she did with a force that caused several passersby to look up and stare in concern.

"You and your jokes," sneered Carolyn. "Everything is always such a lark for you. Can't you get it through your thick head what's about to happen?"

"If you would simply shut up and let me think about it, I probably could," said Margaret as she seated herself once again at her dressing table. "On second thought, keep on ranting. I don't want to think about it."

"I should never have listened to you," Carolyn said as she lit a cigarette.

"Lynnie, put that thing down. You know you don't smoke," said Margaret.

"See? You're making me crazy. Marg, I'm going to be sick. I'm serious. My stomach feels awful. I'll never make it."

Margaret's look of disbelief angered Carolyn still more. "It's all your fault," she bellowed.

"My fault? *My* fault! I wasn't the one who wanted to make her stage debut—how did you put it? Leave *my* mark—on the London stage. I've already done that."

"There is a difference between a mark and a blemish," snapped Carolyn.

308

"Keep it up, Carolyn. Just keep it up and when Judgment Day comes, not only will you be an ugly old woman selling apples on the street, but I'll be standing near you, dressed as Snow White and telling the folks: 'Pass her by. Pass her by.' "

"It's Evelyn Randolph's fault," said Carolyn as she plopped herself on the new gold velour sofa the producer had provided to match the draperies and rug that made a sitting room of what had been a very plain concrete and wood box. "We should never have listened to her. I don't need this. My reputation is assured. I'm a star in radio, in theatre. I don't need international status. You know that, Margaret. If only you had just said no, we wouldn't be here."

"Carolyn, if you don't shut up, you're not going to be here. I'm going to throw you out that window there."

"What's the difference where you throw me, out the window or to the lions—those godawful British reviewers waiting out there," whined Carolyn, panic in her voice.

"Remind me never to share a dressing room with you ever again. We're far too old for that. If we were both alone now, you'd be playing with your beads and me with myself and we'd both be feeling a helluva lot better."

"Your mouth is disgusting sometimes!"

"Please, miss, don't go holy on me now. You're about to play a hotblooded woman who has lusted—do you hear? —lusted for a man who is not her husband. Try to pretend you know what lust is."

Carolyn's half-smile was her only response.

"Oh, great!" said Margaret. "She's doing a Mona Lisa on me. Okay, let's have it. John got back from Paris last night, right? How did it go? Although the grin on your face says he went pretty good. I hope you joined him."

"Absence does indeed make the heart grow fonder," said Carolyn airily as she brushed her hair.

"Listen, Lynnie, when I want homilies I'll tune in Kate Smith. I'm talking about you and John."

A knock interrupted Carolyn's response. When she opened the door, there was yet another delivery boy buckling under the weight of yet another basket of flowers. Automatically, Carolyn handed him a few shillings after instructing the boy to leave the basket with the many others on one side of the room.

"If you should die here and now from stage fright," said Margaret, "the family would at least save a fortune on flowers. And with the reviewers about to bury us alive, death is a possibility."

"Margaret, sometimes your charm escapes me. It truly does."

"We were speaking about you and John, if your addlepated little pea brain can remember. I was asking . . ."

"You were prying . . . again. By the way, you know James came in with him. He said he couldn't wait to see June Allyson play Lavinia in *Mourning Becomes Electra*. Whatever do you think that man was talking about?"

Margaret was laughing. "Frankly, I'd kill to see that myself. June in my role, Peter Lawford or Van Johnson—that's good, Van—as Orin, and Cass Daley, no, Martha Raye as Christine."

"I still think you should have played Christine opening night and I Lavinia. You have aged far more than I have, you know."

"Who wouldn't with you as a sister? Honestly, Carolyn, you are driving me crazy." To emphasize her point, Margaret ran to the window. "She is driving me crazy, world! Crazy. Do you hear?" she screamed into the evening.

"Where is your precious Evelyn Randolph now that you need her?" said Carolyn sarcastically.

"Sitting out front with the rest of London. They're all there with their hatchets . . . just waiting and ready. I can read the headlines now: 'Mourning Becomes Electra but not the Tiernan Sisters.' "

"Is all of London really out there?" asked Carolyn with something sounding suspiciously like a tear in her voice.

"I think Jack the Ripper sent his regrets. And Henry the Eighth. Otherwise, everyone," replied Margaret. "By the way, who are the flowers from? You didn't even look."

Carolyn got up from the sofa and checked the card attached to the gladioluses. "Oh, how nice. How very nice," she said and sat down again. Margaret stared at her sister in disgust.

"Carolyn, who are they from?" she screamed.

"You don't have to scream at me," wailed Carolyn. "I'm just so distracted. They're from Augie and Arthur. Oh, I wish she could have been here. She could have massaged my temples and held my head."

That's it. Sel*fless* to the end. You realize, don't you, nothing but Arthur's health could have kept Aunt Augie away? She would have been here two weeks ago, for Christmas, if she felt Arthur could have managed a transatlantic flight. Now come on, Lynnie. Buck up. I mean, we're really such a sketch, carrying on as if this were our first play."

"Representing our entire country, our most famous playwright, and hundreds of American actors in one of the most difficult plays ever written is worse."

"Ah, Lynnie, you do have a way of saying all that should remain unspoken. Whose friggin' idea was it for us to do O'Neill?"

"Yours! Evelyn suggested we do our *Much Ado* but you said . . . oh, no. How could two American actresses dare to do Shakespeare. So here we are, two American actresses about to make fools of themselves before all of London, my husband, his friend—and I would say yours, too, given the attention he paid to you at Christmas—and our children. . . ."

"Would you shut up? And he did not pay any particular attention to me. James Carrington is a very nice man, somewhat lonely I think, who happens to have charm and culture and is willing to share it with those among us who have precious little. Now, Precious Little, are you or aren't you going to tell me about you and John?"

"His trip was wonderful. He completed his research in Paris and Germany. He said James introduced him to all sorts of writers and artists in Paris. Isn't that strange? He hardly seems the type."

"We're talking about John," said Margaret caustically.

"Yes, John says James has the most spectacular apartment on the Ile Saint-Louis. You have to take a cagelike elevator up to it, past a concierge who John says bears a striking resemblance to Quasimodo. Only Quasi is named Marie. Anyway, this sprawling apartment is like a railroad flat. Strange. The kinds of places we in America no longer would dream of living in are quite the rage in Paris. John says you never saw so much Empire furniture and polished red mahogany woods, ebony too, and beds shaped like gondolas."

Wordlessly, Margaret picked herself up and again crossed to the window. This time, her scream caused a London bobby to inquire from the street if everything was all right "up there."

"I'm going to redo the apartment when I return," continued Carolyn, unruffled. "Lots of soft, muted colors, like the beige silk I'm wearing to the party after the opening. Unless, of course, I decide to go in black. Lots of black."

"To match the color of your eye. I am warning you, Carolyn," said Margaret, mustering all the menace she could manage.

"Right. John and me. Well, it was nice. Better than nice. It was lovely. It's been lovely ever since John came to London. It's like being kids again . . . dating. Only we're married, which means we can make love. And we did . . . yesterday. It was really beautiful. And different. Only nothing else is set between us. Not yet. We really haven't had time to talk, as you know. Now don't look so shocked, it's true. First he took off to do the research in Vienna. Then he came home for Christmas, staying at the Dorchester. And that was no time for talking as he was out with the kids most days. Then it was Christmas dinner and James was there and then they were off again and we were in rehearsal and here we are."

"But you're happy," said Margaret.

"Let's say I'm content. Or happy with the progress we're making but not happy yet with the marriage. We have a lot to talk about, which we will do over the next few weeks."

"Take my word for it. You're happy," said Margaret. "Say it to yourself over and over and then click your heels three times and you'll be back in Kansas."

"Better there than here," said Carolyn, shivering. "Marg, I'm frightened. I think having the children out there for the first time has me even more terrified. They're old enough now to see what we do. Maybe even understand it. I guess in my heart I'm hoping they'll see the work it takes to achieve—not success, I don't mean that—but something that approaches 'special' or perfection, although I know there is no such thing. In my heart of hearts, I am hoping if they can see this, then they can understand why we've been such errant mothers."

"You truly astound me sometimes," said Margaret. "You are so right although I never knew you thought of yourself as an errant mother."

"Oh, come on, Marg, what else are we? Here we are, grown women continuing to dress up like little girls in their mother's clothes and pretending to have tea in a dollhouse."

"If Stella Adler could hear you, she'd throw herself off a stack of books by Stanislavski."

"But it's true," continued Carolyn. "I'm out there 'playing house' before what I hope will be a packed house while my ten-month-old child is in the care of a nurse. I tell myself, as

I have ever since Thomas and Marti were born, that it's quality, not quantity, that counts, but I'll go to my grave believing a child deserves both."

"We did okay, and both our parents were onstage and out of the house a great deal," argued Margaret.

"If you remember, we went with them. Even as kids, Mama lugged us around, kept us in cradles in their dressing room."

"What a time for the galloping guilts," said Margaret, annoyed.

"I'm not all that troubled by it. I accept this is who I am. As a matter of fact, I forgot to tell you, I'm going to do some kind of thing for television when I get back to New York. John is going to write it and Franklin Killerbrew . . ." Carolyn stopped in midword.

"It's all right, Lynnie. You can say his name. Avoiding it doesn't make him go away."

"If you went out more often, it would. My Lord, Margaret, a hundred men flock about and you turn down ninety-nine of them."

"But think of that one I don't!" Margaret said with a salacious smile. "And I'm only looking for one," she added, the grin gone from her face. "Just one. A nice, settled, attractive man without complications. No wife. No secrets in his closet named Bruce. Just a nice and, I hope, passionate man. Lynnie, Franklin Killerbrew is in the audience tonight. No one told me; I just know it. Those flowers to both of us from him were not sent from Hollywood. How do I feel about it? Well, dear heart, it seems to me in every girl's life there should be a Franklin Killerbrew and in every woman's life there should be a time when there no longer is a Franklin Killerbrew. It's one thing to playact in a dollhouse but quite another to live in one. I want a home, not a dollhouse, Lynnie. So it's over. Really over. It has to be or else my life is."

"Ten minutes, everybody. Ten minutes!"

The call was loud and clear over the loudspeaker. Carolyn Tiernan sat quite still although it was obvious from the way her lips were moving that she was in prayer. Another knock on the door interrupted her and Margaret as they each went through their last-minute preparations. "Knock 'em dead, kids," said John as he burst into the room. "Boy, what an audience! It's a goddamn who's who in England. I've never seen such celebrities. And when Elizabeth and Philip entered their box . .."

"Elizabeth and Philip?" echoed Margaret dully

"My gawd, didn't anyone tell you?" gushed John. "There s royalty all over the place. Even the Queen Mother is due any minute. It's the most damned exciting thing I've ever witnessed. Aren't you excited?"

Carolyn's response was to rush past John to the toilet where the sound of her retching could be heard even as the five-minute call was sounded. Margaret, after a moment of shock, ran to the door, threw it open and screamed into the hallway: "No. No. It's a mistake. Tell everybody to come back tomorrow . . . next week. No, make it next year. Olivia de Havilland and Joan Fontaine will be so much better."

"You were quite good, you know. Quite good indeed!" said James Carrington as he and Margaret walked along the deserted Victoria Embankment.

"Control yourself, James. Don't get so carried away," Margaret replied, amused.

"Don't mock me, Margaret. Just because a man my age has all his hair doesn't mean he has all his faculties."

Margaret laughed. "There is nothing old about you, except your intentions, which I suspect are strictly dishonorable."

"Frankly, they weren't until this very minute. But now that you mention it, why not? No fool like an old fool."

Margaret stopped walking. Turning to face James, the wind off the Thames caught her sharply on the cheek. Its bitter cold stung. "Listen, James Carrington. I really find it quite boring and annoying listening to you describe yourself constantly as old. If you must do it, do it around someone else."

"June Allyson would never say such a thing!" he responded with mock injury. Again Margaret laughed, something she found herself doing often with Carrington. She slung her arm through his and continued to stroll away from the Savoy and up past Waterloo Bridge. She felt content and despite the very late hour, not at all tired. The last of the revelers at the Savoy Grill had departed, taking with them only some of the evening's excitement. The ovation at the final curtain was something she would never forget. It had lasted a full ten minutes. And, to look up and see the Royal Box leading the applause had made both her and Carolyn cry. Already Evelyn Randolph, after reading the ecstatic reviews of the normally reserved British press, had announced an extension of the run from its initial three months to mid-July. Their dressing room had been a bedlam of well-wishers and press until Carolyn cleared it for a special moment to be shared just by family. Margaret could still see the halo of wonderment, pride too, each of the children had worn. It was only as they were dressing for the party at the Savoy Grill that Margaret realized James Carrington, not a family member, had been seated in the room as if he belonged there. Somehow, she was bothered and not bothered by his assumption. Which was exactly how she felt at the party later when he acted as if he were her date when he was not. It wasn't in what he said; although it was, and it wasn't precisely in what he did; although it was that, too. James Carrington was just *there*, and at that awkward moment, he had saved several people from embarrassment. Had he known? Had John told him anything of her life? Margaret didn't know. But coincidences can not only be incredible, but strain one's credulity.

She had been standing at the buffet tables watching as Garland heaped her plate with Colchester oysters, Aylesbury duckling, and Beluga caviar, explaining to her and Michael Wilding that if Picasso could have his blue periods why not she her fat ones, when there was a commotion at the Grill's entrance. The whir of white silk and sable flying toward Carolyn, carrying with her the eyes or the camera of every single person in the room, was Dietrich. But it was not she Margaret saw but the man directly behind her. His eyes locked with hers. His head tilted in acknowledgment and then he moved on to greet Carolyn and John. Although he never approached her, Margaret could feel his presence in the room. Wherever she stood and whenever she looked up, his eyes were there even though he was not. Garland said nothing, but from the way she clasped Margaret just under the arm and steered her toward Noel Coward and Crew, as she lovingly referred to her "audience," Margaret could tell she understood the situation. Strangely, Margaret felt James Carrington did too. He was at her side, introducing himself as a family friend and acting most comfortable in a show business setting, which she found surprising for a banker. Eventually, Killerbrew approached the table where she had seated herself with Carrington, Ralph Richardson, and John Gielgud. He raised his champagne glass and said: "Well done, Margaret!" and left. The lack of warmth in his voice had chilled her to the core.

"Franklin," called Carrington to the back of Killerbrew. "I daresay if you want my bank's cooperation in financing your postwar version of the European theatre, you damn well should say hello."

"Jimmy? Jimmy Carrington? What the hell are you doing here?" Killerbrew said as he turned, smiling warmly at the man. "I thought they lock you up at night with the rest of the valuables in the Morgan vault."

"Won't you sit with us," asked Carrington politely. "Perhaps you and Margaret would like to talk."

It had been an odd thing for Carrington to say, Margaret realized. Killerbrew's response, however, seemed to please the banker.

"No. We've said it all. See you in Paris Monday, Jimmy. Good-night, Margaret. Good-night, all."

And he was gone.

As she and Carrington continued to walk along the Embankment, Margaret, snuggling deeper into her full-length, well-traveled sable, looked at her escort's face as it appeared under moon and lamplight. He must have been quite handsome once, she thought. Now he was distinguished-looking. He had turned up the black velvet collar on his Chesterfield to ward off the wind that had whipped his carefully parted salt-and-pepper hair into a rather attractive mass of disarray. She liked his eyes best. They were clear although dark. There wasn't a hint of guile or deceit in them. And unlike most Englishmen, he was not thin-lipped, just thin.

"What do you know about Franklin Killerbrew?" she asked.

"That he is a shrewd businessman about to enter the European market by opening a chain of movie theatres if we or some other bank will lend him the financing."

"Surely he has enough money of his own to do that," said Margaret.

"A shrewd businessman never uses his own money, Margaret."

"What else do you know about him?" Margaret asked as she sat on one of the benches overlooking the Thames. The entire setting of the Embankment and its vistas of the city reminded her of Brooklyn Heights and the walk she once took along the Promenade.

"Don't you think it's rather chilly for you to be sitting?" asked Carrington.

"Don't you think you might answer my question?" Margaret asked as she lifted her black crepe gown so that it wouldn't collect still more dirt from the pavement than it already had accumulated as they had strolled along.

"Actually, I know his wife much better. She, too, is quite the shrewd businesswoman. She has a great many holdings in Europe. Now stop looking at me that way. It doesn't matter what *else*, as you put it, I might know about Franklin Killerbrew or to be more precise, about Franklin Killerbrew and you. Whatever I didn't know, I learned tonight. He, or again to be precise, you—meaning the two of you—are none of my business. Frankly, on a business level, I like the man immensely. That *is* my business. Do you still have business with him, Margaret?" asked Carrington, the meaning of his question very clear.

"No. I've closed out my account," said Margaret emphatically.

"Good show! Now perhaps, if you will allow it, we can invest your assets properly," said Carrington. As Margaret stared at him in surprise, he added, "By the by, are you aware it's nearing four in the morning? Why don't we have some breakfast somewhere? Kippers and cupcakes. I've always wanted to have such a treat."

"Shouldn't you be getting some sleep?" asked Margaret.

"My dear girl, certainly you know we older folks don't require the same amount of sleep we used to. Just give us a double shot of prune juice and we can keep going for days. Figuratively and literally," added Carrington with a twinkle in his eyes that made Margaret feel warm deep down inside.

When James Philip Carrington returned to his apartment on the Ile Saint-Louis late Sunday night, it was with a mixture of sadness and loneliness. At forty-seven, Carrington had no illusions about himself. He knew that to a certain kind of woman, who might not be Deirdre but who would replicate her in all other ways, he was considered Quite-the-Catch. He was not interested in that kind of woman. James Carrington did not believe for a second that he would fall in love at his stage of life. He also didn't believe a woman like Margaret Tiernan would find him anything more than a good long-range investment. That didn't appeal to him either. He had been

317

enough of an investment for Deirdre. She already had the house in Oxford, the Bentley, the AT&T stock . . . and her jewelry bought with his money. So much for investments that paid off for others, he had decided. Not that his hadn't been a perfectly civilized divorce. Deirdre had been exceedingly polite. As she said when she made her final intentions known, "James, you are such a nice man. You've always been such a nice man. I should be marrying you now when most women my age are ready for a nice man. But, I married you at twenty-one and sacrificed exciting for nice. I want now what I didn't have then, James," she explained.

He had understood. He was not angry with her. As he persistently had explained to Margaret, Deirdre had never intended to be unkind. She just wanted excitement. He was still contemplating Margaret's reply: "And what about you, James? Don't you want some excitement?"

He remembered how he had taken her hand and how she had allowed him to hold it as he explained. "I realize to equate banking with acting is something no one in your profession could understand, but, Margaret, I dearly love my work. Finance fascinates me. Money management is a marvel. The making of money per se means nothing to me as I'm comfortably fixed for life. But money, as a game, that's exciting and exacting! Our friend Killerbrew understands that; his wife, even more. She has a great many European investments and will double her money in a very few years. That I helped her with this excites me, Margaret."

She listened and understood without understanding banking at all. But still she pursued her thought. "But what other than work is exciting to you?" He looked at her carefully, calculating whether she could be trusted with information he deemed more confidential and important than what GM or IBM was planning for the future.

"I am not a poetic man. Although I love thoughts . . . words, I am not very good at expressing myself, but I love the spring. I like walking along the Seine or the Thames just before the city awakens. I enjoy strolling through Paris in August when everyone is away on vacation. I like reading the *Sunday Times* and dawdling over breakfast. I enjoy boating and fishing and having a few friends in for dinner. I'm afraid," he concluded with a heavy sigh, "Deirdre was right. Not very exciting and yet . . . now that I have it, I will change it for no one."

She heard his declaration and said nothing. He remembered that as he sat now in his living room looking at and feeling its heaviness. How he hated its furnishings, done more by Deirdre for others than for themselves. All that heavy tapestry collecting dust along with compliments. And draperies that shut out light and noise—or life itself. Awful heavy Napoleonic furniture which Deirdre so proudly paid fortunes for when she discovered it in "out-of-the-way" antique shops that were deliberately *in the way* along Saint Germain des Prés. The initial *N* surmounted by a laurel wreath and an imperial eagle were not his idea of warmth and charm. But he had accepted that a home was a woman's domain, to be done with as she saw fit. And Deirdre had made it so altogether clear that giving up her cherished home in London—the one that looked exactly like this apartment in its heaviness—was a terrible, jolting experience. To rent *their* home to strangers! And worse, so much worse, when those strangers turned out to be *actors*, American actors, named Carolyn Tiernan. Dreadful. Deirdre was heartbroken and vowed that even if he were transferred back to London, she would never live in the Rutland Street house again. Not now that it had been made impure by others. What's more, she resented Evelyn Randolph for having suggested Carolyn Tiernan as a possible occupant. They should have waited for someone more suitable, she insisted.

It was very strange, thought Carrington, coming to a realization after so many years of marriage and then months of pining for what once was but now wasn't, that he didn't like his ex-wife very much. What he had missed, he now saw, was marriage itself. He did not like being single. He hated rattling around every elegant aspect of his gilded, paneled, and mural-ceilinged apartment. Evelyn had suggested he move and said so at the dinner party she had given for the second-night opening when the Tiernan sisters had reversed roles in *Electra*. But he thought it would be easier to throw out the furniture as he threw open the windows and let light back into the room and his life.

Oh, that dinner party of Evelyn's, he thought as he lit his pipe. A sit-down dinner for sixteen. Only Evelyn could do that at a table meant for twelve. She had not seated him next to Margaret, who seemed surprised and annoyed to see him, but next to yet another "available" Englishwoman who owned an art gallery and a stable of horses, to which, Carrington was

319

certain, she bore an uncanny resemblance. She even whinnied when she laughed. Later, over demitasse, Margaret asked why he hadn't mentioned he had been invited when they were together the previous evening. He had not seen the necessity, he replied. She reacted angrily. "How foolish of me to have thought you might have wanted to be my escort," she said and then flounced away. He followed, not knowing quite what to say or do. He apologized and said what was on his mind: that he hadn't thought she would care to accompany him. She looked at him and said, "Perhaps I was wrong, James. Maybe you are too old. Certainly that last statement gives every sign of senility setting in." Again he was confused by her anger. Not knowing what else to do, he asked if he could see her home. She declined, saying she had no wish to ruin his evening as hers had to be cut short due to her exhaustion. But she invited him to have tea with her and Carolyn between performances tomorrow and if he were not leaving early Sunday for Paris, to join the family then at Carolyn's for Sunday afternoon dinner. Cheerfully, he accepted both invitations.

He had not known the traditional Sunday family dinner in many years. In many of the homes to which he and Deirdre had been invited, the children ate separately in a different room and time. Not at the Ollsons', where around the circular dining table, the children threw food and insults at one another. He could see they were performing for him, and Carolyn's outrage made their performance that much more vigorous and, for him, enjoyable. How well he remembered when he used to send his own children off to their separate rooms until they could learn to behave properly. He had to suppress his own laughter when each child returned, looking appropriately contrite, only to fall away in giggles within minutes.

James Carrington envied John Ollson, although he was well aware there was more to a marriage than ever met the public eye. Still, his wife was a beauty and most naturally displayed a lovingness toward Ollson that Carrington was particularly sensitive toward these days. And the girl . . . Marti, a dear who so obviously wanted everyone to be together. Even Vinnie, who Margaret had explained was a troublesome child at times, had been particularly playful. Still, the boy had looked meanly at him when he took Marga-

320

ret for a walk in Hyde Park between the Beef Wellington and the dessert.

It was a nice family. It had been a nice day and a good weekend. Its cheer would warm him through the night, but the remainder of the week would be twice as chilly because of it.

Carolyn panicked when the doorbell rang. You're being foolish, she told herself. It's only John.

Only John indeed. Only my whole life perhaps. Only a time for talking. At his insistence.

She had been in no hurry, enjoying both her success on the London stage and her new romance. And that's what it had been—a new romance with an old husband. They had been "re-courting" with after-theatre dinners, afternoon strolls, and afterward, lovemaking. He had been treating her very differently. But perhaps that was the central difference between men and women. Even his relationship with the children had improved, although he was hardly ever in London because of his assignments, and even when he was, she had still not allowed him to move into the house. This was now the bone of contention between them; the reason he was there this day, now pounding on the lion's-head knocker on the heavy mahogany front door that complemented the red brick of the Regency townhouse.

"I thought you had run off with Rex Harrison," he said when she finally opened the door.

Good! He is as nervous as I am, thought Carolyn as she led him into the living room which so much resembled the Murray Hill townhouse her mother had decorated. When he was seated, she offered him tea.

"Scotch and soda will be fine," he replied.

"At this hour?" she asked, regretting her question as soon as it escaped her thoughts. He answered with a long, studying look which sent her to the liquor cabinet to fix his drink. "I was at school today," she began nervously, "some slight problem with Marti. Her teachers say she shows more interest in boys than she does in her books. Nothing drastic like flirting, just tomboy stuff. If only she would work up to her potential. She tests in the top ten percent of her class, you know. There is no such problem with your son, however, you'll be happy to learn. Head of the class. Strange, isn't it? Two children, twins, and yet so different."

321

"You're doing it, you know," said John as he sipped from his glass. "You're doing exactly what you've always done—put the children before us. Next you'll start talking about Margaret or the grosses at the theatre."

"Well, I know you have this tendency to forget but they are your children!" said Carolyn nastily, "although I'm sure if you went upstairs right now and woke John Junior, he'd greet you with a scream of terror rather than a smile of recognition."

The silence between them was tense. Carolyn used it to think. Finally she asked: "Have I really done that? Have I put the children before you? And even if I have, don't all mothers do that?"

"I don't care what all mothers do," said John, "or how their husbands react. I am telling you I do not want the leftovers in your life!"

"And just what have I in yours?" said Carolyn, literally rising as her voice rose to the attack.

"What the hell are you talking about? Whose idea was it I leave Killerbrew Studios and produce for you?"

"I mean since the war. Ever since you've come home, who has come first in your life?"

"Me! Dammit. And that's how it should be and how it's going to remain," said John angrily. "And that's how it should be for you."

"No. Wrong! That's not how it is for any mother."

"That's bullshit!" said John.

"Don't get vulgar in my home," demanded Carolyn, the tone of her voice annoying even to her.

"More bullshit. You can be so full of it. Grow up, Carolyn. Vulgarity is like obscenity—neither has anything to do with words. I've been telling you that for three years now."

"Oh, yes, I know," said Carolyn, as she walked about the room. "It's killing people that's obscene. It's concentration camps and mass murder. It's how the white American army treated Negroes in that same army during a war that supposedly united the country. Yes, I know. God knows I know. You've told me often enough. Well, my dear husband, how about the way you've treated me and your children? Hasn't that been obscene? Your daughter feels that because you leave her she must be lacking something and your son doesn't really give a damn one way or the other. Have you thought of the price they may pay one day for *your* war and for ours? Either you're married, John, or you're not. Children don't

322

understand in-between. Or in your case, a father who is there when it is convenient for him."

"You're making me the villain, dammit. Tell them the truth and they'll respond properly."

"And just when did you become an expert on children, John? And how? By osmosis? How could you know what it means to be a father when you never had one yourself? And maybe that's part of the problem. How can you give when you've never been given to?"

"I didn't come here to fight," said John. "I came to talk."

"Oh, I *am* sorry," said Carolyn, dripping sarcasm. "But you see, I didn't preplan how I would react. No one gave your silly, dull wife a script or directions to go with the scene. And if they had, I'd have torn it up. This is strictly ad lib, off the cuff, and straight stuff."

"Now if you could do that with all the crap you've been force-fed all your life, we might just get a marriage together," John said attacking. "All that bullshit you've been taught by the church and which you've practiced, has nothing to do with reality. And don't you give me that cautionary-Carolyn look. This isn't blasphemy; it's life. Get that through your head now or we have no place further to go."

"I'm listening," said Carolyn as she sat herself down in a wing chair facing John.

"Not with that look on your puss. You're not listening, you're already too busy defending. You clear your mind of all that Catholic crap or no dice."

When he saw she was as there as it was possible for her to be he continued. "I want a wife who is also a woman and then a mother. I see nothing wrong in that request. I'm not asking you to give up the children for me but I'm demanding you not give me up for them. I am all too aware I've left a lot to be desired as a father. You were right: I had nothing to give them. I was too resentful. Of too many things. The war changed me. We both know that. But, only one of us seems to realize it changed me for the better. Carolyn, so many died in the war, but I was born in it. I will never again be the man I was. You either live with that knowledge or we divorce."

"I will never divorce you!" said Carolyn vehemently.

"Then I will divorce you. Make no mistake about that. Excommunication is just a word invented by people in power to retain that power over powerless people. When I say I will divorce you it is not a threat but, as our friend James

Carrington would say in his business, a statement of purpose. I didn't get born to die in my marriage. I won't be a James Carrington, a man who withered away in his marriage. But let's stick to us and our purpose. I have never objected to your work. You know that. Actually, I'm proud of you and what you've accomplished. You're good. So damn good that every time I see you work it gets me right in the gut. Well, that's how I'm beginning to feel about my work. Just as you wouldn't quit, I wouldn't . . . can't. It's me, now. It's what I do best. It's the best part of me. The difference between us is: you could slow down now while I'm just shifting into high gear, accelerating. It's not just the articles or the film or the book I'm about to do. No, it's all those things three times over again and then some. Carolyn, I'm never going to just observe, read about, life again. It was awful doing that. It's awful because then, when it topples around you, you have the guilt of having done nothing. But when you participate, when you can do what you must do—talk out about what you have seen, what you think and feel, then, *then* there is a life. Shit! You either understand what I'm saying or not. I have no further words to explain it. My work is what you see before you. I'll be pursuing it as I pursue myself the rest of my life. That means traveling, experiencing, moving about. You can either live with that or you can't. Only you can decide. But, if we are to remain married, you must understand and accept just what I have understood and accepted about you from the day we met."

John drained his drink and rose from his chair. He started for the liquor cabinet but stopped midway to look at Carolyn, and continued. "I was a damn good father before the war. I can be a good father, although an unusual one I admit, again. But you must remember I was a child when we married. Not chronologically but emotionally. I was a child until a year or so ago. Sorry about that. I married you under false pretenses. I looked and acted like a grown man but I wasn't. I didn't want John Junior because I first had to raise myself, be my own baby. I needed all the nurturing for me then. And I also felt that so much had been taken from me in the war that I had nothing to give him. I don't feel that way now. In fact, I feel I can probably give him more now than most fathers can ever give their sons. Now, I know you feel other men came through the war and returned intact, husbands and fathers as they were before. But I am not other men. I am me. I love my children in my own way. It's not a Norman Rockwell pretty-picture way but it is mine."

"What you are saying," said Carolyn dully, "is that you will not change."

"No. I am saying I have changed. That's the point. And now you must decide if you want to, and can, live with those changes. Carolyn, I'll be changing the rest of my life now. Why can't that be true of you?"

"What do you mean?" asked Carolyn, defensiveness again in her voice.

"You have been exposed to all kinds of people, life-styles, and still you persist in this good-little-Catholic-girl notion. Carolyn, I *do* believe in God. And I believe He created us—all parts of us—to use. And to enjoy. I am speaking of our bodies. They are not to be denied. How can you believe sex is strictly for procreation, particularly when what we've been doing these past weeks has hardly been what anyone would call *procreating*. We have been having sex."

Suddenly, Carolyn was crying. "Funny," she said in stifled tones, "I thought we were making love."

On his knees by her side, John took both of Carolyn's hands in his. "We were! Don't you see that? We were. And making love is having sex. Not always; sometimes they're not one and the same, but they can be. And it's okay. Because I love you. Yes, I do. You know that. I love you even for the things I dislike about you. Like your Catholicism, or your cockeyed view of it.

"You are such a good person, Carolyn. Truly good. I saw that the first time I ever saw you that day at the train station. Your beauty and your goodness. You care about those you love. What's more, you're there for them. Not many people can do that. But you can't see beyond your own nose and our own family. Carolyn, dearest, listen to me. There's a world out there that needs your love and your caring. There are babies born to Catholic mothers who can't feed themselves, let alone more children. What about those babies, Carolyn? What about understanding why they are born? You perform on a stage above rows and rows of people. But you don't live among those people. I must. And I must give them a voice, a protest, words to speak so others may listen. I know that sounds very grandiose but I mean it."

John was stroking Carolyn's hair as her head rested on his shoulder. "I want you to be my wife and my woman. I want

325

us to make love when we feel like it, and *how* we feel like it, and not as some organization prescribes. Carolyn, I learned one thing in those camps. Life is now. I'm not preaching hedonism but living. Nor am I saying one should live without consequence. I'm not that kind of person. But I believe in the guilt of omission more than I do in any other form of guilt. And sex, or lovemaking, when it is denied between two people who love is an act of omission. I will not have that in my life. I need you, Carolyn. Are you listening? Do you know what I'm saying? *I need you.* Not for 'fucking,' Carolyn. Not for that dreaded, hated word. I can do that with anyone. But I need *you* for all that you are and I need you to want me. Totally. Wholly. Completely."

"I do! I always have," said Carolyn, almost pleading to be believed.

"Have you ever had an orgasm, Carolyn?"

The question stunned her. "I don't know what you mean," she said, confused.

"An orgasm. Have you ever come during our lovemaking?"

Mentally, Carolyn tried to sort through all Margaret had told her and all she had absorbed in pulp fiction. Rushing waters, cascading rocks upon beaches, rolling thunder. Were these euphemisms for an orgasm?

"I'm not sure," she finally answered.

"Carolyn, if you had one, you'd know it," said John. "An orgasm does not require any guesswork. Women do have them. Why not you? Why are you depriving yourself?"

"Who in God's name made you an expert on female anatomy?" Carolyn yelled angrily. "How do you know what I don't? Did I miss a particular issue of *Ladies' Home Companion* or *Good Housekeeping* that did a feature on *You and Your Orgasm* that you read? I guess I'm just not up on the latest. I've been too busy with raising three—no, four—children, to keep up with new phenomena."

"It's not new, Carolyn," said John impatiently. "It's as old as the oldest profession itself."

"A bad analogy, John. I'm not your whore."

"Ah, that you would be! What could be wrong in that?"

"For me? Everything!" Carolyn said angrily. "Now that I've listened to you, it's your turn to listen to me. 'Cause God knows for years I've listened to everyone else. To you. To Margaret. Even to Augie. Everyone telling me each in his or her own way how life is for living. God, of all the boring

326

clichés that's the worst! What else is life for? But you all insist I'm not living mine and if I am, I'm living it wrong. Well, perhaps so . . . for you, for them. But maybe not for me. Why is it I can accept how each of you decides to live? My sister moves her life into a beach house with a man who cannot or will not marry her. My aunt moves her life into an apartment with a man who also cannot marry her. Why is it I can understand and accept how they live even though it is foreign to me and what I believe in, but they can't do the same for me? Why would you all change me? What is it *I* threaten in all of you? Why is it, John, you and everyone else are so certain that what I feel, what I believe in, is no longer applicable in this day and age? Perhaps you are all right in what you believe, but it is what *I* believe that matters to me.

"Now certainly, John," said Carolyn as she circled his chair like a cat about to pounce on its prey, "you, of all people, should understand that. You, who must now live as you see fit. John, here's what is so strange. I agree. You should. But don't you therefore agree that so should I? Listen and listen good, John. I refuse to change to suit you or our marriage. Your face tells me that bit of news surprises you. It would have surprised me a few months back too. But you are not the only one who has changed.

"During the war, John, when you were missing and I didn't know if you were alive or dead, I'd lie awake nights wondering what I would do without you—how I'd survive. I couldn't imagine what life would be like if you didn't return. My need for you was that enormous. Well, then you did return, only you didn't. I mean, your body did but not the person. And I was as alone as I had been when I didn't know where you were or how you were. For a while, I clung to the shell that was the man I had married. But, John, this past year or so, when you began your changes, your new life—one you never bothered to ask me to join—I didn't fall apart or die. And then, when I read your script and saw how you viewed me, well . . . that saved me from becoming a Madge Carter. You, John, without being aware of it, helped me to change my life. In coming to London, in choosing to do this play, to live in this house, I've proven to myself—and that's all that matters—that not only can I survive without you but I can do it quite nicely."

Carolyn paused long enough in her pacing to face John as he sat spellbound in his chair listening to her. "You've been a

327

selfish bastard. Yes, bastard. And frankly, I'm tired of being—or of having been, strictly past tense—the little woman waiting for you till you found yourself. It would seem, John, we have both found ourselves to some extent and like you, I have found *me* a remarkable and rather exciting discovery. With still a great deal more excavating to do. It is absolutely wonderful not to live in fear anymore.

"Now, on to what has always stood between us in our marriage, or more precisely in our bed. You knew when you married me who I was. I tried to change. Yes, I have, although I'm sure that surprises you. I am not as stupid as you wrote me to be in your script, John," said Carolyn, with tears once again burning in her eyes. "Don't you think I can see sex as an act of love? Don't you think I can feel how it need not have anything to do with procreation? Are you so naïve as to think every time I am with you I am thinking of having a baby? All right, I have never had this thing you call an orgasm. It's not my fault. But I have had joyous feelings while we have been in bed. Yes, I have felt them and because I have, I have also been tortured by what is called 'fleshly pleasures.' They contradict all I've been taught regarding right and wrong, all I have held dear to me. I have tried to bend. And it's been hard for me. And you just might recognize that and give me credit for having tried. I do wish I could be more casual, more 'fun-loving' in bed. But I do not wish to be your whore. I am not that woman, John. Nor will I ever be."

Carolyn was trembling from head to toe. It was the longest she had ever spoken without having had the words written out for her in script form. She felt naked, vulnerable, and yet freer than she had ever been before. John was smiling at her and unless she was mistaken there was a look of pride on his face.

"Boy, do we have troubles ahead of us," he said, not looking the least bit troubled. "If we get back together, we'll both have to compromise . . . a lot. But I said it before and it bears repeating right now. I love you, Carolyn. Frankly, up until this moment, I never realized quite how much and all the reasons why. I'll fight for us if you will."

"Dammit, John Ollson," said Carolyn, fresh tears flooding her eyes. "You forget I'm Irish, so prepare yourself for the biggest and best damned fight you've ever had. Because now that I need you less, my friend, I love you more. Much,

much more. And John, one last thing: I'm very proud of you."

The phone was ringing even as the bellman brought Margaret's luggage into her bedroom. It was still ringing as she dug into the bottom of her purse to find several shillings for his tip. It stopped ringing just as he bowed his way out the front door. As she reentered her bedroom, discarding clothes along the way, the phone rang again. Ignoring it, she entered the bathroom and drowned out the phone's incessant peal with the water she sent rushing with a flick of her wrist into the oversized bathtub the Savoy provided its guests. Margaret was sure the caller was Evelyn Randolph seeking to put her mind to rest. The producer had been greatly opposed to Margaret's two-day holiday in Paris.

"Suppose the weather is bad and planes can't take off or land? What then?" she had asked, reasonably worried. Evelyn had not been at all reassured when Margaret avowed she would swim the Channel if necessary to return by curtain time Monday night.

Margaret needed the bath to both relax and revive her. Not that the hour-plus flight from Paris had been exhausting but the two days had. More so emotionally than physically. James Philip Carrington was not to be taken as a "moment's madness." Nor was he a "merry madcap." He had proposed his April in Paris holiday on the promise she would find Paris beautiful. It was not mentioned but was naturally assumed she would stay with him, something Margaret had yet to do in any sense of the word.

From the first, she had doubts. As late as Sunday morning at the London airport, she thought to cancel the trip. As she stood by the phones, ready to call before he left to meet her at the airport, she asked herself why it was easier to spend a weekend with a man one wasn't interested in than with a man with whom one was. The answer had her first on line to board the plane. Scared of involvement or not, she would go.

Only Carolyn knew of her whereabouts although Evelyn Randolph certainly suspected. Margaret, other than with Carolyn, who was openly delighted with Carrington, was very protective of her relationship with Carrington. Whenever he visited London, he made it known to those who asked, it was on bank business. Since neither he nor Margaret was in the habit of public displays of affection or frequenting the more popular or notorious night spots, their relationship went un-noticed by the usually very suspicious British press.

It had almost gone unnoticed by Margaret. "He's crept up on me," she said to Carolyn when discussing him a few weeks before the Paris trip. Carolyn's response had surprised her. "Don't be sure if the reverse isn't also true." He had laughed when she told him this. He laughed often when with her. At little things. In little laughs. Nothing ever hearty or totally consuming. Like their lovemaking. At first, she had been very disappointed. Upset, she had even phoned Carolyn and said somewhat sadly, "The earth doesn't move, nor does the goddamn bed sometimes." It must be his age, she concluded at first. She learned otherwise. It was just his style and she was not used to a man who took his time, and hers, to make love gently and lovingly if not passionately.

She hated herself for comparing him to Franklin Killerbrew; to his hard-muscled body and the way he had used it force-fully and totally in bed. Yet she found a comfort with Carring-ton that was satisfying in a way she had never before experi-enced. He was *there*, totally, and there was no rushing off to be with another for the sake of business or propriety. He was without complications. She was his ties. And he was thought-ful. When she had complained of feeling like an interloper in the Ile Saint-Louis apartment, he had packed his bags and hers and moved them to a charming little hotel on the Left Bank overlooking the Seine. He had shown her his Paris and he had shown her lovemaking when it followed a mood, a feeling, rather than an animal urge.

On his part, James Carrington was oddly not nervous. He felt very practical about "the affair." Either they wanted the same things or they did not. The weekend might answer these questions, or at least begin to. A realist, James Carring-ton, although he hoped Margaret would fall in love with Paris, treasured no such hope that she would also fall in love with him. It would be enough if she were "fond" and "caring" and "respectful." At least that's what he told himself and largely believed.

On Monday, he took her to the Place Vendôme and into number 14 where La Banque Morgan was located just left of the Ministry of Justice and a door down from the Ritz Hotel. She was suitably impressed by the parquet floors, the highly polished-till-it-shone wood counter with the marble insert and its series of gilded glass cages, behind which stood the formally dressed tellers. She took note of vases filled with freshly cut flowers. Introducing her as Margaret Tiernan, a prospective investor, he took her upstairs where it was so hushed, respectfully quiet, she could hear the parquet floors creak as she walked. Carrington's office was next to the president, Nelson Jay. It, too, suitably impressed her. A Louis XV desk stood at one end of a huge, wood-paneled room with tall windows from which hung heavy green draperies. The large marble fireplace was aglow with a freshly made fire the flicker of which was caught and refracted by the chandelier overhead.

When he was satisfied that she had glimpsed his life, he whisked her out of the bank, past Elizabeth Arden and Schiaparelli, and into Van Cleef & Arpels where, over her objections, he bought her a tiny grasshopper made of emeralds. She felt anxious from the moment he clipped it to the lapel of the black Dior suit she had worn that day. It was not an engagement ring but it was a link, a tie of some sort. It disturbed her. Throughout the rest of the morning, as they walked from the Place Vendôme to the Place de la Concorde, past the Tuilleries and the Louvre and over to the Left Bank, where despite the chill April wind they sat out front of Les Deux Magots and watched Paris on parade, she still felt a gnawing discomfort.

What is it I want? Margaret asked herself querulously as the phone rang again. She again drowned out its insistent ring by adding more hot water to the tub. The two days had been basically serene, safe, and sane. There was a moment when she had felt: this is what it would be like to be married. That, too, had unnerved her. "Your discomfort, Margaret Tiernan, is strictly self-made," she said aloud as she soaped herself for the fourth time. "And you had better understand and solve it quickly or give up the man and the relationship." She considered what she had just said and then added: "The hell with that. Haste makes waste. Take your time, Margaret. Fools rush in and in the past so did you. Now be a wise man and have a little fear."

She thought about Carrington and how he had acted. Again, the word *there* flashed through her mind. In quiet but very definite ways, *there*. She thought about his insistence that *should* she—and that was nice; he was taking nothing for granted—should she decide to visit again, she was to bring Vinnie. From the way he had said it, she knew it was not a gesture but a condition, a demand even. He was saying subtly that he was prepared for that responsibility should they strike a responsible bargain. Vinnie was not to be treated as excess baggage. The problem, if there was to be one, would not be with Carrington but with her son. She remembered how his face had remained impassive when she told him where she was going and why. Now, as she lay in the tub reflecting on that moment, she wondered if she had been right to be so honest. Yes, she decided. Given her past problems with Vinnie, henceforth there would be no lies and he would handle what he could. What he could not, they would work out. Or try to.

She suddenly remembered it had bothered her that he had shown no concern or interest in her plans. She thought then he was more excited about his own weekend, which would be spent with his Uncle John and Thomas and Marti at Brighton. But now, knowing what an actor Vinnie could be, she was no longer certain. She did recall that he expressed more disappointment about his Aunt Carolynnie remaining at home with John Jr. than he did about her going off to Paris. Figuring Vinnie was never easy and to guess about any of his reactions was foolhardy, she decided, just as her eye caught the face of the wristwatch she had purposely placed on the sink's edge so she could check the time. Five-thirty. Best to dress and leave for the theatre. Reluctantly, she left the warm safety of the tub and wrapped herself in a bath towel. Again the phone rang. Still wet, she ran to it in the living room where her first words when she lifted the receiver from its cradle were: "Yes, Evelyn, I'm home and the show must go on. And it will!"

"Where have you been? I've been calling you for hours!" said Carolyn impatiently. "Hours, do you hear?"

"Is anything wrong?" Margaret asked, alarmed.

"Don't tell me you haven't opened your mail! Margaret. Open your mail. Now. Open it. Do you hear?"

Carolyn's hysteria took Margaret to the letters piled on her desk where the maid always placed them. The various envelopes with their scrawled "Margaret Tiernan's" looked remarkably like other fan mail. Then came the very white invitation-like envelope. Using her thumbnail, she opened it. It was the Royal Crest embossed on the top that caught her eye first. Then, the entire six-by-four-inch, white-on-white card came into focus. Signed by the Lord Chamberlain, the words were . . . commanded by His Majesty . . . and Margaret Tiernan & Guest.

"Holy shit, it's an invitation to meet the goddamn King and Queen of England!" screamed Margaret. "Carolyn, Carolyn, I'm coming," she yelled toward the phone. "Carolyn, my God, we're being presented at court," she gasped to her sister.

"Not if the Royal Family could hear how eloquently you express your pleasure. The last thing they're looking for is another royal scandal," said Carolyn coolly.

"Listen, you old fart, we, us, you and me—Royal Scandal and Royal Pain in the Ass—are invited to meet the King and Queen. What do we wear? What do we do? What do you say: Hiya Queen, love your crown."

"That's why I called," said Carolyn, excitement gathering in her voice. "We'll need clothes . . ."

"Yes, absolutely," interrupted Margaret. "Can't go bare-ass."

"And protocol," added Carolyn.

"I'll ring Room Service and have them send it up."

"Would you stop that," screamed Carolyn. "We are meeting the Queen."

"And it's a *her* and not a him. What a switch in my life-style!"

"Can't you be serious?" asked Carolyn.

"No. Not for a minute. Lynnie, can you just hear Mama?"

"You bet I can. She's saying right this minute she hopes we won't talk to any strange men and she's asking God not to let her daughters make damned fools of themselves. Margaret! Margaret Tiernan! We are going to the palace. To the ball!"

"I'll bet you a year's wages, Lynnie, you fall flat on your pratt when you curtsy. You always were a klutz."

Augusta Monahan was sniffling as she read the *New York Times*.

"Gussie, either cry or blow your nose but that noise is driving me nuts," Arthur Abel said as he sat next to Augusta on the couch, looking at the newspaper over her shoulder. The dateline was May 14 and Augusta was looking at the AP photo and story of Carolyn and Margaret being presented to King George, Queen Elizabeth, and Queen Mary.

"I'm just so proud," said Augusta, her voice wavery and her eyes wet.

"I wish I could have taken you there," Abel said.

Augusta put down the paper and looked at the man many thought to be her husband and just as many knew to be her lover. "You've taken me to far better places and don't you forget that, sir. They've been to the palace but I," said Augusta, giving Abel's thigh a squeeze as she eyed him lecherously, "have been to Paradise."

The living room rug was covered with newspapers spread about Marti and Vinnie, opened to the coverage of the previous day's presentation at court. "I don't see what's the big deal," said Thomas, impatient with the talk that had been turning the Rutland Street house upside down. "It's not like they're real or anything."

"What are you talking about, jerk," said Marti without looking up from *The Times* picture of her mother and aunt.

"We're Americans," explained Thomas. "We don't believe in kings and queens."

"You're so dumb sometimes, Thomas. It's fairies and Santa Claus we don't believe in," sneered Marti. "Kings and queens are for real. We don't have any because we're a democracy."

"Marti, you ever hear of Parliament? England's a democracy, too," corrected Thomas.

"I know that. But it was once a monastery."

"Monarchy, Marti," corrected Thomas. "You mean *monarchy*."

"It doesn't matter what it's called," said Marti, trying to save face. "It's being invited to meet the Royal Family that's important. It's an honor. You," continued Marti, her voice dripping disdain in Thomas's direction, "would only get excited if you were being presented to Joe DiMaggio."

"This picture of your mother stinks," interrupted Vinnie. He was squinting at the photo of Carolyn as he lay flat on his stomach on the carpeted hardwood floors. "She's either got the sun in her eyes or a bad case of cramps."

"It can't be the sun," said Thomas as he bent down to look over Vinnie's shoulder at the picture. "The reception was held indoors . . . in the palace staterooms."

"What are staterooms?" asked Marti.

No one answered.

"They are magnificent, out-of-a-fairy-tale rooms that could only be in a palace," answered Carolyn as she entered the

334

room, having overheard the children from the kitchen where she was supervising the evening's menu.

"Come on, Mama, tell us about it," begged Marti.

"Again? You've already heard it a dozen times."

"So what's one more? C'mon, Aunt Carolynnie," urged Vinnie.

"All right," said Carolyn as she wiped her hands on her gingham apron and sat herself on one of the blue-and-gray-striped damask side chairs that matched and flanked the upholstered sofa. "Well, you all saw the silver Rolls-Royce that drove us to Buckingham Palace. Oh my, no matter how many times I say the words I keep getting excited. Buckingham Palace! And those huge black and gold gates—you know, the ones we saw leading into the outer courtyard where we watched the changing of the guard. Gorgeous. Just gorgeous. And I'll never forget the view of the palace from the car's windows. All that white stone and those tall windows. As I recall, we had to pass through these arches first to reach it, but I'm not certain. I do remember, however, being helped from the car by a liveried attendant and that we had to give our personal card—that's sort of like a calling card that businessmen have in America—to this man in court uniform.

"Then," Carolyn said, leaning back in her chair, her eyes closed in remembrance, "we were in this hall . . . this incredible grand hall. In fact, it's called the Grand Hall as well it should be. It had this huge domed ceiling and a chandelier . . . well, I'd hate to be the maids assigned to wash its crystals. That's a month's work right there. But how it shone! And all over the place, particularly going up the stairs—or were they just on the walls—damask walls, by the way—these huge gold-framed paintings of past kings and queens wearing velvet and ermine robes. Your Aunt Margaret—your mother, Vinnie—in her true fashion, nearly disgraced us all by asking one of the court attendants if there was a gift shop where she could buy one of the robes as a souvenir. Luckily, the man said nothing. But that didn't stop my sister. Oh, no. We are walking up the Grand Staircase and all along the walls are still more large paintings of the Georgian royalties. Family pictures, in other words. Well, your mother, Vinnie, my sister, takes one long look and in a very loud whisper says: 'And we thought *our* relatives were an ugly bunch!' I could've died."

"Are our relatives ugly?" asked Marti seriously.

"Not your grandparents and certainly not Augusta, but the rest, it's true, did not win prizes for their beauty," admitted Carolyn.

"How come we never see them?" asked Thomas.

"It's like this, kiddo. Sometimes, just because you're family doesn't mean you're peas in the same pod. I mean . . . people don't always match. Like socks. You'd think socks are socks, right? But if you took an argyle and tried to match it to a ribbed or a plain sock, you couldn't. Well, that often happens with family. Some members are argyles, some ribbed, still others are quite plain."

"And which are we?" asked Marti.

Carolyn sighed. "I'm afraid despite my rather clever analogy I can't answer your question as I've never quite thought of myself as a sock *but*," she added, proud of the image that had suddenly come to mind, "I would say we are silk stockings."

"Why don't you just get on with it?" Thomas groaned.

"You mean with the description? Yes, where was I?"

"On the staircase," Thomas reminded her.

"Right. Did I tell you about the huge mirrors in gilded frames that were hanging over these enormous marble mantels which were lined with china urns, figurines, and clocks? Oh, my. Such beauty. And speaking of beauty, you should have seen the people. Didn't the newspapers estimate about twenty-five hundred showed up. Such clothes. Such elegance. Your mother, Vinnie, was gorgeous. Everyone stared at her. Imagine that incredible coloring of hers set off in a pink silk dress, belted at the waist. . . ."

"Ah, c'mon, Ma. Who cares about dresses?" said Thomas petulantly.

". . . and a series of large fan pleats that began at the waist," continued Carolyn unperturbed. "And listen, bub," she added, turning to Thomas, "this is my story and in it, people wear clothes. Now, as I was saying. To top off her whole look, your mother had on the most wonderful wide-brim pink straw hat with a pink rose."

"The papers said you wore a Hartnell," said Vinnie. "Is that like a dress?"

"It is a dress, darling. Norman Hartnell is the name of a designer. And I purposely chose him because, if they were honoring Margaret and me, I felt I should honor them by wearing an Englishman's clothes. If you know what I mean." Carolyn paused. "No, I can see by the look on your faces you

336

don't. Anyway, I wore a Hartnell. A very feminine and fussy floral-print organdy. In soft blue."

"Ma, we saw you when you left the house, remember?" complained Thomas.

"And Queen Elizabeth was in pale blue too, only hers was crepe and trimmed with ostrich feathers. Queen Mary wore cream lace over cream silk and to this moment I couldn't tell you *what* Princess Margaret wore because it defied description! And King George was in his uniform looking much like the Admiral of the Fleet." As soon as she said it, Carolyn exploded with laughter. The children looked to her for an explanation but none was given. Carolyn continued to laugh as she heard Margaret whispering in her ear: "What do you think, Lynnie: When he enters the Royal Chambers and sweeps Elizabeth into his arms and into their love nest, does he beat his chest and proclaim: 'It's down to the sea in ships we go'?"

"Did I tell you about the string band that never stopped playing?" Carolyn asked, picking up the thread of her story. "I never did see exactly where they were located. The palace is *that* huge! But I do know we had gone through a series of rooms. . . . Oh, those rooms. There was one with crimson damask walls and a large but very graceful chandelier hanging from the ceiling. The windows overlooked gorgeous gardens. Then—and my memory is a little fuzzy here as it all happened so quickly—we were in an all-white room. White paneled walls and an elaborately molded ceiling, also in white but with lots of gilt edging. Then we entered a room where everything—I mean *everything*: the walls, the curtains, the carpeting, the upholstery—was all in blue. And my sister—your mother and your aunt—she starts singing—singing in the palace!—'We'll have a blue room, a new room, for two room, where every day's a holiday   .' Well, I thought to die. I'm still not sure she could have been stopped if the string band hadn't suddenly, and mercifully, struck up the English national anthem and the Royal Family entered—except for Elizabeth and Philip, who were off in Paris or about to be."

"Did you stumble when you curtsied?" asked Marti.

"Hadn't I told you? It turned out we didn't have to curtsy so all that worry, and practice, was for nought. A simple handshake was acceptable. Except my hands were sweating and I was afraid to take the Queen's hand until I remembered

337

I was wearing white gloves. I swear I was so nervous that had I not been introduced by the Lord Chamberlain, I don't think I could have spoken my name. But not Margaret. Oh, no. To this minute I haven't any idea what that girl said to the King but after this shocked look passed over his face, he laughed and laughed, causing everyone to look in our direction. And then he repeated whatever it was Margaret had said to the Queen, who didn't look at all amused. Next I knew, we were in the garden drinking tea. After that, I remember nothing, which may or may not be a blessing, depending on what else Margaret Tiernan said or did," added Carolyn with a mock shiver.

"Why didn't Daddy go with you?" asked Marti, watching her mother's face for a reaction that might differ from her words.

Although the question came suddenly, it did not disturb Carolyn. "Your father and I discussed it and we decided it was best he did not go because he felt a very particular way about the manner in which he would be attending if he went. The invitation was addressed to me, to Mrs. John Ollson, and it was in recognition of my work as an actress. Your father felt—and I quite understand this—that if and when he is ever presented in court, it will be in recognition of his work. He does not wish to be known as Mr. Carolyn Tiernan."

"I don't understand that," said Marti, honestly confused.

"And, my darling, I hope you never will. But in a nutshell, it only means a famous woman has to be sensitive to her husband who is just as good but not as famous. Otherwise, his feelings can be hurt."

"Were Daddy's feelings hurt?" asked Marti. "I thought maybe he went away again because he was still mad at us."

"Marti, Daddy was never mad at you. I've told you that and he's told you that. Daddy felt this would be a good time to finish his research so he is in Madrid. The day after tomorrow, he'll be home."

"Home is not the Dorchester Hotel, Mother," said Thomas cuttingly. "Our teacher said a hotel may be a residence for some but it is not a home."

"I said your father will be home the day after tomorrow and I meant *home*, which means *here*, in this house, where he will remain until we all return to New York July twenty-first for the opening of his film."

"Daddy's going to live with us again?" asked Marti, the expression on her face expressing her delight.

"Yes, dear," said Carolyn, beaming back at her daughter.

"Yeah, but for how long this time?" said Thomas, the derision in his voice challenging her statement.

Carolyn turned to face the son whose bitterness toward his father's absences frequently dripped onto her. "Well, that depends, Thomas. If we're all honest and decent and kind to one another, who knows? Let's hope, forever."

"Why can't we go home right after you finish the play July fourth?" asked Marti.

"Your father and I thought it would be nice to take a vacation. Mr. Carrington has offered us his house in Paris and asked us all to come as his guests. It seems the lights of Paris will be turned on again. . . ."

"Paris has had no lights?" asked Thomas, aghast at the notion.

"Paris has had lights, it just hasn't been flood-lit—that means its famous buildings have not been lighted so they can be appreciated at night—since the war. This July, the Eiffel Tower and the Place de la Concorde and the Arc de Triomphe will all be lit and alive again."

"Are just you guys going?" asked Vinnie, trying to look unconcerned.

"We're all going. You, your mother, all of us," said Carolyn, injecting as much cheer and excitement into her voice as she could. "Don't you think that will be fun?"

"Sure . . . for some people," said Vinnie.

"Well, I think if you just try, you'll be one of those people," said Carolyn. "Now, I've got to check on my quiche. It's very hard trying to be a famous actress and a Cordon Bleu cook. But if your Aunt Augusta can make an apple strudel, I can do a quiche."

When the children were alone again among the newspapers, Thomas said, "What do you think, Vin? Do you think Carrington's her boyfriend?"

"Look, I already told you, Thomas, I don't care. But I don't think so. He's an old bag, remember?"

"Well, you're wrong," said Marti with a know-it-all smile. When their attention turned toward her with inquisitive looks, she continued smugly. "I overheard Mama and Aunt Marg talking."

"She means she was listening at the door," sneered Thomas.

339

Marti's face reddened. "I just happened to be passing by," she explained haughtily.

"Shut up and get on with it," demanded Vinnie.

"I can't do both," said Marti annoyingly, "so which shall it be? Should I put up or shut up?"

"Put up and fast or you'll get the worst Indian burn of your life," threatened Vinnie.

"Well, Mama said . . . she thinks Mr. Carrington is ideal, although I don't know what she means by that. Ideal at what? For what? She says he's very well thought of and very well established."

"Like the British Museum," said Vinnie sarcastically.

"Look! Do you want to hear this or not?" asked Marti. Satisfied that both Vinnie and Thomas did, she continued. "Mama also said she thinks Mr. Carrington will make some woman a fine husband. But Aunt Margaret said she wasn't sure whether he was right for her, which is why she didn't invite him to be her escort to the palace and also why she is kind of scared about spending the month of August with him."

"My mother is spending a month with that man?" asked Vinnie, trying not to appear upset.

"Well, that's just it. She isn't sure. She doesn't want Mr. Carrington to get any wrong ideas."

"About what?" asked Thomas.

"About *them*, stupid," continued Marti. "Aunt Margaret says she likes Mr. Carrington a lot but not as much as he likes her. And she said something about not being rushed, and Mama started talking about how there are all kinds of love, and that's when Aunt Margaret started crying and yelled, 'Damn him!' I thought she meant Mr. Carrington, but when Mama said, 'You have to forget him,' I guess she was talking about someone else. And then Mama said, 'You, yourself, said it's over. So give yourself a chance.' "

"At what?" asked Thomas, still confused by much of what Marti was reporting.

"I'm not certain but Aunt Marg was pretty upset and she and Mama cried a lot together."

"What's new about that?" said Thomas. "They're both waterworks."

"Was that it?" asked Vinnie.

"That's all I heard," Marti said.

340

"What happened? Someone catch you at the door?" asked Thomas. "So what do you think, Vinnie?"

"I don't. Why should I? It's got nothing to do with me "

Margaret felt like such a fool crying as if she were being booed instead of cheered by an audience that had been on its feet for five full minutes. Carolyn's arm was around her waist. With her free hand she was waving to their admirers, smiling as if this were the happiest moment of her life. Which it was and wasn't to Margaret. Never before was she so sentimental about a play's closing but never had there been such circumstances that made the production and its six months so distinctly memorable. And it could have continued for another year had not Carolyn insisted on returning with John to New York and to their life there.

It had been a wonderful dream, a fantasy time, thought Margaret as she bowed deeply to the still cheering audience. But what was once real was still all too vivid in her mind. She remembered how she had felt when she first came to London. But I'm not that girl anymore, she suddenly realized as the love of the audience swept onto the stage and held her in its grip. The tears vanished. Gesturing to Carolyn, she stopped to pick up the flowers that had been thrown to them from all parts of the theatre. Giving half to Carolyn, she began to toss them back into the audience. Carolyn followed suit. The roar that greeted their parting gesture was the sound they took with them to their dressing room.

When Carolyn had closed the door behind them, she took Margaret into her arms. "Thank you for the best year of my life," she said softly, "for giving me someplace to go, to think, to be. And to accomplish."

"You did it yourself and you should be as proud of that as I am," said Margaret as she kissed Carolyn lightly and then just as lightly extricated herself from her sister's embrace. Carolyn was glowing, looking her most beautiful and relaxed. At her dressing table, Margaret stared at her reflection. Why wasn't she glowing? Why the tension lines that not even pancake makeup could hide? She wished she could skip Evelyn Randolph's closing-night party. She wished she could be more certain, more confident, of her own wishes. She wished she was not faced with the entire family's going to Paris and to James Carrington's on Tuesday. Suddenly she felt a rush of panic followed by a rush of anger toward Vinnie. He did not want to go, he had informed her. And why hadn't she told him? he had demanded.

Indeed! Why hadn't she? Imagine being afraid of one's own child, but she had good reason to be. James Carrington had courted her son as carefully as he had courted her. But Vinnie had remained unreachable. When Carrington offered him friendship, Vinnie gave him a body but never the entire little person.

"Are you going to marry him?" he had asked in direct confrontation.

"I don't know. He has asked and I'm considering it," Margaret replied.

"Well, remember this: just because you say 'I do' doesn't mean I do, too. I don't want him as a father."

"Why? He has been good to you. He likes you. He wants you to be with us. And Vinnie," Margaret added, shocked at hearing herself pleading, "the man loves me. He is offering me, both of us, a good life."

"I already have a good life and it's not in Paris. If you marry him, I'm staying with my family."

"*I* am your family," Margaret yelled. "*I* am your mother."

"Oh, bullshit! Since when have you been my mother? Aunt Carolyn's been more that than you."

She made a terrible mistake then. Since his words felt like a slap in the face, she slapped his. She then stood there shaking, urgently reminding herself she was the adult and he, the child. Not just a child but *her* child. She looked at him. If her slap had hurt, he was not showing it. Only defiance was etched on his face. His eyes burned as they bore through her. There was a power about him that she had not noticed. But he is only eleven years old! she said to herself, almost as a non sequitur.

"What do you want from me, Vinnie? Tell me. Maybe I can do it and finally put an end to this barrier between us."

Despite the tears he saw in his mother's eyes, Vinnie, without changing a facial muscle, replied, "You know what Rhett Butler said to Scarlett, don't you? Well, that goes double for me."

She couldn't remember what else had happened or been said. She wasn't certain whether she imagined that she had slapped him again or that it had really happened. For days, she had walked around in a fog. He didn't speak to her, nor did she to him, although she kept saying to herself: He's your child. C-h-i-l-d!

"Margaret! Margaret! Where are you?" asked Carolyn. "Haven't you heard me calling you?"

"I'm afraid not," said Margaret, swiveling in her chair to face her sister. "I was lost in my thoughts."

"He'll feel differently once we're all in Paris," Carolyn said.

That her sister was reading her mind no longer surprised Margaret. It had happened too often to be unnerving.

"When we're all together, a family, Vinnie will come around. All he needs is time. You'll see," said Carolyn, convinced of her own words.

But Margaret was not. Carrington offered no opinion. He had felt it best from the first not to interfere. He offered Margaret his emotional support but not advice. He had not been that successful with his own daughter and, according to his wife, although he did not share her opinion, with his son either. He had only assured Margaret that he would do everything to help Vinnie through whatever adjustment he had to make. He also suggested that perhaps it might be wisest not to separate him from his cousins. He offered different perspectives and argued all sides of the issue but never on his own behalf. Except to tell Margaret he loved her and that he truly believed they could have a very fine life together.

"Like a good wine, my dear, our marriage will improve with age," Carrington had said, jesting most seriously. "You'll be bored by the same clients that bore me and stimulated by the people who truly are Paris. I want a home and I can give you that. It will not be someone else's beach house or a lavishly furnished suite in a posh hotel but your home, and if you want, you can fill it with hammocks and fly your red cape from the flagpole."

There was no doubt in Margaret's mind that James Carrington loved her. There was also no doubt that she loved him in a way that was quite new and unsettling to her. He did not arouse feelings Donald Malloy, Franklin Killerbrew, and several strangers in passing had. That both bothered her and didn't bother her. She missed the excitement but not the anxiety those feelings aroused.

As she sat looking at herself in her dressing room mirror, Margaret remembered the anxiety. She felt Franklin Killerbrew's presence in her hallway; his smell in her bed. She

343

remembered his eyes as they had attacked her own at the Savoy Grill after the opening of *Electra*. And she remembered the way he consumed her totally, in bed and out. Involuntarily, she began shaking. If she married James Carrington, she would never shake again. She would gain a sense of security she had never known with a man. There was only one problem, however. She could lose her son. Win some, lose some, they said. Only there were certain things a woman couldn't afford ever to lose and therein lay Margaret's indecision.

To John, a phone ringing in the middle of the night was a sounding of an alarm that something somewhere was not well. Sleepily, as Carolyn faintly stirred beside him, he reached for the ringing intruder into his sleep, hoping as he lifted the receiver from the bedside phone that it was a wrong number. The clock on the nightstand read four. In three hours' time, the family would be up, preparing for the boat train to Paris.

The crackling of the connection, the in and out of the operator's voice, brought him fully awake. Killerbrew, was John's first thought. Something about the picture. Then he heard the operator, her voice coming as through a tunnel, asking for Carolyn Ollson. An Edna Sternberg calling. He told the operator he would take the call. The party on the other end agreed.

It was such a poor connection and Edna Sternberg was in such poor shape that it was difficult for John to hear and to understand. But the distress in Edna's voice was plain even if her words were not. Heart attacks and death. Like salt and pepper. Twins in the night. Shaken but collected, John reassured Edna, calmed her as best he could, with the promise that the family would be on the first flight to New York that morning.

Since all their trunks and baggage had already been packed for the trip to Paris, it merely had to be relabeled and redirected, which John and Mrs. Worthington arranged. Evelyn Randolph used her considerable connections to arrange tickets on Pan American's Constellation service to New York that morning. Just as the plane was soaring into the skies and over the Atlantic, she was talking to James Carrington in Paris, informing him of the events that had taken the family back to New York.

The passengers on the plane kept remarking to one another how well behaved the Tiernan children were. Throughout the fourteen-hour trip, they talked and played quietly. Death didn't have the same finality for them it did for their elders. They watched their mothers sitting side by side, scarcely talking and hardly eating. They could feel, as well as see, the deep concern on their faces. Without being told, the children understood that on this particular trip, their mothers were not to be disturbed any more than they already were.

There were two limousines waiting at La Guardia. One took Mrs. Worthington and the children over the Triborough Bridge and into Manhattan where their apartment was already being made ready by building employees, while another took the sisters and John into the city via the Queens Midtown Tunnel. It was only when the cars passed directly by the house in Murray Hill where they had all once lived, that Carolyn began to cry. As they sped down Fifth Avenue toward the Village, Margaret felt the lump in her throat building into a scream. Internally, she let go, trembling and shivering as the car finally stopped at the brownstone on Ninth Street.

Edna Sternberg opened the door. The very old-looking man sitting on a wooden bench looked up at the new arrivals. It took him a moment to recognize them. When he did, his tired red eyes flooded with tears. His arms went out to them. Before they could reach his embrace, his wail pierced each of their hearts.

"Gussie. My Gussie is gone!"

The man collapsed on the floor and Edna Sternberg was at his side instantly. But neither Carolyn nor Margaret could move or speak. It was John's quiet crying that broke through the tourniquet both sisters had placed around their feelings. Arthur Abel had lost his Gussie. They had lost their Aunt Augie. Whose grief was greater could not be measured by something as simple as tears.

The simple service at St. Patrick's Cathedral was followed by burial at Gardenwood Cemetery on Long Island, the site of the Abel family plot. It was a Jewish cemetery and a rabbi officiated at graveside. Neither Carolyn nor Margaret had any objections to Arthur Abel's wish to have his Gussie buried near him so they could one day be together in eternity. The space to the right of Arthur's future resting place was reserved, however, for Rose Abel, still dead but breathing in a Long Island nursing home. Somehow, no one questioned Augusta's right to be buried in the Abel plot. By his side in life; by his side one day in death.

As the rabbi officiated, Arthur Abel stood between his daughter, Edna, and his son, Harold. He was no longer crying but standing as straight as a man his age could in final tribute to a woman he had loved. John had at first stood between Carolyn and Margaret, but once the service began, he stepped back allowing the sisters to cling to and support each other. Just behind John stood James Philip Carrington, who hadn't asked but took it upon himself to fly in from Paris to be with Margaret if she needed him.

Margaret felt as if a hand had reached within her and was twisting her guts, yanking them out piece by piece. She did not remember feeling the same kind of loss with her own mother. But Augie had been more than an aunt, even more than a mother. She had been a friend, a confidante, someone who had shared herself as an equal. Carolyn was sobbing uncontrollably. When the rabbi asked each member of the family to throw a clump of earth on the coffin, she began screaming: "No! Not yet. Please God, no!"

Margaret turned Carolyn toward her. "Let her go, Lynnie. Let her rest in peace."

"But, Marg," said Carolyn, tears streaming down her face, "I never got to say good-bye. I never got to tell her how much I loved her."

"Then tell her now, Lynnie. Tell her now," said Margaret, cupping her sister's face in her hand.

Carolyn took a clump of earth and as she threw it on the coffin, she said, "Good-bye, Aunt Augie. Good-bye, dearest one. I love you . . . you and your apple strudel."

Arthur Abel insisted on observing the traditional mourning *shiva* for the woman who was not his wife, yet was. That afternoon, following the funeral, as they sat on the hard wooden benches provided for the mourners, he excused himself and went into what was still so recently his and Augusta's bedroom. When he returned, he gave both Carolyn and Margaret identical little packages, each wrapped in pink paper with a red ribbon.

"Gussie once told me, if anything ever happened to her,

even before her will was read, you were to have these," he explained.

Together, Carolyn and Margaret unwrapped the packages. Each was a little jewelry box and in each lay one of the white pearl earrings Augusta had loaned Carolyn for her wedding day. Beneath each earring lay a sheet of Augusta's pale blue stationery on which a brief message was written in her large, firm strokes.

As John, James Carrington, Arthur Abel, and Edna Stern-berg listened, Carolyn, taking the hand Margaret offered, read aloud Augusta Monahan's legacy.

"I leave you, my dear children—and that's what you are: my dear children—with the one 'thing' I own that has mattered to me and this one thought which, thank God, I learned. Life is like love. For either to be complete, it must be shared."

BOOK THREE
1954–1965

1

Thomas Tiernan thought it was all ridiculous. Such carryings-on and over what?—a stupid television game show where people tried to guess who or what you were. It's bullshit! thought Thomas as he watched the panelists go "four down and six to go." All that secrecy and security! You would have thought from the way they had been guarded and sneaked into the studio that they were the First Family. Well, mused Thomas, to misguided millions who believed that crap they read, they were.

Of course Marti and Vinnie thought it "crazy" and it was, but not the way they meant it. Their "crazy" was far different from his, which meant insane. All of them. All of us. The crazy kids who want autographs or to cop a feel, and who thought that they, the Tiernans, had the answers to all teen-age problems. Now that was a laugh!

Thomas felt sick when he realized it would all begin again tomorrow. Usually, he had Sundays to himself and just as usually, shortly before he went to bed, his anxiety level would rise as he thought of the rehearsals that would begin the next day for that week's episode of "Tiernans & Company." Five years and still going strong! Which only proved how stupid people could be. How could anyone believe he, Vinnie, and Marti, with the help of a trusted butler/chauffeur/bodyguard could come up against and defeat crime, was beyond him. Yet, "Tiernans" was a permanent Friday-nights-at-eight American pastime. Or so the network thought. And so did Franklin Killerbrew.

Thomas Tiernan may have been the first actor in television history who wished his show would fail. But as it concluded its '53-'54 season, it was still among Nielsen's top five rated shows. And the fan mail and the number of fans that arrived weekly at the doorstep, both at the studio and at the apartment, proved that their popularity was not waning. Not one of them could make a move without Bruno, the bodyguard who had been hired to protect them.

In the barely functional dressing room the game show staff had assigned to them, Thomas could hear Marti and Vinnie down the hall in makeup laughing as each was being "prepared" to be adored by millions. As he paced, Thomas wondered why they always found it all such fun. What was wrong with him that public appearances such as this felt like a wound that was constantly being opened and could therefore never heal. Why didn't he love having his eyes "heightened" by liner, or the shine removed from his forehead. Those faggots in wardrobe and makeup drove him nuts. Not that any came on with him, but their voices and their gestures made him uncomfortable. Not Vinnie. Not Marti. Both joked with them. With everybody. On their own set, the crew hung out in Vinnie's "hole" as he called his dressing room. No one ever congregated in his. Which was fine. In five years, Thomas hadn't found many actors he liked. The actresses with their pretensions, particularly the young ones, were worse. But all that was part of the fun for Vinnie and Marti, and Thomas could not understand it. Well, no one was going to redden his lips or rinse his hair that was "sooo blond" it needed to be toned down for television. Not once he left all this behind.

Thomas was at that age most parents call "difficult." It wasn't that he, like most teenagers, thought he knew it all, but that they knew nothing. By "they" he meant Marti, Vinnie, his mother, and in particular his father and aunt, both of whom continued to be a constant embarrassment. It was one thing to act crazy as Vinnie did because you're a star, but it was quite another to *be* crazy. As far as Thomas was concerned, his aunt and his father were certifiable and he hoped he would never be judged for their actions. He cringed as he imagined one of the panelists tonight asking the dreaded question: "Are you now or have you ever been a member of the Communist Party?"

"No!" One down and nine to go. Only my aunt and father have been suspected of that and with the positions they took it is a miracle either of them were working. Well, his aunt wasn't and probably never would again. Not in America. And his father? Any day now he expected to hear that John Ollson was a new columnist for the *Daily Worker*.

Soon this will all be over, Thomas thought as he continued

to pace the cubicle. Remembering the applications in his bureau drawer at home made him feel better. His college entrance boards would decide whether he would be attending Harvard or M.I.T. Certainly they could not question his grades, which had been excellent at the Professional Children's School. The top fifth percentile. On his mathematics Regents' exam, he had scored ninety-seven. Now, if they would forgive him his family, their past and his present, he had a good shot at being accepted at both colleges. He particularly hoped for M.I.T. as aeronautical engineering was the coming thing. At last he could learn "how go?"—the question he was told he most asked about his toys and "things" when he was a child. But if M.I.T. didn't accept him and Harvard did, then he would consider law.

Hearing the raucous laughter coming from the makeup room made Thomas wonder how the family would react when they learned of his plans. One more year and finished! He could hear Franklin Killerbrew's roar now. Tough! The old man had made a fortune on Tiernans all his life. From Tots to Teenagers. The success of "Tiernans & Company" had allowed him to set up an independent production company with his father. K.O. Productions. Christ! What bullshit! K for Killerbrew; 0 for Ollson; and a K.O. Production is a Knockout Every Time. Or so said the ads in *Variety*. Well, fuck them. What they did with their lives was not his concern. He now had plans of his own and they damn well weren't similar to theirs.

Everyone had plans. As far as he could see, Vinnie's never changed. To get laid. Marti, too, was "having fun." God only knows who she was chasing or who was chasing her this week. She was just too damn "big" for her age. It was embarrassing. *Jugs* is what the stagehands called Marti's breasts. And she was forever bouncing about as if unaware *they* were bouncing with her. And she knew. Did she ever know! He had seen her at one of Vinnie's "parties." Some party. A group grope is what it was. It was fucking disgusting watching her try to smoke while she turned green from coughing. It was all Vinnie's fault. He had some kind of power over her. The two were much more like twins than he and Marti ever were. Vinnie had no respect for ethics or morals of any kind. And he's got my mother wrapped around his little finger. "With her pea brain that isn't hard," Thomas decided.

The first guest on the game show—he bronzed butterflies—

was replaced by a little blonde whose tiny voice was no match for her oversized breasts. A Roller Derby skater, she whispered into the ear of the show's host. Roars of laughter came from the clued-in audience. Now what the hell is funny about that? Thomas wondered, when it's really sad. Why is some dumb girl wrestling on roller skates considered funny? Thomas shook his head and then put his hands to his temples and pressed upon them. Either I'm crazy or the world is, he thought. Or else the world I'm in is making me crazy. Is it them or me?

This was the question that haunted Thomas. Whether at home, alone in his room, at the TV studio, or at school, he wondered about the "them" and "me." He was constantly troubled not only by the differences between him and his immediate family, but between him and the people he met, at work and at school. Smoking in the bathroom, "making out" in the hallways, circle-jerks. None of it made sense. Not to him. Why not? Why everyone else but not him? Vinnie said he was a prick, but if anyone was that, it was Vinnie. His "exile"—and those were Vinnie's words for his year in Paris with his mother—sure as hell hadn't improved him. What the hell do they teach kids in Paris, Thomas wondered. To drink and to fuck? And his sister, forget about her cock-teasing. The girl was mindless. A ninny. She was barely passing at school and even his mother had said it would only be with the help of the saints that Marti would get a diploma. And yet Marti was unconcerned. To her a synonym for college was jail. The girl had absolutely no ambition to do or be anything more than what she was. And then we have my mother, thought Thomas. The sanest of the bunch, which sure wasn't saying a lot. A seven-year-old kid at home, yet she was still gone for a week, twice a month, traipsing out to Brooklyn for her ninety-minute TV show, produced, of course, in association with K.O. Productions. Thomas was certain that if Franklin Killerbrew could think of a way to use John Jr. he would, and that his mother would allow it. Only the kid wouldn't. He was so shy he cried when crowds assaulted the family. And the poor little guy thought Mrs. Worthington was his mother. What a crummy setup for a kid. Living with strangers. Not just Worthington but Bruno and Annette and Carole, the girls who answered the phone and the mail and who kept careful records of the family's appointments with the press.

354

Of all the problems in Thomas's life, that was the worst. Strangers in his dressing room, in his home, asking him personal questions or such dumb shit as what are your favorite colors. And date layouts. Oh, God, those dumb teenage magazines! And posing with teenage girls—models he didn't know and didn't want to know. They were like Vinnie. All they talked—actually joked is a better word—about was sex. He dated one—took her out to see what all the noise was about. She was fourteen, maybe fifteen, he couldn't remember. She had been a "pro," as she called it, in her business since she was ten. He remembered her parents had gone off to bed when they sat down on the sofa in the living room to begin the obligatory necking. And then suddenly, she was on the carpet, on her knees, in front of him, trying to take him in her mouth. He had been horrified and outraged and had yanked away from her, leaving her apartment still hard and still unzipped. And she couldn't understand what he had been upset about. Christ! He barely knew her.

It would have made a great anecdote for one of those dumb ladies' magazines that were constantly doing stories on the "perfect" family. Oh, God, how he hated them! And Vinnie, lapping it all up, would, after he charmed everybody, turn to him and say: "What do you care what they print? It's all a game. Play it by whatever rules you want. Invent. Nothing they write or say has anything to do with you anyway."

But Thomas didn't see it that way and when he explained that it had everything to do with "my good name," Marti had whooped with laughter and called him pretentious and pompous.

His mother insisted he didn't have to participate in the publicity. Or the series, either. When the show was first offered to the family in 1949, Marti and Vinnie had found it "thrilling." Everything then was "thrilling" to Marti. Vinnie was "thrilled" because it would keep him out of Paris, away from his mother, and in New York. But Thomas hadn't been thrilled, particularly when his mother had said, "Thomas, if you're not certain, don't do it. But once you agree—once you say you will—you *must* give it your best."

Good ole Mom, thought Thomas, always the show-must-go-on bullshit. Yet he had wanted to do it. He had been excited just seeing the Tiernan Tots' features on Channel 13. Five o'clock every night, he and Marti would watch the "tots" through the "snow" that continually fell on the channel from

New Jersey. And then when the features were sold by Killerbrew to stations throughout the country, they had become "stars" again despite their retirement. A part of him then wanted to see where all "this nuttiness," as he had described it, would lead. Now, five years later, he knew.

Thomas thought back to what his father had done and typically it had been nothing. He had disappeared and left the decision solely to him. Which is what his father maintained life was all about and one might just as well learn that early on. His father had learned of the contract signing when he was on the road promoting *War Without/War Within*, his precious novel which won him the goddamn precious Pulitzer Prize and brought even more goddamn magazines to their doorstep.

"And how does that make you feel about your father?" the gushing goof from *Ladies' Home Journal* had asked. He had been tempted to tell her but he didn't. Nor did he tell her how he really felt about his parents' marriage, which was held up to millions of women as an example of "togetherness without the ties that bind." He fully expected that one day his parents would receive the Good Housekeeping Seal of Approval. Idiots! All of them. Well, one day he would be free. The money he had earned over the years had been placed in trust funds and, beginning at age eighteen, he would be a very wealthy young man. And wealth, as everyone knew, meant freedom. From family and all the crap that surrounded them.

That he felt so alienated from his family both angered and pained Thomas. As he waited for his call in the dressing room, he remembered the first time he had felt the pain of being different. It had also been a Sunday. He had been alone in his room trying to read the next week's script when suddenly he couldn't see for the tears in his eyes. Although it was one of those rare times when both his mother and father were at home and Marti was in her room playing her dumb Patti Page records over and over again, he had felt entirely alone. He couldn't describe the feeling but it was the worst he had ever known. It felt much like his recurring nightmare during which he would think himself awake but unable to move. He would scream for help and yet no one—no matter how nearby they were—could hear. Finally, by sheer will, he would force himself into full consciousness. He would lie in bed sweating as he trembled from fright, from the awareness

356

that he was alone. This Sunday night as he waited for his "line" to be guessed, Thomas relived his realization of that Sunday night not so long ago: that in his life, no one was there and that if ever he needed help, he could only call on the one person who would always be there—Thomas Ollson. Yes, Thomas Ollson. Not Thomas Tiernan, because he was someone else's invention, and not him. Not really.

"We're ready for you now, Thomas," said a pretty young woman holding a clipboard to her breast as she smiled warmly from the doorway. Standing to examine himself in the full-length mirror, Thomas couldn't escape the fact that he was his father's son. He straightened his red-and-blue-striped silk tie and tucked the blue shirt—"Don't wear white on camera!" he had been cautioned—into his gray flannel pants. A final brush of lint off his navy blazer and he was ready. Vinnie, dressed identically, smiled at him in the hallway. Thomas noted that Vinnie had his black curls combed "nonchalantly" onto his forehead, as if they fell there naturally. But it was Marti who surprised him. When she had arrived at the studio, her hair had been in a ponytail, and she was wearing those godawful toreador pants and a stupid sweater that shed every time she shook. Now, with her hair falling about her shoulders, and wearing a soft, full pale blue silk blouse nipped into a black skirt by a bleeding blue-into-black waist-cincher, she looked beautiful. As the elevator took them down to stage level, Marti fastened a strand of pearls about her neck.

They were grouped together just behind the partition that served as a curtain when John Daly said: "Would the Mystery Guest sign in, please!" The director cued them and together, the Tiernans walked onstage to a roar of recognition that hurt Thomas's already hurting head. Still, he managed a smile through the perfect white teeth that were so well known all over America.

"I just hope it isn't that dreadful Kilgallen woman who guesses them," said Carolyn, whose loathing for the columnist went as unabated as the columnist's baiting of the senior Tiernan family members.

"Mama, what's dreadful mean?" asked John Jr., who was sitting on his mother's lap, his head on her shoulder as he watched the TV screen.

"Not nice . . . bad," explained Carolyn to her half-awake child.

"Why is she not nice, Mama?"

"Yes, Mama, why is she not nice?" mimicked John, amused at Carolyn's predicament. As she so often told the children, if you can't say anything nice, say nothing at all.

"Can we please watch the show," answered Carolyn. "I've kept you up so you could see everyone on television. Isn't it exciting?"

John Jr.'s response was a yawn. He failed to see why his family on television was anything special since one or the other always was.

"John, adjust the contrast, would you? And I think the picture is too bright."

"I am not moving. We've already adjusted the set twelve times—by count—this one night. By the way," added John as he snuggled up next to Carolyn on the sofa facing the combination TV and stereo on the far wall, "your daughter is the image of you. A knockout!"

Carolyn, pleased, patted John's hand. "Actually, she's much prettier, but thank you. And thank God for sparing her my hips!"

"I like your hips," said John as his hand slipped under Carolyn's rump. She slapped at his hand as her eyes motioned to John Jr. Unfortunately, or fortunately, her seven-year-old was asleep and so John's hand continued to squeeze and fondle affectionately.

"The hearts that girl is going to break," he said as he gazed at his daughter on the screen.

"Let's hope it is their hearts and not hers," replied Carolyn. "She may look mature but she is very young."

"You'll be saying that when she's thirty," John said as he nibbled at Carolyn's ear.

As if she didn't notice, which she did, Carolyn continued talking, although more to herself than to John. "She's a lot like Margaret was at that age. Too young to act so old. And she's such a child." Carolyn was recalling her recent conversation with Marti, who had been talking earnestly about dating and saving "it" until "the right man comes along." To which Carolyn had said: "Well, I do hope you'll take Mr. Right by the hand and lead him to the altar before he leads you astray." And Marti had said quite honestly that she hadn't the vaguest idea what she would do with or about her virginity until the time came to decide.

"I don't suppose there is anything I could say that would influence you?" Carolyn asked, knowing full well there was not.

Carolyn could still see Marti's expression and could still hear her amused reply. "You mean . . . why buy a cow when you can get the milk for free? Right? Well, Ma, it's like this. For companionship. You know how they say: man does not live by bread alone. Well, milk isn't all it's cracked up to be either."

With that, Carolyn had turned it over to God. Let it be His problem, she decided, knowing she would continue to worry anyway.

"You've certainly picked a strange time, John Ollson, to get romantic," Carolyn said as she brushed John's lips away from her ear.

"There are no strange times between consenting adults," he responded, as his tongue slipped in and out of the creases of her ear.

"Would you stop! You know that gets me crazy. Haven't you any work to do?"

"As a matter of fact, I do," said John as he picked himself up off the couch. "I must review my notes for tomorrow's interviews. But how about a rendezvous in an hour?"

"With or without your notes?" teased Carolyn.

"For what I have in mind, I don't need any notes. Nor do you. You've learned to take direction quite well, my dear," he said as he lightly kissed the top of her head.

"I guess the years of training have finally paid off," she responded sarcastically. "By the way, not to ruin the moment, but . . . has Edna been able to open any more doors?"

"A few. She's called a number of Arthur's old cronies and those who are retired are willing to talk. But on the whole, no one is too anxious to blow the lid off hospital care for the aged. If Arthur were alive, I'd get a helluva lot more cooperation."

"If Arthur were alive, you wouldn't have his notes. Remember?" said Carolyn.

"True enough," John said as he stretched and yawned. "See you in a bit," he said as he disappeared down the hallway toward the room that was once Augusta's but was now his den.

John Jr. felt heavy asleep in her lap, but it was a nice heaviness, Carolyn decided. She could feel him there, and she liked that. Her youngest and her last. Soon he would be too old to sit on her lap. She would miss that. As it was, with two weeks out of every month spent at the NBC studios in

Brooklyn, she felt she had not enough time to share her son's childhood. And he was so different from her others. Such a quiet child. So shy and not at all mischievous or even adventuresome as boys his age normally were.

Carolyn looked up at the blindfolded Kilgallen who had just established that there was more than one celebrity guest. Happily, she asked if they were the Ritz Brothers, which made the audience scream with laughter; John Daly, too. In fact, all but Thomas were laughing. He seldom laughed. He was an odd child, but the psychology books assured her that his closed door at night and his need for secrecy were part of normal teenage development. She hoped so. But there was no way to know as Thomas didn't talk, not to her and certainly not to John. Like Marti, he looked so much older than his age, but then he was already, at six feet one, an inch taller than his father. And serious. Too serious. If only he were a little more like Vinnie, who seemed to take nothing very seriously. Always the joke, the one-liner, the smart retort. He was a dazzling child; both handsome and pretty. His manner was electric and drew people to him constantly. And yet, he had brooding eyes. The Irish in him, Carolyn had decided. By all standards, Vinnie should be the odd one of the lot, yet he seemed to have the most friends among the three children. He was constantly invited to parties to which he took a more than willing Marti, and left a more than willing Thomas at home. But Thomas was a loner. Even this summer, when Marti and Vinnie were off to Margaret in Paris—Vinnie more by demand than by desire—Thomas was staying at home—catching up on his studies, he had said by way of explanation.

The applause coming from the TV set captured Carolyn's attention once again. Good! Arlene Francis had guessed their identities, as well she should. She had known the children all their lives. As they rose to say good-night and to greet the rest of the panel, a moment of fear passed through Carolyn. Oh, God, what would they do when they came to Kilgallen after all she had written about Margaret, John, and herself. Fine! Really good! Carolyn was thinking as Thomas and Vinnie shook her hand and passed on to Abe Burrows. Oh, no! Please God, tell me that what I just saw didn't happen! But it had. Carolyn could see that from the absolutely stunned look on Kilgallen's face.

*   *   *

Franklin Killerbrew was standing in front of the DuMont television set that had been built into one wall of his den, and he was laughing. She may look like her mother but she's her aunt all over again. Only Margaret would have looked into Kilgallen's face, stared at her outstretched hand, ignored it, as Marti had, and moved on.

Although Killerbrew had been alerted by his publicity staff that the Tiernans would be the Mystery Guest on "What's My Line?" he had not been prepared for Marti Tiernan. Which is why he was standing in front of the TV set. From the moment she had come on screen, he was so startled that he had left his club chair to be closer to the tube to see if there was any distortion to his set. There was none. There was also no child there. Nor was there a girl or a woman, but a breathtaking someone about to move gracefully from one stage to another. The beauty was unmistakably her mother's, but the jaunt and the attitude—a sort of saucy, sexy arrogance— were strictly her aunt's. He remembered the first time he had seen that attitude and how another aunt had silently demanded the girl uncross her legs, pull her skirt down, and behave properly. It was a bittersweet remembrance that made him both angry and sad.

Now, there it was again. Blatant and mocking. Unaware, Marti Tiernan was proving that history does repeat itself. As he returned to his club chair and the highball glass filled with bourbon and soda by its side, he thought: I can use her. Not now. No sense in competing with Natalie Wood. But in a year or two . . . move over Monroe and Taylor.

"She is very beautiful."

The voice surprised him, particularly its softness. Nancy never entered his den unless there was some major social event she wanted to make sure he remembered. In recent months—or was it years?—that hadn't happened very often.

"She reminds me of Margaret."

So she had seen that too. Often Nancy surprised him.

"I'm sure you must have plans for her."

He ignored her double entendre, hoping she would go away but knowing that if she had entered his sanctum she would not. She sat quietly observing him as he pretended to take interest in the show's last guest—a lady dentist.

"You know, Franklin, you've held up well. For a man your age, you're still very attractive. But not my type," she added as he looked at her wonderingly. "No. Not my type at all, as

361

I'm sure you've guessed since we have not—how shall I put it?—*lain* together—yes, that's nice; I like the sound of that—lain together in years."

When Killerbrew continued to stare at the television screen as if she wasn't there, Nancy Quentin Blanchard perched on the edge of the club chair in which her husband was sitting.

"Franklin," she crooned in his ear, "I've got good news for you."

Killerbrew didn't budge. Not a muscle or an eyeball. Until Nancy began to laugh. Not a mocking or an arrogant laugh but a deep from the gut good-natured howl.

"Franklin, darling, the news really *is* good. I'm leaving you. Yes," she said, with his full attention now. "Leaving you. As in divorce! Now, Franklin, you are one man who looks ridiculous wearing a stunned expression. It doesn't suit you at all. You're implacable, remember? Or is it unflappable? Whatever. Yes, my dear, after all these years, how does that song go? 'The Masquerade Is Over.' Now for the best part. You're not only getting your freedom, but your studio. Your lawyers will be notified that I have instructed mine to give you first refusal on my Killerbrew Studios stock. Nice of me, no?"

Nancy was up from the chair's arm and pacing back and forth in her aquamarine silk robe. She was aware he was watching her although he still had not spoken. "California community property law is very explicit on what's to be done. I'll take no less; I want no more. I do not want the house; I'll have no need for it. If you want it, it's yours, after an evaluation of its worth, of course. Other than that, I can think of no other details to be discussed. Except it was very sneaky of you, Franklin, to set up K.O. Productions in John Ollson's name. Was that to be your ticket out of the marriage?"

Killerbrew rose slowly from his chair. Bennett Cerf was saying "Good-night, Arlene," and Arlene was about to say "Good-night, Abe," when he flicked off the set, again slowly, as if it took great thought to engineer the on-off button. Then, even more slowly, he turned toward Nancy, and slapped her with such force she spun back against the wall.

"Sit down, *darling*," he said quietly, as he went to the humidor that rested on the bar. Slowly he unwrapped one of his favorite Havanas.

"You should never have done that," Nancy said as she

362

rubbed her cheek, now crimson from the force of his blow. "I was being nice about everything."

Killerbrew turned on her with a fury that in all her years of marriage to the man she had never seen.

"It's too late for *niceness*. Where was it when I needed it?" he yelled at her.

"If you mean when you wanted to marry Margaret Tiernan," said Nancy Quentin Blanchard as she faced her husband squarely, her posture demonstrating she would match him blow for blow if it came to that, "I wasn't ready to divorce you. I needed you. I don't anymore."

"You coming out, Nancy? You telling the world you suck cunt?" asked Killerbrew derisively.

"You needn't say it with such disgust, Franklin, particularly since it's one of the things you do best. I'm moving to Europe. *Where* in Europe is none of your business. *Why* isn't either, but surely you know that James Carrington has helped triple my assets. You know of the gallery in London and now the one in Rome. Soon there will be another in Paris and later in New York. But then you don't know much about art and galleries, do you, Franklin? The barbarians of Hollywood *make* pictures; they don't paint them."

"Who is she, Nancy?" said Killerbrew. "That's the crux of this."

"How clever of you, Franklin. Only it is none of your business."

Suddenly, Nancy's attitude changed. He watched her venom disappear into a softness that made her look vulnerable; something he could never recall in her before. "There is someone, Franklin, and I'm damn lucky. At my age to be in love is rather remarkable, isn't it? And happily in love. Even more remarkable, she's a very nice person. She even makes me feel like a very nice person, which we both know I am not and have never been. But that doesn't mean I can't be. I know we've had ugly times, Franklin, and that our best times would be another's periods of truce. But it's over now. I'm not going to do movie dialogue and say 'Let's part friends' as we both know that isn't possible. But, now that I'm leaving, it's easier to say this. I do admire you, Franklin. I even like a great deal about you. Except your weakness. Now don't look so injured. I'm not going after you or—how do the young folks, bless their young, young hearts, say today?—putting you down, but had I loved anyone the way you loved that

363

woman, I'd have killed for her. In short: you fucked up, my dear. Well, so be it. As I said but minutes ago, you've held up well. A man as attractive as you should have no problem. But then you never did. My, when I think of our mad, impetuous youth, between us, we must have had half of Hollywood."

"At least," admitted Franklin, smiling at the improbability of the past thirty-one years of what had passed for a marriage.

"But you never had me!" said Nancy Quentin Blanchard triumphantly.

"No, I never did," agreed Franklin.

As she rose from where she was sitting, Nancy Killerbrew tightened the sash around her robe. At the door she stopped and then walked back to where Killerbrew was standing. As he remained immobile, she reached up, took his face in her hands, and kissed him on the cheek.

"Good-bye, Franklin. I hope the rest of your life will be as good as mine."

He looked to see the sarcasm, the derision, on her face, but there was none. To his amazement, there were only tears.

Charlene Quarles was dressing silently. Of the game show staff, she was the only one who remained in the CBS studio on Fifty-second Street. But then, she was the only one "working" overtime. Her cigarette lay in a tin ashtray on the side of the dressing table and its smoke filled the cubicle that had room only for an old, ugly couch and an end table. The former was still damp, as was Charlene as she continued to think about herself and the boy with whom she had just thrashed about on the couch. So unlike his cousin, who had avoided her eye when she came into this very room to tell him they were the next guests to appear. Charlene felt very pleased with herself. Only one out of every four male celebrity guests had refused her "services" and that Vinnie had not—not in the fullest sense of the word—gotten his "jollies," was not of import to Charlene, as she had. Several times. If he were saving his for someone else, Charlene didn't care.

As she slipped into the shoes with heels that made her a full three inches taller, she said to the half-dressed boy, "Maybe I'll see you around this summer. You gonna be in town or are you doing stock or something?"

"I'm going to Paris next week," Vinnie answered. "My mother lives there," he explained.

"Your mother? Oh, yeah. Margaret Tiernan," said Charlene as she connected the two. "Hey, whatever happened to her?"

That Margaret Tiernan had never felt quite so happy and complete would have surprised the people who saw tears running down the face of the elegantly dressed woman who strolled ever so slowly along the Quai d'Orsay toward Les Invalides. It was not unusual in Paris to see such a woman crying to herself as she missed an errant husband between the hours of *cinq et sept*. But Margaret was no such woman and James Carrington was no such man. Margaret knew exactly where James would be at five, six, seven, and at any hour of the day. This early autumn evening, chilled but not yet cold, he would be sitting, glen-plaid scarf wrapped about his neck, on the small bedroom balcony of the townhouse they had purchased on Rue Monsieur overlooking the sculptures and the gardens of the Musée Rodin. No, thought Margaret, there is never any mystery as to the whereabouts of James Carrington. After the close of the business day, he returned to his wife and the four-story home that had become famous among their small circle of friends for its collection of various art forms and artists.

As she walked along the Seine's Left Bank, the Arc de Triomphe at her back and the spires of Notre Dame before her, Margaret felt anew her love affair with the city and the river that divided it into delicious sections of varying tastes and designs. Paris was a place to *be*. It made quiet but insistent demands that one notice a sunset, a sky, and a style. She was not hurrying home for that reason and for another, even more important. She wanted to savor the moment, to live with it alone first before sharing it with James. Over and over she fed on the knowledge that she and only she had.

She anticipated the evening ahead. First, she would be with James and she could envision—not so much his excitement—but his pleasure. Then she would call Carolyn and hope that Marti would be there so she could share her happiness with "my darling; my sister's child and my own." And that is how Marti felt to Margaret—like her own. More so than Vinnie. He had made the past summer unbearable. He would be unbearable now. She would not allow that. No, nothing and no one could take away from this, from the now, from the miracle.

Why did she have to think about Vinnie? Always, no matter where or when, he was inescapable, lurking at the back of her mind, all too ready to make an impromptu appearance. Her guilt. Her ever-present guilt. A mother's legacy and curse, Carolyn had said. But he had been so awful, Margaret defended. From the beginning, from the moment he stepped off the plane with Marti, he had been argumentative. She did not mind when he vented his hostility toward her but when it reached out to touch—no, to scathe—James, that she would not tolerate. James had done nothing to deserve such treatment. From the moment of their marriage, James had tried with Vinnie. When they bought the Rue Monsieur townhouse, they had given the third floor over to Vinnie and told him he could do anything he wished with the space. They even installed a pantry next to the bathroom so he could serve himself and be his own independent person if he so desired. Did he want a dog? James had asked. Was there a particular school he would prefer to attend?

But from the start, Vinnie made it clear he wanted nothing and that nothing would satisfy him. It came as a relief to Margaret when Killerbrew put together "Tiernans & Company," and Vinnie made it clear to her he welcomed the TV offer as a condemned murderer would a reprieve from the governor.

It was terrible realizing you wanted your own child out of your house and out of your life, but Margaret lived with that guilt as best she could. Summers, when Vinnie visited, were usually pleasant enough. But this time . . . if only she had known what had been on his mind she would have acted differently. He had provoked a confrontation and the resulting separation. He had engineered and nursed it for Lord only knows how long. She didn't blame him but why should she blame herself?

James had taken Marti to Versailles for the day and she found herself alone with her son, who said he wished to talk rather than tour. She was pleased. Vinnie seldom sought her advice or opinion or consultation. Nor was he doing so now, it turned out.

"Why didn't you tell me my father was a fag?" he shot at her without warning.

"What makes you certain he was?" she asked, borrowing time so she could think as he spoke.

"That's the buzz. I heard it at school; I hear it on the set. That Sonny Stevens, cowboy star, seen most any night on the late show riding his horse into the sunset, was more likely to be riding off into the bushes with some guy."

"That brief little bit of bitchery does a disservice to one of the nicest and dearest men I ever knew—a man, by the way, who loved you."

"But he dug guys, didn't he?" asked Vinnie, his tone insistent.

"Yes," she admitted, her voice quiet, her feelings raw as she remembered the man and his death.

"How could you? How could you do that to me?" Vinnie yelled.

"Do *what* to you? I gave you a father!"

"A father who's a fairy? You gave me shit! As always. Do you know how many bad jokes I hear almost every goddamn fucking day of my life about my father? People want to know if it's hereditary. They also want to know how you managed it. Did you pose as John Wayne or somebody equally butch?"

"I never want to hear you say another word about Sonny Stevens to me again," said Margaret in a voice she hardly recognized as her own, so awesome was it in its threat. "He does not deserve your malice or your contempt. He was a father to you when he didn't have to be. Do you understand?"

Vinnie stared at her, the beginnings of an understanding slowly dawning on his face. "Who was he then?" he asked finally.

"If by 'he' you mean who was your father, his name was Donald Malloy. He's dead now. He was killed in the war. He never knew about you because I didn't think he should. I no longer know if I did the right or wrong thing. Times were very different then. I was young, although I refused to believe it; impetuous, and not in love with the man, although at one time I thought I was. Since I refused to have an abortion, it was arranged for me to marry Sonny."

"By Franklin Killerbrew," interjected Vinnie.

"Yes. By none other than himself," said Margaret wearily.

"And what was *Uncle* Franklin's stake in all this?" asked Vinnie with such sarcasm Margaret realized he had put two and two together but got four and a half rather than just plain four.

"*That* is none of your business. Your father was Donald Malloy. He worked at the studio. He was bright, energetic, fiercely male and independent and an Irish Catholic from a less than grand background. You could even say he was a self-made man."

"Who made you," added Vinnie bitterly.

"Yes, you could say that too," said Margaret.

"You should have told me all this a long time ago instead of letting me find out through the gutter."

"You are right. I suppose another of my mistakes was thinking you were too young—that you weren't ready yet—that the world wouldn't care and so wouldn't talk. I guess that's what I wanted to believe so I believed it. Wrong again. I'm sorry."

"Sorry is shit! You're always sorry about something or other. Are you sorry about all the times you left me with Aunt Carolyn to go off on your own? Are you sorry for having given birth to me?"

She wanted to say something that would ease his pain and then hers. She sought for words, for anything to express what she had felt and what she was feeling then. "I was never sorry about anything," she replied, knowing immediately he would not understand what she meant. "I am glad for you, that you *are*. I just couldn't be all you wanted. It was too much. I was too young. I needed my own life. That was not a crime. You were never neglected. You were never unloved."

"I never came first," he said sullenly.

Margaret nearly toppled from the chair in which she was sitting. She had no response to the punch of the unwanted but spoken truth. She said nothing when Vinnie went on to inform her of his plans. He would leave for London in a week, tour the British Isles, and then return to New York for the fall season. She agreed, but only in part to his demands. By the end of the day she had arranged for Bruno to meet Vinnie in London and act as his companion and watchdog. She also arranged quarters for both at Evelyn Randolph's.

Carolyn was appalled by Margaret's acquiescence to Vinnie's demands. She was certain that if she spoke to her nephew, acquainted him with the "true facts"—from another's point of view—he would come to a different understanding. Margaret didn't think so. Someday, perhaps. But definitely not now.

At the end of the day, before James and Marti returned, Margaret went to Vinnie's room with her own demands.

"Regardless of what you feel toward me, I insist while you are in my home, you are to treat my husband with the respect he both deserves and has earned. I will not allow whatever exists between you and me to create tension in my husband's life. He is now first. Is that clear?"

Margaret shuddered as she remembered the look of hatred and hurt that mingled and meshed on her son's face. As she turned off the Quai and onto Rue de Constantine, she felt her spirits sink. No! she screamed internally. I will not allow my guilt to lacerate me anymore. Still, she couldn't stop the memory of the feeling that pervaded when Vinnie's plane taxied down the runway at Orly and took off for London. She knew then that he was flying not just out of Paris but out of her life, and her sense of loss was as great as when Augusta was laid in her final resting place.

Napoleon lives on through his monument, thought Margaret as she walked down the Boulevard des Invalides where he was entombed, and Augusta lives on in my marriage. How happy Augusta would be if she were here this day! Life is like love and for either to be complete it must be shared, she had written. And it had been her words, her "bequest," that had made Margaret realize she should and would marry James Carrington. She often thanked Augusta for her part in the past six years of contentment that came and went and came again like a gentle summer breeze. Not that the adjustment to marriage and to their life together had all been easy. There were those days when a nondescript but insidious boredom crept along the white-tiled entrance hallway, past the living and dining rooms, up the staircase, and into the brown and beige, earth-toned bedroom she shared with her husband. It would accompany her, uninvited and unwelcome, as she breakfasted on a tray before the recessed fireplace that kept the bedroom free from the dampness that so often hovered over Paris. Not that she missed her work—yet she did. A contradiction? Perhaps. An ambivalence? Definitely. But it was not worth thinking about, given the mood of America that made her return to work there highly improbable. Margaret felt about America the way she felt about her work. Ambivalent. She did not want to return to its current insanity, yet she missed it. She could never be an expatriate like so many she had met in Paris. Never. In fact, she looked forward to her Christmas visit. It would be her first return to America since that awful period in '52! Such had been the country's outrage at her statements from Paris on the House Committee on Un-American Activities. Which is why Carolyn, sans Thomas, who refused to leave his studies, had brought Christmas the past two years to Paris. Thomas and Vinnie. Two of a kind but only in one respect. They both divided the family.

"I'm going to throw the switch," said Margaret aloud as she turned onto Rue de Varenne. "I am going to forget about Thomas and Vincent Tiernan and allow nothing—nothing, I say!—to spoil this moment. This is my day."

Some passersby looked at her oddly. Well-dressed women of obvious means did not talk aloud in the streets. She nodded at them and smiled as if to assure them that she was not a minor disturbance that would disrupt their day.

The stone walls that lined Rue Monsieur, keeping the private homes from public view, were already in shadow. The sun was at that very moment making its final farewells to the day. It was a sad hour, a time of remembrance of things past, thought Margaret as she quickened her pace. Now she wanted her husband, to be at his side, to feel his happiness when she shared what she had just that hour learned. She needed to hear Carolyn—to hear her chatter delightedly as she had from childhood whenever something occurred to please her. Oh, how they would hug each other if they were together now! Thank God those awful stupid months of estrangement were over.

Again, despite the attempt not to throw the switch to times past, Margaret's mind moved to the days in 1950 and 1951 when she avidly followed the proceedings of the House Committee on Un-American Activities in the Paris *Tribune*. She remembered her disgust and the feeling of revulsion in her stomach when the Rosenbergs were sentenced. As far back as 1947 when Robert Taylor had testified before the committee on *Song of Russia*, she had thought Taylor and the committee were both ludicrous and misguided. But it had moved from ludicrous to downright dangerous when that same committee called Dashiell Hammett in '51 and Sidney Barasch in '52 to testify. Ridiculous! Barasch, a communist? *Waifs in the Wind*, Red propaganda? It was too ridiculous to take seriously except that it was happening. And it was happening to her: the committee let it be known through Franklin Killerbrew that they would be most pleased if she would come to Washington to talk to them about Barasch, and her relationship with him over the years.

She had not known what to do until the day Barasch appeared before the committee, refusing to answer any questions as a matter of principle rather than politics. That Thursday morning, Barasch was discredited and humiliated. That Thursday evening, he had not only lost his reputation and his professional standing but his right eye—the result of an attack by a mob of hooligans outside his Washington hotel. The following Wednesday, in weekly *Variety*, a full-page ad appeared that reverberated throughout the world. Its copy denounced the House Committee on Un-American Activities and all those who supported it. It further decried the witch hunt that threatened to destroy creative thought and freedom itself. Finally, it urged everyone who considered himself or herself to be an artist and an American, to join in a denunciation of the committee. The ad was signed by Margaret Tiernan.

Almost immediately, the house on Rue Monsieur was besieged by worldwide press. From the wrought-iron gates that separated stone wall and street from courtyard and home, Margaret calmly announced that she had said all she ever intended to say on the subject. When asked if she was or had ever been a communist sympathizer, she repeated what she had just said, closed the gates, and returned to her home.

The right-wing members of America's fourth estate labeled her "unfriendly" and made strong hints about her "leftist" friends and the likelihood of her own politics. Why, asked Hedda Hopper, was a woman who had gained so much from a trusting industry and a trusting public living in Paris unless . . . unless . . . The point was made. Worse, it was remade and made again many times in the year that followed. Matters were not helped but worsened when John Ollson, in *Collier's*, wrote a vitriolic attack on the committee and the Americans who supported it—"who fed the fever that was making America's mind sicker and sicker." Immediately, he was called a "pinko" and as Lee Mortimer asked in his column: "Hasn't that always been apparent ever since his 'Letters to My Unborn Child' article in *Esquire*?"

The publication of John's article so soon after Margaret's press statement turned public and media attention toward Carolyn. Her biweekly "Front Row Center" had easily made the transition from radio to television and since its inception in spring 1949, the ninety-minute Monday night offering was consistently among the twenty top TV programs. Within days of the *Collier's* article, Carolyn was threatened with immediate cancellation by her sponsors—makers of dentifrice and deodorant. Either she denounce and disassociate herself from her husband's and sister's politics or her show would pay the consequences. Strangely, the children were not so threatened. Perhaps, thought Carolyn, the profits of sponsoring Number One were greater than the debits of political overtones or fallout.

Carolyn Tiernan was "invited" to appear before the House Committee on Un-American Activities. Before the committee could learn of her willingness, or lack of it, to testify, she called a press conference.

Carolyn Tiernan chose the RCA Johnny Victor Theatre on Forty-ninth Street for what became the season's most spirited performance. Before cameras, microphones, and scores of reporters, she announced: "I am not and never have been a communist. Regarding *Waifs in the Wind*: It was the second worst script—*A Prince Awaits* was *far* worse—I have ever read in my life. I assure you that the final print is more the product of two young girls' imagination than it is the workings of a writer. I also assure you, *Waifs* was purely a capitalistic enterprise and we, my sister and I, were well paid—although today I don't think there would be enough money in the world for me to make such a loathsome picture with such a loathsome title—by the great capitalist and filmmaker Franklin Killerbrew, upon whose original idea *Waifs* was based. Let me repeat for those who might be just the least bit slow. *Waifs* had absolutely no artistic aspirations, let alone political ones.

"Finally, I wish to remind everyone that my sister, Margaret Tiernan, was one of the founders of the Hollywood Canteen. The records will show she served there almost every Saturday night for two years. The records will also show she and I raised millions of dollars in war bond drives. And my husband, lest everyone forget, was in the service of his country for three years. This," said Carolyn as she held up a black, clothbound book, "is a Bible. Many of you who have written—nauseatingly I might add, now that we're all being so honest—of my religious beliefs, know what this book of God means to me. Therefore, I swear upon it that neither my husband nor my sister was or is a communist. Now, gentlemen, and ladies," added Carolyn as she saw several women in her audience, "I will answer whatever questions you may have that apply to me and only to me."

Carolyn Tiernan defied the Powers-that-Be and walked a very thin line between Heroic Stature among some and Safety to others. Because she never directly attacked the committee and its work—although it was pointed out by several members of the press that she did not endorse it either—she was not vilified and her show was not canceled. Only two things upset Carolyn. The first was herself; that she had used her religious beliefs publicly to prove a point. Although she had obviously planned it, later she felt it had been a theatrical and almost sacrilegious gesture. The second was Margaret. Never had Margaret been so angry with her. Through telephone and letter, an outraged Margaret poured out her anger. How could Carolyn dignify those accusations? How dare Carolyn speak for her? And if she was to speak, why not denounce, decry, declaim the true dangers?

Carolyn was stunned by Margaret's anger. And hurt. John took her part. When in Paris on assignment, he urged Margaret to end the sisters' version of cold war by picking up a telephone. He cut Margaret by saying: "You of all people should understand the courage it took for her to do such a thing; you who knew her when the sum total of her political awareness could be placed—with room to spare—on the tip of a needle. Besides," John added more softly and supplicatingly, "I would think you'd be damned before you'd allow this committee to come between you and your sister."

As she stood before her local patisserie wondering whether James had bought bread or whether she should, she smiled as she recalled how John's words had shaken sense into her head. Lynnie had taken on the House and proved it to be the house of cards that it was. My little sister, my older-but-not-wiser Lynnie, did that, she thought as she decided that they could live without bread if James had not purchased it on his way home.

Suddenly she remembered what else John had told her that day, and the pain it had caused. Public and internal pressure had forced Franklin Killerbrew to remove all pictures of her from the studio's walls. According to John, to walk through Killerbrew Studios today was to see no trace of the great star who had once been the major money-maker for the studio. What hurt Margaret most was realizing that it was not the removal of her pictures that bothered her but the fact that they would no longer be a constant reminder of what she had been in Franklin Killerbrew's life. She had not known until that moment that she still cared. Now, two years later, what difference?

Two years later . . . another life in another lifetime, she thought. Their style of living was so much simpler . . . easier. Then, before the changes in James's life, they had had to employ a cook and a couple to care for the house and all the entertaining he was expected to do as part of his job for the bank. Now, they had the house and their lives to themselves with the only outsider being Mathilde, the woman who came in each morning for three hours to clean and keep the household in some form of order.

She had not known of the difficulties James was having at the bank because he hadn't told her. He was not in the practice of bringing his work home unless he felt it would be of interest to her or in the form of a person who had to be entertained. It took her a long time to realize they were no longer being asked to prepare or attend dinners for visiting American manufacturers and financiers. It took a "friend" to tell her of the rumblings at the bank caused by her "political action." Later, she was to learn that the rumblings were more like an earthquake. But James had said nothing. He simply informed her one day that he was leaving the bank to become the vice-president of a French investment company at nearly twice the money but at half the hours he had spent at the bank. If he suffered about leaving what had been a lifelong career, he never let on. Instead, he spoke of the change and the advantages of such a change when a man is at the half-century mark and thinks nothing new is likely ever to happen again in his life.

As she thought of her husband, his past and her own, and the something new that was about to happen in both their lives, Margaret fought the tears about to fall in both sadness and joy. Throughout, from the time they had met, he had always been so supportive and so giving. When friends during that terrible period became enemies or strangers, he raged against them rather than rued their defection. Whereas others in the world were having their loyalties questioned, she never had to ask about James Carrington's.

Why is it, thought Margaret as she opened and walked through the wrought-iron gates into her courtyard, that loving someone can be sweet and sad? Often, she ached for

James Carrington. She wanted life to be everything it hadn't for him. She wanted to make up for Deirdre and that fool daughter of his and finally for the son he had so loved and then lost. And didn't they share *that* in common. Funny how she felt his protector even as his love made her feel protected. She remembered when she had hidden behind his knowledge, afraid to come out and display her ignorance. They had just bought the house and he said, "Do with it what you will." Which, of course, was kind but foolish since she knew nothing about decor. So he had taught her by taking her to museums and design centers. For a year, as he educated and allowed her to cultivate her tastes, they had lived in a house whose only furnishings were a double bed that sat majestically on a raised platform.

Now standing in the entrance hall, inhaling the aroma of the fresh flowers so artfully arranged by James in the huge crystal vase that sat alone on the waist-high teak table that looked so elegant in its white-tiled space, she was drawn into their living room. She browsed through it, wanting that moment of reacquaintance with objects that held memories of other times and people, before finding James where she knew he would be. Off-white walls and off-white carpeting. How impractical it had seemed but how bright and alive and new. Which is exactly what they had wanted in their lives. Even the Danish furniture, so startling in its design that as many people hated as loved it, spoke to this need for the new. All the couches and chairs in the room were of birchwood and covered in an off-white nubby-weave fabric. And the main thrust of this room wasn't the usual fireplace or the French doors that led to their tiniest but prettiest of gardens, but the paintings—the Mirós and Jackson Pollocks and the terribly expensive Mondrians. They set the room aflame with warmth and vitality in an interior design for living rather than effect.

Her dining room was a gallery, a showcase for new painters and sculptors whose work they collected on their weekend rounds of not just Paris but Lord only knew how many cities they had visited in the past few years. Even the birchwood boat-shaped table Florence Knoll had designed for conferences but which they used for dining was part of their excitement over introducing new forms to their home and their lives. For a moment she sat in one of the six Eero Saarinen plastic-shell, foam-rubber-upholstered chairs that surrounded

375

the table. She recalled that Christmas morning not too long ago when Carolyn sat in one of the chairs across from her and asked, "Is it enough?" And Margaret remembered her reply. "Oh, yes, Lynnie," she had answered, understanding the full implications of Carolyn's question, "it's enough. It's more than enough," she said with a fullness that had made Carolyn reach out and hug her.

It was with that feeling of fullness that Margaret climbed the stairs. From the stairwell, she could see into the bedroom and to the tiny balcony where James Carrington sat, his whiskey and soda in his hand, staring out at some part of life he never ceased to find a miracle. In that moment before he felt her presence, Margaret observed the man she had married, his back held straight and his face turned toward whatever was out there. Again the tears rushed to her eyes and spilled onto her cheeks. He was not alarmed when he turned and looked at her because the tears were falling into the widening abyss of a smile that took over Margaret's face. She was laughing and crying and crying and laughing and as he rose to hold her he thought it must be someone else who was saying: "James . . . James. My darling James. We are going to have a baby."

There was no question in Carolyn's mind that the worst day of the year was January 3. No matter that the twelve days of Christmas didn't end until the fifth of the month, in the world in which she lived, the holidays ended with a thud, more than a crash, the day after New Year's. But the effects were felt on the third. A dreary day in January. A dreary month in New York. Dreary weather. Dreary winter. Dreary.

All right, Carolyn girl. Get up. Get busy. Get an early start and take down the tree. Pack away the ornaments carefully so that this one year none break. Do anything but sit here thinking. A good and wise decision, thought Carolyn as she rose from the empty breakfast table where she had been dawdling alone over her coffee. John Jr. had skipped off to school with visions of sugarplums still dancing in his head. Christmas—at least what it had become—was definitely for the children. John Sr. was snug-a-bed where he would remain after having worked till the wee hours correcting the galleys on his *Health Care and the Aged* book that was due at the publisher's this morning. Thomas and Vinnie were at rehearsals and Marti, who should have accompanied them, was in bed, nursing the cold she had picked up on her ski weekend.

Marti and ski weekends. Already. And without a chaperone. Just with the trust of her loved ones. Oh, yeah? Says who? thought Carolyn as she plopped down again in her chair. Certainly not by me, although I make a great show of pretending otherwise. The curse of being a modern mother. I don't envy Margaret one bit. I couldn't go through it again. By the time Margaret's child is a teenager, I'll be an antique, belonging to another era. Pre-Victorian . . . Maybe I should call Margaret. Maybe that would cheer me up. Maybe another cup of coffee.

"Hey, gorgeous, pour me a cup, too, while you're up."

Carolyn was surprised and pleased. She hadn't expected to see John until noon or thereabouts when he was due downtown at the publisher's.

"You're up early," she chirped, pretending to a cheerfulness that wasn't there.

"Couldn't sleep. Flop sweats. The book is a bomb," John replied as he sat down.

"It's wonderful and you know it. I couldn't believe what I read."

"If I weren't your husband, would you have read it? Don't bother to answer. The truth of the matter is: people who don't need to read this book will; people who should, won't. It will be a critical success and a financial failure. Happily, I've a rich woman who will keep me and see me through my hour of need."

"Call her," said Carolyn sourly. "Maybe she'll see me through mine, too."

As she seated herself across from where he was sitting, John stared at his wife as she stirred saccharin into her black coffee. "The blahs, the blues, or both?" he asked.

"You got to admit, it wasn't exactly the best Christmas ever."

"Agreed," said John. "And here I always thought practice makes perfect."

"I wish I could take it so lightly. No, really, I do," she added when she saw he thought she was being sarcastic. "I wish I could find some humor in all this. But I'm worried and upset and angry and confused. I also feel torn. A part of me wants to be with Margaret in Paris; still another part feels I should stay here and try to piece together the fragments of a

377

family; and still another wants to take you by the hand, pack a bag, and fly off someplace where it's warm and sunny."

"I can be packed in ten minutes. How about you?"

Carolyn sighed. "It takes a woman longer, particularly at my age."

"Age? What's age have to do with this? Don't you know women are at their sexual peak in their forties? Come, peak with me! Let's rush off to exotic lands and do exotic things, you wild and wonderful woman you."

In spite of herself, Carolyn laughed. "This is no laughing matter," John said seriously. "A woman, according to all scientific studies, peaks when a man is already in his decline. Soon your appetites will far outweigh mine. And frankly, I can hardly wait."

Again, Carolyn laughed. "You're impossible. But at least you'll be lively company as we spend eternity together in hell."

"Now that you're laughing, tell me . . . what's bothering you? Margaret? Vinnie? Thomas? Marti? Or all of the above?"

"Margaret should not be pregnant. I know she wants that baby so badly but oh, God, I'm worried."

"But you can understand her wanting it," said John as he moved to her side of the table so he could sit next to her.

"Yes, of course, but John, she will soon be thirty-nine."

"Lynnie, next November is not soon."

"It is when your baby is due at the end of May or early June. John, it's dangerous for a woman to have a child at that age. Dangerous for her and the baby."

"Which is exactly why the doctors put her to bed and told her to remain relatively inactive for the first few months. Carolyn, remember, it was *you* who told me it was not that unusual for a woman to stain in the first few months of pregnancy."

"Not unusual but certainly not good."

"But not necessarily disaster either. Right?"

"Yes," Carolyn conceded. Restless, she rose and poured herself yet another cup of coffee and then sat down. "It's just me. I'm overly anxious. Actually, I'm a wreck. I can't imagine having another baby at forty."

"Thirty-nine," corrected John. "You and Jack Benny, remember."

"Today I feel forty. Every day of that and more," sighed Carolyn.

378

"You look eighteen and twenty-four and thirty-six and . . . forty. All together at the same time. You are still the world's most gorgeous woman."

"If WOR stuck a microphone in here, we would certainly bring a lot more sparkle to radio listeners than Dorothy and Dick or Ed and Pegeen Fitzgerald. Your blarney puts the Irish to shame. In case you haven't noticed, John, I have streaks of gray in my hair. My waist is an inch and a half more than it was when we met. I have lines about my eyes and my stomach muscles are like La Guardia Airport—sinking fast into the ground, and you carry on as if I were some young chicken."

John stood up on his chair, flapped his arms, and yelled: "Cock-a-doodle-do!"

"Oh, shut up and sit down," said Carolyn in mock exasperation.

"You drink too much coffee, you know that?" said John. "I bet that contributes to your edginess. Listen," John said as he took Carolyn's face in his hands and turned it toward him. "Are you upset about Thomas?"

"If you mean about his quitting the show, no. If you mean Thomas himself, yes. You bet I am. And you should be, too. It's wonderful M.I.T. has accepted him. Better than wonderful. And his scores on his entrance exams make me grateful I listened to Augie and Margaret and placed him in a special school. But John, the fact remains he did all of this without telling us. And that's what bothers me. Not that he didn't ask but that he didn't tell. It is his life and I would endorse anything he wants to do with it, but to shut us out like this? To not tell Vinnie or Marti that he was hoping to go on to something else? That wasn't very fair, or nice, of him. And I do think a Christmas dinner is a rather peculiar time to announce your intention. It was one 'gift' we could all have lived without. Among many others of the season," Carolyn added wryly.

"He always was a mite peculiar," said John.

"No. That's not so. He *became* peculiar, during the war and afterward."

"Carolyn," said John angrily, "I'm not going to carry that guilt. Lots of kids' fathers went off to war and came back different people—different fathers. Many adjusted; just as many didn't, I'm sure. But I didn't plan to be away. I didn't plan to be a prisoner. I didn't plan to go from one type of man and father to another. It happened. I accept my responsibility; understand I was not and could not be all he might have wanted me to be as a father. But I won't be guilty about it. There's another side to this, Carolyn. Between what you and I provided, that kid has had more advantages than ninety-nine percent of all other kids in this world. He has never wanted for a damn thing. He has had excellent schooling and damned supportive parents. I don't pretend I have loved him with all my heart. Frankly, I never found him all that lovable." Noting the shocked expression on Carolyn's face, John added: "I didn't and that's the truth of it. But you did. You gave him as much as you gave any of the others."

"Let me understand this," said Carolyn, trying to sort through her emotions. "Are you saying you don't love your own son?"

"No. I'm not saying that. I love Thomas in the way—a very peculiar way that has no basis in intellect—fathers love their sons or mothers their children and I suppose vice versa. But . . . I don't always like him."

Carolyn sighed.

"You're doing that a lot. Sighing," he explained when she looked at him uncomprehendingly. "Speak. Don't sigh."

"I was thinking of how angry Killerbrew was when we notified him of Thomas's decision and how quick he was to offer Vinnie a film for the summer. A film that hasn't even been written yet. And Vinnie's response: 'We'll see.' I don't understand that. All the boy has talked about is making the transition from TV to films and now it's 'We'll see.' "

"He's afraid Killerbrew is looking for another James Dean rather than a Vinnie Tiernan," said John.

"And now this . . . this . . . this *moving out* of his," spewed Carolyn. "It's not right. He's not eighteen yet. If Vinnie wasn't in pain, he wouldn't be doing it. Everyone thinks he's such a bundle of laughs but he's not. It's not natural for a child to refuse to see or speak with his mother. Nor is it natural for a child to live alone."

"First, Lynnie," said John soothingly, "Vinnie is not a child. Yes, I know, he hasn't turned eighteen but he is not a child. Some kids grow up faster than others. That's Vinnie. He's moving out, Lynnie, and there is no way to stop him and if you try, you will force him to sever the only family ties he has. Don't do it. The boy loves you and he may need you someday. His mother has already agreed to use the money—

money he earns, I might add—to pay his rent. I say give him your blessing and your support."

"You've spoken with him already, haven't you?" said Carolyn, amazed at what she had just realized.

"Actually, he spoke to me. He has some kind of problem that needs a doctor. Nothing serious," John added quickly as he saw the concerned look on Carolyn's face. "It's man stuff. I'm not exactly sure what it's about but I suspect our lady-killer has picked up some unwanted souvenir of love."

"I'm sorry I asked," Carolyn said. "I was so much better off when I was ignorant of everything. Now I'm only partially ignorant and I must tell you that's much worse. John, why don't they give courses in parenthood at school?"

"If they did, probably no one would have babies," said John as he rose from his chair. "I better get ready for my meeting." He reached down, pulled his wife to him, and then sat her down on his lap as he collapsed again into the chair in which he had been sitting. With both arms around her, he was nuzzling her neck, alternating between little kisses and little bites, bear-hugging her simultaneously, when Marti walked in, her quilted bathrobe mopping the floor as it dragged behind her.

"They don't do that sort of thing on 'Ozzie and Harriet' or 'Father Knows Best,' you know."

Embarrassed, Carolyn quickly pushed John's arms away from her and extricated herself from his lap. "Your father was just leaving to get ready for work."

"That's not what he looked like he was getting ready for at all." Marti laughed, although she had been considerably surprised by the scene into which she had stumbled.

John kissed Carolyn lightly on the top of her head, rumpled Marti's already quite rumpled hair, and left. Marti continued to stare after him with a quizzical expression on her face.

"Martha Tiernan Ollson, would you tell me what you're doing walking around on an ice-cold floor without slippers or socks? You already have a cold. Would you like to try for pneumonia? What is it with you kids today! Why do you have such an aversion to shoes? Not to mention that bathrobe. It's so old the lining is shot. I can't understand it. You earn a fortune and you walk around looking like a pauper."

"Could this pauper have some breakfast without the wisdom of the ages poured on her cornflakes, please? And my

381

feet aren't cold. I just ache all over but I think it's from the skiing. God, that's hard work! Did you ever try it?"

"Your father and I, many years ago, talked about it when we both were living in California. But it was just one of those many things we thought to do but didn't."

"From what I just saw, I'd say you've managed quite well."

"Marti, really!" said Carolyn stuffily.

"I don't believe it. Ma, look at me," Marti said as Carolyn averted her head. "Why, you are! You're blushing. You know, that's kind of sweet. Actually, it was all kind of sweet . . . seeing you and Dad like that. I didn't think that sort of thing happened at your age."

"At *my* age? What's that supposed to mean?" Carolyn said, her face now flushed from anger rather than red from embarrassment.

"I mean . . . Oh, c'mon, Ma, you know . . . sex. I just didn't think at your age, you and Daddy . . . I mean . . . you don't still, do you?"

"Marti, I'm barely thirty-nine. Now, I know at seventeen that seems ancient but I assure you, it isn't. Actually, if we're being frank, a woman is first at the peak of her sexual powers in her forties."

"Well, I guess that means we won't be seeing much of you over the next decade," said Marti, mischief written all over her face. "You have a lot to look forward to."

"And just how would you know?" asked Carolyn. "On second thought, don't answer that. I'm not sure I want to know."

"You mean if I'm 'intact' or not? Hold on to your beads, Ma, but I am. Surprise! Although for how long I don't know. It seems like everyone but me this weekend was shacking up and having a good time. I don't know why I was so dumb to think the girls would share one room at the lodge and the boys another. I must say the way they were carrying on about it made me very curious. One thing I did learn: men are obsessed when it comes to sex. It's all they want."

"Marti, that's my line. I'm the one who is supposed to tell you that."

"Was Daddy like that?"

"Marti, that's a terrible thing to ask your mother! And just why are you asking me all these questions?"

"Well, who should I be asking? Honestly, Mother, you're

such a prude. Aunt Marg didn't backtrack or beg off when I asked her about sex last summer."

"Your Aunt Marg was never one to backtrack or beg off from sex *any* summer," snapped Carolyn.

"If I didn't know you better, I'd say you were being bitchy."

"Don't use that word in my house! And you're right, I'm being bitchy—and a bit jealous, too. But I always envied your aunt. She was such a lively, freethinking, high-spirited girl."

"Now that's funny, 'cause she said she envied you for being—how did she put it?—rooted . . . anchored in fundamental good sense."

"Margaret said that?" said Carolyn, stunned.

"She equated herself with a balloon that flew off in every which way without first checking to see if she could get back. She said you always helped reel her in."

Carolyn's eyes grew misty. "She didn't tell you, I'm sure, how a balloon helped an anchor to save her marriage."

Marti looked stunned. "It was right after the war, wasn't it?"

"I'm surprised you noticed."

"Ma, kids notice the damnedest things. I knew Daddy didn't feel the same way about us as we did about him when he returned."

"Marti, I've told you before and I'll tell you again. It had nothing to do with you."

Now it was Marti who was close to tears. "But I never felt that. I missed my father and I always felt I had failed him in some way."

"You know, Marti, you should talk to your father about that," said Carolyn. "It's a weight you needn't be carrying on your mind."

"Ma, you didn't answer me before, do you and Daddy still do it?"

"Marti, it is only half-past nine. Don't you think this mother/daughter heart-to-heart is unexpected enough without doing it at such an uncivilized hour?"

"It didn't seem all that uncivilized when I walked in on you and Daddy. What's the matter, Mom, don't you like sex?"

Carolyn's normal response to such a question from anyone other than Margaret would have been outrage. That her daughter would one day ask her such a question had never entered Carolyn's mind. That they were now discussing sex dismayed yet pleased Carolyn. There was a moment when she wanted to say: "It's none of your business," but looking at Marti's face, she had the distinct impression that it was.

"Well, you might say something, Ma. Obviously, since Aunt Marg is pregnant, there must be sex after thirty."

"There is lovemaking after thirty-five and, I would suspect, after forty—I'll let you know when I get there—and even after fifty. In fact, since we're being so truthful today—it must be the new brand of bran flakes—I know there is lovemaking after fifty because your Aunt Augusta was mad about Arthur Abel. Your Aunt Margaret would be much better than I at talking about this. I am, as you say, a prude. But, I can tell you, when it's with someone you love and trust—that's very important . . . the trust—it gets better and better."

"Mom," said Marti as she reached her hand across the table to touch her mother's, "why is this so difficult for you to talk about?"

"Marti, the world has changed so since I was a girl. People didn't talk about these things then, although Margaret seems to have had some kind of heart-to-heart with our mother that I didn't. I regret that. I also resent it, if you want the entire truth. When I think of the differences between your aunt and myself, more and more I'm convinced babies get switched at the hospital and one of us belongs to some woman out there who is at her wits' end now with her whoever-is-this-person's daughter."

Marti laughed. "You know, kid, you're pretty okay even if you haven't read *Catcher in the Rye* and you don't think Tab Hunter is the cutest thing in the whole world."

"Marti, I don't want to pry into a private conversation, but is there anything Margaret told you about sex that we can discuss?"

"That's what's so terrific about her, Ma. Aunt Marg said she could only speak for herself and that I should then talk to you. The only advice she gave was: after listening to all sides, do what I felt was best for me because I would have to live with it and the consequences. But I have a feeling you wouldn't agree."

"In other words, you think I'll tell you what's right and what to do."

"Sort of. Yes, I suppose so," Marti admitted.

"You've written the script, cast the characters, and directed the action without ever asking me for my interpretation."

"I'm sorry," said Marti, meaning it. "Go ahead. Surprise me. Tell me you think it's perfectly all right for a girl not to save it for her wedding night."

"I cannot tell you that. I believe what I believe and you, little girl, know exactly how I feel on that subject. But, as I have learned, times change and one cannot expect one's children to remain rooted or anchored in the past. I cannot live your life, although I admit I would love to. Find a mother who wouldn't want to meddle and I'll show you a mother who doesn't give a damn about her kids. But I've learned over the years that each person has to find what's best for her. So that puts me in agreement with Margaret. Marti . . . do you need help? I mean . . . do you want to see Dr. Garber or someone younger . . . you know, a gynecologist?"

"Mom, I did. A long time ago, actually. I may even be the first girl who received advice and 'props' at sixteen and never used either." Marti laughed. "I was like a Girl Scout." When Carolyn looked at her blankly, Marti explained: "Ma, their motto is: 'Be prepared.' "

"I'm glad you waited," said Carolyn, thinking out loud. "There's a big difference between being prepared physically and being prepared emotionally, being mature enough. I'm sure men think you are both."

"What burns me is: they expect me to sleep with them. Like this past weekend. If he hadn't taken the attitude that it was his right, I might have. I liked him enough, Lord knows."

"Who is he?" Carolyn asked. "No, on second thought, don't tell me. I don't want to know."

"I'll tell you anyway. Now don't look at me that way. I won't mention any names. But he's a director—not Kerry Jones—very handsome and distinguished-looking with his gray hair."

"Gray hair?" shrieked Carolyn. "Gray hair? Marti, how old is this man?"

"What difference?" said Marti impatiently. "And it's only a few streaks of gray anyway. Don't make it into something disgusting like Vinnie did—which is pretty funny considering that woman *he's* been running around with. Why, she's even older than you!"

"What do you mean *even* older than me. Oh, forget that! What woman? No. Forget that too. I don't want to know. This has all gotten out of hand. I'm going to pretend none of the last few minutes happened. You are not dating a man with gray streaks and Vinnie is not running around with a woman who is—as you so delicately put it—even older than me. What's more, I am not about to fall on my knees, beat my breast or ask the Blessed Virgin to forgive us all. Nor am I going to faint. No. I'm going to get up now, Marti. I'm going to bathe and then go to Bonwit's, Bergdorf's, and Bendel's where there's not a trace of reality to bother me.

"I don't suppose," Carolyn continued as she busied herself clearing the breakfast table, "you've given any thought to this summer and your future. I couldn't convince you, could I, to spend a delightful year or three in a convent, could I?"

As her mother sponged the table free of crumbs, Marti got up from her chair and hugged Carolyn from behind. "Oh, Ma, I do love you and thanks for the offer but no nunnery. Actually, I thought we'd both be in Paris for the baby's arrival. I've even asked that they write me out of the last two or three shows so I can do that."

"But after that? Do you know? Do you want to act, or should we try to buy a college and get you in that way?"

"First I want to meet Gerard Philippe and Louis Jourdan. Beyond that, I haven't given the future much thought."

"Well, dear, as they say today, you are certainly keeping all avenues open," said Carolyn. "Now, would you please go to your room like a good little girl and put some shoes on and leave your old mother to her illusions and delusions."

As Marti gave her a final squeeze, Carolyn looked at her daughter out of the corner of her eye and asked, "You don't suppose Vinnie and that woman are just friends, do you?" The expression on Marti's face was all the response Carolyn needed. "I didn't think so. Well . . . win some, lose some."

It was like being the camera and the picture it was taking at the same time, John thought as he observed and participated in the family farewells. Suddenly, the images came clearly into focus, stunning John and hurting him at the same time. When had all this happened? Is it a sign of aging when what's past seems like only yesterday? But wasn't it just last month, maybe a year ago at the most, when Thomas asked, "How go, Da-da?" and Marti was struggling between two boys who wanted to hold her in the place designated for girls. And certainly, John Jr.'s birth had been but a minute ago.

Only in film can you stop action and move from fast to slow motion, thought John, surprised by his feelings of loss and sentimentality. His children were grown or growing, leaving behind their childhood and their parents. John stared at his older son standing off to the side of the picture. Tall, erect, and proud; a handsome eighteen-year-old soon to enter college, leaving one life for another. Some of the press didn't believe that, but John knew that with the last "Tiernans & Company" Thomas Tiernan the actor would die, so that Thomas Ollson the man, the person, could live.

They were standing in the middle of Studio 3B at NBC. Dress rehearsal was but minutes away and Carolyn's and Marti's plane to Paris but hours. The third from the last "Tiernans & Company" marked John Jr.'s debut as an actor, an idea born in Hollywood where Franklin Killerbrew kept an ever-watchful eye on the future. John's youngest thought it all great fun but also an annoyance. Missing "Superman" and the "Adventures of Rin-Tin-Tin" on TV each night was too great a price to pay for this lark.

John's inner lens focused on John J., as he was now called, sitting atop Vinnie's shoulders, delighting in the danger and the thrill of his perch. John J. was laughing and looked laughable buried beneath his coonskin Davy Crockett hat which he wore even when forced into the bathtub. He was a happy child, John realized. The baby gets the breaks. He had outgrown his initial shyness and was an eager, bright child although still drawn to the sidelines rather than the center of attention. It was his decision not to accompany Carolyn to Paris but to remain with his father so that he could "keep up" in school. Straight A's and rising and the kid wants to "keep up."

Click. Another picture. Thomas impatiently checking his watch. Not out of concern for his mother possibly missing her plane, if she continued to emotionally dawdle, but discomfort with the scene. Thomas wanted to do "a wrap." He had said his good-byes. Now, somewhat petulantly for a stern and severe eighteen-year-old, he said, "Ma, the limo is waiting downstairs. He'll get a ticket for double-parking if you don't hurry."

Click. Carolyn . . . turning toward her elder son. "We can well afford the price of a ticket," she snapped curtly and returned to Vinnie, smoothing away, as was her habit, the curls that flopped seductively on his forehead. Her darling Vinnie, off to California as soon as the season ended. On his own. To do what? There was still no script, no plan for a

387

production. Just a contract held by Franklin Killerbrew stipulating that this Botticelli beauty of a boy be available for work in Hollywood beginning July 1. She worried. John could see that worry etched on her face even as she smiled encouragingly at the nephew who was every bit a son to her. He was returning her smile, reassuring her that he and it, whatever "it" was, would be all right.

As Carolyn turned from Vinnie to her "baby"—"Aw, Ma, don't call me that!" John J. complained—John saw the look of loss flash across Vinnie's face. He looked even thinner today than he usually did. It was a look that caused teenage girls to scream and swear their undying devotion, but to John, the camera had caught the boy's fragility.

It was strange, John realized, being so near and yet feeling removed from one's own family. Not that he didn't feel close, just separate, as if he were a reporter covering a story objectively. It was something he did not want to be with his own family. He reached up to John J. and the child tumbled from Vinnie's shoulders into his arms. John held him as Carolyn reminded him to mind Mrs. Worthington when Daddy wasn't home, and said she would miss him even though he always forgot to wash out the bathtub when he was finished. "One of these days, young man, I'm going to take that ring around the tub and put it through your nose," Carolyn threatened. John J. giggled.

The lump in John's throat surprised him. Why had he failed to realize this would be the last time they would all be together until . . . when? Who could say? Different people heading in different directions. As it should be, he told himself. Yet it's difficult.

Marti had reached up and taken John J. from his arms. She was kneeling in front of the child, promising to write him every week and asking if he would please do the same.

"I'll see if my schedule permits," he said with great solemnity. "And if it doesn't," he said brightly as he thought of something, "I'll ask Annette or Carole to write for me."

Marti laughed and hugged her baby brother to her. "You do that," she said and then stood to face Vinnie. "I'll say hello to your mother for you," she said softly.

"And I'll say good-bye to the dirty ole man for you," he responded. Marti laughed. Click. A new picture but with the same people. Tears now in Marti's eyes. Her fingers played with Vinnie's and then they entwined. She looked from him

388

to Thomas. She took one hand and placed it on her brother's shoulder.

Thomas removed Marti's hand and turned so he was facing her squarely. "I think you should come home afterward. I don't like the idea of you alone in Paris."

"I'm not alone; I'm with Aunt Margaret," replied Marti.

"That's what I mean," said Thomas. As Marti stepped back from him angrily, Thomas grabbed her hand. "Just remember: you know where to reach me this fall if you need anything."

Although still angry, Marti again reached out for her brother. This time, Thomas returned her hug. Marti's eyes were swollen with tears. As she turned to walk away, Vinnie caught her by the hand.

Click. Forever caught in one's book of memories an embrace of such love that all were held in its grip. John J. was the first to speak. "Hey, why don't we all ride to the airport?"

"They announced dress rehearsal in ten minutes," said Carolyn. "Haven't you heard, no matter what, the show must go on?"

John J. had a one-word response: "Why?"

Carolyn laughed. As she knelt before her youngest she said, "It's a question, kiddo, I've often asked myself. And if I ever find the answer to it, you'll be the first to know. Oh boy, I'm going to miss you," she said as she gave him a final hug.

"Break a leg, Mama."

Through the beginning of tears, Carolyn laughed. " 'Bon voyage' would have done nicely, John J., but you made your point. Thank you."

A final touch of this one's face, of that one's hand, and the family picture was torn into separate parts. John could feel it as he led the way off the set. John J. was sitting in the special chair marked *John J., Star* that the producers had rigged up for him, and Thomas was standing next to him. From behind a camera, Marti yelled out: "Hey, Vinnie? Remember what I once told you: don't take any wooden nickels."

Standing alone, center stage, Vinnie, assuming the stance and intonation of Bogart, replied, "Here's looking at you, kid."

Carolyn was debating whether or not to be evil. She knew Margaret could never resist taking a pack even though it was loaded with sevens. Carolyn, faced with a decision—whether to meld a pair of eights with a joker and go out with her

389

discard or to throw a card she knew Margaret was holding in a pair—chose to be evil. The look of glee on her face when Margaret pounced on the pack of cards that comprised the discard pile was not lost on her partner. But then, not much in the dynamics between her mother and her aunt was lost on Marti. Measuring her own hand, Marti realized that no matter how many canastas Margaret could make from the pack, she would be stuck with more than four sevens and so penalized fifteen hundred points if either she or her mother could end the game with a proper discard.

Margaret just loved to pick up cards, even though this late in the game it was a grandstand play. She didn't need the overkill but she delighted in it because it had been Marti and Carolyn who taught her and James canasta, which they played most every night. Carolyn looked at Margaret's gloating face and remembered how even as a child, Margaret could be suckered at cards. She was always the Old Maid and she never won at War, which made her invariably start another—one without cards.

Carolyn watched her beaming sister from across the dining table which they were using for the card game. Never had Margaret seemed happier or more fulfilled. Particularly *fulfilled*, thought Carolyn as she looked at Margaret's belly swelling like a wave over the boat-shaped table. She was two weeks late, but unperturbed. On doctor's orders she had remained calm and thin. Her skin shone as did her hair and eyes. Even Carrington, who was not going through hormonal changes from carrying a baby, looked younger and healthier, thought Carolyn.

It had been a lovely three weeks in Paris despite Margaret's inability to tour or shop. But as Marti browsed through the city on her own, Carolyn and Margaret browsed over the recent events in their past. So Thomas was off to college and John J. was doing well at school! Margaret's pleasure at the news was unmistakable. Her pain at the brief message Marti delivered from Vinnie was also unmistakable. It had fooled no one.

"Lynnie," Margaret said almost passionately during one of their conversations, "this time I'm going to get it right. My baby will come first, although I'll never neglect James. But there will be no career—not that there has been any lately—and no public life as Margaret Tiernan." As if to prove her point, Margaret had filled the bookcase in the fourth-floor

390

guest room—study with books on babies written from A (Dr. Ashkenazi) to Z (Dr. Ziedler) and had read them all. What had been Vinnie's apartment was now a nursery, with a room adjoining it to house a nurse or governess should she and James decide one was needed.

"I will be good this time," Margaret insisted. "This baby is wanted, and I hope it's a boy so we can have a son to replace the one we both lost." It was such a pitiful statement to Carolyn; a mother admitting she had lost her child. But Margaret wouldn't talk at any length about Vinnie; only about the child she was expecting. Her fervor made Carolyn think perhaps forty was not too old for her to begin another child.

"Forget it, Ma!" Marti advised when Carolyn mentioned the idea in passing. "Have a play on Broadway instead or buy a dog. But no baby. Why don't you just let Aunt Margaret do all the work and you have all the fun playing aunt. Besides, I don't think my father would be too thrilled having to go through the entire ordeal all over again."

"What do you mean, 'ordeal'? Your father never thought of you as that," defended Carolyn.

"You're right," Marti replied. "He never really thought of us as much of anything when we were young."

Further recollections of that particular conversation were interrupted when Carolyn noted the glint in Margaret's eyes as she debated before discarding.

"You're not!" said Carolyn aloud, thus breaking a rule of the table—not to talk until a play was concluded.

"The hell I'm not!" roared Margaret as she melded six sevens. If her partner could add one, they would earn twenty-five hundred points and win the game. If he couldn't, and if Marti or Carolyn could discard and go out, they would be minus twenty-five hundred points.

James's face revealed nothing. Nor did Marti's until she picked up a card and without looking at it, melded three nines, discarded the card she had picked, and closed out the game, thus "sticking"—as it was called—Margaret and James.

Margaret screamed. She protested. She howled. Carrington sat in his chair rigidly, saying nothing, which in effect was saying everything. Margaret howled repeatedly and screamed again. And again. But the last was different. Carolyn looked up in the middle of her laughter and saw Margaret gasping for breath, her face contorted by pain. She watched help-lessly as Margaret tried to rise but couldn't, falling back into her chair like a weighted balloon. She was trying to speak but couldn't.

"James, call the doctor," commanded Carolyn. "Marti, get Aunt Margaret's suitcase from her room. Margaret—Margaret!" snapped Carolyn. "It *is* the baby, isn't it?" Margaret nodded that it was.

Noting that James hadn't moved from his chair, Marti, after laying an assuring hand on his shoulder, went to the phone and found the listing that had been marked with a red feather for the doctor. Yes, he said when reached, he would meet them at the hospital. James was finally free of his stupor and was already in the driveway warming up the Citroën for the twenty- or thirty-minute drive—depending on traffic—to the American Hospital, about five miles from their home in the heart of Paris. In forty-five minutes, Margaret was in her private room in the hospital, breathing heavily and pretending the pain was nothing.

"I hate haggard-but-brave performances," said Carolyn. "Now scream, damn you, or you'll turn from blue to purple."

Margaret screamed. And she screamed. The baby that had not been in any great hurry to make an entrance into the world was now showing great impatience. James was told to make a brief good-bye, which he did with a tenderness that made Marti want to cry from happiness for her aunt and loneliness for herself. And then Margaret shooed James from the room "to do what you expectant fathers do best—Expect!" When James had left for the waiting room, Margaret took Carolyn's hand, clutching it whenever the contractions choked her. Seeing the pain etched on her sister's face, Carolyn put an end to any further thoughts of ever having another child.

"We will be right outside waiting with James," Carolyn said as she kissed her sister.

"Just keep your hands off him," warned Margaret "I know your type."

Marti giggled.

They asked if she wanted a shot for the pain but Margaret refused angrily. No shot. No anesthesia. Nothing to put her out, to make her unaware of the miracle that was soon to be. She would be awake for her child's arrival in a world she would make safe and loving. Still, whatever they administered at a certain difficult point in the delivery made her groggy. She could hear them urging her to push. *Push!* Bear down, Margaret. And then she heard nothing. Absolutely nothing but a hush, a stillness, that terrified her. The baby was stillborn. It had to be. And then the slap. The crash of flesh on flesh. A cry. A small, pitiful, but miraculous cry. Urgent and insistent and wonderful. And then she dissolved into another world where if there were dreams, she would never remember one of them.

Standing on the bedroom's balcony, James Carrington was watching Margaret and Marti as they sat side by side on the sculptured slab of white stone—one of three—that served as benches in the garden. Neither was talking and both seemed, despite their proximity to one another, in different worlds. But not too different, thought Carrington as he marveled again at the resemblance between the two women. It was not physical as much as it was attitudinal. Their coloring was sharply different, particularly with Margaret's hair still auburn and Marti's almost charcoal-colored. It was the set of the jaw, the tilt of the head, an arrogance that really wasn't that at all but which looked to strangers as if it were.

The sky was threatening but the weather report had promised clearing. At last. August had been so dismal. Normally, he and Margaret never spent the month in Paris but somewhere else in Europe where a vacationer could feel both warm and mentally stimulated. No beachfront for them, but a city or an island with treasures to be explored between basks on the beach or in the water. But this August, they were at home, which was the only place Margaret ever wanted to be these days. As he gazed down on the women, Carrington wondered if Margaret was warm enough. As if reading his mind, Marti drew the shawl tighter about her aunt's shoulders. He could see Margaret's hand patting Marti's in a gesture of gratitude. It was a scene reminiscent of many between Carolyn and Margaret. Now it was Marti, as Carolyn had gone home six weeks ago, at Margaret's insistence.

Carrington thought about the baby and his eyes clouded over with a fine mist. The nursery was just above the room in which he was standing. It was all pink and blue and sunny and bright, which the day was now becoming. Thank God for September, thought Carrington. A strange month. The beginning and the end. A midpoint between two seasons, it showed the best face of both, often giving false hope to the

393

people who judged from its warmth and beauty that the winter would be mild.

From where he stood, Carrington heard Marti ask: "Shall I begin reading?" Without waiting for Margaret to answer, Marti picked up *Marjorie Morningstar*. "As you will undoubtedly remember, we left our heroine yesterday once again faced with the dilemma to have a joyous Noel or not to. You know, a piece on earth. You *are* paying attention, Aunt Margaret, aren't you?" asked Marti with mock teacher/pupil overtones. "You don't seem to realize our heroine has a real problem. To be an actress and a virgin or just an actress. Or just a virgin. Should her 'charms' be given to Noel Airman or should she save them for some nice Jewish fella who would appreciate it only if he married it first. God, it's hard to believe people believe this crap," editorialized Marti. "But they do. Christ! *I* do."

Even in this speech, she was so much more Margaret than her mother, thought Carrington. Yet, she was the middle ground between the two. It was no wonder she had half the eligible men in Paris calling for dates. What was a wonder was how few she accepted and how even fewer were the ones she saw again.

"Hey, you two down there," called Carrington, 'I'm going to do some marketing before the stores get packed with Saturday shoppers."

"Why didn't Mathilde do it yesterday?" asked Marti

"*Why* is a question one does not ask Mathilde Bergot," said Carrington. "Nor is *when* or *what* or *would you* or *could you*. One just remains thankful she shows up each day and is able to distinguish between floor wax and car wax."

"Well, don't worry about a thing," called Marti. "We're going to be busy planning our wardrobe for our big evening tonight."

No, thought Carrington, as he headed for the stairway, I won't worry about a thing. And certainly not about Evelyn's art gallery opening tonight on Rue Jacob; the first social event of the fall season. He would not even be attending if Marti had not insisted and Margaret not resisted. But worry? No. Needless to do that. Every doctor had assured him of that. Just time was needed. Time. But how much time, he would ask. A simple question. Except no one had the answer

James began to walk briskly toward the Seine along Rue Monsieur. Although the sky had cleared somewhat, he clutched his umbrella. The more the memories washed over him, the quicker James Carrington walked.

He could still see the doctor in his green surgical gown as he strode toward him in the waiting room. When he stood to meet him, he could feel Carolyn by his side. And then he couldn't. Somewhere in the recesses of his memory, he could see—or did he imagine—Marti sitting her down on a couch and drawing her mother near. The long hallway was no such distant or indistinct memory. That he remembered, as he did the nursery they passed with the faces of parents pressed to the glass as they babbled at babies who were so welcome in their world. And then a room. A strong smell of disinfectant. Here, too, babies. His own. In a basket. It was the oversized head he saw first and then the hands with the three missing fingers. He took a deep breath as the doctor slowly drew the blanket off the infant to reveal flippers where feet should have been.

He did not scream. Not out loud. He did not cry. Not audibly. But he did pray to Whomever or Whatever that this child be spared—that it die. Three days later, his prayers were answered. A malfunctioning digestive system saw to that.

At first, Margaret remained calm when the baby was not immediately brought to her. She accepted the first day's lie—that there were minor complications and that for the baby's safety, it was being kept in isolation. On the second day, when she was able to walk about, Margaret was no longer so accepting when she was denied visiting privileges with her own child. It was then decided that James must tell her. Carolyn waited outside, allowing the beige wall to support her much the way she had held up and supported James Carrington for the past forty-eight hours. Marti stood nearby, feeling helpless for both her mother and her aunt.

As he reached the Pont des Arts, James Carrington remembered bitterly those first few days when Margaret came home from the hospital. She had immediately gone to the refrigerator and made herself a sandwich. What of? Who could remember. But a sandwich. Later, a cake. And then ice cream. Twenty pounds in two months. A gain for a loss, explained the doctors.

He had pleaded with her to talk to him. She did but about inconsequentia. When spoken to, she responded. But she was not responsive. She would pass the nursery and act as if it hadn't happened. She drifted from day to day, from meal to snack to meal again. In their bed, she allowed him to hold but not comfort her as she remained removed from reality. "The baby is dead. Accept it!" he had yelled at her in frustration one night. She had looked at him and simply said: "I know; I have."

He was not supposed to have heard Carolyn's confrontation with Margaret. And that's what it had been.

"You are not going to do this!" Carolyn had begun. "I've played this scene, remember? How dare you steal from me?"

The device didn't work. Margaret looked at Carolyn and said, "Lynnie. I hear you. I'm here."

Carolyn finally collapsed. Her sobs could be heard throughout the house. He watched from the hallway as Margaret patted her sister's shoulder, offering her the comfort they were all trying to give her.

"Marg, please listen to me," urged Carolyn as she both talked and cried. "You remember how when Mama and Daddy died, you said you no longer believed in God? Remember how you questioned how a loving God could do such a terrible thing to children? Ask it again, Marg. Scream it. Yell it. I won't even argue 'cause I myself don't understand it. Tell Him you hate Him, think He's cruel and unjust. But don't keep it locked up inside. Please, Marg."

"It's not Him, Lynnie. Not Him," said Margaret soothingly. "Go home now, Carolyn. Go home to your own family. To John J. It will be all right."

And two weeks later, James remembered as he stepped off the bridge onto the Right Bank, Carolyn had left for home but it was not all right. Margaret was but half herself, spiritless, as slow in wit as she was in movement.

It will change, the doctors insisted. In time.

The Louvre loomed before James. It was his retreat and refuge. In the museum's works of art, he could forget himself and the work of art at home, of which there could never be a reproduction made. Not of the original. Not of the woman he had married.

As James Carrington climbed to the second floor where glass and fabric ropes put distance between art and art lover similar to the distance between James and Margaret, he thought about the opening of Evelyn Randolph's art gallery that night and how Margaret had consented to attend. A start . . . a beginning . . . a step . . . a hope. Maybe.

As Margaret examined herself in her bedroom's full-length mirror, she decided the "full effect" of the Dior whale-gray dress she was wearing was "to make me look the perfect date for Moby Dick." Marti, helping Margaret to dress, went to the heart of the matter.

"Nervous?" she asked.

"I don't have earrings to match," Margaret complained as Marti fastened the strands of pearls around her neck.

"Oh, yes, you do. Mama sent these a few days ago." Marti opened a little black velvet box. Margaret stared at Augusta's pearl earrings, remembering her aunt's last words. Life, love, and sharing. After a long silence, Margaret adjusted an earring to each ear. She would go to the damned opening; she had promised she would when she realized that the scope of her life was decreasing in direct proportion to the increase in her disinterest and depression. And if she found herself boring, ungiving, dispassionate and passionless, how must James be finding her? What of him and his past few months? No baby, no wife, and no woman. His life, too, had slipped away, but unlike hers, not by choice. It was those very realizations that had brought Margaret, dragged by Marti, to the House of Dior and into this "damn tent of a dress."

"You look fine," said Marti.

"You lie, you scheming wench," replied Margaret. "The one who looks *fine*, as you so delicately put it, is the svelte one in the mirror. You see her, don't you? She's wearing that little black nothing cut to *there* in front and in back."

"I'm not so sure Mother would approve," Marti said as she marveled at her image in the mirror.

"Too bad. She has no one but herself to blame. You prove what can happen when a mother insists her child eat all her vegetables and drink her milk."

"If the two of you would stop with your mouths and start with your feet, we just might get to the opening before it closes," said James as he entered the room. In his gray flannel suit, he was a near perfect match in color to Margaret, right up to the face; only his was flushed from excitement whereas Margaret's was from anxiety. "The cab is still waiting. If you don't hurry, we could buy the damn thing for what it's going to cost in waiting time."

Muttering and grumbling, Margaret was pushed and prodded until she felt herself wedged between Marti and James in the back seat of the taxi. As they drove the short distance from the Rue Monsieur to Rue Jacob, the *au courant* place to be arty, Margaret's sole question brought roars of laughter from James and Marti: "All I asked was whether or not food would be served. I hardly see the humor in that," said Margaret meanly. Except as James and Marti continued to laugh, she did see the humor, black and bleak though it was, and a smile eased the tension on her face.

"Only champagne, dear," James said as he patted his wife's knee consolingly. "The chic never eat."

"Chic shit!" stormed Margaret as the cab came to a stop before the gallery. "Or shit on the chic. Take your choice."

To the untrained observer, it would have seemed that the family's entrance into Jacob's Ladder went unobserved. In truth, within seconds, word filtered from the Celebrated to the Notorious and on to the Well-Connected and the Well-Hung that the Tiernans had arrived. Margaret, taking a quick look around, growled under her breath, "It looks like a reunion of the passengers on Noah's Ark. There's two of everything." Marti tried to keep a straight face as she gazed upon the Perfect and Imperfect of Paris, all in attendance, many— particularly some of the more secure "women"—in formal wear, which was not unusual except it was men's formal wear.

James was already mingling with Vadim and Bardot, shaking hands with Montand and Signoret, exchanging pleasantries with Danielle Darrieux and René Clair. If one judged by the caliber of celebrity who attended gallery openings, Jacob's Ladder ("A Stairway to Heavenly Treasures," read the brochure) was a great success. Particularly for James Carrington, who reveled in mingling with the "masses," and at that moment, with Paris's top fashion model, a gorgeous gargantuan of six feet who, rumor maintained, was really a Steven and not a Stephanie. It was with great pride and not a little of a pixie's pleasure that he introduced an impressed Marti to Gerard Philippe, whose business affairs James had frequently been privy to when he was employed at the Morgan Bank. Margaret clung to his side, smiling dutifully but hardly responding when people asked questions. She was left stranded, however, when James went off to greet Josephine Baker, whom Margaret insisted she did not recognize. "How could I when for once she doesn't look like a walking fruit stand."

There was a momentary flash of panic when Margaret realized she was alone in a room filled with people and a voice was all but screaming: "Margaret! For God's sake, Margaret Tiernan, it's you! And what a sight for sore eyes you are. Although in that dress you're enough to make one's eyes sore."

Turning to face the familiar voice, Margaret stared into a face she both knew and yet didn't know. "The name is Margaret Carrington," she said coldly.

"Ah, but I knew you when!" said the woman triumphantly. "You don't recognize me, do you, Margaret?"

The woman was smiling at her warmly, encouragingly. Oh, God, Margaret pleaded silently, don't let this be happening. Don't let me be that far away from myself. As the woman continued to smile teasingly at her, Margaret yelped in recognition.

"Evelyn. Evelyn Randolph! My God, what have you done to yourself! I mean . . . you've changed," Margaret stammered as she remembered the once free-flowing shoulder-length brown hair with strands of gray that had framed Evelyn's face. Now, she was sporting—and that was it! connected Margaret; she was *sporting*—a modified and very flattering version of the poodle cut. And her hair was an iced blonde, not brassy, but bland and it totally suited this new face. And new body. "My God, the weight I've gained is the weight you've lost," Margaret said.

Evelyn was wearing black corduroy pants, belted in back in the new Ivy League style. A sheer, frilly white blouse, unbuttoned just to where cleavage was obvious but not too obvious, made her look "right" for her own gallery. Amazing, thought Margaret, Evelyn Randolph has gone from being attractive—in both a physical and mental sense—to being a stunning woman who could have stepped out of the pages of *Bazaar* or *Vogue*. She reminded Margaret of someone but she could not think who. What matter? This was Evelyn Randolph who was guiding her up a spiral staircase to a huge room above the gallery where dozens of paintings sat on the floor, leaning against walls. There was no desk but instead a conversational grouping of three chairs around a drum table on which was placed a bud vase holding a single red rose, a sterling silver cigarette case with matching lighter, and a lead crystal ashtray.

As Evelyn lit a Gauloise, she looked at Margaret and beamed. She didn't say "you look wonderful" or make some sympathetic comment about the baby, about which Margaret was certain Evelyn knew, considering the press attention it had been given.

"Well, as you can see, I'm now in the art business and having the time of my life pretending with the Pretentious and conning the Cognoscenti. Margaret, you won't believe it but the art world makes the theatre seem . . . *sincere*. Yes, that's the word, sincere. There is so much phony shit in the art world that if it were ever collected you could start a prefab manure business. But it's also rather wonderful, particularly when you find a new artist who has something new to say. Not unlike finding a new writer. And opening a gallery, mounting shows to present artists' works, is no different from mounting a production. A bravo is a bravo and a painting sold is like tickets purchased."

"You know, James and I collect. In fact, I noticed that many of your artists are those already displayed in our home."

"How is home?" asked Evelyn, her voice giving no indication of previous knowledge about Margaret's current life. "I hope you've gone fat and lazy from sheer happiness."

"It's not fat," said Margaret looking down. "Call it avoirdupois. It sounds so much nicer even if it doesn't look any better. You know, until this week, I was unaware of how 'mature'—that's what the saleslady at Dior called my figure— I've become. But then I haven't exactly been aware of very much recently."

Evelyn reached across the table and touched Margaret's hand. "I would have written but I feel in situations such as yours, it's often kinder not to reopen wounds by making a polite and sincere attempt to say something meaningful when there are no words to ease the pain. But had I been living here, Margaret, I'd have called."

Moved, Margaret, looking away from Evelyn, asked, "Do you live here now?"

"Yes and no. I seem to be living in many places which is so strange for a nester like me. But we have galleries in London and Rome and home is wherever we make it."

"*We?* Have you married?" asked Margaret.

"Sort of. But that's another story to be saved for later, when the dragons downstairs have all gone back to their crypts and castles. Margaret," said Evelyn in a voice softer than Margaret had ever heard from her, "my life has changed rather dramatically. For the better. As you can see, I'm happy. Really happy. Maybe you've heard the talk."

"No, I haven't," said Margaret, looking down. "You see, I've been out of touch."

"How *out of touch?*" asked Evelyn, her voice now that of the producer she once was, who wanted answers when she asked questions.

"Very," said Margaret simply. "Not a breakdown. Just a drifting, a depression, a drifting depression."

"And now?"

"It comes and goes. Mostly, it comes, which is more than I can say about me," added Margaret, trying to make a heavy moment lighter.

"Get help," said Evelyn. "I'm sure there are fine doctors here in Paris."

"I've seen doctors. They say I'll snap out of it and that I'm really in great shape physically."

"I'm not talking about your physical state but your emotional well-being. Your head, Margaret. Psychiatry. What you see before you is the result of couch work three days a week for three years." When Margaret looked askance, Evelyn said, "Freudian analysis is no longer a bugaboo or something for the idle rich. Actually, Margaret, although John was not aware of it, he was receiving psychotherapy from Dr. Fielding at the V.A. hospital. Margaret, psychiatry really helped me. It made me understand and accept who I really am. If you wish, I'll ask my doctor in London to recommend some doctors here. There is no reason a woman like you should ever be unaware or out of touch. Goodness, Margaret, you're one of life's *happenings*. So happen!"

Margaret said nothing but simply stared again at the woman who had once been such a close friend. Her gaze was returned with friendly firmness. "It's up to you, Margaret. It's your life."

Yes, thought Margaret, as she unconsciously began to finger her earrings. It's my life.

Late in October, after many misgivings, Margaret, hidden in her sable coat and sunglasses that made a cloudy, dark day seem even darker, sneaked into the offices of Dr. Franz Ochinclausin, an Austrian-born, Freudian-trained psychiatrist. His office looked exactly as she had imagined it would. Dark, but not too. Wood-paneled with paintings either pastoral or whimsical in mood. At the center of the room was a massive mahogany desk with a leather-tufted chair at its side. When she went to sit in it, the doctor, with a wave of his arm, motioned her to the chaiselike leather couch on the far wall.

"It is necessary," he said when he saw her reluctance.

She had not counted on "the couch," about which she had heard so much. She had come to talk to him, to hear an objective voice sort through her problems. Gingerly, Margaret sat down. As the doctor observed her every move, she kicked off her shoes and shifted to a reclining position, her head resting on a brown leather pillow that seemed sewn to the head of the couch. Ochinclausin had seated himself behind her where she could not see him.

"I never did like it when people snuck up on me," she said, hoping to produce a laugh. She only heard the sound of a pencil speeding along on notebook paper. "I mean it is so much nicer to meet people head on. Face to face." More scratchings on paper were the response. "You must be wondering why I'm here. Frankly, at this moment, so am I! You see, I know my problems. I just don't know how to work free of them. I'm depressed, but the plain and simple truth is . . . I've reason to be."

"You feel abused."

A voice at last. And not just a voice but *his*. "No, not abused. Well, maybe yes. Abused. When you've lost a baby, a baby you so much wanted, you do feel abused . . . kicked about. You see, I gave birth to a deformed child not long ago."

Silence.

"Mercifully, the baby died."

Silence still.

"That was in June and since then, I can't seem to get interested in anything. If I go on this way, I'm afraid I'll lose the one thing I've got left—my marriage. God knows I'm no joy to live with. Sexually . . . well, there's nothing to say about that because there's nothing happening there."

Silence.

"Hello out there! Can you hear me?" Margaret asked as she shifted to see the doctor's face. "Oh, good! You're still there. I thought maybe you went out for a quick bite."

"Do you often have the feeling people don't listen to you or ignore you?" asked Ochinclausin.

"When they don't reply or give any sign that they're listening or even alive, I do," said Margaret.

402

"Then what you're saying is: you feel you must always have people's attention."

"I'm not saying that at all. You're saying that," snapped Margaret. "I find people usually speak quite nicely to me, and as for attention, I've often had quite more than I've wanted."

"You have felt besieged and beleaguered then."

"Sometimes. But that's not important."

"You think those feelings are not important?"

"What feelings?" asked Margaret, suddenly confused. "Listen, I came here to discuss my depression, the loss of my baby, the loss of me. I'm not bewitched, besieged, beleaguered, and bewildered."

"I beg your pardon?" said Ochinclausin

"Forget it. It's not important."

"You seem to think much of what you say is not important," offered Ochinclausin.

"Doctor," began Margaret firmly. "Either I am not making myself clear or you're not listening. I've lost a baby. I'm worried about losing a husband. I have a son, eighteen years old, who could only send me a sympathy card signed 'sincerely.' He doesn't talk or write to me. I feel I failed him. Just as I feel I failed James in not giving him a healthy child. I walk around all day feeling I've failed this one and that one I'm inundated with guilt. I know all that. What I don't know is how to rid myself of it."

As Ochinclausin wrote furiously on his pad, Margaret continued: "I'm an actress—or I was an actress—and although I made some very good choices—that's actor's terminology—as an actress, I think I made some bum ones as a mother. You see? Again, an overwhelming sense of inadequacy. Problems, I know; solutions, I don't."

"You feel you must always have answers at your fingertips."

Margaret sighed and said nothing and still she heard the scribbling behind her. Angry, she lay on the couch staring at the brown ceiling.

"When did you first notice your feelings of resentment?" the voice behind her asked.

Looking at her watch, Margaret replied, "I'd say about thirty-two minutes ago. Listen, doctor, I came here to talk, not to find a Boswell."

"Please lie down, Mrs. Carrington," said Ochinclausin as Margaret sat up.

"Not on your life, bub, I've had enough," said Margaret as she slipped into her shoes.

"Very well. I feel we've made some very good progress this first session. I will see you next week at this same time," said the doctor as he took off his glasses and closed the pad in which he had been writing.

"Not unless you intend to catch one of my old flicks at a local theatre," said Margaret as she scribbled out a check for two hundred francs. "Thanks for everything, doc. And has anyone ever told you, you really have a terrific way with words!"

Margaret was pacing in her living room, furious, which delighted Marti. With words, gestures, and any other device she could think to use, Marti was encouraging her aunt to vent her anger.

"Damn fool. Thrown away money," muttered Margaret.

"It's only money. Think of the time you've thrown away over the past few months," said Marti. "Now don't give me that look. You've thrown away time. You put yourself on the cross and hammered in the nails."

"With just cause."

"Oh, bullshit! Did you or did you not do everything the doctors told you to do once you began staining? Yes, you did. You damn well did. There was absolutely nothing in your actions that could have caused what happened."

"Except you forget it was *me* who gave birth to that *thing*," screamed Margaret. "Explain that."

"I can't," Marti screamed back. "Nor can any other woman who ever gave birth to a *thing*."

"Do you think they, too, were glad their *things* died?" asked Margaret, the tears streaming down her face. "Yes, you heard me. When I learned about the baby, the flippers, the head, I was so glad it died. It's wonderful, this 'mother love,' isn't it?"

"I would have wished the same," said Marti firmly.

"And you know what else?" ranted Margaret. "Your sophisticated aunt, Margaret Tiernan, atheist, shook her fist and damned Him in heaven. This was after she prayed to Him, of course. I didn't tell you that. But yes, I did. When I was on the table, when I didn't hear any cry coming from the baby after I was delivered of it, I prayed to God for a sound, any sound, of life. And when that baby cried, Margaret Tiernan thanked God for His goodness. And then when that same

404

baby died, she both blessed Him for answering her prayers and hated Him for giving her this . . . this *baby*. Oh, how I cursed Him. I still do. The rage I feel for the gift I was expecting and then the disappointment when that gift arrived and was exactly what I didn't want."

"What *no* woman would want," yelled Marti. "And everyone turns to God, whether they believe or not, in times like that. So what? Maybe you do believe after all."

"I don't know what I believe or what to believe," said Margaret bitterly. "I don't know where to put this ache, this pain, this rage," she added, her face illustrating the words she had used.

"Put it the only place it belongs: to rest," said Marti. "It does not belong on your shoulders."

"You know, your sophisticated aunt even thought for a while she was being punished for her sins. Divine retribution for my wicked, wicked ways."

"Name a wicked way. I defy you."

"I once was very much in love with a married man. I urged him to leave his wife. He didn't."

"If you're talking about Franklin Killerbrew, that was his problem. Why do you look so surprised? Of course I know about you and Killerbrew. All of us kids did. People in our business talk. Talk? They delight, revel, feed off, grow, on talk."

"Vinnie knew?" Margaret asked blankly.

"I just told you, we all knew. Really, Aunt Margaret, for this great sophisticate you seem to think you are, you are truly naïve. From the time the TV series was a hit, we were bombed with every rumor ever created about Mother, Father, and you. Name it; they said it. Right down to your alleged onetime lesbianism."

"If only that one was true I wouldn't be in the mess I'm in now. I'd not have had a child who died and another who acts as if I had, or wishes that I would."

"I'm sick of that also. You and Vinnie, I mean. Dammit, Margaret, look at me when I'm talking!"

Margaret looked at her niece, amazed. So now it was Margaret and not "Aunt." She wasn't sure how she liked that. "I'm listening."

"I understand how Vinnie feels. I'm not him so I can't say whether he is wrong or right, although I think he is dead wrong and I've told him so What is it you exactly did that

405

was so awful? You had to work. Whatever the reasons—financial or selfish or any combination thereof—you *had* to work. It wasn't as if you were a Vanderbilt or a Rockefeller. Yes, you could have had round-the-clock servants to raise him. You also could have sent him, as so many of your fellow actresses did, to a boarding school. But you didn't. Instead, you sent him to your sister and best friend. And all she did was treat him like her own. Better. She adored him, and he worshiped her, as you know. And he received as much attention from my father as we ever did. And love? Vinnie is still my best boyfriend, my buddy. So I ask you, does that seem like a life of hardship?

"You're so full of shit sometimes, Margaret. You did what you had to do and some of it was terrific and maybe other parts of it weren't. Name ten parents throughout history who didn't make mistakes. But I was there. Remember that! I saw your face when we all came off the boat at Southampton. I saw the look of love when you clasped Vinnie to you. I remember you in the park, explaining ever so carefully how my father wasn't Vinnie's father but how he loved Vinnie anyway. And you know what, Aunt Margaret, you looked pretty damned good to me."

Margaret was looking at Marti with an odd expression. "Yeah! You're fuckin'-A right! I'm terrific. You've convinced me. I'm a goddamn Margaret the Marvelous."

"You better believe it!" continued Marti. "So take that avoirdupois and your guilt and either drown them in the Seine or flush them down the toilet."

"Tell me, little girl, when—no, more important—*how* did you get so smart?" asked Margaret.

"As you said, Aunt Margaret, I was a good girl and ate all my vegetables." As her aunt laughed, Marti threw her arm around her shoulders and with great assurance said, "Believe me, kid, when you've been around as long as I have, you know a kid like you is making too much of too little. Vinnie will come around. It may take a year or two, but things will change."

406

2

Things certainly did change but, thought Margaret, what Marti hadn't said two years back is that they change for both better and worse. And often, they changed faster than a person could. Look at her own life. Whoever would have thought she would be the "Managing Director" of Jacob's Ladder. And loving it. Loving "acting" again. And that's what it was—acting. Some of the junk she had to peddle as art took all her "talents" to sell. Evelyn had offered her a part-time job at the gallery two years ago during the pre-Christmas rush. Although she knew Evelyn needed an assistant like she needed an extra anxiety, she accepted, knowing work would take her mind off "things"—such as the food she was finally denying herself. Shortly thereafter, as if the shock of finding herself a member of the "working class," as she jested to James, wasn't enough, she was "startled to the socks" one evening before Christmas when Evelyn walked through the door. At least it seemed like Evelyn from the determined stride, the lithe body, the iced-blonde hair, but it wasn't.

The shock of recognition had been twofold. Suddenly, Margaret not only knew who the woman was, but whom Evelyn had become.

"Hello, Margaret," said the woman as she extended a gloved hand in greeting. "I can see from that 'I'll-be-damned!' expression on that gorgeous puss of yours that Evelyn hasn't told you, although she certainly has told me about you."

"Nancy Killerbrew, you do show up at the oddest times and places!"

The laugh was gutsy, obviously recalling Margaret's reference and delighting in it.

"You *did* drive a mean car, Margaret. By the way, it's not Killerbrew anymore. I've taken back my maiden name, although God knows the only place this ole broad will be maiden again is when she is made-in-bed." Again Nancy

407

laughed heartily. Seeing the confusion on Margaret's face, she said seriously, "I'm not that woman anymore, Margaret. She's gone and I must say, the new one is a helluvan improvement."

Which was how Margaret learned that Franklin Killerbrew was no longer married. Too well she remembered with disgust the feeling of hope, of "Now!" that had flashed through her mind. But it was *then*, she had silently screamed to herself as Nancy Quentin Blanchard looked at her curiously, surprised that Margaret hadn't known of the divorce. Hadn't James told her? No, he had not. Hadn't she read of it in the newspapers? No, there was a period when she was too filled with her own self to read about others, Margaret explained.

Nancy invited her to dinner, but Margaret declined. "Frankly, Nancy, my head doesn't turn that fast. You've changed and the people around you have too, but obviously I need some time to catch up with all this."

As Margaret proceeded to close up the gallery for the night, covering various sculptures with cheesecloth and others with wide strips of clear plastic, Nancy's response rang out as clearly as it had two years before. "I understand. I also understand about us. You, me, and Franklin. How we lived. Margaret, it takes two to strike a bargain, even a bad one. Whether it was me, you, or Franklin, we knew how the beds were made before and even as we slept in them."

Which of course was true, as Margaret could finally see. The Killerbrews had been at war when Margaret entered as both ally and foe. To both. Still, it had been hard for Margaret to wipe the slate clean and start anew. Those first times when she had to deal with Evelyn and Nancy together, Margaret maintained a distance that had nothing to do with their affair, which was different from what she had imagined. They were so gentle with each other . . . comfortable and comforting. It was very odd. Now that Nancy was what they called "out," she was softer and more feminine. And Evelyn . . . well, that Margaret would never understand. As she told James, "Evelyn Randolph did more—so to speak—for the boys during the war than all our Bundles for Britain."

It had bothered Margaret to learn that James had helped Nancy set up her galleries. When she asked why he had not told her, he said, "Frankly, I couldn't see where it was any of your business or how it could concern you other than negatively. You must remember, my experience with Nancy, personally and professionally, has been very rewarding. She has been a client and a very good friend."

That summer Margaret had seen just how good a friend. She had been working as an "assistant" and "showpiece" at the gallery for almost eight months when James suggested they spend the first two weeks of August on Lido. Jacob's was closed for the month, as was just about everything in Paris during August, so Nancy not only approved of the vacation but suggested James and Margaret visit her and Evelyn at their villa near Rome en route to Lido. Despite Margaret's misgivings, they went and enjoyed the three days. When had Nancy gotten a sense of humor? What happened to the "dragoness of the castle"? And finally, when and where had she gotten such heart?

They had been on Lido just a day when James, after strolling on the beach and swimming when he wasn't sunbathing, complained of chest pains. They were in their room preparing to go to dinner and Margaret didn't hesitate but rang for the house doctor and a taxi. At the hospital later, it was verified that James had suffered a mild heart attack—a "warning," as they put it, but nonetheless a heart attack. Frightened, Margaret called Evelyn for emotional support, but it was Nancy who drove half the night from Rome to Venice and then arrived on Lido by way of a hired private launch. And she stayed until Margaret had collected herself and James was assured he could travel without danger.

The phone ringing in the gallery at that late hour startled Margaret. It was, as she suspected, a wrong number. As soon as the line disconnected and Margaret heard the dial tone, she rang James at home. "I'm leaving momentarily," she said. "Warm up the coffee and that motor of yours. Mama's got a helluva hunger tonight." She heard his laugh and felt secure. But then James always had that effect upon her. Even after the scare . . . the "warning."

She remembered him coming to her shortly after their return from Lido. It was early fall and he had joined her in the garden after dinner. As they sipped their demitasse, he explained how he had been over all their accounts and found there was enough to last them forever and a day . . . "or, to be more precise, for as long as my love will last for you." She had called him a corny old fool in need of new dialogue, but he was not to be deterred. He was, he explained, a fifty-six-year-old man who was going to retire immediately and live life as he always thought it should be lived—at leisure. He would read, garden, attend the Comédie Française and the Opéra, tour the museums of the world, and travel. With and without her.

She was amazed by his ability to stare calmly at his own mortality and not feel threatened by it. So unlike herself or Carolyn, who had phoned that December and wailed: "Now that I'm *really* past forty, it's all downhill. Half of my life has been lived and what have I accomplished?" Margaret told Carolyn to look up the answer in *Who's Who in America*. When Carolyn remained distressed and dismal, James took the phone and said, rather harshly for him: "It doesn't matter where it's all gone to, Carolyn, but where it's going."

James's retirement had changed the entire rhythm of their lives. Despite his heart condition, he became less dependent on her. If there were something he wanted to see someplace—even if that place was another country—he went. Sometimes without her, but more often with her. For the remainder of 1956 and into the spring of '57, they traveled periodically, their affairs and the house managed by Marti and Mathilde Bergot. They never rushed through cities or airports but lived at leisure and in luxury. It was all as serene as it was scenic. Thus, the shock, when they got home after their one prolonged absence "doing" Australia, of finding their house surrounded by photographers who seemingly never slept, was more than just mildly upsetting.

Oh yes, thought Margaret, as she put on her coat and wrapped a scarf about her neck, things certainly change. Just as Marti had said. Only she hadn't said the changes would be as much in her as they would be in anyone or anything else. Suddenly, Marti Tiernan was a star. Not the star she had been in the United States. Not a Tiernan Tot or Teenager, but a French film star, which meant . . . an American scandal. She had appeared apparently in the nude in a film directed by Charles Chauverant, and all of France wanted to paint her. Among other things. It was those "other things" that were alarming to Margaret and what matter if, as James said, her niece was no longer a child. Margaret was not quite sure *what* Marti was at that time. She was up most mornings at five for the hour's drive to Eclair Studios in the Paris suburbs and did not return to the house—when she did return—until nine or ten at night. And the house was under constant siege. Suddenly, to Margaret's horror, the phone that frequently rang and which she often answered had a much more active fantasy and sex life than she did.

Marti's burst of film activity and fame, combined with James's constant pursuit of his mind's interests, made Margaret feel like a slow child always struggling to keep up. She did not like the feeling. She, Margaret Tiernan, slow? The pacesetter and rebel? Which was why she decided to become the Managing Director of Jacob's Ladder when the position was offered to her in the spring of this year. It was, Margaret decided, a sure sign of change and age that she was now managing affairs instead of having them.

As she double-locked the doors to Jacob's Ladder and stood on Rue Jacob, Margaret felt a chill that had nothing to do with the rather mild December weather, but with the weekend that was almost upon her. The weekend and all those guests! Although every possible detail for the wedding had been thought out and covered, including very separate rooms at the Ritz for some of the very separate guests, she was terribly nervous. The weekend marked the first time she would be seeing Vinnie since that awful summer in '54. My Son, the Star. Or Superstar as the press and everyone else now refers to him. A good thing she had thought to add more security guards to protect the house this weekend. Between Marti's and Vinnie's fame and infamy, they would earn their pay. God knows the house and everyone in it will be under siege by the press, none of whom would be particularly interested in her. As she began to walk briskly toward Rue Monsieur, Margaret realized she was not too thrilled with that last observation. Not too thrilled at all.

Evelyn Randolph whooped as she whirled Carolyn about in a dance of delight that caused travelers at Heathrow Airport to stare. Carolyn was dying to do likewise. Although Margaret had told her of the changes in Evelyn's life, the physical ones were startling, particularly since she had not seen Evelyn since 1948 when she and Margaret were doing Mourning Becomes Electra.

Evelyn had recognized Carolyn as she waited with John J. in tow for the BEA flight to Paris. "One would never guess looking at you that you had been flying all night. You look gorgeous!"

"My father says my mama always looks gorgeous—that it's part of her talent."

411

Evelyn turned her attention to the boy who was already his mother's height and who shared her coloring. Pale, almost translucent skin. But his father's blue, blue eyes.

"And of course your father is right," said Evelyn. "Do you remember me? What a stupid question! How could you? You were only a year or so when we first met. How old are you now?"

"Almost eleven."

"Are you married?"

John J. giggled at the question. "No . . . divorced."

It was Evelyn's turn to laugh. Carolyn observed some of the changes in the woman just from the raucous rather than the refined laughter she had associated with Evelyn. Some change, thought Carolyn. Not just in her but . . . my God, here I am waiting for a plane to Paris, talking to a woman and her lover, who only happens to be a woman also, but not just any woman but the former wife of my sister's former lover—and really, this is all too much for me.

"I'm Nancy Blanchard. We've never met but I have a feeling we're well acquainted," she said, not bothering to hide the humor she found in the situation.

Ah, Lord, if only I were that sophisticated, thought Carolyn. "I know," she finally replied, trying to comprehend that this elegant woman, in a cream-colored suit with a small, cinched-in waist, was a lesbian.

"Like it?" asked Nancy.

"I beg your pardon," answered Carolyn.

"The suit. I saw you staring at it. It's from Dior. There's this wonderful new about-to-happen designer there, Yves Saint Laurent, and if you like, I'll take you to meet him."

This conversation cannot be happening, thought Carolyn, feeling absurd and awkward in her rumpled gray skirt and somewhat smelly white blouse which had seemed perfect for all-night transatlantic plane travel but hardly the thing to wear when meeting Nancy Whatever-she-now-called-herself.

"It's marvelous that we're all on the same plane," gushed Evelyn. "It just adds to the excitement. God, can you believe it, Carolyn? Where does time go? Speaking of 'going,' where's John? Of course he's coming, isn't he?"

"Yes, of course. But driving from Rome *if* he makes it. My husband, the great social commentator of our day, is doing a TV entertainment documentary on Loren and Lollobrigida and the effect of Italian film on America. Not to mention *their* effect on him. He has assured me his work with Lollo and Loro is all basically social commentary, to which I say: That's a lotta pasta!"

When their flight was announced, the women and John J. boarded the plane, Carolyn with some difficulty as there were certain fragile Christmas presents she preferred to carry than to check through with the luggage. Carolyn was looking forward less to the occasion than to the family's once again all spending Christmas together. Well . . . almost all. She was still furious with Thomas and still upset that her last words to him before Christmas had been angry ones.

After making sure John J.'s safety belt was securely buckled, Carolyn relaxed into her seat. As soon as the plane was airborne, she pushed the button at her side that allowed her to slide deeper into the cushioned seat and her thoughts. Christmas. In Paris. A homecoming, of sorts. Such a change from the usual. But what was unusual anymore? It's a different time, a different world, she kept reminding herself. Her TV show was gone. Canceled by costs and ratings. Only occasional guest appearances now. But that was fine. She was now free to do that marvelous play for Broadway. Lord knows the script was no problem. Nor was John J. But the fact that he wasn't a problem was what prevented her from giving a definite "Yes!" to an anxiously awaiting producer. This child was so different from the others. Despite his bad beginnings, this child was seemingly complete. He was confident, secure, even though he was not a scene-stealer and preferred the background to the limelight. Carolyn felt afraid to risk this completeness. Would there be, could there be, a bad effect on this child if she were out of the house six nights a week?

John, of course, had been no help at all. The decision was hers. If she could draw analogies from his relationship with his son, she should do the play. John bounced about the world at will—*his* and none other's—and when he came back he resumed with John J. as if he had never been gone. The two shared a camaraderie she had never seen between a father and son. Their relationship was proof she could do the play if she wished. Aye, there's the rub, thought Carolyn as the plane flew through wisps of white clouds that opened and closed on the sea below. Do I really *wish* to do theatre again? Sometimes, I don't believe myself. What happened to the girl that was? To all her ambition. Where was the actress who panicked if she didn't have a new show to do every year or every two years at most? Now . . . yes, she wanted to do the play but, now, there were other considerations. Like John J. and like John. She wanted to be home when he was. At least that's what she thought this week. By next, she could change her mind again. And why not? If everything around me can change, why can't I?

She thought about that last statement. The Russians had launched Sputnik and changed the world forever by changing fantasy to reality. Somebody named Elvis-the-Pelvis was swiveling his hips and Lord only knows what else on television, and while some parents thought it disgusting and that rock 'n' roll would ruin the morals of the country forever, others laughed as they remembered the uproar when they, as teenagers, did the jitterbug and men wore zoot suits. And here I sit with two women, lovers, going to see my sister and my daughter who is an international star and scandal, threatened with excommunication—her films banned by many churchmen—and I worry whether or not to do a play. Meantime, I have a son, who, like his cousin, is removed from his family. Only his cousin maintains some ties, at least, to those he loves. But maybe that's the difference, thought Carolyn with a sudden and sad realization. Vinnie loves while Thomas does not. At least it would appear he doesn't.

With that thought, Carolyn pressed her face to the window so that neither John J. nor the two women across the aisle could see the tears sliding gently down her cheeks.

The jerky motion of the train as it tumbled down the track tossed Thomas in his coach seat. His face was pressed to the window and an observer would have thought he was lost in his admiration of the countryside. Not so. Thomas was lost in thoughts that tossed him about far more than the train. In his lap was the most recent layout in that men's magazine that had caused him, again, such embarrassment. In his head was his anger, his feelings of mistreatment and alienation. The argument with his mother had been harsh and she, like him, had been unrelenting.

And he could not forgive Marti any more than he could his father, who no matter what he said otherwise, gave every indication in his work of being "leftist." And Vinnie. Since Thomas himself had been the manufactured victim of numerous imaginative minds at magazines and newspapers, he had no idea if a tenth of what he read about his cousin was true.

But certainly that picture of him, unshaven and unkempt as he resisted arrest by officers who had picked him up for drunken driving, was real. There can be no faking that. Any more than there can be this, thought Thomas, as he turned from the landscape to the six-page layout of Marti that had been brought to his attention—somewhat snidely—by several of his classmates.

An earlier layout shocked Thomas who had never thought Marti would go bare-ass in a film or in a magazine. Now, there she was again as she bared her soul and everything else for the public, but more likely, Thomas thought, for Charles Chauverant, the film's director and Marti's lover.

Thomas wondered if Reese had seen it and if so, how had she taken it? How could anyone take it? All that top-heavy cheesecake spilling off the pages and into one's fantasies. Probably Reese would adjust to this latest family trauma better than he. But Marti wasn't Reese's sister. Reese didn't have to overhear locker-room jerk-off bullshit about how so-and-so would like to do you-know-what to Marti Tiernan. Reese didn't go to bed knowing men all over America were coming all over Marti's breasts.

Thomas had given Reese his two-door Chevy convertible to drive to Bridgeport while he took the train to New York. He had reached a decision: never again would he live in the Central Park West apartment. He was using this Christmas recess, with the family grouped in Paris, to take the remainder of his things without incident. Then, he would train it back to Bridgeport, pick up Reese and the car, and spend the rest of the Christmas holiday meeting her friends and family, and trying to forget he had severed the cord; something he had been trying to do, at least symbolically, from the moment he had entered M.I.T. Using his real last name had been a beginning. Not buying the M.G. or the Mercedes he really wanted was part of that beginning. The less ostentation, the greater the chance for anonymity. He chose not to live on campus but instead found a one-bedroom apartment with a bow window overlooking Commonwealth Avenue in Back Bay. It was just a thirty-minute walk or a ten-minute drive over the Harvard Bridge to campus. He furnished the apartment with solid antique wooden furniture and never had classmates in for drinks or dinner.

Keeping his past identity under wraps was and yet was not possible. Many recognized him instantly while others thought they did, and still others, not TV devotees, had no idea whatsoever that the young man with the blond crew cut was once a major star. When wearing his khakis with the blue tie and hat for his weekly Air Force R.O.T.C. training, he looked like any other good-looking boy from the Midwest.

Thomas had made very few friends in his first year at M.I.T. and was considered an "egghead" by his peers, who envied and yet objected to the amount of time Thomas spent at Barker, the engineering library on campus where he lost himself in space—both the space he hoped to conquer one day and the space that rose up above him to the library's domed roof, with its carved geometric patterns. It came as no surprise to anyone at the semester's conclusion that Thomas was first in the class. Given his antisocial yet always pleasant behavior, it was also no surprise that he did not pledge a fraternity or go out for any of the team sports on campus. That he didn't have a girl was also predictable to his classmates, who believed Thomas lived a monastic existence off-campus in the apartment they knew of but had not seen.

His was hardly a monastic existence. Thomas met numerous girls but his goal, unlike that of his fellow freshmen, was not "getting laid," as that experience was not new to him and hadn't been new for several years. Thomas took out many girls and took several of them to bed. But never just for the bedding. He was looking for *a* girl, *the* girl, and a year ago, just before Christmas, he had found her. Or to be precise, she was found for him.

There was one student at M.I.T. with whom Thomas developed a good relationship. Joe Walsch also hoped for a career in aeronautical engineering and also marched once a week as part of his R.O.T.C. training on the West Campus during spring and fall and in the gymnasium during the winter. His sister was first to date Thomas but she didn't like him, not as a "date," anyway, as she explained to her brother. But she knew this Wellesley girl who she thought would be perfect and no, she insisted, Theresa Tomlinson was not "a dog" but a "smart cookie" with a lot of "moxie." From the first, Thomas was in agreement with Joe Walsch's sister. Reese Tomlinson was exactly as described in her high school yearbook: "Pert & Perky." She was also petite, at a little more than five-feet-four and one hundred and sixteen pounds. She wore her light brown hair short and ducktailed in the back, which was the current campus rage. She wore Bermuda

416

shorts with knee socks at all times. She had not been with Thomas ten minutes when she announced: "You're the best-looking man I've ever seen." He looked at her in amazement and found she was looking at him in the same way.

The best thing about Reese Tomlinson was her ability to make Thomas laugh. She didn't think his family's "antics," as she called them, were as awful as they were funny. "Of course, I'm not related to them . . . *yet.*" It was the "yet," spoken on either their third or fourth date that had also amazed Thomas. He had not known till then that she was assessing him as he was her for "futures." But then Thomas didn't know that Wellesley girls attended college more to get a husband than a degree. Reese was a notch above the usual Wellesley girl as she also planned to continue her schooling after obtaining her undergraduate degree in liberal arts. "I just know I'd be good with kids, and maybe someday I should teach."

She was certainly good with Thomas. She even relaxed him into toggle coats and skinny, tight Ivy League pants. For their drives about the Boston area, she bought him a tan corduroy cap, with the *de rigueur* Bermuda buckle in the back, to match the tan melton jacket he now wore as though it were a badge of their love. That love was put to the test when Marti's first *Playboy* layout appeared. Reese's parents had been almost as outraged as Thomas. Reese, their only child, who had used that advantage to attain almost everything she wanted, told them to "cool it." They got her meaning even if they did not understand the words. Reese, "the mouth of Bridgeport," simply said, "Look, if I were built like that, I wouldn't hide it either." Of course Reese wasn't serious. She was not the kind of girl who would take her clothes off for anybody unless it was Thomas. That he didn't care she wasn't "busty" like Marti was a miracle as breasts were big on campus in '56, when she and Thomas met, Monroe and Taylor still being the criteria by which all girls were judged.

Thomas had been shocked at the picture of his sister stepping out of a sunken pink bathtub, her body shimmering from water and her hair, pasty wet, away from her face and falling to her shoulders. He had heard she was making a film but had not heard it was *that* kind of film. In reading the text that accompanied the pictures, Thomas learned that Charles Chauverant was to Marti what Vadim had been to Bardot. In *all* ways, if one could believe the article. The picture of

Chauverant showed a Beatnik with black turtleneck sweater, black pants, and lots of gray-streaked, long, stringy hair. Thirty-six, twice divorced, and the father of one legitimate and one illegitimate child, the article said. They had met, it revealed, at a posh gallery opening in Paris, through Margaret Tiernan (of course, thought Thomas disdainfully), Marti's aunt (my aunt!).

When Thomas brought his outrage to his mother, he found that Carolyn was also shocked but not outraged. Her concern over Marti's exposure was nothing in comparison to her concern about her involvement with Chauverant. She understood Thomas's embarrassment. All too clearly she could hear the crudities and the vulgarities of his classmen. Still, as they discussed Marti's actions, Carolyn, in an unguarded moment, said what she was really thinking. "She certainly is one of God's most gorgeous creations!" Thomas mistakenly took his mother's observation as an endorsement and became even more enraged.

Les Enfants Américains, after its European release, made a star of Marti long before the film came to the art houses where foreign films played in America. *Jeune Fille*, her second film, made "Marti-Mania," as Earl Wilson called it, rampant in the United States. Also rampant was the criticism which rivaled and often exceeded Thomas's. Although the film was as artistically well received in Europe as it proved to be financially in America, the explicitness of its simulated and suggested sex scenes was vilified at Sunday sermons throughout the country—which only added to the American grosses and to "Marti-Mania." *Jean et Jeanne et Jean*, Marti's latest film, involving a ménage à trois, would only add to the controversy and Marti's stardom. As would her wedding, which was taking place this weekend in Paris and which Thomas had flatly refused to attend. Carolyn had been furious with him but her imploring clichés—"She is your sister, your *twin* sister"—had fallen on hardened hostility.

"You can choose your friends but not your family," he countered. "But as an adult, you can also choose not to be party to that family when it continues to be a poor moral example."

"How dare you judge us all?" Carolyn said over the telephone, her voice quivering from anger she didn't think it possible for a mother to feel toward her child. "What gives you the right to play judge and jury? To play God?"

"I give me the right, Mother. After all, it is my life."

As the train went from daylight into the darkness of the tunnel that would end at Grand Central Station, Thomas thought about his mother. She was a victim of her family and her own inability to be firm when firmness was needed, he decided. Once he had seen her as a martyr but now he saw her as weak, spineless, and totally lacking the courage of her convictions. If she still had any. As the train ground its way to a lurching halt, Thomas realized that he loved his mother but he really didn't like her.

As Reese Tomlinson turned on Stratfield Road, the Church of Our Lady of the Assumption faded from view but not from her mind. She had worshiped there as a child and she knew she would be married there as well. It would be a lovely wedding. All white and pink; the moment she had waited for most of her life. After a choir of angels sang, the audible sighs of relief would be heard coming from her parents. Reese laughed at the thought. What would her parents have done had she chosen to be a "career woman" and shunned marriage? Worse, suppose she had been ugly and no boys had called, what then would they have done? The shame of having an unwed-by-twenty-two daughter would probably have caused them to walk hunched and bent for the rest of their lives. They might even have given up the two-story white colonial house with its pretty green shutters and screened-in porch and moved from Bridgeport to someplace where their shame would not be known. Reese wondered if there was a city in America where parents whose daughters hadn't made "matches" could live with some shred of their dignity intact. Again, she laughed. Reese often found humor in the moral or value systems of society, although what she found funny her parents and peers often did not.

The M.D. license plate on the Chrysler at curbside on Brooklawn Avenue was evidence her father was home and preparing to go out on call later. The driveway leading up to the house was therefore clear so Reese drove the Chevy to the garage doors and parked. Just before turning off the car radio, she heard a local disc jockey comment on a news item that had preceded his broadcast.

"So Marti Tiernan gets married tomorrow in Paris. You know, at some weddings, the guests wonder if the bride will

419

wear white. I hear at this one, the guests are wondering if the bride will wear anything at all."

Reese flicked the switch on the radio, happy to know there wasn't any way Thomas, who had already been subjected to so much teasing which he took as torture, could have heard the broadcast. Although Reese understood how it could and would upset him, she also felt, and told Thomas so, he was being overly sensitive. Often she marveled how such a traditionalist could come from such an unconventional family. But wasn't that her mother's cry and the curse that she maintained she bore throughout her life? How could she, Louise Tomlinson, have raised such a rebellious daughter? Some rebel! All because I *thought* I might want to work, might want a master's degree in education. My God, thought Reese, think how Mother would react if she knew her daughter, at twenty, was no longer a virgin! If the church didn't excommunicate me, Mother would.

Again Reese laughed but it was not the laugh of derision but of love. Her mother, like Thomas, was a traditionalist and always had been, which is why Reese, as a teenager, had to take a thirty-minute train ride twice a day to attend the Academy of Our Lady of Mercy in Milford, Connecticut. "I will not allow you to have anything less than a proper Catholic upbringing," her mother had explained as she packed her lunch then packed her onto the train each morning, "and since there is no Catholic high school in Bridgeport, off you must go." So off she went and it was wonderful. A full thirty minutes away meant miles apart in those years. With the other "good little Catholic girls," she learned to smoke and drink beer. She also found there were "good little Catholic boys" with heathenish or hedonistic ideas on their "good little minds." She liked that.

Even Thomas had laughed at her conventional—or so her mother thought—education and upbringing. That he could laugh, and did, but usually only with her, was part of what endeared Thomas Ollson to Reese. The boy who looked and acted so straitlaced was capable of much charm and gentleness, she knew, even if no one else did. As she smoked a Viceroy, her last visceral pleasure before entering a house of rules and regulations, she thought about her first meeting with Thomas.

She had been upstairs waiting in Shafer Hall, Wellesley's own Tower of London, with its own turrets and towers, when the girl "on bells" rang up to announce: "There is a Thomas Ollson waiting." As soon as she hung up, Reese put on the one thing she was not wearing: shoes. High-heeled shoes. The signal from "on bells" had been received. Had the girl said Thomas was waiting *down*stairs, the buzz word was *down*, which would have meant flats. She remembered feeling good that Thomas Ollson was tall. When Reese saw Thomas sitting in the living room just off the "bells desk," she felt really good. Instantly, she recognized him: her teenage idol, in person. He laughed when she told him and warned: "I really don't fight crime. I not only don't pack a gun but my fists don't pack a wallop either."

So her first impression had been of his good looks and his humor. It was only after several days that she saw his intensity. His classmates had dubbed him, unaffectionately, "Mr Perfect," such was his insistence to be the best. The hours he labored over his term papers and his studies were far beyond normal. He acted as if it were up to him to prove he was different from those members of his family whom he considered a disgrace. He did not believe, as she continually argued, that he was judged for himself and not for Marti or Margaret, Vinnie or his father.

Reese could not remember whether it was on their fourth or fifth date that she fell in love with him, although certainly she had been smitten with a crush from the moment she laid eyes on him. He had taken her to the Totem Pole for dinner and dancing. At first, he would only dance the "slow ones," but after he loosened up she got him to try the Bop and the Slop. He was awkward but only because of his compulsive desire not to call attention to himself. When he had taken her to his apartment on Commonwealth Avenue, she saw still more dimensions to the man. The furniture was strong and sturdy, solid stuff, made to last a lifetime. Which was exactly how she saw Thomas Ollson. But the sofa and chairs were soft yet with a firmness to give support where support was needed. This, too, she felt was like him. When he took her to bed the first time, he had not wanted to take her virginity also. They could caress, fondle, hold, and do things to one another that would be acts of love without desecrating—his word— her purity. To which she said: "Fuck it!"—and meant it both figuratively and literally. He laughed at first and then said rather seriously, "I would prefer, if you don't mind, that you don't use that kind of language." She did not mind only because he did. When they did make love, it was, as she had been forewarned, painful at first and then exquisite. Never had she felt so alive and so cared for . . . loved. At no time did she experience any guilt about the physical relationship she enjoyed with Thomas. But then Reese couldn't separate it from the emotional and intellectual relationship between them.

She had been pleased when he agreed to meet her parents this holiday but not as pleased as they had been. Yes, they had some misgivings about his family, but given his own misgivings, which Reese had relayed to them, they felt hopeful about their daughter's choice for a husband. And that's what Thomas is, thought Reese, as she climbed out of the car: my choice for a husband. Because he needs me. Because he's lonely. Because I'm the one person he says he trusts. And . . . because I love him for being gruff and grumpy when he really is a dear and honest man looking for stability in what he feels has been an unstable life.

At the last moment, John had decided to add footage to his entertainment documentary on Italian sex symbols of the cinema and spent several unplanned days interviewing as he filmed Anna Magnani and Silvana Mangano. Since the footage with Magnani was wonderfully witty and wry, he had not minded missing the opportunity to drive the rather long distance from Rome to Paris and was more than content to be luxuriating in the first class section of the Air France Constellation that was midway between the two cities. Only Franklin Killerbrew was upset by the change in plans as he had been looking forward to the drive through the Alps and the countryside which he had seen previously only from the air.

John sneaked a look at his sleeping partner, a pillow lodged between his head and the plane's window. He was trying to imagine how Killerbrew would look to Margaret and now that he thought about it, how she would seem to him. It had been nine years, John realized. It was hard for John to judge Killerbrew's changes as he saw the man so frequently. Not only were they invading television, meeting constant opposition from networks that resented an outside producing team doing what they felt they could do better ("If you can, why aren't you?" Killerbrew would ask), but now, as good friends, they were constantly invading one another, challenging convictions and politics.

John noted that the perpetually tanned face now had deep creases around the eyes and mouth. His hair, although abundant as ever, was salt and pepper. The similarly colored mustache added age but it also added a look of rakishness. Italy proved, if further proof were needed, that Killerbrew could charm into bed ladies half or twice his age. And Killerbrew had proven, if again further proof had been needed, that in a country where nothing is urgent and everything can wait, that one word or look from him sent everyone scurrying.

It was John who had insisted on Killerbrew's being invited to his daughter's wedding. He was not about to slight or offend his friend and partner. Strangely, only Carolyn had offered some weak resistance which vanished when Margaret said it was quite all right. Killerbrew himself had questioned the advisability of his attending and had seemed pleased when told he was wanted by all concerned. John wondered, now that he knew, how Killerbrew would react when he learned that his former wife would also be a guest. Hopefully he would take it as well as John had taken the news that his former sort-of/kind-of lover, Evelyn Randolph, was now Franklin Killerbrew's ex-wife's lover.

As the plane approached Orly and the stewardess asked that they fasten their seat belts, John thought how strange it felt having a child old enough actually to be getting married. How could that be when he was still so young and so recently married? And even if that last wasn't true, that is how he felt. Someone here was definitely getting older. It had to be Marti. Those pictures in the magazine proved it. And how thrilled Killerbrew had been with those pictures, and with Marti's success in foreign films. As he told John, from the beginning he had wanted to sign Marti but didn't know what to do with her, considering how strong her all-American, girl-next-door image had been. Now that she had shed that image, and along with it a great many former fans, he had no such problems. Nor would this marriage to a much older man hurt her career in America. Hollywood sex symbols are expected to marry and marry and marry. It's the price they pay—and Americans demand that they pay—for being beautiful, sexy, and wanted. Certainly the public delighted as they pretended to sympathize with the "plights" of the Monroes and Taylors. Killerbrew always understood the love/hate relationship America had with its stars. Now, with Marti Tiernan,

Killerbrew saw a way to parlay that ambivalence into profits. Provided he could lure her to Hollywood. One of his lures would be Vinnie. Could Marti resist costarring with her fellow sex symbol and cousin in an epic that would feature a cast of thousands? Suppose it was biblical in theme? Wouldn't she make a perfect Delilah or Salome? And the husband? Killerbrew wasn't worried about him as he was already giving the marriage two years at best. The director was a notorious "chick-chaser," and in two or three years Marti would be an old woman in his eyes.

What a pity Marti and Vinnie were cousins, Killerbrew had complained with joking seriousness. Otherwise, what a coupling on the screen! Both had a presence that comes but a few times in a celluloid century. If Vinnie hadn't had it, Killerbrew had confided, he would have "thrown the kid's ass off the lot months ago. What a little snot he can be. I once asked him—not that it was any of my business—what was going on between him and Margaret and he answered: 'You don't ask me about me and my mother and I don't ask about you and my mother. Got it?' I got it and have been left with it and him ever since."

John nudged Killerbrew awake. "Fasten your seat belt, sir," he said in a saccharine imitation of the stewardess. "Given what lies ahead these next few days, it might not be just the landing that's bumpy."

She was through the revolving doors, and the heels on her western-style boots were leaving tiny marks on the floral rug as she sped past the wood-paneled walls with their inlaid mirrors and silk-shaded sconces, when one of the patrons at what had to be the tiniest bar ever in a hotel lobby said aloud: "Isn't that the Marti Tiernan girl?"

Before anyone's head could turn fast enough, the girl, indeed Marti Tiernan, was past the marble pillars and the concierge's desk and into the Ritz Hotel's elevator demanding to be taken to three. The operator, an elderly gentleman in formal regalia, was used to nobility, both real and imagined, and not to film people, as he called them with considerable disdain. Still, he did not hesitate but quickly closed the brass gates and took Marti to her destination. There was something about her confident manner, worn as comfortably as her outlandish garb, that made it seem most unlikely to the old guardsman that his passenger was a crasher. And had she been, she would never have gotten past the hawks at the front desk, he reasoned. But imagine, a serape, gaucho hat, blue jeans, and boots in the Ritz! And after ten o'clock. What was the world coming to! Who could she be other than a guest of that equally strange person who had checked in a few hours ago. Some young American star, he had been told. Well, certainly times had changed since the Douglas Fairbankses and the Charles Boyers. Obviously, thought the old gentleman as he opened the gates to let Marti out on three, clothes no longer make or bespeak the man.

Marti all but skipped down the silent plush-carpeted hallway humming the same tune she had been whistling when Mathilde Bergot had knocked on her door thirty minutes ago to announce that a Mr. Nickels was waiting for her in Room 312 at the Ritz. She did not know a Mr. Rickles, Marti had replied as she attempted to focus on last-minute items still to be shoved into one of the seven already bursting suitcases for her honeymoon on Corfu.

"No, Mademoiselle Marti. Nickels, not Rickles," she corrected. Whatever the name, Mathilde Bergot was indignant, not yet used to the calls, mainly obscene, that had begun shortly after Marti's first fling with fame, and which continued to come no matter how often the telephone number was changed. But this one was different. This one had actually called her by her name . . . Mathilde Bergot.

"He said to tell you Mr. W. Nickels—the W for 'wooden' —awaits and you should get your derriere there *tout de suite! Incroyable!*"

Recognition caused Marti to grab Mathilde Bergot roughly by the shoulders and as she danced about to yell, "Say it again. What room? Where? Did he say anything else?" When the housekeeper said no, Marti dismissed her but not before shrieking she should call for a taxi immediately.

Before Marti could knock a second time, the door was flung open and there stood Vinnie, grinning and beaming at her as he stood barefoot, his tan feet showing beneath frayed and faded blue jeans. As she looked up, she took note of the hard muscular body that pushed against the tightness of his snug electric-blue T-shirt. As she looked at her cousin, and he at her, Marti began to laugh. Standing in the hushed hallway, her laugh, never exactly quiet, sounded shrill and out of place.

"It's you!" she said between sputters of laughter. "No, not

425

you, but you," she started to explain again. "You should be at the Y and not framed by a 'salon.' Look behind you. It's all oak-paneled and Louis and Napoleonic and Empire and elegant and Marie Antoinette and majestic. And you. You're jockey shorts."

"It's nice to see you, too," said Vinnie as he yanked Marti in through the door and back into his life. "And I'll phone Babe Paley right now and tell her she's got fierce competition for the number one slot next year on the Best Dressed List. Or, should we now say, on the best undressed list. How is everything on the pampas, by the way?" asked Vinnie as he surveyed Marti's attire.

She didn't respond. Vinnie didn't speak. For a while they stood looking at each other shyly. Then Vinnie opened his arms and Marti snuggled against him. "I was so afraid you wouldn't come," she whispered.

"And miss your wedding? Not on your life. I only wish I could go on your honeymoon and watch."

"Watch!" echoed Marti, outraged.

"Yeah," whispered Vinnie conspiratorially. "Watch old age creeping up on you."

"Vinnie!" cried Marti as she slapped at Vinnie's chest. Breaking free from him, she stood back and looked at him full length. The regular workouts at the studio gym had altered his former thinness to a tense tautness. "Not bad. Of course you could use a little more work on your lats but your pecs are fabulous!"

"The world is saying similar things about *your* pecs. Where the hell did they come from? I don't remember seeing anything like that when Aunt Carolyn used to bathe us all together in the bathtub. Do you remember," began Vinnie, a smile again about to form at the corners of his mouth, "when Thomas got angry at you and said he would knock your tits off?"

"If you're about to make another foul reference, some crude joke at my expense, don't!" warned Marti. "I've heard them all. Including the one that says . . . The Tiernan Tots have turned into the Tiernan Tits."

"I wasn't going to say anything *that* crude," said Vinnie with a contrite expression. "I was merely going to suggest he wouldn't make so brash a statement today. Not unless he's a lot stronger than he looks. Besides, he couldn't do it even if

426

he wanted to. I hear there's a movement afoot to make them a national landmark."

"Vinnie!" protested Marti. But she was laughing and she was also aware the banter was covering the gaps between the years that had passed.

"You heard Thomas isn't coming to the wedding?" asked Marti.

"No. Who would I have heard it from? As a matter of fact, as soon as I checked in, I phoned the desk to see if he was registered but thought, when they said he wasn't, that he was staying at the house. What happened? Is he sick?"

"Yes, sort of," said Marti. "Of me. My 'cheapness,' he calls it; says it embarrasses him; that we all do and always have."

"Does it hurt, Marti?" asked Vinnie softly.

"Not as much as my feet. Can we sit down now, Vinnie? Remember: I'm getting married tomorrow."

"And you and I are celebrating that fact tonight," replied Vinnie as he rang one of the buzzers attached to the phone. Within seconds, a man in morning suit appeared.

"You rang, sir?"

"Would you bring in the caviar and the *pêches melba* now. And the popcorn for Madame, too. No, it's Mademoiselle, still. And the popcorn for Mademoiselle."

"And the wine, sir?"

"Yes, and the wine," answered Vinnie to the servant, who bowed and left.

"Peach melbas and popcorn?"

"Like in prison movies. A last dinner before execution."

"But this is not my execution," said Marti.

"Well, we'll pretend it is. Your final exams weren't your execution either but when you were depressed over them, usually the night before, I'd take you to Rumpelmayer's and we'd stuff ourselves on cakes and *glacés* and coffee mixed with hot chocolate. Do you remember?"

"There are some things you don't forget," said Marti. "And to answer your question of a moment ago, yes, it hurts that Thomas isn't here. He seems to have written me off his list."

"You're in good company. Although with me, I can't say I blame him," mocked Vinnie.

"If you're good for half the stuff I read about you these days, you're crazy. Do you get drunk often?"

"Hell, no. Only on special occasions like this. Like I've ordered us a dozen different wines and I thought we would

427

take all twelve and mix them together and then drink it."

"Like when we were kids," said Marti excitedly. "Oh, Vinnie, I had forgotten that. The time—oh, God, was Mama mad!—when we emptied the milk, the orange and prune juice, the sarsaparilla and cherry soda and some bottle of—what was that stuff?"

"Pancake syrup."

"And we poured it in a pitcher and had the nerve to serve it to everyone at dinner as a brand-new drink we invented."

"I still don't understand why your mother was so mad," Vinnie said thoughtfully. "Imagine trying to stifle a child's creativity. But then, what do I know about the whims and madness of mothers?"

Vinnie had seated himself on the floor in front of the pearl-gray silk-covered sofa and its marble-topped coffee table. Marti was facing him, also on the floor, her legs crossed under the table. She did not look up as the servant laid six peach melbas, a punchbowl filled with popcorn, and a silver bowl of caviar on the elegant table. She kept her face free of expression until she assumed that the waiter had gone.

"Six? Six peach melbas? Are you mad, flipped your wig?"

She knew exactly what he would say.

"You used to be good for at least two sundaes the night before an exam."

"Vinnie, a wedding is not like an exam. One you take because you have to; the other, unless you're pregnant, you do not. And I am not pregnant."

"Marti, if you can't have one big bang before the wedding, when can you?"

"Vinnie, dear, the 'big bang' comes after the wedding with most people."

"If you're going to tell me you're being married in your mother's white gown, I'll vomit," said Vinnie.

"Not her gown, but a suit," replied Marti, remembering the argument with her mother much too clearly for the night before her wedding. "And not exactly white but off-white, as in cream."

"Very honest of you. And chic. Somehow, given what I've read about you recently, I was expecting you to wear something from Frederick's of Hollywood."

The popcorn Marti had stuffed in her mouth came flying out as she struggled to breathe, laugh, and speak simultaneously. "I'm also wearing Aunt Augie's pearl earrings. A gift

428

from my mother and yours. Which reminds me. Have you called your mother?"

"What are you, my answering service?" said Vinnie, the smile on his face not masking the anger in his voice. "Yes, I've called her. All sorts of things I've called her. You want to hear some?"

"You are still holding on to the past," Marti said in amazement as she shook her head from side to side. "And don't give me that look. You couldn't have expected me to come here—at *your* request—without the subject coming up."

"My mother, God love her and goddammit, comes up just about all the time and on every fucking channel and Late Show in the Los Angeles area. Since Killerbrew peddled her ass—nothing new there, right?—to TV, it's the goddamn Margaret Tiernan Show just about every goddamn day," Vinnie spat out before draining the wineglass he had just filled.

"Listen, prick. I'm not into a repeat showing of *I'll Cry Tomorrow*. Drunk scenes bore me almost as much as drunks themselves. So cut the crap."

"Do you know," continued Vinnie as if Marti had not spoken, "that Killerbrew once had the nerve to ask what was going on between me and my mother? You should have heard what I told him. Only the old bastard said in that smug way of his, 'I'll tell you whatever you want to know since what you probably *think* you know is garbage.' I told him I wasn't interested in discussing the 'subject'—and that it was none of my business. And he stood up—all eight feet nine inches of him—and said: 'Then act that way.' "

"They loved each other," said Marti softly. "Had it been possible, they would have married."

"Tough shit! So his wife was a dyke and her husband a fag. As the saying goes: you can't have everything."

Hearing the bitter edge to his voice, Marti leaned across the coffee table and slipped her hand into the crook of his arm. "Vinnie," she said softly, "it was so long ago. Does it matter? Look around you. You haven't done so badly."

"Some things you can't see," Vinnie replied as he stared directly into Marti's eyes. For the first time since her arrival in Vinnie's room, Marti saw something in his face that made her stomach cramp, and not from the sudden chill of the vanilla ice cream she had just spooned into her mouth. "What is it?" she demanded as it seemed Vinnie was about to cry.

"*It* is a crock of shit, which is why I say eat up and drink

429

up," said Vinnie, returning to what she now realized was a pose. "You're right. Dead right. It's a good life. A great life. We have it all, you and I. All the advantages. Big houses, big cars, big money, and in your case, big tits," added Vinnie as he looked with mocking lechery at the man's shirt that hid her endowments.

"Listen, my friend, rumor says you don't do so bad in that area—only a little lower—yourself," said Marti.

"As I said: we got it all. Ain't fame a bitch, Marti?" asked Vinnie, now wearing his most charming smile.

Marti wasn't as stunned by the question as she was by the tone of his voice. "I like it," she said finally. "I like it a lot. It's all like this," she explained, waving her hand around the room, pausing to point at the melted sundaes and the popcorn, the caviar that had gone untouched. "An extravagance. Not real and yet, well, as real as the peach melbas. They're here, aren't they? Here! And once eaten, or once melted, they're gone. Finished. But while they're here . . . divine. I even like the work, the hours of waiting for the set to be lit, for the makeup to be just right. And the cars that await and even the planes they will hold just because you are who they think you are."

"And who do *you* think you are?" asked Vinnie.

"The luckiest girl in the whole world," gushed Marti, "the girl who has everything. And after tomorrow, who has even more."

"Does he still have mirrors covering the walls and ceiling of his bedroom?" asked Vinnie sharply.

"How do you know about that?"

"His apartment is famous in Hollywood circles. More so even than the Arc de Triomphe. In fact, insiders call his bed that, or his technique. I forget which."

Marti's face had reddened. "I've heard about it all. Charles has told me. What was, was!"

"Men don't change just like that," snapped Vinnie.

"You're wrong. They do. Don't look at me as though I'm a naïve little girl. I know all about his former orgies. He's told me everything. He doesn't treat me like a child. I know what he's done and that's all over with. He says he's never known anyone like me before; someone who so stimulates and satisfies him. And I . . . well, Vinnie, I truly do have everything, for at last I feel there is a mature man in my life who loves me and is willing to take care of me. I need that. I always have."

"Who's taking care of your money?" Vinnie asked bluntly.

"The same management firm that handles yours," said Marti angrily as she rose from the floor. "What a disgusting insinuation. What's happened to you?"

"Not to me but to a few dozen actresses who have married men who have produced and directed them into bankruptcy. We got one in Hollywood now—she should have millions—whose only assets are her name, her talent, and her health, which if he keeps feeding her those 'vitamin pills' he pushes, she won't have much longer."

"How did we get into this?" said Marti agitatedly. "I know," she said as she began to pace, "we tried to cover too much too quickly. Thomas, your mother, us, but why are you telling me this the night before my wedding?" screamed Marti as she turned to face Vinnie. "There are always victims, in all walks of life. I'm not one of them. I don't understand. If something is wrong with you, tell me. Please, Vinnie. What's wrong?"

"Wrong? You want to know what's wrong?" stormed Vinnie. "Okay, I'll tell you what's wrong," he said as he stomped about the room angrily. "They forgot to send up cookies with the peach melbas."

"Vinnie, how many girls do you ask up for dessert during a week?" asked Marti, not sidetracked from an idea despite Vinnie's histrionics.

"Enough," replied Vinnie sullenly.

"Anybody special?"

"Not any*body* or any*thing*. In California, the sex is like the sun. It's there almost every day."

"I would think that could get pretty boring without a change of season."

"Stop being so fucking poetic or making with the elliptical allusions. Am I lonely? How could I be? I've got girls coming in through the window. In fact, I had to move. I now live in the topmost part of Laurel Canyon. To get there, you gotta die and get permission from Saint Peter. Ever since that record . . ."

"I heard it. God, was it awful."

"No worse than Tab Hunter's 'Young Love,' " said Vinnie defensively.

"No better, either."

"Yeah, well . . . it got me a Gold Record. One million six

431

hundred thousand copies were sold of 'Young Enough to Know Better; Old Enough to Learn.' "

"Nonetheless, it was a lousy song. It certainly did, however, give your mother a start when she first heard it; said it reminded her of something she said many years ago."

"Was there anything that woman didn't say many years ago?"

Marti turned her back and walked away from Vinnie toward the windows overlooking the Ritz gardens. "No, she said it all. Only I seem to have heard it and you didn't."

"As you yourself said, kid, it's past. Let it go. We're two of a kind. Both of us. We've got it all."

"Do you, Vinnie?" asked Marti as she approached her cousin.

"Sure I do. What else could a man want? What else is there?"

"Don't you know?" asked Marti. "Don't you really know?" She placed her hand on his shoulder. "Where is the love?"

Angrily, Vinnie turned from her. "It's in this," he said as he shoved his spoon into the remains of the ice cream. "This is love, kiddo, and if you can't see, taste, or touch it, it don't exist."

Marti's hand moved from Vinnie's shoulder to his cheek. "Can you feel this, Vin?" she asked softly as tears slid down her cheeks.

Vinnie's hand reached up and covered Marti's as it lay on his cheek. "Yes. Yes, I can, Marti. But it can't be love because it hurts so bad. So awfully bad."

John and James had both warned Margaret if she so much as moved an eyeball, she would be banished from their presence and not allowed back into the living room until the wedding began. Margaret, after again voicing her many concerns about the caterers and whether there would be enough food, was banished. Which she decided as she headed for the kitchen was just as well. Best she should double-check the details herself, an opinion not shared by Mathilde Bergot and the caterers, who had been victims of Margaret's double and triple checks throughout the morning. Banished again, Margaret, muttering "there would never be enough," set about finding something to do. There was nothing. It was, after all, a quiet "family" wedding. As Marti had dictated, a few friends and loved ones.

Marti . . . thinking about her niece gave Margaret the idea to "comfort" her. Hadn't Carolyn needed her the morning of her wedding? But Margaret had seen Marti earlier that morning, appearing anything but in need of comfort as she nibbled on dry toast, frequently dunked, doughnut-style, into her *café au lait*. Marti had smiled absentmindedly at Margaret, said something innocuous, and went on reading the *Tribune* as if nothing unusual were happening that day.

"Carolyn?" screamed Margaret as she ran up the stairs to the third floor where John and Carolyn were lodged. "Carolyn? Where the hell are you?" demanded Margaret as she burst into the bedroom.

"In the shower, trying to get rid of a headache."

"Wouldn't it be easier just to ask him to leave?" yelled Margaret to the form she could see outlined behind the shower curtain.

Carolyn's shower-capped head poked through the curtain. "Listen, garbage mouth. I want no nonsense from you today. None. There's been no rehearsal for this little production. Leave it to one of *my* children to have a do-it-yourself wedding. Do you realize I have no idea of what's about to happen?"

"I do," said Margaret glumly. "We're about to have a famine. There are only some dinky little canapés. It looks like we're cheap."

"Would you just stop!" screamed Carolyn. "Oh, Lord, my nerves! I'm just so nervous."

Margaret sat down on the toilet seat. "I really don't understand why you're carrying on so," she began as though she were calm personified. "It's just a simple little wedding in which the players recite lines they have written themselves. No problem. It's all, as Marti so dearly puts it, 'family.' So what if that little 'family' includes half the perverts of Paris, the beatniks and the boozers, strumpets, whores, and harlots? It's just your typical Hollywood party. And what difference, I ask, does it make that among the guests are my former lover and his former wife who was my former enemy before she 'married' *our* former friend and producer . . ."

"Who was my husband's former lover," Carolyn said as she turned off the water and stepped out of the shower and into an oversized bath towel. "Oh, beeswax!" she said disgustedly as she saw the astonished look on Margaret's face. "Did you really think I didn't know about John and Evelyn?

433

Really, Margaret. What kind of a fool do you take me for?"

"I give up. What kind of fool are you?" said Margaret as she toweled Carolyn's back.

"*Some* kind of one, I assure you. Imagine *that* grouping in *our* home. And you didn't cover half the list. Let us not forget we have one son arriving who has not seen his mother, or spoken to her, in many years. We also have one other son who is not coming. Both are certain to make worldwide news by their appearances or lack of same. Then let's not forget we have Charles Chauverant's first wife—she must be about twelve by now, I would guess—and his second child by his second wife. She, of course, is not coming as she is skiing the Swiss Alps but it was lovely of her to send that horseshoe wreath of flowers. Then we have Chauverant's eighteen-year-old daughter—illegitimate but what difference, eh?—a cross between Bardot and Loren who thinks *my* husband is simply *très charmant*. Now, let's add all this up and see what we have. One wedding, not in a church, of my only daughter to a man old enough, well almost, to be her father, who is a two-time loser. His best man at the wedding is a transsexual, although I absolutely refuse to believe he—or *it*—is really the eighteen-year-old daughter's mother. Oh, Lord, how will I ever get through this?" moaned Carolyn as she sat down on Margaret's lap on the commode.

"This can't be happening. I'm not old enough to have a daughter getting married. *I* just got married. What do I know about children? I'm still a child myself. Margaret, we're just babies."

"I got news for you, sweetheart, baby weighs a ton," complained Margaret as she shoved Carolyn off her lap.

"I do not!" said Carolyn huffily. "My weight hasn't changed in years."

"I must admit, for a woman your age, you do have a pretty good body," Margaret said as she watched Carolyn slip into a sequiny midnight-blue dress that had a matching jacket.

"It's not a 'pretty good' but a damned good body and you know it, Margaret. You can't live on nine hundred calories a day and not have a damned good body. There'd be no point in living if you didn't."

"Do you know you have a mole—it's really ugly—just to the right of your right tit?"

"It's not a mole but a beauty mark!" yelled Carolyn. "Oh,

you can be so evil. You never hear me making remarks about *your* body . . . what there is of it."

"Thin is in, my dear," said Margaret as she pirouetted before the mirrors, her chiffon skirts swirling about her, a mass of brown hues colliding and coalescing. Carolyn looked at Margaret as she sat on the edge of the bed putting on her black pumps. Although Margaret's figure was decidedly better than her own, due no doubt to the dance classes she took regularly with Marti, she now looked older than she did. The penalties of Margaret's life were etched deeply about her eyes and flickeringly about her mouth. Yet, Carolyn realized, in ways she could not define, Margaret was more beautiful at forty-one than she had ever been.

"Lynnie," began Margaret tentatively as she studied her face in the mirror. "Do you think . . . Listen. I'm worried about . . ."

"Marg, you look great and he'll think so too," replied Carolyn as she stood up to check the seams on her stockings.

Margaret looked at Carolyn and shook her head in disbelief. "You always know, don't you."

"Some things, yes. Others, no. For example: something I've always wanted to know which you wouldn't tell me."

"I know what it is and I still don't think we should discuss it."

"Oh, c'mon, Marg, tell me. That time at the palace, what did you say that made the King laugh so but which the Queen didn't think was at all funny."

Margaret studied her sister's face. "Remember. You asked for it. I simply asked the old boy if he had heard about the girl who always wanted to know if all she had heard about His Majesty's Navy was true, and so she put out to sea."

Carolyn's sigh said it all. "Margaret, I'm going to pretend I didn't ask, and you're going to pretend you didn't tell, and both of us are going to deny it ever happened, because I refuse to be associated with that kind of story when a Bob Thomas or a Gerold Frank does our unauthorized biographies. Lord, as if I didn't have enough to contend with right now! Why can't you comfort me? In fact, I insist you comfort me. Margaret, you're a trouper. Pretend you're on top of all this. Act as if we really are those Tiernan Sisters people write about. Tell me how, after all we've been through these past years, we are winding up with such a wedding in a room full of such people."

"Well, my dear," said Margaret airily, "it only proves that life, although seldom simple, often complex, complicated and furiously frustrating, when in the hands of two reasonable, well-adjusted, and highly sensitive and intelligent women, can be rich and fulfilling."

"Margaret," said Carolyn severely, "with the Christians about to be fed to the lions, I would suggest that if you know how to locate these two women, you do so immediately!"

From the beginning, Marti had been firm about what she did and did not want at her wedding. It was to be small and simple, uncluttered and uncomplicated by unwelcome guests. There would be no press admitted. As Chauverant's office announced, the media would be allowed fifteen minutes of the couples' and the family's time immediately following the marriage. It was John who had suggested they set up a bar for the press by the gates outside. And it was James who had insisted food be available too. "The press is always so much more docile when they're loaded—with both liquids and solids," he explained. Still, although Marti's request for privacy was honored, it was not totally appreciated. As the family's nemesis wrote in her column: "Grace Kelly, certainly a bigger star at a much more important wedding, was much more gracious to the people who made her."

Marti raged at that one. "No one made me but my husband-to-be," she complained to Margaret.

"My dear, the whole world knows how he made you—on screen and off—so there's no need to shout about it."

The wedding went exactly as planned. The couple walked down the staircase, through the tiled entranceway, and into the living room where, before a roaring fire, they were married in a civil ceremony. There was no father to give the bride away, as Marti felt that had happened a long time ago. There were no ushers or bridesmaids. Nor was there a receiving line afterward. Marti rejected that despite Carolyn's urgings that they extend a welcome to their guests. No, Marti had insisted, there would be no forcing of confrontations. How people would mix and mingle would be left solely to their discretion and decision.

Since Marti wanted to be married in a living room that looked like a living room, there were no rows of rented folding chairs. People either sat on the low Danish modern couches and chairs or stood about the room watching the proceedings. Margaret was seated next to Carolyn, James to her right and John to Carolyn's left, when she saw Vinnie enter the room minutes before the ceremony. For a second, he leaned against the white wall and his black curly hair and black eyes gave her a look that was both haunted and haunting. Still, Vinnie took Margaret's breath away. He was a combination of Donald Malloy and Carolyn Tiernan. Their eyes locked. Instantly she rose and walked to meet him as he came toward them. She was smiling and trying not to cry. And then she was hugging him. His body was there, pressed to hers, but she could feel that he was not. Rigid and removed, he played the scene convincingly to the observers but he had not played it from within. Crushed, Margaret released him and sat down. She watched as Vinnie politely exchanged pleasantries with James and then warmly greeted John before lovingly embracing Carolyn. With no room on the couch and no chair available, he sat on his haunches nearest to John. The hand that covered hers was not Carolyn's, as she first thought, but James's. He had felt her anguish. Looking up at his face, Margaret relaxed. This was real. James Carrington knew who she was. Now *and* then.

As Marti was married, Margaret's mind played with the idea of Vinnie's marriage. Whom would he finally choose? And when? She hoped it would be soon. There was an urgency of need about him. He seemed as ill at ease among these people as she had been when she first had to venture into Hollywood society. A costar for Taylor and a best buddy of Monroe? Vinnie? It didn't seem likely although the press maintained it was true. The last thought Margaret had before Marti made her marriage vows was: Carolyn is right. We are too young to have children who are so old. And then her thoughts were interrupted by great cries which announced to the waiting press that Marti Tiernan Ollson was now Mrs. Charles Chauverant. Champagne was served and toasts were flung from all corners of the room. Before Carolyn or Margaret could compose themselves, Marti was enveloped by well-wishers.

The moment between Marti and Vinnie did not go unobserved. When two such beautiful people come together in an embrace of such pure affection and gentleness, it affects everybody. A fleeting rush of feeling hovered over and hushed the room. When the cousins parted, it was Vinnie with the tears running down his cheeks and Marti with the smile. As

Nancy Blanchard and Evelyn Randolph fought their way toward Marti's side, their greeting was interrupted by John J., who told his sister the ceremony had been "neat." He then solemnly shook hands with Chauverant and was about to return to Alysse, Chauverant's younger daughter, when Marti grabbed him.

"If you don't give me one big hug and two big kisses, this wedding is invalid," she said to him.

John J. giggled. "That gives me a lot of power. I sure know what Mother would like me to do."

"Never mind that!" said Marti quickly, realizing that out of the mouths of babes often come words that strike others dumb. "Do I get my hug and kisses or not?"

John J. threw himself into Marti's arms and then shyly shook hands with Vinnie. "Thanks for sending me your album," he said solemnly.

"Thank you for not telling me how you liked it," Vinnie replied.

Again John J. giggled. "You're a good actor," he said sincerely.

"You made your point, kid," said Vinnie as he threw his arm around John J.'s shoulder. "Now don't push it."

As Carolyn approached her daughter, Evelyn and Nancy were congratulating her. The incongruity of the elegant and regal Nancy Quentin Blanchard saying *mazel tov* was not lost even though Marti at that moment had turned toward her mother.

"There's so much I want to say . . . to wish for you," Carolyn began.

"Mama," said Marti as she held Carolyn at arm's length, "you've said it all our lives and in so many ways." As mother and daughter embraced, John approached. "Well, Dad, you're finally relieved of all responsibility," Marti said without thinking, a smile coating her words.

"Had you not said what you just did, I would have agreed," said John calmly. "But it would seem you still do hold me responsible, Marti."

Carolyn was shaken by the exchange and Marti was dazed by it. Margaret, nearby, about to descend on Marti herself, decided it was no more bizarre than anything else that was happening that day and should be taken no more seriously or lightly. As the crowd about Marti dispersed, Margaret approached and guided her niece toward the windows where the early afternoon sun shimmered on the blending of cream silk and shades of brown chiffon as the women held one another.

"There is something I feel I must tell you," began Margaret as she cried unashamedly. "Your mother and I . . . well, you know we've always been so much more than sisters. And now you. You're not just my niece or my sister's child or the daughter I never had. You're all that, more, and beyond that again. I'm here if ever you need me," said Margaret as she tilted Marti's chin upward so she could see into her eyes. It was a beautiful moment, one Franklin Killerbrew caught with an inner camera; a picture forever to be carried near his heart.

Both women saw him approach just as Carolyn did. And James. And John. And Vinnie. And Nancy Blanchard, who spilled her drink on Evelyn's Dior *sac* dress. For a moment, the tension was thicker than the buttercream icing on the seven-tier wedding cake.

Involuntarily, Marti stepped the slightest bit aside. Margaret stared at the man as he approached. Killerbrew stopped two, perhaps three feet from her. His eyes were guarded; his face expressionless. She looked at him, he at her. And then slowly, his arms opened as they once had in the hallway of a hotel in New York City and Margaret flew into them once again, crying: "Oh, Franklin. Oh, my God, Franklin. How I've missed you!" And he held her and he kissed her, on the cheek, the mouth, and on the cheek again. They hugged and again they kissed as they delighted in being together as they never had been before. There was no threat to anyone in their acknowledgment of each other. Nor was there a promise or a portent of things to come. It was simply, and finally, the greeting of two people who were once lovers but who now were friends, which did not make the love they felt for each other any less. Just different.

He was awake yet dreaming, drifting through a sensuous sleep that was but wasn't. His eyes flickered as they opened. Yes . . . look up . . . up . . . up. As he focused on the up-above, he remembered. His room. Her. The others. Smoke-filled it had been. The *sweet* smell . . . of success.

He saw himself, reflected and refracted over and over again. A hall of mirrors. A wall of mirrors. A ceiling that dances with images and fantasies that were as real as they were imagined.

He was on his back, he saw, his hands under his head and both cradled by a pillow of satin. The smoothness in his hand was her hair. He could see her now in the mirrors. Hair upon hair; chestnut turning into auburn and now nearly black. A mixture of hair. A texture of hair. In his hands.

The face, *her* face, was hidden, but the mirrors revealed her raised buttocks, held high, inviting entry, a welcome sign to travelers and strangers. He turned his face to the left and now he could see her in profile. She was beautiful. Even with her face distorted with the immenseness of him in her mouth, she was beautiful. Even with the spittle, the dribble, running down her cheeks and chin, she was beautiful.

The walls have ears, they say. Not his. His have eyes. As does his ceiling. She was everywhere he could see and everywhere he couldn't. Bobbing up, down, around, about, she was trying to make him give what he couldn't . . . hadn't. Not for hours. Not ever.

He turned his gaze to the right. The others. She . . . the blonde . . . was watching, like a child at play . . . with herself, as his chestnut/auburn nibbled and gnawed. At him. On him. For a moment he wondered . . . but only for a moment . . . who were these Others? What matter. He watched, as she watched, as still Another nibbled at her nipple, making himself harder as he did.

He turned his attention away from the mirrors, from the Others, and looked at the girl. His girl. She looked up as he looked down. Her eyes locked with his as she took him deeper and deeper into her warm, wet cavern. She moved up slowly, her eyes never leaving his, as she emptied herself of him. He watched as her tongue flicked about, over and under her prize. And his. She would not stop. He would not let her. Hand upon hair, he pushed her down . . . down . . . on him. She moaned. In unison, the Other moaned, too, and as he turned toward this other moan, he saw her crawling along the carpet toward him. When she reached the bed, her tongue flicked onto his thigh, moving closer to where she could meet and then kiss the girl . . . his girl . . . his chestnut/auburn as she glided about him. Together, they caused a series of sensations that enveloped him. Mouths and tongues probed and penetrated as they urged him toward a peak he could climb but from which he could never jump.

Another moan. Another sigh. His eyes opened to see the girl, not his, penetrated, deeply, hurtingly. Strokes and shoves and writhings in rhythm. He watched as they, the Others, toppled off the peaks. And still his girl held him securely, devotedly, worshipfully in her mouth. But he wouldn't sate her. He couldn't. He never could. Which is why he was famous and envied. The Endless Lover. A man with a beginning, a middle, but no end. A man who made up wonderful stories. Except there was no climax to them. Unless he wrote his own . . . took matters into his own hands. Which is exactly what Vinnie finally did. And so his cries were added to those that reverberated almost nightly in the famous bedroom of the house high atop Laurel Canyon.

Margaret's cries reverberated throughout the house. A keening wail, it came from within recesses of the ravaged woman that left her half in and half out of her mind. Her face ashen, her eyes pools of pain from what they had seen, she fell to her knees.

"Cut! Print it!" called Chauverant. After the initial startled silence, the set on *More Blessed to Give* burst into applause. There were cries of "Bravo!" and other exclamations for the artistry just witnessed. If Margaret heard, she made no sign. Unable to get up from where she had fallen, she allowed Chauverant to lift her bodily. Dimly she heard him repeating: *"Bien*, Margaret. *Bien*."

He led her through and past the cameras and the cables from the room they had been using in the empty farmhouse to another where the wardrobe mistress wrapped a shawl about her. After another pat on her shoulder, mumbled words she felt rather than heard, Chauverant returned to his set and his last day of filming.

Margaret trembled. Although it was June, it was chilly in the country, chillier than it had been in the poorly heated Studios de Boulogne where filming had begun on the ice-cold first day of spring. As she was combed and coddled by the elderly lady who served as her dresser and secretary, Margaret relaxed, feeling much like a child in need of a mother's care. This had not been filmmaking as she had remembered it. Cukor had never worked in such a fashion. Nor had Hawks or any of the greats she remembered. Who ever kept an actress on a set ten, twelve hours, through countless takes of the same scene? Chauverant had broken her down, robbed her of every technique she had mastered, and in doing so had attained what *he* wanted. Had she been any good? She had no idea, no objectivity, so deep had been her immersion in her role.

She was surprised when the chauffeur awakened her. She could not remember getting into the limousine for the hour's drive back to Paris. For the first time, she felt to the fullest extent the fourteen years that had elapsed between films.

As soon as she came through the front door, she was greeted by the familiar smells of supper. Tomato soup, probably with pieces of sausage, and spaghetti made with James's secret sauce.

"You have exactly an hour before I come to feed and fondle you," called James from the kitchen.

"How about some fondle now and feed later," Margaret yelled back. His face flushed from the heat of the kitchen, James came toward her. In his arms, she nestled and rested as he stroked her hair.

"I hear you were bloody sensational!" he said. Seeing the surprise on her face he explained: "Chauverant called shortly after you left the studio. He said your last scene not only brought down the house but you with it."

"They may call this the new wave in filmmaking," said Margaret grumpily, "but there is nothing new about it. It's all a rehash of the Spanish Inquisition."

Carrington again gave Margaret a fatherly hug and then, after he about-faced her, a slap on her rear to set her in motion. "A bath will help. Then some wine, candlelight, and guess what I have made as a surprise for dinner?" he added with an impish smile.

As she luxuriated in the tub, Margaret could feel her body returning to herself rather than still belonging to the woman she had played. How she had hated Jessica Drake when she first read the script! Such a dreadful woman. Still, today, when Jessica entered that bedroom and saw the lover she thought she had bought, owned outright, in bed with a younger woman, she had been devastated. Jessica's need had been so total. Her despair was therefore all-encompassing.

All this, thought Margaret, despite the film's not being what it seemed on the surface. When Chauverant had approached her with the property shortly after his wedding last year, she had instantly refused. His proddings to at least read the script were reinforced by James. So one wet, rainy winter afternoon, she read *More Blessed* and was outraged by its anti-American statement. Jessica Drake represented the ugly

442

American who bought love and then misused what she felt was hers and hers alone. Chauverant's film was a study of French/American relations, which had been and were increasingly hostile, but in different ways. Chauverant's script condemned not only a certain kind of largess but giving in general when strings were attached. It asked whether the receiver is beholden to the giver and if so, for how long. Ever since the Marshall Plan many French citizens had been asking this very same question.

Margaret had instantly rejected Chauverant's offer and he just as instantly refused to accept her decision. To her surprise, James thought the film worth making. So did John, who felt that in the script's ugliness there was a question and a truth that needed to be asked and heard. He pointed to Jessica as a symbol. She, like the country she represented, was suffering from a huge cancer, which, if left undetected, would become terminal. Still she had hesitated. Franklin Killerbrew had struck the final blow.

"You scared?" he asked in a long-distance phone call from London where he was preparing a new low-budget film "of exceptional taste and dignity."

"Damn straight I'm scared," she responded. "The repercussions could be very loud and carry all the way from America to here. I don't want anything in my professional life to become personally disturbing to James."

"Wait. Let me get out the violins to underscore your bullshit."

"It's not bullshit. Besides, people don't even remember who Margaret Tiernan is."

"The hell they don't, you phony!" growled Killerbrew. "I knew you were scared. You think you're a has-been. You've been in Paris too long. Didn't anyone tell you that in every drag show in Hollywood, a queen can't get off the stage unless he does a Margaret Tiernan along with a Mae West and a Tallulah. You're a goddamn cult figure."

"You mean a fag hag," said Margaret, surprised and dismayed and pleased all at the same time. "Well, I'll be damned. If Carolyn knew she'd choke on her beads."

"Do it, Margaret. It's a great role," urged Killerbrew.

Suddenly Margaret had an insight. "What's in it for you?" she asked, onto a game in which she was an unwitting player.

"Marti. I get her for my exceptionally tasteful and dignified

443

low-budget pictures. I get to put her in clothes and an American film for the first time."

"What is this, a swap meet? Besides, she'll never do it. She won't leave Chauverant after just being married."

"We shoot at Pinetree Studios in London and she's home every weekend," said Killerbrew in a tone of voice that informed Margaret that Marti had already agreed.

And thank God Marti had, thought Margaret as she dried herself in a terrycloth robe that she kept next to the shelf of towels over the hamper. She shivered as she remembered those first few days on the set at the Studios de Boulogne. Not that she had been surprised Marti would be there. No. But she was surprised at the manner in which Marti was there. She sat next to Chauverant on the set and sometimes even at his feet. She said little but seemed content when he absentmindedly fondled her hair or patted her head. As if she were his dog or a child in need of Daddy's praise. And when too much time went by without her rewarding her in some fashion, Marti became petulant. It had been very disturbing to observe. She had never thought of Marti as being dependent. But then she had never thought of Chauverant as being a serious filmmaker either, or that a time would come when she would be happy to see Marti leave her life. But when her niece left for London a week into the shooting of *More Blessed*, Margaret relaxed both internally and on the set. Marti's absence, she felt, was best for both the film and Marti's marriage. Certainly on those rare times on weekends when she did see Marti, the girl looked happy enough, adjusted to this new arrangement in her life. As for the gossip: Margaret had heard there was a young girl in Chauverant's bed the morning after Marti left. She disbelieved it. Chauverant acted like a man consumed with passion but not for women or *a* woman but for his film. Through the years, she had known and greatly admired this kind of man.

As she collapsed on the double bed in the bedroom, Margaret's thoughts turned briefly to Marti. She wondered how her niece would react once she was permanently home in a few weeks and Chauverant was locked up in the editing room most days and probably many nights. She feared Marti would have difficulty being alone and feeling deprived, although neither would be true.

As she heard James coming up the stairs, Margaret's wondering shifted from Marti to herself. How would she cope now that *she* was alone and without? The thought disturbed her. But that's not true of me either, she protested to her inner voice. I didn't even want to make this film, she argued with herself. I was content not working. I will be content again.

James had lain down beside her on the bed. When she curled up against him, he placed his arm about her protectively. As she burrowed into him she said, "I feel very strange."

After a brief silence, so typical of James, she thought, who always measured and weighed before speaking, he said, "I should imagine you would. I recall when I left the Morgan Bank, I felt that a life was ending. And it was. I felt afraid because I was not certain of the future even though I had someplace to go. Which you don't. In other words, you've just left your own Morgan Bank and you have no certain place to go," James concluded, repeating himself to make his point.

"But I have *here* to go," protested Margaret.

"No. You have here to *be* and that is quite different," James said in his "logical voice," as Margaret referred to it. "There is a very big difference. For some, to be is enough. For others, there must be a place to be and to go. Methinks you are now in that category and quandary, and," added James loudly as Margaret began to interrupt, "that is not bad unless you make it bad. I can't believe, Margaret, you thought you would never act again."

Suddenly, Margaret sat up in bed. "Well, I'll be damned!" she said aloud to herself more than to James. "That's it. I'm afraid I'll never act again; that no one will care or ask me to. For chrissake! Can you believe it? I'm carrying on like some goddamn ingenue who has done her first bit and is now waiting for her phone to ring."

"Isn't it nice to be able to feel that way again?" asked James from where he was still lying.

"No!" Margaret said meanly although she was smiling. "No, it really isn't," she said as she lay back down and snuggled against James again. "There is absolutely nothing nice about the usual normal neurotic behavior of an actress."

Vinnie was confused. Why am I standing? he wondered as he slowly reentered the room he had never left. Beneath him, he felt his world coming apart. An earthquake! A sudden paranoid panic swept over him. No. No earthquake, he told himself. No natural disaster. Just the unsure footing of feet—his—on a mattress. Standing on a bed of shifting springs. Mirrors and music above his head. Below . . . who was she? This girl . . . kneeling at his unsteady feet, her tongue flicking above his toes, up his arch, and over his calves. And down again. Her hand, greased with her own wetness, was massaging his groin, moving gently over the objects she so loved to take ever so slowly, one at a time, into her mouth. As she now looked up at him, her eyes implored and begged. Suddenly he remembered what she wanted. That was why the rubber sheets had been placed on the beds in the room. For her and for the others who enjoyed variations on a well-known, perhaps too well-known theme. So many variations; as many as there were reds and yellows, pills of power and promise, washed down with whatever one chose to drink.

Images in the mirror. A man. Who? Not like him. Hairy . . . Ugly . . . Watchful of the girl as she whimpered and beseeched for favors he would not, could not, give. She fell away. Onto her back. She arched her body, raised it in a pleading, supplicating motion. The earthquake intensified as the man, the sole survivor of the evening, dropped onto the quivering flesh, burying his bearded face into that part of her that pulsated and throbbed, moved the world as though it were a volcano erupting.

His vision again clouded. Falling . . . falling . . . into a welcome wet abyss. When he came to, he saw in the mirror now facing him that he was atop and into and out of and into her. Over and again. Her body arched to meet his every thrust. Their rhythms matched the music coming from the sky. Warm sensations . . . vibrations everywhere. A mouth and a tongue sliding down his spine. Lower . . . lower. Deeper. Still two bodies blended into one. Warm and wet. A feeling never experienced before as he rested deep within her. A feeling. Filled and bothered. Yet stimulated as he probed and felt probed.

He tried to bring himself back from wherever he was. He opened his eyes and looked in the mirrors all around him. A picture he had not seen before. Three people. Locked together. He saw himself rise up to plunge into the girl, this girl, once again. And as he did, the man, the hairy man, once again plunged deep, hard, without question, into him.

* * *

446

Carolyn stumbled into the kitchen. Through half-seeing eyes, she saw the bright red light and felt instantly grateful to the man who had made coffee earlier that morning and left the electric percolater on warm. Holding her coffee mug with both hands, she sat down heavily in a chair by the kitchen table and finally allowed herself to look out the window. Rain again. The rainiest April on record, the forecasters said. Depressing. Very.

As she reached for her saccharin tablets, Carolyn decided "to hell with it," and used real sugar instead. A potential Tony nominee deserved a treat, particularly on a Tuesday morning after her first evening performance of the week. And a rainy, rotten Tuesday morning at that!

The clock over the refrigerator read ten-thirty. *Today* was already yesterday for the early morning TV show. Vaguely, she wondered how John's interview had gone. Ever since *Family Affairs* had opened Broadway's '58 season, it and they, individually and collectively, had been both revered and reviled by press and public. The continuing controversy pleased John who had both written and directed the play. Nearly eight months into its run, *Family Affairs* was still standing room only and the subject of cocktail party chatter. His greatest triumph had also been hers. But the reviews for her performance, the wide acclaim, gave pleasure, but not enough in comparison to the pain. Particularly the pain of opening night.

But I will not remember that now, decreed Carolyn as she opened the *New York Times* John had left neatly folded for her. Just as always, she opened to the theatre section first, a habit which annoyed John, who maintained the real news began on page one. No doubt, agreed Carolyn, but until she awakened gently to the "Merman-isms" of her world, to the inconsequentia of the Rialto, she couldn't face the bald-headed barbarian Russian leader who was coming to address the U.N. this fall or the bearded barbarian who had come down from the mountains to change both Cuba and the West forever. A review by Bosley Crowther made her laugh. The theatre and film pages of the *Times* always soothed her internal troubled waters. They gave her a sense of security. There, almost daily, she could read about one of the Tiernans. Look! Margaret's film was still playing at the Art and the Gramercy. Now that it had won the New York Film Critics Award as the Best Foreign Film of 1958, it would undoubtedly run forever.

447

Too bad Margaret had not been eligible for Best Actress honors, she thought. Still, even if she had been, and had Hollywood nominated her, Margaret wouldn't have attended the award ceremonies. She was still that bitter about the industry's position on Joseph McCarthy.

On another page, Carolyn saw the advertisement for the double feature starring Marti in what had been her first American film—a damn good one, thanks to Killerbrew!—and Vinnie in his first—and, she hoped, last—Western. Carolyn couldn't keep up with Marti's career. From Paris to London and on to Hollywood. One film after another; contract upon contract. It seemed every time she picked up the newspaper, Marti was being announced for another film. But always there too, often side by side in the ABC theatre listings, was *Family Affairs*. With her name above the title! It was reassuring; at least on mornings like this, it was.

Carolyn's depression was something she was learning to live with. When she had first read John's play shortly before Marti's wedding, she had thought it "honest" and "important" —words of intellect and no feeling. It wasn't until she began rehearsals last August that she started to get into Frieda Schneider. And then . . . Frieda Schneider got into her. She became the German-born Jew who survives the camps and then fourteen years later follows a trail that brings her to America and to the daughter she smuggled out of Germany at age three who had been raised in upper-middle-class WASP gentility.

Carolyn had not known or suspected and, as she later admitted to Margaret, not cared that there remained a "Jewish question" in upper-middle-class America. John raised that question and gave disturbing answers. He, and the play, were labeled by some as communistic, Zionistic, and Antagonistic. Their mail reflected the hatred toward Jews that still existed in many pockets of America.

After the play's opening, the drabness of Frieda Schneider crept into Carolyn's bones and ached like a nagging arthritis. Each morning, she awakened semidepressed and lethargic. John understood and made few demands on her, although at times she wished he would, thinking that perhaps their union might bring her back to her own reality. Not that her reality was perfect. Far from it. It hadn't been since opening night, although she had to admit, as John said, that the problem started long before that.

448

So I'm going to remember it again, thought Carolyn as she buttered her Ry-Krisp. But only for a moment, she told herself. No sense in dwelling on it. In spite of her admonitions, she started to cry. This damn play! she thought angrily. It destroys me. She knew she was being unfair and that the play was not at the root of her upset. It had crystallized opening night. Marti had come in from Hollywood where she had been making a film, and Vinnie had accompanied her to the opening. Chauverant arrived from Paris two hours before curtain. At the last minute, Margaret did not come as James was feeling light-headed and dizzy. To Carolyn's surprise and pleasure, Thomas had phoned to say he not only would attend but was bringing a Theresa Tomlinson and her family. She didn't have to ask why. Somehow, she knew. It was arranged that the families would meet after the opening, but while one family grouped and waited in Carolyn's flower-laden dressing room, the other never appeared. No note. No explanation. Nothing. It wasn't until the next morning when she finally reached Thomas by phone in Boston that she learned of his outrage. At her. At his father. At his father's manipulation of her talents to further his misguided thinking. When he called her a fool, John grabbed the phone and spoke very harsh words—all of which she heard; none of which she could recall. They did not hear from Thomas again, except at Christmas, in a note that said he would be spending the holiday with the Tomlinsons. She had not understood. Not any of it—although John seemed to.

As the rain quickened and rattled against the kitchen window, Carolyn looked out on the darkened day and wondered if it really was sunny in sunny Spain. She wished herself there, next to, even starring with Marti and Vinnie in Killerbrew's biblical epic that featured the Hollywood casting directory. *Anything* to get away. Was that what Marti was doing? Carolyn wondered suddenly. Was her personal life less fulfilling than her professional one? On mornings like this, and with unanswered questions like that in her mind, Carolyn felt a sense of extreme separation and loss. The family was scattered throughout the world but it was more than distance that separated some members of it. Although John insisted it happened in the best of families, Carolyn had difficulty accepting it in hers. She lived with a sense of foreboding, an anxiety similar to the one she felt when the children first went off to school on their own, and later when they were allowed to stay out past midnight on their first dates.

Only John J. gave Carolyn a sense of security. He would be graduating this June, the youngest by almost a year in his class, and yet its valedictorian. This child was quite unlike either of her others. He loved his Saturday afternoons at the movies but had no desire to be a part of them. He would become excited each time Marti's or Vinnie's face was on a magazine cover but he never bought or read the magazines. Even with her current success, he had attended opening night, declared it "real good," and had not asked to see it again. John J.'s enthusiasm was confined to satellites and rockets, rock 'n' roll, and the great outdoors, which Carolyn found strange for a child raised on Central Park West in New York. She had not argued, however, when John J. asked if he could spend the summer at the Wildwood Nature Camp, which the Massachusetts Audubon Society operated.

Where this child comes from and who he takes after I'll never know, thought Carolyn as she turned her attention to the woman's page. The article on Mollie Parnis caught her eye. She was halfway through its second paragraph when a headline next to the column she was reading jumped at her. At first, she dismissed it as a bizarre coincidence. Many people shared the same names. But inwardly, Carolyn knew from her trembling hands that this was no coincidence although it certainly was bizarre.

THERESA TOMLINSON TO WED
THOMAS OLLSON

Dr. and Mrs. Morgan Tomlinson of Bridgeport, Connecticut, have announced the engagement of their daughter, Theresa Ann Tomlinson, to Thomas Ollson, son of Mr. and Mrs. John Ollson of New York City. A June wedding is planned.

Miss Tomlinson, a senior at Wellesley College and a graduate of the Academy of Our Lady of Mercy in Milford, Connecticut, will receive her bachelor's degree in the humanities this June. Her father, Dr. Morgan Tomlinson, a general practitioner for twenty-seven years, is associated with St. Vincent's Hospital of Bridgeport, Connecticut.

Thomas Ollson will graduate this June from M.I.T. with a degree in aeronautical engineering. Following a brief honeymoon in Bermuda and Hyannisport, Mr. Ollson will assume his commission as a second lieutenant in the United States Air Force and will be stationed in Bartow, Florida.

The future bridegroom is the grandson of the late Thomas and Victoria Tiernan and the son of writer John Ollson and actress Carolyn Tiernan.

On Carolyn's tiled kitchen floor, a brown puddle of coffee was spreading about the pieces and splinters from her broken coffee mug. She looked from it to the paper and back again, as she wondered, Which mess should I clean up first?

There were many things that made John angry but most were philosophical rather than personal. The anger John felt toward Thomas, however, was deeply personal because Thomas had hurt the person John loved most, not only by announcing his engagement to the world and not to them, but by his refusal to discuss it with his mother when she called. Which was why John didn't phone or write but presented himself a little after six one evening at Thomas's doorstep. Although his son's expression upon seeing him was one of surprise which quickly turned to distaste when he realized there was about to be a confrontation, he did not avoid it.

Without a greeting, John entered the handsomely furnished apartment, taking note not of it but of Thomas's refusal to be hospitable or conciliatory. A straight-backed, hand-carved maple chair was offered; Thomas sat in its exact replica. As they sat face to face, John was temporarily thrown by Thomas's composure. He was obviously neither contrite nor concerned. Quietly, he sat waiting for John to speak and when John hesitated, Thomas said coldly: "Please. You've traveled a long distance to say something. Say it, as I have my final exams to think about and they do take priority."

Thomas was making no attempt to hide what he felt toward his father. The contempt was visible. John shook his head, amazed that this stranger could be his child.

"I look at you and wonder who is this person," he said. "I don't know you."

"Why should that come as a surprise? You never did. You never had the time or the interest," said Thomas with an icy calm.

"I did not come here to defend or discuss my fatherhood."

"You can't separate whatever you've come here for from that," snapped Thomas. "Before you can address yourself

451

to anything further, you must address yourself to that."

"I didn't come here to 'address' but to talk. And let me make something very plain from the start. I don't give a shit what you think of me because whatever you feel, you can't dislike me as much as I now do you."

"Wanna bet?" said Thomas, still icy in his composure. "I dislike everything you *think* you stand for. All your bleeding-heart liberal bullshit. You and your kind are dragging this country into ruin and you've been doing it for years. You and Margaret should have been put behind bars. But you're worse than she is. You operate under the guise of caring. She is out-and-out selfish. In that respect, she is more honest than you. How come you *care* so deeply about issues and not about your children? You never did care about your children, did you? Or do you lie about that to yourself also? And of course you *cared* about Mother," said Thomas, the contempt now oozing out and coating his every word. "Sure you did. You used her as you misused her. She's been your pawn. You play her, take advantage of her gullibility. The pity about my mother is . . . she's very nice but not very bright. Her permissiveness has created perversity."

"On that last point we agree," said John. "Let's talk about your perversity and how you have insulted your mother. First by not informing her of your engagement and second by whatever the hell you'd call your stunt on her opening night."

"Let's get straight who insulted whom," said Thomas angrily. "Had I known she would be appearing in such blatant Zionism, such Jewish propaganda, I would never have subjected the Tomlinsons to it. Although they have far too much class to say anything, I know they were deeply offended by it."

"Why? Did it cut too close to their Catholic cores?"

Thomas paled. His fists clenched. For a moment, John thought he would either be asked to leave or be thrown out bodily. Instead, Thomas returned to his cold composure. "The Tomlinsons have been in this country since the late sixteen-hundreds. They and their ancestors helped to build it. Dr. Tomlinson even today nurtures it in his practice. They are respected as good, God-fearing people."

"The implication being that we are not."

"Let us just say the Tomlinsons never were called before the House Un-American Activities Committee. No one suffered 'emotional difficulties' in a loony bin. Nor have their films been banned because of nudity and immoral content. No one in their family tree got impregnated by a stranger and then married a homosexual to save face. Nor is there anyone who has been arrested for drunken driving and for assaulting an officer. I think that just about covers everyone in the family, doesn't it?"

When John sat silently looking at this man who he continually had to remind himself was his son, he heard Thomas add: "You, each of you, is an embarrassment to me. I wish it were otherwise. I wish my sister had had better influences. I wish she had known someone like Reese. I wish I could have helped her more. The point is, *Father*, our lives have taken different turns. Just as you went your own way years ago, I am going mine. I have found a wonderful girl. For the first time that I can remember—think of what I just said: the *first time* that I can remember—I am happy. We intend to be happy. Our intentions do not include being harassed by continuous embarrassment brought about by people to whom I'm related only by birth."

"And what about your mother? Is she to be crossed off your list? If she's even on it. Tell me, did you intend to invite her to your wedding or just notify her of it afterward?"

In a somewhat softer tone Thomas replied, "I'd like her to be there but I doubt whether she will come without you. And after this meeting, which you initiated, I doubt whether you and I will ever have anything further to say to each other."

"You will hurt her terribly if you ask her to choose between you and your wedding and me. And that's what you will be doing if you invite her without me."

"I doubt whether she will be all that hurt. Once before I asked her to choose. Yes, in London," said Thomas to John's astounded face. "It was shortly after she left you. Had she any guts or convictions whatsoever, she would never have taken you back. And when I suggested she not, she made it very clear that if ever she had to choose between the two of us, she would choose you. I have never forgotten that. I never will. Nonetheless, I would like her to be at my wedding. You can tell her that. Also tell her that despite all, I have feelings of love for her. Now please go. I can't imagine this has been any more pleasant for you than it has been for me. But it's done, finished, over with. There is nothing more to say, but then we never did have much to say to each other anyway."

It wasn't until John was on the street that he began to feel sick. He looked about for a hotel or coffee shop whose rest room he might use. There was none. The people who were passing by thought John was some disgusting drunk regurgitating what had sickened him. They were partially right. John was not drunk and it was not liquor but his feelings he was vomiting all over the front lawn of the house on Commonwealth Avenue that housed the man looking down on him from his third-floor windows.

The navy-blue tablecloth had been one of the wedding gifts her mother had mocked but now, as Reese completed setting the table for her "intimate" New Year's Eve dinner, she thought it added just the right touch to the festivities. Her white bone china with the gold and blue trim looked perfect on the cloth. As did her Waterford crystal, the Rogers Bros.'s silver cutlery, and the Steuben glass bowl in which roses were floating.

It was a lovely table, Reese decided, pleased with her doings. A lovely way to end what had been a perfectly lovely year and begin what she was sure would be an even lovelier one. Normally, Reese hated the idea of New Year's Eve. She never had understood people celebrating out with the old and in with the new as she treasured every moment of each day. Reese was the first to admit she had never had a "bad year" or a "bad time" and wondered if she was shallow because of it. Her life had been and still was one unending fairy tale. In 1959, she had married the prince and he had whisked her off to paradise, although she was aware most people would hardly call Bartow, Florida, paradise. Their mistake, thought Reese.

As she waited for Thomas to finish dressing and join her in the living room, Reese poured a small glass of sherry before seating herself in front of the heavy oak coffee table where "Our Wedding Album" was kept on display. They had said she was a beautiful bride and Reese supposed if pictures could be trusted she had looked pretty. But not beautiful. Pert & Perkies are never beautiful, she thought to herself without bitterness as she again looked at the picture of the glowing girl in the white embroidered organdy wedding dress. It had been in the new style, short in front and long in back, and it had made Reese look longer, taller, and even thinner. Over it, during the ceremony but not at the reception at the

Brooklawn Country Club, she had worn the long-sleeved embroidered fitted jacket which closed so simply but elegantly at the neck with a pearl button.

And hadn't Thomas looked splendid in his Air Force uniform! It had been a lovely day, a lovely ceremony. Everything had been perfect. Well, almost. The picture Reese was staring at was the "almost." It had been taken looking down over the priest's shoulders, past the kneeling Reese and Thomas, and into the first pew. There was a recognizable face. It was drawn and tearstained. It was the face of her mother-in-law who had not been expected to come but who did come—only for the ceremony. Reese had been touched by the gesture and had tried to persuade the woman to stay, but to no avail. She had simply wished her daughter-in-law "all the best," kissed her son on the cheek, and walked away to a waiting car, driven, Reese suspected, by John's father.

In the six months since the wedding, Reese frequently tried to effect some sort of reconciliation between Thomas and his family but had been rebuffed by her husband who insisted she did not understand. He was right. She did not. Her relationship with her own family was close. When she and Thomas rented this wonderful old house on Oak Street, the Tomlinsons had driven down from Bridgeport to assist in the unpacking and the arranging and rearranging of furniture. Her father had even stayed to help Thomas paint the exterior of the house: a bright white that sparkled when the sun reached it through the huge old oak trees that lined both sides of the wide street. Because Thomas was basically a city boy, her father had shown him how to turn over the ground for the azalea bushes on the front lawn. Family is family, thought Reese, a part of you always. Ever. Thomas did not agree.

The house was indeed the princess's castle, thought Reese, who had fallen in love with it from the first. Although it was much too large for their needs, it was not only a five-minute drive from the base where Thomas was stationed and less than an hour from Tampa, but also old, in a regal, Spanish sort of way. It spoke of substance and tradition. With Thomas's Early American antiques, it had the feel of permanence. It also made her the envy of the officers' wives, most of whom lived in small apartments.

As Reese closed the album, she hugged her knees to her

455

chest and felt wonderfully warm and content. Thomas found her that way when he entered the room. He said nothing as he refilled her glass and poured some brandy for himself into a snifter. After he raised his glass in a silent tribute to her, he leaned across the sofa and kissed her lightly on the lips. He lingered about the corners of her mouth before moving to her eyes.

"If you keep that up, it'll be a toss-up as to who comes first—our company or me," said Reese laughing. Thomas shook his head in mock disapproval. She knew he disliked vulgarity but she was also aware there were times when she could get away with it.

As he drew her close, she played absentmindedly with his fingers waiting for just the right moment to speak. She felt him stiffen slightly when she suggested that this evening would be the perfect time to call his mother.

"Thomas, she should know," Reese said softly.

"You just want the world to know," he answered.

"Yes, I do. I'm that happy. But your mother . . . this time . . . should know before the world does. Please, Thomas, it is New Year's. We are beginning a new decade. Call and tell her. Give her that."

Thomas saw the earnest pleading in his wife's eyes. Without a word, he raised himself from the sofa and walked toward the hallway where the phone rested on a small slab of heavy oakwood that had been affixed to the wall, over which hung a mirror with a matching wood frame. To be certain he would not have to speak to his father, Thomas said to the operator: "I'd like to place a long-distance call—person to person—to Mrs. Carolyn Ollson. The number is . . ."

They had been waiting for the elevator when they heard the phone ring in the apartment. They had decided not to answer it because they were late. Now, as Carolyn sat in the Edwardian Room of the Plaza Hotel, she wondered who might have been calling. Having spoken to Margaret earlier that day, Marti the night before, she could not imagine who had been calling at nine on New Year's Eve. Unless it had been Vinnie. He did call at odd times.

The dinner at the Plaza was not usual New Year's Eve doings for Carolyn. Normally, she and John preferred a quiet dinner at home, but when Franklin Killerbrew, in New York en route from Spain back to Los Angeles, had invited them to dinner, they had naturally accepted.

The evening had been fun. People at the Edwardian Room were simply too elegant to abuse New Year's Eve. Only Franklin was, as the expression went, three sheets to the wind. But nicely so. How much calmer he had become, softer too. Time does change things, she thought as the waiter poured steamy black coffee from a silver pot into her cup. All night long Carolyn had been fading in and out of the past and present. Twenty-five years ago, Franklin Killerbrew was this monster. Or so he had seemed to two young girls. Now he was her husband's partner and best friend. He was her friend too which sometimes surprised her, given her onetime disapproval of his relationship with Margaret. But that was a long time ago. She looked across the table at Killerbrew and was surprised. He *looked* his age, soon to be fifty-seven. Every day of it. Yet, every head turned when he walked into the room. That presence is still there. She stole a look at John as he engaged in a discussion with the woman Killerbrew had brought with him to dinner. Still the handsomest man in the room. More so than ever. Instinctively, she reached for his hand under the table. He took it with a gentle squeeze and held it in his lap.

It had been a pleasant dinner, a nice conclusion to what had been an uneven but generally not pleasant or nice year. Not even the Tony Award could ease the ache of the situation with Thomas. And Vinnie: in and out of trouble, seemingly so confused for someone so young. No, she corrected herself, it is mainly the young who are confused. Still, she was certain that so much of what bothered Vinnie would become meaningless with the passing of years. He's just rebellious, she would say in his defense.

Marti was as much an enigma to her these days as Franklin Killerbrew. Couldn't he see that this tall, imperious woman who was his date bore a startling resemblance to Nancy Blanchard? Who knows what people do or don't see anymore, thought Carolyn unhappily. Look at her own relationship with Marti. Throughout Marti's week-long layoff from M-G-M's *Haphazard* at Christmas, she had been distant, as though a married woman no longer spoke candidly with her mother. If so, why hadn't she stayed in Hollywood? Why travel three thousand miles to be a stranger? Except she wasn't a stranger with John J. Oh my, but that had been funny!

Carolyn laughed out loud.

"Does she do that often, John?" asked Killerbrew. "I have awfully good connections with the Motion Picture Home for the Aged, should you need them."

"I was just thinking of something John J. said. That's my youngest," she explained to Katherine Christianson, Killerbrew's date. "He's a freshman at the Collegiate School, majoring—or so I thought—in basketball rather than girls or scholastics. But recently, when my daughter was home, she asked what he was doing New Year's Eve and he, after giving me a suspicious look, announced he was taking a date to a school party. I, of course, protested. Dating at twelve—although he'll be thirteen in a few months—is a little young for my tastes. So this child of mine looks at his ancient and archaic mother and asks, 'Just what do you think could happen?' When I don't respond, he looks to heaven and says, 'I should only be so lucky.' Which makes my daughter scream with laughter but me blush. I certainly never talked that way to my parents. I probably wouldn't now if they were alive. Anyway, this kid then adds: 'Not that I would know what to do. Talk about performance anxiety!' "

As John and Killerbrew laughed, Carolyn explained to Kate Christianson that that was an acting term. The woman smiled dutifully, obviously not thinking the exchange at all funny. Killerbrew tried to help. "It's what Carolyn here has at the very mention of her making a picture. We want her to re-create Frieda Schneider for the screen and she is suggesting we turn what is an Oscar-winning role over to her sister. Now some would call that unselfish but those of us who know, and love, Carolyn Tiernan the actress, know it's performance anxiety. Still, I got to tell you, she's a pretty good broad."

A rather unsteady Franklin Killerbrew rose to his feet. With his bourbon and soda in hand, he looked directly at Carolyn—were his eyes moist or was she imagining it?—and said: "A toast! To the second most beautiful woman I have ever known."

Although Katherine Christianson blushed and tried not to look embarrassed, Carolyn realized, with a stab of pain, that things had not changed for Franklin Killerbrew and perhaps never would. As she stared at the man, she realized she had not imagined anything: his eyes were wet. Spontaneously, Carolyn picked up her wineglass. "To the excellent taste you have always had, sir. I and the world's most beautiful woman salute and thank you."

Margaret was finding it impossible to be in the double bed alone. It was a helluva way to see in a new year. As anxiety swept over her, Margaret remembered what the doctors had said: the immediate danger was past but it was not gone. It would never be gone again. It would be instead a constant companion on which one would have to keep an open eye.

Unlike the other, this heart attack had been no "warning." When she had finally arrived at the American Hospital in the ambulance with James, he was unconscious and looked more dead than alive. That had been two days before Christmas; two days she could no longer recall. She had slept at the hospital and had refused to leave until doctors had assured her the crisis had passed. Carolyn had offered to fly over immediately but once Nancy arrived, it had seemed unnecessary to ruin Carolyn's Christmas, her first with Marti in several years.

It had been the worst Christmas since she had left Killerbrew so many years ago that the exact number was meaningless. She was convinced James could die at any time. Which was true but, as Nancy reminded her, it was true for any of them. There were no written guarantees regarding life and longevity.

Evelyn had arrived on Christmas Day and had cooked dinner, which Margaret remembered eating—although what she had forced into her mouth she could not recall. They had been marvelous to her, Margaret recalled as she lay sweating yet chilled in her bed. Which is why she hated herself for the feelings she discovered she had about their sharing a bedroom in her home. There was even a moment when she felt physically threatened and had to force herself not to bolt her bedroom door.

This night, the first of a new year and a new decade, she would have welcomed Nancy and Evelyn in her house. Even in her room! She missed their noise. They were always laughing or fighting. They so obviously delighted in each other, which Margaret found delightful. Why then was she drawing the line at what transpired between two adults behind closed doors? She, of all people! Was she naturally repelled by the idea of lesbianism or threatened by it? She tried to imagine making love with and to a woman. She couldn't. Not even in fantasy. Sex without a man's body, without that extension of

459

him that both needed and fulfilled her, was simply not of interest. Even with Franklin, oral sex was a matter of foreplay for her.

Franklin . . . how strange and yet how nice that Carolyn and he should now be friends.

Again a rush of panic enveloped her. Franklin wanted her for a film. She had consented since it would be shot in England and James would accompany her. But that had been before the heart attack. She didn't like the tone of James's conversation earlier that evening. "Margaret," he had said as firmly as his strength would permit, "I want nothing to change. Not in your life and not in mine. At least not any more than it has to. I refuse to be an invalid and I refuse to let you play the invalid's dutiful wife. If you so much as hint at another retirement, I'll leave you for another woman, a young girl who would be very happy to 'accommodate' an old man knowing he might kick the bucket in a matter of days or months."

"I don't care about making a film," she protested weakly.

"But I care and whether you will admit it or not, you do, too. You're not the type to sit back and grow old gracefully. And I would dislike you for it if you could. I'd much rather watch you do what comes naturally: grow old *dis*gracefully. *That* becomes you."

Just as she had earlier in the hospital room, Margaret cried. James Carrington was the best thing that had ever happened to her. He had given her a new life. For his sake, she would not sacrifice it. To do so would be to dishonor him. She would follow his lead: live to the fullest. But please God, she prayed silently, something she found herself doing with increasing regularity, let it be with him for many more years to come.

Still crying, Margaret rolled onto her side, clutching the pillow she would pretend was James. By doing so, she hoped she would finally be able to sleep.

Marti took the pillow from the stewardess and hugged it to her. Aware she was being watched by the other passengers in the first class section, she crammed the pillow between the headrest and the plane, turned away from her unwanted audience, and tried to sleep. Again, nausea attacked her. She rushed from her seat toward the lavatory and as the plane

460

suddenly pitched, she fell to her knees. She could hear the whispers of "drunk" all about her.

The stewardess gently assisted her back to her seat, taking special pains, as she was taught to do with celebrity passengers. The seat next to Marti was empty, the man accompanying her having chosen to sit behind her, so that Marti could stretch out if she desired.

Not even the Miltown had calmed her. Her hands shaking, she reached into her purse for another. She swallowed it without water, feeling it stick to her throat momentarily before making its descent to the cavern of her stomach. Again, she felt nauseous. Her heart was pounding and as Marti lay inert in her seat, her head on the headrest now, she decided if she listened to that—to the beating of her heart—and nothing else—not a thought, not a feeling—she would be fine. Listen and forget. Still, over the sound of her heart fighting to break free of her body, she could see the judge, hear him speak in Spanish something only her lawyer could understand. But she comprehended from the smile on her lawyer's face and from his congratulatory handshake that what they had come to Mexico for that morning had been accomplished. Now, as the plane was making its final approach to the Los Angeles airport, Marti, despite her attempts not to, was hearing all the fears and doubts, all the resentments and rages she felt toward the man who had failed her and from whom she was now declared legally free.

As the plane landed, the few passengers on board cheered. She wondered why until she heard the yells, the screams, of "Happy New Year!"

Like peanuts, the pills of every size, shape, and color had been placed in bowls about the room. Maryjanes and Bloody Marys were served with whipped cream and K-Y by the most famous "waiter" in Hollywood, a man who "served" nude. Goliath was his nickname and it was fitting.

As he distanced himself from the entanglement of bodies, Vinnie could not remember what he had taken and whom he had had. The orgy had been endless in its variety and spice. Still, he was bored, although one could not have suspected that from his seemingly aroused state. It was shortly before midnight and, from somewhere within, Vinnie felt the need to leave, to not be in this room when a new year and a new decade began. Unsteadily, he weaved into the host's guest bedroom where clothes were thrown haphazardly on the bed and floor. He had neatly folded and placed his own on the floor of the closet next to a shoebag. As he was slipping into his jeans, he heard a girl ask if he wanted company in the closet. With the door shut. Or open. Standing up. Or lying down. He was leaving . . . going home. Would he give her a lift back to Hollywood? She would make the ride interesting, she promised.

In his new Thunderbird convertible, as the car sped up the San Diego Freeway, the girl placed his fingers inside her. She moved about languorously, making little sounds of pleasure each time a bump in the road added to the motion she was creating inside her body. He could feel and hear her pleasure.

He was doing seventy when she unzipped his pants and pulled them down so that he was totally exposed. Unsteady and unsure from the drugs, with his legs now confined by the discomfort of the pulled-down jeans, his driving became more and more erratic. He watched the road with one eye and her with another as she pulled a jar of Albolene cream from her handbag. It smelled sweet and felt cool yet incredibly hot as she slowly worked it into him. She did not attempt to bring him to orgasm. Her hand acted as if she were spastic and as if it could move up and down only with the greatest of concentration and with the slowest of motions. He was throbbing all over when they reached her apartment in West Hollywood.

His pants remained about his knees as he struggled from the car and into her apartment. There was no time to pull out the convertible couch. In seconds, he had thrown her to the floor and was atop and into her, driving with the speed and force that her hand had purposely denied him. He tore at her as she tore at him. Her fingernails drew blood on his back. He screamed in pain, which brought her to orgasm. She screamed for him to plunge deeper, farther, harder into her. She pulled herself from under him and turned onto her knees, panting, looking like a dog. Frantic, unsatisfied, she abused him verbally, commanded that he take her, hurt her, destroy her. His plunges into her were not enough. She berated him for being inept. She called him a fake and a faggot, which caused him to rise up and without warning or saliva or caring, plunge into her rectum. Her scream shook the room and him. She continued to scream as he continued to rock her with a ramming motion. She was crying and screaming and attempting to break free of his grasp. When she did, he threw her to the floor. Pinned on her back, she was no match for his strength as he pushed her legs up and entered, pounded, pulverized that part of her unused to penetration. She spit as she clawed at him. She punched his face screaming obscenities in her pain. Her rage brought his to the surface. As he plunged into her, he struck her repeatedly, first breaking her nose and then her jaw. He saw the blood appear at her nostrils and then come streaming from her mouth onto the carpet. He knew she was screaming but he could only hear himself as he experienced for the first time in his life an orgasm inside a woman. His last conscious thought—before the blare of the police siren and the neighbors' cries of "Happy New Year!" drowned out all further thinking—was a question: Was she spilling more blood than he was semen?

3

The knock on his door surprised Franklin Killerbrew. Dorothea Wolfe had always buzzed on the intercom to announce guests or give a message. That had been her way, but it was not Pamela Washburn's. His new secretary, efficient and pretty—her one advantage over Dorothea Wolfe, who had taken her retirement, pension, and gold watch two months ago—liked to "look in," as she called it, on her employer from time to time.

"Miss Tiernan called," said the young woman as she stood in the doorway between their offices. "She's running late and should be here in ten to fifteen minutes."

Killerbrew nodded and returned to the golf club he was fondling. In the old days, no one who valued his acting career was late for a meeting with a studio chief even if it meant leaving a day early. But that was the old days, Killerbrew reminded himself. Then, he had held tennis rackets and not the less physically demanding golf clubs. At least his office had remained the same. He had refused to modernize to the starkness of the steel and glass that were becoming the new status symbols in Hollywood office decor.

Killerbrew's stomach hurt. With Marti Tiernan due in a matter of minutes, he was experiencing a feeling of déjà vu. The month and the year were different, but his gut said the situation would be similar to scores that had preceded it. Although Marti hadn't sounded upset or in need, the divorce was but a month old. It was one of the more exhausting months that he could remember.

He had been sleeping off his drunk when the phone rang in his suite at the Plaza Hotel and the voice of John Ollson sobered him instantly. He listened even as he ached, the chain of events becoming clear as his mind unfogged. Margaret, first to awake in Paris, was first to hear the news on the radio about Vinnie and Marti. Distraught, she called Carolyn who despite the early morning hour and her distress was instantly clearheaded. John, upon learning from Carolyn of Vinnie's imprisonment in a Los Angeles jail, called Killerbrew. Within the hour, Franklin was in a taxi headed for Idlewild and the first flight to Los Angeles. With him was Carmine Abruzzio, a "nurse" who would assist in the care and feeding of Vinnie Tiernan once Killerbrew had arranged for his release.

The boy behind bars who faced Killerbrew later that day looked nothing like the beautiful film star who graced fan magazine covers month after month. Although he had been tended to by medical authorities, his eyes were vacant and looked out, as if from a great distance, from cheekbones which were purple from where they had been hit. Bail posted and paid, Killerbrew took Vinnie to his sky-high Laurel Canyon retreat, surrounded it with hired private police, and left him to the ministrations of Carmine Abruzzio, who made a thorough search for pills, pot, and booze before closing the door on Killerbrew.

When he had reached his own house, Killerbrew called Margaret in Paris. That proved to be as disturbing in its own way as confronting Vinnie in a jail: hysteria was not something he associated with Margaret. She was nearly incoherent as she asked what she could do. He didn't reply as he knew she was asking the question of herself. James was in the hospital; her son in and now out of jail and both needed her. Again, she was being asked to choose, she ranted. Only there was no choice. She could not leave James. Not in the condition he was in. Killerbrew agreed but his reinforcement of her decision did not seem to comfort her.

Killerbrew drove to the Los Angeles airport where he met the day's last plane from New York. After briefing Carolyn on Vinnie's physical and mental condition, he drove her to the Chateau Marmont where Marti was not taking any calls. The desk informed them, however, that Marti had been seen by the chambermaid and was well. Carolyn demanded the passkey to Marti's bungalow. To his surprise, Marti had not barricaded the door with double locks or bolts. When Carolyn entered, she found Marti much the way Augusta had found Margaret that afternoon so many years ago when the girls learned that their parents were dead. Marti, however, was able to react. As soon as she saw her mother in the doorway, she rushed to her, releasing such pent-up pain that her screams caused several guests to phone the front desk in concern.

Killerbrew's thoughts were suddenly interrupted by a loud, insistent buzz. This time, Pamela Washburn had used the intercom. "Mr. Reading is calling from New York."

"Take a number and tell him I'll call back," said Killerbrew sourly. Damned financiers on Wall Street. They were taking over the goddamn industry. All this pressure from three thousand miles away and for what? To add youth to the Killerbrew roster. So M-G-M had signed Connie Francis. That didn't mean he should sign Brenda Lee. Girl singers-turned-actresses were a tricky business. Doris Day was the rarity. Certainly Patti Page hadn't set the screen on fire and the Clooney girl, despite some good advantages—and starring in a film with Crosby and Astaire was one helluvan advantage—hadn't brought in big bucks at the box office either. So Brenda Lee could sing. What did that prove? Why couldn't his silent partners remain silent as in the old days? He knew what he was doing. Hadn't he been the one to wrest Marti Tiernan from European films? And she owed Killerbrew Pictures two more features—one to begin in April. She and Vinnie on the lot at the same time. Again the stockholders had been irate. Vinnie Tiernan was a risk and a washout in pictures. Killerbrew didn't think so. Yes, the press had been as vivid as propriety allowed in describing the "love nest" and true, photographers had certainly captured Vinnie's disordered state at the stationhouse, but, Killerbrew reasoned, hadn't all the years of notoriety bolstered rather than hurt the young Errol Flynn? Killerbrew argued with Wall Street that Vinnie's bad press could actually enhance his worth to the studio, which had options on him for three more pictures. He was another rebel without rhyme, reason, or cause, and the closest thing to a James Dean in all of Hollywood.

The girl would be no problem, of that he was sure. From her hospital bed, she had been making sounds—or her lawyer had been—about a lawsuit. There was no doubt she had a case *if* she had been allowed to present it. All past tense. He had seen to that just this week. Just thinking about it made Killerbrew feel good. It was a scene he had played many times in the past and he relished his expertise. He had walked into her room in the hospital and not given her a chance to speak. Not that she could. Her jaw was wired shut, the result of its having been broken in three places by Vinnie.

But her eyes were clear and almost free of the black and blue circles in which they had been encased.

He didn't ask but told her she would drop all charges against Vinnie Tiernan. In exchange for her "kindness," all hospital, dental, and plastic surgeon bills would be paid. Plus, the day she took the first plane out of Los Angeles, she would be handed an envelope at the boarding gate filled with bills totaling fifty thousand dollars. As Killerbrew calmly explained, she would be taking an all-expenses-paid pleasure trip from which she would never return.

As the girl's eyes met and locked with Killerbrew's, he continued in a harsh, guttural voice. If she did not "take a trip," he would produce testimony in court from at least one hundred men with whom she had been intimate. As her face registered disbelief, Killerbrew took a packet of pictures from the breast pocket of his blazer. He held them up one by one before her eyes. Wasn't it true, the old saying that one picture is worth a thousand words, he asked as he presented her in various—how shall we say, he asked—*compromising* positions, "although I do admire that breed of German shepherd greatly."

It had been a brief but highly effective visit to a shut-in. It had also been predictable. The girl would take the money and run. On the way home from the hospital, Killerbrew visited Vinnie, who was watching "Bat Masterson" as if his life depended on it, which Killerbrew realized in some respect it did. Without liquor or drugs of any kind, Vinnie was showing signs of strain. Only Marti's visits relaxed him enough to eat a full meal, all of which, if Marti stayed the night, he retained, rather than regurgitating as usual. Some people, Killerbrew knew, would be outraged that Vinnie would get off "scot-free." Just looking at the boy, Killerbrew knew that could never be the case. He also knew that as soon as Vinnie was no longer frightened and felt back in control, he would throw Carmine Abruzzio out of the house. This wasn't the old days, rued Killerbrew, when a studio could control a star's life. Which was why he decided not to tell Vinnie what he had accomplished at the hospital. The longer he thinks he is in jeopardy, the longer he's likely to remain in line, reasoned Killerbrew.

Suddenly Franklin Killerbrew felt depressed. He was not relishing Marti's visit. He did not want to know what was bothering her or whether his intuition was correct. He wondered if this was how parents felt when they and their children reached a certain age. When is enough, enough? And like it or not, in some ways he had not intended or foreseen, Vinnie and Marti were his children. They, like their mothers, were family, the only one, he now acknowledged, he would ever have. He felt it even if they—or in particular, Vinnie—did not. He had tried to get the boy to speak openly with him but Vinnie wouldn't respond. He had told Vinnie bluntly that he knew from just asking around what his problem was and that it could be corrected with help. Vinnie just looked at him blankly and said, "The doctor Uncle John sent me to years ago told me I'd outgrow it, that a lot of young guys have this problem at first." Vinnie's laugh had haunted him ever since.

I'm too old to be a father, thought Killerbrew as he looked at the calendar. Fifty-seven on Thomas Alva Edison's birthday is proof positive that my days of wet-nursing are, or should be, behind me. Suddenly, he laughed out loud. "Franklin, you know you're getting old when the only thing you want to make is pictures."

Marti's hands were sweating as she parked her white Corvette in the studio parking lot. After placing the ignition key in her shoulder bag, she took out a hairbrush and smoothed her hair about her shoulders. A last deep breath and she opened the car door, swung her legs to the pavement, and began what looked like a march toward the main entrance of Killerbrew Studios. From her stride, it was not apparent that only an hour ago, she had been immobilized by cramps and hot-and-cold sweats. It was also not apparent from her appearance that she had been immobilized ever since her divorce a month ago. There was as much bounce to her step as there was to her hair, and the bright red of the silk blouse tucked tightly into black slacks gave off sparks of life that covered the depression with which she was learning to live.

Marti announced herself to Pamela Washburn even before she had closed the door behind her. She was shown at once into Killerbrew's office. As she walked toward him, he came from behind his desk to meet her, his eyes never leaving her face. Even as they lightly hugged, his hands were checking her body for tension. Although her face was showing no distress, it did seem paler and more drawn than usual. He offered her a choice of beverages but she declined.

"Well then, spill it. What brings you here?" Killerbrew asked as Marti flopped into the chair by his desk. "It's got to be one of three things: you hate the script; you hate the director; or," he added after a long pause, "you're pregnant."

The astonished look on Marti's face said "Bull's-eye!"

"How on earth did you know?" she asked, stunned by his perceptiveness.

"Call it a studio head's intuition combined with years of experience and one lucky guess. How far along?" he asked, coming directly to the point.

"Nine or ten weeks," Marti said as she coughed on a cigarette she could barely hold comfortably, let alone smoke. "It happened around Thanksgiving."

"Chauverant?" asked Killerbrew.

"The one and only." Marti sighed. "And you can interpret that exactly as stated."

"Does he know?"

"No," said Marti as her mouth tightened. "Only Margaret knows. And now you."

"I suppose it was your aunt's idea that you come here?"

"Don't say it so snidely. You should be flattered."

"I didn't realize Margaret was advocating abortion these days."

"You know better than that. Margaret is not advocating anything other than me doing what I want. And what I want she seems to think you can help provide with the least medical risk. I want a doctor, not a quack; I want dignity, not humiliation; respect, not condemnation. I have enough problems to deal with without adding others."

"Do you think maybe this should be discussed with Chauverant?"

"No. I do not. It is not his body. It is not his life. It is not his decision to make."

"But it is his baby."

"Yes, along with several others, recognized and acknowledged or refuted and resented. Look, Franklin. My body is my business. *Only* mine, as I'm divorced. Almost five weeks divorced. A baby changes nothing between me and Charles, but if I were to have it, it changes everything for me. I don't want his baby. Can't you understand that?"

"But it's also yours."

"I'd resent it. I'd look at that baby and hate it for all the

469

things it would get—'cause *I'd* see to that—that I didn't. Certainly not from Charles."

Killerbrew was looking calmly at Marti Tiernan, resisting his impulse to leave his seat and go to her. With her lower lip trembling, she looked like a child in need of comfort. She reminded him of the last time he saw Monroe: a little girl in a woman's disguise wearing a mantle now being placed on Marti's shoulders. Killerbrew worried that the weight of it would do to Marti what it had done to Monroe.

"Have you spoken to your mother about this?" he asked.

The question caused Marti to flinch. "No. Hardly," she said in a whisper. "This is not something I can discuss with her. It was difficult enough with the divorce. Not because I failed or he failed or it failed but divorce is difficult for Mother to handle because of her *religion.*"

"Still, as I recall, she stayed with you for a week and didn't seem terribly upset or destroyed by your choice and decision."

"Yes, she was wonderful," agreed Marti, tears now beginning to form at the corners of her eyes. "But this is different. She would see abortion as killing . . . as murder. And I feel the only one who would be killed or murdered if I had this child would be me and my life. My mother simply could not condone an abortion."

Killerbrew did not contest the point as he suspected Marti was right. In part. Carolyn would not condone such an act but she would, he felt—but realized Marti did not—understand. "You're absolutely certain about this," he said.

Marti's tears now fell softly, which disturbed Killerbrew more than it seemed to disturb her. "As certain as any woman can be in this situation," she answered in a nearly inaudible voice.

This time Killerbrew did rise from his chair and go to Marti's side. Awkwardly, he rumpled her hair. "It's okay, kid. We'll do what's necessary."

Marti reached up and took his hand from her head and held it to her cheek. She wasn't able to say anything, but nonetheless, Killerbrew heard her clearly.

On the second ring, Carolyn came instantly awake. There was a part of her these days that lived in fear of the family telephone. Its ringing sounded an alarm as the number was known only to family members and was for emergency use only. The clock by the telephone read two-twenty when she said a tentative hello into the receiver.

"Mama?"

For a moment, the voice sounded as if it were coming from down the hall, from Marti's old room.

"Marti? Marti, is that you?"

"Yes, Mom?"

"What's wrong?" asked Carolyn, trying to keep control of her panic.

"Nothing. I just wanted to talk to you, Mom."

The "nothing" meant *something* to Carolyn, who sat up in bed aware that John was awake and watching her.

"Ma . . . is everything all right?"

The voice, although Marti's, was not hers at all. Even as she answered a question ridiculous under the circumstances since it was Marti who had called her in the middle of the night, Carolyn sought to analyze what was different about Marti's voice.

"I just wanted to say hello," Marti said. "Ma . . . is it all right? You're not angry I called so late?"

"Of course it's all right, dear. I wasn't doing anything but sleeping and I can always do that," said Carolyn, trying for a lightness she wasn't feeling. Her fears were telling her that Marti was either drunk or on . . . "Marti, have you taken anything? I mean . . . your voice is sort of funny."

"A Miltown. Maybe two. I forget. I still get anxious, Mom."

A silence fell between the wires connecting Marti in Los Angeles and Carolyn in New York; a quiet Carolyn didn't know how to conquer. She had put her small talk to bed with her earlier that evening. Now, she wished John would write her dialogue but he was simply staring at her. Finally, Carolyn heard herself say: "Marti, there is nothing to be anxious about. We're here; Vinnie's there."

"Mom . . . I feel so lonely . . . so all alone now. It feels so awful."

"Now, Marti, you listen to me," Carolyn said harshly and she hoped convincingly. "All women feel that way after they've been divorced. You must remind yourself you have family and that you're not alone."

"You're right, Mom. I'm sorry. I shouldn't have called. Don't be mad, Mama. Please. I'll call you tomorrow. You go back to sleep."

"Marti! Don't hang up," said Carolyn frantically. "I'm awake

471

now. Wide awake. Why, sleep is the farthest thing from my mind. And besides, I wanted to talk to you anyway. I was thinking, why don't you come home for a while? Wouldn't you like that?"

Carolyn was fully aware her voice was that of a mother coaxing a child. She was responding to the quality she now recognized in Marti's voice, hoping her role-playing would help her daughter through whatever this was about.

"I can't," said Marti, sounding as if she were going to cry. "So many pictures to do. Pictures, pictures, and more pictures."

Marti's voice sounded drowsier and more drugged by the second. Panicked, Carolyn asked, "Marti, try to remember. How many Miltowns did you take?"

"Two . . . I'm sure," Marti said, not adding there had also been a Seconal. "I'm just nervous."

"About what, dear?" Carolyn asked, trying desperately to coax an answer that would make some sense of this phone call and Marti's distress.

"About life. Yes . . . life. The meaning of it. What it's about and why . . ."

Terrified, Carolyn placed her hand over the receiver. "John, she's taken something and sounds awful. I don't know what to do. I think she's in trouble."

John grabbed the phone. "Marti? It's me . . . Dad. How's it going?" he asked with a bravado that sounded false even to him.

"Going? Nothing's going. It's all gone. Gone."

"C'mon, Marti. What's that supposed to mean?"

"My life . . . *a* life . . . as it once was . . . gone."

Now it was John who placed his hand over the receiver. "Call Vinnie on the other phone," he whispered. "Tell him you don't like the sound of what's happening and for him to get over to Marti's immediately. If you can't reach him, call Killerbrew."

As John inveigled Marti into further conversation, Carolyn, her agitation so great that she misdialed twice before reaching Carmine Abruzzio, prayed silently for her daughter. It was only when Abruzzio said Vinnie was there and he would awaken him that Carolyn heard herself breathing normally again.

Vinnie's voice was filled with concern rather than annoyance. He listened as Carolyn quickly briefed him. She was still talking when he interrupted to say he would be on his way to the Marmont in five minutes. He would call back only if Marti was in danger. Yes, he would also call Killerbrew if that was the case. If Carolyn did not hear from him within an hour, she was to be assured all was well. Or as well as can be, added Vinnie.

Back in the bedroom, Carolyn took the phone from John. "Marti? I just want you to know I'm here. Any time of any day. Do you want me to come out? Do you need me there?"

The voice, just down the hall but very far away now, said: "No, Mama. I'm going to sleep. I just wanted to be tucked in. Nightie-night. Sleep tight. Don't let the bedbugs bite. May the sandman bring you pleasant dreams."

It was only when Carolyn heard the dial tone that she put the phone back in its cradle. She looked at the clock. Two thirty-five. Vinnie had said within the hour. She would wait up till four. Just in case. As she lay miserable in bed, she felt John's arm slip under her neck and around her shoulders. She turned toward him and allowed her feelings of helplessness to be enfolded in his arms.

March 8, 1960

Dear Mother Ollson,

We would have written sooner but we have been so busy with our move from Bartow to Big Spring, which contrary to its name is not very big at all. Thomas will be stationed here for the next six months and I'm still getting used to our little apartment on base. It's a big change from the beautiful house we were in. Well, that's the Air Force for you. Or for Thomas, anyway. For me, I'd be happier in a big city. El Paso is closest to Webb—that's the name of the base we're on—but even that's one hundred and fifty miles away. One thing we learned as we drove here from Florida, Texas is very big.

Thomas tried to call you New Year's Eve but you were out. We had some wonderful news. We still have it. But with the move and one thing and another . . . well, you know how time flies. Anyway, what we both wanted to tell you is: We're having a baby. And yes, it's wonderful. We are so excited. The baby's due sometime in August but whether it's the beginning, middle, or end of the month, I don't know. Isn't that awful? My parents spend a fortune on my college education and I still can't calculate properly.

Anyway, we are very excited. Thrilled says it better. And we know you will be as happy for us as we are.

We hope you are well.

With our fondest regards,
Reese and Thomas

Reese had written the letter three times before deciding it finally had the right tone and she could mail it. Thomas did not care to read it but then he hadn't cared about sending it either. The explosion of headlines about the family on New Year's Day had hardened his feelings once again. She hadn't even raised the question of telling his mother until they were driving from Bartow to Big Spring. Then he had said neither yes nor no. Now, when she asked, he said nothing—which to her was permission. Of all things on Thomas's mind, his mother was probably the last, Reese thought. Just as he had thrown himself into his scholastics at M.I.T. Thomas was now involved with the same intensity in learning his "snap rolls" and "Cuban Eights" and all the other techniques of pilot training. He had little time for anything these days, which made life dull for her, what with a movie or two a week on base and no social life at all to speak of. Thank heaven, she thought, for "Maverick," "Rawhide," "Hawaiian Eye," and the Ed Sullivan and the Garry Moore shows.

Watching television for more than an hour or watching anything for any length of time bored Margaret, which is why she found it amazing that James could sit, as he now was, on the set of *Nature's Way* for hours. And be interested! Not that he was there every day but still, what was the fun in watching? I could never do that, she thought as the director was about to cue the action. But then I don't have to and he does.

Margaret and James had arrived in London with an early spring. The filming at Pinetree Studios proved to be sedating for Margaret. After the first week of rehearsal, she found herself less involved with James's every sigh. She stopped searching his face for signs of exhaustion or overexertion. She let him live as she resumed living; this suited James, who had been insisting he was fine. And other than looking thin, he was, Margaret realized.

To make life as simple and easy as possible, they rented a suite similar to the one Margaret had occupied when she first met James at the Savoy. As the weeks went by, much of the gnawing anxiety Margaret had lived with since Christmas diminished. When she awakened in the middle of the night or first thing in the morning, she no longer looked to see if the man lying next to her was still alive, although she found she still listened for sounds of troubled breathing. She would be doing that forever, she was certain. But mainly, the anxiety she felt now was about Vinnie. Her horror over the facts of his arrest remained unabated and unresolved. Killerbrew had told her of Vinnie's refusal to seek psychiatric help, but given her own experience with Dr. Ochinclausin, she was of two minds about Vinnie's decision. Still, she knew he needed some kind of help, something to resolve his problems. Certainly he would accept nothing she offered as a remedy. Her letters remained unanswered. Despite his refusal to acknowledge them, she wrote every two weeks.

Margaret's anxiety lessened further when she learned that Marti had moved in with Vinnie. Given what Marti was going through, it was a good move for both, Margaret felt. Perhaps they could give each other the support both needed. And soon Carolyn would be there, having chosen to play *Family Affairs* for three months this summer in Los Angeles rather than London as previously planned. A good and wise move, Margaret knew, yet resented as well.

"You're acting like a child," James had chastised. "A jealous child."

He had been right but recognizing that fact hadn't made her feel any less angry toward Carolyn. After the months of braving it alone, of seeing James through, Margaret had looked forward to Carolyn's shoulder to lean on. Now she felt . . . cheated.

"As I said: just like a child," James said smugly.

"How would you like this *child* to show you what-for," she replied, making a fist and shaking it just under his nose. "And don't you dare laugh at me. I see it and I'm telling you to put that smile away this instant. It would be a helluva thing for me to find out that you married me for my logical mind."

"You can rest assured I made no such mistake," James said in solemn ones, leaving her both angry and in giggles at the same time.

They had enjoyed London. On her free days, she accompanied him to the galleries. They also "reenacted the scene of the crime" and went late one evening for a stroll on the

Victoria Embankment. Days when she was required to work, James, when not at the studio, lunched with former business associates or friends. Frequently, he took in a matinee and just as frequently, when Nancy and Evelyn were in town, he lunched with one or both. Although he strictly obeyed doctors' orders, James was active and involved, particularly with the stock market which he dabbled in for pleasure rather than profit, although he obtained both.

Margaret marveled at James's adjustment. She first saw it as courage and in a sense she still did. But mainly she realized it was something more: something that made this man not just a survivor—that would never be enough for James—but a partygoer. A reveler. They were strange words but in James's case they applied. If life was indeed, as the cliché insisted, a banquet, well then, Margaret decided, James was its toastmaster.

When the director called lunch, Margaret found James sitting behind the cameras and cables reading the real estate section of the newspaper. When he became aware of her standing before him, he quickly rose and without asking wrapped first a sweater and then an arm around her shoulders. No sooner were they seated before a hot lunch served in her small, spare dressing room than he said as he spooned split pea soup into his mouth: "I think we should move to London."

"And give up our home?" she said, horrified. "Our way of life? You must be insane. I won't hear of it." Suddenly, she was angry. "What is this, some sort of coming-home-to-die routine?"

"If you mean," he said quietly, unperturbed by her anger, "a sort of return to the womb, no, although there is a certain sense of that since I was born and lived a good part of my life—but not the best—in London. No, moving here just seemed to be a bit of practicality and extravagance all at the same time."

When she looked at him quizzically he continued: "We'd be nearer your work and that would mean no more hotels and living out of suitcases. It would also mean a new beginning for me, for you, for us. And that's what I find exciting. Beginning something new. A new life. But if it upsets you so, we won't do it. It just seemed rather exciting to me."

Margaret looked lovingly and with considerable wonder at this man who never failed to surprise and delight her. A new life. A new beginning. And with death constantly staring them in the face. Only he refused to see it; and he was right. "You wouldn't miss our home and Paris?" she asked, her voice soft and wistful.

"There is only one thing in the world I would miss should I lose it and I am looking directly at it. And I see she is warming to the idea by the second."

"You know me so well," she said, fighting back the tears which would require a fresh bout with the makeup artists if they fell on her rouged and powdered cheeks. "It's just . . . well . . . we've been so happy in Paris. So safe and secure and serene. Even the stone wall and the wrought-iron gates that separated us from the world always seemed so right to me."

"Margaret, you no longer need them," James said softly. "The best safety comes from within and the truly safe person doesn't need walls or gates. Danger is often within oneself and then ascribed to the world outside."

"James, you're a regular Fulton Sheen. Sometimes your profundity . . . well, I gotta tell you. It's better than a Sominex. Snore time. Boy, can you be a horse's ass. A stuffed one!"

"I love it when you sweet-talk me," said James grinning delightedly. "I take it then from your response that we will sell the house and move?"

"James, m'ducks. If I know you, you've already stripped and sold it. 'Fess up."

"Well, there is this flat, a duplex I've seen, just off Hyde Park near where Carolyn lived, that would suit us fine. A spiral staircase to the upstairs and a skylight. Yes . . . a skylight. Two fireplaces, one in each bedroom, and where are you going?"

"To check the local phone directory. I don't suppose the Seven Santini Brothers have branches in London and Paris. Do you?"

Marti slowly lowered herself onto one of the upholstered concrete slabs that served as furniture in Vinnie's multilevel living room and checked her watch. Her mother was right: there *was* time. Still, as she sat with her hands folded across her stomach, Marti felt anxious. Her bag was packed, standing in readiness by the door. She had written a note to Vinnie telling him where she would be if he arrived home in time to meet her. The note was already Scotch-taped to the front door. As far as Marti could tell, nothing had been overlooked.

477

Within minutes, Carolyn would be arriving by taxi "to see you off and through," she had said gaily, while her father would come directly from the studio where he was working on the film adaptation of *Family Affairs*. Undoubtedly, he would be bringing John J., the studio "go-fer" for the summer, with him. Just the thought of *Family Affairs* was soothing to Marti. The film would begin shooting next spring. By then, she would be more than ready to essay the best role of her life. And wasn't it typical Killerbrew genius to cast her as the daughter to Carolyn's mother!

As she sat waiting, Marti looked about the home Vinnie had turned into her castle and impregnable fortress these past months. Only once had she come off the mountain, so to speak, and that was when Carolyn had opened in *Family Affairs* and had achieved her first Hollywood stage success. Vinnie had driven her to the Huntington Hartford Theatre, but had not come in. Having just finished *Storms*—an apt title considering the constant storm of controversy about him—he felt reclusive.

He and his house were one and the same. Reclusive . . . hidden from public view. She remembered the first time she had seen the extremely modern house with its series of stone and cement levels built into the top side of a small mountain. She remembered thinking . . . this should belong to a movie star, and how she had laughed when she realized it did: it belonged to Vinnie. I wish he were here right now. This second, thought Marti. He should be. If it weren't for him . . .

Marti's mind drifted to that February night months ago when Vinnie had pounded on her door, demanding she let him in even as she tried to ignore his presence. Upon entering, he had taken immediate control, deciding just how much was too much Miltown to be washed down with a Seconal and white wine. Somehow he managed to carry her to his car and then drive her to the house atop the canyon. But she did recall sobbing and blurting out what she planned to do the following day and why. Later, in what was to become her bedroom, she lay with her head on his shoulder, his arm about her protectively, and listened as he talked. Although his exact words were now lost to her, Marti was certain Vinnie, ever so plaintively, had said, "Marti, a real live someone to love must feel so much better than an audience or a career. I wish I had that." And later, had he said, or did she imagine it: "What better way to lose the loneliness than

478

to have a child?" Was it he who had convinced her that life wouldn't be over but would actually begin anew with a baby, or had that been the recesses of her own mind speaking? Or both. He had argued then for her life and what he thought she needed for it then. If only he could be so eloquent about his own, thought Marti. But Vinnie's actions spoke louder than his words. Almost daily, he took off at breakneck speed on the Sportster 900 Harley-Davidson. How she hated its noise. And its danger to which he pretended to be oblivious. He would career recklessly about the canyon, and when she accused him of wanting to kill himself, he laughed and said there were easier, less painful ways, if that indeed was his intent.

She didn't know his intent as he seemed to have none. Except to drive his "bike" and to see how much liquor his system could hold before he became incapacitated. Once, when he was more than just a little "high," he had said wistfully, "I'm a star with no sky in which to shine." It was his way of admitting, she realized, that there was no demand for his services. Not in films. Not even onstage. She assured him, although she really didn't know it for a fact, that once the industry saw what was bound to be favorable public response to *Storms*, his phone would be ringing off the hook. He looked at her in the same way he had when she suggested he read Margaret's letters—with mild disgust and a who-are-you-kidding sneer. He went to his room and she knew that his loud slam of the door was to close her out of his life.

Although she did not want to relive the experience of that night, Marti was there again, in her bed, awakened by the awful noise of glass breaking. At first, she thought someone was smashing the windows encircling the house in an attempt to break in. She yelled for Carmine Abruzzio and then remembered Vinnie had discharged the man, claiming that with her there, Abruzzio was not needed. Vinnie's screams threw her from the bed. She ran toward the noise which she realized was coming from the bedroom down the hall Vinnie never used. At least not since she had arrived. In the dark, she tripped on the little steps that popped up unexpectedly throughout the house. Her ankle! Still, she flung herself into the room and what she saw made *her* scream. Vinnie, with a hammer in his hand, was pounding on the walls of the room. Walls made of mirrors. Glass was on the floor in jagged piles. Some slivers must have cut his face as there were streaks of blood dripping onto his T-shirt. Unaware of her presence, he picked up the hammer that had fallen and flung it straight up at the mirrored ceiling. It crashed and smashed and as it fell to the floor it took part of the ceiling with it.

It was not the room that shocked Marti. She had lived in one similar to it for almost a year. The shock was seeing Vinnie, out of control and seemingly out of his mind, crying as he screamed in some sort of frustration she could not understand but which she could feel. For a second, she thought to run to her room and to protect herself and her body. Then, with a strength she didn't think she had, she threw herself at Vinnie and wrestled the hammer from him. He stood there staring at her in nonrecognition, his eyes glazed and wild. And then suddenly, he fell into her arms and sobbed much as she had the night he had taken her from the Chateau Marmont to his home. She wasn't sure how to comfort him so she babbled on about Chauverant and how she had wanted to take a hammer to him. Yes, to him but not to his room; the room that had been theirs. She had needed for so long to smash and hurt him the way she felt hurt and smashed herself. No, it was not about other women. That she might have been able to tolerate. That would even have been human. No. It was Chauverant's lack of attention and his lack of caring and his love on the dole. His work was his only real wife and mistress. That they had been together at Thanksgiving was only because she had spent two full days in flight to have thirty-six hours together. But he wouldn't do the same, no matter how much she had pleaded, when she was at Carolyn's in New York over Christmas.

And so they had talked. Through that night and so many others when, and only when, Vinnie was talking. It now seemed so ironic that she was so happy, so full of life—Yes! *Full* of life!—because of him. Yet he was so empty. She was filled with excitement about the new life about to unfold and only because he had been the one to take her by the hand and cross her over from one street to another. But he couldn't do the same for himself and he wouldn't allow her to do it for him. Not her or Carolyn—and Lord knows how Mother has tried, thought Marti. Despite her own terror of her Hollywood stage debut, she had spent hours with Vinnie before her opening trying to break through.

My mother is a helluva dame but a late one, thought Marti as she checked her watch. Come on, Ma, hurry up. There are some curtains that cannot be held for anyone and this, I fear, given the way I am now feeling, is one of them.

As if on cue, the sounds of a car crushing the gravel in the long driveway leading up to the house drifted in through the open windows. A car horn honked. As she eased herself off the cushioned slab and walked to the door, Marti took a long, slow look at the house that had been her home the past six months. She knew it was stupid but she said nonetheless: "Take care of Vinnie." Who in their right mind talks to houses? she asked as she opened the front door to find her mother standing there, waiting to take her daughter's suitcase in one hand and her daughter's hand in the other to the waiting taxi.

Vinnie was speeding up the winding roads of Laurel Canyon when he came around a blindman's curve and was nearly sideswiped by the taxi that was going just a little faster than it should at its occupants' request. The hot August wind combined with a hazy sun had stiffened and scorched his forehead. He had been out on his bike almost five hours, riding up and down the coast, stopping to either race with other bikers or swill some beer. He was a familiar face to the motorcyclists although none realized the man they knew as Rick under the well-trimmed full beard was Vinnie Tiernan. Since many of the bikers did not want questions asked of them, they didn't ask any of Vinnie. His anonymity was thus preserved, and with it, his precarious and often fleeting sense of well-being.

There were days when Vinnie thought to just keep riding, not stop, not ever. But by sunset, realizing Marti would be waiting at home, he returned, never speaking much about his day, but preferring to ask about hers. He wondered as he biked up the final approach to his house what he would do now that Marti would soon be leaving? With the house empty, himself empty, maybe he should leave the country, take a job in European films. They wanted him even if the M-G-Ms and Columbias didn't. At least not now. His agent had said just the other day that he was certain he could land a lead in a play coming to Broadway, where no one seemed to care what you've done or whom. But the idea of performing before an audience terrified Vinnie. That he had already given too many performances before too many people was part of his problem, he realized.

481

At the front door, as Vinnie removed his skintight leather gloves, he read the note hanging at eye level. Within seconds, the gloves were back on his hands and he was on his motorcycle, racing down the hills, once again hoping to catch Marti before it was too late. If he had done it before, he could do it again, he decided as he took a curve on a forty-five-degree angle.

"I wish you'd turn that awful thing off," Carolyn said grumpily as she continued to do her nails.

"It's just a game, Mom," said Marti, amused by her mother's annoyance.

"Frankly, I prefer hide-and-seek or kick-the-can to a 'game' —as you put it—where women pull one another's hair and fight and kick each other. I'll never understand why your brother loves it so."

"Because it's just another variation on the good guys versus the bad guys. Like a Western movie. Look. See that girl? The one with the nose like Ichabod Crane? She's dressed in black which means she's the bad guy. She beats up the good guys. Look! The girl in white. The big blonde. God, she is big, isn't she! Anyway, she's a good guy and she'll make sure Ichabod will get hers at the end of the game. I don't know why you're so upset, Mom. It's really nothing more than a morality play on a banked track rather than a stage."

"How foolish of me not to have recognized that," said Carolyn caustically. "I still think it's—oh, my heart! Marti, tell me what I'm seeing isn't true."

The camera had zoomed in on the Ichabod Crane girl, "Little Iodine" Behrens, screaming at a boy in the audience who was screaming right back at her. The crowd was egging the kid on and Behrens was milking the situation for all it was worth.

"She could put you out of business," Marti said, still amused. "C'mon, John J. Give it to her. He's such a little ham. Imagine him going around saying he doesn't want to be in the business and the moment our back is turned there he is on television."

"Please turn that thing off," said Carolyn. "He couldn't ask like other boys his age to be taken to Brown's for a sundae or Disneyland on his last night in Los Angeles. No, he has to see the Roller Derby. Such chicanery!"

"If Vinnie didn't mind I don't see why you should."

"Vinnie would do anything for that boy, while I'm not quite so giving. Nor is his father. As you can see, he remained here despite his promises to go along."

"They weren't promises; they were threats. Dad knew very well John J. wanted to go alone with Vinnie. And by the way, Mom," Marti said as she flicked off the TV, "*chicanery?* Doesn't that word date you?"

"What dates me more than anything is you! Imagine making me a grandmother at my age. Have you any idea how embarrassing that is? Although your father thinks it's sexy. I swear that man gets more perverted with every passing year."

"How nice for you," said Marti, giving the line her best lecherous reading.

"What's even nicer," Carolyn said, ignoring Marti's obvious intent, "is that he's next door packing while I'm here doing my nails. You know, if I were running an airline, I'd have a manicurist on board. I bet she'd make a fortune."

Suddenly Carolyn sighed and looked miserable. "Are you sure you're going to be all right? I just hate leaving you now."

"Then stay. I've already told you I'll be fine. Just fine. But if you're not convinced, I repeat, stay."

"If it weren't for John J. going back to Collegiate, I would. But he may need me."

"Not unless you answer to Fido or Rover, he doesn't. Why don't you break down and buy that boy a dog?"

" 'Cause I know who'll end up taking care of it. Besides, I don't want anything with more than two legs in my house. Do you remember when Vinnie brought home that hamster for your birthday?"

"How could I ever forget? It was the first time I realized as a child that grown-ups get afraid, too. I'll never forget thinking that as I hid in my room and you and Aunt Margaret were carrying on outside. Till then I thought mamas and aunts were never afraid of anything."

Carolyn's derisive laugh was counterpoint to the crying that had begun quietly in the other bedroom. Just as Marti knew they would, the soft cries soon became deafening roars. When Carolyn offered to look in, Marti refused and was off the couch and in the bedroom before her mother could move. Seconds later, Marti returned with a baby in each arm.

"I still don't understand how you had twins when they're supposed to skip a generation," said Carolyn. "And I also don't understand how you manage to carry both at the same time."

"Mom, they only weigh about nine pounds each. Let me enjoy it while I can. Lord knows in a matter of weeks they'll be too heavy."

"How are you going to manage when I'm gone?"

"Very nicely, I assure you. Now stop that!" said Marti, annoyed. "How did you manage?"

"There was a big difference. I had your father, your Aunt Margaret—from time to time—Aunt Augie, *and* outside help."

"Well, Dorothea Wolfe will be staying with them when I go back to work next month."

"Dorothea Wolfe is a hundred and twelve years old. How do you expect her to run after twins?"

"I don't! They're only a month old in case you haven't noticed. They won't be running for at least another few weeks. And by then, I'll have a full-time nanny."

"Well, I still don't see why you're waiting a month to have Dorothea Wolfe come in."

"Because I want to be alone with my babies. Soon enough, thanks to those damn preexisting contracts, I'll have to leave them, although my agent is already negotiating to have a nursery of sorts built into all of my dressing rooms or trailers. Now, since you're leaving tomorrow, wouldn't you like to hold one of your grandchildren? Which do you want? Allison or Mark?"

"Don't make me play favorites. And since I can't tell one from the other without the wrappings, you choose."

The bundle placed in Carolyn's arms was Allison, or Ali, as John J. had already dubbed her; she was named for Augusta. She had more hair than her brother although she had been born seventeen minutes later. She also cried more as if being second meant she needed more attention, lest anyone forget she was every bit as important as her brother. No one did.

"They look like absolutely no one I know," said Carolyn.

"They have the Tiernan coloring. Black hair and dark eyes."

"You forget there's some Chauverant involved," said Carolyn.

"You're right. I forget and let's keep it that way," Marti snapped. "I told you when we discussed this months ago, other than fathering these children through a quite common— no double entendre meant—act, Chauverant has nothing whatsoever to do with my babies. I have waived child support in exchange for his giving up all rights to them."

"Shades of your Aunt Margaret. Next you'll be making their legal names Tiernan. Haven't you learned anything from your aunt's experience? One day, your children may resent your decision to be both father and mother to them."

"I doubt it. My children are named for Augie and Margaret—people who gave me love. That's what matters. *All* that matters."

Although she was thinking, Ah, that life should be that simple, Carolyn said nothing but continued to look down at the pinched little face of the baby whose tiny hand was clutching her fingers.

"When I see something so small and precious, I think I would gladly die to spare it any pain," she said softly. "But I tried that once. It didn't work. Somehow there seems to be no escape from the pain that living brings. A parent can only hope the joy outweighs by far all the difficulties."

"Mom, have I outweighed all the difficulties?" asked Marti as she sat down next to Carolyn. "I mean, for all the trouble I've caused, was I worth it?"

"Oh, God, how can you ask?" Carolyn said, her eyes filled with tears. "Marti, I look at your babies and I look at you and I think . . . I'm so glad she had these children. And you know why? So someday, they will give to you all you give to me. Yes, there is pain, but Marti, the joy! The pure unmitigated joy!"

"Mom, that night I called you so upset . . ." began Marti, her head resting on her mother's shoulder as her baby, Mark, rested on her breast.

"I don't want to talk about it," said Carolyn.

"You knew, didn't you," pursued Marti softly.

"Not then. Later, this addlepated brain put it together."

"Would you have hated me?"

"You? Never! What you planned to do? Yes. And I thank God and Vinnie daily that you didn't abort a human life."

"But you never said anything."

"Marti, you learn as you get older that often there is nothing one *can* say, particularly to a child who is not a child to anyone else but you. Also, times and people change. Your Aunt Augie taught me that more than anyone else. Even more than Margaret. Not that I will ever feel differently about abortion but obviously a lot of women are beginning to.

485

I understand but I don't approve. And it's not necessary that I do. I guess what I've had to learn—particularly to keep my marriage intact—is: the only approval that matters is your own because in certain things that apply to one's life, it's all that can or should matter."

"Mom," Marti said as she squeezed her mother's hand, "I just hope my kids grow up to like me as much as I *like* you. *Like*, Mom. That's so different from love. But you know that, don't you."

"Yes," said Carolyn, thinking of Thomas as she spoke, "I guess I do."

Mr. and Mrs. Thomas Ollson
announce the birth of
Karl Ollson
August 9, 1960 6 lbs. 7 oz.

The birth announcement was among the mail waiting for Carolyn when she returned to New York. A month later, it was followed by a letter addressed in what was now known to Carolyn as Reese's free-flowing and rather extravagant manuscript handwriting. Carolyn waited until John J. had left for Collegiate and she had taken Mickey (named for Mickey Mantle, who else? she informed those who inquired) for his morning walk. The schnauzer, now twelve weeks old, had been waiting for them in their secretary's care ever since it had arrived—a gift from Vinnie—the day before they did. Of course John J. had predictably fallen madly in love with the puppy. The love was ongoing but the devotion lasted a week. To her amazement, Carolyn became the doting mother, annoyed with herself for acting with Mickey—but only privately and certainly not in front of John J., who she still hoped would assume his responsibility with the dog—as she would with her grandchildren if they were there. Once, John had caught her baby-talking to Mickey and he had whooped with laughter until he yelped from the impact of the pillow Carolyn had thrown at his head.

Now, with Mickey asleep in his bed between the sink and the refrigerator, Carolyn, a second cup of coffee in hand, sat down at the kitchen table to read Reese's letter.

Dear Mother Ollson,

Thomas and I apologize for the announcement we sent without a note but . . . Boy, were things hectic!

You have a wonderful healthy grandson whose lungs predict a great future with some opera company. As you may have noticed from the postmark, we have been transferred . . . again. We are now at George Air Force Base in Victorville. California. We are about forty miles north of San Bernardino. That might help you to locate us. Karl and I have only been here a week having flown in from Bridgeport where I've been staying since the end of July. Thomas thought it best for me to be with my family and at Dad's hospital when baby arrived. Of course that made it difficult for both of us as we don't really like to be separated. But . . . the Air Force sort of cooperated (considering all their rules and regulations, they really did cooperate!) and Thomas was with me when Karl arrived in this world. Unfortunately for Thomas, because of the baby, I remained in Bridgeport while he packed up our old homestead and moved to the new. Now you can understand why no note was attached with the announcement. Talk about people being in different places doing different things at different times! But we are all together again and that's wonderful.

We are sending you a picture of your *other* grandson. Isn't it a coincidence that Karl was born the same day as your other grandchildren. We read about Marti's twins and we hope you will congratulate her for us. By the way, the picture of Karl doesn't do him justice. He's really the sweetest little thing and he sends his grandma his love

With our fondest regards,
Thomas and Reese

Reese downed two Anacin tablets with a slug of orange juice and proceeded to dress the turkey, grimly determined that nothing would ruin the family's Thanksgiving. As she used her forearm to wipe the perspiration off her forehead, Reese acknowledged that the previous evening had been chaos and disaster but not her fault. That they should invite another couple to dinner and then drive the hour to San Bernardino to catch a sneak preview had been her idea, yes, and it had been a good one, she defended to herself as she smoothed sage over the bird. Anything that relieved the monotony of Victorville was a good idea.

Maybe it was the heat that had affected Thomas yesterday, mused Reese. Except it was always hot and dry in Victorville and Thomas was used to it by now even if she wasn't and never would be, she feared. Desert country is not Bridgeport. No winds there blow layers of dust across everything, always, ever, as they do here. Endless whirls of wind whipping up endless swirls of dust in endless heat. Monotonous. For her. But not for Thomas. He was in endless ecstasy learning to fly F-104s, fighter jets. Well, that was him, reasoned Reese. Nothing would ever talk her out of her intrinsic fears of flying and fighting. Put the two together and she was an anxious military wife who was particularly nervous the days she knew Thomas was airborne.

But last night had been a disaster and she had seen it coming. Perhaps she should hang a sign in the dining alcove: No Politics Allowed at Mealtime. As soon as that idiot, Marie Banks, admitted she had voted for Kennedy for President, Thomas had put down his fork and had looked as if he had been stabbed. If he had not asked Barney whether he, like his wife, had also voted for Kennedy, things might not have gotten out of hand. But Thomas had and Barney did and the combination thereof brought a discourse on the dangers of JFK that took Thomas from the fruit compote through the coq au vin. Weren't the Bankses aware that Kennedy was no match for Khrushchev or Castro; that although JFK was ambitious he was not bright? Nor was he shrewd enough to handle the emergencies of the day. And they were emergencies! Thomas had declared as he pointed a fork at Marie Banks. Nixon, however, had he been elected President, was a man of proven strength. How Barney Banks had hooted at that! Which had enraged Thomas. He went into his "declining power" speech and the threat of misguided liberals who were making our great nation weak and impotent. America ten years ago, five years ago, maintained Thomas, would never have permitted a fat old drunk to take off his shoe and bang the table at the U.N. as Khrushchev had.

Although Reese was in agreement with most of what Thomas had repeatedly said about American domestic and foreign policies, she had learned not to discuss her views with their friends. Thomas's zealousness had lost them several bridge partners and dinner companions as far back as last February,

488

when they were still in Bartow and he had been raging publicly against the criticisms that "outside forces" had leveled at the training manuals of the Air Force. "And why were there these 'protests'?" Thomas had asked, giving the answer as he did. "Because someone dared to tell it right. Dared to say: thirty of the ninety-five persons who revised the English translation of the Bible for the National Council of Churches were members of subversive groups." Reese could still remember the looks some wives gave their husbands when Thomas would talk of the "menace" that was creeping insidiously into their lives daily

And later, when they were at Webb Air Force Base and Francis Gary Powers had been shot down in his U-2 plane over Russia, Thomas had been all for going to war "here and now! To stop the cancer before it spreads." When even his fellow airmen had laughed at him, Thomas enjoyed the last laugh, although it was not humorous but bitter. Only a month after the Powers incident, fifteen hundred leftists in the Orient staged an anti-American snake dance when President Eisenhower was a guest in their country. Suddenly, those who had laughed were listening as Thomas spoke of the "handwriting on the wall—the decline of U.S. respect and power."

Which is why he had campaigned at Webb and at George for Nixon. Thomas felt, as he said last night at dinner, that Nixon would restore American supremacy or at least the possibility of it throughout the Mideast and Far East. It was then that idiot Marie Banks—I'm never going to ask her to this house again, thought Reese; she knew what she was doing—asked in that so sweet Southern drawl of hers: "But didn't your daddy actively campaign for Senator Kennedy?"

That, of course, had *really* sent Thomas off the deep end Reese had been so angry that she intentionally did not serve her famous Boston cream pie which she had made that day It was definitely too good for Marie Banks.

The arrival of Mrs. Needham cleared the tension. As the baby-sitter made idle conversation with Marie Banks, Reese wrote down the name of the theatre in San Bernardino where they could be reached in an emergency. It was with an actual thrill of anticipation that Reese applied fresh makeup. As she told herself, going to town was a big event in Apple Valley life, where there was little to do but tend house, baby, and husband. A night on the town, a chance to dress up—and with buttered popcorn as a bonus—was something to anticipate!

How could I have known, wondered Reese as she stuffed the turkey with chestnut dressing. Who could ever have thought such a coincidence was possible? And in San Bernardino? Poor Thomas. She wondered if his head hurt this morning as hers did. Certainly he had tossed about just as she had most of the night, and he had been up and out of the house by five forty-five. Given the way he drove and the emptiness of the roads at that hour—or at any hour of the day in Victorville—combined with his rage, he had probably driven the ten miles from Apple Valley to the base in five minutes. She hoped he would either work off or work out his anger before he came home. They had so much to be thankful for this Thanksgiving. Karl was a beautiful baby. And Thomas was excelling, as she knew he would, in his training program. And she had finally gotten back to her pre-baby weight if not her dimensions.

The sudden thud on the back door of the one-story ranch house announced that the pitching arm of Lonnie Detweiler was in good shape since the newspaper thrown from his bike had hit the door instead of a window, drainpipe, or the carport. She was not going to look at it, Reese decided. If those awful pictures had made the morning edition, why should she be the first on her block to know it? Besides, she didn't need to see any pictures. She had been there. Oh, please, God, Reese prayed, let it *not* be.

She had been so certain from the nondescript advertisement that had appeared twice that week in their local newspaper that the pre-Thanksgiving Day sneak preview was the new Paul Newman movie. She had adored Paul Newman ever since her parents had taken her on her birthday to see *Picnic* on Broadway, thinking it was a wholesome musical about a wholesome family on a day's outing. It wasn't, much to their consternation and Reese's delight. Marie Banks also loved Paul Newman, which today, as Reese reflected on that bit of information, made her decide to leave Paul Newman forever to that Woodward woman.

The theatre was packed even though they had arrived early and had sat through the last twenty minutes of *Solomon and Sheba*, which had seemed ridiculous even to starved-for-excitement Reese. When the screen finally darkened, an expectant hush fell over the theatre. Then, a gray light turning to white, then gray again, as clouds rushed and gathered on screen. Torrents of rain fell. Out of the winds came the logo: Killerbrew Studios presents: *Storms*. Starring . . . Vinnie Tiernan.

The audience went wild. Screams of delight mixed with yells of derision. Catcalls and cooings. As she felt Thomas tense, she heard Marie Banks whisper across her husband in girlish glee, "Isn't this just the most wonderful coincidence? I do declare!" Only with difficulty did Reese suppress her impulse to ram her box of popcorn into that sweet Southern mouth.

Was the film any good? Reese realized she could remember almost nothing about it. Throughout, she had felt her heart pounding as she watched Thomas out of the corner of her eye more than she did the screen. He was sitting as he marched in formation: straight and rigid. Dimly, she remembered thinking how little resemblance there was between Thomas and Vinnie. On screen, Vinnie often looked Italian, and unlike Thomas he was not a commanding presence but a hypnotic one. Reese found he moved her although she was unaware of anything he was saying: such had been the extent of her distress. It was his eyes. No, his mouth. Actually, it was his entire face.

After what seemed like a week, the film ended. At first the audience seemed stunned. Then, there was a smattering of applause. And then, nothing. No catcalls or jeers, but no cheers either. Thomas grabbed her arm just as the film was ending and whispered to the Bankses to meet them in the parking lot. They sped up the aisle while the theatre was still dark and ushers prepared to hand out preview cards. At the door they collided with others rushing to leave before the stampede for the exits began. Reese knew she would never forget the moment when they all seemed to tumble through the doors at the same time into the bright lights of the garish lobby.

"Thomas, my God. Thomas!" The voice was loud and filled with surprise. Delighted surprise.

She turned in its direction just as Thomas did and was confronted by the most beautiful girl she had ever seen, far more beautiful and softer than any of her pictures revealed, on screen or in magazines. With her was the man they had just watched on screen.

"I can't believe it. Thomas, say something It *is* you. isn't it?"

The distinguished-looking older man with them growled that this was hardly the place for a family reunion and swept them all toward the parking lot where an enormous limousine stood waiting. As did the photographers. Before he could fully comprehend what was happening, Thomas was sandwiched between Marti and Vinnie as flashbulbs popped. They stopped when Thomas said in his most authoritarian voice: "The next person who takes my picture gets his head cracked and then his camera."

Somehow, in all the confusion, introductions were made, although Reese still did not know what the older man had to do exactly with the film or the Tiernans. She heard Marti suggest they find some place quiet to have a drink; Thomas declined. Reese was disappointed. Marti was quite unlike what she had imagined. She was wearing a simple gray dress, although it was cut down to *there*, and carrying a black leather coat. Marti had seemed so genuinely glad to meet them. She was so warm and friendly until she realized that Thomas was not. Unrelentingly not.

What had Marti said that made Thomas snap: "I don't think so"?

What had Thomas then said that made Marti's hand fly to her bosom as if to cover her cleavage and then stop just before it did?

Why had Vinnie Tiernan then said: "You're such a shit!"?

And Thomas, making as if to swing at Vinnie. Would he have if that man hadn't come between them?

She remembered the look on Marti's face before she backed away and disappeared into the limousine. Reese also remembered the look on Thomas's face as he stared after her. He was looking in as Marti looked out. Their eyes seemed to be tearing into one another when Thomas roughly grasped her by the elbow and steered her off toward their car. And then that strange man—who was he? Reese asked herself, annoyed that she hadn't listened when introduced—running after Thomas and Thomas replying, "No, Franklin. I'm not interested. Not in any of them. What they do and how they do it is of no concern of mine until it enters my life or is forced into my face as it just was."

The scene, of course, had not gone unnoticed by Marie Banks, but when she began to comment on it on the drive back to Victorville, Reese snapped: "Can it, Marie, unless you want to walk the forty miles back to Apple Valley."

Reese, as she put her turkey in the oven and set the temperature at 350 degrees, still couldn't believe she had actually said that to a neighbor and now former friend. But then, had someone told her she and Thomas would ever go to bed without speaking to each other, she would not have believed that either. Yet, that is what had happened; both angry with themselves and each other but for different reasons. Why couldn't Thomas observe simple social amenities with his family? How did a hello, how-are-you, a card at Christmas, compromise one's values? It is so damn hard to believe, thought Reese, that this same man, this Thomas Ollson, was the one to suggest as a Christmas present that they fly in *her* parents so that the entire family—*his* words: family—could be together for the holidays. And *really* together, as he wouldn't hear of them staying any place other than in their home.

As she mashed the potatoes, Reese heard the back door open. She was surprised to see Thomas home this early. In his usual to-the-point fashion, without saying hello, he said, "Reese, I'm sorry about last night. I was set off at dinner— and then the movie—and I guess, the surprise of what happened then got to me. I didn't handle it very well. But honey, I'm not those people anymore. I'm just not! And I don't want anyone to think I am."

The look of pain on her husband's face pained Reese as well. A considerable part of it she understood as he handed her the newspaper opened to a picture of Marti that concentrated on her dress, or that part that accentuated what was in it.

"I know, Thomas," she said consolingly as she slid into his arms. "I know. Now why don't you sit yourself down and I'll get you a cold glass of milk and the biggest and best piece of Boston cream pie you have ever had."

4

The memo on his desk annoyed Franklin Killerbrew. It made
sense yet it didn't. Sure, they had a point: Carolyn Tiernan
wasn't a proven box office draw. But shit, thought Killerbrew,
this property would carry itself with a real-life mother and
daughter playing mother and daughter on screen, particularly
with Marti Tiernan in her first deglamorized role. But *they*
didn't see it that way. As the memo dictated, when *Family
Affairs* went before the cameras in April, *they* wanted Carolyn Tiernan out and Margaret Tiernan—now that she was
again a proven draw—in.

Even as Killerbrew conceded that their position made some
sense, he resented their mistrust of his judgment. They had
challenged him on Vinnie Tiernan and he had proven them
wrong. *Storms* was the studio's biggest hit in two years and
had reestablished Vinnie as one of the industry's major names.
And who had him on their back lot right this very minute?
And why? Because he, Franklin Killerbrew, had gambled on
what he knew was a sure thing, and had won. Only *they*
didn't see it that way. Their representatives visited the set
daily to make sure Vinnie was there and coherent.

They weren't totally wrong about that either, conceded
Killerbrew as he chewed on his pipestem still wishing it was
the cigar doctors had made him give up recently. *Storms* had
not only reestablished Vinnie on screen but off, and he was
once again that famous partygiver and -goer. The stories that
filtered down from the house on the hill were disturbing, not
because of their orgiastic flavor—Killerbrew remembered that
period of his life quite well and without either regret or
longing—but because they showed Vinnie's lack of caring and
discernment about who came and went (so to speak, thought
Killerbrew, aware of his own double entendre) and what they
often took with them from the house without asking. Yet,
despite Vinnie's "grinding" social calendar, Killerbrew's daily

check of the productions on the lot showed the boy to be on time. His director insisted Vinnie's lines were learned and that he was always prepared.

Despite his many efforts, Killerbrew found Vinnie uncommunicative. But not rude. He often seemed far away, lost in thoughts and vague images he could not verbalize. In his trailer, he either watched television or played rock records. His only guest was Marti when she wasn't working or was between takes. Often, she would leave the twins in Vinnie's care.

Marti. Shit! Sure as shit, thought Killerbrew, she would be upset. All she had talked about, other than the babies, of course, at dinner recently had been her fear yet excitement about working with her mother in *Family Affairs*. Damn! If Marti's upset, think of how Carolyn is going to react, thought Killerbrew.

Throwing his pipe on the desk, Killerbrew rose to pace the room that had been his office for almost five decades. He'd be damned, he decided, if he'd be the one to tell Carolyn. Let John have that miserable task. Killerbrew stopped as suddenly as if someone had called his name. In that split second, he realized that his days of running a studio were over. Strangely, the fact didn't disturb him as much as it surprised him. And pleased him, too. In the old days, the *real* old days, how a Carolyn Tiernan would react at being replaced—dumped, actually—for a bigger name would not have bothered him. Which is why I was so goddamn good for my pictures, my studio, and this town. But now, you've gone soft, Killerbrew, he said to himself as he sat down again behind his desk. In the gut and in the head, he added as he pressed down on his intercom. Almost immediately, Pamela Washburn stood in his doorway. "Get me John Ollson at his New York office. And when that call is completed, would you come in, please? There's a memo I want to dictate to our board of directors and the head of our New York office."

John was surprised but pleased by Killerbrew's decision to resign from the studio. Now his partner was free to devote all his time to the growth of K.O. Productions. Even with Killerbrew's part-time association, K.O. was second only to the growing David Wolper organization in major independent television productions. Like Killerbrew, John would have liked someone other than himself to tell Carolyn about the studio's decision. He knew how she would react despite her having lost the past several roles she had created onstage to film actresses of lesser talent. He also knew that rather than be pleased that her replacement was Margaret, she would act as if salt had been rubbed in her wounds.

John was right. When he told Carolyn, she looked at him in disbelief and then ran to her room. She remained behind closed doors, except for meals which she continued to prepare for her own sanity rather than for the welfare of her men—as she referred to her two Johns. When she was finally able to speak, she railed against Killerbrew, choosing not to understand that the control of the studio that bore his name was in the hands of power brokers on Wall Street. Despite John's explanations, Carolyn consulted her agents and lawyers to see if she had any recourse. She also was made to understand Killerbrew's position.

"I feel like a mother who has learned that the court has awarded custody of her child to someone else," she cried in John's arms one night. "Frieda was my invention. You wrote her for me. I made her into what she was for you and us."

John watched as Carolyn went through the various stages of mourning for her "child." He knew it was over when Carolyn came into the kitchen one morning as bright and sunny as the early spring day that shone outside their windows. The answer to this strange but very welcome behavior lay in the lead article in the drama section of the *New York Times* which Carolyn placed before him. It announced: "Carolyn Tiernan will star this fall in a new Broadway production by a young Southern writer. . . ." Before John could finish the paragraph, Carolyn interjected: "My role makes Blanche DuBois look like Heidi."

A day later, Killerbrew, acting as president of Killerbrew/Ollson Productions, called. "I always said a K.O. is a knockout every time," he said to Carolyn. "So how'd you like to be knocked out?"

If she agreed—and the deal was contingent upon her and Margaret's joint approval—K.O. would produce for NBC and its major greeting card sponsor a two-hour TV version of Noel Coward's *Fallen Angels,* starring the Tiernan Sisters. Killerbrew didn't have long to wait for Carolyn's answer. He didn't even have time to explain that production would begin taping in London in late June, one week after the conclusion of *Family Affairs,* and end two weeks before her Broadway rehearsals began, when Carolyn began screaming her yesses over and over. Which, of course, had been Margaret's reaction also.

"You're both incorrigible hams," Killerbrew said. "And I just better add Alka-Seltzer to the overall budget knowing in advance the way you will both chew up the scenery."

So much for Carolyn's depression, and all would have been well if it had ended well, thought John, only nothing ever ended, it just continued in a new way. The very next morning after Killerbrew's call came a brief letter to "Mother Ollson" announcing she would be a grandmother again in September. And ·that same afternoon brought an ecstatic phone call from Marti. She was one hour ahead of the final edition of the *New York Post* in telling her parents that just an hour ago she had married Sydon Silverman, California's noted diamond dealer.

As he sat on the carpeted floor, holding the crystal prism to the light, his smiling face was full of wonder. A happy child in an adult's body. The clusters of people who passed watched in fear. They knew who he was but not what he was doing. Grown men do not sit on the floor of the Steuben Glass Room at Bullock's Wilshire no matter how rich and famous.

Pretty prism. Pretty colors. Pretty world.

Now the crystal obelisk was held up toward the fluorescent light. He spun it carefully, watching closely as the reds and oranges sparkled past the yellows and blues. Now the crystal egg; now the prism again.

So pretty. So perfect. A perfect, pretty present for a perfectly pretty bride.

No silver for Silverman but crystal for Marti. To refract and reflect her beauty. A wedding present. Yes, absolutely I wish to make a purchase, he said to the store's general manager as he helped him to his feet with the aid of a uniformed guard. He would like the obelisk, the egg, and the prism. A card? Yes, that would be nice.

Dear Marti: I love you. I'll be here should the Silver(man) tarnish. Love, Vinnie.

Marti was not at London's Heathrow Airport to greet Carolyn although the rest of the family, surrounded by press, was. In the limousine, when Carolyn asked about Marti, Margaret looked out the window while John suggested somewhat testily that she ask Marti herself since they would be at the hotel

497

in a matter of minutes. As soon as she had unpacked her essentials and washed her face, Carolyn took the elevator three floors up to Marti's suite at the Savoy. The sounds of babies crying told Carolyn she was at the right place. Her knock was answered by a young woman who announced she was: "Miss Jennings. Elizabeth Jennings. Companion." Marti was changing the babies. "Go right in," she instructed when Carolyn was already halfway into the children's room.

Even though Marti's casual "Hi, Mom!" was wafted over her bent back as she changed Allison—or is that Mark? Carolyn wondered—her tone of voice told Carolyn something was wrong. As soon as her daughter came to greet her, Carolyn could see from Marti's eyes that something was indeed wrong. Very, very wrong.

"You look like hell," said Carolyn.

"I feel like it," Marti said miserably.

"Do you want to talk about it?"

"Not in front of the babies," said Marti. "Don't look as if I'm crazy. They may not understand words but they pick up feelings. If I cry in front of them—and I'm afraid I'm going to—it will upset them."

Marti waited until Miss Jennings, companion, had replaced her in the bedroom before she sat down next to Carolyn on one of the pink silk couches in the living room. "By the way, hello," she said as she took Carolyn's hand.

"I'd ask how you are, but I already know so give me a hug instead." As Marti fell into her embrace, Carolyn could feel her daughter coming apart, piece by piece. It began with staccato breathing, little short breaths that became gasps. The softest little sounds, whimpers actually, became little cries and then sobs. Its end came quicker than its beginning. "Mom, it was so awful, so very awful."

"What, baby?" asked Carolyn.

Marti didn't explain, she just replied: "I'm getting a divorce, Mom. Just as soon as possible, I'm getting a divorce."

Carolyn had met Sydon Silverman when Marti arranged her schedule to allow two days in New York before leaving for filming in London. It was not, from Carolyn's viewpoint, the perfect match. Silverman was divorced, the father of two children—one of whom was John J.'s age—Jewish, and truly old enough to be Marti's father. On the positive side was his obvious love of children as evidenced by the great displays of effusive affection he slobbered on Ali and Mark. He was also generous if that monstrous diamond on Marti's finger was any indication. And that was the problem, or part of it anyway, according to Marti. Silverman was generous to a fault, giving his money away freely to the horses, the bookies, merchants, and realtors. His creditors were sending calling cards from the other side of the globe, and Silverman had thought nothing of asking Marti for loans.

He had seemed so settled and secure when he was courting her, Marti explained. Without any form of cheap ostentation, he commanded the respect of waiters in the restaurants they frequented. He was known at all the major art galleries in the Los Angeles area. At concerts, the ushers knew exactly where his seats were even before he presented his season tickets. His home in Encino was spacious and elegant but again, like the man, not ostentatious. It begged for her presence, he had insisted. It needed her children to make it a home, he had argued. It needed a woman to make it whole, and he did, too. That he was something less than a creative or thrilling lover hadn't mattered, Marti told Carolyn. She had experienced that with Chauverant and it had blinded her to the deficiencies in the relationship.

Silverman had gone through more than one hundred thousand of Marti's dollars in their four-month marriage but that wasn't why she had thrown him out. That he was penniless would not have been a problem had he not had a child's attitude toward money and her. It was gimme, gimme, gimme. Quickly she found herself doling out money the way some mothers dole out cookies to their children. She waited and worried when he returned late from an "exhausting" day but she never knew what he had found to do in London that exhausted him and when she asked, his answers were so evasive they exhausted her. Worse was *her* coming home after a day of filming and finding *he* wanted pampering and comfort—and a hot meal—when she was so obviously the one in need.

As Marti unburdened herself, Carolyn found she was only partially listening. Not that she was uninterested, yet she was. Silverman and Chauverant, although worlds apart, were one and the same man with one and the same failing in Marti's mind. There was nothing Carolyn could say that would make her think otherwise. And besides, Carolyn hadn't liked or approved of either. Carolyn knew that although she could comfort her daughter, she couldn't make things right

499

for her. To her surprise, Carolyn realized she no longer felt she had to. Like Margaret, like herself, Marti would have to right her own wrongs and find her own answers. As she caressed Marti's hair, hoping to soothe her hurt, Carolyn realized it was strange to suddenly comprehend that your child's life belongs to her and not to you. Strange . . . and yet oddly liberating.

As Carolyn sat next to James on the set of *Family Affairs* at Elswood Studios, she was thinking how often life imitated art and vice versa. Marti, in her final scenes with Margaret, looked haggard and drawn. Audiences would credit that to makeup but Carolyn knew that no makeup had been required. *Family Affairs* had run a week over its production schedule due to Marti's emotional "difficulties." Franklin Killerbrew tolerated Marti's absences because she was brilliant. Despite her personal problems, Marti was so much better than any other actress with whom Carolyn had played onstage. She had defined her character's every nuance and understood her every motivation. Ah, if only life would imitate art here! thought Carolyn. As for Margaret in the role of Frieda Schneider, that, too, had proven a miracle. Margaret's interpretation differed from Carolyn's and was no less or more brilliant. It was, however, perfect for the screen and Margaret, despite the grueling schedule of filming *Family* by day and rehearsing *Fallen Angels* at night with Carolyn, was thriving.

As she sipped the tea James had brought for her, Carolyn watched John standing to the left of the set, mouthing the dialogue along with the actors. He still took her breath away. Twenty-five years. It hardly seemed possible. But if her own years with John had seemed unreal when celebrated at the party Margaret and James had given for them, hearing James say that he and Margaret would be observing fifteen years of marriage this fall had totally stunned her.

"Marg, we're getting old," she wailed.

"Speak for yourself, you old bag. I, myself, am younger than springtime."

"I would say after careful inspection, then, that spring will be a little late this year. Either that, or we'll have none at all," replied Carolyn.

In private moments, Carolyn thought how both she and Margaret had "managed." Yes, that was the word: managed to make it despite the obstacles they themselves had put in the way of their marital success. They had both succeeded. As she looked at John and thought about how he continued to both comfort and excite her, a little laugh bubbled up and out of her, causing James to stare at her for a moment. And now I'm the one who requires more of John than he does of me, although he does quite nicely, thank you, Carolyn told herself. Thinking about just how "nicely" made her laugh again.

"If it's dirty, tell me," James whispered in her ear.

Carolyn turned beet red and laughed still more loudly. "It is dirty and I will not tell you because I don't want you getting overstimulated. Besides, from what I hear you're dirty enough."

"It's a rotten rumor," said James in injured tones, "and I must stop spreading it."

Carolyn hooted, which caused Franklin Killerbrew to say from his position just behind the camera, "Would you be still. Don't you realize there are Academy Awards at work here?"

Carolyn fled the set, deciding the time was exactly right to reach John J. at Wildwood Nature Camp where he was spending the summer again. As she waited for the transatlantic operator to put through her call, Carolyn thought of the Special Academy Award she should present to John for his outstanding performance over two and a half decades. This time, Carolyn didn't giggle or hoot but roared with laughter even as she heard her youngest child say: "Hi, Mom."

"The nominees for this year's Best Supporting Actress are . . ."

As the audience at the Santa Monica Civic Auditorium for the 1963 Oscar award presentations grew still, Carolyn remembered *to the second* where she had been a year ago when the same award had been presented. On stage at the Longacre Theatre. Attempting to be very Southern and very neurotic. Offstage, by agreement, the prop manager was set to flash the "win" sign if Marti's name was called for *Family Affairs*. As he accidentally dropped his card, Carolyn dropped her line, and if audiences could have simultaneously watched mother and daughter on different coasts, they would have been hard pressed to decide who had played her "mad scene" best.

As Patty Duke raced down the aisle to collect her award for

The Miracle Worker, Vinnie was remembering his own "mad scene" a year ago in Rome. An old-fashioned Roman orgy it had been. Afterward, when he had returned to his room at the Hotel de la Ville, he lay awake, hating himself for not naving escorted Marti to the ceremonies that were still in progress in Hollywood. Certainly the producers had been more than willing to give him the three days off from filming, understanding that the publicity Vinnie would receive at the Oscars would help their film more than the additional dialogue they hoped Gore Vidal would write. It was he who had opted not to go; he who had not wanted a confrontation with his also nominated mother. And then she hadn't attended after all. At the last moment, as the papers stated: "Margaret Tiernan had been unavoidably detained."

Along with the audience, Margaret, as she waited hidden backstage at the Civic Auditorium, laughed at one of Frank Sinatra's witticisms although she had not understood it. Nervous, she would have laughed if someone merely said hello, how are you. More nervous perhaps than even the year before when only a transatlantic telephone cable kept her in touch with the Oscar proceedings. A year ago, she was lying in bed, James holding her hand as her own held the telephone. Waiting . . . waiting . . . waiting for the information to be relayed by Franklin. She didn't expect to win but then she hadn't expected to be nominated for *Family Affairs* either, believing Hollywood would neither forgive nor forget. It was Killerbrew who thought otherwise, who had convinced her to come to Hollywood for the festivities. Just as she had completed all arrangements to fly the polar route directly from London to Los Angeles, James had suffered a mild heart attack; "nothing serious," lied the doctors when they knew any attack at James's age and in his condition was serious. So she had sent her regrets to the Academy and the press, sympathetic, wrote of her "dedication" to her husband rather than to her work. That was a year ago, thought Margaret, as she wondered what the press would write of her after this night.

As the camera did a slow pan on "Mother Ollson" and her husband, Vinnie to his left and James Carrington to her right, Reese thought of the *Look* magazine article of a year ago. She remembered the writer calling from New York shortly after

502

the nominations had been announced and it was revealed that the "Tiernan Family" had racked up a goodly share. The writer wanted to come to Victorville and interview Thomas, who had been most insistent that he was "unavailable." The writer came anyway and had camped on their doorstep. Thomas remained adamant: no interview. He was in the military now, a private citizen who did not want his private life made public. He was not, he emphasized, a Tiernan anymore. Yet, when the article appeared a week before the Oscar ceremonies, there had been unauthorized pictures of Karl and Kristan as they played in the front yard. There was also a picture of Thomas as he had once looked when part of "Tiernans & Company" and as he looked today in his orange flight suit. And just how that picture had been taken as he stood near one of the fighter jets on George Air Force Base was beyond Thomas.

After considerable consultation with his lawyers, Thomas decided not to sue the magazine for invasion of privacy. A suit, he realized, would only fan the flames of the family feud that had been strongly intimated in the magazine article. Reese had not been surprised last year when Thomas had refused to watch the awards show with her. She had not expected that he would.

As she now watched the same show on the same channel, Reese thought what a difference a year makes. Although he made no comment as the pictures of his family flashed on and off the screen, Thomas, as he sat by her side, wore a look of stone on his face. *That* she expected. It was the look Thomas always wore whenever his family was mentioned.

As Ethel Merman concluded her medley of Irving Berlin songs, bringing a rousing response from the Civic Auditorium audience, Carolyn remembered how she had been applauded by the cast when she came offstage a year ago, as if she, and not Marti, had just won the Oscar. There was champagne and caviar, all the signs of a party, only Carolyn was depressed. She had missed a great moment in her daughter's and her own life. Not even the knowledge that she could see it later, repeated on newscasts, could make her feel better. She remembered closing herself, but not her dressing room door, to the party in her room as she watched the remainder of the telecast. Her heart pounded then as it was pounding now. It was criminal that John hadn't won for best screenplay. Margaret's loss to Sophia Loren was somehow easier to take. Certainly Margaret's winning during the past year both the British Oscar and Italy's Donizetti—or is it the Donatello? What difference? It's an award, isn't it?—had compensated somewhat. Plus the Emmy nomination for *Fallen Angels*. Neither of them had won but still, Carolyn thought as her anxiety heightened, there was much to be grateful for.

John Ollson was holding his wife's hand, pretending an interest he didn't have in the actual award ceremonies. A year ago he had been a nominee in the Best Screenplay category. He had wanted to win, wanted the further validation for the truths in *Family Affairs*. Still, he had not been nervous, at least nowhere near as nervous as he was now waiting for the "big event." Strange how there can be more difficulty in waiting to pay homage to a loved one, he thought, than there is in wanting others to pay homage to you.

Vinnie, sitting at his uncle's side, had been summoned to the mount, as he called it, by his agents and advisers, who cautioned that this was one industry event which he had to attend. Like it or not. He understood their reasoning and even agreed with it, despite the position it put him in. If he could be somewhere else with any plausibility, that's where he would be. But given the occasion, he was where he should be, his reason dictated even as his stomach revolted. Beneath his formal wear which made him look quite unlike himself and his image, Vinnie felt his body turn cold and wet.

Backstage, Marti was fanning herself with a program. Wearing a pink ball gown designed by Balenciaga, her hair flowing freely to her shoulders despite Ernie Adler's insistence she wear it up, she was attracting her usual lion's share of attention. As she fanned and paced, Marti was mouthing her lines. Never had she felt quite so nervous. Everything has to be *perfect*, she kept telling herself. Yes, the words were all written on cue cards just above camera two, but she wanted not to read or recite but to speak them from somewhere within. As she was talking it out to herself, she was dimly aware of being led toward the stage. The lights awakened her. That was Frank Sinatra, she realized, announcing: "Here to present the Irving Thalberg Award . . ." Applause. Applause. Walk tall, from the center of the body. Smile.

As she was promised, the words were there before her on cue cards. "The Irving Thalberg Award . . . the industry's highest honor . . . presented to a filmmaker of distinction and devotion. . . . This year, the recipient of this award will receive it from his discovery and five-time Oscar nominee and Academy Award winner . . . Margaret Tiernan."

Since her presence had been a secret to all but the immediate family and the director of the telecast, there was a gasp and then a silence that greeted the slender woman who walked with assurance toward center stage. The short hair was different from what most remembered, but the long-legged stride was not. That belonged unmistakably to "the horsey one." At first, the smattering of applause was perfunctory. Then, as shock gave way to recognition, roars of approval barraged Margaret, causing her to step back a foot or two. On its feet, the audience was waving and whistling, stomping as it cheered and clapped.

Carolyn, too, was standing, unaware of the tears that were streaming down her face and that she was being superimposed in the upper lefthand corner of TV screens in homes and at the auditorium showing a stunned Margaret Tiernan. When members of the audience became aware of the director's "added attraction," they turned toward Carolyn and applauded her. Louder and louder came the cheers. Margaret, flustered, tried to speak but couldn't. Instead, she cried. When she finally stopped, so did the audience reaction. Suddenly, as if becoming aware that this was her moment, Margaret looked into the audience, singling out for herself faces she remembered. In an almost inaudible voice she said: "Thomas Wolfe was wrong. You *can* go home again. And it feels so good to be back."

Again the ovation swelled but this time Margaret silenced it by beginning her prepared speech extolling the virtues of the recipient of the Irving Thalberg Award. Midway through words that felt uncomfortable in her mouth, she stopped. She signaled the camera to follow her, an act that caused the director in the control room to scream in frustration as she walked into the wings. When she came out, she was on the arm of Franklin Killerbrew. At center stage, she explained: "If you knew this bum for as long as I have, you'd know he was never a man of words—unless he either wrote or dictated them. Ladies and gentlemen, a great filmmaker and a great friend, this year's Irving Thalberg Award winner . . . Franklin Killerbrew."

The distinguished-looking white-haired gentleman, trim and tanned, bore a remarkable resemblance to Cary Grant. As the audience rose in tribute to him, he placed one arm protectively about Margaret and squeezed her to him. As the applause continued, he smiled into her face rather than into the camera. On the TV screens in the Civic Auditorium, people saw what viewers on the ABC-TV network were privy to: a look and an embrace of emotions too numerous to define or label.

"Some things never change," said Thomas Ollson disgustedly in Victorville.

Time makes for such wonderful changes, thought James Carrington as he proudly watched his friend and his wife acknowledge all they had meant to each other over the years.

It seems like old times, said Vinnie to himself bitterly.

All things in time, thought John as he saw, as if they were visible, the distances Margaret and Franklin had traveled to reach this place in their lives.

"Time for bed," said John J. to an already snoozing Mickey in New York where it was almost midnight.

"Time heals all wounds," said Carolyn to Augusta Monahan and her mother as she felt her family about her. "Well, almost all," she corrected as she thought of Thomas somewhere out there beyond the red eye of the television camera.

"Where did this *thing* come from?" Margaret asked as the limousine drove up to the Beverly Hilton Hotel for the post-Oscars Board of Governors Ball. "It wasn't here yesterday."

"Margaret, twenty years is not yesterday," said Carolyn as she viewed with distaste the klieg lights and the several hundred people behind roped barriers she would soon have to face.

"How very profound of you, Lynnie. Really, John, you've done wonders with her. Such insight she has into reality! Imagine, twenty years is not yesterday, she says. Listen, if you guys will just wait right here, I'll dash down the street to my room at the Beverly Hills Hotel. I want to write down those immortal words in my diary."

"The only thing that hasn't changed in twenty years is your mouth," said Carolyn.

"They're both wrong," John said to James. "What hasn't

506

changed in twenty—make that thirty—years is the childish way they speak to each other."

"It's unresolved sibling rivalry," offered James. "Either that or both are suffering from severe regression."

"You'll be suffering from a severe *de*pression—the one I'll make in your chin with my fist—if you keep that up," cautioned Margaret. Then turning to Carolyn, she said brusquely: "What have you to be nervous about?"

"Meeting Marti's new man. God, I hope this one is younger than I am."

"Almost anyone would have to be, my dear," sniped Margaret in her bitchiest voice.

Carolyn didn't have to ask what was making Margaret nervous. Although Vinnie had done his job well backstage at the Civic Auditorium, posing for family pictures for the photographers, even a "two-shot" with Margaret, he had been remote although always polite. That he was attending the ball Carolyn attributed to his good sense. Still, deciding to leave nothing to chance, Carolyn had taken Vinnie aside before they had all separated into two limousines and said, "This is your mother's evening. She's earned it. Don't do anything to ruin it." The look that appeared on Vinnie's face stayed with her throughout the drive from Santa Monica to Beverly Hills.

As the Hilton Hotel doorman opened the back door of the oversized Lincoln Continental, Carolyn grasped Margaret's hand. "Okay, waif, it's into the wind with us," she said as she pulled Margaret with her into the glare of flashbulbs. Before Margaret could think about the huge crowd of press that would only be allowed outside the hotel, she found herself next to Carolyn waving to the fans, even those "up past their bedtime" who hadn't the vaguest idea who they were.

"The Gish Sisters? But of course," said Margaret as she signed the autograph album of one teenage boy she saw as one big adolescent pimple. "Here, Lillian, you next," she said to Carolyn as she handed her the boy's book.

Once past the throng and in the hotel, Margaret, standing with James and staring into the huge International Ballroom, said, "This, my dear, is your typical *intime* Hollywood party. Here, when someone faints, they yell out: 'Is there an agent in the house?' A small difference but an important one."

The ballroom was on three tiers, the first with a hardwood floor for dancing. The sixteen hundred guests were lighted to their very best advantage by ten huge crystal chandeliers whose light mingled and played gently with the inlaid mirrors on the walls throughout the room. As they were pushed, and pushed their way, through the clusters who milled about second-guessing or complimenting the award winners, Margaret, dismayed, whispered to Carolyn: "I don't recognize a soul. Where is everybody?"

Carolyn, having lived through similar feelings at last season's Tony Awards, patted Margaret's hand reassuringly. "They've taken a hot bath, a glass of hot milk, and gone to bed."

"If that's all they've taken to bed, times have indeed changed," groaned Margaret.

"We have a table somewhere up there," said John as he pointed toward the third tier which, like the rest of the accessories in the room, was a garish yet grand pink, red, and gold. As he searched above the heads of the standing guests, he spotted Franklin Killerbrew waving at him. Sitting to his left was Vinnie, to his right, Marti, and to her right . . . "Carolyn, how would you define *mature* as in mature-looking?" asked John hesitantly.

"He's that old, eh?" said Carolyn, reading John to perfection.

"Oh, my God, he's Carl Sandburg!" Margaret said as she caught a glimpse of Marti's date. "Or Arthur Fiedler. I'm not sure which."

It was the full head of white hair worn just below his shirt collar that made Philip Charper look considerably older than he was. When he stood for the introductions, his leanness indicated a man of forty rather than the originally feared eighty. Introduced by Marti as "Dr. Charper," he had been quick, in deep, resonant, and rather commanding tones, to explain the "doctor" was a formality, confined to the classes he taught at the Center for Psychotherapeutic Research and Development and the patients he treated. As a psychotherapist.

"Well, you certainly have come to the right table," chirped Margaret gaily. Marti and Carolyn glared.

"Oops, sorry," Margaret said, covering her face with a napkin.

Carolyn kicked her under the table.

When she peeked out from under the gray linen, Margaret saw Killerbrew trying to suppress his laughter and Charper looking anything but amused. He was actually staring at her as if studying a laboratory specimen. As Margaret bristled, Carolyn, to relieve the tension, said, "Shall we dance?"

'I'd love to," replied Margaret. "but this time you lead and let me be the girl."

"Would you stop!" said Carolyn exasperatedly. "Really. whatever will Dr. Charper think of us?"

"I should think the shoe would be on the other foot," replied Margaret watching Charper's face for some kind of response. "Tell me, doctor, are you somewhat nervous about meeting the family?"

"Not in the least," Charper replied coldly. "From what I've read and observed I feel I already know you."

Now it was Vinnie who was staring at Charper. "That's funny. It must be dual déjà vu. For I'm getting the decided impression that I've also met you. *Many times*," added Vinnie, making his contempt clear.

Charper tilted his head ever so slightly in Vinnie's direction as if to acknowledge a point scored by the opposing team. "Marti, why don't we dance?" he asked, standing before Marti could say yes or no. As they worked their way through the crowd to the dance floor below, Margaret muttered, "What a charming man. He makes a lobotomy seem a preferable alternative to psychotherapy."

"I'd be quite happy to perform one on you with this butter knife," said Carolyn. "In case you haven't quite gotten the picture, Marti is involved with this man."

"Lynnie, I've gotten the *picture* and the picture is a fraud. a copy, a pale imitation of the masters."

"Maybe we should dance, Margaret," said James

"Listen, but, thanks to Y. A. Tittle here, my feet have already taken enough abuse."

Vinnie was suddenly on his feet, explaining he was to meet his date at the elevators and would return just as soon as she arrived. When he was out of earshot, James turned to Margaret and said, "Instead of making wisecracks, why don't you make conversation with your son?"

Margaret stared in disbelief at James. Tears stung her eyes In one quick motion, she pushed back from the table, stood, and then dashed for the ladies' room, knocking aside several standees as she did. For a moment, no one spoke. Then Carolyn, after folding her napkin and placing it on the table, excused herself.

In the ladies' room, Carolyn hoped no one would think it terribly peculiar that she was stooping to look under the door of the booths. When one woman stared at her curiously,

Carolyn, embarrassed, explained matter-of-factly: "I'm looking for a beige dress."

The woman nodded. "Of course, darling," she replied. "But don't you think you'd have better luck at Robinson's or the May Company?"

The laughter from the last booth against the wall identified Margaret. "Come on out of there, I want to talk to you," said Carolyn.

"No, you come in," Margaret said, her voice sounding more childish than womanly.

Carolyn looked about to see who could observe this even more bizarre behavior on her part before she did as Margaret asked. When certain she was alone, she rapped on the door and Margaret opened it.

"Won't you sit down?" Margaret asked grandly as her arm waved in the direction of the toilet seat. "I realize, it's a little small but the rent is cheap and the hotel supplies all the utilities, including toilet paper."

"That's enough!" said Carolyn, ending Margaret's make-believe merry-making. "You should do as James says: talk to Vinnie."

Margaret sat down heavily on the seat she had offered to Carolyn. "I can't," she said, the tears she was holding back evident in her voice. "I don't know what to say. What *is* there to say?"

"Marg, you haven't seen him in four years. Try 'What's new?' for openers."

"And he'll say 'Nothing,'" said Margaret as tears began to ruin her makeup. "He'll be civil, even polite, and that's all he'll be. Christ! I'd prefer his rage to this . . . deadness."

"If it matters to you, and it obviously does, ask him outright to meet for lunch or a duel at dawn. Anything. But try to open the lines of communication."

"And what if he says no?" asked Margaret miserably.

"Then you have several choices," replied Carolyn knowingly "You can either feel terrible the rest of your life or angry for his ingratitude and selfishness. You'd be amazed but you can even feel both. At the same time. You can hate yourself for your mistakes and you can hate him for his unforgiving nature. You can do most anything except forget the situation exists."

Margaret stood to face Carolyn whose own eyes were filled with tears. Forgetting her own anxiety, she clutched Carolyn to her and stroked her hair as if it were pain that could be smoothed away. When Carolyn was composed, Margaret kissed her lightly on the cheek. Holding her at arm's length she said: "Lynnie, I do love you dearly but . . . we must stop meeting like this."

Carolyn's raucous laughter caused the other women now in the ladies' room to stare in the direction of the last booth against the wall. As Margaret and Carolyn exited, Margaret looked at the stunned expressions and said in their direction: "It's really quite all right and not at all what you think. You see, we're not really sisters."

At the table, Philip Charper was "addressing" James, John, and Marti on the new humanism that was about to change the entire nature of the therapeutic community. Franklin Killerbrew was chomping on his unlit cigar and Margaret instantly knew from his expression that the cigar was standing in for Charper. When he saw her looking at him, Killerbrew rolled his eyes heavenward. Margaret winked at him as she said, "How about a dance, big boy? This is our night, you know."

Carolyn was sitting quietly, holding John's hand under the table, alternately watching Margaret and Killerbrew on the dance floor and her daughter gazing up at the man who continued to lecture rather than talk. Although she was aware that John's questions, asked in a calm, modulated voice, were meant to puncture Charper's pontification, no one else seemed to be. She was thinking that absolutely nothing else could add to the tension of the evening when Carolyn saw Vinnie with his date. Remembering a New Year's Eve at the Plaza with Franklin Killerbrew, her hand flew to her heart and as she shook her head in disbelief, she gasped, "Oh, my God!"

John looked up just as Vinnie arrived. "Everybody," he heard his nephew say: "I'd like you to meet Katherine Christianson."

And as if once hadn't been enough, John heard Carolyn repeat: "Oh, my God. My dear, dear God!"

What had seemed like a wonderful idea at the time she thought of it, now loomed as a chore and an act of masochism to Marti After last night, she was not feeling kindly disposed toward anyone, least of all her luncheon guests. As she waited for Carolyn and Margaret to arrive, Marti lit a cigarette she still couldn't hold, let alone smoke, comfortably. When exactly had it gone wrong? she asked herself. Certainly not at the Civic Auditorium. That had been a dream come true, right down to her having met Patti Page who was singing "Hush, Hush, Sweet Charlotte," one of the five nominated songs. It was strange but nice to gush over someone when so many were gushing over you, thought Marti as the first effects of the smoke hit her head. No, she reiterated for herself, that part of the evening, with Margaret and Franklin and the family, had been thrilling.

Not so thrilling had been the party and Philip's attitude toward her afterward. In bed, he had turned away from her. She had found his silence as punishing as his unusual physical rejection. That morning, before leaving to teach his weekly class, he had lashed into her family, calling them children and her an infant. They were too much a part of her, he insisted. They stultified her growth, did not give her the space she needed to fully mature. He blamed her "underdevelopment" on the overdeveloped individual egos of the family.

She tried to argue and then reason with him but Philip always made her logic seem ridiculous. "You don't have to live with your family physically, Marti, to still be in their home and under their roof. But you have yet to cut the cord." She looked uncomprehendingly at him. She was twice married, she argued, twice divorced, the mother of twins, a homeowner, one of the three leading women in films, and his lover. And she hadn't cut the cord?

"Despite everything you seemingly have and are, the externals in other words, you are a child," Charper said before he slammed out of the house.

We should have left the damn party when he wanted to, thought Marti as she ground out the cigarette in a shiny, sculptured tin ashtray, one of many in the living room decorated in Mexican style. Philip had wanted to leave the Hilton shortly after Vinnie and his "date" arrived. Certainly he had been right about that. Things had gotten rather tense at the table, Marti now admitted. First her mother, like a broken record stuck in the same groove, kept muttering "Oh, my God!" as her father looked from Philip to that Katherine Christianson woman wide-eyed and with head shaking in disbelief. Then there was Franklin chomping on that stupid cigar as Vinnie had the nerve to light up a reefer. In front of everybody! And James, acting like Fred Astaire, whisking Margaret off to the dance floor whenever someone said something with a double or a hidden meaning, which was just about every other sentence. Thank God, Thomas wasn't there to see us all, thought Marti with a shudder.

She had seen some humor in the situation . . . then, but not Philip. Oh, no, not Philip. But of course, she had to admit, he had taken much of the abuse which peppered him in thinly veiled hostility. "And how many times have you been married, Dr. Charper?" is not the kind of question one usually asks at a first meeting. Marti assumed that the reason Margaret had screamed immediately upon asking was that her mother had given her another swift kick. Not that Mother was much better, thought Marti. "Only twice?" was hardly a proper response to Philip's reply to Margaret's rudeness. Maybe Philip is right. Maybe there are dynamics within the family I don't understand, thought Marti. Maybe I should have called off this luncheon.

Even as she thought this, Marti checked the table on the patio. From behind the plate-glass doors of her living room, she could see the kelly-green tablecloth with its avocado napkins and white plates with green trim—a perfect match for the springlike April day. It will be just the least bit cool eating outdoors but it will be a treat for Mother and Margaret, Marti decided once again, given how they can't avail themselves of such pleasures in New York and London.

In the kitchen, Marti gently opened the oven door to look at her handiwork. The cheese soufflé looked beautiful as it rose majestically in what was beginning to be a golden puff. As she closed the oven, she tried again to remember whether Margaret loathed or loved spinach. She bartered with God as she hoped it was the latter. Otherwise her beautiful spinach, mushroom, and bacon salad would be a disaster and God, said Marti, last night was enough of a disaster without having a repeat performance of any kind. With that, Marti opened one of the cold bottles of California white wine, poured herself a glass, and then collapsed on one of the bright blue couches, hugging a grass-green pillow to her.

Margaret was once again concentrating on the final approach to Marti's house. One wrong turn and she and Carolyn would be lost again. Bel Air had certainly gotten bigger, much bigger, in twenty years.

"Do try and get it right this time," said Carolyn as they reached a familiar fork in the road that they had taken twice and twice had gone wrong.

"Would you like to drive?" Margaret asked, ice dripping from every word.

"Don't be disgusting. You know I don't drive," said Carolyn equally icily.

"Then shut up unless you can *finally* follow those damn directions and tell me exactly how to reach where we're going."

Carolyn put on her bifocals again and looked at the drawing Marti had made for them the night before. "Just follow these arrows," Marti had said, "and you'll find the house easily." Sure, thought Carolyn, if you're an Indian you can follow arrows. But we're New Yorkers. "You try," she said to Margaret, shoving Marti's map in her direction.

"I can't even remember my name today so how do you expect me to read a map that would have confused Vasco da Gama?"

Carolyn looked at Margaret but didn't know what to say. What can you say to someone, particularly your sister, when her son is with her one night, agreeing to see her the next, and then takes off for Acapulco, leaving her to discover this bit of news from his answering service? When Margaret had told her this an hour ago, Carolyn had reacted as if slapped— and she wasn't the one who had been.

"More and more I'm coming to the conclusion we should have been nuns," Carolyn said with a sigh.

"It must be up that road to the left," said Margaret as she put down Marti's map and started up the engine of the rented Oldsmobile. "The map shows three forks in the road and we've taken two so it has to be that one. If not, it's back to the Beverly Hills Hotel and a massage."

"There it is!" yelled Carolyn excitedly. "It's *that*," she added, not knowing what to call the huge gray stone walls that surrounded the property bearing the elusive address.

"It looks like Sing-Sing. All that's missing is the tower and an armed guard."

"It's to prevent trespassers and kidnappers," offered Carolyn by way of explanation as Margaret pulled the car over to the call box by the massive iron gates that wouldn't open until Marti buzzed them in.

"After last night, don't be too sure they weren't just erected to prevent us," grumbled Margaret.

In the annals of Great Disasters, Marti would forever rank

her little luncheon somewhere between the *Titanic* and the *Hindenburg,* although no lives were lost—just tempers. First the intercom hadn't worked and if she hadn't heard the horn on the Oldsmobile blaring—which she hadn't for almost five minutes, she was pointedly told—her aunt and her mother might still be standing in the roadway, which in retrospect seemed like a good idea. Then, once they were buzzed in, Thor, the guard dog, had somehow gotten loose and terrorized her mother, probably because her clothes bore Mickey's scent. Of course their being forty minutes late had resulted in a burnt soufflé that collapsed even faster than her spirits upon its arrival on the luncheon table.

"Spinach? You know I can't eat spinach. When did you ever see me eat spinach in all the years you lived with me in Paris?"

"We're eating outdoors? But darling, it's so nice inside. No bugs to bother us. No nasty little ants and frogs that leap about and little birds that leave their little calling cards. I'm sure we'd all be so much more comfortable indoors. Besides, you know your aunt can't take the sun."

And then for dessert in popped Ali and Mark in their usual high spirits, spitting and spilling, knocking down everything in their usual uninhibited fashion. The twins had been surprised and hurt when Carolyn disciplined them. As had been Marti, who did not ask but ordered her mother to stop immediately. Her children were *her* children and she gave them the total run of the house. If things got broken, they were only, after all, *things* that could be replaced. That had caused yet another "discussion" which began with . . . "Oh, is that Philip's teaching?" and ended with a lecture on "this new permissiveness," as her mother referred to anything that varied from her own ideas of child-raising, and "the effect it would have on society in later years."

Marti had replied too quickly and rather badly with: "I don't see that the old way worked very much better unless you've received a loving letter from my brother that you've forgotten to mention."

And that had been the best of it! Margaret had asked if she had known that Vinnie was intending to fly off without a word and Marti had been offended by the question. Again she had answered too quickly and rather unwisely. No, she replied, and even if she had she would not have told Margaret. Margaret's "Whose side are you on anyway?" had elicited a frustrated "No one's!" which made Margaret look confused and hurt. But that hadn't given her the right to say: "What makes you both take up with such awful people?" Even her mother had bristled at that, although it was evident from what she said later that she shared those sentiments where Philip was concerned.

As she sat sipping warm white wine Marti still couldn't believe she had invited her guests to leave. Yet, her words still resounded in the room.

"I refuse to sit in my own home and listen to you both criticize me and the man I may marry."

"Live with him, but don't marry him," Margaret said without a moment's hesitation or thought.

"When she wants your opinion she'll ask for it," her mother snapped. "Don't do either. Just take your time for once"—it was the *for once* that had enraged Marti—"and rush into nothing. Be certain. You have the children to think about."

"Plus you, right?" Marti replied angrily. "Your feelings and your possible embarrassment."

So everybody had left angry with everybody, and whereas her mother and aunt were stuck with each other on their drive back to the Beverly Hills Hotel, she was stuck with a bunch of wilting spinach and an even worse looking brownish lump of soufflé which even Thor wouldn't touch. Smart dog, thought Marti. He had been trying to tell her something from the moment he had attempted to prevent Carolyn from entering the house. She should have listened

Katherine Christianson didn't understand Vinnie but didn't feel the need to. That she understood herself and the circumstances was enough. Vinnie was fulfilling her wants and needs . . . often. That their affair had lust but not love was perfectly acceptable to Katherine. She was not demanding love any more than she was looking for it. Not that she would have turned her back on a romance, a bona fide love affair—hardly! —but she just wasn't holding her breath waiting for one. At forty-six, Katherine settled for what she could get and what she got with Vinnie was a good fuck. Plain and simple. Actually, not plain or simple, but certainly the best fuck a woman her age could ask for.

Katherine Christianson was a realist. After a marriage that had ended in divorce after nineteen years, she took what she could get. She never thought Vinnie was more than a toy or that his feelings for her were any deeper than a puddle after a sudden summer shower. Vinnie was a "tweenie"—her euphemism for someone who helped her through her betwixt-and-betweens. She had already informed him she would have to leave Acapulco at the end of April because she was scheduled for a paint job the first week in May. Whether she would or wouldn't see Vinnie again after the apartment on Park Avenue was totally refurbished hardly mattered. It was now, when her nerves were so frayed by the decisions of which fabrics to choose for the draperies and the sofas, which colors should dominate the nine-room apartment, that she needed his tranquilization, which was hardly tranquil but certainly did take her mind off things. In many ways, Katherine found great similarities in the way Vinnie and Franklin Killerbrew made love: neither did. They fucked, which was just as valid an expression *so long* as they didn't—and again, neither did—pretend that it was something else.

As she looked out the windows of their suite at the Pierre Marquis Hotel, Katherine searched for Vinnie among the tan bodies on the beach below. At the water's edge she saw him in his white Jantzen briefs talking to one of the many beach boys who "serviced" the area. Katherine didn't question Vinnie's buying whatever was for sale in the beach drug traffic. Vinnie's excesses were just that—Vinnie's. She remained uninterested in the pills and powders; a double martini was all the stimulant or tranquilizer she needed.

The brown-skinned boy was shaking his head no to Vinnie, but Katherine knew it was only a temporary denial. Soon, a mutually agreeable price would be reached. As Katherine turned away from the window, she directed her attention to the condition of her skin, which had dried much too quickly in the glare of the Acapulco sun. Gently, she eased a combination of oils into her pores. The slow, steady movement of her hand on her body made her hope Vinnie would return early from his afternoon "hunt" for his evening activities. Katherine ignored any feelings she had about Vinnie's appetites, having decided that whatever dangers he was courting were not her concern. Besides, her interest in Vinnie was purely social—but not as in "social worker." He was a stimulating if rather inconsistent lover—and wasn't that a stimulation in itself, never quite knowing what he wanted or would want. An unexpected bonus was discovering he was conversant with Mahler and Sibelius and could quote—*quote, mind*

517

you—passages from *The Magic Mountain* and *The Trial*.

If she allowed herself, which she decidedly did not, she could be upset by his abuse, or at least his attempted abuse of her At times, he would act like a puppy, seeking her approval. More often, he would be highly critical of her, picking apart her every move, her every sentence, her every motivation. In bed, he could be sweet on occasion using words of tenderness to urge her along. But again. more often, he abused her verbally, calling her by all sorts of vile names that seemed to arouse him. There were times she distinctly felt he disliked her. Other times, when they were just talking, playing their let's-not-get-too-personal game of people, places, and things—but not us, he seemed to appreciate and respect her opinion. Had it mattered, Katherine Christianson would have asked questions about Vinnie, or at the very least made him question himself. But she didn't. She was more than content with what she already had and wasn't searching for more.

May 5, 1963

Dear Marti,

How I loved your letter! Oh my, but the vision of you sweeping across the desert on a camel does make me laugh. You, who could barely stay on a horse . . . on a horse? on your tricycle! . . . when you were a kid, bouncing about the Sahara, is a sight not to be believed. Or is it? Are you doing your own cameling or are you using a stand-in? By the way, Franklin says you should not be depressed over this "adventure film." He says it will "expose you" to a whole new audience. Frankly, as your mother, I think you've had quite enough exposure.

As your mother . . . we come back to that *again*. Which is why your aunt Margaret and I sent the roses. Guilt and regret. Your mothers—note the plural—had an attack of the old-fashioneds and meddled. That we are forgiven shows you have a good heart and darn good business sense. Continue to coddle Marg and me and you will come into a good deal of money one day. How's that for bribing one's affections?

What can I say about your aunt's and my behavior? Margaret feels so rotten she's been punishing herself by eating her spinach three times a day. My penance is to take at least one of my meals on the grass in Central Park. With the bugs. And the birdies.

518

Oh, my darling, someday you will understand that mothers meddle even as they hate themselves for doing it. That both Margaret and I were upset is no excuse (not at our age) for our behavior in your home. You were right to throw us out, although I must say it took your father to make me realize it. I, for one, prefer a somewhat more familial approach to being rebuked by one's own daughter. Your father says I'm lucky you didn't set Thor on me.

Your aunt, my sister, that five-time Oscar nominee and Academy Award winner, Margaret Tiernan Carrington, and I fought all the way back to the hotel. Such carryings-on! I was insisting she had no right to speak to you that way and she was screaming she had as much right as I did—which gives you a pretty fair indication (not that you needed one) of how your aunt feels about you.

I just noticed I keep referring to Margaret as "your aunt" which tells me I still haven't accepted how she feels. Your aunt—oops! Just did it again—thinks of you as her daughter and not as her niece. Her daughter and her friend, she said. I don't mind the "friend" but I do the daughter. You're mine, all mine. So there!!! And you can't have her as your *sister* either. Which shows you what kind of a nice person I am.

Now that Margaret and James have gone, the house seems very quiet. Your father, too, left this morning, this time for Birmingham. Why Birmingham? That's what I asked. Your father, God love him, is off to participate, both as a private citizen and as a TV documentary maker, in the demonstrations planned by Negroes and civic leaders to desegregate public facilities. How a blue-eyed, blond Swedish-American gets involved in a black cause was beyond me until he explained. Your father has never forgotten the treatment of Negroes in the army during World War II. He has never understood how you can ask people to fight for their country, die for it even, and then deny them all that country has to offer. In listening to him, he made me realize how much I don't know. The theatre, like New York City, is very insular.

That's not all the news regarding your father. What a man of surprises! He and Franklin have expanded their organization, and guess who will run their London operation? If you said Evelyn Randolph—which I doubt you did—you win the prize. Yes, Evelyn and Nancy were here all of last week to finalize the arrangements. I gather Nancy will continue to operate the galleries in Rome, Paris, and Madrid while Evelyn returns to her former love: producing.

And that's not all!

Guess who will run the London gallery—manage it as an equal partner? Right! James. Against Margaret's wishes but she's wrong (see? I can't stop meddling). James, just as he insists, should be active. That man, despite his heart attacks, does more in one day than I do in a week. He ran John and Franklin ragged in Los Angeles, wanting to see as much as possible in the few days he and Margaret were there. He's amazing. Just amazing. And an interesting man. When John was giving me his impassioned view of the Negro question—that's how your father puts it—in America today, James was translating for me in very clear and precise English. Meaning: He has the dispassionate overview; a historical sense of things even as they are happening. Which is far better than Margaret's and my *hysterical* sense of things.

Speaking of hysterical—by now you should be able to follow the bouncing ball mechanism of what I call my mind—I should tell you I've been offered a "seat" on a new TV game show. I think it's called "I've Got a Truth" or "What's My Secret?" Who knows, they're all the same to me. Margaret says I'm perfect—that every game show has one dummy to make the Arlene Francis character look good. Anyway, they're doing the pilot next week and since absolutely nothing of any interest has come my way in the form of an intelligent script—which reminds me I must tell you about what's been offered to Margaret and me—I'm going to do it! It certainly did make Arlene an American institution.

Margaret and I were offered a "script" that makes *Baby Jane* look like *Little Women*. I would play this really beautiful (typecasting, obviously) but strange (no one asked you to make a comment here) woman who operates a resort on the moors just outside London. What do you mean there are no moors in London? Do you want accuracy or profits?

Back to the strange woman. She operates this "resort" with her "husband" (quote marks to be explained) and they offer their guests a choice between the American and the European Plan. If the guests knew in advance what kind of activities the "resort" had in store for them, they'd insist on the Blue Cross plan and forget about food altogether. I never encountered so many poisonings, hatchet murders, and strangulations in one film in my life! And I only read far enough to realize my "husband" would be played by Margaret. Not all the money in the world (and that's what the producers were insisting we could make with the percentage they were offering) could convince me to do a film like that. Your aunt (she's quite crazy, you know) wired back that if they could get Joan Crawford (yes, that feud rages on) to play my role, and if they wrote in a scene where she would get to kick Joan around a living room the way Bette Davis did, she'd consider it. She (you won't believe this!) got a wire back saying they thought that could be arranged.

So what will your aunt do while James is managing the gallery? A talk show for the BBC. I've warned her against it. I mean . . . when was the last time you heard anyone say . . . Faye Emerson. She's not exactly on the tip of everyone's tongue.

By the way (and how's that for a smart segue into a new topic), I had another "Dear Mother Ollson" letter. Yup, Reese is pregnant again. Number three. And Thomas, she writes, is thinking of working at Convair (they're in the San Diego area) in their missile development program after his discharge, which I think is a year from now. She always writes as "we" which is sweet of her. I have the feeling she is a nice girl and that makes me happy for Thomas. He should have someone good in his life. He needs that. Don't we all?

Something good in my life just came in. I can always tell by the way the door slams (no matter how many times I tell him to close, not slam it) when my youngest child is home. "Youngest child" is now well over six feet and is about to become handsome. At the moment he is still awkward-looking. About thirty pounds would help. I'll donate fifteen of my own, gladly. He's off to camp again this summer but with changes. He's going to be a junior counselor and not a camper. Where does time go?

How are my grandchildren? How I admire your taking them with you. And to think you had an air-conditioned nursery written into your contract. And in the desert. Only in the movies. Speaking of which (I'm doing it again) I had a brief note from Vinnie. From Acapulco. He starts a movie in July. In Hollywood. And isn't that a switch? I didn't think anyone filmed there anymore.

I must go. John J. just poked his handsome head in the kitchen and asked what's to eat. I told him I would look if he

521

would walk Mickey. Food is the only means of barter that works with that boy.

I leave you with these immortal words (I've been practicing them all week in preparation for the TV pilot) . . . Is it bigger than a breadbox?

My love for you certainly is that and more. Much more.

Carolyn . . . also known as your mother
Your *real* mother

When she answered the telephone, Carolyn was surprised to hear John J.'s voice. Now that he was "all grown up," he didn't call once a week from camp anymore. Once a month if she was lucky, with a letter or two in between.

"You are due home tomorrow, no?" asked Carolyn.

"I *was* due home tomorrow," John J. answered. "That's why I'm calling. A few of us are going to Washington when camp breaks, and I want to check it out with you."

"Well, thank you for that, I'm sure, except you did say a few of us *are* going. I mean, my ears aren't failing yet, are they?"

"Now, Ma, come on. It's just for a day or two and it's really something I want to do. So don't be an old fussbudget."

Carolyn loved the word. Her youngest was the only person she knew who used it. "Well, the fussbudget here would like to know who you are going with and why."

"I'm going with Robbie and Jeanne."

"Robbie and Gene," repeated Carolyn, feeling ridiculous because now that she had names she still knew nothing. "How are you getting there?"

"We'll hitch or take a bus."

"Now JJ, I don't want you hitching. We've been over that many times."

"Ma, there's three of us," said a young but very patient voice. "What can happen?"

He's got you on that one, thought Carolyn, but then that boy always had you one up on something. "Listen. What's the big deal suddenly about Washington? You hoping to get in a game of touch football on the White House lawn with the Kennedys?"

The giggle was pure John J., the boy/child, rather than this new John J., the boy/man.

"We're going for the March, Mom."

Till that second, the March in Carolyn's mind had been

just another of John's involvements in the "Negro Question," only this time he was joining ranks with Brando and Heston. "But why?" she heard herself ask, honestly confused.

"What do you mean 'Why?' It's important. That's why!" John J. replied.

"Aren't just Negroes mainly marching?" asked Carolyn.

"I don't think so but what's the difference? This affects all of us."

This affects all of us? How? thought Carolyn but didn't ask. She would have to ask John. She would also have to ask why their son felt the issue was of importance to him.

"What do Robbie and Gene's parents think of this?" asked Carolyn, knowing her question was irrelevant.

"Robbie's folks are in Europe and won't be back until the day after tomorrow and Jeanne's parents don't like it but they said it's okay."

Carolyn was always amazed and considerably proud of John J.'s truthfulness. He never bent the truth or told it in halves. "I don't suppose there's any chance of my convincing you to hook up with your father and drive with him to Washington. He's one of the speakers, you know."

"Yes, I know, but no. I want to go on my own."

Carolyn understood. On his own . . . something she and John had encouraged—at John's insistence—for years. With such celebrated siblings and parents, they had felt the sooner John found himself and his place, the better he would be. In the past year or so, despite his closeness to his father, John J. had begun to step out of the shadows. In school, he was the acknowledged intellectual leader. Athletically, he was, as he said, "pure *klutz.*" Socially, he was out of the house most Friday and Saturday nights but since he was always home by the established curfew of midnight, she didn't question and he didn't volunteer any information on what he was doing. She trusted this boy although she was sure his sexual attitudes must have changed by now

As John J. continued to explain some of his ideological reasons for wanting to march *on* Washington (he said *on*—not *in*, thought Carolyn), she recalled John's sex education talk with their son just four years ago. He was twelve, late for most kids to be birds-and-bees'd, but not for John J. She almost laughed into the phone as she remembered John imitating their son's voice as he said at the crucial point in his lesson: "Would you stop! I'm going to throw up." And then later . . . "I'm never going to do that. Ugh! Put my thing in there? Never. It's disgusting." John had assured him it wouldn't be one day and Carolyn thought John J. must be approaching that day rather rapidly. She was certain half the phone calls that came for him were from girls. Girls who called him! That certainly wasn't done in her day, she had said to John J., and he had replied: "Ma, in your day, they didn't have telephones."

"Do you have enough money?" she asked, realizing the question was an acceptance of his request. She knew his answer before he spoke. Of course he had money. He had always had money, even before he earned it for the first time on his own this summer. Vinnie had "staked him" years ago, giving him a check for one thousand dollars because "no one should ever be dependent on others for money." At first, she had been upset by Vinnie giving so much money to a child. None of her other children, no matter how much they had earned, were ever in control of their money until they reached eighteen. Yet Vinnie, so much a child himself, had known exactly what her child would do. John J. came home after school one day and announced rather proudly: "I am a member in good standing at Chase Manhattan" as he brandished his savings account passbook.

With his money, and Vinnie's intervention, John J. had the telephone company install a private phone in his room. Had she not been through Thomas's teenage quest for privacy, Carolyn would have not only misunderstood but not permitted this. But, it proved to help rather than hurt. Each month, John J. paid his own bill by money order and once, when he questioned a charge, he went downtown to talk to one of the supervisors personally.

From the giggles that came from John J.'s room about nine o'clock most Wednesday or Thursday nights, she knew Vinnie was calling. Vinnie always got giggles while she and John—Marti, too—got laughs. Also arriving weekly, even more punctual than the phone calls, was a check from Vinnie for John J. This, too, was deposited. Carolyn now suspected that John J. "could buy and sell us all."

"Listen, kiddo, would you mind if I told your father you're going? That wouldn't upset you, would it?" said Carolyn, taking pains not to step on her son's pride. "I mean, it wouldn't chop you down any if I asked him to look out for you."

"Ma, there's going to be an awful lot of people there, and

Dad will be up on the rostrum while I'm down on the lawn somewhere, but tell him if it'll make you feel better."

"Gee, thanks, John J. You're a peach!"

Again, the John J. giggle.

"So listen, Lewis *and* Clark, when do I roll out the welcome mat for you?"

"The day after tomorrow, unless Jeanne and I decide to hang out and see the city. But we'll be home by the weekend because Jeanne's parents have a place at Lake Mahopac and the family is having a thing for Labor Day."

A "thing." How descriptive, thought Carolyn. "Well, call me when you get to Washington."

"You mean that's it?" asked John J. "You're not even going to tell me to take a sweater?"

"John, take a sweater, okay? And don't feel I'm neglecting you but you see, I went through this with your sister—a ski weekend—when she was seventeen, and I'm just too old to go through it again. You want sage words of advice from your mama? You got them: Don't get pregnant."

"I won't, Mom. I promise. But if *you* want to, feel free." Again the giggle.

"John J. One second. I want to talk to you very seriously before we hang up."

Here it comes, he thought, resigning himself to what he assumed would be *the* lecture. "I'm listening, Ma. Fire when ready."

"The fussbudget here loves you. That's it. Signing off."

"Ma, hey wait!" yelled John J. "I mean, hey . . . listen. I mean . . . See you later, alligator."

As tears stung her eyes, Carolyn replied: "After a while, crocodile."

"*Please*, I don't want to discuss it!"

"Marti, you cannot go through life avoiding confrontations. An adult faces responsibility; discusses things as they come up," Philip Charper said firmly.

"I've faced enough today," said Marti miserably.

"And just what have you faced that millions of women haven't every year when September rolls around and school opens?"

"I'm not every woman," cried Marti. "I'm me and I've never been a mother before. And it was nursery school, remember that."

"And remember it was *your* decision," Charper said coldly.

"Well, maybe I was wrong. Maybe my mother was right. Maybe the twins are too young."

"Your mother. Always your mother. Marti, *you're* a mother, which means you should act like one. Maybe if you did, you could see my point."

"I don't want to talk about it," said Marti. "You and Vinnie have never gotten along and I refuse to be placed in the middle."

"You are in the middle whether you like it or not and, if you'll stop acting like a child for a moment, you'll see that whether Vinnie and I do or don't get along is not what's important here. The man should not be allowed to act the way he does in your home. It is bad for the children and it's bad for you."

"Stop it, dammit! Just stop it!" screamed Marti.

"That's it, throw a temper tantrum. It's what I expect. But not with me around. Marti, I'm going to do what all parents should do with petulant children when they are irascible—leave you alone to think about your actions. When you're ready to talk, call me."

With that, Philip Charper was gone, leaving Marti at the dinner table. First Vinnie; now Charper. Gone. In anger. What a mess! *I'm* a mess, thought Marti as she started to cry. Lord only knows why Philip puts up with me.

It was a thought that had been darting in and out of her mind ever since the summer when Philip had visited the set on the Sahara where she was filming *The Sands of Time.* It was a ridiculous, sprawling, adventure epic, the kind of film no one but the public liked. "Why are you doing this?" he had asked disgustedly after watching a day's shooting. He could not understand that contractually she had no choice. Everyone has choices, he argued. It's the neurotic personality who thinks she does not. The idea of "owing a picture" was foreign to him. And as he spoke, it became foreign to her. She should have a choice, should have more control over her work. And her free time. He was being ignored. When she wasn't playing an Arabian princess by day, she was playing mother at night. There was little time left to play "woman" to his "man." He left the location two days earlier than planned and when back in Los Angeles he did not even write. Which is why she hurried home, stopping off only for a day in

London to see Margaret and James and two days in New York with Carolyn.

Had she not been so desperate to see if there remained any ties to be reestablished with Philip, she would have stayed on in New York, as Carolyn was crazed from the latest crank letter John had received. "But why?" Marti asked. "Why this one when we've all gotten them before? This isn't the first to call Daddy a nigger-lover." Happily John had been in full control and done exactly as instructed in the past: given the letter to the FBI.

Marti was struck by her own incongruity. In New York, she hadn't felt at all menaced by the death threat and had taken charge of her mother's emotions. She had been a calming, "mature" influence. Yet, home again, she felt anything but calm and mature when Philip remained distant on the telephone. When he finally drove out to the house Labor Day, he was not warm or effusive. He had some questions he wanted to ask, he said, and he asked them. What was her "incessant" filmmaking about? Was it an indication of "compulsive behavior," some possible "defense mechanism to avoid feeling"? She did not understand what he meant and stupidly argued that "an actress often acts in films for which she has signed before a script has been written."

To which Philip replied: "No one should be that insecure or . . . stupid."

He was right. Undeniably right. She could finally see that. She couldn't miss seeing it as the very next day she was due at Paramount for wardrobe fittings on *Vanilla Fudge*.

"Just what merit can a film with that title have?" asked Philip.

"It will be a big box office success," she said weakly and then withered under his disgusted look.

It would change, she said. *She* would change. As soon as her contractual obligations were all honored, she would advise her agents she wanted script approval and no more than two films a year. At the most.

Charper was pleased by her "growth" as he termed it, and the past week had seen the labor of Labor Day bear fruit. They had grown close again. Until tonight. She had not been expecting Vinnie for dinner but these days one didn't really "expect" Vinnie ever. He dropped in or dropped out at random. She had heard when visiting the wardrobe department at Paramount that Vinnie had been working "high," but tonight, when he had arrived unannounced for dinner, it was obvious he was low. Very low. As he sat down opposite Charper, Marti noticed that his eyes were red and watery and unless she was imagining it, there was the slightest twitch appearing and then disappearing—like a neon sign—under his right eye. Still, he was playful with the twins who were playing on the floor with their toys as dinner was being served to the adults.

At first, despite Philip's obvious annoyance at the interruption, Vinnie had been his old self . . . funny. Uproarious actually thought Marti as she brought the incident back into focus in her mind. Over the artichokes, he imitated his German director and his *zaftig* German costar. Then, in the middle of a laugh, he started to cry. Not just cry but sob. It frightened the twins. Ali was first to cry; then Mark. Before Marti could reach them, Vinnie was on the floor with the blocks and other toys surrounding them. He cooed as he calmed, wiping away their tears with his smile, explaining how Uncle Vinnie had been "making-believe" as he told a story. That the twins understood.

"You see, Marti?" Vinnie said as he got up. "That's all it is—another scene. And you and I both know I'm expert at playing scenes."

She had felt as if her heart and other vital organs were being ripped from her. As she choked back her tears, she hugged him. In monkey-see, monkey-do fashion, the twins hugged his legs and hers. Soon, they were all on the floor—all but Philip, that is—hugging and tickling and laughing and loving. Everything was better, or so it seemed, until they were seated again and Vinnie went to light one of his "funny" cigarettes. Philip ripped it from his mouth before the match had been scratched.

"Not in this house! Your behavior is not only repugnant but irresponsible. Suppose the police were to barge in. Everyone would suffer for your indulgences."

"But, Philip," Marti pleaded. "Why would the police barge in here?"

"If you weren't such a child sometimes, Marti, you would know there is often a fine line between doing and dealing when it comes to drugs." His eyes confronted Vinnie; his voice was icy calm.

Vinnie rose from the table and walked to his Jeep without saying a word. Stupidly, all Marti could say was "I'll call you tomorrow." When she returned to the table, Philip began his lecture. And he was right. Only she had not wanted to listen or discuss it. Vinnie *was* putting them all in jeopardy. But worse, what kind of jeopardy was he again putting himself in?

As she sat at the dish-laden dining table, Marti shook her head in self-flagellation. Would she never grow up? She must start making adult choices. She looked at her watch and wondered how long she had been sitting there. "Well, if he's home, he's home," she said aloud as she dialed Philip Charper's number.

As he veered off the main highway, Thomas found the dusty road leading toward Victorville deserted. The drive back from San Diego had taken close to three hours; time enough to be alone and think through the months ahead and those that had just passed. Although he was tired, Thomas felt hopeful. The opportunities for a new life, another *kind* of life, were there. All he had to do was say yes to the people at the Convair Aerospace Division of the General Dynamics plant and the job, upon his discharge, was his. He had even found the perfect place to live—if there was such a place anymore in this day and age.

Thomas shuddered as he thought how much revolved about *ifs* these days. Reese would love the Rancho Santa Fe community. No ifs about that. It was wooded and secluded and the perfect place to raise children. *If.*

There are and always will be ifs in life, Thomas reasoned, hoping to allay the anxiety that always rose within him these days when he thought about the children. The tract of land he had seen earlier that afternoon was on a ridge overlooking the Black Mountains. The streets were lined with eucalyptus trees. No traffic would pass by the house they could build by August. A golf course was minutes away and his drive to work at the Kearny Mesa plant would take no more than thirty minutes. "Reese," he would say, not to convince but to assure her, "it's a very exclusive area. One has to earn the right to live there. It's safe."

She would stare at him, he knew, and he could already hear her echo . . . "Safe?" She would laugh, a mocking expulsion of breath and sound that would contain a paragraph of words and nights upon nights of nightmares.

Kelly Ollson had been born the day of a nightmare, the day John F. Kennedy had been assassinated. She had been the joy in a day of unrelenting horror. Reese had just gone into labor when word reached the hospital that the President had been shot. As he told the Tomlinsons, who had come from Bridgeport to care for Karl and Kristan, so he told the staff at the hospital: Reese was to be told nothing until after the baby's birth. He knew she would suffer as he had from JFK's death. Not that either had admired him politically but they had respected his office and his status as head of the country and of his family. Of course he had been right to keep the news from Reese. She wept when told of the murder. She mourned, as Thomas did, as if . . . Again . . . if. If what? If he is truly dead then there is no chance of Camelot. Somewhere within us all is there a wish to return to the Camelot we once knew or thought we knew? Was that why he had called his mother when his own nightmare occurred so shortly afterward? She had offered to take the next plane from New York. Why hadn't he let her?

Thomas pulled the station wagon off the road. As he sat behind the wheel of the parked car, he defended his position. Had Carolyn come out, it would have added an extra strain on Reese . . . on him. And there were always "circumstances" to be considered: Vinnie, recently arrested for driving on the wrong side of a highway and then booked for disorderly conduct and possession of drugs. His father, recently arrested in some godforsaken Southern town for disturbing the peace during what civil rights leaders called a peaceful demonstration to integrate a lunch counter. And Marti, recently married . . . again, to a doctor, and didn't all actresses number among their many husbands at least one professional man? His course of action had been correct, Thomas decided again. Not permitting his mother to be with them at this time had been a wise move. Calling her had not been.

"Mother? This is Thomas. Yes, Thomas. Yes, everything is all right. I mean . . . No. It isn't. Mom . . . Kelly . . . Reese."

The words had frozen in his mouth. Although he had wanted to tell her then, he couldn't. Had not Mrs. Tomlinson taken the phone, Carolyn might still not know. It wasn't just his mother. Even at the base for weeks afterward, whether he was addressed by the formal Lieutenant Ollson or as Thomas, he couldn't respond to the expressions of sympathy. His words were only for Reese and she needed all his consolation and comfort.

Reese had been rolling the ball to Karl just outside their

530

front door and catching it, when she heard Kelly crying in the house. Since Mrs. Tomlinson was napping, Reese went to see what the baby needed. She lifted her from the crib, was cooing to her when she heard the screech of tires and the slamming of *something*—a thud of some kind—that turned her cold. With Kelly in her arms, she went running to the door. As a car careened down the street and into Apple Valley, she saw, in the road, her child . . . Karl, bloodied and lifeless. She screamed as she ran toward him; screamed as she knelt beside him with Kelly still in her arms. She was still screaming when her mother and the neighbors called an ambulance for Karl and the police for the hit-and-run driver.

At the hospital, he held her as they waited and waited. An interminable wait. A blood clot in the brain. Possible paralysis. Multiple fractures. But would he live? And when it became fairly certain that he would, the question was: would he walk again? It was a question they were still asking these many months later.

Reese had blamed herself. Reese continued to blame herself. She should not have left a four-year-old alone. Not for a second. She would never leave any of her children again, she promised irrationally, not as long as there are people who hit with their cars and run from responsibility. Not all of Thomas's words could convince Reese she wasn't to blame and that he didn't blame her too.

Did he? Often he wondered. Someone *had* to be blamed. Someone had to pay. But who? Not Reese. Never her. Not his girl, his wife, not the mother who put her children not only before herself but before him, too. And wasn't that how it should be? he asked, sure of the answer to his question.

Karl was home now, immobilized by a cast that began at his hip and ended at his ankle.

"We don't know, Lieutenant," the doctors would say when Thomas questioned them as to whether Karl would walk again. "There is so much medical science doesn't know. But we are hopeful."

Thank God someone was. Too often, watching Reese, her eyes blank or else filled with fear, seeing his son, his joy as protected, encased, as his body, made Thomas lose the hope that things could and would be all right again. They must be! Thomas said to himself. "They must be!" Thomas said aloud to the One he had been praying to ever since the accident.

On the car radio, Patsy Cline began singing "I Fall to Pieces" just as Thomas did.

Having cooked and served the twins their breakfast, Marti began cleaning up their slops and spills so she could relax over her own toasted English muffin and coffee. The next hour was hers as the twins, under Miss Jennings's careful supervision, were restoring their room to some semblance of order. An impossible task for four-year-olds but good training nonetheless. By ten, Marti would drive Ali and Mark to the neighborhood playground where they would shove and shovel in the sandpile with other children or play on the sliding pond under her watchful eye.

Hers would not be the only eye that watched. Despite her presence in the park these many months, the nannies and governesses never failed to note and make comment on her appearance. It was as if she were violating some Beverly Hills code tending to her own children. Their sentiments were shared by Marti's agency, who was pleading she return to work. But as Philip had said, if there's a job worth doing, then it's worth doing well. But if it's not worth doing well, then it's not worth doing. Marti, finally free of contractual agreements made two and three years ago, no longer was rushing into anything that didn't display her talent as blatantly as her tits.

"Well put!" her agent at Ashley-Famous had enthused as he eyed Marti's husband sitting casually smoking his pipe, pretending indifference as Marti did the talking. "Yes, sir. Very well put, Marti," the agent had added. "In fact, we'll get right on it—let the word get around town that you're looking for something meaningful for your next film. Good. Something heavy should follow *Vanilla Fudge*."

She left the meeting feeling pleased she had listened to Philip and spoken up for herself. Two weeks later, when a script arrived that was already a remake when Yvonne De Carlo remade it, her pleasure turned to disgust. It wasn't as if she were a Monroe. She *had* an Oscar to prove she was an actress. She had been acting since childhood.

Vinnie advised her to take the money and run. But she didn't need money and could not understand Vinnie's very determined decision to do just that. Philip could, however. "He has neither your aspirations nor your talent." But Marti knew that wasn't true. Talent, Vinnie had; it was the aspiration that was missing.

At the bar, where the "adults" took their breakfast, Marti saw the previous day's *New York Times* just as Philip had left it, its bright red pencil markings and blue underlinings telling her what Philip felt was important for her to read. He had done this ever since their marriage, helping to educate what he felt was a good but untrained and undisciplined mind. At first, the names of the various world leaders were unknown to Marti, as were the diverse issues on the editorial pages, but now, she was cognizant of if not conversant with both.

In the evening, when he returned from his practice, Philip would have the *Los Angeles Times* similarly marked for her "night classes." Tuesdays and Thursdays, after dinner, they would discuss over brandies what she had read and her comprehension of the issues involved. When Philip felt her logic was wanting, he would tap on his snifter with his pipe—his signal that he wanted her to rethink her position. Philip had recently added to the Tuesday night discussion an examination of the fashion pages of both the east and west coast editions of the *Times*. It was time her wardrobe changed. Christmas trees were fine at Christmas but out of place the rest of the year. Give it to Goodwill became his battle cry. She listened, particularly after she made the fashion pages for the first time in a gown he had selected for her to wear to a dinner of the American Psychological Association at the Roosevelt Hotel.

"You've ruined me," she complained facetiously after the picture appeared. "I'll never make Mr. Blackwell's Ten Worst Dressed List again."

Also given to Goodwill were the tin Mexican ashtrays along with several Mexican "prints" both on the walls and on the floor. In their stead, beautiful ceramics of various colors and crystal ashtrays from Baccarat and Tiffany in New York were set casually about the various tables in the living room. "No one is born with good taste," Philip said. "It is acquired and it can be bred into children and adults with thought and patience."

As Marti leafed through the *Times*, trying to decide which blue-underlined issue she should tackle first, she lit yet another cigarette. Long gone was any awkwardness in smoking and she had the beginnings of a smoker's cough to prove it. Often she awoke in the middle of the night and only a cigarette helped her return to sleep. The habit annoyed Philip and he did not accept her insistence that it calmed her nerves. Besides, he argued, what had she to make her nervous? He was right, of course, but wasn't he always? Wasn't everything in her life nearly perfect at last?

No, she thought as she inhaled deeply. Not everything is perfect. Not by a long shot. The palpitations proved that, along with what Philip called "free-floating anxiety." He would not allow her to take tranquilizers but he insisted she could tranquilize herself if she would just "explore the recesses of your mind—get in touch with yourself." She tried. Every morning, as part of her "quiet time," a fifteen-minute period Philip insisted she set aside for meditation, she tried to sort through the panic that would sometimes envelop her. But it was nebulous and undefined. The only time it disappeared was when she was with Ali and Mark.

"You cannot let your children define you," Philip cautioned. "You must have an identity beyond and apart from 'mother.' " She could not tell him that he did not understand her feelings. He was unconcerned that the children shied away from him. "They'll approach me when they're ready," he said. She wanted to reply: "Will you do the same?" but didn't. He was not good with children, which probably explained why he had not had any with his previous wives and why he was not anxious for her to conceive just yet.

The gardener rapping on the glass doors interrupted Marti's thoughts. "Morning mail, Mrs. H.," said the old man as he brought in the usual scripts and flyers. The only letter of interest was from John J. Like a child eating candy when she shouldn't, Marti looked about to see if she were being observed. To hell with the *Times* this morning; she'd rather read what JJ had to say.

August 18, 1964

Hey Marti!

They say better late than never but the way I write letters, they could be wrong. But seriously, folks . . . thank you belatedly for your graduation present. The stereo is neat and I'm having it shipped directly up to Cornell as soon as I decide where I'm going to live.

Mart, I would have written sooner but as Mom may have told you, I took off for the dude ranch the day after graduation and since arriving I've been working my city slicker's ass off.

Up at dawn and out with the chickens. Only there's no chickens here. Come to think of it, there's no dudes either. Just a lot of dudesses all wanting to ride . . . not horses, kid, but dudes. But don't get the wrong idea. Success is not spoiling Rock Ollson here.

Actually, it's a lot of work with as much play as you want rolled in. It's fun but not quite what I had in mind. I like being around the horses but I haven't learned much about them. I mean . . . I couldn't treat any kind of illness if one got sick. Which reminds me, did Mom tell you I've pretty much decided to major in animal husbandry? Mom thinks that's when you matchmake between cows and bulls but it isn't. Actually, I'm not too sure what it is but it will require my working on farms most summers in between semesters. Sounds like fun to me.

Speaking of fun, Vinnie is coming up for the weekend. A friend is loaning me his car and I'm driving down to Denver to pick him up at the airport. He called last night—wanted me to hear his imitation of Julie Andrews in *Mary Poppins*. I told him to hold it for one of the campfires. He said he wouldn't—didn't like the lighting or something like that.

I wish you'd come up. Bring the kids. I'd teach them to ride. You, too, although Mom says I should stick to the difficult and leave the impossible to the Lord.

Hey, gotta go. Again, thanks for the noisemaker. My neighbors are going to love you for it

I love you, too, for it and everything else

JJ

For the briefest of seconds, Marti wondered if she could take the twins and join Vinnie and John J. The panic the thought induced told her it was not a good idea, although the panic did not tell her why. She missed not seeing Vinnie more than she did. Since he and Philip were so vocal in their dislike of one another, Marti found she was reluctant to invite Vinnie to the house. Although the situation was never discussed between them, Marti knew that Vinnie understood from the way he suddenly started appearing one or two mornings a week at the playground. And didn't that cause a buzz among the nervous nannies! He always arrived like a Santa Claus with enough oranges and apples to feed all the kids, not just Ali and Mark, who clung to him in the way she would have loved to see them cling to Philip. Of course the

535

twins would drag them both to the seesaw demanding Vinnie balance one while she balanced the other. It was not her favorite game as the twins fought over who got Uncle Vinnie while she was the reluctant booby prize.

I wish he would marry, Marti suddenly thought. Some nice girl who would give him what he needs. Her next thought disturbed her. What does he need? She didn't know and not knowing suddenly raised a new wave of panic within her. Not knowing what Vinnie needed made her realize that the same was true of herself. Except she needed Philip. She knew that. He allayed the anxiety. And yet . . .

And yet what? Marti asked herself as she pushed aside the *Times*. From somewhere within the "recesses" of her mind that Philip insisted she explore, she "got in touch" with the feeling ("Go with your feelings, Marti," Philip always urged) that in some way Philip Charper was part of her panic, her nameless anxiety that seemed to be increasing rather than decreasing. Recognizing this, Marti picked up the discarded *Times* and began reading the article starred on the front page. That had to be important. Very important. Read it, she commanded herself. Read it she did.

This is not like me, thought Carolyn as the limousine sped north on the eight-lane highway. Don't think about it or you'll turn this car around again, she advised as she settled herself into the lush gray interior of the Cadillac.

Thirty minutes ago, Carolyn had been halfway to the airport, her ten-day Nielsen multi-city promotional tour for the network and "The Name's the Game" completed. An airline ticket to New York via Los Angeles was nestled in her handbag. What then had prompted her to stop the car and phone the number on the change of address card she had received several months ago? The season, she decided. It had been a Christmas thirty years ago—thirty! Now that was sobering—when she knew she would marry John Ollson. And that marriage had produced three children. It was that simple fact that had pushed her into the phone booth. It was pushing her now toward a destination the exact location of which was scrawled on the back of the American Airlines ticket that was supposed to deposit her in Marti's arms before she flew home to be with her Johns for Christmas.

Due to the Saturday morning shopping traffic, the trip took forty-five and not the thirty minutes she had been advised.

As the limousine crawled past the secluded estates, she saw that palm trees and olive trees punctuated a landscape freely dotted with bougainvillea, oleander, and azalea bushes. The grass-carpeted golf course looked exactly right, Carolyn thought, for the storybook setting.

Children were playing ball in the streets as fathers swept up leaves or affixed holiday lights to rooftops or fir trees on front lawns. Suddenly, the limousine veered up a curving road and onto a ridge that faced the Black Mountains.

"This is Las Planideras, Miss Tiernan," announced the driver through the glass partition in the huge Cadillac. "The house should be coming up on your right."

The wide, spotless street was bordered by eucalyptus trees and the rambling ranch-style homes were set back on lawns that rivaled the grassy green of the golf course. It was the shock of blond hair Carolyn recognized first. He had been bending over, tending to one of the many azalea bushes under his bow window when the little boy by his side tugged at the sleeve of his tan chino jacket and pointed at her car. When he stood, Carolyn's heartbeat quickened. She saw but did not hear him yell toward the house. As she stepped out of the car, a woman appeared in the doorway, a baby with blonde curls on one arm while a pixie in pink clung to her hand.

It was the familiar voice that spoke first: "Karl, go wish your grandmother a Merry Christmas and give her a kiss."

Without a word, the boy hobbled toward her, one leg quicker and more sure than the other. As she watched as if from her own dream, Carolyn heard the child say, "Merry Christmas, Grandma."

It was an ugly day and Carolyn's mood matched the dreary morning. The wind whipping sleet on the kitchen windows was as disquieting as the thoughts that had been whipping her mind ever since her return from California more than two weeks ago. John could say that none of it was her business and although he was right in theory, in practice he was not. And they both knew it. Whether either of them liked it or not, what one's children did, even long after they were married—whether it was for the first time or the third time—always remained their business.

When Carolyn reached across the kitchen table to answer the intercom, the sleeve of her bathrobe knocked over her coffee cup. "Damn!" she muttered as she mopped with one hand and held the phone with the other.

"And a good morning to you, too," replied John cheerily. "I was going to stop work and join you for your morning coffee but the 'damn' in your voice tells me my typewriter would be a better, although this morning a most unwilling, companion."

"Cut the jokes and do come in here. I'm depressed," Carolyn complained.

"Of course you are. It's January third. You're always depressed on January third."

"I just knew there had to be a good reason." Carolyn sighed.

"I'll be right in," replied John. As he came down the hallway from his den he was chirping: "I can't imagine what's bothering you on such a gorgeous morning. By the way," he said as he entered the kitchen and immediately poured himself a cup of coffee, "I called because John J. did. He's on his way in from Ithaca. He and this friend of his . . ."

"Gene?" asked Carolyn dispassionately.

"That's the name he mentioned, yes. Anyway, he and Gene are going to shack up here—that's what he said; don't look at me funny, I write the language, not invent it—a few days to catch some exhibit at the Museum of Natural History."

"Call the supermarket. Have them deliver the store. Make it two stores in case this Gene person eats like our son," Carolyn said as John sat next to her.

"Hiya, cutie," he murmured as he nuzzled her neck.

"Please. Have you no respect for a woman my age? God, it really should be you, and not me, going through the change. Have you ever considered what it's called: menopause. Say it slowly and what have you got: men-o-pause. So it should be men doing the pausing and not us women. But you just get more *immature* every year."

"You weren't complaining last night," John said into her neck where he was still resting.

"A gentleman, John, never mentions what transpired the night before. But it was fun," said Carolyn as she squeezed John's thigh affectionately.

"A little higher and to the right, please," he whispered as he nibbled her earlobe.

As Carolyn slapped at John, she began laughing.

"Ah! Look, folks. Carolyn Ollson is laughing. A first for

538

January third. She's ruining her Guinness Book of Records' mark. Fifty years shot as the all-time January third grump. Who knows, folks. Given what's just occurred, we might even get through the morning without discussing Thomas and Marti or Marti and Thomas."

"That's just it," said Carolyn. "I have finally figured out what's been bothering me. The pieces are finally in place."

"And you're going to tell me, aren't you," John groaned. "Well," he said, rising, "let me pour another cup of coffee then."

"It started from the moment I stepped out of the limousine," said Carolyn, talking to John's back. "I suddenly, just this morning, realized the children didn't have a lick of dirt on them. Not a lick. John, children get dirty but not these kids. Kristan and Kelly had on matching pink and white frilly party dresses. At ten-thirty A.M.! Dolled-up, they were. Like little dolls and not like little girls. And that dear little boy. John, a boy of that age should be in dungarees and not gray flannel pants and a white shirt."

"Carolyn, they dressed the kids up for you. That's not unusual. Parents do that all the time to show off their kids."

"But you should have heard the dialogue. 'Krissy, say hello to Grandma.' 'Kelly, give Grandma a kiss.' 'Krissy, you do not cry when you fall but you pick yourself up.' 'Krissy, we do not leave dirty cake plates on the table.' 'No, Karl, you cannot walk like that.' 'No, Karl, do not limp.' 'Walk for grandma, Karl. Walk straight!' It was awful," said Carolyn, shuddering as she remembered.

"Carolyn, I'd like to have a dime for every parent who talks to their children that way."

"Like a pair of drill sergeants parading the troops? John, the boy limps. He has made a remarkable recovery from what I hear was a ghastly accident. But he limps. Only according to Thomas he does not, will not, and must not."

"Lynnie, it's the military. It does that to some people."

"And it makes robots out of their children? Their wives, too?" asked Carolyn incredulously. "Do you know—yes, you do, 'cause I've told you, but now I understand why I keep telling you—Reese had a full lunch prepared for all of us. Lunch. And a clean house and clean children. My gawd, the house and the children were so clean you wouldn't believe one was lived in and the others were alive. This girl, this dear

539

imp of a girl, had lunch and a household fixed and ready to go all within an hour of my calling. How did she do it?"

"What makes this conversation very strange," John said, "is your questioning the very things you were raving about when you first came home a few weeks ago."

"I know. But I think the reason I kept on about them is that I was searching for an understanding."

For a moment, Carolyn grew silent as she recalled the tenor of her meeting with Thomas. He had been friendly, almost warm and certainly not cold. He had been solicitous about her health and interested in her travels for the network. He had even made some interesting comments on her panelist abilities on "The Name's the Game." But not once did he ask about "the old neighborhood" or his family. Not once. Which was tactful and not unusual.

"But now I would prefer that he had ranted about you or Marti," Carolyn said aloud.

"I beg your pardon?" said John, confused.

"Oh, I was just thinking about Thomas and how much more real the whole thing would have been if he had been nasty or ugly or . . . anything. But no, he was perfect. That's it!" said Carolyn as she found yet another piece of her puzzle. "He was perfect. Reese was perfect. The perfect wife and mother. And she and Thomas live in a perfect house in a perfect community with . . . what else? . . . perfect children. You just know that if they had a Mickey, the dog would go down to the nearest filling station to relieve himself rather than make a mess anywhere. And Thomas . . . Thomas was the perfect host and . . . a perfect stranger.

"At least Marti wasn't perfect," continued Carolyn. "Boy, was she ever not perfect! When she wasn't running herself down, Philip was. In that terribly assured manner of his, he was forever correcting her, as if rehabilitating some socially disordered child."

"You're just angry because Philip wouldn't allow you to stay at the house," said John as he rumpled Carolyn's hair.

"Well, I have every right to be!" replied Carolyn huffily. "What is this nonsense about symbiotic relationships? I never ever heard of such a thing until Philip Charper. Now, he has filled Marti's head with the 'stultifying symbiosis'—meaning me, Margaret, too—that has 'stifled' her all her life."

"And she believes it?" asked John.

"I don't know. She's like a pot about to boil over. She says nothing but I have the feeling the words are simmering inside. She smokes like a chimney and seems incapable of making a decision on her own. Like lunch at the Bel Air. A simple thing like that and she was a half hour late because she couldn't decide what was proper to wear. This from a girl who wore nothing and didn't think it improper. And when I try to suggest or say anything, I'm lectured about invading space."

"Forget it, Lynnie," said John. "It's like Newton's Law only this is Charper's horseshit."

"Charper would say you simply are not in touch with your gut feelings—what a dreadful expression—if he could hear you. He would also insist you are not being *open*; that you are *copping out*. John, he and Marti talk not in words, but in jargon. I don't think a sentence is spoken without one or the other screaming 'Cop Out!' at the other.

"Do you know the only time she was real, the old Marti, was at the playground with the twins. Despite the noise of the children, she was peaceful for the first time. And patient. And she talks to Ali and Mark. In real words and with real, not *gut*, feeling. Do you know I sat on a park bench with my own daughter and when I wanted to talk with her about me, about her, us, she steered the conversation to political or social issues? She was exactly like Thomas except she was an *imperfect* stranger. Very imperfect. This gorgeous, talented child moping about, acting as if she were deformed or retarded. I never thought I'd live to see the day when I would wish with all my heart for one of my children to get divorced."

"She's going to be all right, Lynnie," said John with a sureness that surprised her.

"You and Margaret say the same thing but I wonder," Carolyn replied, fighting back tears.

The sound of the front door opening and then slamming announced the arrival of John J.

"Hey? We're here. Anybody home?"

"We're in the kitchen!" John yelled.

"Waiting for you," added Carolyn.

"Come on in," yelled John.

"Not before you take off your wet things. The floors were just done yesterday so leave your shoes outside," demanded Carolyn.

"Too late, Ma, we're here. Everybody," said John J., "I'd like you to meet my friend."

541

Carolyn stared at the long red hair and the bright blue eyes accosting her. As she continued to stare Carolyn remembered the summer camp, the Washington march, the skiing weekends, the trips to Bar Harbor, Maine, and the family cabin, and as she remembered she heard a voice moan: "Oh, my God, my dear, dear God. Gene is a Jeanne."

To which another voice, John's, replied: "You always did have an amazing eye for detail, didn't you, Lynnie?"

"I don't give a shit—do you hear?—not one shit what the fucking woman or what anyone else at the fucking marathon had to say," screamed Marti as she dashed from the car through the rain to the front door of the house in Bel Air. "I don't need strangers analyzing me or my life," she continued to yell as she fumbled with her key in the lock. "From now on, my life is not open to a bunch of strangers."

"Marti, do try to control your emotions," Charper said calmly. "You're going to wake the children."

"Well, if I've just woken up, maybe they should too," said Marti as she threw her raincoat on the floor.

"Marti, how many times have I told you not to throw things just anywhere. Now go and hang up your clothes," Charper said with all the patience one might bring in talking to a truculent child.

"Don't tell me what to do. Don't ever tell me again. Fuck off!"

"You're being very hostile," said Philip.

"You're damn right I'm being hostile," Marti yelled. "I have every reason to be hostile. This is it, Philip. No more encounter weekends. No more five-hour drives to trust walks and hot tubs and communal *kvetching*. No more marathons or sensitivity training groups or rap sessions or any of that shit. You go but not me. I will not leave my children on weekends once a month and particularly now that I'm making a film."

"Have you learned nothing?" asked Philip. "What is a film? What compulsion drives you toward being this plastic person, this persona, rather than someone who is real, who can give and take and love?"

"Oh, stop that garbage. Philip One film in one year is hardly a compulsion."

"But what kind of film?" persisted Charper "It's irrelevant. It has no basis in human awareness, no reality factor whatsoever."

"The reality is plain to me. It brings me back into humans awareness. I was among the top box office names in the industry when we married. My career needs activity."

"Your career or your ego?"

"Oh, fuck off with your Freud and your nouveau shrink shit."

"Marti, can't you hear your displaced hostility? Dig, Marti. Dig deeply and discover who you are really angry at," Charper urged.

"I don't have to dig, Philip. I know. At me. For leaving my kids for bullshit. I don't need to sit on a floor and scream or be screamed at. I don't need to learn how to touch or be touched. What I actually need *is* to touch and be touched; something you haven't been exactly good at for quite some time now."

Charper's face blanched. "That's fighting below the belt."

"So to speak. Yes, you might say that. Actually, that's actually what you should say. I am talking about what's happening, or not happening, below the belt between us. Among other things."

"You know how I am when I'm going through something emotionally," said Charper nastily.

"Philip, you're always going through something. You spend your life taking your own and everyone else's emotional pulse. And Philip, it's boring."

"Marti, I think you've said quite enough. I suggest you go upstairs to bed."

"Don't speak to me as if I were a child. Not in my house."

"Your house?" echoed Charper. "Marti, this isn't your house. It's *our* house. We're husband and wife. There is no mine and yours. Just ours. Now why don't you sit down and tell me what it was that upset you so at the women's group."

"Nothing upset me. Except the group itself. Can't you understand I don't want to sit around and hear how a bunch of women hate their mothers."

"Yes," said Philip as he sat down on one of the living room sofas. "That would be very difficult for you," he added as he lit his pipe.

"Stop that now I do not hate my mother."

"Are you certain? Are you so sure this little display you're

543

now engaging in isn't your frustration—your anger at having been kept a little girl by your mother?"

Marti looked at Philip as though he were someone she was meeting for the first time. "Yes, Philip, I'm very sure," she said coldly. "In fact, let me give you my . . . *gut* feeling. My mother loved me. She still does. Yes, I did resent her for a while. Everything always seemed to come so easily to her—marriage, motherhood, and a career—while I have always had to struggle. But I have discovered in talking with her, that what seemed easy, never was. And it never will be. Not for her or for me. That lesson learned, it's time to move on."

"You're rationalizing," said Charper, his voice assuming its normal superior tone. "Your mother, and your aunt, castrated you, robbed you of your own individual sense of womanhood."

"No, Philip. Not them. Not ever. Only the men in my life. Each and every one of them. And I've allowed it."

"I suppose you're including me in that neat little package of yours?"

"Particularly you, Philip. In fact, I know it's late but I'd like you to leave this house. Tonight. I'll help you pack a suitcase but I want you to go. Philip, I'm getting a divorce."

"What you do is what you do but I'm not leaving this house. I don't seem able to make you understand, Marti," Charper said as he kicked off his shoes and put his feet up on the coffee table. "This is my house and I have no wish to leave it, particularly on a rainy night such as this. Now if you want to leave, feel free. But before you do, dear, would you be a good girl and turn the clock ahead an hour. We went on daylight savings time yesterday while one of us was learning to delve further into his unconscious and the other was avoiding a confrontation with herself."

Marti stood by the bar, perhaps ten feet from where Philip was sitting, and stared at her husband's face. She looked about the room measuring each piece of furniture and bric-a-brac for its worth. Then she turned and walked up the stairs to the bedrooms. When she knocked loudly, it was a startled-from-sleep Miss Jennings who told her to enter.

"I know it's late and I apologize for disturbing you but I'm taking the twins and leaving. Now. Tonight," she added as she watched the woman's face struggle for comprehension. "Tomorrow, I want you to pack as much as you can of the children's clothes into two suitcases and take them and yourself to my cousin Vinnie Tiernan's house." When she was certain the woman understood, Marti closed her door. When she entered the twins' room, she saw that Mark had kicked off his cover as usual while Ali slept with her head practically hidden under the pillow, her way of avoiding "loud talk" when she didn't want to hear it. Marti picked up Ali first, hugging her until the child awoke. Then she sat her down on the edge of Mark's bed while she awakened her son.

"Listen, big fella, we're going to Uncle Vinnie's," Marti said brightly.

"Now?" asked Mark, rubbing his eyes. "It's dark out."

"Scaredy-cat. He's afraid of the dark, Mommy, but I'm not," said Ali.

"None of us is afraid of the dark," Marti said as she quickly dressed her children. "Not anymore."

From halfway up the canyon, Marti could see Vinnie's house on the topmost hill, shining like a beacon against a backdrop of black sky laced with gray storm clouds. Although the rain made driving hazardous, there was a sureness in Marti's driving. Her grip on herself was as firm as her grip on the wheel. By her side, Ali had fallen asleep. Mark, watching the dark, was wide awake.

With all the lights on at the late hour, Marti expected to find numerous cars parked about Vinnie's home. But there were none. Nor was there an answer when she rang the doorbell and pounded on the brass knocker. If Mark hadn't leaned against the oak door for support, his weight opening it, she might have left, raced back to a hotel where her face would have been her credit card.

As she entered the silent house, Marti repeatedly called out for Vinnie. Every part of her was silently screaming a warning. She placed the sleeping Ali on one of the cushion-covered stone slabs in the living room and told Mark to watch over her. "Call if you need me," she told the frightened child as she mounted the steps leading up to Vinnie's bedroom.

She saw him immediately reflected over and over in the mirrors of the room. He was sitting up in the center of the bed staring at his reflections. A gun was at his side.

"Vinnie, didn't you hear me?" asked Marti cautiously.

As if it took his greatest effort, Vinnie turned his attention from the mirrors to the voice that was summoning him. A smile of recognition replaced his look of annoyance.

"Hey, Marti. Hey," he said as he tried to get up but fell over into a sitting position again.

"Vinnie, why are all the lights on and what are you doing with that gun?"

"Bugs, Marti. Everywhere. Green and yellow bugs. They were nice at first. But they're not nice now. I saw myself in a bug, Marti. Really, I did. We are all bugs. No, really, Marti. But then the bug wanted to see me in it. And that's no good."

"Vinnie, I'm here with the twins. We're going to stay for a while."

For a moment, it seemed to Marti as if Vinnie had not only heard but understood her words.

"Mi casa es su casa," he replied. "But tell Ali and Mark not to touch the bugs. Or the lights, Marti. The lights. They keep away the bugs."

Marti left Vinnie's room and hurried down the hallway to the room that was once hers. To her relief, the telephone was where it had always been: on one of the polished wooden pedestal tables. Hurriedly, she dialed a number she commanded herself to remember. The moment she heard Franklin Killerbrew's voice, Marti relaxed. Then, she cried.

As the studio-provided limousine crawled up the canyon roads, Marti felt anxiety gather in the pit of her stomach. It made its reappearance every night at this time as Marti drew nearer the house and the problems, potential and present, that lived there. Still, she had done it, hadn't she? She was proud of herself. The morning after she had left Charper and discovered Vinnie in his disordered state, the remaining eight weeks of filming on *Oh, Yeah? Who Says?* loomed like an Everest, the other side of which she would never reach. Today, she had not only reached but passed it. Forever. It was "in the can," along with her marriage, only the latter was garbage while the former had distinct possibilities.

She would not have managed without Killerbrew's intervention. From the moment she called, he had taken over. Within twenty-four hours, Carmine Abruzzio was back from New York and ensconced as Vínnie's "companion" much as Miss Jennings was to her own children. Doctors whose nurses and secretaries did not have Hedda Hopper's private number were brought to the house for consultation. All agreed Vinnie's "motor mechanisms" were fine but that overdoses of lysergic acid diethylamide had caused some mental confusion.

The media, of course, had made much of what they termed the latest in Tiernan Traumas. Her divorce was noted without surprise but with considerable sarcasm. The media also revealed that Vinnie had been "released" from *Motion Sickness* the very afternoon she and Philip had driven to their encounter weekend in the Big Sur area. "Artistic differences" had read the press release the studio issued and that is what the press printed although the word in Hollywood was: Vinnie had been fired as he could not sustain his characterization or remember his lines.

Of course Margaret had called as did her mother but Vinnie would speak to no one except John J. And what they had spoken about, she did not know. But Vinnie, she noticed, could be with JJ as he was with Ali and Mark—this other person, this gentle, childlike being without guile but with great humor. He could also be, she discovered as the days went by, still another person; one who would awake screaming in the night, fighting off his multicolored bugs.

There was a part of Marti that felt she was doing wrong; that she should not be subjecting the twins to possible danger by leaving them in the house with Vinnie. A stronger part of Marti refused to accept this even though it believed it. Vinnie needed her as did the twins. As did *Oh, Yeah?* For a while, Marti felt torn from within and without. But her confusion ended each time she realized there would be no Ali and Mark if there hadn't been a Vinnie and his intervention five years ago.

There were no such doubts this early summer evening although there was the anxiety—but that was about Vinnie's life, not her own. Not that her problems had been solved, but somehow in finishing the film, in doing her job, in coping with the various loose ends in her life, she had gained confidence. She could now take the next few weeks, the next few months even, to make decisions; some simple, others not simple at all.

"I have problems," she had confided to Franklin Killerbrew.

"Name ten people who don't and I'll bet their current address is Forest Lawn," he replied matter-of-factly.

"But I don't want to be dead to be at peace," she answered with a resolve that had surprised her as much as him.

"Let me know if I can help" was all Killerbrew said, but Marti knew his one sentence was worth another's thousand paragraphs. Franklin had urged her and Margaret to place

547

Vinnie in a private treatment center but neither could see the immediate need for it. Now, as the limousine rounded the final curve that would end in Vinnie's driveway, Marti acknowledged that perhaps neither she nor Margaret wanted to.

It was Franklin Killerbrew's car she saw first. What was it doing there and who did the Volkswagen belong to? As if hearing her unspoken questions, Killerbrew appeared in the doorway waiting as she tentatively stepped from the limousine onto the gravel driveway. He didn't wait for her to ask.

"Vinnie's missing, Marti. This is Bill Foster, formerly of the L.A.P.D.," he said, indicating a baldish heavyset man with a red face. "He's helping us to comb the hills."

Marti stared at Killerbrew trying to comprehend his words. "Comb the hills?" she echoed.

"Carmine was in the house while Vinnie was in the pool with Ali and Mark," explained Killerbrew. "When the kids came in to watch the 'Lucy' reruns, Vinnie wasn't with them. Both his bike and his car are still here, Marti. As best as Carmine can tell, Vinnie's out there somewhere in his bathing suit. We don't even know if he has a shirt with him. We don't know anything actually but we're going out looking."

Marti continued to stare at Killerbrew as she fought to control her panic. Seeing the strain on her face, Killerbrew took Marti's hand and said, "Hey, kid. Not to worry. I'm an old hand at treasure hunts. We'll find him."

"Franklin," Marti called to Killerbrew as he and Foster walked to the beetlelike car, "wait just one second, please. I want to find a sweater for you to take to Vinnie."

"I simply don't understand it. All this talk about how there are simply no roles being written for women. One hardly has to be a genius to see that Paul Newman could not have played Mary Poppins. Julie Andrews has become quite the star in America by playing in roles written for women."

"I think you've missed the point," said Margaret dryly. "One would hardly call Mary Poppins or Eliza Doolittle real women. My point is: no one writes of women, about women, or for women. In other words: those issues confronting women."

"But, my dear," argued the actress facing Margaret, "the paying public doesn't want to see themselves up there. They want larger than life creations. They want fantasy; women much like the ones Tennessee Williams creates. Albee, too."

548

"They are not women but creatures, machinations of a very particular male mind. They have nothing to do with me," said Margaret testily.

"Thank God they do with me. And I have the Tonys and the critical raves to prove it!" replied the actress, winking directly into the camera. "Margaret, darling, if people wanted *real*, they could stay home and invite the neighbors in for a rum punch or a game of gin."

"*That* is an elitist point of view which I refuse to accept," said Margaret on the attack. "You are assuming all people are dull or that what they feel or experience in their lives is not dramatic or interesting."

"Well really, Margaret, let's face it. How interesting are the lives of most people? Which is exactly why they pay outrageous prices to go to the theatre. And at fifteen dollars a ticket, they don't want to be confronted by themselves onstage."

"Medea could be a Hilda Schlockhauser or a Mary Brown. She is any woman who is left by her husband for another woman."

"Medea! Don't be ridiculous. Next you'll be saying Lear is Uncle Sam, the Umbrella Man."

"Exactly!" thumped Margaret triumphantly. "Lear is Everyman. Nora in *A Doll's House* is every woman who begins to question the mores and values that have been imposed on her from the day she was born."

From the control room just up above the set where Margaret and her guest were going at it, Carolyn was watching Margaret earn her press-won reputation as Tough Tiger Tiernan. "Tiernan-Talk" was now the top rated 7 P.M. TV show in London, both with viewers and with the London literati and European jet-setters who reveled in Margaret's hard-edged interviewing style. Although Margaret's aggressiveness often made her wince, Carolyn could see exactly how it pushed the program to its success. "She's terrific!" whispered Carolyn to John who was also watching from behind the glass, enthralled by the live drama taking place just below.

"Cue, Margaret! Five minutes to close."

The clipped command, spoken by the director from the booth to his floor crew below, caused Carolyn again to become aware of the persistent growling of her stomach. Having just arrived in London on this first day of summer for two weeks of vacation from "The Name's the Game," her "inner

549

clock" was talking hunger and sleep while London time dictated that dinner was an hour away. She hoped the restaurant James had chosen was French and not English as the idea of overcooked vegetables was not something she could cheerfully deal with this night. They should have eaten at home, particularly with James feeling tired and not looking well. Perhaps the nap would revive him, Carolyn thought somewhat worriedly.

The ringing of the telephone in the control room surprised her until Carolyn remembered it could not be heard beyond the glass where Margaret was making a final assault before declaring an end to the battle with her guest. At first, Carolyn refused to believe the man who tapped her on the shoulder and then whispered that the call was for her. Who could be calling her here and why? A rush of panic passed over Carolyn. Ever since Thomas had enlisted in the war and was scheduled to go to Vietnam as a fighter pilot, every unexpected phone call was a cause for alarm.

Carolyn picked up the receiver as if it were a live mouse or rattlesnake. Cautiously, she said hello. At first, when she recognized the voice, her face registered delight but as the voice continued, the delight turned to horror. Dropping the phone, Carolyn's hands flew to cover her face, then her head, as if she could protect herself from what she had just heard. John caught her as she spun from one end of the control room to another, her hands pressed firmly over her mouth stifling her screams.

Margaret had just said her good-nights and was walking off the set with her guest, leaving the director to shoot the two empty chairs over which the credits would be superimposed, when she looked up to the control room for her usual A-OK signal. When she saw John holding on to Carolyn, heard the silent screams through the soundproof glass, she knew that what she had long expected had occurred. As if doused by icy water, she calmly opened the door and stood in front of it, her controlled presence challenging Carolyn.

When she saw Margaret standing as if nailed to the floor, Carolyn's hysteria abruptly ended. She tried to turn away from Margaret but John turned his wife toward her sister. Breathing deeply, calming herself by sheer will, Carolyn walked to Margaret, whose eyes suddenly flooded with tears. Seeing the pain in Carolyn's eyes caused Margaret to shut her own and to shake her head from side to side as if that could deny what Carolyn was about to say.

"Margaret," said Carolyn as she placed her hands firmly on Margaret's shoulders. "It's very bad news." No sooner had she said the words than Carolyn began to cry. "Margaret, Franklin Killerbrew is dead. Franklin, Margaret. Dead."

Shocked, Margaret pulled away from Carolyn's grasp. "Franklin?" she whispered.

Carolyn advanced on her, clasping her firmly again by the arms. "Yes, Margaret. Franklin's dead. He was killed . . . shot to death by a man who thought he was a bug . . . a big green and yellow bug."

BOOK FOUR

1917–1919

BOOK FOUR
1967–1973

1

It was more than just the glare of the late November afternoon sun shimmering on ruffled ocean water that was causing John his temporary difficulty in seeing. As he stood on the glass-enclosed patio looking down at his children as they played on the beach, the echoes of other children and other beaches reverberated through his mind.

Not so many years ago, he, a child of twenty-two, had walked a girl, also a child, along sands not so very far from here as her sister pretended indifference as she waited on a Santa Monica pier. John remembered how those children talked that day, yet how they hadn't. They had had to learn—and they did—to use words that contained content and feeling.

And then there were those other children, those with dirty hands and bloodied faces who ran or dropped along the sands of foreign shores. Like little children, they were playing soldier, only for many the playing was for keeps. They, too, had been too young, too unprepared for the aging processes of life. Some got a chance to learn. Others . . . did not.

But the best beach of all, thought John, was at Nantasket. With my children, *all* my children, watching as they dared one another to dare the waves. A prelude to each daring life? Perhaps. But a foolish dare, as life had proven to be more than equal to it. As his eyes focused on the blanket two hundred feet below, John could see Marti watching as Ali and Mark played fetch with Mickey, the only jet-setting schnauzer in America with homes in Trancas and New York. From the distance, Marti's back and shoulders did not seem broad. Not in comparison to the burdens she had carried, and continued to carry, for the past two years. As if hearing her name called, Marti suddenly looked about. John noted that the famous face was hidden from public view by wraparound sunglasses. An almost needless precaution, thought John, considering the remoteness of Trancas. Its position, just out beyond Malibu, made it also beyond the reach of tourists, gossips, and the press. Marti lived at the top of a small hill, a dune really, and from the road, her home seemed to be at the top of the world.

It was a gorgeous house, found and paid for by Marti without advice and consent. No concrete walls separated it from reality. Only glass, an alarm system, and Mickey, when he was in attendance, as Thor had remained with Charper and the house in Bel Air. The children went to the local public school, which was basically private as the residents of Trancas were among the very privileged. Even there, however, Ali and Mark were confronted by classmates with things they didn't understand but of which unwittingly they had been a part. Like murder . . . insanity . . . and by reason of.

She had dealt with it, thought John, as he watched Marti throw back the ball that had bounced onto the blanket where she was sitting. She had not withdrawn the twins from school but had insisted they cope with life as it was and with explanations which she could give and which they could or could not comprehend. Although she was the most written about star in the world, Marti lived a reclusive life. However, unlike her famous neighbor to the north, Steve McQueen, she was not in hiding. She did her own marketing and when not working, chauffeured her children to and from school.

She also chauffeured her other "child" to and from the private home where he continued to live. As John's vision again became blinded, he saw that other "child" sitting by Marti's side, his knees drawn to his chest and his arms encircling his knees. He, too, was watching Ali and Mark but unlike Marti, he was watching them silently. Again, as if aware someone were eavesdropping, Marti suddenly raised an arm and flung it protectively around Vinnie's shoulders. With both their backs to him, John, if he squinted hard, could brush away the memory of the same two children sitting similarly on that other beach in Nantasket with matching red pails by their sides.

Almost three decades ago. Realizing that took John's breath away. His daughter . . . thirty years old. Not possible. But then, she was not possible. Where had this Marti come from? Or was Margaret right? Had she always been there but unknown to both others and herself? He didn't know her. Perhaps he never had. She had grown up to become this "thing" and suddenly John realized that he, too, like the public had bought the image. The beautiful but troubled Marti Tiernan. Well, she had been that but obviously, she had been much more. The world had cracked open and while others—Margaret, Carolyn, himself, too, to an extent—had fallen into the gaping hole, Marti had not. But why? How?

As Marti sat staring at nothing, her eyes focused on some shimmer on the waters in the distance, she was also wondering . . . why and how. Why was Vinnie still as he was and how long before he might be as the doctors assured her he could be. With luck. And prayer. I don't believe much in luck anymore, thought Marti. Make your own. It's better. She was teaching Ali and Mark that. Don't wait for luck, opportunity, or others. You want something; get it yourself. *For* yourself. It was worth losing the house in Bel Air to Philip Charper to learn that. It was worth three marriages and three divorces to say to hell with depending on anyone but yourself. I don't like it but I do it, thought Marti, still angry that she had to. She was also angry that her weekend was soon to be interrupted by her father. She had no idea why he had called and asked to see her. Of course she would not say no, not because of "duty" but from curiosity—her own. But Friday was never convenient. That was the day her nerves were taut, often stretched beyond endurance. She would drive out to Santa Barbara—not before phoning The Home first to see if Vinnie's weekend privileges were still intact—and then worry all the way there whether he would be eight, twelve, or thirty years old. If he was not catatonic or agitated in some physical manner, they would have him ready for her. Stan, the male nurse, would be at his side, his suitcase packed. Vinnie didn't need to take anything as she kept his room outfitted with clothes and toiletries. But Stan, big, burly, beefy Stan, he had to pack his things—including the Thorazine, the Valium, and the Elavil, just in case Vinnie "went off" and needed sedating during the weekend.

And then drive back, making childlike conversation with a child. Except when he was there, really there, her cousin and friend. That didn't happen often but at least now it happened. Yet, every time it did, it brought about the violent behavior, not immediately but eventually. And then the drugs. Drugs to treat drug abuse. It seemed ironic to Marti but she didn't question it. She had investigated scores of private "homes" before settling on the one in Santa Barbara so private that it had no name. She had seen the insane and those

557

made insane, temporarily or permanently, by drugs or some other trauma. Since she had never been able to sit through *The Snake Pit*, she was not about to let Vinnie live in one, no matter how nicely it was painted pink and lavender or white. She had found The Home just as she had found the lawyer who represented Vinnie—by seeking out and then interviewing the best. What she didn't know, she learned. When she didn't understand, she asked for explanations and then asked again when she still didn't understand.

There was still much she didn't understand, thought Marti, beginning with why her father was about to visit and ending with her own personal boredom. Scripts lay piled on her bedside table. She had no interest in them. It was far more important to her agent, publicist, and public that she maintain her number one box office position than it was to her. She had no difficulty understanding she was whoever she seemed to be to others, but she could not be that for herself. Her career gave her money and nothing else. And money, she really didn't need.

What do I need? asked Marti of herself, reaching into the box of Oreo cookies and giving one to Vinnie as she nibbled on another. Her mother might have said "a good man" but Marti knew that wasn't the case. She had forced herself to accept the invitations of three different men over the past year. Each time, she felt obliged to be pleasant, a "good companion." She didn't have to worry about being pleasant or good in bed. It never got that far. Marti's body told her it was as much closed off to that possibility as her head was. "There are no openings for men in my life," she had recently said to her mother in a phone conversation and then had laughed at her unintended double entendre. So no wonder she was bored; no wonder she had said yes when her agents called and said Bob Hope wanted her on his Christmas trip to Vietnam to entertain the soldiers. Why not? Her mother knew why not. You don't leave family at Christmas, she had argued. But Marti thought that ridiculous and said so. "I do not want my kids waiting around for birthdays and Christmas to have good things happen or to feel, even *be,* loved. They should have that all the time." Marti hadn't added how as a little girl she always believed, no . . . she hoped, that on her birthday or at Christmas, her father would love her. But although he was usually physically there on those days, as she remembered it, his love was not.

John's eyes again focused narrowly on the arm draped so casually over the semislouched shoulders of his nephew. Certainly if Vinnie could be made to feel safe, this girl, no, corrected John, this woman could do it. She had that kind of determination. John hoped it didn't extend to her announced and highly publicized decision to accompany Bob Hope to Vietnam. Suddenly, John felt weary. He wished he had not come to question and object to one of Marti's actions. His resolve returned when he realized he was not doing so as a father but as a private citizen who had made quite vocal his abhorrence of American intervention in Vietnam. His participation in the antiwar demonstration in Washington last month had cost K.O. Productions several contracts. They were gradually being eased out of the independent syndication market and John suspected he was a name on hidden government lists that were not labeled *The Great Society*.

As he kicked off his loafers and removed his socks, John's worry drifted from Marti to Evelyn. He had uprooted her from London to send her to the Los Angeles office and although she insisted her arthritis would be forever grateful to him, he wondered if the dwindling K.O. accounts could afford the size of its staff and office. Not that money was a problem with Evelyn; Nancy's new gallery on Robinson was still quite the rage of Hollywood, but he felt obligated to her current salary plus percentage of profits and not a penny less. As he walked down the steel steps leading to the beach, John knew Evelyn would make light of his self-imposed guarantees.

The first to realize John had arrived was Mickey who raced into the wind to greet his old friend" from the East. As the dog yapped his way up the cool sands ne was followed by Ali shrieking in recognition as she ran with her arms already outstretched toward the Piggyback Man, as she called John. Through the rose tint of her sunglasses, Marti saw John stoop to scoop up his granddaughter. She heard him say as he whooshed her into the air: "You're getting too heavy or I'm getting too old for this."

Too old? Her father? Impossible, thought Marti, instantly rejecting the idea as false. But suddenly, as she stared at him unobserved, she realized that John had indeed grown older. She wondered why she had not seen this before. His hair was more white than it was blond but it seemed to enhance rather than detract from his overall attractiveness. He was still slender and straight, with no slouching. The upright walk of a young man. Only the lines about his face, the now deep set of his eyes said otherwise. Marti was pleased to see that unlike other Hollywood "moguls" his age and older, John was wearing neither a Nehru jacket nor denims. And no stupid gold medallion hung about his neck either. Her father had not gone "mod" or "hip" and that pleased her.

"Mama, look! It's Grandpa," yelled Ali as she danced about the blanket. As she saw her daughter's excitement, Marti was pleased that she had not transmitted any of her negative feelings about her father to her children. Both Ali and Mark had what she herself had never known: adoring grandparents who thought they were firm disciplinarians but who were true libertarians where the twins were concerned.

Vinnie looked up at John and smiled. "Hello, Grandpa," he said shyly.

Marti was quick to correct him. "Vinnie, that's not your grandpa. You know that. He is your Uncle John."

Vinnie's face reflected his struggle for comprehension. Without a smile he repeated: "Uncle John."

The look on her father's face did not escape Marti. She watched as he turned away from Vinnie's gaze and stared at the sea. Suddenly he looked even older. Neither of her parents dealt well with Vinnie. Both had difficulty with his in-and-out states. Happily for all, the children did not. She often marveled how they accepted Vinnie as a peer when he presented himself that way, and also, when he was "there," as the Uncle Vinnie they knew. Mark still hadn't moved from Vinnie's lap but sat there gazing adoringly at his grandpa as he offered him his slightly nibbled Oreo cookie.

"Why don't you guys take the Frisbee and play by the water?" Marti asked as she took the toy out of an all-purpose beach bag she had brought with her. "Come on, Vinnie, you start and I'll join you in a bit."

"But I want to stay here!" Ali pouted.

"Grandpa and I want to talk," explained Marti.

"That's why I want to stay. Why can't I hear? How will I know what you're talking about if I'm not here?" asked Ali, perfectly secure in what she believed to be her rights.

John was smiling when Marti replied, "Little girl child of mine, if I wanted you to hear, I'd ask you to stay." When Ali's face began to crumble Marti said, "Now don't you go all gushy on me. Do I cry when you and Mark start telling secrets to one another? Do I insist you tell me everything?"

"You mean you and Grandpa want to tell secrets?" asked Ali, her face lighting up again.

"That's close enough to it," replied Marti. "So what do you say, kid? Do you scram now?"

"I like secrets," said Ali as she pressed her cheek to John's. "Will you tell me a secret later?"

"I'll tell you two," John said as he hugged her.

"Me too?" asked Mark, his lower lip beginning to tremble at the thought of being left out.

"Of course," said John. "Special man-to-man secrets."

As the kids bounded down the beach, Marti said to Vinnie firmly, "You're in charge. Watch them." Vinnie looked at her dumbly for a second and then nodded his head. As he, too, went toward the water, John said, "It's like having another child, isn't it?"

"No. It isn't," said Marti with a vehemence that made John look directly at her. "He is an adult who has regressed to childlike behavior. He is not to be encouraged in that behavior. When he doesn't remember, he must be made aware of what he has forgotten . . . corrected, almost trained to be who he is. It may not look it today," she added with a sigh, "but he's better. Much better. He does go in, but he will come out. It's part of this flashback thing. They tell me he was himself for several days this week. They insist that when he becomes comfortable with himself, he will stay centered in the present." As she saw John watching her intently, she continued. "He becomes easily enraged when he is himself. Which, by the way, the doctors maintain is good. It's his inability to deal with his rage that drives him back into the past. He keeps returning—or so they say—to a traumatic time in his life. When he confronts it—in the flashbacks, that is—instead of feeling and venting his anger, he snaps off, breaks with reality. At least, that's what they tell me."

"You keep saying 'they' as though they were the enemy," said John softly.

"A remnant of my happy marriage to Philip Charper," Marti said sarcastically. "I still find it very difficult to put any faith in the words of head doctors, although the opinions I have just distilled for you are those of the entire staff at The Home and not just the psychiatric team."

"Do you believe them?" asked John, more for his own corroboration than Marti's.

"If I hadn't seen him come back, so to speak, I wouldn't.

561

But there have been times when Vinnie is all there, or should I say right here."

"Does he still remember nothing?"

"He has now remembered everything *but*. The doctors aren't sure he will ever remember that because he was totally gone when he shot Franklin. Gone in the sense that he really thought he was shooting a green and yellow bug."

Involuntarily Marti shuddered. As if she had pressed a button in her mind, she suddenly faced her father and asked, "Why are you here, Dad?"

"I need a reason, don't I?" John said more than asked, knowing both knew the answer.

"It's a little late for either of us to pretend you would just drop in for a chat or to see how things are," Marti said, her voice intentionally clear of any emotion.

"Marti, why don't you say what you feel? Perhaps Vinnie isn't the only one with an inability to deal with his rage."

"Dad, please, let's not fight."

"Why not, Marti? Maybe we should. In fact, maybe it's long past due. Are you going to hang me forever?"

Marti looked at her father, stunned by his words because in some way that she had yet to grasp, she knew they were true.

"When are you going to understand I did the best I could?"

"It wasn't good enough!" snapped Marti, her voice harsh and unforgiving.

"It was all I had."

"It was precious little," Marti said. "What I can't understand is why you ever had children if you didn't like kids."

"Didn't like kids? What the hell are you talking about?"

"Oh, come on, Dad. Just because late in life you've become a doting grandfather doesn't mean you liked kids. Certainly you never liked me or Thomas."

"I loved you both as best I could. Don't you remember?"

"I remember your avoiding us . . . me."

"When?"

"When you came home from the war," said Marti.

"Doesn't that tell you something? Use that head of yours. I was sick. Sick at heart. Sick to my stomach. Sick in the head. I had nothing inside to give. I was half-dead. And I guess I didn't want to love anybody deeply. Not even your mother. I think . . . oh, God, Marti, when you see what I saw, what I lived through, it's more difficult to love, because you are so

562

afraid it will all happen again and happen to those you love. I couldn't love you the way I once had, the way you seemingly wanted, because . . . I just couldn't. Can't you understand?"

Marti was silent. In her mind, she was replaying her father's words. "You mean it wasn't me?" she asked at last in a soft voice.

"It was never you, although when I felt you turn away from me, I was angry. With you. I needed you, Marti."

"But I was a child," Marti protested.

"So was I," replied John.

"No, you weren't. You were . . ."

"Just a little older than you are now when I came home from the war," interrupted John. "Tell me something, Marti, do you feel old . . . mature at thirty? Or are there some days when you feel like a kid, when you're scared and helpless and wonder why you feel that way when the whole world knows that at thirty, one should never be scared or unsure, but complete."

Suddenly Marti was in tears. "I'm afraid every day. Not so much for me but for Vinnie. Oh, shit . . . yes, for me too. I don't know what I want anymore. Nothing seems quite so clear as it once did."

"Marti, this will sound like a crock, but that's the very beginning of clarity."

"Dad, *did* you like me?" asked Marti, returning to the source of what was now hammering at her forehead.

John looked at her until she matched his gaze. "I never knew you." When Marti started to look away, John cupped her chin in his hand and turned her head back toward him. "Marti, that was more my loss, or as much, anyway, as yours. I loved you but I didn't know you. You have to know someone to like them. But I like you now, Marti. These past two years, watching you take charge—not just of Vinnie but of yourself, your life, your children—that's been a wonder to me. If you only knew how many times I have stood back and thought: Who is this girl? I still wonder. Where did the strength come from? Was it always there? The family was in shock, falling apart. You, for more reasons perhaps than any of us except Margaret, should have fallen apart, too, But you not only didn't, you emerged. And you didn't throw the fact that you took charge—that you hired the lawyers for Vinnie; that you personally found a home for him—in anyone's face."

"I wanted to," Marti said, feeling as if she were about to cry again.

"But you didn't, and that's another reason I like you," said John. "Look, Marti, I know this is an abrupt segue, but I'm wondering . . . how committed are you to going with Hope to Vietnam?"

"What do you mean?" asked Marti, confused. "There's no signed contract, but he has my word. Why? Is there some project you'd like me to look at?"

"No, that's not what I meant. Marti, this war in Vietnam is immoral. We don't belong there."

"Oh, Dad, look! You know I'm not political. I haven't the vaguest idea why we are in Vietnam. But I do know why I'm going."

"Marti, just listen for a second. I'll try to explain without lecturing. When we had our Civil War, we hated foreign interference. And rightfully so because those foreign interests were serving themselves and not us. It's the same here. As I said: we don't belong in Vietnam. The Vietnamese have a right to fight among themselves, to work out their own problems just as we did over a century ago. They've been at war twenty years, Marti. Twenty! Most of which have been spent trying to get rid of foreign control."

"Dad, I don't see what this has to do with me and Bob Hope," said Marti impatiently.

"It has everything to do with you and anyone else who gives some sort of tacit 'agreement' to our involvement in Vietnam. Marti, you are a celebrity. As the papers say: a great star. You have influence. People will interpret your going with Hope as a vote of confidence in American intervention in Vietnam. And Marti, that's wrong. We're there under the guise of heading off the communist threat. But there is no threat. We're just saying there is one to maintain our foothold in Southeast Asia. If Vietnam topples to communist influences, it doesn't mean the rest of the world will."

Marti looked at her father's face. It was afire with an anger she couldn't understand. "We are going to overcommit ourselves," he was saying. To what? she wondered. "If we're not careful, we won't be able to retreat without losing face," he argued. Impossible, she thought. We are the greatest face on the world map.

"We're risking human lives, Marti. We're negating the suffering any kind of war brings. Not only to our own men but to innocent victims . . . people, like you and me, only without power. Vietnamese people. Please, Marti, don't go

564

with Hope. To go with him, I tell you, is to give your support to our involvement."

"No, it's not," said Marti emphatically. "I am going as a citizen, a very successful citizen, to pay back something. I'm going to give of myself . . . and to get. But my going has nothing to do with the war. The fact is, I don't even understand the war."

"That's just it, Marti. Perhaps if you did, you wouldn't go. Anyway, I don't want to belabor my point. I only ask that you reconsider or at least think about what I've said."

"Will you and Mom come to stay with the kids at Christmas regardless?" asked Marti.

"One has nothing to do with the other. Of course, we'll be here should you decide to go."

Together, Marti and John watched the Frisbee game at the water's edge. Mark's determination was matched only by Mickey who leaped high into the air in mainly vain attempts to intercept the passes of Vinnie and Ali. When Marti spoke, it was to the horizon.

"I hated you the most when others admired and liked you the best. I thought this wonderful man who does wonderful things was ashamed of me because I wasn't wonderful. Oh, Dad, how I needed you to make me feel wonderful. I never knew how to do that for myself. It seems I always needed others to define me. I know this sounds crazy but if I could have loved you less, I would have hated you less. Why did I feel it was me with the lack instead of you?"

The tears in John's eyes reflected the pain in his voice. "I did that to you?" he asked tremulously. "I never meant to. Not ever," he said when Marti didn't answer but stared down at the sand. "I'm sorry. Truly, truly sorry."

Although Marti couldn't speak, the hand that found its way into John's said it all. She felt it squeezed and then she felt it resting comfortably, easily, most of all peacefully, in her father's. "Guess what? I have a secret to tell you after all," she said. "I love you."

Margaret decided the wind on her back, pushing her south down Park Avenue, was a sign. If she couldn't continue, the wind would press her onward. Unfortunately. She had awoken that morning convinced she had the first signs of flu. She was somewhat disappointed that she felt considerably better once up and out of bed, her sinuses clearing as the weather did. A last-minute panic over Christmas shopping also seemed a likely excuse not to keep her appointment except when she checked, her shopping was completed. Even the tree had been purchased and it stood naked in an uncluttered corner in her living room. If she had not traditionally decorated the tree Christmas Eve, she could have busied herself with that. Sometime after three, Margaret began to feel nausea rising and falling with her resolve. By then she realized her body would play as many tricks as her mind would allow. But she could allow no further delaying tactics. She had done that for too long.

The walk from her residence at the Lowell on Madison and Sixty-third to Park and Sixty-first took her ten minutes instead of the five it would have taken had she not felt ambivalent. The office she was going to was at the side of a stately old apartment building, private, or as private as anything on Park Avenue could be in midafternoon. Her finger on the doorbell brought an answering buzzer that unlocked the door when she pushed it.

The anteroom was a vestibule with two black leather-upholstered chairs separated by a glass and chrome table on which there was no reading material whatsoever and a small sign that read: THANK YOU FOR NOT SMOKING. The carpeting was an industrial salt-and-pepper tweed and the walls were covered in a similarly colored nubby fabric. No sooner had she seated herself than the inner door opened and the man standing in the doorway smiled her into his office, which was of the same design and color as the vestibule. Except that over the industrial carpet was an exotic rug—either Indian or Iranian. There were no draperies to further darken the almost dark but cozy room; only Levolor blinds which completely covered the twin windows—probably overlooking an alley, Margaret thought—on one side of the room.

She became aware that he was watching her as she looked with distaste at the black leather chaiselike couch against the wall facing his desk. Deciding if he could be so impolite as to stare, she could also, Margaret looked the man full in the face. She was surprised when he returned her gaze comfortably. She was also surprised at his casual appearance: coatless, rolled-up sleeves, tie at half-mast. He was young, or youngish, and nice-looking in an unobtrusive way. Sitting down, she said, "I'm sure you're wondering why I'm here."

"I have the distinct impression you're wondering that far

more than I," he said, his amusement evident in his voice.

"Well, yes, I suppose that's true. I must tell you straight off, I'm not at all sure I believe in this process."

"There are days when I, myself, have that same feeling," he replied, still amused.

"Listen, if I hadn't tried all else, and had all else not failed, I'd be in Martinique or . . . the Bronx. Anywhere other than here. First I tried a gypsy fortune-teller, Madame Rosa. Nice gal. Gives great leaves. She had a ball!"

No response.

"A ball? Like in . . . I had a ball . . . a crystal ball. Well, never mind," said Margaret as she saw he was not about to react. "Anyway, she looked into her leaves and said, 'I see a tall, dark man,' and I said, 'Quick! Give him my number!' " Margaret looked up at the face looking across at her. "She didn't laugh either. O-kay, moving right along. Next we have my sister. She's the good one. She suggested I try the church. And I did. The priest advised I let go and let God, but either God didn't get my change of address card—you see I recently moved back from London—or God doesn't make house calls anymore. I mean . . . you know how hard it is to get a god when you need one. Particularly on weekends."

"You use humor a lot, don't you, Mrs. Carrington?"

"I beg your pardon," replied Margaret, confused.

"Use humor . . . as a defense, a shield, a guard against feeling. What are you protecting, Mrs. Carrington?"

Margaret was angry. She was about to lash back when the truth of the words she had just heard struck again at her. "And here all this time I was fool enough to think I had a humorous outlook on life."

"One doesn't negate the other. You may. In fact, I would already make the assumption that you do and that this outlook of yours has served you as well as it has not. I am just suggesting you may sometimes use your wit as a device, a defense against feeling whatever is troubling you."

"Message received. You want me on the couch now or later?"

"Maybe never."

"You're kidding," said Margaret. "I thought all of you Sanforizers worked with the couch."

"What makes you think you need to be shrunk? Maybe you just need to work through some immediate difficulties. I have no problem with our working face to face. Do you?"

567

It was as if a pin had been pulled. All the tension left Margaret's body. She became aware that she was still wearing her coat, her only concession to being indoors having been the removal of her scarf and the opening of the top buttons on the "fun-fur" she was wearing. Standing, she removed the coat, folded it, and sat holding it in front of her.

"Another shield, Mrs. Carrington? The coat," he explained as he saw the puzzled look on Margaret's face. "You're holding it between you and me, guarding something that's either very precious or frightening. Which is it?"

"Frightening. Only because it's so awful. If it weren't, I'd have been able to talk to Carolyn—she's my sister—"

"The *good one* is how I believe you referred to her."

"Yes, well, that was a joke," Margaret said. "At least I thought it was," she added as she looked at the face that obviously didn't think it was a joke at all. "Carolyn would never feel as I do now. She's much nicer . . . more charitable . . . loving."

"Mrs. Carrington, what makes you so awful?"

Margaret looked up at the man and as her eyes looked into his she said: "I hate my son." When he didn't respond she continued. "He killed a friend of mine. A former lover. A man I would have married a long time ago had it been possible. Anyway, my son killed him, although the courts declared it was by reason of insanity and it was. Nonetheless, he killed a man I loved and he helped to kill my husband."

"That certainly sounds like grounds enough to hate someone, son or no son."

"Mothers don't hate their sons. Mothers, or at least good mothers, love their children no matter what."

"Mrs. Carrington, to be blunt, that's a crock of shit. The biggest crock of shit I've heard in at least"—he checked his watch—"forty minutes."

Margaret's mouth fell open as her eyes registered shock. "Doctor, psychiatrists do not say *shit*."

"Why not? We certainly hear enough of it. I really suggest you take a look at some of the stereotypical thinking you indulge in, Mrs. Carrington. And by the way, my name is Jeffrey Dellarobe. You can either call me Jeff or doctor—I prefer Jeff—and with your permission, I'd like to call you Margaret unless you have some objection."

"Where do we begin?" was Margaret's response.

568

"Wherever *you* want. Wherever you feel most comfortable."

To Margaret, that was a funny response. Not ha-ha funny but funny in that she really didn't want to begin anywhere as nowhere in the past two years had anything been comfortable. Still, she began talking, reliving—beginning with the control room in London. Shock. Horror. Guilt. In that order. Thank God it was not James, as she had thought, who was dead. But it was Franklin, *her* Franklin. When she could absorb that, she felt that not only he had died, but a part of her as well. Her youth, which she knew intellectually was long gone, but now . . . when he was laid to rest, a treasured fantasy, some part of her past that was always present, was laid to rest with him. Not that she had ever thought to relive those years but it had been comforting knowing that they and Franklin were there.

No, she replied when she heard the question, she could not recall what she felt when Carolyn told her it had been Vinnie who shot Franklin. Actually, she wasn't sure she felt anything. But later, yes, later she felt Vinnie had killed Franklin to kill her . . . purposely. Of course this was irrational as doctors kept testifying Vinnie was paranoid and also amnesic. Her son, she was told, to this day had no knowledge of what he had done.

James had been wonderful. The flight from London to Los Angeles had been difficult for him as he was unwell. And she was guilty about that too. She should have insisted he remain in London but selfishly she wanted him with her. "I needed him. Oh God, how I needed him. And he was there. Even when he finally fell asleep—with that terrible turbulence we had most of the flight that was a miracle!—he fell asleep with his hand covering mine. And throughout the month in L.A. . . . the funeral and the inquest, he was always . . . *there* . . . in some way, his hand was always covering mine."

Margaret stopped talking for a moment, choosing instead to regulate her body with the breathing exercises she had learned some months ago during her brief study of Transcendental Meditation. It was silly to feel guilty, wasn't it, particularly since James had been in failing health for so many years. But so many *good* years! Such very good years, she repeated just in case Dellarobe didn't realize how good they were. James had no fear of death, she explained. Only she did, more of his death than her own. In fact, when they were back in London, he was insisting he would welcome his time away from her so he could compare notes on her "performances" with Franklin before she arrived to give them both hell. She slapped at him then, threatened her well-known knuckle sandwich. And he laughed—his wonderful, quiet, but—for James—hearty laugh, and then clasped her to him. It wasn't much of a clasp as his strength was gone. At least his physical strength was but his other—his real strength—that remained. When he died, he ordered, she was to live. There is nothing else, he maintained, and then explained how ever since his first attack, ever since he had conquered his anxiety and realized he could "go" any day, every day had become his best day.

She had seen that. Not that he wasn't sometimes depressed or despondent, but mainly, he celebrated life. He said one week before his death, so terribly soon after Franklin's: "You must mourn when I die. If you don't, I'll come back to haunt you. But you mustn't make it a lifetime occupation. Black doesn't suit you, nor does mourning. You *are* life, Margaret. You always were and my hope is you will always be. You're active, not passive, and I must say—if you'll forgive the momentary lapse into dirty old manism—I have found that most refreshing."

She was laughing as she imitated James's accent. Laughing until she explained how what he had said wasn't entirely true. She had certainly been passive the entire time she was in Los Angeles. She couldn't take charge of herself so how could she take charge of her own son's welfare. More guilt. And at Franklin's funeral, everyone else had such a clear idea of where it should be held and how it should be observed, whereas she, who had been closest to him, went along with plans made without her. Thank God it had been private, or as private as anything could be in that area known as Hollywood, which seems to encompass everything as far east as Las Vegas and as far south as Acapulco. Throughout, she had the feeling that she was simply a featured actress in a movie. That's about how much reality it had to her. At graveside, to her left were her sister, John, and Marti. To her right . . . that's what was so strange . . . Nancy Killerbrew. Yes, that day, Nancy Killerbrew. Not Nancy Quentin Blanchard. She was crying. *Sobbing* better describes it. It was so strange realizing this woman, once enemy, now friend, had loved him in some way not in Margaret's ken, a love combined with hate.

She never felt Franklin's death. In Los Angeles, there were other things to distract her. The lawyer for one. He had been obtained by Marti and he was one of the nation's top criminal attorneys. He wanted her endorsement. After all, she, not Marti, was Vinnie's mother. Technically that was true. But only technically, given all that Marti had done and continues to do, said Margaret.

Marti . . . a miracle. She is my niece, as my sister points out regularly, she heard herself saying lightly to Dellarobe. A little friction on that point. If you knew Marti, you could well understand why one would be possessive of her. She had been in the house when Bill Foster—"I had met him years ago"—brought Vinnie out of the hills and called an ambulance to take him to the hospital. Foster also called the police, described in detail where the body could be found, and then told Marti she should contact the lawyer immediately.

The law, explained Margaret to Dellarobe, dictated that a police guard was to be maintained outside Vinnie's room at the hospital and immediately upon his regaining consciousness, his rights were to be read and he was then to be arrested. But there was one complication; a rather major one. Vinnie never became fully cognitive and at the inquest a month later, when various psychiatrists, for the state and otherwise, testified that Vincent Tiernan was not capable of standing trial and must remain institutionalized for an unknown period of time, he was not indicted and all charges were dropped.

It was Marti who went searching each day for an institution for Vinnie, Margaret continued. It was Marti who found The Home in Santa Barbara, not she. She could not. Yes, she had seen him once. Only once. James took her into his room. They had warned her he vacillated between hysteria and catatonia. He was silent until his eyes met hers. Then, he sat up in bed and started screaming. Just screaming. No words. Just screams. She ran from the room with Carolyn trying to hold on to some part of her. It was Carolyn who cried in the hallway, not she. It was James who asked the doctors what could be done and whether there would eventually be a recovery. Not she.

They left for London soon thereafter, but they couldn't leave behind what had happened. The press saw to that. For weeks, the murder and the "scandal" flipped between page one and page three news. All that had been hidden for so many years was finally common knowledge. "And that's what it was . . . common. 'Son Kills Former Lover.' What headlines! What revelations! I, Margaret Tiernan, had been the paramour—only they don't use that word anymore—of Franklin Killerbrew. They made something ugly out of something that had been bittersweet, brutal, and yes, beautiful."

No matter where she was, the British press hurled questions at her. Of course it became impossible to continue with her TV show. How could she be the interviewer when it was apparent that not only her viewers but many of her guests wanted to interview her? So she quit, which was better than being asked to leave, which is what happened to Carolyn when the producers of "The Name's the Game" decided that the family's notoriety interfered with the lightness, the gaiety, they wanted on camera for the game. And wasn't that, too, her fault? Margaret asked.

The "fun fur" Margaret had been clasping slipped from her lap to the floor. Looking at it she said, "That's how James went . . . he just slipped away from me. The trip had tired him and God only knows how the events of those weeks must have exhausted him because he never spoke of it. But he showed it. By the time we had returned to London, the summer was half-gone, as was James. We would still take our daily walk in Hyde Park but for a briefer period every day. And then one night—just after dinner—when I had finished the dishes, I found him in the living room 'asleep' in his chair."

That funeral too did not seem real to her, she explained. What she remembered most was that once again others were crying. Evelyn . . . Nancy . . . Carolyn. "Even as my sister's arm encircled my waist, holding me up as the coffin went down, she was crying. But Marti couldn't approach me. Her grief was what mine would have been had I allowed it. She had loved James as he had loved her. When we all lived together in Paris, they built a very special bond. I think he was a father figure to her and she was the loving daughter he had hoped for but didn't get. His daughter, by the way, did not come to the funeral, although she sent me a very *nice* handwritten note. And Deirdre decided that James had long been dead for her, so why pretend to a loss when there wasn't one. I'm sure Deirdre thought her note a comfort to me. I *know* my reply was not a comfort to her."

At first, she could not leave the house, she explained. No,

she didn't mean she couldn't leave it to shop or even to visit with friends; she couldn't leave it. To go on. To begin anew. Every picture, every piece of sculpture, every tapestry or Knoll design was James. They kept him alive. Or so she thought until one day she realized quite unexpectedly that they did not but she could. In her mind, no matter where she lived and with whatever accessories, James Carrington would be there.

It was then she decided to return to New York, to dispose of the apartment and all its furnishings. Except the artwork. That was too precious. Not for its actual resale worth. Oh, no. There was no market price one could establish that could come near the value she attached to the paintings.

She found the two-bedroom apartment at the Lowell rather quickly and had been persuaded almost instantly to take it by the fireplace in the living room. Some of her best memories, Margaret explained, involved fireplaces and people. Then, too, it had a wraparound terrace and a concierge and attended elevators. From the moment she set foot in the lobby, the Lowell had given her a feeling of permanence and security.

And she had done exactly as James ordered: gotten on with it. Madison Avenue above Fifth-seventh Street was one long gallery. The Whitney Museum was just a half-mile or so from the Lowell and the Metropolitan and Guggenheim were up just a bit farther on Fifth. And the theatre that season had been wonderful. So many new ventures in the '60s, although watching a bunch of long-haired, scruffy-looking children take their clothes off was not her idea of theatre. But still, she went out, explored the budding SoHo area and this new Chelsea. She even accepted a few invitations from men she had known or men she met through John or Carolyn, but that was pointless. She had had the best, the very best, and she was not in the market for poor substitutes. And sex? Suddenly—it must be the changes one goes through—but sex didn't seem very interesting. The same was true of the scripts she had begun receiving again.

"So my life was very full—or so I told myself—except I felt very empty. The best way I can explain is: somewhere in the Bible, I think, Jesus says, or someone says of Jesus, 'I am in this life but not of it.' Me? I'm of this life but not in it. I'm walled off from it. I seem to feel nothing. Except hate. Which brings us full circle, doesn't it?" she said to the man sitting opposite her, his face reflecting concern and caring. "Hate.

573

How I hate my son. Which makes me a terrible mother and an awful person, don't you think?"

"Margaret, what I think is not important. What you think is. If I told you I didn't think you were awful for hating your son but only experiencing a normal reaction, would it make a real difference? Would you feel better about yourself because of what I say? You must give yourself permission to hate. Or to love. Or to feel anything else for that matter. You must accept who you are. Equally as important is that you must accept that this is how you feel. It's not so awful and you may not feel it forever. Margaret, all mothers are not the same, just as all people are not the same. You are who you are and I would suggest you acknowledge and permit who you are and what you feel. Your feelings don't make you a bad or unfit person or mother."

"I tried," said Margaret agitatedly. "All my life I tried. I wasn't perfect. But I tried. I gave him what I could. I loved him the best I could. I made choices, yes. Many I wouldn't make again. But who doesn't feel that way about something in their lives? Who wouldn't, if given the chance, change something?"

"Exactly, Margaret," said Dellarobe. "Who? Who feels that he or she or life has been perfect?"

"He was always unforgiving, unrelenting, and uncompromising. But why should I hate him so now when I didn't when he was a child?" asked Margaret with more anguish than she had allowed herself in a very long time.

"Margaret, there's a passage in a book called *I Never Promised You a Rose Garden*. I can't quote it exactly but I think it says: 'Measure your capacity to feel pain and that is your capacity to feel joy.' I would say to you, Margaret: Measure your capacity to feel hate and that is your capacity to feel love. I'm sure you have often heard how closely linked the two emotions are."

Margaret was silent as she absorbed Dellarobe's words.

"You've suffered a great many losses in a very short time, haven't you, Margaret," Dellarobe said softly, almost persuadingly.

Margaret nodded her head. "Yes . . . a great many." she replied and then, as if admitting to the truth of her words, the losses rushed in to surround and attack her. In the next twenty minutes, Margaret cried two years' worth of tears.

* * *

Marti shivered as she sat bundled in a blanket on her glass-enclosed patio watching the whitecapped breakers pound the rocks and the shore. The noise of the waves, filtered through the glass, reminded her of another noise; one that had turned her cold then, as the memory of it did now.

Cu Chi . . . her third day in Vietnam. The plane had just begun its takeoff and was roaring down the runway when it suddenly U-turned, starting on the ground and ending in a deep, spiral climb in the sky. She had heard the gunshots and later, when the plane landed again in Bangkok, she had seen the bullet holes from the small-arms fire.

Marti's feelings about what she was doing in Vietnam changed that day. What had seemed till then to be a joyride, a "swell thing" for a bunch of movie stars to do, became a nightmare. Now, when the troupe left the Erawan Hotel each morning after a luxurious breakfast served, if one wished, on a luxurious terrace, she was keenly aware that the bus they rode to the plane or the bases where they played had grills over the windows just in case "things" were thrown. Those "things," she realized, could range from grenades to bombs.

It was then Marti began to use the steno pad she had found attached to a tape recorder when she opened her luggage at the Erawan Hotel. The note, written on K.O. Production stationery, read: "For what you see, think, and feel." At first, she thought of the gift as useless, as some projection of her father's needs rather than her own. That changed with Cu Chi. Then, the recorder and pad became needed friends, "people" she could talk to without judgment.

Marti had never thought of herself as brave and the diary she made of the steno pad proved to her she was not. Her unpolished prose told of her terror as helicopters flew her from Phan Rang to Cam Ranh. A direct quote of instructions re-created her terror each time she read it. "If shot down, stay with the copter."

The realization that death was a possible unannounced "special" guest on the Hope tour made other discomforts laughable. Suddenly, being awakened at five in the morning to be driven from the hotel to the airport where a C-130 plane would take them into Nam didn't seem all that bad. At least, she could be awakened, whereas all the noise in the world—which she heard at many of the bases where they played—could not awaken the dead. The incongruity of it all bothered her. She, in a revealing satiny gown, bringing holiday cheer as jet bombers flew off to bring their "cheer" to the enemy in North Vietnam. And later, at some marine camp, the name of which she could not remember, the irony of Hope doing his comedy "bit" as calls to units in the audience demanded that they report immediately for combat patrol and do their "bit."

As her diary noted, Marti never knew if she were the only member of the troupe to experience discomfort. Not the physical—no one could enjoy the bucket seats of the C-130 or the less-than-seats in the C-141—but the emotional. Wasn't anyone else bothered by the fact that they were bringing cheer to audiences who often showed up still muddied, still armed, still frightened by the war they had just left?

So much of what she was experiencing felt like an M-G-M Mickey-and-Judy B movie with "let's put on a show in the barn" as the big finale. Everyone had the spirit. Even the inside of the transport plane was decorated with scraps of tinsel and ratty Christmas trees. There were days when she felt she was playing the two-a-day on the RKO circuit. Only it wasn't the Palace but makeshift stages in such towns as Plei Ku, Phu Cat, Lai Khe, indistinguishable from each other. There were twenty-two in all scheduled for the fourteen days in Nam and they played thirty-five shows, many of which were impromptu. Although her notes told her of impressions, Marti could not see distinguishable faces. All the soldiers meshed into one. Young. Very young. Children. This was wrong, not as it should be. Wars were fought by grown men. She remembered that from the war films she had seen as a child and as a teenager. When had it changed? She realized it hadn't and that it was always thus. *She* had changed. She had gotten older and as she did, the soldiers got younger, although they hadn't; not really.

Her diary hinted but did not say what she really felt toward the end of her first week in Vietnam. Now, of course, as she looked back she was incensed, enraged at her own duplicity and what she personally believed to be the duplicity of the tour itself. She was a beautifully wrapped present in Bob Hope's bag of toys. She was part of the fantasy they unfolded twice a day for the boys. Comic relief, you could call it. An escape, a pretense that the war didn't exist, at least not for that moment. She understood how others could feel that what they were doing was right. Bringing a little Christmas cheer to the cheerless was certainly a Christian thing to do. But she worried about the illusion, the sham she and others created. Perhaps one should see the reality of murder, not only of others but what could be their own. Maybe soldiers should have constant reminders of why they are fighting, killing, and dying. All this she asked of herself in her diary.

Marti had read several of her entries many times. They continued to affect her even now, nearly three weeks after her return. Often she found herself troubled. When she wasn't cranky, angry over something intangible, she was weepy, also over something unknown. The hospitals she had visited in Nam remained uppermost in her mind. Had she not searched through so many hospitals for Vinnie—had she already not seen the unspeakable—she would never have been able to accompany Hope on his rounds of the wounded. Her diary would never let her forget Raquel Welch who spoke more with the boys in the hospitals than she did with members of the troupe, her shyness disappearing when the need of others appeared. Only this week, Marti heard that Welch had called several of the wounded men's parents to advise them of their sons' well-being.

Her own well-being was shaken severely on December 23. A sunny afternoon at Udorn Air Base in Thailand, her diary began. Udorn . . . busy and bustling, a little city of narrow roads, always crowded with broken-down buses and jitneys. As usual, the show had drawn a huge crowd and her comedy sketch with Hope got huge laughs. The show closed, as it always did, with Barbara McNair singing "Silent Night." But it was afternoon. In the sun. It made no difference. Boys . . . men . . . men who really were boys, Hope, Welch, herself— all joined McNair as she sang. Voices swelled as they wished to sleep . . . to sleep in "Heav-enly pe-ace." The impact of those words hit her for the first time that day and, before thousands, Marti had wept.

When she came off the stage, she thought at first that the sun and the emotional experience were combining to play tricks on her. Of course, through her mother, she had known Thomas was somewhere in the Vietnam area but at Udorn? With captain's bars on his shoulders? And smiling at her as he said words so foreign to the Thomas she had known—that he was *proud* of her, proud of what she was doing for her country. At first she couldn't respond as she was somewhere else, still sleeping in heavenly peace. But he was not asking

577

for responses. He led her away from the crowds of photographers recording the brother/sister reunion for "the folks back home." She saw the officers' quarters, the one-story units made from logs which Thomas called "hootches." She saw the base gymnasium, its swimming pool and movie theatre, and she thought of the weekend she had spent at Grossinger's once and hadn't it, too, had "hootches"—cabins of some kind made of logs just off the main house? She couldn't remember. She couldn't think as she was too busy smiling at the men introduced to her so proudly by Thomas—his men as a flight leader of the Triple Nickel Squadron. Thomas, a leader now, and no longer a follower of family traditions.

He spoke and he spoke. Of moral responsibility, patriotic duty, and of the war we had to win. Of our "position" and our "posture" in Southeast Asia. Of why the people of South Vietnam must have the right—which the United States is helping them to obtain—to determine their future without external intervention.

She tried, she truly tried, she told herself for weeks later, to understand him. She couldn't. Particularly when he said he would sign up for yet another year when his tour of duty was up in January. "And I will keep on extending my tour of duty until we have won the war."

"How does Reese feel about that?" she asked. "I mean," she stuttered when she saw the dumbfounded look in Thomas's eyes, "how does she feel being alone, with three kids, and you in danger and all?"

"You should ask her when you return. But I believe she feels proud. Very proud. She understands that I'm here so she can be there, with our kids, safe . . . not just for today but always. This war, as you know, Marti, isn't just about Vietnam. Hardly. This war is saying 'No!' loud and clear to the communists. It's letting them know they cannot take another inch. If we give in here, we eventually give in to the takeover of all of Southeast Asia."

"Dad doesn't think we should be here at all," she said, sending up her trial balloon with caution.

"Yes, I read he had participated in the antiwar protest in Washington; he and your brother," said Thomas shaking his head. She had noted "your brother" but couldn't challenge him as he continued to talk. "I wasn't surprised. Nor was I embarrassed. The man has nothing to do with me. Not anymore. He really seems like something that happened a long

578

time ago. He was my father. *Was*. An argument could be waged he will always be my father and biologically that is true. But I believe that for a man to always be another man's father, it has more to do with fathering and feeling than it does with a biological act. I have been fatherless most of my life. Now, as an adult, as a parent, my childhood is long gone, past, although not forgotten. Don't you agree?"

As Marti pulled the blanket around her thinking she really should sit inside by the fire, she remembered that moment with stunning clarity. She did not respond to Thomas's question because she felt he would not understand. Yes, she felt older. But older didn't mean more mature. Yes, she had children of her own. But some days she yearned to be someone's child and was so glad she was. Yes, ever since they had spoken that day on the beach, she needed her father less—yet needed him more. But in a new way that was still quite strange but no less wonderful. She looked at her entry for December 23. It ended: "I have a brother. A twin brother. His name is Thomas. I feel no closer to him than he feels to our father. But I know he is my brother, whereas he does not know our father is and always will be our father."

Suddenly she was weeping again. Her eye had caught another of her entries and beneath its seeming banality—"People get hurt in war; many even die"—was her most vivid remembrance. The wards of the hospitals she had visited came back into focus. It was there she began to make use of John's gift by recording messages from the wounded to take back to wives and families. In the spontaneous tapings, she could hear the fear and the courage in the voices and words of the wounded. Over and over she played the tape with the Southern boy, Taylor. She had recorded his message and had then forgotten to turn off the recorder. When she returned to Trancas and began her daily playbacks of memories, she heard Taylor discuss life and death—his own—without either Thomas's or John's sureness. This boy soldier didn't know why he was in Vietnam; just that he was and according to the credos and ethics with which he was raised, he was supposed to be where his country said he should be. Still, as his thoughts spilled onto the tape, so did his questions and doubts. It wasn't just that Taylor admitted he was afraid to die but that he didn't understand exactly what he was being asked to die for.

Carolyn had cried when she heard that tape. Her father

579

looked grim but said nothing. He didn't have to as the tape had said it all. As she watched the rain splash against the glass of the patio, Marti began to feel the tears to which she had become accustomed splash down her face. When she heard her mother's voice yoo-hooing from the living room, she was glad of it and quickly picked herself up from her chair and her mood to join her by the fireplace.

"You're home early," she said as Carolyn rubbed her hands before the fire.

"They ran out of ways to explode me out of a moving train. One moment I'm trapped between Napoleon Solo and Ilya Kuryakin and the next I rub a button on my jumpsuit and I jump—right through the roof of the train—don't ask why I don't hurt my head—leaving an explosion behind that would kill half of Anaheim, Azusa, and Cucamonga but which is to be continued next week."

Carolyn laughed delightedly and Marti was again amazed at the ease with which her mother had "graduated" from Broadway to guest shots on television's "Man From U.N.C.L.E." and "Run for Your Life." Work is work, Carolyn argued, grateful that producers no longer thought her so-called notoriety of two years earlier would detract from the plot. "Of course that's largely due to the absence of any plot whatsoever and I really think they use me to distract viewers from that tiny little lack of what used to be the nuts and bolts of a dramatic offering. However, as TV people out here tell me: Who would be fool enough to confuse a TV audience with something as mundane as a plot? Not me. Not now that they're writing a sequel for me in which I'm joined—are you ready—by my sister in crime . . . yes, the once again ever popular Margaret Tiernan."

"Marg is going to work?" said Marti, pleased and surprised.

"You bet your bippy, as they say out there in TV land," Carolyn replied. "What's more, she is coming next week to play Minerva: Madame of Menace in a two-parter on 'Batman,' and there's talk she may commute every four or five weeks if the character proves to be successful. Can't you just see it? Better still, can you hear it? Margaret, working in TV where they care nothing about perfection but everything about getting it done in a week. It's going to be a nine-point-two on the Richter scale, I tell you. Now, what have you been up to all day?" asked Carolyn, aware from the circles of black underlining Marti's eyes that she was still reacting to her Christmas.

"Mom, when you met Reese," began Marti slowly, "what did you feel about her? How do you think she really feels about seeing Thomas one month out of every year—you know, that time between his extension of duty? I mean . . . if it were Dad, how would you feel?"

"Angry. I already gave at the office, as they say. He went once. He nearly died and so did I and so nearly did our life together. But in those days, Marti, if your country needed you, you went. Yours was not to question why; yours was but to do or die. Or so they said . . . then. Now, the whys and wherefores are uppermost in most people's minds. Me? There's not a day I don't think of not just when but *how* Thomas will come home. That precedes the right or wrong of it. If you want to know more, your father was right. Go talk to those boys' wives and mothers."

"Your mother really is not the one to answer your questions about war," said John as he entered the living room unnoticed. "Despite all my efforts, she continues to hold *Variety* to her bosom as a safeguard against enlightenment just as a virgin holds a cross to her breast to ward off vampires. Where have I failed? Where *have* I failed?" John said feigning distress. "By the way, not to pressure you or anything, but I did speak to my agent about your tape with Taylor and although it isn't much, it's enough for her to think you might have the beginnings of a book."

"Oh, Dad, come off it. Me? A book? You're talking to the girl who majored in the mambo and the cha-cha in high school. My senior year I wore a button that read: "Perez Prado for President. That was my entire youthful consciousness: Patti Page and Perez Prado.""

"Considering who is in office now and who is planning to run for the job," replied John, "I'd say Patti Page and Perez Prado are as good a ticket as any."

Marti sighed. "What the hell, if Mother can be Tanya Troubleska on 'U.N.C.L.E.' and Margaret the Madame of Menace on 'Batman,' certainly I can talk to your agent about a book. It seems to me they're all connected and one is no more foolish than the other," Marti added with a smile that surprised even her.

The lobby smelled of disinfectant. Friday was the one day of the week the super mopped the tiled entranceway with a concoction of bleach, ammonia, and Janitor in a Drum. He would not miss the smell, the building, or the apartment, thought John J. as he placed his keys in the super's mailbox as previously arranged. What was even more surprising, he would not miss Jeanne.

Upper Broadway at six-thirty on a Friday night in March was its usual assortment of Hispanics, blacks, middle-class whites, and students shopping for wares or selling them. Jeanne had bought her dope there from one of the pushers who hovered on or about the university: a teenager known fondly as the Columbia Connection. His mother hated the neighborhood and like most women her age did not feel safe in it. Only once Carolyn had visited his apartment in one of the few new high rises in the neighborhood and had not been pleased despite its built-in air conditioner and laundry facilities in the hallway.

John J. understood. The area around Columbia University was a melting pot and he found it fun even if the pot threatened to boil over at times. But as he asked his mother: What wasn't at a boiling point these days? Jeanne, of course, thought it was part of the revolution: a time when the system would be destroyed by the pot, filled with boiling people, fired up—Jeanne spoke in that kind of rhetoric—demanding change. Her views were popular with the Mark Rudds on campus. Jeanne was a member in good standing in SDS, although John often thought her opinions left no room for a democratic society. Autocratic, maybe.

If John J. had become disenchanted with Jeanne, she more than matched his displeasure. To her, John J. was a phony, a tightrope walker trying to walk the line between both sides of the fence, a member of the establishment disguised as a radical. But he had never been a radical. Even at Cornell when he became involved in the SDS, he was not among those first to burn their draft cards. His participation was to march in peaceful protest on Willard Straight Hall. He had also written several letters, thinly disguised editorials actually, for campus and local newspapers which logically gave evidence why the United States should not be in Vietnam. This had been and remained his way: to work within the system for change.

When John traced the erosion of his relationship with Jeanne, it began with his transfer during his sophomore year at Cornell to prelaw at Columbia. Jeanne had mistakenly interpreted his act as budding radicalism, fostered by his involvement in both the civil rights and the more recent antiwar marches in Washington. Jeanne could not understand how anyone today could be politicized without being part of the radical left. Thus, the people in positions of power on campus that Jeanne admired, he thought self-serving and misguided. When he attended their "lectures" with her, he was bored by their rhetoric. They had fought bitterly when he said her so-called free thinkers were actually trapped by their own rather narrow views of freedom. It was either their way, John realized—which meant loosely structured but rigidly liberal—or no way at all. There was no middle ground. You either agreed or you were one of the pigs.

"Money is an evil, a tool of the system to control the masses." John J. understood how that was true in part but he also saw, as he pointed out to Jeanne, how money—her parents' money, loathed as it was—paid for her tuition and her student discount fare each summer to Europe. And her status symbol backpack filled with the bare necessities was also filled, he reminded her, with a thousand dollars in traveler's checks, all courtesy of the system's money. If you're going to renounce, John J. told Jeanne, it takes more than words.

To John J. money was a convenience and he felt no anger or guilt about the manner in which his parents earned it. His father's works were among the most lauded on campus; he was one of the established few thought to put his money where his mouth was. His mother was just a name to his peers. Few knew what she brought to her work, even that which was silly to her. His aunt was a heroine in certain campus circles. The more politicized women revered her position during the McCarthy years. The unpoliticized and the uninvolved revered her Minerva: Madame of Menace and never missed those Thursday nights when she guest-starred on "Batman."

By seven, John was standing in front of Teacher's where he had promised to meet Margaret. He enjoyed his bimonthly dinners with his aunt, although he wasn't sure how much he would enjoy this one as he knew what would be uppermost on Margaret's mind. As usual, she was prompt, the taxicab drawing up before the restaurant minutes after he had arrived. John J. could see the driver knew who Margaret was as he leaned over the partition to shake her hand, smiling in a way not often associated these days with cabbies.

She was wearing the mink she had received for being one of the first "legendary ladies" in a fur association's upcoming ad campaign and she looked warm but wrong for the West Side. The thickness of the coat was such that John could not feel Margaret when she hugged him to her. Instantly, she was recognized. The student body at Teacher's lifted their beers and booze to her and then, as one, gave her the Bronx cheer . . . raspberries, salutations fitting Minerva. Margaret bowed deeply and hissed back at her audience. John J. could see she was loving every minute of the attention and appreciating that the form it took was a tribute to her TV villainy.

Once seated in a booth of hard unupholstered wood, Margaret eased off the mink, although it never entirely left her body. The pale pink of her blouse matched the coloring of her cheeks. To John J.'s Heineken, she ordered a white wine. When the waiter had left, she tilted the green-shaded lamp hanging overhead toward John's face so she could study it.

"For a man who just ended a relationship, you look pretty good," she said. "Or are looks deceiving?"

"No, I'm okay. No hassle. I just need to find a new pad—you know, someplace to crash when I'm not staying with the folks."

"Another den of *inequity*, is what your mother would malappropriately say," said Margaret.

John laughed for it was true. His mother had never quite condoned his rather free living arrangement with Jeanne. She continued to think of it—although she never spoke of it—as living in sin. "Which is exactly how Jeanne viewed my staying with the folks—as living in sin. Jeanne saw luxury's lap as sinful. Did you ever think the day would come, Aunt Marg, when to be rich was to be a pig—something shameful?"

Margaret didn't respond immediately. "It's an extreme," she said finally. "Like all others, it will pass. It's relevant to the times. We're a society that is suddenly examining our haves and have-nots. I understand how many believe the haves have by misappropriation but what I fail to understand is why those who do not have feel they should be given whatever it is they lack just because they've been, or think they've been, denied it. I worked for what I got. I'm still odd and old-fashioned enough to believe that's how it should be. Perhaps I'm missing an important point but why should I feel guilty for what I have? Why should I make restitution to

584

any minority group? Out of fear? It's pure extortion . . . blackmail."

"Aunt Marg, I don't think it is you, the individual, they are talking about," said John. "It's the governments, the banks, the big business interests that have played Robin Hood. Only they've robbed the poor to give to the rich."

"I'm afraid we're heading for big trouble in this country," said Margaret. "Heading? How foolish. We're there. While the revolution continues, we now have another. Tell me, what will you do if you're drafted next year when you graduate?"

"I'll serve although I'll protest every inch of the way. But I don't believe it will come to that. I should get a student deferment until I finish law school and then let's hope this mess in Vietnam will be over."

"Have you decided yet which branch of law you're going to practice?" asked Margaret as she sipped the cold wine the waiter had just set before her.

"Right now I'm afraid the simplicity of my plans will sound grandiose. But I think I want to practice for the American Civil Liberties Union or the Legal Aid Society. Something that serves the people instead of just some small faction. What about you, Aunt Marg? I can't quite see you as Minerva: Madame of Menace forever."

"I know what I want. But whether I can get it is another story. Your mother and I have had several meetings with the Council on the Arts and quite a few foundations. I'd rather not be too specific now because depending on their largess, or lack of same, we will begin something new either on a fairly ambitious or somewhat modest scale. But it will involve youth and I'll be doing it for pleasure and peanuts rather than something as 'piggish' as money."

John J. beamed at his aunt. "You're too much. Too fucking much."

"No greater praise hath any man. And so eloquently put! Your mother would be so pleased. She would feel your eloquence is worth the fortunes she has spent on your education."

John laughed, happy under his aunt's adoring gaze. As she reached across the table to touch his cheek with one hand she produced a tiny gift-wrapped package with the other.

"Happy birthday, m'love! And so many, many more. It's not a little something so I won't say it is. Actually, it's a very big something and I wanted you to have it on the special occasion of turning twenty-one."

When John J. opened the box, he found gold ball cuff links. "They were James's. I want you to have them and I think he would have too. It doesn't really matter whether you like them or not—I mean it does; but it doesn't. What matters is: I want to give them to you, as I gave them to James on our fifth wedding anniversary."

John J. swallowed the lump in his throat. As he played with the heavy gold links, he said, "They're the real McCoy. Well, that's what they should be. They're you, aren't they?"

As the waiter took their dinner orders, Margaret said from behind a menu, "Tell me about Vinnie. I think it's best if we speak about him before the food arrives. How did you find him last weekend?"

"I didn't. I mean this time around he wasn't there to be found. He was really inside himself." As he saw his aunt's face change mood, John added: "The doctors explained it all for me very precisely. Vinnie's at his worst whenever he has a flashback, which is happening less and less, or when he is forced to confront himself or something in the past. Instead of dealing with his feelings, he runs from them. In his case, that means withdrawal . . . catatonia. Just as he used drugs to sedate his feelings, the doctors insist he's now using this withdrawal to avoid whatever churns within him. They're trying to grow him up. What that means," he continued as he saw the confused look on Margaret's face, "is they are trying to return him to that point in his childhood when his emotions, instead of being accepted or voiced, were denied. When he learns how to deal with these repressed feelings, relive them and deal with them in a different, more productive, fashion, the doctors feel he'll come out on the other side. And they do believe that, Aunt Marg."

"So tell me what else you did on your fabulous weekend in Hollywood," Margaret said, purposely moving the conversation away from what was always so disturbing.

John J. looked directly at Margaret and said, "Hang in, kid. He's going to make it."

Margaret nodded appreciatively but said nothing. To take up the slack in the conversation, John told Margaret about the Factory. "Or the Daisy. I'm not sure which. One once was where the other now is. Anyway, it's a private disco for celebs. Marti and I did the scene my second night in town.

586

You should have seen her. In a silver micro-mini and silver boots up to her knees and a hot pink handkerchief top! When she did the Funky Chicken, she *was* the Funky Chicken."

For what seemed like a long time, Margaret was silent. When she finally spoke, she was shaking her head as if to free it from disturbing thoughts. "I was somewhere back in the golden days of Hollywood," she said of her silence, "and I was trying to imagine Clark and Spence, Mae West and Garbo doing the Funky Chicken. And that I couldn't makes me firm in my belief that there is a God."

John J. laughed. "You really are okay, aren't you?"

Knowing what he meant Margaret replied, "Yes, I really am. So okay actually that the good doctor Dellarobe says it is pointless for me to continue with him. At least I think he said pointless although it may have been useless. Small difference so what difference?" Margaret said gaily. "I did my best, JJ, I truly did. Not only knowing but feeling that has saved my rather kicked-around ass. Yes, I could have been a better mother but I'm sure most mothers feel that. But he could have been a better son and I'm sure most mothers feel that way about their sons too. If I hurt—and it's fairly certain that I did—he also hurt me. Horribly. Talk about restitution or retribution—I have been paid back in full. The debt is cleared. I owe nothing. The anger is gone and with it the hate. What's left is my concern. Knowing he is in some kind of horrible pain pains me. I would do anything in my power to alleviate his pain except take it for myself. Which is what I think he has wanted. I love Vinnie. He is my son. I wish to God he was also my friend. Like you are. Maybe someday; maybe not. JJ, for the first time in my life I'm doing what I never believed was possible: I'm letting go. Letting go and letting God."

2

"I'm so fucking sick of your fucking silence, man. It really bugs me."

"Shit, Lettinger, why should you care if the dummy talks or not? It's no skin off your ass."

" 'Cause it sucks, Wheeler, and you know it. The goddamn guy sits around taking it all in and giving nothing back."

"What do you want Vinnie to give back or to say, Kyle?" asked Mike Greer, in response to Lettinger's attack on Vinnie.

The question, as intended, upset Lettinger, whose mother, a well-known political figure in California, seemingly had done her talking only to voters and special interest groups.

"Shit, Mike, the goddamn creep is always sucking up attention, always getting our fucking pity. For what? What the hell is he anyway? Just some burnt-out speed freak who killed a guy. Shit, if he were a nigger instead of a fucking celebrity, he'd have been locked up and the key thrown away."

"You're so full of shit sometimes, Kyle," said Florie Feingresher. "What the hell do you think you are—some underprivileged child? Your folks don't exactly live on skid row. And you, schmuck, took that silver spoon—you know, the one you were born with in your mouth—and shoved it up your nose. With cocaine. Face it, freak. None of us here are street niggers, although you sure do your best to talk like one."

"You know, Florie, sometimes you sound like someone's fucking mother," said Wheeler. "You run the same rap. How they gave me everything. They gave me shit. And you got the same thing. Every one of us here got royally fucked over, only you got royally fucked as well. And by your ole man."

Florie's face crimsoned. Although she herself had told the group of the sexual abuse that had begun when she was nine, unless she brought it into the discussion she became enraged when anyone else used it to whatever advantage.

"Would someone tell me what's going on here today?" demanded Sandy Shimon. "I mean, this is all bullshit. Why is everyone on everyone's back? What's going on?"

"What do you think is going on, Sandy?" asked Mike Greer softly. "In fact, why don't we all take a break—get into ourselves—and see if we can figure out what's going on."

As each member of the group reacted to his order, Mike Greer tried to decide if holding the group outdoors had been a mistake. Maybe they still needed the safety of an enclosure. But that had been his purpose—to introduce them to the outside world, even though it truly remained outside the grounds and gates of The Home. The end of therapy for these people would occur when they would feel safe to express their feelings any place, anywhere, rather than drown them in drugs or alcohol or behind a brick wall. Still, from all he had read in his clinical psychology course when completing his work on his Ph.D., many people in treatment—even those not—felt threatened outdoors.

Why was Lettinger so hostile this day? It couldn't be just the change of environment. Why wasn't this perfect spring day comforting to the group? Greer didn't have answers. He tried to recall his own internment in the rehab center ten years ago. How did he feel those first few times when he was given a new freedom? Resentful. That was it. Resentful. He had not wanted to grow up once he realized how neglected his childhood had been. And wasn't the point of therapy here at The Home "to grow" each already grown "child" into a mature adult?

"I don't like it out here," said Sandy Shimon, tears running down her face. "I think we should go inside where no one can hear us."

"What are you afraid someone might hear, Sandy?" asked Greer, knowing the answers.

"Her uglies, man," Lettinger said. "That's what she's afraid people will hear. She's got a problem with hostility."

"Listen, asshole, when I need a therapist I got one here so eighty-six your shrink number," replied the girl. "Sure I got a problem with hostility. You'd have one too if you grew up in a house where actions spoke louder than words."

Greer was watching Shimon's face hoping she would take yet another step toward the front door of The Home. In the past year, she had worked free of the depressions which she used to relieve with amphetamines and sex. She had been a battered child and teenager who was now more afraid of her own hostility and anger than those of others. When Shimon's rage would begin to surface and be expressed, she would be homeward bound. The same was true for all of the group members, Greer knew. Once their bottled-up rage was uncorked, unplugged, freed, they'd be likewise. But true to the textbooks, each resisted change and he, the therapist, was the enemy, the one who poked and prodded them into movement when complacency was often all they desired.

"Why don't we have a topic," suggested Wheeler. "We always do better with a topic. I suggest we discuss moving the group indoors and to hell with all this fresh air and sun."

"Everyone here who agrees, raise your hand," said Florie Feingresher, her hand already in the air. When all but Vinnie's hand waved in response, she said, "Majority rules. Let's go, Mike. Back into the dungeon."

"I would think all of you have been in enough dungeons—particularly the ones you've held yourselves in—to last a lifetime," said Greer.

"Now *that's* heavy," Lettinger said mockingly. "I mean, that's *really* heavy."

"That's so deep, Mike, that I think we should end the group right now. On that note," said Sandy. "In fact, I suggest we all head down to the pool for a swim."

"You know, Sandy, you got a real bug up your ass. You can never sit still," said Florie. "You always gotta be doing something. How come?"

Sandy looked about the grounds as if seeking an escape. "I'm going to be sick!" she said.

"No! You're not," Greer insisted.

"No, really, I'm going to throw up or scream."

"Neither, Sandy," commanded Greer. "They're both copouts. And you know it. Tell us how you feel. Right now. Sandy How do you feel?"

"Like a fucking firecracker about to go off. Mike, please," the girl pleaded. "That pressure is happening again. I can't breathe. I gotta do something—push-ups, swim. I can't stand it, Mike. Please. It hurts."

The girl was crying as was Florie Feingresher. Marcia Galente, a little farther along than Vinnie, was trembling. Each member of the group was reacting in his or her own way to a feeling they had all experienced and which they had sedated rather than feel. Lettinger, big, tough-talking, loudmouth Lettinger, reached out to touch Sandy's hand. "Shit, girl. Tell the motherfuckers to go fuck themselves."

Sandy Shimon, her face pale, her voice now a whisper, suddenly spoke. "They were crazy bastards. Nut cases. Bona fide crazies. Nobody in their right mind beats on a child. Nobody. A kid can't do anything to protect herself. There's no place to hide or to go. And my mother, she has to pretend it isn't happening and . . . oh God, I'm so frightened all the time. So frightened. She would buy me new dresses. Every day or every week new dresses to hide old and new bruises."

"Sandy, what did she buy you for the bruises inside, the ones that couldn't be covered by clothes even if they showed?" asked Greer quietly.

There was no response.

"Sandy," Greer tried again. "What did she give you for the pain . . . the real pain?"

"She gave me shit!" the girl exploded.

"Say it again only louder this time, Sandy," urged Greer.

"She gave me SHIT!" yelled the girl.

"Shit! Shit! Shit! Goddamn shitty shit-shit. Shit!"

The voice broke through the tension and the group's concentration. They looked, as if not believing what they had heard, at the man who seldom spoke, and when he did, never above a quiet monotone. Greer, acting as if nothing unusual had occurred, casually said, "What was shit, Vinnie?"

Greer noted the dilated eyes, the frenzied look, the bits of spittle at the corners of the man's mouth. "Vinnie, what was shit?" he repeated.

"Everything the bitch ever did. Everything. I got shit, shit, and more shit."

"How does that make you feel, Vinnie?" asked Greer.

Vinnie looked at Greer and then around at the group members. Suddenly he was on his feet as if to bolt. Again, Greer's words were flung at him. "How does it make you feel, Vinnie?"

"Bad," came the one-word response. And then came the tears followed by sobs, gut-wrenching sobs which only lost their audibility when Vinnie was surrounded by the arms of the members of the group who went to hold him.

Karen Kramer had sent a two-page outline and the transcript of the "Taylor tape," as it was now called, to five major book publishers, instructing each they had but one week to bid on

Marti Tiernan's *Those Who Wait*. Although no proof of Marti's ability to write was submitted by the agent, four of the five houses fought in six figures for the right to publish her book. Several facts made the bidding brisk: the book, interviews with family members of those who served in Vietnam, was timely; and, more important, Marti Tiernan was a "name" and not just any "name" but a huge one. Curiosity alone would sell her book. Combine that with strategic talk show appearances and an automatic best-seller was waiting in the wings. And if she couldn't write? There were editors who could, and slap-and-paste had produced many a celebrity's best-seller.

On March 31, the day Lyndon Johnson announced he would not seek another term in office, Marti Tiernan affixed her signature to a six-page document that said, in effect, that Grant & Lowe would publish if she could produce *Those Who Wait* by year's end. Publication would be nine months after completion of the manuscript, but privately the publisher hoped to have the book in the stores sooner to cash in on its timeliness. *Wait* was not considered a difficult book to do. Marti would meet with perhaps a dozen to fourteen families around the country and talk to them about the war, and the men and boys they had serving in it. It was expected Marti could accomplish each interview in four or five days and that transcripts of the tapes could be made even as she was interviewing her next subjects. Since the format was to be the simple question-and-answer technique popularized by *Playboy*, Marti and her editor, William Flannigan, would have little to do but organize and cut. As Flannigan had told the Grant & Lowe board of directors: "We can have this book typeset chapter by chapter and thus ready for publication within weeks of its completion."

Having done exactly as Karen Kramer instructed—arranged for her first interview prior to contract signing, which Kramer had insisted was a mere formality—Marti found herself in San Francisco April 1. Parting from Ali and Mark certainly was sweet sorrow, she told herself as the Western Airlines jet bounced her northward toward San Francisco. Although excited about beginning a book, *her* book, she had left the twins with considerable trepidation. Prior to Carolyn's arrival to baby-sit for the week, Marti had sat down with Ali and Mark and explained her new work and why it was taking her away. She could still remember their expression—a sort of bored "So?" Hadn't her work taken her away before?

Once settled at the Mark Hopkins, Marti drove her rented car to the Valleyview Housing Project where Bettylu Laitham lived. It was a neighborhood . . . of sorts, as was the area in which the Mark Hopkins stood firm, but they were disparate, sharing in common only their mailing address: San Francisco. As Marti parked, she was aware she had passed through many disparate neighborhoods in her life but until now had never really seen them.

In a two-bedroom apartment with cracked walls and faucets that continually dripped, leaving rust marks on otherwise scrubbed white sinks and bathtubs, Bettylu and her two children lived in stark, spotless simplicity. Both preschoolers, the children stayed most days at the project's child-care center when Bettylu did her day work, as she called it, a euphemism for cleaning house. Another job, this one full time each night from seven to two, paid the bulk of her rent and drained most of her patience and energy as she served the public at one of the better hotel restaurants in the city. As Bettylu explained, had it not been for the neighbors who "looked in" on the children when she was at work, she would be a welfare recipient, something she wanted no part of.

To work with Marti, Bettylu had arranged to do her "day work" mornings and talk with Marti in the afternoon. When first contacted, Bettylu had been "thrilled" to speak with Marti Tiernan, the movie star. And that Marti brought a taped message from her husband was just as thrilling. Later, when asked to be a chapter in Marti's book, Bettylu agreed readily because her ego was flattered. A chapter in *a* book that would be *a*bout her was more than she could resist.

By the second day of interviewing, Bettylu was resisting. By then, Marti Tiernan's glamour had worn thin as had Bettylu's patience and hospitality. And why? "Because, girl, you haven't any idea how it's going down out there for black folks." When Marti replied simply: "Tell me," Bettylu did; not in the Tiernan tongue but in street talk purposely chosen by Bettylu for its shock effect and the distance it maintained between her and Marti.

Did Marti know that proportionately more blacks were drafted than whites despite the fact that there were far more whites of draft age than there were blacks? Did Marti know that the front lines in Vietnam proportionately had more black boys than white? Was Marti aware that white boys got deferments because they were in college? And does Marti believe, as so many Americans seem to, that this is right—that those in the process of being educated are of more value than those who are not? And wasn't that discriminatory—or hadn't Marti thought of that—since everyone knows "us black folks don't get us no education as we be too poor or too damn dumb to make the grade—so to speak. So we go fight a war while the young massas play at home . . . in the schoolyard. It does seem like, doesn't it, Miss T., that our black boys ain't worth a whole lot to this country since they be sent off to be killed. But! They be worth something to us. They *are* our most precious natural resource."

The questions that poured out of Bettylu along with her anger Marti recorded but did not answer. On the eve of the last day of interviewing, Bettylu demanded Marti call her sister-in-law in Gainesville, Georgia. "If you want to know how some of us feel, talk to one who has given and lost."

Clarrysa Browne spoke in a soft Southern voice with none of the anger audible in Bettylu's diction and choice of words. She had been on her job, working as a companion to an arthritic elderly woman, when her sister arrived unannounced accompanied by a white man in a business suit. Instantly, Clarrysa understood without being told. She had already begun screaming when the man, from some local government office, was saying how sorry he was. Her screams caused the professor whose mother she was caring for to ask her to leave "because your personal affairs do not belong in my home."

Clarrysa Browne took a deep breath before speaking again. "They sent my Randy home in a box. A plain box. Soon—I don't remember how soon—they sent me a check for ten thousand dollars. Insurance, I guess. Must be required 'cause I know the government don't give black folks nothing it don't have to. Now some might think that be mighty generous and maybe it is but I don't feel all that grateful. I mean . . . how do they come up with a price tag on my husband's life? Who decides? And is it the same for everybody? I mean I can't help wondering if white mamas and wives get the same or more. I know it can't be less. But why ten thousand dollars? Why not ten hundred thousand? Randy was twenty-three. If he had been twenty-two, would I have gotten eleven thousand dollars? I mean does the price go up or down as one ages? My papa says it's all hush money but it don't seem to have had a hushing effect on me. I don't know if Bettylu told you or not but I got a two-year-old son. He's got a dead daddy and a check—*we* got a check—that's supposed to have paid for his daddy's life. I sure hope he thinks so when he gets older or he sure be likely to be one angry and mean child."

Marti was still shaken when she reached Bettylu's apartment the next afternoon but from the moment Bettylu opened the door, Marti saw her own upset was nothing to that of Bettylu's.

Marti's "What's wrong?" brought a look of such hatred that Marti felt personally threatened. As Bettylu tumbled into a chair, she pointed to the TV screen. As she stood watching, Marti, in seconds, understood. When she tried to reach out to Bettylu, her hand was slapped away.

"You're going to kill us all, one by one," she said. "Each and every one of us. But why him? Why Martin?" asked Bettylu, her eyes brimming with tears. "Why a man who told us that fighting and killing will accomplish nothing more than still more fighting and more killing."

"Maybe Martin was killed . . ."

"Don't you *dare* call him Martin!" screamed Bettylu. "He's *Dr*. King to you. Do you hear?"

"Maybe that's why Dr. King was killed . . . because his political position was ultimately more threatening than militancy."

Bettylu turned her stricken face toward Marti. "Sometimes it's so hard to see, to hear, who is really there talking to you. You just can't see or hear beyond the color of the person's face," she said as she cried. "And sometimes it's so damn hard not to want to hurt back."

When Marti returned home, she played the tapes for her father and then read him Clarrysa Browne's words. She wanted to know if there was truth to the women's accusations and became angry when John would not say yes or no. Instead, he turned on the tape recorder and made Marti listen again. "What's important is what's here, *on tape*. You have successfully captured the feelings of two women. In one respect it doesn't matter whether or not their words are totally or only in part or not at all true. That they believe them to be true is what's important, is what will shape or disfigure this country. This should be the point of your book," said John with a passion that stirred her.

* * *

595

At six-forty-five, Carolyn was awakened by an unobtrusive voice that bid her "Good-morning, this is Tuesday, April thirtieth, the temperature is forty-four degrees, and you are tuned to Radio WINS in New York City." Reluctantly, Carolyn kicked off the bedcovers and staggered barefoot toward the kitchen for the coffee John would have made before leaving for NBC and his guest appearance on the "Today" show. It seemed to Carolyn that John was doing far more political commentary than documentaries for K.O. Productions. An inside governmental source had told John his CIA dossier had him down as an undesirable. Another said the word had been spread to the network heads by those close to LBJ that John be "phased out" of their programming plans. Yet, since April 1, "Today" had asked John to appear twice: the first time, shortly after Johnson announced his decision not to run, and now, as the student demonstrations at Columbia ended their first week. John was a good guest, Carolyn had to acknowledge, as he certainly spoke his mind, but she often wished he was less honest because the mail his opinions drew was often threatening. She was eager to hear what he would say today.

By the electric coffee maker, neatly folded in half, was the morning *Times*. Its headline shocked Carolyn out of her still semisleepy state.

1000 POLICE ACT TO OUST STUDENTS FROM FIVE BUILDINGS AT COLUMBIA: MOVE IN AT UNIVERSITY'S REQUEST

Gripping the paper with a tense hand, Carolyn's eyes flew over the copy.

A handpicked force of 1000 policemen moved onto the Columbia University campus early today and began ordering student demonstrators out of five buildings the students have occupied in a tense week-long protest.

Tense, indeed, thought Carolyn, and the situation didn't need police to make it even more so. As she read on, her heartbeat quickened as her hands grew cold.

As the hour for the police assault approached, tension mounted sharply on campus as groups of students held

596

informal meetings. At 1:45 A.M. when word reached the Mathematics Building

Oh, my God! My dear, dear God!

that "a bust" or police raid was imminent, student demonstrators began strengthening their barricades and girding themselves for the assault.

The newspaper fell to the kitchen floor as Carolyn's hand flew to her mouth. Her brief, sharp cry frightened Mickey, now at home in the East, as he sat in his usual place under Carolyn's chair at the kitchen table. Carolyn rushed to the telephone but once there didn't know whom to call. In her bedroom, she tore through her closet looking for clothes to wear. But to wear where? To see whom? To do what?

Frightened and frustrated, Carolyn collapsed on the floor of her walk-in closet. "God, please," she prayed, "tell me what to do. It is my son who is locked in up there, and I'm scared, dear Lord. I'm scared."

On May 1, after three trying weeks of asking questions of herself and of others not directly concerned with the book, Marti stood in William Flannigan's office. She had just come from the hospital where JJ was recuperating from the concussion he had suffered when a policeman's club battered him senseless onto the ground. Marti had been shocked when she heard from her mother that her brother was one of those involved in the riots at Columbia. JJ with his button-downs and his medium-length hair, always washed and brushed into a casual style, hardly looked or acted the revolutionary type. In fact, she knew him to be a moderate, or as moderate as a campus liberal could be.

Although she still didn't understand all the issues, Marti could see and so understand the police brutality that had been involved. That was not pardonable. On her first visit to see JJ he had explained why he had been there in protest. It seemed, or at least it did according to JJ's research, that Columbia was one of twelve universities performing secret research for the Pentagon, and that, he was most insistent, was reprehensible for a place of learning. There should never be governmental interference in higher education. What gross manipulation was taking place? JJ had asked. Then, too, how could a university be insensitive to the neighborhood in which it was situated? How dare they plan to build a new gymnasium when Harlem needed new *everything* essential to basic human survival? Other issues, like the students' right to restructure the university, Marti could not understand, but it had not taken special understanding to react with horror to the seven hundred uniformed men who even Mayor John Lindsay said "used excessive force" to subdue children . . . students.

With so much to understand and with so little understanding, Marti told William Flannigan that there was a larger, more comprehensive book to be done: one that would seek the reactions of scores or perhaps hundreds of Americans to the issues confronting the country today. Yes, the book would include the Bettylu Leithams but it would also include those who fought both actively and passively for and against the war. It was to be a book of "whys and hows and what do you really think about X, Y, and Z. This book," Marti explained, "would be titled *A House Divided: A War Within*, and it would seek, by means of a nonscientific sampling, to reveal the kind of nation we are, in our schisms and unities."

William Flannigan was impressed by Marti's passion. She was obviously someone whose awareness, and lack of same, had been aroused, and that could change a "movie-star book" to a worthwhile document with every bit of the sales potential of the former. Even more. Which is why Flannigan had the contract amended within twenty-four hours, with a new expense budget affixed so that Marti could travel the length and breadth of the country.

A week later, using JJ's contacts, Marti was in a small Canadian province talking to several boys who had fled the draft. From there she drove down to Detroit where she spoke with auto workers and others of the blue-collar class. It was not easy. To many, she was a slumming movie star. To others, she was the daughter of that fink whose anti-Vietnam-war talk was traitorous. It often took Marti several days just to be "a regular person."

On the road or in the air through most of the spring and early summer, Marti was lonely, although exhilarated much of the time. Her nightly phone calls to Ali and Mark helped yet hurt. Hearing their voices and encouraging them to speak their minds alleviated her anxiety about their well-being but it also accentuated her sense of aloneness and . . . guilt. Now she knew firsthand how Margaret must have felt so many years ago entrusting the care of her child to others.

Summer was better. With school out, Marti rented a trailer and packed Ali, Mark, and Miss Jennings into it. Throughout July, they saw America while she talked with it. At the end of the month, ten pounds lighter but feeling so much heavier from thoughts and feelings she had yet to sift and sort through, she returned to Trancas for a week's rest. Some of the transcribed tapes were waiting for her. In the evenings, after Ali and Mark were asleep, Marti read and edited them, seeing to her amazement that her book was taking shape on its own.

The day after her return, Marti drove to Santa Barbara to meet with Mike Greer, with whom she had been in constant touch throughout her touring, and to have lunch with Vinnie, whom she had also spoken with from various points in America. Vinnie was doing well, Greer assured her, making slow but steady progress now. He was sustaining two one-on-one therapy sessions per week and Greer hoped to increase it to three, and then four, as soon as he felt Vinnie's ego-strength was such that he could not only tolerate but support it.

Marti thought Vinnie looked worse, not better, and Greer agreed, explaining: "As the patient begins to really feel rather than repress, he feels worse, not better. The material, after all, is painful. Not until a patient comes to the other end of the tunnel does 'better' or 'feeling good' become the norm."

Vinnie, explained Greer, was first remembering his recent past, his excesses and his losses. He was reacting painfully to what he was finally acknowledging had been a painful adult life. Because he was still resisting an exploration of his childhood, Vinnie still had little understanding of the whys. But he was taking care of himself, assuming responsibility for his body, his feeding, and his room. It was not, however, advisable that Margaret visit yet. When informed of Greer's opinion, Margaret, appearing downtown at the Ahmanson Theatre as Alexandra Del Lago in *Sweet Bird of Youth,* was accepting and simply said, "When he's ready, I'm ready."

When Greer took Marti to see Vinnie, he acted angry. As the three walked to the dining room, Vinnie refused to talk until Greer said, "Cut the crap, Vinnie. Instead of acting like a rejected kid, why don't you just tell Marti you missed her and that you're pissed off she went away and left you."

"Are you going again?" asked Vinnie hostilely.

"I must—got another couple weeks of interviewing in the

Southeast," Marti replied. When Vinnie's face hardened, Marti exploded: "Dammit, Vinnie, I miss you too but it makes me mad as hell that you're so goddamn nonunderstanding and self-involved. I have a job to do. Why can't you just plain accept that instead of punishing me with that face of yours, 'cause frankly, I don't need any more accusatory looks. I see them every time I look in the mirror or at my own children. So stop it!"

And Vinnie did. When they lunched together, he evinced interest in her work and asked questions that surprised her by their incisiveness. He had not known about JJ's concussion and was annoyed it had been withheld from him, particularly by JJ himself, who had visited during the summer. What was he, asked Vinnie, a child who couldn't be told the truth? The question created a tension until Vinnie broke it with: "Yeah, I guess that describes a certain part of me." Although he made no mention of the events leading up to his placement in The Home, Marti could see Vinnie was better. Later, she asked Greer whether Vinnie could slip back again and was distressed to hear that he could; that in fact, she should expect it and therefore not be upset when it happened.

When Marti left on the last leg of her touring, Margaret volunteered to baby-sit on one condition: "That when your mother joins me in midmonth following her musical debut on the Kenley circuit in *The Sound of Music* she will not be allowed to wear a nun's habit in this house, or to once, once I say, tell me to climb every mountain or fjord every stream."

Assured that the children would be in "good if somewhat strange hands," Marti put her energies to the remainder of her work. From Louisiana on to Arkansas and into Kentucky, and finally Illinois, she questioned, the people answered, and she absorbed—often more than her tape recorder. By the time she had reached Chicago on August 25 for a brief reunion with her father before flying home to California, she was exhausted, physically, mentally, and emotionally. Suddenly she would have fits of inexplicable weeping. John understood, although he said nothing as he comforted her. They were lunching in John's room at the Drake when Marti tried to sort through her feelings.

"It's all been too much, too fast. I feel engorged with words—other people's words; other people's feelings—and mine are undefined. I just seem to hurt all over without knowing why."

"Don't you think that is exactly how many people feel?" asked John. "Do you really think people have been able to digest and define how they feel about first Dr. King's assassination and then Robert Kennedy's? Do you think they can assimilate these student riots, make heads or tails out of the issues involved when many are blinded by the beards and beads, externals that are threatening because they are new? And the war. Who understands this war clearly, without equivocation? People are confused, Marti. Perhaps more so than at any other time in history."

"And I'm mirroring their confusion and my own, although so many seem so certain of what they believe," Marti said. "There are those who passionately, fervently, believe in America and the American Way of Life. They are not politicians mouthing rhetoric, Dad, but people; some quite poor and others quite plain and still others like the vast majority, who believe 'My country, right or wrong.' They love what they believe America stands for. They cannot understand anyone dodging the draft or refusing to fight for their country. So many of these people are so touching. They mean nobody any harm. And the others, those who are angry, those who believe 'America: love it or leave it!'—don't understand that the American Way which they protest they love is rooted in dissent. And still others, not like you, not like me, truly feel war sometimes is a necessary means to an end. They stand firm in a belief that we, as a nation, must stand firmly someplace, sometime, against the threat of worldwide communism. And they see that time as now and that place as Vietnam.

"Listen to this," Marti said suddenly, jumping up to where her tape recorder lay on the bureau by her shoulder bag. "It takes just a second but listen."

The *on* button first brought a silence and then static. Finally, a young male voice said without emotion: "Well, even if I do lose my arm, I don't see it as all that big a deal. I mean, my family gets crazy when they see me. But I'm not sorry. I mean I'd hate to lose my arm but I'm not sorry about having gone over there. As I see it—and I did see it!—if the commies take over in Nam, they'll keep right on taking over. They gotta be stopped somewhere."

John's sole response was: "Will he lose his arm?" To which Marti nodded her head up and down, signifying he would.

Later, after dinner, this time in Marti's room, she was

again groping for an understanding of what she had seen and heard. "Throughout the country, people label the ills as 'drugs' or too much sexual freedom, too much violence on television, a breakdown of the family. No one seems to connect them, seems to see they are all interrelated. No one wants to realize there is a breakdown in this so-called American Way so many hold so dear. It is not working, and Dad, I find that so sad. Why is it we all, me included, affix labels to people which instead of helping to identify only act to separate us from one another? It's black or white, Christian or Jew, rich or poor, straight or gay. Always a label. Always a separation by externals. But Dad, in talking with people, I saw no matter what their obvious differences, fundamentally, they are the same in that people want to live peacefully and with some sense of dignity, hope, and worth."

Again Marti was crying and again it was without any real knowledge of why. John had drawn his chair closer to hers and dimly she heard him say, "Marti, I think you are seeing for the first time how very difficult it is for people to have such very simple and very basic needs fulfilled when it should be so easy."

In a sentence, John had crystallized for Marti much of what she had been feeling. She now understood why he was so much in demand as a speaker on college campuses and also why he was reviled by the many who thought him "anti" when he was actually "for"—but for the people rather than for any particular labeled system.

"It's going to get worse before it gets better, Marti. The wounds will not only grow deeper, but they'll fester, become infected and the poison will spread before they heal."

A few days later, as she sat on her patio, one eye watching the twins playing on the beach, the other on the portable television that sat on a glass-topped table, Marti watched as her father, a guest commentator, described the rioting that had just taken place inside and out of the Chicago convention center where Democrats were nominating a candidate to run opposite Richard Nixon for President. In "living color," Marti saw how much worse things could get as the Chicago police billy-clubbed the dissidents, pummeling them into bloodied dispersion and impotence. This was not the American Way, she decided and then thought: Or is it? Is this what it has become?

It was with pieces of her puzzled mind still missing that

Marti put the twins in the car and drove to Rancho Santa Fe to do what Thomas had suggested almost a year ago at Udorn in Thailand: speak with Reese about the war—his, hers, and theirs.

Cupping the glass with her hands, hoping to stifle whatever noise the ice cubes might make as they clinked against the crystal, Reese slowly raised the glass to her lips and sipped. As she looked down at her sleeping husband, tears as hot as the vodka was cold ran down her face. She had been awakened by his trembling which shook the bed as well as her. It had only ceased, as had his very faint whimpers, when she had covered his body with her own.

Suddenly, Reese was sobbing, ashamed for not being "the good little soldier" and angry that she was asked to be that. As her own trembling began, she wanted to scream in frustration at her sleeping husband: "Hold me! Stop me from being frightened." Instead, she sipped still more from her glass. What could he say? What would he do? He had already said it all when he had once again extended his tour of duty for another year without consulting her. Another year of active duty. Active for him. For her? But then, that was part of being a good little soldier.

She had made one demand when she learned of his extension: that this time, unlike the others, they spend one week of his month-long leave without the children. She needed time alone with him. At first he had objected, wanting the family to be together, but he relented when he heard her determination. She met him at the Royal Hawaiian Hotel in Honolulu, the last week in January; her parents baby-sat with the children. From day one, her fantasy of a romantic interlude was shattered. They were no longer those two kids from Boston or Bartow. He was a Captain in the Air Force. A tired Captain. At first, she thought the extra pounds she had gained—what was there to do when there was nothing to do except eat?—made her unattractive to him. He slept; she dozed. He ate voraciously; she nibbled. He swam in the ocean; she waded. And then, almost miraculously, as the creases in his face disappeared, he reappeared, devouring her not just with passion but with love. He held her as though she might slip through and out of his life. She had loved his loving her; loved his needing her, and loved him as she always had. Everything was idyllic until their last day in the lush suite at the hotel. He noticed her taking a pill and asked about it. She was surprised, not by his asking, but by her carelessness. Or was it intentional? Had she wanted him to know she was practicing birth control? Had she hoped that would lead to the discussion she so much wanted to have? If so, she was only partially successful as they left Hawaii angry with each other but unable to talk because the plane was waiting. So were their children, who were as anxious to see their father as he was eager to see them.

It was only after they had been home a few days and the excitement of being a family again had worn off that Reese realized they had not talked. Not at all. Except . . . he trembled; she held. He whimpered; she held. They made love; he climaxed. She understood he needed time, time to heal himself before he could help her heal whatever was hurting her. Her and the children.

Her glass empty but not her mind, Reese found her way in the dark down the stairs to the living room where she poured herself another shot from the Smirnoffs bottle, adding a single cube from the fridge at the wet bar.

"I wish you'd stick to sherry."

Thomas's voice startled her. The glass fell to the Formica bar, breaking in half.

"How long have you been drinking vodka?" he asked as he tied the belt on his robe about his waist.

"I do not have a drinking problem if that's what you're implying," said Reese archly. "You know I only drink wine and only at dinner. It's when I can't sleep that I take some vodka. It's better than a pill."

As soon as the word was out, spoken, thrust between them, Reese knew they were going to talk. As she mopped up the spill from her broken glass, Thomas fixed her another drink and one for himself. He took his scotch and water to the Barcalounger she had bought him as a homecoming present. He knew it was a gift of love as it was the sole distortion in a carefully furnished room of antiques and Early American reproductions. When he was settled in, he patted his lap, designating that she should sit there. Suddenly, she was aloft, floating above the room, as he tilted the chair back and up. It was the most relaxed she had felt in days and suddenly, her face was again awash with tears. He stroked her head and her hair much the way a mother would to comfort her child.

"I am not a good soldier and I'm sick of pretending that I

am," she began in explanation. "I pretend for the children but I hate pretending. Thomas, you should have consulted me before you extended your tour of duty. Marriage is a partnership."

"I had to do this, Reese," Thomas said quietly.

"I don't think I can handle it anymore, Thomas. It's killing me. The worry. The constant worry. I wake up, it's there. Center forehead. I go to sleep. It's there. It's always there. In the middle of my mind I see you. And God help me, *how* I see you! It's always in flames or dead.

"I tell myself to keep busy," said Reese, wiping her tear-streaked face on the sleeve of her bathrobe. "So I do. Take the kids to school. Clean the house. Take Kelly to the playground. Make lunch. Pick up the kids at school. Have a snack. Play with the kids. Make dinner. Watch TV. This is your life, Reese Tomlinson.

"Mother says to get out more. Where? Some of the neighbors occasionally do invite me to dinner. Most don't. I'm the extra person no one knows what to do with. They can't invite a 'date' and they can't discuss the war, God knows, not with the way some people feel. To most around here, I'm a reminder of something unpleasant. And what's so awful, to me, is that they are a reminder of something that was . . . *is* so pleasant. Us. A home. A husband and wife. A family.

"Thomas, when I see a couple, a husband and wife, I feel so jealous, so bitter, that I usually have to look the other way. Why isn't he serving? Why isn't she alone when I am? Awful thoughts that make me feel like an awful person. Thomas, it's so hard being alone," she said, free of tears, her eyes now looking directly into his as her head rested on his shoulder.

"Reese, don't you think I know that?" Thomas said quietly. "I'm alone every day."

"But that's *your* choice. *Yours!* It's what you have chosen to do to yourself. And to me," she said, angry again.

Thomas turned his face away from hers. "Yes, you've made your point. My choice, although my heart tells me I have no choice—that this is something I must do. But let me .ell you something, Reese, none of that makes my choice any easier. Yes, I believe in what I am doing but that doesn't make it any less painful to be ignored by my own men. They can't see me as me. To them, I'm their flight leader, their protector. Big Daddy. They need that. It gives them courage but it isolates me. The buck stops here," said Thomas as he poked his chest

605

with his finger. "You have your mother, Reese. Someone to talk with. And let me tell you, someone is better than no one."

"I'm too angry to feel sorry for you," spat Reese. "You should have consulted me. More important: you should have considered the children. Don't look away. And don't you dare tell me this is all for the children. Tell them that when they have nightmares. Go ahead. Tell them that after Kristan has seen the TV news and is too young to understand you're not in every plane that's shot down. Tell that to your son who is without a father on father-and-son day in Cub Scouts. You know what his father is to him? A tape that comes once every ten days or two weeks in which your voice tells him to study, walk straight, compete, and be good. 'Take care of everybody,' you tell him. Dammit Thomas, he's a child. We should be taking care of him; not him, us! I think your son equates your commands with love. And your darling Kelly. She didn't even know who you were when you walked through the door. And she needs to know. Thomas," pleaded Reese, "look at how you felt about your father for putting his beliefs before you."

"It's not the same," protested Thomas, "and you know that, Reese."

"But a child doesn't. Nor can a child assimilate the pros and cons he or she hears at school about our 'involvement' —that's the word they use now, Thomas—in Vietnam. A child only knows that some of his friends' parents think you're one of the bad guys. They ask me questions and I try to explain but lately I seem to have lost the answers myself. And I'm so afraid they pick up on my resentment or my fear. Oh, God, Thomas! Sometimes when I see other fathers playing with their children, I just start to cry. It comes over me and I can't control it and I know it frightens the children. But Thomas, they . . . you . . . are missing out on so much. Sometimes—I can't help this, Thomas—sometimes I think how will I manage if you get killed. How will I? How will they?"

"Is that why you're on the pill?"

"Why else? You know what my religion has meant to me. But the conflict between the pill and bringing another child into this world who might be fatherless was no contest. The pill won hands down. And God will forgive me. He will understand. I cannot have a baby by myself! I can hardly

606

stand being my own baby myself. And Thomas, it is by myself. Slowly but surely, these new words are taking on new meanings. The hawks are being chased by the doves and that frightens me because I know you and I know me, and we're not hawks. We're people! It frightens me, I tell you. Everything frightens me and I can't understand how I can be so afraid and you're not."

Thomas pushed her off his lap so abruptly as he stood that had he not grabbed her arm, Reese would have fallen.

"Are you crazy? Are you fucking crazy?" he yelled at her.

"Thomas! Shush! You'll wake the children."

"I don't give a shit. Maybe you should awaken them so they can hear this. Are you out of your head, Reese? Not afraid? What do you think I am—some kind of fucking psycho? I'm scared shitless every goddamn day out there and for better reasons than you, because no one I know of ever got killed by worry. In case you've forgotten, I'm the one who could get blown to bits. I'm the one that if taken by the enemy could come back in a basket. No. Strike that. Given what I've seen, make that several baskets. One for each piece they cut off, bit by bit, or to be blunt . . . piece by piece.

"Now *you* look at *me*, Reese," Thomas commanded. "Don't you think I know the best years of my life are passing me by? Don't you think I know whereas you and I can make up the time we've lost, I can never make it up with the children. They grow, they change, and I miss out on both. It hurts. Everything hurts. Okay? You understand. It hurts that I, Big Brave Captain Thomas Ollson, am afraid. It hurts that some of my men die. It hurts that I've learned to hate; hate people I only see from the sky. I never thought I could kill somebody. Not ever. God knows, you, who know me better than anyone ever has or ever will, know the idea of killing is horrible to me. But, Reese, when you're over there, and it's kill or be killed, you kill. It's incredible but we do have this instinct to shoot when someone shoots at us.

"And you know what's the worst, Reese?" asked Thomas as tears began to spill onto his cheeks. "The water buffaloes. That's right, you heard me," said Thomas as he looked at the amazement on Reese's face. "The water buffaloes. No one ever tells you about the animals you have to kill. The water buffaloes carry the cannons for the enemy. We fly in low over them, bombing or firing, and they explode. A head here, a limb there. Pieces of buffalo everywhere. They never have a

607

chance because they don't know about enemies and running for cover. And that gnaws at you. But you know what gnaws even worse, Reese? That you care more about the water buffaloes that you've killed than the enemy, some of whom are boys no older than fourteen, fifteen, even twelve, Reese. How do you hate, let alone kill, a boy of twelve even though you know he would kill you with that rifle in his hand?"

Reese went to Thomas. As she wrapped her arms about him from behind, she laid her head on his back.

"Some days, Reese, the only thing that gets me through is you."

She turned him around so they could cling to each other. She felt his chest heave as he cried from within.

"Then why, Thomas?" she asked. "Please, tell me again. Why?"

"Because with all my heart I believe if we don't fight it here, right here and now in Nam, we will have to fight it somewhere else someday soon. The times it gets the hardest is when you realize you and just a handful of others know that. Reese, we're losing lives daily and losing face and who knows, maybe even losing this war. And it's so frustrating. If only they would let the military fight the war, it would end. Quickly. But it's the businessmen and the politicians that are running this war from behind their desks and none of them seems to realize if you're going to be in a war, you might as well have an all-out war or else all of this terrible dying is for nothing. Nobody likes war. Oh, God, Reese, how I hate it. You'd have to be a psycho not to. But if you get into one, you should try to win it as quickly as possible. Otherwise there's just no sense to any of it.

"But that's what's so goddamn crazy—what makes you think maybe it's your marbles that have gotten scrambled—half your country disagrees with you and so you're only getting half the supplies, support, and help you should."

"Then get out, Thomas. Please. Get out!" implored Reese.

"I can't. I just can't. I know how to live with fear, Reese. I've learned that. But I don't know how to live without honor. And it is honorable that we be—that I be—in Vietnam. For all of our sakes. I need you to understand that, Reese," Thomas said as he clutched Reese to him. "Oh, God," he moaned, "I just plain need you."

* * *

To break the silence that lay as heavy in the car as the enchiladas and tacos she had just eaten lay on her stomach, Marti turned on the radio. As if on cue, Dionne Warwick was insisting she'd never fall in love again.

"That comes right to the point, doesn't it?" asked Mike as the song continued. "You ever gonna fall in love again, Marti?"

"Don't act smart with me," cautioned Marti. "It would be taking unfair advantage for one thing as I'm rendered helpless by heartburn. Calling those things *hot* tamales is an understatement."

"You eat too much and you're getting fat," Greer said, not unkindly but as a statement of fact.

"Listen, Greer, this isn't one of your encounter groups where everyone is encouraged to 'talk straight.' Sometimes a little lie can be a lotta kindness. Honesty isn't always all it's cracked up to be," she added, feigning an annoyance she was not feeling. She had gained weight—the ten pounds she had previously lost plus five. "It's nerves," she said in defense. "If you had a book coming out in a week or so, you'd be a wreck too."

"Shit, with all the editing I helped you do, I feel as if I do have a book coming out in a week," said Greer. "I was a goddamn midwife for chrissakes."

"Yes, you were," agreed Marti, reaching out with her hand to pat his thigh. Taking one hand off the wheel, Greer caught hers and placed it firmly on his thigh, and when both his hands were not required on the wheel, he covered hers with his own.

Marti leaned back in the bucket seat, closed her eyes, and tried the impossible: not to think about The Book or her relationship with Mike Greer. Both were upon her; the book looming as this "thing" that could destroy and devastate. She often wondered why she had never felt so about any performance in any film she had made. Not even her father's insistence that all authors suffer from such prepublication anxieties helped. Nor did the fact that *A House Divided* was a Literary Guild selection.

Since completing her work on The Book, Marti had had little patience to read the scripts that had piled up on her desk. Her agents habitually hammered home the point that her career would not withstand yet another year's layoff from the screen. She couldn't seem to care. Margaret told her this was normal and that she should make no decision until she was well rested. However, with her anxieties either awakening her or keeping her awake, Marti was constantly tired. And like Margaret once did, she had begun to feed her frenzies; something she hoped would end when The Book made its appearance and was either well received or rejected.

Which was sort of how she imagined Mike Greer was feeling in regard to her. Although he had not said anything, she felt pressed as if he wanted a commitment. Life was easier, thought Marti, although nowhere near as much fun, when Greer was just Vinnie's therapist and friend during those more and more frequent times when Vinnie was capable of friendship. Greer was only two years older than Marti but often seemed much younger. His sense of fun and play was greater than hers. Actually, when she thought about it, it was greater than anyone's except her aunt's. Had there not been the traces of scars on his wrists, she would have thought he was one of the fortunates; one of those born happy and whose life had remained that way.

That was not the Mike Greer case history, although his early years had been idyllic as the only child to a happy couple who became increasingly unhappy as he got older. Their divorce came as a surprise to no one except him. He was twelve and was not consulted but he saw his father every weekend and during the summers when his mother would "take tours." He never understood what a tour was until she came home with a husband. A year later, his father remarried. At fifteen, he had half-sisters and half-brothers and felt like a "fifth wheel"—unwanted by both parents, a bad reminder of what once had been. Jealous and resentful, he began "getting a buzz with booze" but was happy to graduate to hard drugs as they didn't "hurt the head or the stomach." By sixteen, he was "hitting on and hustling Hollywood Boulevard, selling my ass—which is really selling your soul—to get high." He kicked around and was kicked around the Beverly Hills circuit, "performing" at house parties until he found himself one night at the Tropicana Motel on Santa Monica Boulevard with "five hundred dollars in my pockets but nothing else. I mean . . . I had nothing else. Inside and out."

It was then he slit his wrists.

Later, at a rehab center similar in style to that of Synanon, he was made to realize, although he never could remember, that it was *he* who picked up the phone in that motel room and asked the switchboard operator for help. Which he received. On his twentieth birthday, he completed his continuation courses and graduated from high school. His father, well connected, "helped" him into UCLA where he worked nights at various low-paying—but paying, nonetheless—jobs and days at his studies. He graduated cum laude and was accepted into graduate school without difficulty. His father continued to assist him financially although he helped himself by parking cars at the Cock & Bull, just toward the end of the Strip leading into Beverly Hills. There he saw many of his former clients although they never saw him. Nor did his mother. As she had divorced his father, so she had divorced herself from him. Like Vinnie, his mother had been at the eye of his inner storm. Unlike Vinnie, he had allowed that storm to blow itself out. He had followed her one day into the Hamburger Hamlet in Westwood Village and in the middle of her ever-so-dainty consumption of her bacon/cheeseburger, he took aim and unloaded his verbal rifles. She sat there dripping ketchup on her plate and the tablecloth. The sight of that made him laugh. She looked ridiculous. But she *was* ridiculous, he remembered telling himself then, and it hadn't been worth making himself seem equally so to the onlookers just for the momentary high. "Revenge feels sweet . . . for about a minute and a half. And then it's gone and a part of you has gone with it," he had told Marti.

Marti had realized at the time Mike Greer told "my story," he was committing himself to something she wasn't sure she wanted but wasn't sure she did not. When she tried to recall exactly when they had begun to "formally date," she couldn't. Perhaps they never had. He had become a frequent visitor on Sundays, usually arriving late for supper and then driving Vinnie back to Santa Barbara that night, thus saving her the time the following morning to work on The Book. Vinnie enjoyed his company, as did she. Mike Greer had the happy facility to make them talk and make them laugh. He often seduced Vinnie into talk of the past where his remembrances were verified, or challenged, by Marti's. She found it fascinating to see how two people could go through the exact same experiences but have totally different reactions to it. She remembered Margaret as *there*, truly *there*, at every important moment in their lives. Vinnie had obliterated any such memories.

Vinnie was now in therapy three times a week but not with

Mike. "It's more important he has me as a friend," Greer explained. "Besides, I'm too emotionally involved." When he said that, Marti did not respond although she knew Greer was referring more to his involvement with her than with Vinnie. Nor did she respond in any way whatsoever when Greer began staying over Sundays so as to avoid the long drive at night back to Santa Barbara. Somehow, what she remembered, was that it had seemed right, nice, having a man in the house. She could not recall exactly when he was not only in her house but in her bed. Just that it had gradually graduated to that and that, too, had seemed right, nice. It wasn't so much the sex, although that was certainly as satisfying as she had ever known it to be, but the sleeping together that made the experience different from any she had previously known. Of course she had slept with her husbands but never the way she slept with Greer. He was a cuddler. He was also a man who didn't withdraw when he withdrew from her. He literally *stayed the night*; a big, lusty man who was tender, silly, and goofy all at the same time.

"Hey, Chubs, you letting me in on what's going through that head of yours or is this game night?" asked Greer, startling Marti from her reverie.

"Mike, I don't want to get serious," she replied.

"Fine. We'll keep it light. Heard any good jokes lately?" he asked teasingly.

"You misunderstand. I mean, I don't want *us* to get serious. I like us as we are."

"Marti, do you hear me asking for something else or different?" asked Greer as he tried to watch the road to Trancas and Marti at the same time.

Marti did not respond immediately. She knew from the way Greer made love to her that he was in love with her and that he was afraid neither to show that love nor to offer it on a continuing basis.

"I'm in a funny place at this point in my life or maybe it isn't funny at all," Marti began. "But for the first time, I'm beginning to feel something I think is me. I'm also feeling something I think is labeled freedom. Now I know all the jargon. *Dr.* Charper used to blithely say . . . when one is free one is unafraid to make commitments . . . to love. Well, we all know what I think about *Dr.* Charper. That same sweet man used to say: when one is free, one no longer needs to bind or be bound by love. Oh, Christ, how I wish I hadn't

612

repeated that! My stomach hurts enough. Not that the rhetoric is necessarily wrong but like all rhetoric, it isn't always right for all people. It obviates the fact that some people need to bind or be bound in order to survive, and as the saying goes . . . whatever gets you through the night.

"Except I guess I don't really subscribe to that anymore," said Marti, thinking aloud. "Drugs got Vinnie through just as my marriages got me through. Actually, it's not at all about whatever or whoever gets you through the night. That's pure and simple horseshit!"

As the Mustang veered off the main highway onto the road leading up to Marti's house, Greer said, "Slow down, Marti. Just take a deep breath and think what it is you're really trying to say."

They were standing in the living room when Marti turned to Greer and said, "I want to make it through my nights in the absolute right way for *me*. I want to know . . . no, make that I want to *feel* 'cause I already know, that I don't need a man to survive. Mike, having you around is wonderful. Shit! That sounds wrong. It's almost denigrating. It minimizes you and us. What I mean is: you're terrific and we are often terrific together. But I'm still learning how to be committed to me and that's all I want right now. Which doesn't mean I want just me and a good book for the rest of my life but that's all the commitment I want for now. I need to take one step at a time."

To her absolute amazement and total nonunderstanding, Mike Greer was standing before her with a big, silly, what one would even call "goofy," grin on his face. She didn't need a verbal reply as his face said it all. Not just to her but to Vinnie who had come to the head of the stairs overlooking the living room to see what all the noise was about.

At first, Mike Greer didn't give that much attention to Vinnie's attitude, thinking it was just another phase, perhaps even regressive, in his therapy. Normally, when the two met "on campus," which is how they referred to The Home, they either talked or joked and shared something that resembled friendship. But suddenly, Vinnie was cool, either just nodding or grunting a hello as they passed in the hallways or in the meeting or dining room. When Mike Greer finally asked, Vinnie's therapist could not offer any explanation for the attitude. Still, Greer knew there was something.

Understanding Vinnie's behavior from what had once been his own, Greer decided to confront Vinnie in his room one night. Vinnie was lying fully clothed on his Hollywood bed reading *War and Peace*—which Greer found ironically amusing—while his personal TV was "suffering through" *Peyton Place*—which, given what Greer knew about Vinnie and his family history, he also found ironically amusing.

Despite his pretending otherwise, Greer knew Vinnie was aware he was standing in front of his bed waiting to be acknowledged. When he continued to be ignored, Greer exploded: "What's going on with you?"

Vinnie looked over the top of his book. "Nothing," he replied, his eyes remaining as guarded as he obviously intended to keep his feelings.

"Don't give me that bullshit. This is me, Mike Greer, remember? If you're angry about something, say it."

"When I'm angry," said Vinnie into the pages of his book, "you'll be the first to know."

"I doubt it," sneered Greer as he positioned himself against the chest of drawers. "I doubt if you've got the balls to say you're angry when you are."

"Hey, man, don't push me," Vinnie said, putting the book down as he raised himself up on the bed. "When I've got something to say, I'll say it."

Realizing that both were posturing and nothing was being accomplished, Greer tried another tack. "Come on, Vin. We're friends. If something's wrong or if I've done something that's pissed you off, tell me."

The closed look on Vinnie's face turned to open hatred. "You're using me to hit on Marti," he said coldly.

"What do you mean 'hit on'?"

"You're fucking her. Don't deny it."

"I hate to sound like a kid on some street corner defending his turf but . . . what's it to you if I am, Vinnie?" As he saw the confusion on Vinnie's face, Greer attacked. "I asked what's it to you? She's over twenty-one. Hardly a virgin. But even if she were, I don't see where that would be any of your business either."

"She's my cousin," said Vinnie angrily.

"Exactly! Your cousin. And probably your best friend. Probably even the person you love most. So what?"

"So plenty. I don't want to see her get hurt!"

"Bullshit! *You* don't want to get hurt. And in your fucked-

614

up way of thinkng, or not thinking but reacting . . . any guy who comes along threatening to be more important to Marti than you, hurts you."

"What the fuck are you talking about?" Vinnie demanded, a buzz beginning in his head as his vision began to blur.

"I'll tell you. You're acting as if Marti was your lover or your wife, and she's not. You are acting like you own her and you don't. You don't want me around her because it hurts your ego—your distorted ego. You can't stand the idea of another man *having* Marti. Face it, Vinnie. Face it once and for all. Face it and then get the hell out of this place and back into the real world where you belong. You always have to be *the* man in your woman's life. First it was your mother. You wanted her to love only you and you alone. Love you best. You wanted to be the focal point of her life. Well, hello, Dr. Freud! And now you've transferred those feelings to Marti. You want to be Numero Uno in her life. Come on, Vinnie, work! Isn't that right? Don't you want to be the One, the Only One?" demanded Greer, moving close to Vinnie as he pushed home the point that he hoped would push Vinnie over one more, perhaps the last, hurdle.

"Get the fuck out of here!" snarled Vinnie.

"I'm not going nowhere. I'm in your life, Vinnie, and you can't push me out any more than you could any of the men in your mother's life.

"Hey, Vin," said Greer moving in for the psychological kill. "Why don't we pull out our cocks and see whose is bigger? Legend around town says ole Franklin Killerbrew had one helluva piece of meat."

Mike Greer saw Vinnie leaping at him; saw the face that wasn't a recognizable person's any longer and the eyes that were more animal's than man's. He braced himself as Vinnie threw the entire weight of his body at the terrible green and yellow bug he had to destroy before it destroyed him.

Carolyn had just landed on Boardwalk which had Margaret cackling gleefully as just her previous turn she had built a hotel on the high-rent property. As she was greedily collecting Carolyn's money, the radio flashed the news bulletin. Margaret's shock was so great that Carolyn instantly moved to her side. Mark, without asking, knew the Monopoly game was over and began placing properties, houses, hotels, and Community Chest and Chance cards into the box. Ali, fright-

615

ened by the sudden turn in emotions, watched as her grandmother led her aunt onto the patio, her arm about her waist.

"Kids, we're going for a walk on the beach. We won't be gone long," called Carolyn through the open glass sliding doors. Seeing the upset on Ali's face, Carolyn gently added, "It's a friend, Ali. A very good friend of your Aunt Margaret's. But everything will be fine. Why don't you turn on the TV and if Grandpa comes home before we do, tell him where we are."

Carolyn and Margaret walked silently for a while, neither remembering to protect her skin from the late summer afternoon sun. After they had strolled a short distance Margaret said, "Maybe after James, maybe after I finally cried for him, there was nothing left over for anyone else. But you know, she was very good to me."

"Yes, I remember," said Carolyn, "particularly after the opening in London, at the party, how she whisked you off protectively when Franklin arrived and was being Franklin. It was almost as if she were older than you."

Margaret sighed. "She was. Much older, although not chronologically. She was the oldest and wisest and at the same time the youngest and dumbest woman I ever knew. Did I ever tell you when James and I returned to London after the inquest, she was the only one who came to call and not pry. She cared. She really cared."

Margaret was crying now. "She got her wish. She's over the rainbow now."

Carolyn stopped abruptly, her sandals spraying sand as she did. "Margaret, Vinnie is not Judy Garland. Do you hear? I refuse to let you lump him with her or Dean or Monroe or Clift or any of those people. He is getting help. Whether he wants it or not, he has people who truly care about him. He is not being exploited. And he is better! And Marg, one thing we have both learned despite our meager mental abilities: no one gets helped unless he helps himself."

As Margaret wiped her tears with a red handkerchief she had pulled from the back pocket of her trainman's overalls, she said, "Lynnie, why do I think our children are nothing like us—that life was easier when we were young? We didn't struggle the way they do."

Carolyn laughed. "Oh my, but we do forget! First there was me, confused about men and sex, crawling into bed with

616

you because it was so much safer than crawling into bed with the man I loved."

"Why, you louse! And here all these years I thought I was more than just a one-night stand. So much for my beautiful memories!"

"We don't need memories, dummy; we have each other. Now where was I? Yes, I was unhappy, unsure of me and my body. And then you . . . so seemingly sure and confident. Remember? And how that all changed after my wedding and your discovering once you returned here how Mr. Malloy was not what you thought. Do you remember how you felt?"

"Big mouth! No wonder we have crazy kids. John wasn't exactly sane either."

"Hardly," admitted Carolyn. "From press agent to producer to soldier to writer. Changes upon changes. And when you're young, everything seems so much bigger. More confusing. It's only when you get older that you can step back and see things proportionately."

"Lynnie, if you're going to turn out to be one of those wise old women everyone quotes and calls a marvel, tell me now so I can do a Norman Maine and walk out into the ocean and disappear."

"We're both wise . . . or wiser," said Carolyn.

"Yes, but only one of us is a legend in her own lifetime," Margaret said, rankling Carolyn with what Carolyn felt was an unfair slight.

"You will be a very dead legend in her own lifetime if you ever mention that again. I'm surprised you're not wearing the damn thing on the beach now. It's only eighty-seven degrees. Now what was I saying?"

"If you keep asking that, I'm going to start worrying about you."

"Yes, I remember. It was something about both of us being wiser—which is why we're here. Still, there are some things one never does understand. Like a daughter who marries and marries. Yet, that same daughter becomes a best-selling author—off promoting her book—while her brother, who speaks to no one in the family, has become a decorated war hero. While still another brother graduates but does not attend his college graduation and has no intention of continuing on to law school despite his hard-earned acceptance. Our JJ. Who would have thought that he, too, would wind up confused as to where he wants to be and what he wants to do? Yet, it's not unusual. John changed directions many times and now, so has Marti. My husband, the political pundit."

"*Pundit?* Carolyn, this is me, Margaret. What do you know from pundits? Pandas maybe; pundits, no."

"I read it in the *Washington Post*. It means . . . a learned man, a teacher; one who gives opinions in an authoritative manner. Webster's New Collegiate Dictionary, 1969."

"Oh, Lord," sighed Margaret. "Just when I had gotten used to her quoting from the collected works of Pat Boone, she quotes Webster."

"Well, it just seems each person must struggle to find his or her own way and that the way can keep changing," continued Carolyn unperturbed by Margaret's verbal intrusions.

"And turning philosophical to boot!" said Margaret, her eyes rolling up toward the heavens.

"Oh, do stop! I'm simply saying if we, two actresses of some note . . . "

"But only one a legend," Margaret interrupted.

". . . could move from theatre to film to television, although I do think 'The Dating Game' asking you to appear was a bit tacky . . . "

"Funny you should mention that. Given the last few men I've been introduced to, I've been thinking of reconsidering my refusal and giving the show a whirl," said Margaret.

"I wouldn't put it past you. I swear. Anyway, where was I? You keep making me forget my place. Yes, right. I remember. I was simply making the point that we have been flexible. We've grown and we are continuing to grow. By the end of this year, we will begin a whole new chapter in our lives . . . a school, a repertory company. In other words . . . the beat goes on."

"I can't stand it. I just can't stand it!" repeated Margaret feigning agitation. "From the works of Pat Boone and Webster, fine! I can handle that. But Sonny and Cher?"

Carolyn stood her ground, looking squarely at Margaret, determined that her sister's humor wouldn't cloud the point she was making. "We found ourselves, Margaret," she said softly. "Many times. And that's the beginning, middle, and end of it. So will our children."

As the sun shining behind Carolyn lit her hair, Margaret thought her still the most beautiful woman she had ever seen. Almost shyly she took her hand. "Lynnie, let's do something foolish. Let's run into the ocean with all our clothes

618

on. Let's do it for Donald and Franklin and Augie and Arthur, James and Judy and Marti and Vinnie. And for fun. For just plain good old-fashioned fun."

From the patio, John watched as two "mature" women, screaming and laughing, scampered into the ocean, splashing water and spray about as they did. There was no doubt in John's mind that what he was witnessing was among the most beautiful sights he had ever seen.

3

Quiet on the set! Ready? Lights . . . action . . . camera!

Vinnie slowly picked up two suitcases and walked toward the front door, his face reflecting his fear of what lay beyond it.

Cut! Vinnie, why didn't you put one bag down, open the door with your free hand, and walk on out as you're supposed to?

Because I'm afraid, godamnit. I'm not ready.

Of course you're ready. You've been rehearsing this for days. Now come on. We don't want to add still more costs to this production.

Vinnie sat down in the canvas-backed sling chair, one of two in the small living room of the two-room apartment. I am not going anywhere, he told his director. I'm not ready to do this scene, he insisted to his coach. Screw the costs, I'll pay for them as I've paid for everything.

The knock on the front door disturbed Vinnie's conversation with his inner selves.

"Who is it?" he yelled.

"Opportunity, *putz*, who else?"

"Why don't you use your key, moron?" answered Vinnie.

"Cooperative to the end, aren't you?" Mike Greer said as he let himself in. "The landlord asked me to look around before you checked out—make sure you are leaving the place the way you found it."

"I guarantee it's as depressing as it was when I moved in," said Vinnie.

The apartment, although small with its cell-like bedroom and kitchenette, was not depressing. Purposely furnished in Contemporary Cheap, it resembled many of Santa Barbara's bachelor units, as they were called, right down to the orange nylon carpet with matching fiberglass curtains. The Home's intent was to replicate the apartment of any young person starting out in Southern California. A ten-minute drive or a

620

fifteen- to twenty-minute walk to The Home, it was part of the program's reentry process. When a patient was deemed nearly ready to return to his family or to "the other side of the wall"—as group members referred to the world at large—he was given this apartment first. Here, he learned how to go it alone but with the knowledge and thus support that friends and a surrogate family were but minutes away. It was a seemingly simple procedure of doing simple things for oneself— like the marketing and the cleaning and the cooking—and yet for all its simplicity, many found it a mass of complications. They, unlike Vinnie, did not receive "diplomas" or "discharge papers"—again the terms of group members—but had to "repeat the course."

Mike Greer was fixing coffee for both himself and Vinnie. As he watched the anxious movements of his graduate, he felt as if he were the one who would cry. It would be tough out there, more so for Vinnie than for others. They had their anonymity, which Greer realized was worth more than all of Vinnie's money. Yes, he could buy himself physical security—a home, two homes—but with his known face and past, he could not buy a chance to begin anew.

As Greer handed Vinnie his black coffee, he said, "It's fitting that you should be setting out on your own today." When Vinnie looked at him uncomprehendingly, he added: "Shmuck! It's October twelfth—the day to discover America. Why not?" he asked of Vinnie's incredulous expression. "If Columbus did it, why not you?"

"Get a piece of paper. Write down the numbers one to a hundred and I'll give you a list of reasons why not, beginning with . . . I'm afraid."

Greer sat down next to Vinnie on the rust-colored sofa bed. "You're ready," he said, his voice no longer feigning brightness. "Absolutely ready. That you're afraid is good, not bad. I'd worry if you weren't anxious. After four years plus, you should be scared."

"I'm still so fucked up," Vinnie said, putting his cup down and then his head, into his hands.

"Sure. You and everybody else out there. But you know it and that's a major difference. You have enough inner resources and knowledge to cope with your shit now."

"Mike, how do we know I won't have another flashback?" asked Vinnie miserably.

"We don't. But we don't know whether or not we have a big

621

motherfucker coming up on the Richter scale tomorrow or next week either. But we live anyway. There are no guarantees. That's all been explained to you. No one knows yet how long chemicals, such as the ones you were taking, might cause flashbacks. I'm betting that won't happen because you don't need to flash back anymore, Vinnie. You don't need to live in the past. You've got a free future ahead."

Vinnie took a deep breath and exhaled loudly. "I wish Marti were here," he said sullenly.

"So do I but she isn't," Greer said with an almost equal sullenness. "She's not and she hasn't been, at least not physically, in a long time now. But, Vinnie . . ."

"I can tell from the tone of that 'but Vinnie' that you're getting set to talk like some fucking therapist," interrupted Vinnie.

"I am a 'fucking therapist' and what I was about to say is: Marti is still there for you even if she is not here. *Capisce?*"

Vinnie thought about Marti, her frequent letters and just as frequent phone calls, always made prior to the twins' bedtime so they could speak with their uncle. He understood that Marti's move back to New York had moved her away from him only physically, as she was still the person closest to him. When she had first left California, Vinnie had felt abandoned. Mike Greer had helped him to realize it was more Marti's proximity to The Home that he missed than he did Marti herself as "herself" was always around in letter, feeling, or phone call. And hadn't that always been true, too, of JJ? Always around, although in reality, hardly ever.

Mike Greer wished his own feelings toward Marti were as clear as Vinnie's. He missed her and although they, too, stayed in touch, it was without regularity or even anything approaching frequency. With her move to New York, prompted by both her literary success and the mutilation murders of Sharon Tate and her friends, their relationship had changed, moved on. It would take his feelings some time to catch up with these changes, Greer realized. Philosophically, he insisted to himself, their separation coming as it did when her book, after five months, was first ebbing off the best-seller list, was for the best. Film-Star-and-Best-Selling Authoress and drug counselor/therapist do not a successful match make!

"What time is your plane?" asked Greer checking his watch.

"I'm okay. I have an hour," Vinnie said as he lit a

new cigarette with the one he had just smoked to a butt.

"Vinnie, there's no reason for me to shit you. I don't get paid by the cure. You're okay. You can make it. Just by keeping it all out front where you can feel and so deal with it."

"I can't do it here, Mike, and I can't do it in New York either. There's too many people watching. It's really terrific," said Vinnie sarcastically. "Thirty-two years old and starting over. A brand-new me."

"Stop complaining. That's very in today—men going through changes, giving up one career and moving to Tahiti."

For a moment, they sat silently. Then, after snuffing out his cigarette, Vinnie rose. "Why the hell JJ chose Nashville to crash in is beyond me," he said.

"Maybe he just plain likes it and maybe you will too. Vinnie," said Greer soberly, "it may just be the first stop on what proves to be a very long trip. Take the time to enjoy it. Don't be in any hurry. Remember: no matter where you are going, you, Vincent Tiernan, a.k.a. Vinnie, a.k.a. my friend, have already arrived."

At the door, Vinnie once again put down his luggage, this time to put his arms around Mike Greer "I love you, you shithead."

"Tell it to Minnie Pearl," said Greer as he hugged Vinnie as tightly as he held back his tears.

John J. hadn't chosen Nashville; his Triumph had, breaking down and threatening not to recover just inside the city's limits. When he learned from the garage that it would take several days to *import* the needed parts and then fix the auto, John took up residence at the Downtowner Motor Inn, "within walking distance," boasted the motel's night manager, of the Grand Ole Opry. Which indeed the Downtowner was and JJ walked to and by the Opry thinking the landmark an ugly and undistinguished old building and hardly reeking of tradition.

John J. would have been the first to admit he did not know a Loretta Lynn from a Loretta Young. To his untrained ear, the Nashville sound was all twang and sentimental twit. Still, when he did attend the Opry much against his better judgment on a Saturday night, he was taken with a "family feeling" that cloaked the crowd that had assembled. He fully expected there to be a communal fish fry after the evening's festivities and was disappointed when there wasn't.

Within a few days of his arrival, John J. was ready to push

on. Unfortunately, the Triumph was not as it continued to reject transplants of parts not made specifically for its body. There was little in Nashville proper to keep John occupied. Its main street had the usual string of department stores and movie theatres, but at night it was desolate. Activity in Nashville centered around western bars and booze, neither of which interested John J. In other cities John J. had passed through, he found people talkative if not always friendly. Conversations sprang up over lunch counters, at gas pumps, and in lobbies of motels where he stopped. Not in Nashville. Not unless you were in the music industry.

When Vinnie stepped off the American Airlines jet from Los Angeles, unrecognized, largely due to the heavy tortoiseshell glasses he wore, instead of being whisked off, as he had imagined, to John J's "crash pad," he found himself in a Triumph speeding south toward New Orleans. Too tired to complain, Vinnie slept sitting up, relaxed, even if his body wasn't, in the knowledge that he was safe; that no one could detect his presence in the car.

They checked into the St. Louis, a small but elegant hotel in the French Quarter. Their room, on the balcony, overlooked the gardens. Through the gauzelike draperies they could stare down into the dining room that also used the lush foliage as part of its decor. After three days, they checked out of the St. Louis and into a small, clean, and very inexpensive motel in the Quarter or within "proper" city limits. They were following a pattern which John J. had established early in his own version of the Grand Tour. In each city—other than Nashville— he first lived first class, enjoying the privileges money could buy, which he soon learned provided him a very different view of a city from that afforded to the "less fortunate"; a term rich folks used which John J. found as funny as he did offensive.

Vinnie was certain no one other than John J. would have thought spending Christmas in Miami Beach "a hoot!" Particularly no one with JJ's Irish Catholic background. But as Vinnie, now well disguised by a trim beard and aviator sunglasses, had to admit when he walked on Lincoln Road among the huge floral displays of Christmas wreaths and all their trimmings, JJ had been right. Miami Beach, with its look of Christmas but its sounds of Yiddish and its sprinklings of Spanish as spoken by its Cuban population, was not just a "hoot" but a "happening." Santa Clauses on street corners sweating beneath a tropical sun were something one expected to see only on "a trip" induced by drugs and not by the Miami Beach Chamber of Commerce.

They checked into the Doral Hotel, a towering monolithlike building that rivaled the Fontainebleau Hotel for dominance on Collins Avenue. Their French Regency–style suite overlooked the Dresden blue of the ocean. This time, happily, thought Vinnie, JJ had no plans to see how the "less fortunate" lived in Miami Beach. "I'm on vacation," he declared as he plopped down on the sand, his body supplicating the rays of the sun.

"From what?" asked Vinnie sarcastically.

"From touring. That's very exhausting, you know," said JJ, meaning his words.

"Try work. It's even more exhausting," Vinnie replied.

John J. gave Vinnie an odd look and Vinnie was pressed to explain, even to himself, where his remark had come from. After he had apologized, as they lay on side-by-side lounge chairs by the hotel pool, Vinnie began asking questions of John J. that hadn't seemed important over the last two months they had been traveling.

"I don't know what to work at," explained JJ. "I don't know what I want to do anymore. Law suddenly seems ludicrous as there seem to be two sets of laws for the two different classes of this country. Suddenly, the law and the lawyers are not there to solely protect the innocent. The guilty, even if they are not rich, can now hide behind the law. It's all gotten out of hand."

His original idea, to become a farmer of some sort or a veterinarian, seemed in this day and age not to be "very relevant or important. And God knows, what we do must be that!"

The last statement was said with such vehemence and hostility that Vinnie automatically said what he was thinking: "Why? Where is it written and who says?" It was then he learned that Marti was researching another book; this one a study of attitudes—be they political, social, spiritual, sexual, or economic—on college campuses. She was "measuring" the '60s and in particular, the effect the decade had had on the nation's young. John was appearing on the PBS network in "Ollson Observes," a weekly commentary on American life. And on January 2, the papers would announce the formation of The Tiernan Company, a school and theatre group headed jointly by Carolyn and Margaret Tiernan that would be funded in equal parts by a grant from the Lyceum Foundation and the public sector.

"We come from a most accomplished family," said JJ with a bitterness that surprised Vinnie.

"Feeling the heat?" he asked. "And I don't mean the sun."

"It is a tough act to follow," JJ said as he turned on his stomach so that the sun could bake his back. "When I was in the hospital, with the concussion—remember?—I was the only one of the injured who had paragraphs written about him in the *Times*, the *News*, and the *Post*. And the lead line always was . . . John Ollson, the son of writer/political commentator John Ollson . . . or John Ollson Jr., whose mother is . . . and whose father is . . . It was never just me or even about me. It seems I'm always somebody's son or brother or nephew."

"Why now?" said Vinnie, raising himself up on one arm to look down at John. "Why is this first bothering you? And what about your scores at college? No one bought them for you with the family name."

"But I did it for the family name," said JJ. "Christ, I had to. Thomas, whom I hardly know except by name, gets decorated and by Westmoreland, no less. Marti gets an Oscar and is rumored to be Dad's rival for a Pulitzer—and so on. I mean . . . did I do it to keep up? For them? Or did I do it for me? I wish I knew. I wish I could go somewhere, be something and somebody, without the pros and cons, the pulls in both positive and negative directions because of the family name.

"It's really funny if you think about it," John J. said as he flipped over on his back and then sat up, yoga style. "Some guys my age would kill to be in my shoes. I've got it all—including the bread you gave me over the years—to drop out. But I don't just drop out. Hell, no. I do it in style. In a Triumph sports car. In first class hotels. Dad said: 'Take notes.' I say: What for? Let him and Marti do that. The only notes I need are in my head."

"So?" asked Vinnie.

"So nothing. So I do nothing. And I'll continue to do just that until I know what I want. Meantime, I'm getting a helluvan education. This is a big, wide-assed country with an equally big and unflinching mouth."

To his own surprise, Vinnie heard himself say, "JJ, when you push on, I'm going to stay. I don't know exactly why—

maybe 'cause the weather is similar to California and it all seems easier, more comfortable here. But I think I've got to put down roots and put them down on my own. So I'm thinking of finding a place in the Gables or maybe even up around Lauderdale."

"And do what, Vinnie?" asked John J.

"I don't know but I don't think that's as important as my wanting to do something."

A few days later, after breakfast, when JJ and Vinnie stopped by the front desk, they found that Carolyn, as she promised during the Christmas Day phone call, had sent the mail that had accumulated. "None of it looks important—except maybe the notice of the year-end sale at Abercrombie's," Carolyn had joked.

"Jesus H. Fucking C. Christ!" said JJ as he read and then reread the form letter that had his name typed in at the top. The people in the Doral lobby, not used to such language, or at least not used to hearing it in eighty-dollars-a-day-and-up elegance, turned to stare at the young man who was cursing as he stared at his letter. Wordlessly, he handed it to Vinnie, who after reading it could find nothing of solace to say. What is there to say to a buddy when on the eve of a new decade, he receives word he is to report for his physical and then his induction into the United States Army.

When John climbed to the third floor of the four-story building on Forty-seventh Street just off Tenth Avenue, he found Carolyn and Margaret in the middle of the huge empty room talking with architects and carpenters. The blueprints were spread across a wooden plank that rested on wooden horses. From where John stood, it was an incongruous sight. All of it. Beginning with two women of the theatre, the screen, and television, discussing wallboard and plaster where in time they would be discussing Stanislavski and Strasberg. Then, too, in their full-length minks, bundled in scarves and turbans against the frigid February air that sneaked in through every loose brick in the building—of which John estimated there were thousands—they did look out of place amid the wood shavings, chipped bricks, and denim-clad workers.

The building had been "a steal"—the real estate agent's words—because, as Margaret so aptly put it, "everything of any worth had been stolen from it." The boiler lay sleeping, undoubtedly dreaming of its younger days when it had fire and potency. The plumbing had always been primitive and remained happily so. What pipes hadn't burst from the cold made their arthritic discomfort known by their screeching noise. But the building was air-conditioned, thanks to the age-old putty that had rotted and fallen away from the windows, thus allowing a steady breeze to cross-ventilate the space.

Still, it was perfect and they all knew it. The first and second floors were already well on their way to completion. The stage was built and the four hundred seats in what would eventually be a theatre were soon to be installed. On the second floor, two laboratorylike classrooms had been made out of the single space. Each had an amphitheatre feel to it and was perfect for either lectures or in-class workshop performances. At the current rate of progress, the two lower floors would be ready and the school open in early spring. The third floor, for more private classes, individual or small study groups, would take considerably more time. And noise, Margaret had pointed out when they began making plans to teach in April. Fall was the target date for the completion of the two-hundred-seat Augusta Monahan Theatre on the top floor. The executive offices were also planned for that level.

As he watched Carolyn knowledgeably discuss building logistics with the architects and carpenters, John was again surprised by her expertise. Carolyn, who couldn't balance her checkbook, who had little or no regard for money, was suddenly this businesswoman fighting over hidden costs and "prices for a Rockefeller but not a Tiernan Rep Company!" It was incongruous, at least to John, that *his* Carolyn would gravitate more toward the administrative than the creative end of the new business. Margaret was setting the curriculum and hiring the men and women who would teach lighting, scenic and costume design, and stage management.

John's was a "command performance" this day, having been summoned by the Tiernan Sisters to discuss what known or respected playwrights they should invite to join their teaching staff. Had "Ollson Observes" not been in the K.O. producing hands of Evelyn Randolph, John would have been frantic and probably in his office at the PBS studios at Columbus Circle. The show, after all, was weekly and current. It required a constant perusal of the issues the nation's newspapers addressed, as it was those very same issues to which John would speak come airtime on Thursday night, when the show taped at the WNET studios on Ninth Avenue. Happily, thought John as he approached the group in the center of the room, Evelyn had cheerfully moved to New York and Nancy had just as cheerfully invited herself to the board of directors of the Tiernan Company and became its chief in-house financial adviser and fund-raiser. In her spare time, she opened a gallery, stunning her Suzy-columned friends by shunning Madison Avenue for a loft in SoHo.

No sooner had John joined the circle than it broke; the architects and carpenters moved off in one direction, leaving him and the women standing in the middle of the room. As he handed Carolyn the morning mail which had arrived as he was leaving, he said to Margaret, "They want you, Lynnie, and Marti for 'Girl Talk.'" When Margaret looked pained, John said, "It could help Nancy in her fund-raising. Just give it some thought before saying no."

They both became aware of Carolyn's silence simultaneously. It was physical as well as verbal. Only the letter moved, trembling when the hand that held it did. Wordlessly, Carolyn handed the letter to John and Margaret.

February 10, 1970

Dear Mother Ollson,

Two days ago I was informed by the Air Force that Thomas was shot down over North Vietnam in late December. They had just received word that he is being held prisoner by the North Vietnamese, although exactly where they do not say.

I would have called but I am not feeling my best for obvious reasons. This has been hanging over my head like a sword since December as I had not heard from Thomas since then. Which was very frightening as his year's extension was up and . . . well . . . You can figure out the rest. I'm sorry to be curt. My own feelings are too raw to be much concerned with anyone else's.

The children send you. No . . . they don't. They really don't send you anything. Why should they? They hardly know you.

Sincerely,
Reese

John took Carolyn's hand. "She's just upset, Lynnie. She's very upset. But it's not really about you."

Carolyn's eyes were dry as was her voice, which sounded raw and raspy when she said: "John, we must get JJ out!"

John put his arm around Carolyn and drew her to him. "JJ is all right. He is not going to fight in Vietnam," he assured Carolyn while thinking . . no, his fight will be at home, here and forever.

"John? Do you promise?" asked Carolyn as she tightly gripped his hand

It was Margaret who was softly crying for a boy she had hardly known, or liked, since his childhood. That the news hurt, surprised her. She had not known she had feelings for Thomas—"But he's family!" a voice inside persisted in reminding her—any more than she knew that somewhere deep down she had always believed he and John, he and Carolyn, he and she, would all one day work things out. Now, there was the distinct possibility that that hidden fantasy might never come true.

February 16, 1970

Dear Vinnie,

I've been sitting here at my desk for twenty minutes trying to find a way to begin this letter. It's been a very long time since we've been in touch.

Or has it? I sometimes think even in our silences we communicate, reach out, and hurt each other.

What to say? I've recently learned I use humor, make jokes, when I'm upset or nervous. And I'm both. Upset because of Thomas. Terribly upset. I can't even think about it. My imagination runs away from me and I imagine the worst. And I'm nervous because . . . well, I don't know how you will receive this letter.

By the way, please don't be angry with Marti for giving me your address. It was right after she spoke with you—told you about Thomas—that I asked and she gave it to me. Be assured, should you not wish to correspond, I will not bother you, and your whereabouts will remain secret.

I just don't know where to begin. I look back and all I can see are the years that have passed. How long has it been since I've seen you? So very long. Too long. It seems to me it's not right or wrong anymore, although you may not agree. I've accepted and yes, forgiven myself, for my shortcomings. I have also accepted and forgiven *you* for yours.

If that last statement of mine hasn't sent you through the roof or back to drugs, I'll continue.

I miss you and I realize—yes, admittedly rather late—that

I've always missed you. Even in my good times—and oh, Vinnie, was I fortunate 'cause I knew truly good times with James—I missed you. I always had the feeling I had lost something or left something behind. Like . . . have you ever left the house and thought . . . I've forgotten the key or my wallet? Something. And it gnaws at you until you can remember what it is.

That's what I mean when I say I've always missed you.

Oh, dear, I'm beginning to cry. No, that isn't meant to elicit your sympathy although there is a healthy (or unhealthy) measure of self-pity in that statement. It's just . . . I realize I've missed out on a great deal. Fault? Mine? Yours? Yes! So what? All that is the past. We can't change it. Nor can we erase it. Nor can we, as people love to say, "wipe the slate clean." There's been too much bitterness and anger and hurt for that. And maybe we shouldn't wipe our respective slates clean. Maybe they should be there as reminders. Maybe by respecting the past, we can make better use of the present and the future.

What I am trying to say, undoubtedly quite feebly, is that I would so much like us to have some sort of present and future. A beginning would be to hear from you. However, should this not be possible at this time, I will understand. I shall not like it. But I will understand.

In short: I am standing at the Lost & Found Department and inquiring about a son I misplaced. I hope you can tell me where he is.

> Love,
> Your Mother

John J's eyes fluttered open and again, as most mornings, his first feeling upon awakening in the army barracks was of cold. He had been cold ever since he had ridden the IRT to the army induction center on Whitehall Street. It was a bleak, windswept morning when he appeared for his physical. As he lay shivering in his bunk, John J. remembered. Breathe! Cough! Urinate into the bottle. He couldn't. Nor could several others who stood around the urinals, bottles, like extra appendages, dangling from their penises and hands. They needed a specimen, they insisted. Wasn't he enough of one? Wasn't that what the draft was all about? he had silently asked .

If only he hadn't been silent. If only he had voiced his anger and his fear *then*. Why hadn't he declared himself a conscientious objector during the psychological evaluation? Why hadn't he declared then that he could not, would not, carry a gun; would not, could not kill?

That is what they would ask if he waited for his hearing. And that could be in weeks or months. He didn't have either. Nor did he have the heart to undergo the grilling, the doubting of his sincerity. Worse, the doubting of his manhood.

In just a few weeks, he would complete his basic training and turn twenty-three. He would leave Fort Dix for a month's leave and then be scheduled to report to Fort Benning in Georgia for an additional eight weeks of "advanced training."

Trembling beneath his army blankets, his body chilled from within, John J. bitterly dissected the term "advanced training." A euphemism for learning more sophisticated—*advanced*— ways to kill. Ever since boarding the bus that took inductees from Whitehall Street to Fort Dix, he had felt he was being killed, slowly but very surely. It was as if the army was determined to stamp out whoever he had been prior to induction.

It was not possible, although in one respect he had wished it were. He tried to keep his identity a secret but his superiors at boot camp knew who both his father and his brother were. He was buffeted between abuse and respect, neither of which he had earned. The boys with whom he bunked and trained initially gave him the space his entire physical manner demanded but that ended when they learned Marti Tiernan was his sister and Vinnie Tiernan his cousin. Their celebrated status superseded in people's minds any right he had to privacy. Besides, a draftee has no rights, as his commanding officers kept reminding him.

His mother, in highly charged, emotional phone calls, kept insisting his father would get him out; that he was in the process of "using his pull" in Washington at that very moment to obtain his release. His father was realistic although also emotional. There was no one who could change John J's status. It was too late. If prior to being inducted he had pleaded insanity, homosexuality, or religious beliefs that prevented military service, there would have been no problem.

On the parade grounds at Dix, as they marched with the wind at their backs or in their faces, he remembered telling Margaret he would serve if drafted, but protest every inch of the way. He had been naïve. There was no one to whom he could protest. That inalienable right he had lost as soon as he

632

was inducted. He didn't mind the marching or the hikes or the calisthenics, although his body often did. But you can quiet a protesting body, whereas you can't always quiet a protesting mind.

The agony and his inner protests began with the "war games." Sport for grown men. Hand-to-hand combat. No arm-wrestling but judo holds—defense mechanisms against a knife, a gun, or any form of hand weaponry. The realization, deep from within, not reasoned but felt, that this "game" was to prepare him for an actual attack by a real man with a real knife and a real intent to kill, staggered him. He had never really thought about anyone killing—least of all him. The chill that invaded his system turned to a sickening cold the first time, at another "game," they placed a bayonet in his hands.

He stared at the mechanical dummy hanging before him waiting to be gored and he wondered what, if any, was the real difference between them. Weren't they both motorized and mechanized to serve the army's interests?

Parry and thrust! Thrust! The blade on the end of the bayonet is *thrust*, damn you, thrust, into the dummy's guts. And turned. Like a corkscrew!

It made him sick. No matter where he was or what he was doing, the image of a bayonet thrusting into a man, blood and guts spilling everywhere, remained fixed in his head. He could not kill. Could not thrust. Could not. No matter how those in charge insisted that men under fire, men whose lives were in danger, would respond in kind to that danger. Because the survival instinct—the kill-or-be-killed credo—would win out. John J. didn't think so.

He asked himself if he was afraid of dying and the question made him laugh. One of the few times he had laughed since the bottles and the buses at Whitehall Street. Of course he was afraid. Terrified! All men were. *That* was the survival instinct. That is what the military counted on. That was the principle behind kill-or-be-killed. You took a life to save your own.

But that principle didn't work for him. He, and others, saw that during another "game." For this one, he was costumed in a football helmet and hockey-type gloves. He was given a pugil stick. It resembled a broomstick but with padding on both ends. The object of the game was to defend against being hit and knocked down as you attempted to hit and knock down your opponent. With your stick. With all your strength. Hit or be killed. Hit or be killed.

633

Repeatedly, he was knocked to the ground, battered on the body and the head. Repeatedly, he picked himself up, the anger the military counted on to surface remaining dormant. He couldn't use his cudgel. He couldn't bear any kind of arms in any of their "games." He didn't like what they played or how. Nor did he like the outcome. He couldn't understand how the winner could feel all that much different from the loser. He wasn't even certain if there was a winner. Survival at any cost? Not if the cost, the price for being the winner, is oneself—some part of you that dies so that the "whole" of you can survive.

There was no point in bucking the system now, thought John J. as the sounds of reveille broke throughout the camp. No point in petitioning the higher-ups for a spectator seat at their games. After his and his team's training, he realized he didn't even want to sit on the bench. He was not a mascot or a cheerleader. Nor was he one who could administrate, help the team to win the "games" by performing useful tasks on the sidelines. As a conscientious objector would have to do. No, he could not do that because the game plan, as well as the game, violated every principle he believed in. And whether those principles were founded in Jesus Christ or not, didn't matter. Not to him. They were his principles and he was not about to call on a higher-up to validate that which was right for him.

Again John J. realized, as he slowly lifted himself off the bed and onto the cold planked floor, that in a matter of weeks his basic training would be over and so would be the life he had always known. When he was supposed to be betwixt and between Forts Dix and Benning, he would actually be betwixt and between those who would understand and those who never would. Not ever.

It's just a game, Thomas reminded himself constantly. A game. A game. A game. How one plays—no matter what the rules— determines who wins. It might be their "Las Vegas," but his life would not be decided by a roll of the dice. No. He would beat the odds, beat them at their own game. Despite the deck being stacked against him. All it takes is strategy. Forget about luck. Trade that for a will to win. But oh, God, if only I could stand up straight. Or breathe. Forget that! Play your game. Do you hear, Ollson? Play your game!

Thomas had been flying an escort reconnaissance mission over Dong Hoi when his Phantom Jet took a 57-millimeter antiaircraft shell in its wing. Fifty miles from the border of South Vietnam, he and his "gibs" ejected themselves from the burning plane. Thomas could still smell his own singed hair but he couldn't remember the parachutes. His own had opened—his being alive was testimony to that fact—but Dickey's? He never did learn what happened to Pierce Dickey, his "running mate," as he used to call the boy from Beaufort, Texas.

When Thomas tried, he could remember staring up into hating faces. With long bamboo sticks, they poked at him as one would a slimy snake. He had been slimy. Wherever he had fallen, he recalled, was marshy and muddy. It made a soft bed for his half-conscious, semifeeling body. When he awoke again, he was seated on a stool and it was his turn in a game he hadn't asked to play.

He was in "Heartbreak Hotel" playing "Twenty Questions." To which he only had one answer. "I am Thomas Ollson. I am a Captain in the United States Air Force. My serial number is . . ."

They penalized him for incorrect answers. Just like in the old "Truth or Consequences." You didn't tell the truth so you have to pay the consequences. Which were grave. Even, some might say torturous. Twenty wrong answers to twenty questions lost the game and . . . fingernails and . . . the function of the kidneys. He never won at their game but he never lost at his own. The North Vietnamese learned he was the kind of prisoner of war they hated; a man who would pay the consequences to keep his own truths.

From "Heartbreak Hotel," they moved him to that area of Hoala Prison known to Americans both as "Las Vegas" and the "Hanoi Hilton." The little buildings of two and three rooms all bore the names of hotels on the Strip. He was confined to the "Gold Nugget" where the rules of the house dictated you did not speak *in any way* to the other *guests* in the other rooms. Through tappings on the wall, hand signals, eye contact, they always found a way.

And then he was asked to sit in on another game. In this one, he was to be a pawn, moved into place by the North Vietnamese before an American antiwar delegation. He refused. He absolutely refused. He did not pass "go"; did not collect two hundred dollars, but went directly to a stool in the Heartbreak Hotel courtyard where he was forced to sit—that means *sit*; no standing to stretch *a* muscle—for three days and three nights. It rained two of the three days The rainwater was the only nourishment he received.

From the courtyard, they moved him to "Calcutta"—as in Black Hole of. It was a room without a view. Without a window of any kind. There was no room for one. What "architect" builds windows into a six-by-two-foot space? Calcutta had one advantage, the enemy claimed. It was far from the madding crowd. Quite far. Fifty yards to be exact. Calcutta was indeed very solitary confinement. Men were known to go quite crazy from the quiet.

He was an example of how not to play the game, his fellow prisoners were told. They knew otherwise; so did Thomas. In the "hole," he trained himself not to notice the crick in his neck, the ache in his lower back, the bites of the bugs, the stink of his own stench which drew vermin of every kind If it hadn't been for the dysentery, as unrelenting as the interrogations and the demands that he see American antiwar delegations, he would have been fine. Well, almost

As his body weakened, his resolve strengthened. He made up his own game to beat them at theirs. It consumed his waking hours, consumed his thoughts and his energies, drowning out all else. Focused on his "game," he felt no pain, no deprivation . . . nothing. He was writing his autobiography, beginning with his earliest recollections and describing each in full. Without aid of pencil and paper. All in his head. Visions of sugarplums named . . . Mama and Marti and Mrs. Worthington and Aunt Margaret and whistling rings that glowed in the dark—courtesy of three boxtops, one quarter, and the box number in Battle Creek, Michigan. Thomas wrote his book nonstop and as he did, he held the trump card, the one that he was sure could win him the game. Only occasionally did his mind wander. Only occasionally did every part of him cry out to . . . stand up straight! Breathe! But only occasionally

It was the smallest house on North Bay Road and that it only had eleven rooms made it a white elephant on the Miami Beach market where bigger meant better. Hardly a mansion, by no means an estate, it was, said the agent with practiced gaiety, a "villa-ette." Once the proud possession of an old gentleman who lived a reclusive life behind the gray stone walls that separated the house from the narrow Bay Road, the house, complained the agent, had no "image," no lore, to make it seem exotic to the buyer. Otherwise, it would have been sold long ago.

Vinnie, the moment he saw the length and breadth of Biscayne Bay but a hundred feet from the glass-walled living room, knew the house was his. The patio just beyond the living room with its umbrellaed picnic tables reminded him of a house of long ago, on an ocean in Malibu. Except this one was nicer. Each of the bedrooms faced the bay as did the dining room. There was even an already-built dock for the boat he didn't already have. An inner courtyard, running from the gray stone walls to the house, was filled with tropical trees and foliage. It also had a ridiculous reduced-in-size replica of the Fontana di Trevi.

Vinnie had looked at numerous apartments and houses in various parts of the Miami area. Coral Gables had seemed too cliquish; Coconut Grove, too chummy. The houses on the little islands on the causeway between Miami and the Beach were too removed from a reality with which Vinnie wanted to stay in touch. He wanted a house that would be sequestered but near everything. That was Villa-ette.

Several days after the agent had shown the house to a bearded Vince Malloy, he received a check from Vincent Tiernan's lawyers. If the agent connected one Vince with the other Vincent, he made no mention. A house sold is just that: sold. Commission granted!

As soon as the pedestal bed he had ordered arrived from the department store, Vinnie left the Doral Hotel and moved to his new home. The necessities of household life had been ordered directly through the pages of the *Miami Herald* and his once bare cupboards and closets were now stocked with cooking and cleaning utensils, linens, and sundries of all kinds.

Unlike his house in Laurel Canyon, the decor Vinnie chose for Villa-ette, as he now called his home, was neither stark nor simple. He took his decorating cue from the azalea bushes that rowed three sides of the house. Flamingo pinks and reds, mixed with grays and blacks, gave his living and dining rooms a sultry tropical look. "And sexy," Marti declared when she visited during her three days of intensive interviewing on campus at the University of Miami.

The "and sexy" surprised Vinnie as sex was something he occasionally thought about but seldom felt the need to pursue. Mike Greer had urged him to date but Vinnie was happy for the moment being alone. That fact was evident to Marti who wasn't the least subtle in her delight with Vinnie's physical and mental states. Throughout her stay, she kept muttering as she watched Vinnie, "The Pope should declare it a miracle." He laughed, as did she, for both knew it was no miracle; just the fruition of several people's hard work, but mainly his own.

On her last night in Miami, Vinnie prepared a special dinner that culminated in peach melbas. The gesture touched Marti, especially when she realized how far he had come since that night at the Ritz Hotel, the eve of her first marriage. Coincidentally, the phone rang just as she was talking about Chauverant and her neurotic need for him, for any man who would make Marti Tiernan feel good about Marti Tiernan.

The caller was Mike Greer. He was calling to tell Vinnie his good news. Before he could, Marti grabbed the phone and said, "I was just saying how I don't need a man to make Marti Tiernan feel good about Marti Tiernan. However, I sometimes do feel the need for a man to make Marti Tiernan feel good. So why don't you come right over." She expected he would laugh at her lechery but he didn't. Instead, caustically, he suggested she try her local service station. As if stung by one of Miami's many men-of-war that often ruined the ocean water for bathing, she dropped the phone into Vinnie's hands.

Mike had called to joyously announce his appointment by the Los Angeles Council on Mental Health as director of a new bureau on drug abuse and its prevention and treatment. As if Mike were in the room, Vinnie popped the cork on the champagne that had been chilling and toasted Mike's new success. The phone call ended without Marti and Mike speaking again. Just as it was evident to Vinnie that Marti "had problems" where Mike Greer was concerned and possibly vice versa, it was equally apparent she did not want to talk about it.

Now, as he sat at his desk in his blue and green bedroom, Vinnie again turned away from the letter he had been trying to write and looked out the window. Somewhere out there, he realized as he looked northwest, Marti and Mike were weekending. It was either Vail or Sun Valley, he couldn't remember which, only that they would be skiing if they weren't shouting at each other, as Marti had said. The sun, Vinnie noted, was sparkling on the docile bay. He had been told that spring in Miami was even better than spring in Southern California and it was, he decided. The days were continually warm and cloudless. The sun's intensity was bright but bearable, which he knew in another month or two it would no longer be. With a long, last look at the view and a long, deep sigh, Vinnie returned to his letter.

". . . and it is strange, not only being in school again but enjoying it. If I do well as a nonmatric, I'll matriculate in the fall. At the moment, I'm taking nine credits. That's three courses, including trigonometry and classical civilization. If I pass all three, I'll only need one hundred and eleven more credits for my bachelor's degree. Funny how at my age I'm first excited about 'education' . . . about school, the things I didn't much have as a kid."

Again Vinnie looked up and away from the letter he had been writing for what seemed like days. The "didn't much have as a kid" had brought the bile to the surface. Again. A part of him demanded he crumple and shove the unfinished letter with the others in the wastebasket by the desk. Some stronger part of him said no; finish the job at hand.

"Anyway, come the fall and I'll be a freshman at the U of Miami—nice campus with a lake in the middle. Lots of pretty buildings and pretty people."

Once more, Vinnie stopped. When he picked up the pen again, his hand came down hard on the paper.

Look! I really don't want to write this letter. At least a part of me doesn't. I figure if I tell you that, maybe it will make writing the damn thing easier. So you ask me—just as I ask myself—if it's so damn difficult, why do it? Good question. I have to. I must. For me. It's been hanging over me ever since your letter arrived almost two months ago. I could have killed you for writing. My first feeling was: Why the fuck is she bothering me now when I've got enough to deal with? A week or so later, when I reread your letter, I felt different. I'm not saying I loved it or that it warmed my heart but . . . what you said made sense. It was honest. I realized I didn't want any part of it because I don't want any part of you. I'm trying to get past you.

A lousy thing to say, right? Well, I still have a lot of conflicting feelings where you're concerned. But one thing I now know—which is why I'm writing—is that to get past you, I must do just that: forget about all that happened— No. Strike that! Not forget but accept. Accept and understand. And not just your part in it but mine.

It's damned hard to let go. Damned, damned hard. When you live with anger, hate, for as long as I have, you don't know

639

at first how to live without them. They're like your best buddies. When you kick them out of your life, you're alone . . . lonely, without company. I've had to learn how to live without my best buddies. I'm still learning how to live alone. No. Strike that, too! I'm learning how to live with *me*. And if I can do that, I'm not alone. Not ever.

I don't know what if anything we can ever be to each other. I don't know what if anything I want from you. But as I keep telling myself, a letter is only a letter. I don't have to see you. That's not said to hurt you. It's just the God's honest truth. I'm with me now, making things right for *me*. It's a self-involvement but a necessary one.

Listen. Marti told me about what you and Aunt Carolynnie are doing and I think it's great. About Thomas . . . you know, it's been so long since I've had any feelings about him that it's hard for me to feel anything now. But JJ. That's something else. I ache for him. Shit! How I ache for him. Had I known he was going to make a run for it, I'd have gone with him. What the hell is the difference between Florida and Canada anyway—except sixty or seventy degrees Fahrenheit.

Thanks for your letter. Seeing how difficult it was for me to write this one, I can appreciate how difficult it must have been for you to write yours. But you know, in reassessing my life, I look at yours and you always did have a helluva lot of balls. Now that I've stopped resenting that, I can admire it.

Regards to all,
Vinnie

As he began to write out Margaret's address on an envelope, Vinnie got up from his chair and walked to the open glass door of the terrace that surrounded his bedroom. He didn't feel good about the letter. Only angry. He tried to be his own analyst. What was he angry about? What was he resenting? The answer, he realized almost immediately, was in the letter, itself. By communicating with his mother, he was giving up his "best buddies" once again and he didn't like it; didn't like feeling vulnerable.

Back at the desk, he became aware of the folder in which he kept bills. Still to be paid that day was the month's mortgage payment on the house, the payment on the small boat that now rested at dockside, and the analyst he now saw twice a week at Mike Greer's suggestion. He had taken charge of his own affairs in recent months and knew exactly how much money he had and how much had been spent in recent years on The Home and lawyers' fees. Despite huge outlays of money, he remained a very wealthy man, one who, if he chose, need never work again. He owed that to his mother, he suddenly realized. From the time he had been a child star, she had wisely invested his earnings and had protected most of his money in trust funds.

It was what his analyst called "an insight." In looking at his financial picture, he saw that contrary to what he had wanted to believe, his mother had taken care of him. At least in this fashion. Suddenly, Vinnie broke down. His sobbing was convulsive. It was not about Margaret—not directly—but about Franklin Killerbrew, who had made him the primary heir to all his considerable holdings.

Pleasant but nothing spectacular. A house. A three-story, one-family house. Brick. Very solid. In a very solid neighborhood. Perfect.

John J. watched as the elegantly dressed woman moved about the empty rooms with an innate style that seemed wrong for the white-collar community of Rosedale. If the real estate agent noticed the disparity between his potential buyer and the neighborhood, he was not about to say anything. The woman was asking intelligent questions about carrying costs and taxes. It didn't strike him as unusual that the woman didn't ask about public schools or churches nearby, as in this day and age many families chose not to have children or God in their home, although that wasn't so true of Rosedale. Its small-town mannerisms and mentality made it much farther away than the advertised ten minutes to bustling downtown Toronto.

Convinced upon inspection that the heating unit in the house was new and would be well able to heat the three stories through the eight months of Canadian winter, the woman smiled on—not *at*, but *on*, thought John—the agent and announced that the house would be suitable and that she would like to take immediate occupancy. Her words were followed by the quick action of a handwritten check for half the asked-for amount. As the agent looked at it, all traces of his carefully etched boredom erased from his professional manner, the woman asked for the keys. He dropped them in her hands as he continued to stare at the check. The woman turned, winked at John J., and then elegantly escorted the agent from her house.

"It's in my name but it's all yours. Gladly," the woman said as she shuddered. "Although I've yearned to live most everywhere, Canada has always begun and ended for me with Montreal. Actually," she said as her eye cast yet another appraising look around the vast space meant to be a living room, "it's quite a fine house. Well built. Can your name go on the front door?"

"It must," John said. "The Canadian government insists on it if I'm to maintain my Landed Immigrant card. But your buying the house for me buys time at the very least. Since I don't have to be listed in the phone directory, it will take some doing for reporters to find me. I really appreciate what you've done, Nancy. I realize you not only didn't have to but have put yourself on a limb by doing so."

Nancy Blanchard laughed. "JJ, the rich are never on a limb. The worst that could happen would be some controversy. Frankly, I would welcome it. I used to be quite controversial, you know. Or maybe you don't, actually. I miss being the object of scorn and envy. Your aunt and I used to be such a good feud and that was such good fun. Now that we're such close friends, it's just not the same." Nancy sighed. "Where did I go wrong?"

She was intentionally keeping it light and John J. knew that. "Thanks, Nancy," he said softly. "For everything."

"Your family has meant a great deal to me," she said in an entirely different tone and manner. "Actually, I think of us all as family. I hope you don't mind. I'm not very good with words, I'm afraid—that's always been my failing—but I've always been quite fond of you. It would have pained me had you gone to war and pained me even worse had you not returned. Speaking of return, I must get to the airport. Your father is meeting my plane at Kennedy. Any message?"

John reached into his pocket and withdrew a small package, awkwardly wrapped in foil and tied with a black ribbon. "Tell him this is for Father's Day. It's on loan to him. Tell the ole man it's the only thing I own that matters to me which is why I want him to have it."

The smile on John's face said one thing while the tears in his eyes told Nancy another. "Come on," she said. "Drive me or we'll be late."

John J. did not go into the terminal but left immediately after depositing Nancy Blanchard at the Air Canada entrance. His good-bye was as awkward as his hug. Nancy was halfway through the doors when she heard JJ calling through the open car window: "Tell my mother . . ." His sentence remained unfinished. She saw his pained face before he looked away and then drove off. It didn't matter. She would finish his sentence for him when she saw Carolyn.

The signs of summer were all about and JJ was glad to see them. The Canadian winter had been extremely cold and made even colder by his emotional state. Yet, he was one of the fortunates. He had a job and money. As important, unlike many of the boys who had either dodged the draft or dodged service once they were inducted into the army, he had a totally supportive family. They had actually taken more abuse for his action than he had.

It had been an awful day in mid-April, quite unlike this sunny one in June, when his parents, on his mother's insistence, had driven him in the rented car to Buffalo. Had she had her way, they would have driven him clear into Canada. His father's good sense had prevented that. She didn't give "a whit" about public reaction or her career, she had stormed, but his father, cooler, more logical, stated she now had a repertory company and the lives of many children to consider and thus could not risk offending those whose monies supported the Tiernan Company Players. She understood that; understood that the car they would rent would be in Nancy's name so there would be no trace of their having participated in their son's escape.

But they had participated. Carolyn had flown into a frenzy of participation. Funds from her account were transferred into one opened in John's name at the Bank of Toronto. Down jackets, down comforters, snow boots, thermal underwear, sweaters, and the like were bought and sent directly to the row house on Huron Street where the underground had arranged for him to live. Jeanne had been invaluable in securing that. He had not seen her since leaving Columbia but she had responded immediately to his call. Within a day, she advised what he would need to "make a life," as she put it, in Canada.

To obtain Landed Immigrant status, "like a Green Card here in the U.S.," she had explained, he would need to score fifty points with the Ministry of Immigration. A job offer was worth ten. If he could convince a Canadian company to hire his services, he was halfway home. His father saw to that instantly, arranging for JJ to work as a production assistant for the Canadian Broadcasting Company in Toronto. Other points, Jeanne advised, were awarded for schooling—one point for every year in some institution of higher learning. Bring diplomas as proof. Then there were extra points awarded if one had studied French. John had. Bring transcripts. Last, if one could find Canadian businessmen or leaders to write letters of recommendation, they, too, scored points. John could and they did. When John J. left his parents and drove across the bridge in the used Chevrolet he had just purchased off a lot in Buffalo, he knew before meeting with immigration officials he had enough points to remain, and work, legally, in Canada.

He was indeed, as he kept reminding himself when others didn't, one of the fortunates. In more ways than many knew. He hadn't been among the "resisters" for more than a few weeks when he realized he felt differently from many. He was not among the guilty, among those who walked hangdog. He did not feel that he had done anything wrong or that he had wronged his country. Quite the opposite, he felt his country had wronged him; had forced him to make decisions that would forever alter his life and quite possibly harm the lives of those he loved. He wasn't wrong about the last. When the press learned of John J.'s desertion, much was made of it. Except by John and Carolyn who had decided not to discuss it publicly. A statement was issued that simply read: "The John Ollsons have one son in service and one who is not. They are equally proud of both."

The statement created a controversy in itself. That Marti and Margaret when questioned not only endorsed but applauded the statement only fanned the fanatical flames on both sides of the issue. Retribution came in ugly letters and gift-wrapped packages of dead animals. The second such arrival prompted John to have all mail other than letters screened, particularly for explosives.

It had been a lonely three months for John J. His job and his desire to fit into the Canadian mainstream kept him somewhat apart from other resisters. He dressed conservatively like the Canadians, wearing jeans only in the apartment. Determined to make the most of his new life, he applied himself at the TV station, learning all he could when he could during his self-imposed ten- to twelve-hour day. His social life was nonexistent as the Canadian girls were slow to warm to Americans known or thought to be resisters. And the American girls who had followed the boys from the States to Canada John J. found to be much like groupies and did not interest him. Thus, he was alone much of the time, although always available, on call to help some newcomer from America. Many was the night when his roommate's name was unknown and remained unknown as he was gone within a day.

Within weeks, John J. decided he did not want to live in the Huron and Queen Street area which housed most of the deserters. It was depressing, similar to New York's Lower East Side. Deciding to buy a house, he was persuaded by his father to let Nancy buy it for him. For safety—a precautionary measure. His father had been filled with precautionary measures. To avoid the FBI, phone calls were never made between John's office or home to Toronto. A special number had been arranged and to this moment JJ hadn't any idea where it was other than, judging from the Plaza exchange, somewhere in central Manhattan. Their calls were not frequent and visits so far not possible, as the watchful eye of the press seemed forever focused on Carolyn.

But within days, thought John J. as he turned off the highway toward downtown Toronto, he would be moving to Rosedale. He would have a house, a garden, and, thanks to the twins' generosity, an aging, although he didn't seem to know it, schnauzer named Mickey who would be arriving via a 727 jet in a few days.

It will be nice to have a familiar face around the house, thought John J., and then laughed at the idea of a dog's face being familiar. But Mickey was a reminder of home, of John and Carolyn, and so would be most welcome. He made a note and attached it to his sun visor after he parked. Buy dog food, it read. Cheered, John J. walked almost jauntily into Swedish Hall where Saturdays and Sundays he volunteered his services, helping new "arrivals" to obtain housing, jobs, and immigration status.

On Father's Day, when John opened the package delivered by Nancy Blanchard, he looked at the gold ball cuff links that had meant so much to his son, Margaret, and James Carrington, and cried.

The persistent ring of the telephone was disturbing Margaret's dream. In it, she was just about to meet in a lingering embrace with . . . with whom? Dammit! With whom? Too late, the shrill ring had her fully awake and angry. As she threw off the covers, she looked at the luminous dial on her clock radio.

Who the hell was calling her on the house phone at three-forty in the morning? she wondered.

In the kitchen, Margaret asked a "Yeah?" into the mouthpiece of the wall phone.

"Mrs. Carrington," said the hotel operator, "there's a Miss Tiernan here to see you. Shall I send her up?"

Instantly, Margaret was awake. "Yes, please," she said more cordially. Back in her bedroom as she slipped into her bathrobe, Margaret wondered what catastrophe was bringing Marti to her doorstep in the middle of the night. She was waiting when the elevator operator deposited a gowned and furred Marti in the vestibule.

"How nice of you to drop in," said Margaret from her doorway as she motioned for Marti to enter. "But if you're trick-or-treating, you're a little late. Halloween was last week."

"Have you any ice cream?" Marti asked.

"What do I look like—your local Howard Johnson's? Next you'll ask if I have any nuts or marshmallows to go with it."

"Oh, God, Margaret, do you? I'd kill for that."

"I really don't believe you or this," said Margaret as she went into the kitchen to check her freezer. "Chocolate or fudge ripple?" she called into the other room.

"Right! Chocolate *and* fudge ripple," replied Marti.

"Do tell me there's a perfectly good reason why you are here in the middle of the night in formal attire about to have a food orgy in which I have the most awful feeling I'm going to participate."

"I was at the Waldorf Towers sleeping with one of our presidential hopefuls for '72 when I felt bored, lonely, disgusted, and that his party platform was a lot better than his party behavior."

"Used and abused, eh?" said Margaret as she entered the living room carrying two soup bowls filled with ice cream.

"I can't believe it. He pontificates on 'the good of the people' and one for all and working together and he is totally selfish and unfeeling as a lover. He wasn't 'working together' with me. Hardly. He was working with himself, for his own enjoyment, and God forbid if I tried to make my own."

"I don't believe you're actually going to accuse a man of treating you like an object," said Margaret wryly as she snuggled into her side chair by the fireplace.

"To *them* . . ."

"You say 'them' like 'them' is the enemy," Margaret said.

"Well, they are. At least they are when they treat me like a thing, like my image rather than like a person. I'm like some prize—some Rubens or Van Gogh that they are collecting. My needs are not considered. And they should be!" said Marti angrily as she thrust some ripple into her mouth. "I'm not a bank for a sperm deposit. Why should I be some passive participant at my own orgasm?"

"Perhaps we should call Germaine Greer or Kate Millett," said Margaret.

"Oh, bullshit! You know exactly what I'm talking about. Now that you're dating again, it can't be all that different for you."

"It's worse," Margaret said glumly. "I bet your presidential hopeful had no difficulty—how shall I say—obtaining and maintaining his political *posture*. Oh, that's good! I like that. The men I date, however, expect me to raise them from the dead. Pick up their spirits, so to speak. Oh, that's good too! It must be the ripple."

"Well, it's still easier for you," said Marti brusquely. "At your age, sex isn't all that important."

"Oh, really! At *my* age. My dear, I'm fifty-four. Not dead. It may take me a little longer to get there but . . . getting there is, as they say, half the fun."

"That's the point. Getting there, or to use the jargon of the day—'getting off' is half the fun. So why aren't we allowed to have it? Why is it they—'them'—have this damned prescribed role they want us to play?"

Margaret sighed. "Well, I must admit I've been very lucky. None of the men I've known, at least none of the ones I've known intimately, have ever wanted me to be what I wasn't. In fact, they were damned glad, and damned lucky if you ask me, that I wasn't a passive woman in bed or out. Which has left me rather poorly prepared for the poor excuse of a male I'm meeting nowadays. If I'm myself, they say I'm castrating them. It's insane. They put me on a pedestal—which is not what I want—and then when I try to come down from that pedestal . . ."

"They get upset. Oh, yes, I know," Marti said excitedly. "But there's a twist to it. At least there is with the younger man. He also has to be on a pedestal and his has to be eight to ten inches . . ."

"Eight to ten inches? Marti, don't be gross!"

"I should be so lucky! What I was saying before I was so

rudely interrupted: men don't want equality. They always want to be one up on you or—as I was saying—eight to ten inches higher."

"You want some more ice cream?" asked Margaret as she headed for the kitchen. "All this talk of sex has given me the munchies."

"I came here for wisdom," called Marti to the kitchen.

"I've only Sealtest or Schrafft's. I'm out of wisdom. Actually, if it's wisdom you want, try your mother. I'm sure she'd just love to discuss sex with you at this hour of the morning. A presidential hopeful, eh?" Margaret said. "Does he walk softly and carry a big stick?" she asked as she poked her head out of the kitchen, her eyebrows doing a Groucho Marx.

"I'm going to ignore that. Just pretend you didn't say it. By the way, have you any cookies?"

"Your kids ate them all yesterday and what they didn't eat they took with them to the airport."

"Oh, God help National Airlines! Mama gave them custard first and then you gave them cookies. For the stewardesses' sake I sure hope it was a smooth flight to Miami."

"You amaze me, sending little ones on a plane by themselves."

"That better be amazement and not judgment I hear in your voice," cautioned Marti, "or you'll be the recipient of your own knuckle sandwich. Need I remind you that the plane seats about two hundred? Which is hardly by themselves. And Vinnie was meeting the plane. I think it's good for them. I don't want my kids tied to my apron strings."

"Your daughter has begun looking at condos so I wouldn't worry about that," said Margaret.

"She is awfully independent for a ten-year-old, isn't she?" Marti said adoringly. "She swears it was Vinnie's idea but I swear it was hers that he fly them to Miami for a weekend as a birthday present." Marti laughed again. Then, quite suddenly, she turned serious. "Do you think there's such a thing as a woman becoming too strong, too liberated?"

"No, but I doubt if any man will agree with that," said Margaret. "I for one, given what I saw in my day, am delighted women are becoming—have become—strong, more aggressive and demanding. When I think back to my early years in Hollywood and the way women were treated, I am retroactively enraged. Worse than like objects. Meat is not an object the way a Rubens is. Women then had no status. No matter how much they earned, they were something to be owned . . .

controlled. And what was so awful—and thank God it's changed or changing—most women then didn't think it should be any different. In looking back, I think the reason so many legendary ladies cracked up or screwed up or did both was that that's how they saw themselves. As objects. As high-priced cunts."

"There are still women who fail to see themselves as equals to men or as *persons* to be prized," said Marti. "And for every woman who is in the process of liberating herself, there is a man who has yet to catch up with her. It's all very depressing. The pill has made us equals except it hasn't. Oh, no. That's a myth. When I was interviewing on college campuses, I found girls dropping the pill and their pants in equal parts. But they weren't feeling good about it. It was almost as if it were something they had to do. And many, although they wouldn't admit it to their peers, were very judgmental of their own actions. There was still that little voice inside that said . . . nice girls don't. And you know, when I interviewed the boys, when they let down privately and said how they really felt, they agreed: nice girls don't but they were awfully glad they now did. A double standard. Double? Triple! Quadruple! The truth is: for all the talk, as sexes, we've yet to move one inch!"

"Again with the inches? Really, Marti, you're obsessed."

When Marti laughed, Margaret continued cautiously. "I have a sneaking suspicion that somewhere in all this Mike Greer is playing a rather big role."

"Mike Greer is your typical chauvinist," exploded Marti. "Only he's not a pig about it. Just piggish. For all his talk, he would like me to be more at home than at large."

"You don't have a home—not the two of you anyway, remember?" said Margaret.

"But he's pushing for one. That's the problem. He wants a commitment. He has sort of intimated that either we move in together—have some sort of understanding that is as permanent as any can be without marriage or . . . or we end. Can you believe that?" sputtered Marti angrily.

"Shocking!" Margaret said, trying not to laugh. "And to think I can remember when it was the woman who pressed for a commitment, who gave ultimatums. My, how the times have indeed changed!"

"I have the feeling you are missing the point," said Marti, exasperated. "Times *have* changed. I don't want to 'settle down' and don't see why I should. Frankly, I'm toying with the idea of accepting North Vietnam's invitation to see their side of things. I probably won't go but I'd like to know I can. Mike doesn't want that. He wants me home and he can't understand home is wherever I am. When I'm with him, then that becomes our home, but when I'm away he and the home belong to the then and not the now."

"A sort of laissez-faire kind of arrangement," said Margaret.

"I knew you'd understand," Marti said happily.

"No, I can't say I do and I certainly can tell you that Franklin, if he were alive, wouldn't and James—he'd have my luggage packed—very neatly of course but packed nonetheless—waiting at the door."

"Are you telling me I'm wrong?" asked Marti defensively.

"Don't be ridiculous. Only you can tell yourself that. I certainly won't judge. I remember all too clearly how people—your mother and late aunt for example—thought I was far too independent and aggressive."

"God, but I hope by the time Ali is of age all of this role-playing and roles and sexist shit are long gone," said Marti.

"I doubt it but she'll write her own book about it, I'm sure."

"I just don't understand why Mike can't leave things as they are. We have a collective life and yet separate lives, if that makes any sense to you."

"In this day and age, my dear, nothing and yet everything make sense to me," said Margaret wearily.

"Do you know why I left tonight; know why I picked myself up, dressed, and left our presidential hopeful in the middle of the night?"

"Frankly no, and if he's who I think he is, I don't care; just give me the key and let me slip back in, take your place until the sunrise. That's not too much for an old aunt to ask, is it?"

"You wouldn't make it ten minutes as a feminist or in the Sisterhood," said Marti. "Those women have no sense of humor about anything."

"If I looked like most of them, neither would I," commiserated Margaret.

Marti's laugh seemed particularly loud given the lateness of the hour. "Well, they'd be pleased to hear I'm giving up men, or at least indiscriminate sleeping around," she added when she saw the "Oh, yeah?" look on Margaret's face. "Really. I've done my sixties thing. And no more. I like me too much to spread it around, particularly for some man who isn't aware or

650

caring of what he is getting. It makes me feel bad when that happens. And it doesn't do a thing for me that a good vibrator couldn't and without messing the sheets. From now on, my diaphragm is what I use to breathe deeply."

Taking the empty plate from Margaret's hands, Marti picked herself up from the couch and went into the kitchen. As she ran the water in the sink, she said loudly, "Fifty-four and you still care about *it*. God, how I wish you hadn't told me that. It's depressing."

"It wouldn't be if you were fifty-four, my dear," Margaret called out gaily.

The dishes cleaned, Marti turned off the tap and dried her hands on a towel that hung limply from the refrigerator's handle. In the living room, she looked at her aunt appraisingly. "You know something, you old lech? You're a hoot. An absolute hoot!"

Margaret cast her eyes demurely downward. "Once, in another such tender moment, your younger brother said I was 'too much. Too fucking much,' is how I recall he phrased it. I was touched then; I'm touched now. To be so thought of by one's relatives in one's lifetime is . . . well, I'm not sure how to express it. I'll know after I ask a question. Marti dear, what the fuck is a hoot?"

Looking at the transcript of Vince Malloy's grades made Vinnie Tiernan feel good. Three As, two Bs, and a C in physical education were, he decided, pretty damned good for a man who not so long ago couldn't remember his own name. Better still, with the spring term, he was a sophomore. It often seemed unbelievable to him but from the time he had begun taking courses a year ago last January, through the summer semester to now, he had completed his freshman requirements. And with an A-minus average!

Vinnie's first impulse upon receiving his grades that day in the morning mail had been to call Mike and then Marti. But he quashed that feeling, deciding he would first celebrate with himself. As he had recently discovered in his analysis, he had never learned to celebrate his triumphs, little or big, or just the miracle of existence, the miracle of self.

It wasn't the grades or the overall average that Vinnie was celebrating with a daylong binge of assorted miniature Danish pastries he had purchased from Wolfie's, but the accomplishment. He had done something strictly for himself. Not as a

Tiernan Tot or a Tiernan. No favors had been asked for or given. The success was his . . . Vince Malloy, the unknown and the unheralded. It felt good. Damn good. In fact, the only thing that didn't feel good in his life, thought Vinnie, was "the goddamn beard." He hated its itch but it was all that stood between Vince Malloy and Vince Tiernan. A few of his classmates had thought he looked familiar but none so far had put the beard on the well-known face and put two and two together to get one and the same man. Vinnie didn't know when if ever he would remove the beard as he had no desire to resume his former identity. In any shape or form.

Over the past year, he had been surprised that Marti's frequent presence in the Miami area hadn't led reporters straight to his door, behind which she often stayed for long weekends. But then the press no longer hounded Marti as it once did, seemingly finding her of less interest now that she was "political" than they did when she was "a star." Still, whether she was speaking out against the war or for women's rights on TV talk shows or college campuses, her speeches were constantly chronicled.

As he sat on the patio dunking a Danish into his coffee, Vinnie laughed as he thought of the uproar caused by just the announced title of Marti's next book. *How to Be Your Own Man* was Marti's Emancipation Proclamation in semiautobiographical style. It was her unshackling from "man"—her statement of independence and strength. Her detractors, of which there were many, decided it was her coming-out party and thus *dyke* was yet another of their descriptions for her.

"It's ridiculous!" Marti had protested as she sat on that very same patio at Christmas. "Every woman has attributes society labels as 'masculine' when they should simply be called human. These qualities should be nurtured and developed. A woman should not look to a man for a completeness she can give herself."

Mike Greer looked at her with great disdain. He put down his beer and very quietly said, "Horseshit! Pure and stinking horseshit. We all turn to one another for completeness. All relationships are about completion of self in some way. Haven't you ever listened to the lyrics of the song 'People'?"

"That's not what I mean and you know it!" Marti said, annoyed. "Most women are raised to believe they can't make it without a man; that their lives are half without a relationship;

652

that they need a man to make them feel better about themselves. It's *that* that's horseshit, my friend!"

Marti and Mike, sharing a room and the week between Christmas and New Year's in his home, had aroused many feelings in Vinnie, none of which was about them so much as they were about him. Similarly, watching Ali and Mark at play on the boat he had purchased and realizing they were not his children even though he felt as if they were, had also awakened dormant thoughts. When they had all departed for their separate lives, he remained troubled and somewhat anxious. For the first time, he confronted the fact that he was alone and that he had been for a very long time. What he could not discern was whether he really wished to change that. Did he want a relationship? A marriage? Children?

That he was experiencing such thoughts and feelings his analyst credited to his newly found ego strength; the same one that was permitting his ongoing, although not very frequent correspondence with his mother. But on that front too he was making progress. This week, when he had an indication his grades might be good or even excellent, he had realized that the last person he wanted to tell was his mother. When he asked himself why, his answer had forced a response to her last letter of six weeks ago. He did not like to write when there was nothing bad to say. His life was good. He was making it on his own terms. To tell her that would be like a pardon, would be allowing her off the hook he had continually kept her on. If, however, he continued to do badly, it could remain her fault. His debilitation had been her punishment; his aloneness his retribution and revenge. No, that too, he had to give up.

As he watched the sun set on Biscayne Bay, Vinnie decided he would go out that evening. No sooner had he made the decision than a voice asked: Where? Another said: And do what? And still another: With whom? These voices and their questions were well known to him. Usually they combined to keep him home evenings in front of the television set. As he had complained to Mike Greer over Christmas, "If only I were really feeling juicy, getting out wouldn't be so much of a problem. Then, too," he added, "if I were only sure of what I wanted . . ." He hadn't finished the statement; Mike Greer hadn't allowed that. "Find out. The way to do that, is . . . to do that!"

"I'm not so sure I'm ready to discover I'm gay," said Vinnie dourly.

"What makes you think you might be?" Greer asked.

" 'Cause I'm not turned on when I see a great-looking woman."

"Are you when you see a great-looking guy?" Greer questioned almost belligerently.

"No."

"So what does that tell you?"

"Nothing," Vinnie said.

"Bullshit. It tells me you're switched off. Or, just plain scared."

"Shitless," Vinnie added. "Scared shitless. You gotta remember I had some pretty rough times with sex."

"Don't show me 'before' pictures. This is 'after.' You want some slap-and-paste therapy? You got it! If you feel good about you, you have good sex."

"You're so fucking smart," Vinnie said. He could still hear Mike's bitter response: "Tell that to Marti," he growled.

This past week, with school on hiatus until the spring term, Vinnie had found himself with considerable time to fill and sharply felt the need for a someone. Confused but resolved to explore possibilities, he had driven to one of the area's few gay beaches. He parked in the municipal lot and sat on the low brick wall that overlooked the beach and the boys and men sitting and staring either at the sun or at one another. He allowed himself to be drawn into several conversations, some of which were dull, others pleasant, still more an unstated but expected prelude to a later assignation.

"I just can't see it," he said later to his analyst. "I can't feel me in bed with a man. It was different in groups. You sort of mixed it up without knowing what was happening, although *you* would say one always knows but one doesn't always want to accept the responsibility for what one knows. Okay, I'll buy that," Vinnie said, sitting up straight on the couch and facing the analyst. "Let's even say I got off—no pun intended—on the times the scenes got bisexual. Oh, shit! I don't know what the fuck I'm talking about. I just know I can't get it up thinking about sex with a man."

"I am going out tonight," Vinnie said loudly to the empty room and the voices from within that might challenge his decision. "Out! To the Beachcomber or the Aztec Lounge but out. Where there are girls . . . women. The truth is: I think I'm a closet straight."

He was mentally sorting through his closet, trying to decide on "a look" to wear—something he hadn't done since his pre-Home days—when the phone rang. He was surprised and somewhat hesitant when the caller asked for him by his real name.

"Yes, this is Vinnie Tiernan," he replied cautiously. Listening to the voice on the other end, his apprehension gave way to excitement. "Yes, yes, I did ask Mike Greer to inquire for me. You see, I had been to both Spectrum and Concept House and neither could use me as a drug counselor because I really don't have any credentials. . . . Sure, I can come in and talk to you. But listen, you *do* understand I'm only a fresh . . . I mean, I'm a sophomore in college and I've more to recommend me in my experience than I do in my education. So far," added Vinnie. "So far."

"Ma!"

Through the eerie sounds of sobbing Reese heard the cry. "Ma!"

It screamed through the blackness and into her soul. "Ma! Wake up. Please wake up."

Karl was crying as she awakened to find her son pushing and shoving at what had just been her sleeping body.

"I'm up, Karl. I'm up. It's all right, baby," she reassured the boy without knowing what had been troubling him.

Kristan, too, was standing by the bed, tears in her eyes, the only expression on an otherwise masked face.

"Was I dreaming again?" she asked stupidly. "Another nightmare. Just a bad dream," she told the children. "Where is Kelly? Is she all right?"

When the children looked at her blankly, Reese said, "Kristan, please see if your sister is all right." Sitting up in her bed, Reese discovered the sheet by the night table was wet; on it, the highball glass lay tipped over. Seeing Karl looking from the glass to her and back again, she said quickly, "The ham . . . it made me thirsty. I must have fallen asleep with the ice water in my hand."

The boy said nothing as he sat on the edge of the bed. "You were crying. Like the last time. Only it was louder . . . worse."

She reached out to touch her son, so much like Thomas in appearance and not at all like him in makeup. "It was just a bad dream," she said again.

"About Daddy?" Karl asked.

Reese sighed. "No," she lied. "It wasn't about anything. You know how silly dreams can be. Real mixed-up stuff."

"He's not going to come home, is he?" asked Karl, trembling.

"Yes, he is!" said Reese vehemently. "Your father wouldn't leave us."

"If Daddy was dead, he wouldn't have any choice," said Kristan, who had just returned to the room.

"But he's not dead, darling," Reese said reassuringly.

"How do you know, Mommy?" asked Kristan.

God, how do I know? asked Reese silently. "It's just something mommies know. When a man and woman are married, and when they love each other, there are certain things they sense about one another without being told. Kristan, is Kelly all right?"

"Sleeping," was the one-word response.

"Mom, suppose Daddy found another family?"

Reese looked at her son, looking lost in the pajamas that were still a size too large for him despite her mother's insistence last Christmas that he would soon grow into them, and wondered what was going through his mind.

"This article I read," he explained. "It said some of the soldiers coming back from Vietnam had new wives and children. Maybe that's what happened to Daddy. Maybe he has a new family and can't come back."

"Karl, we are Daddy's family. He doesn't want any other. He loves us." Even as she talked to Karl, she could see the doubt on his face. It was at times like this that she wished she could crawl into that blond little head of Karl's to hear what he was really thinking. "Daddy, wherever he is, prays for us every day. He needs us just as we need him."

"Mom, if Daddy's dead, would you ever get married again?"

Kristan's question was totally new to Reese. She wondered what the child was really asking, what fears she was really expressing. The doctors she had seen advised her to ask, if she didn't know.

"Kristan, that's such a strange question. Why do you ask it?"

"Just wondered," said Kristan, her face remaining masked. "Why were you crying?"

"A dream. A bad dream," Reese repeated wearily.

Kristan had climbed onto the big queen-sized bed and had snuggled up to her side. Looking at Karl's face, she realized that he, too, wanted that comfort and safety.

"Hop in, kid. There's plenty of room. We'll all cuddle up in this big bed and be snug as a bug. Okay?"

Her voice was as light and as merry as any professional storyteller's. The children bedded down and as their eyes were closing, Reese was cooing: "Daddy'll be home just as soon as he can. And I've got this most terrific feeling that we're going to get a letter tomorrow. And if not tomorrow, then the next day or the day after that for sure. I can feel it in my bones. Just like I do before it rains."

A letter, thought Reese as her hand played with Kristan's fine blonde hair. A single, solitary, lone letter. One. It would be wonderful. In eighteen months, there hadn't been one. Not one. Not a single, solitary, lone letter. Nothing. Not a word. Not a sign. Not. No.

But she wrote. Three times a week, she wrote a letter and each time, before sealing it, she had the children add a few lines of their own to it. Kelly protested. "But I hardly know the man!" she complained, sounding more like an old woman than a little girl who would just be eight in November.

There were nights, such as this one, when Reese, too, felt she hardly knew the man. Thomas was, and had been, so very far away for so very long. The nightmare was the same she had been having for months. In it, Thomas came home . . . in a casket. In several caskets. All unmarked. And she couldn't tell which belonged to her. The only way was for her to open each, one at a time. It was then her screams would start.

Her parents had urged her to come home. She reminded them repeatedly that she was home. In her home. The children, she explained, had enough difficulties without adding a change of schools, environment, and friends. Her parents visited three times a year, two weeks at a time. They made Reese more nervous than she already was with their good intentions and their sympathetic looks that eroded the resolve she was determined to wear. And they criticized. For her own good, of course. Her father, the doctor, actually prescribed sleeping pills; he thought them better than the vodka at night. Her parents were of another generation. They did not understand how people could smoke or drink. And barbiturates were not hard drugs, her father insisted, not morphine or heroin.

Everyone had suggestions on how she should live her life. Her mother-in-law had called several times and offered to stay with the children if Reese wanted to get away. Reese had laughed at her, mocked her good intentions, and asked that she not call again. And she didn't. Reese did not feel the least bit contrite about how she had treated "Mother Ollson." She wanted no part of a woman who condoned her son's decision to disobey the law and run from his duty as a soldier. That family was an insult to her husband and to America. Like father, like son. Criminals.

The thought of Marti made Reese shudder. She could think of no one she hated more. Despite Marti's insistence that she was wrong, Reese knew Marti had intentionally distorted her words in her first book. She had played with Reese's sentences and used them to further her antiwar sentiments. In her letter to Marti, she had demanded to know how she could live with herself knowing she had purposely distorted the truth. She had asked how Marti dare use innocent people who were fighting to protect garbage like her to further her own selfish aims. Marti had replied that Reese misunderstood her intentions and the book; that she was not necessarily anti the war in Vietnam but anti war of any kind.

It was lies and Reese wrote back telling Marti it was just that. To which Marti had answered: "No wonder you and Thomas are married. You complement each other perfectly." That was meant to be an insult, Reese knew, but it did not have the intended effect.

Reese's reverie was interrupted by Karl's muted cries. Reaching across Kristan, she stroked her son's head. His eyelids fluttered open and then closed. The tiny cries stopped. Softly, Reese began singing: "Letters. We get letters. We get stacks and stacks of letters. Dear Perry: Would you be so kind. To fill a request and sing the songs we love best."

Reese lay back on her pillow.

Dear Thomas, she began. Dear Thomas wherever and however you are. How are you? We are not fine. We are not good little soldiers. We are people. Frightened little people. And we blame you: you and your goddamn need to play soldier. Values. Ethics. Morals. Whose? And who the hell gives a damn? No one in this country, I assure you. They've all turned against you, Thomas. And against me. Us. Our children. Thanks to you and your values we live all alone. At least I do. Nowhere to go; nothing to do; and certainly no one to do my nothing with. My husband is a prisoner of war. What the hell do you think I am? The torture inflicted on you can't be any greater than the torture inflicted on me   . on your children. And like you, all I give to people is my name, rank, and serial number. The only difference between us is: the people I meet don't want any further information. In fact, the less they know about me, the happier they are. My feelings? My children's feelings? Don't be ridiculous! No one cares. Guess what we did tonight, the first night of the weekend. We watched "The Brady Bunch," "The Partridge Family," "Room 222," and "The Odd Couple." We laughed. We had ice cream. We went to bed. We had bad dreams. Vietnam? What's that? It wasn't part of "Love, American Style" which I stayed up to see after I put the kids to sleep.

By the way, darling, guess what day this is? Come on, guess! Give up? Well, it's June 25th. We've been married twelve years today. Twelve years since we said our I dos. Only I don't anymore. I really don't, Thomas. I am so angry and hurting and I feel so crazy that I think I hate more than I love you. I don't care where you are. If you're dead, I wish you'd have the courtesy just to let us know.

Reese flung herself out of bed. As she wrapped her robe tightly about her, she looked to see if the children were still sleeping. Assured that they were, she slipped out of the room and down the stairs. If there was ever to be any sleep for her that night, she knew she just had to have another drink.

The television screen was dark. And silent. Then faintly, as if drawing near from a great distance, came the sound of sleighbells. The screen went white, as whirling snowflakes the size of butterflies fell upon holiday shoppers. The camera froze on the face of a young man whose army coat collar was turned up against the wind. The title appeared as the sound of sleighbells faded into a deepening distance. *A Merry Little Christmas*, it read. A Film by John J. Ollson.

They had grouped in John's den shortly after Christmas dinner and watched the one-hour PBS documentary without comment. The film, raw, almost rude in its blunt edges, was a closeup on the lives of those American men who had dissented and deserted to Canada. It painted pictures of people rather than villains or heroes. Confused people and some not so confused. It suggested their future as it depicted life in a country that on the surface was friendly but below was as cold as its winter. It was a film of questions but with few answers. It was about "marking time" and "filling space." It was about anger and alienation, resentment and guilt. And hope.

None of the family wished to watch the round-table discussion on amnesty that immediately followed on the local PBS station because each was involved in reactions that were painful yet curiously joyous. John felt as if he were being held together with rubber bands so stretched that they were close to breaking. Carolyn was sitting quietly, her hand still in Margaret's. Marti nibbled at her bottom lip. The cameras had never focused on John J. but she had seen him in every frame of the film. Everyone had felt him. On screen. In the room. Little JJ had made a big film.

For weeks, John had been unable to reach a decision, to make the commitment others had asked of him. There were so many doubts; fears, too. With one film, his son had turned them all aside. Not gone but aside. There would always be the doubts and the fears. About oneself and one's capabilities. And about others. Particularly about others. Those others who hated and let their hate be known.

"I've come to a decision," John said softly. As each woman turned toward him, she saw from his face what that decision was. A short cry burst from Marti before she burst upon John, enfolding him in a supportive embrace. Carolyn nodded approvingly as her eyes caught John's. Yes, it was right although she hated it. Margaret's hand, squeezing hers, firmly yet gently, was an expression of her concern. They must all be concerned, thought Carolyn. After all, concern is what it's all about, isn't it?

MEMO: TO ALL MEN
FROM: THOMAS OLLSON

This is to advise that there has been no Christmas this year by order of the North Vietnamese, your "hosts" here at the "Hanoi Hilton." Thus, no exchange of presents and no caroling between the "Stardust," the "Gold Nugget," and the "Desert Inn."

Thomas laughed as he put the imaginary memo aside in his head. He was remembering the shocked look on the enemy's faces last March when he and several other senior officers had tried to hold a church service for their men. How quickly they were disassembled. And nearly dismembered. That wasn't funny. But the men, those who had remained, had burst into "The Star-Spangled Banner," which had incensed the gooks and caused brutal beatings. He wondered how many of those men were alive today, and of those that were, how many would dare, even in some silent way, to celebrate Christmas. He had hoped his "hosts" on Skid Row might have allowed him to go "home" for the holidays—"home" being the one large room where he could sleep on the floor but next to an American. Next to someone, some*thing* other than a bug.

He had been a "guest" on Skid Row since March. He had been given opportunities to "check out" but he had declined. Steadfastly. Thomas Ollson was not about to speak to or with American antiwar delegations. Thomas Ollson was not about to repudiate all he believed. Not even when they shocked his sensibilities or attempted to humiliate him in front of his men. They had sought a reaction last spring when they had taken him from his six-by-four "room" at Skid Row and placed him with the others. All others. Enlistees and officers; children and men. From the *New York Daily News* and the *Los Angeles Times* they read the reports of John J. Ollson's defection from the army and his flight to Canada. They read Mr. and Mrs. John Ollson's statement. But they could not read his face. And they had slapped it, several times, verbally and physically, to see if it would say something "quotable." It and he hadn't.

They thought Skid Row was the worst of all possible punishments. Solitary confinement. Aloneness. Men had returned to fetal positions and never dreamed of another white or any other colored Christmas again once placed and left on Skid Row. But Thomas dreamed and planned and wrote. Mainly, he wrote. Aloneness, solitary confinement, was "a piece of cake."

MEMO: TO ALL MEN
FROM: THOMAS OLLSON

As I write this memo, I am reminded of another room, not as small, another Christmas—actually, many other Christmases many years ago. Although it was Central Park West and not by any stretch of the imagination can that be called Skid Row, it was solitary confinement. Although with my family, I lived alone. Once sorry for myself, I now am grateful for that opportunity, for the loneliness, for the feeling of being alone. Totally alone. Had I not had such a solitary experience, I would not be here today, writing to you all. All those many years, alone in my room, alone in my head, served me well. They made me a soldier.

* * *

Remembering, Thomas paused in the writing of his memo.

"Chapter twenty-six, page eight hundred twelve," he suddenly said aloud. Christmas, 1947. Or was it 1946? It's Christmas Day and the man we visited at the mental hospital is coming home for Christmas dinner. Mama says he is our father but he's not the father I remember. Mama says I'm too young to remember how he once was but that's not true. He used to sit with his legs crossed in his easy chair and I would climb up on his knee to be bounced. He was a good bouncer. This man, the one in the hospital, he doesn't bounce.

My mother placed this man at the head of our Christmas table. I was afraid to look at him for too long a time. Not that it would have mattered as he didn't see me.

Looking back, seeing it now, I realize he didn't see anyone. No one. Not just me or Marti. No one. He hardly ate. He hardly spoke. He hardly was. Just like some of the men here after they've visited Calcutta or been on Skid Row. His face sat atop a body atop the head of the table. It was a face in pain. Good God, the man was in pain! Why didn't someone give him something for it? Not a fruit compote, dammit. Something stronger.

I used to tell myself my father was killed in the war. I didn't realize until this very moment, that was true. The war killed my father, and then sent me someone else in his stead.

Dear Karl,

I promise you on this holiest of days I will come back the same man that I was. No, I will come back better. Much better.

Dear Karl,

It has come to my attention, son, that some men when they return from the war, particularly if they have served time as prisoners, are seemingly changed from what they once were. Although I would hope no such change would take place in me, I want to alert you to that possibility. Also, this change, should it occur, will have nothing to do with you.

Dear Karl,

You're old enough to understand nothing remains the same. Nothing. Not a goddamn thing. Life changes people and you can't do a damn thing about that even when you want to. Life is tough and don't believe anyone who says otherwise. It's damn tough which is why I'm always on your case, trying to toughen you up. Not for my sake. But for yours. To take on this thing called life. They say life is to be lived but I wonder if it's not to be fought. At least I think that sometimes.

Dear Karl,

It's Christmas Day and I'm alone in an awful little room that's cramped and cold and crawling with vermin. And I'm writing you because I'm so fucking lonely and upset and depressed and I miss you and everyone else in the family and sometimes it is so goddamn hard to keep going and . . .

Christmas, 1947 or 1946. My father sits in a chair by the fireplace. I am in the hallway trying to decide whether to ask him a question. I don't ask it because I think I know the answer. Today, these many years later, I don't think I had that answer right. My father may have loved me after all. Maybe not a lot. Maybe not as much as I wanted. But maybe as much as he could. "They" can remove love from you just as easily as they can remove Christmas and replace it with deprivation and despair. And death.

Dear Reese,

I have made a decision. I will live so that we can always celebrate Christmas. Together. All of us. Always. Do you hear? That's a command, goddamnit. A goddamn command!

Dear Reese,

Disregard first letter. The only decision worth making is the one I made years ago when I promised to take you for my wedded wife. To love . . . honor . . . cherish. Till death do us part. But let's not think about that. In fact, let's make a very conscious decision not to think about that at all.

They had just finished the Christmas dinner she had prepared a day after the fact and as she cleared the dishes, Mike Greer was pouring Courvoisier into brandy snifters. He had been pleased that she had insisted that she cook for him and not he for her, despite her having been the one to arrive in Los Angeles after a long flight.

She had brought him gifts from the East and the family's blessings. She had also brought the pork chops from a favorite butcher and the bread-and-chestnut stuffing from her mother's refrigerator and pantry. There was something sweetly ludicrous about a gorgeous woman stepping off a 747 with a shopping bag filled with groceries. He had liked that; liked it a lot. It made him feel good. About them.

When she came into his living room, he handed her the brandy. As he lifted his glass in silent tribute to her, Mike Greer reached a decision. He would marry this woman if she was ready. An hour later, as they cuddled in bed, Mike Greer proposed. Instantly, Brooke Canaday said yes. Not once but twice. Just in case he hadn't heard or understood her the first time.

Vinnie was sleeping when the clock radio went off and announced it was five minutes before ten, sixty-three degrees and partly cloudy this second day of January 1972. He was half in and half out of the new day when the third item on the newscast acted like cold water in his face. "Hot damn!" he exclaimed joyously as he bounded off the bed. As the newscaster gave further details, Vinnie was hopping up and down on the cold terrazzo floor even as he dialed the telephone.

"Who are you calling?" asked a sleepy voice from the bed.

"My uncle. He just announced he will enter the Democratic primary in June. Goddamn if he isn't running for the U.S. Congress!"

"Your uncle?" the girl repeated sleepily.

Vinnie abruptly hung up the telephone. If he spoke to John and John was his uncle, who would that make him? He knew who but he didn't want the girl to know. To her, he was Vince Malloy. She liked Vince Malloy. And he wanted to keep it that way and not complicate what had been the best thing that had happened since coming to Miami as Vincent Tiernan. As the girl searched his face for clues, Vinnie decided to keep his identity like his face: hidden from public view.

"What would you like for breakfast?" he asked as he sat on the bed next to her.

"You!" she said as she reached up and slid her arms around his neck.

"Coming right *up*," said Vinnie.

As the girl explored Vinnie's nakedness, she laughed and then said, "So I see. Well, Mother always said one should start the day with a good breakfast."

*   *   *

664

The map was clearly outlined, the man at the car rental agency having taken pains to mark in red the roads she should travel. Marti's hands, which had been sweating from nervousness, were now dry as she became more assured of the Ford's touch and the fact that she was not being followed.

The flight had been an easy hour and twenty minutes. No one had guessed that beneath the blonde Dynel Harpo Marx-like wig was a Marti Tiernan. The owllike glasses helped the disguise. She had purposely chosen to fly into Detroit rather than Buffalo because it was a busier airport and so she was even less likely to be noticed. The car rental had been paid for in advance in the name of Nancy Blanchard. Such had been Marti's precautions. Her planning had begun that night in John's den when her brother's film had prompted her decision.

She had not been able to tell any member of the family of her intentions, which is how they would have wanted it and how it had to be, given the surveillance they were under. Still, Marti was certain that her father knew something was afoot. Why would she have asked him for JJ's phone number otherwise?

She had called John J. from a phone booth in the RCA Building, having left Ali and Mark at the ice-skating rink on the pretext of "running into" Saks. Because she knew JJ's phone was tapped, she identified herself as Mickey's mother, calling to see if Mickey needed anything. JJ had said he would inquire and call her back in five minutes. Which he did from a filling station somewhere in Rosedale. His delight was uncontrolled. He did not attempt to change her mind but encouraged her decision to visit the day after New Year's.

"We'll meet at the Hockey Hall of Fame building at Exhibition Place," he said. "Who the hell would ever think to spot the two of us among hockey pucks?" he added.

That morning, as soon as she had successfully pushed Ali and Mark out the front door and pointed them in the direction of the Ethical Culture School where classes were resuming after the Christmas break, Marti ran up the stairs of the brownstone she had purchased two years ago in Chelsea and took a fast shower. She purposely did not apply makeup afterward. Quickly, she took the shoulder bag from her closet, already packed with necessities only, and walked down the two flights to the kitchen where she found Mrs. Yemen, the housekeeper. Informing her she would be back late that night and no, she could not be reached, she took her brown cloth

665

coat from the hall closet, slipped into it and then, at the front door, stood a second or two longer than necessary so that if anyone was watching or observing, they could get a good look at her. Then she hailed a taxi and told the driver to take her to Bloomingdale's.

She had loved it as it had all felt very 007. At the store, she purchased a horrible purplish coat and took it with her into the ladies' room where she donned her Harpo Marx wig and her new coat—leaving her other in the lavatory stall—and left the store looking quite unlike the way she had when she entered. On the corner of Fifty-ninth and Third, she hailed another taxi and took it to La Guardia Airport. Now, as she drove out of the Detroit-Windsor tunnel toward Toronto, Marti felt exhilarated. In a matter of hours, she would see her brother. In nervous anticipation, her hands started to sweat again. That JJ might like her idea—an idea that had worldwide ramifications—well, best not to think of that, she decided, until we are among the Maurice Richards and Edgar Laprades of the hockey world.

"You would have thought by now I would have learned," said Margaret as she paced the tiny dressing room, waving her cigarette about as if in a bad imitation of Bette Davis. "But no. Fifty-five years old and I'm still being manipulated."

"Oh, do shut up and do put out that cigarette before you burn yourself," said Carolyn impatiently as she fixed the wig of gray and white hair on her head.

"It calms me down," Margaret protested.

"Margaret, you don't smoke, remember?" said Carolyn nastily.

"I can't even remember my name, thanks to you," screamed Margaret. "Why, tell me, *why* am I doing this to myself? I don't need it. I'm a very big star, you know. At this very moment, I could be doing Hostess Twinkie commercials."

"You are giving me such a headache," complained Carolyn. "Now tell me," she said, turning from the makeup mirror toward Margaret, "do I look old enough?"

"Neither of us is old enough for this. Or we're too old. I'm not sure which. You make me so crazy I'm not sure of anything except the date. Do you know what day this is?" asked Margaret evilly.

"It's January third. I am well aware of that without you reminding me."

"Do you know what happens to famous actresses who open

666

on Broadway on January third?" crooned Margaret. "They fall on their famous asses."

"Tenth Avenue is not Broadway. Now stop it. Let me look at you." As Carolyn assessed Margaret's makeup, she shook her head and said admiringly, "You're going to make a wonderful old lady."

"If I live long enough. Any more opening nights with you and I'll die young."

"You can never die young anymore, Margaret. Not ever."

"Do you remember that applecart—the one you're going to wind up behind? Remember how I promised to buy an apple from you? Well, I will. And guess where I'm going to shove it! In fact, if I had an apple, I'd do it right now. It might help your performance—how shall we say—take wing."

"What are you so hysterical about? I honestly don't understand. This is just a little production of *Arsenic and Old Lace*, performed by our very best students. A little theatre offering," said Carolyn trying to be placating.

"My dear dumb duckie. A *little* theatre offering? Exactly! Very little. Only four hundred seats surrounding us. We're like pioneers in a circle and they, D.D., are the Indians. We are about to be scalped by the critics, particularly those who do not write for the newspapers. They'll be so close to the stage they'll see right through our makeup to the pimples and wrinkles. They'll hear every breath, every wheeze. And by the way, Carolyn, you do wheeze."

"It is a rather small theater, isn't it?" Carolyn asked tremulously. "I hadn't really thought about that."

"And because *you* haven't thought about *that*, my glorious career—the one that has spanned three mediums and four decades—will be ruined. And what have I got to show for it, I ask you?"

"That damn fur coat you're wearing! That's what. Honestly, Margaret, it's one hundred degrees in here if it's a degree. Don't you think you might take that legendary mink off your back?"

"It comforts me. It reminds me of Oscars and Tonys and a few Irvings and Bruces if you want to know the truth," added Margaret with a leer.

"Need I remind you, this is a repertory company, a showcase for the young and talented. We are not the stars here," said Carolyn airily.

"Oh, but butter wouldn't melt in that mouth of hers! Who

are you kidding? Who? Not me, I assure you. There is but one reason we are about to go out there and make fools of ourselves. Fools, Carolyn. Utter fools. And the reason is your vanity. Yes! Yes! Your vanity. Your pride that is about to goeth for a fall on your prideful ass. You think I don't know this is your last-gasp attempt, your last hope, your drowning man's third time up before he goes down."

"Margaret, what are you talking about!" Carolyn demanded impatiently.

"You think portraying a sweet old lady who just happens to commit murder is going to win you glorious notices and propel you into this coat of mine—of which you've always been maniacally jealous. Your whole life is one attempt to be a legendary lady at last. Oh, you don't fool me, Carolyn. Believe me. God will punish you."

"He already has," snapped Carolyn. "With you! Well, I've had enough. You're right. We never learn. But I've had it. I want separate dressing rooms. Yours should be in Pittsburgh. Actually, I want a divorce. We've been through this too often for too many years. The magic is gone. Over. We both know it, so why pretend otherwise. It's no good anymore. It won't work. It's finished. Margaret, I want you to go out there and tell all those people to go home."

A knock on their door brought the room to a stunned silence. Who dared to bother them before a performance, they wondered. Without being asked, a young girl opened the door and walked in carrying a huge bouquet of flowers.

"Oh, hi, you two," she said in greeting. "Some lady came backstage and asked that I give you these," she said, thrusting the flowers at Margaret. "They're for both of you," the girl added, closing the door behind her as she left the room.

Margaret opened the door and screamed after her, "Don't bother to knock. Just come right in." She slammed the door angrily and then stuffed the bouquet in an umbrella stand. "Damned impertinence. She must know something. Maybe she heard some talk among the reviewers. Maybe she knows they're going to massacre us and so has no respect for either of us."

"Margaret, she has never had any respect for either of us," said Carolyn with icy calm. "She has always made it very plain she thinks we are has-beens, never-wases, and never-will-bes."

"So what the hell is she doing with us? Why haven't we just kicked her ass out? This is our company, isn't it?"

"And it *is* funded by her father's foundation, isn't it?" sneered Carolyn.

Margaret opened the door to the dressing room and in her sweetest voice called out, "So nice of you to have dropped in. Do come anytime. The door is always open." Closing the door, Margaret muttered, "Cunt!"

Carolyn screamed, "How often must I ask you not to use that disgusting word. It's loathsome, cheap, degrading . . ."

"How would you like a knuckle sandwich with mustard and relish?" asked Margaret as she took the note from the bouquet of flowers. "Cunt!" she said again as she read the card.

"Margaret!"

"Oh, shut up and listen to this, Lynnie. 'To Arsenic *and* Old Lace—and we'll let you two decide which is which—knock them dead. Love, Nancy.' Oh, I always knew that woman would show her true colors again. God, I think I'm going to throw up and if I do, guess where it's going to be. Listen, maybe if you tell me again why we are doing this, I'll feel better."

"Because we must. Once a year, we must trot out our wares. Wares, here, refers not to us but to our students. Our actors and our costume, set, and lighting designers. Our prop men and stage managers. If we are to continue to receive funds from both the private and public sector, we must put our best feet forward."

"Not good enough! I say we sell. Maybe Mary and Ethel would buy in. Boy, what I wouldn't give to see Ethel flying around that stage as Peter Pan. What a hoot!"

"A hoot? Would you please explain?" asked Carolyn.

Another knock on the door again brought the room to stunned silence.

"Do come in, whoever you are who is so foolhardy to destroy theatre tradition, not to mention our concentration, and visit the actors before curtain," said Margaret, her voice dripping sarcasm.

John's beaming face appeared in the doorway. "Just popped in to say good luck to you."

"Good luck? Luck!" exploded Carolyn. "You have the nerve to come here at a time like this and wish us luck? Are you crazy? What a dreadful thing to say! Have we gotten so bad that we need outside forces to see us through? How dare you upset us! How could you do such a thing as wish us luck?"

Before he could respond, John was elbowed into the room by Marti.

"Why are you wearing a black strapless evening gown? This is a school, remember?" Carolyn said angrily.

"Ma, this is an opening night," replied Marti.

"No! No! No! It really *isn't*. Not *that* kind of opening night anyway. This is just a little offering by a little rep company," said Carolyn.

"Ma, your little rep company has in its audience one of the great collections outside of the Metropolitan Museum. There are Mick and Bianca, Jackie and Ari, even the Carpenters, Ma."

"Oh, God!" said Carolyn as she crossed herself.

"And, Ma, the box office is holding two tickets—Row F center—in the name of R. Burton."

"Would you get your daughter out of here?" screamed Margaret.

"*My* daughter? How dare you? What do you mean *my* daughter. For years she was your precious Marti. Now that I don't want her, you shove her back on me. Well, no thank you. No thank you at all for nothing!" yelled Carolyn.

"Ma!" protested Marti.

"Don't you 'Ma' me. Why are you here anyway? This is no time for a social visit."

"Five minutes to curtain, everybody!" yelled a voice outside the dressing room door.

"Up yours!" Margaret screamed back.

"Come, Marti. I think we best leave," said John. "Obviously we have two hysterics here who couldn't possibly deal with the message you have brought from JJ."

John had Marti by the arm and was approaching the door when Margaret placed herself between it and them. In one quick motion, she snapped the bolt on the door just as Carolyn said in a most menacing voice, "If you ever hope to leave this room alive, I suggest you start talking. And fast!"

4

It's ugly but these are ugly times, thought Reese as her eyes focused on the TV on the kitchen counter while her hands automatically washed the dinner dishes. She felt no sympathy whatsoever for the man whose stonelike face appeared, disappeared, and then reappeared on the screen as accusations were hurled by offscreen voices. Actually, Reese realized that she was glad her father-in-law was being vilified. Had she a stone, she, too, would cast it.

Carolyn's face disturbed her as did her entire presence. She was standing by John's side. Tall. Calm. No hint of upset but strong and assured. There was even a righteous attitude that was pouring into the camera and into the six o'clock news. It was unusual for a California newscast to focus on a campaign in another city but John Ollson's candidacy for Congress had become a national issue and even she had been thrust into the limelight because of it.

When the first reporter called the house for a reaction to her father-in-law's declaring himself a candidate, Reese had been caught unprepared. She even had asked: "Why me?" To which the reporter had replied, "Because your husband is a military man and a prisoner in a war your father-in-law feels is immoral for us to be in. He would not see your husband as a hero."

Although the last statement was pure speculation, it pushed the desired button. Reese exploded, denouncing John, and attacking him personally as a father as well as a political candidate. She went on to accuse the entire family of "war crimes" against the country.

What had been meant to be a "small story" for a local newspaper became a front-page, nationwide controversy. For days afterward, Reese's telephone did not stop ringing with requests for interviews and . . . with threats. The hate mail arrived along with the love letters. At school, Karl was terrorized by the children of the antiwar movement. An irony but a fact to be faced. And feared. At supermarkets, women who had never spoken to Reese, spoke to her now, either harshly or lovingly. A cross was burned on her lawn, which made no sense to anyone. WAR-MONGER, splashed in red paint across the garage door, did, however.

Again, the Tomlinsons asked their daughter to come home. Again she reminded her parents she was home. But this time, with sleep becoming next to impossible, she took the Librium her father sent, illegally, through the mail. She also had her phone number changed to an unlisted one. That ended the crank calls. It also ended a hope she didn't know she carried. She awoke one night, sweating, panicked, thinking . . . My God, Should Thomas want to call, he can't reach me. It was only after she reminded herself that a phone was not within Thomas's reach that she was able to return to rest.

The TV screen was awash with demonstrators and placards jostling one another before John's campaign office on Sixty-third Street and Broadway. The Hawks and the Doves were at one another in words threatening to become deeds. Their faces were all ugly, but these were, she repeated as she reminded herself, ugly times. And she was glad they were finally raining down on her father-in-law. She was certain Thomas would be glad too.

Judging by the sun's position in the scorched sky, it was somewhere after noon, Thomas calculated, when they took him from Skid Row to the Camp Unity area which was in another part of Hoala Prison. There, he was placed in the center of a circle, surrounded by forty-five or fifty men, some of whom had been part of the Triple Nickel Squadron. He had no idea why he was in this room or in the circle's center. At the moment, what mattered was . . . people. People upon people upon people. Faces. Forms. After so long in solitary, to see other persons! Although they had all been warned not to communicate, his eyes searched out familiar faces. With a wink here, a half-smile there, the men greeted Thomas.

The gook they called "Rabbit" was suddenly in the circle standing next to Thomas, several newspapers clutched in his hand. In his accented English, he began talking, ever so sarcastically, about the treasured freedom of the press and Americans' right to dissent. And then he began to read, first the announcement in the January 2 edition of the *New York*

Times that reported John Ollson's candidacy for Congress. Then the Rabbit read of the "spring storms"—as the *Post* referred to the controversy that surrounded the candidate. And the threats. "And to think," said the Rabbit, "just because he proposes peace." Methodically, Rabbit read John's antiwar campaign speeches He read slowly, allowing each sentence with its thought to sink into his captive audience's awareness. He read of John's plea for amnesty and he read of the propaganda film being prepared by Marti Tiernan and her dissenter/deserter brother; a film that would focus on the *bravery* of those who dared to defy the draft. Last, Rabbit read the heartfelt and so twice as heartrending rantings of Theresa Tomlinson Ollson.

He stood there feeling naked. He could hear Reese's words above all others; hear her anguish and her anger. He yearned to reach out and comfort her. And then he thought of his father, the man about whom he had written in the last sixty-seven pages of his book. And Thomas hurt for him. His father was wrong. Very wrong. But he was right to take an active role in his government. He was using the system and that was his right, just as it was the system's right to denounce and destroy him.

"And now perhaps we shall hear a few words from Captain Ollson?" said the Rabbit, his voice terrifying in its sweetness.

Thomas said nothing. Rabbit spoke again. "Captain, you are keeping us waiting. Surely you must have something to say about your family's politics; your country's treatment of them and others like them who believe in your treasured freedom of speech. Is there not something to be learned, Captain. by your father's speaking out against the crimes perpetrated by America against the people of Vietnam? Shouldn't you do the same, Captain?" the Rabbit asked as he moved within inches of Thomas's face.

Thomas didn't speak. He screamed when they kicked and broke two of the ribs that poked through his emaciated body, but he did not speak. No matter what they did—all they did—he steadfastly refused

With her head on his chest, his arm about her shoulders, Carolyn could hear John's heart beating and feel his chest rise and fall in his steady breathing. Awake, despite the lateness of the hour and the exhaustion she had felt upon her return from her evening performance at the theatre in *Arsenic and*

Old Lace, Carolyn shivered as she thought of the state of their lives. Immediately, John drew her closer to him as he pulled the quilt covers up to engulf them even more than they already did.

Carolyn was not shivering from the cold but from an anxiety caused by anger. She walked around most days wanting to shake and then scream at anyone who would listen. How could people be so stupid as not to realize John wanted not what was best for him but what was best for the country? How could they think him traitorous? Worse yet, how could they dare think him incompetent! The smears and the smirches were unrelenting. Half-truths and total conjectures were brutal reminders of what had once been brutal times.

The entire family was under attack. Hadn't Margaret defied the House Un-American Activities Committee years ago? Indeed she had! John and his supporters agreed proudly. Hadn't John Ollson Jr. dodged his responsibility? No! boomed John. He had fulfilled it. And hadn't he, John Ollson, always been a critic rather than a supporter of America? One can support by criticism that is constructive far better than if one is a yes man, he countered.

Reese's tirade added to the harassment. Thomas Ollson, in absentia, became news and a hero. Newspapers concocted articles about the "feud" between father and son and made it seem as if theirs were an ongoing ideological war when in truth there had been no communication between the two in years. A feature writer for the Women's News Service cornered Reese in the dairy department of the A & P and later, in her story, made much of the fact that Thomas Ollson had not invited his father to his wedding, so at odds was he with his father's political leanings.

Still, the early polling of the Nineteenth Congressional District showed John a front-runner in the June primary. As of the second week in April, John was within percentage points of catching the incumbent, Charles Rangel. What the polls would reflect now that John's mental competency was being questioned, no one could predict.

Exactly who had leaked the information was not yet known but the news that John had been a mental patient at the Veterans' Hospital in Northport had sent shock waves throughout the country. The "exclusive interview" in one of the weekly tabloids that flourished on trauma and gossip was Item One on every newscast across the country. A ward

674

nurse, or one who claimed to have been a ward nurse, wrote of John's catatonia, depression, and violent states. It was that which Carolyn was reacting to this evening as she lay awake, shivering, even as John held her.

"It isn't fair," she complained aloud.

John laughed, knowing exactly what she meant, although their discussion of the day's events had ended long ago. "Nowhere is it written except on the sound stages of M-G-M that life is fair," he said.

"I'm glad you can laugh at it but I can't. Dammit all, I know you. I'm not speaking as your wife when I say you'd make a wonderful congressman. A wonderful President, for that matter."

John leaned over and kissed Carolyn's breast. "And you'd make one helluva very sexy First Lady."

"More sagging than sexy, I'm afraid," said Carolyn. "What goes up must come down, it would seem," she added as John continued to nuzzle her breast.

"Ah, yes," he said with mocking good humor, "I've noticed that more and more about myself. Particularly the 'must come down' part. There is only one good thing to say about that: it gives me a lot more time to do good work."

"You always did good work," said Carolyn. "Now stop that!" she demanded, slapping his hand. "I didn't mean there. Or here. In bed. I meant in your work. Out there."

"What's the matter? Wasn't my work good here too?" he asked as he lowered his hand to the inner part of her thigh.

"I am trying to have a serious discussion," said Carolyn, feigning annoyance.

"And I'm trying to get laid," whispered John as he nibbled her ear.

"Is that your answer to everything?" Carolyn asked.

"If it were—if I came out and said that publicly—I'd probably win in a landslide."

Carolyn whooped with laughter.

"Ssh!" John cautioned. "If you laugh too loud, Ali and Mark will think it's a party and you know what that means: the stereo and Sly and the Family Bone."

"You mean Stone. Sly and the Family Stone!" corrected Carolyn. "You're really not very 'with it,' John. The kids tell me I'm very hip, you know."

John was again nibbling at Carolyn's ear as his hands roamed about her body. "Why, Grandma, what big hips you got," he growled.

Carolyn again whooped with laughter. "I know," she said. "Be quiet or I'll wake them. God, I'll be glad when Marti comes home from wherever she's traipsed off to and takes those children home. Don't look at me that way. You'll be glad too and you know it. If only they hadn't brought those electric guitars with them! And their records. Honestly, I had forgotten how much noise preteens make."

"Who are you kidding?" asked John. "You're delighted to play grandma."

"But only for a short run . . . a limited engagement. I'm delighted they're here but I'll be just as delighted when they go and I have my peace and quiet again. And so will you. I mean . . . just how much Creedence Clearwater can one person stand? Creedence Clearwater indeed! Whatever happened to normal names like Dick Haymes and Johnny Johnston?"

"You know, Lynnie, the strangest thing has happened," John said, responding more to his thoughts than to what Carolyn had been saying. "Ever since that interview appeared with Reese, I've been wanting to meet her, to explain how things were. Not to exonerate myself because I don't feel guilty. But to clear up some things. Shit! Maybe I am guilty. Maybe I fucked up. I should have made better attempts to reach Thomas. I hurt because he hates."

"You don't know that he does," said Carolyn. "You only have the words of one woman who has every right to be upset. In her place, I might feel exactly the same way."

"And to think I remember when you were just another pretty face," said John admiringly.

"Yes, and you almost divorced me because that's all I was."

"That's not quite how it was. You were going to divorce me, remember?"

"But only because you had already divorced yourself from all of us and were connubialing with others," said Carolyn.

"Connubialing? Where did you ever think up such a word?" John asked, laughing.

"I have my moments," said Carolyn.

"I'll say you do. Is this one of them?" John leered. As Carolyn laughed but did not answer he said, "I know your kind. You want it all nice and legal first. Okay, will you marry me?"

"I already did that, remember? God! It was thirty-six years ago. How is that possible? How could I have married at two years of age? I was but a child, and you? You were a child molester! Anyway, I would do it all again if that's what you're asking. You've improved with age, you know."

"You make me sound like a cheese," complained John.

"I was thinking of a fine claret."

"And I remember when you thought a claret was what Frenchmen wore on their heads."

"I was never that gauche!" protested Carolyn.

"You most certainly were and that's why I married you."

"And here all these years I thought it was purely sexual," said Carolyn.

"It was sexual and it was pure. You kept it that way."

"Well, that was a long time ago," said Carolyn, "and you certainly had your way with me . . . ruined me forever."

"And ain't you the lucky one for it?" John asked as he again nibbled her ear.

"You better believe it!" said Carolyn as she turned more toward John so that they were now facing each other. "Now you tell *me* how lucky *you* were," she said teasingly.

John didn't speak, although his eyes did, and his lips, as he kissed her gently on her eyelids, the tip of her nose, and then her mouth.

"You gave me the freedom to be and then to become," he said finally.

"No. I learned to let you be. You became all by yourself and you made me do the same," she replied.

"Yes. But you had to want it to have it," he countered. "You really would make a great First Lady, you know?"

"No, I don't and I don't see how you can either," she replied.

"Because you've been the First Lady of my life, of our family, and it's just another small step—not even a leap—to being the First Lady for the rest of the country."

"Oh, you flatterer. How you do go on!"

"Makes you feel good, huh?" John whispered almost coyly.

"Yes, it does," said Carolyn proudly.

"Good! Does that mean I can get laid now?"

This time the sound of Carolyn's laughter did wake both Ali and Mark but realizing it was laughter and not danger they were hearing and sensing, they turned over and went to sleep. Which was not exactly what was happening in their grandparents' room down the hall.

"Would you stop that!" said Vinnie as he lifted the covers and shouted down to the giggling form somewhere around his middle. "I just don't understand how you can do that and laugh."

"That's your problem, Vince Malloy," Este said as she came up from below to join Vinnie at the head of the bed. "You don't know how to have fun."

"Gee! And here all these months I thought that's what we were having," said Vinnie sarcastically.

"There is fun and then there is fun-fun. What we were just having was fun-fun," explained Este.

"Fun-fun. Did Scarlett say that to Rhett or it is a new Masters and Johnson technique?"

"Will you be serious! No. Strike that. Don't be serious. That's part of your problem. You take sex much too seriously," Este said.

"Next you'll be saying sex is a laughing matter," said Vinnie.

"Well, if you think about some of the really ridiculous positions we get ourselves into when having it, it is. I mean, it doesn't exactly resemble any moves Balanchine or Robbins would create. Actually, sex should be just as much fun as it is sexy. You just never learned how to have fun in bed."

"I always thought the fun was in the fucking," said Vinnie pensively.

"Well, think again," Este said almost angrily. "You reduce it to just that—fucking—when you say what you just did."

Vinnie grew silent as he thought about Este's words. Sensing she was more hurt than angry, he wrapped an arm about her and pulled her close. They had been together about six months but they were not, as Este kept reminding him, a couple. They were together when their schedules permitted, which was not often. Vinnie's week was crammed with five days of school and three nights of counseling at New Hope House, the residential drug rehabilitation center at the foot of Collins Avenue. Crowding the schedule were exams and term papers. Weekends, however, for the most part were free, and Este would arrive Saturday morning and remain until early Monday when she would leave for her apartment to change clothes for her job at the El Dorado Country Club, a hotel/spa and dinner theatre for the rich. In six years, she had worked her way from desk clerk to assistant public relations director.

Estelle Hollis had come to Miami Beach fourteen years ago—"a Sandra Dee with tits and tochis" as she told Vinnie. A bubbly bubblehead at nineteen, she had left the "line" at the Latin Casino in Cherry Hill, New Jersey, to dance with the "big shows" that back in 1958 frequented Miami Beach. Over the years she had worked the Eden Roc with Lena Horne and the Fontainebleau with both the Sinatra and Ann-Margret shows. She had as active a social life as the Beach's Chamber of Commerce insisted one could. Not that she was ever "loose." Just available, bubbly and bouncy. Then suddenly, as the Beach traffic collapsed, "so did my tits and ass," she explained. The big spenders who had willingly paid for "big favors" were replaced by the nickel and dime set and she was replaced by the teenybopper. She awoke one morning to see a "beach bimbo" in the mirror and "it literally sobered me. This was one blonde who suddenly was not having more fun so I went straight—straight back to boring brown and a straight job. Only I couldn't get one because I lacked skills." Eventually, through "connections," she became a night desk clerk at the Dorado, primarily because she promised but never delivered "the goods"—in this case, her body—to the night manager. By the time he realized he had been had but she hadn't, Estelle Hollis had connected with and convinced Geoffrey Eddy in public relations that her personality was a perfect balance to his. Which it was. Eddy was a dour drunk who hated the sun, the press, Jews, and Cubans. He was not, needless to say, a happy man. Estelle was his late-in-life gift from God. She was sociable, unconcerned with ethnic origins, and a sun lover. Once Eddy hired her, he retired to his dark office while she, a zippy blonde again, zipped about town, promoting the hotel's dinner theatre and celebrity golf tournament and in general having a wonderful time with the press and the public. Although Geoffrey Eddy took the bows with management for the success of the publicity department, he was generous with the hotel's money. Estelle received six-month raises and bonuses. She was now earning more than three hundred dollars per week and sleeping only with men of her choice rather than of necessity.

Estelle Hollis played the tough broad quite successfully for Miami's press. She was a good drinker and a "good sport."

Had she not been so blatantly A Blonde, she would have been termed one of the boys. Only Vinnie saw her vulnerability, particularly on those Tuesday nights when they were together and she wept over that week's terminal illness on "Marcus Welby." Weekends, she arrived not only with suitcase but with cats: Mary and Jane whom she refused to leave for any length of time. Lovemaking always had to be to the strains of lush music and never rock as the latter seemed often to unleash something in Vinnie she did not like. As passionate as she was, that's how turned off she could get when traces of his old violence were exhibited.

"Listen, a fuck is not a fracas," she once said angrily when he became too rough. "You don't have to use that thing of yours like some gun. Nor does it have to go off every time you fire it."

He had looked at her with hatred the first time she probed that particular wound. "Oh, come on," she said, the disgust evident in her voice. "Don't tell me you're one of those men whose ego is wrapped up in whether or not he gets off or not! Spare me. So sometimes you do and sometimes you don't. Big deal. Despite anything you may have read in *Redbook* or *Cosmo*, I'm not always achieving multiple orgasms. So? What the fuck does that mean? Nothing. I enjoy it just as much whether I do or I don't because I enjoy you. I like feeling you inside me—being close in that way. If there's a payoff, a jackpot, great! If not, so what? You men are so childish where that's concerned. I don't feel rejected when you don't or can't. I know it has nothing to do with me."

As he lay listening to the *Nilsson Schmilsson* album Este had bought that day, Vinnie, relaxed and contented, said, "I think maybe we should live together."

"I think you think too much," replied Este.

"I just asked you to live with me," Vinnie said angrily.

"I heard and I'm flattered. I'm also touched. I'm not, however, insane."

"What are you talking about? We're good together. We are good to each other."

"Yes, we leave each other be, respect each other's space." She picked up where he had left off. "And we respect each other's privacy. Boy, do we do that well! Actually, Vince, you've been the best thing that's happened to me since Charlie Crenshaw. He was my steady in my sophomore year in high school. You've restored my faith in men. Actually, what you've done is restored my faith in me. I've been around the town a lot in my day but you make me feel not exactly new but not used either. But the truth is: we don't have it for the long haul. I'm a simple girl with simple tastes and a basic, if not simple, mentality. What you see is what you get. Not many surprises here. But you, kid, you're different. What I see is not all there is. I don't know who you are or what you are. When we met way back then at the Embers I thought you were just another stud looking for pasture privileges. And I didn't care. You were pleasant, handsome as hell, and seemingly not a freak. But when you brought me back here, to this incredible house, I knew something was weird even if you weren't. I still don't know who you are. Not really. I know your name is Vince Malloy and that you really do attend the University of Miami. You also have some kind of night job but what the hell that is, I don't know. There's volumes about you I don't know and I don't ask 'cause it's not supposed to matter. And for what we got, it doesn't. But for living together, or marriage, it does."

Este was sitting up in bed and her breasts were bobbing over the sheet as she talked earnestly. "I listen when you speak, watch you when you move, and there's an elegance about you. And something familiar but I don't know what. I look at your clothes and the way you wear them; the foods you eat and the ease with which you identify things on restaurant menus I can't even pronounce. You've had a helluvanother life, Vince Malloy. I'd like to know about it and then again . . . I wouldn't. I like who you are here. It's enough for me. It's enough for us now. I don't want anything more. If you do, maybe then we should split. Which in my opinion would be a mistake. You see, my friend," said Este as she leaned over Vinnie, her face but an inch away from his, "I think we're both taking some kind of cure and that we're one another's best medicine. Let it go at that, Vince. Let it go."

"I don't know," said Vinnie unhappily. "I just don't know."

"I don't know," said Marti as the plane shuddered from a sudden head wind. "My reaction to Mike Greer is very schizo. Sometimes I feel like I want to kill the guy and other times I think what am I carrying on about? It's not like I wanted to marry him because I didn't. Not him or anybody else. And he wanted 'a little woman' and I'm not about to be that for anyone. Besides, just seeing that fawn he married makes me realize he's not half the man I thought he was."

"That sounds like bullshit to me," said JJ. "According to what Vinnie told me, and even some of the hints you dropped, you were pretty hung up on the guy."

"Now *that's* bullshit," Marti said angrily. "I was never that involved with Mike Greer. Never!" she repeated just in case JJ and half the first class cabin hadn't heard her.

JJ looked at Marti out of the corner of his eye. The tight set of her face made him resist his impulse to say: Methinks the lady protesteth too much. Instead, he said, "Don't look now but they're feeding us again."

Marti groaned. Since leaving Stockholm hours ago, the SAS crew had served dinner, a snack, and now, she presumed, breakfast.

"They certainly are blonde and pretty," said Marti dourly as she looked over the stewardesses.

"Why the hint of meanness in your voice?" JJ asked.

"Because it's a mean job, thought up by mean men who are exploiting women just to make a buck. These girls are objects. Like bunnies in a Playboy Club."

"Jesus! You are so full of shit sometimes. Marti, did you ever think maybe they like being objects? Not all women want to be 'persons' any more than not all boys want to be men. How about a little respect for individual choice? I don't see anyone twisting these girls' arms to do what they do."

"Speaking of girls," said Marti, changing the subject because she knew JJ was right, "what are you doing for female companionship? I haven't heard you speak of anyone since Jeanne, and she was a long time ago."

"When I need a woman," said JJ as the stewardess lowered the tray on the seat back in front of him, "I go out and get one."

"Goddamnit, JJ. You make a woman sound like a bar of soap or a haircut!" Marti exploded.

"Marti, would you fuck off with the feminist shit! You 'ladies' forget that men and women do 'exchange pleasantries' without indulging in 'meaningful relationships.' In case you haven't noticed, it takes two to get laid and I see a lot of girls and women all too willing to service or to be serviced. What is with you? Christ, you sowed your oats. Are you now judging them?"

"I was used by men," Marti said bitterly.

"You also used them, or have you forgotten all you learned from you and Chauverant and you and Charper and you and ad infinitum."

"You're right. I'm sorry," said Marti. "It's just that I'm still reacting to who I once was and who they were to me. And that's all mixed up with my feelings about Mike. But it does seem to me men want certain things from women that women shouldn't give up."

"The same could be said in reverse," John J. said as the scrambled eggs, sausage and bacon were placed on his plate. "Jesus, maybe we should do a documentary on this after we finish the one we're making. I mean . . . this is a whole other war and you're waging it."

"Now that's bullshit. Men made this war eons ago," said Marti as she buttered her croissant. "Ours is a patriarchal society. Women must fight for their rights."

"Oh, God!" JJ groaned. "What rights? Let's examine it closely. Women wanted the *right* to ask men out. Now they have it. They won the battle but lost the war. Sure it was tough on a girl to sit around waiting to be asked out but . . . ask yourself this. What's tougher? Waiting to be asked or being rejected? You women never realized you had all the power: the right to say yes or no. A guy calls, asks a girl out and if she says no, he's got one shriveled pecker and ego. Rejection sucks! Then, too, think of the guy who gets his date and then his girl makes it plain all night she thinks he's a nerd. And on his money! Speaking of money, you've also won that battle and again lost your war. If women were such lowly creatures in men's eyes, why did they pay for their company? And don't tell me to get into their pants 'cause you can do that for five to fifteen bucks on any back street in almost any town in the world. You know, Marti, all those issues that seem so fucking clear to you are really very muddied and muddled and will take years to sort out."

"Boy, could one get to hate a younger brother like you who knows more than I do," said Marti as she sipped at her Bloody Mary. She was grinning, enjoying JJ's tirade and realizing, to her delight rather than the annoyance she was feigning, that he was absolutely right. "And you know, you've come up with one helluvan idea. Why don't we do a film on this new 'war.' We could use a split-screen technique—have the men appear on one side, the women on the other, with both expressing their views on the same subject simultaneously."

"We've exactly five weeks to finish this project and you're talking about starting another," groaned JJ.

"We'll make it. And in plenty of time. It's damn good programming for them to slot our antiwar film on D Day. There's terrific irony in that."

"There's an irony in you saying 'We'll make it' when for the most part you'll be in New York and I'll be in the studio in Toronto."

"You know that nothing but campaigning for Dad could keep me from helping you edit. I'm going to miss out on the final fun," said Marti meaning her words. "All of this has been . . ." Her voice trailed off. It wasn't just the experience of *Soldiers: A War of Their Own* that had moved her but what she and JJ had been to each other. From the first when she had presented her idea to him that day at the Hockey Hall of Fame, he had been enthusiastic. The idea of expanding his documentary to include dissenters and deserters as far back as World War I was exciting, particularly since one now had the years between to see how their lives had been affected.

It was Marti who had made all overseas arrangements and had taken great precautions to ensure their safety. The family was told nothing of their plans, only that she would be away for several weeks on a secret project. It was her idea they fly separately; she from Kennedy to Paris and he, a day later, from Montreal. That way, if either was under surveillance, and both were sure they were, it would be somewhat confusing to have them take off on different days from different cities.

JJ had been nervous. Although France was basically sympathetic toward dissenters, JJ trusted no one outside Canada with his safety. Still, the call of the planned documentary overcame any of his fears. In Paris, it became common knowledge that Marti Tiernan and John J. Ollson were interviewing current and past dissenters and deserters. Therefore their "slipping into" Germany was twice as dangerous because the German government, "host" to a quarter of a million American soldiers, was not hospitable to men like JJ. Marti offered to make the trip to Berlin and Munich alone but JJ couldn't live with that decision. The German dissenters' point of view would be fascinating in light of the two world wars their government had created. Juxtaposed to the French dissenters' vehement antiwar sentiments, the interviews would be doubly pertinent and poignant.

Marti flew into Berlin and her arrival created the press attention on which they had counted. While Marti was interviewed and followed about, JJ entered Germany by train and went directly to Munich where he tape-recorded interviews with those subjects his underground network had secured for him.

They did the same in England where there was a large pocket of American dissenters living in London. Marti flew directly into the city, garnering press attention, while JJ took the boat train and arrived quite unnoticed. From there, they went to Sweden, which prided itself on its "humanitarian asylum" to resisters. Neither Marti nor JJ found it all that humane. Yes, asylum was provided but jobs and housing were not. In Stockholm, "the Venice of the North," Marti discovered that the gaiety of the city was a contradiction to the somberness of the American men who had fled there from the draft or the army.

But the focus of *Soldiers* had not been Stockholm or Munich or any of the cities in which Marti and JJ had traveled, but the men themselves; their lives before and after the fact of their resistance and desertion. Listening to men speak of walking away from the Battle of Verdun or the Bulge and of what had happened after their "walk" of so many years ago proved to be stuff for strong stomachs and strong documentaries. All that was needed at that moment as the SAS jet flew into morning light was to edit the sixteen hours of film into two hours; a job JJ would begin almost as soon as the plane landed and he drove home to Rosedale and the studio he had constructed in his basement. JJ was glad he would soon be home, and he was no longer surprised that he thought of the community outside of Toronto and Canada itself as his home. He would not be glad, however, to see Marti fly on to New York. He would miss her. In the past weeks as they traveled and worked together, she had fallen from the great height of Big Sister to the more comfortable shoulder-level position of Best Friend. He would particularly miss their fights, most of which were mock; exercises to stimulate their intellectual processes. Often, even when they agreed, they pretended not to, just to enjoy the facing off on social, moral, political, and spiritual issues. They had learned each other's weak spots and sore points. As important, they had learned how to laugh with and at each other and themselves.

JJ had been a considerable surprise to Marti. As she had said to him toward the end of their stay in Stockholm: "So many of these men are defeated by their own decision or by events that were not at all of their choice. So many are inundated and weighed down by guilt. Anger, too. But you're not like any of them. You seem to have grown into yourself because of all this. That sweet boy I once knew is now this rough, often brusque, even bitter, but terribly sensitive and decisive man. There is no question mark where your face is."

JJ had not denied her words although he had not been aware of their truth until she had said them. He was thinking of their discussion of two nights back when he heard Marti say: "You're doing it again."

"Doing what?" he asked, confused.

"Going AWOL on me. What were you thinking about this time?"

"You, me . . . Dad. All of us, I guess," said John J. and then, to his amazement, he was crying. It had seemingly come from nowhere and although he had his tears well under control, they were there and visible and he did feel upset. Marti took his hand and held it until he was ready to speak.

"We really are a helluva bunch," JJ began. "And I miss them all. You know, so many guys my age bitch about their parents. I can't understand it, although I know from what you told me, you can. But I'm so proud of Dad and so damn mad I can't be there to help him now."

"I'll help for both of us," Marti said, as tears began to push up from under. "I promise I will."

The stewardess's voice filled the cabin over the loudspeaker. "Ladies and gentlemen. We are making our final approach into Montreal. Would you please see that your seatbelts are securely fastened and that your seat backs are in an upright position. The ground temperature on this first day in May is forty-four degrees with rain expected later this afternoon."

"You know, until recently I was jealous of the position you always had with Dad," said Marti. "He so obviously favored you. I think he learned how to love you from the way he didn't know how to love me and Thomas. . . ."

"I don't think so," said JJ. "It wasn't what Dad did per se with me but that he just *was* with me. It wasn't that he spent more time with me than he did with you because if you totaled it up, it was probably a lot less. But when he was there, he was all there. And without any bullshit. He never told me one thing while he did another. Which was different from Mom. She always read me the litany first and then— God love her!—once she had done her religious duty, she'd close her eyes to whatever it was I chose to do."

"Within reason," corrected Marti. "If you really think about it, Mom's eyes were never closed. Not to anything. Ever. At no time."

Again JJ's eyes filled with tears. "I have thought about it. And thought about it and then thought about it some more. I wish I could have brought her home something special from Europe that would have told her how often I have thought about it."

"But you have, JJ," said Marti, thinking of the cans of film and tape in the baggage compartment. "You have and she will love it."

POLITICAL CAMPAIGNING MADE EASY

A Handbook by Margaret Tiernan
Prepared Especially for
Carolyn Ollson

All the novice (that's *you*, dum-dum) must remember is to say nothing and smile. This will be interpreted by all as a sign of beatitude and no one will suspect you have absolutely nothing of any interest or worth to say.

When newsmen thrust a microphone in your face, do not— repeat: do not say you want to thank all the little people for making this possible because to most, *you* are the little people.

Lastly, do not kiss any babies. With your morning breath you could wipe out half the youth population of the Nineteenth District.

Carolyn laughed as she read Margaret's parting words for the fourth or fifth time that morning. The campaign swing through John's potential district had been exhausting, although she had little to do other than shake the hands of strangers and smile in exactly the manner prescribed by Margaret. Although they were not scheduled to embark on their tour until ten, Margaret had arrived at eight to help Carolyn dress. The twins, with Marti, had arrived at eight-thirty to wish Grandpa luck. Marti was her father's daughter. Both were calm, as if nothing unusual was happening. A little ride uptown—as far uptown as One Hundred Sixty-sixth Street—and then down again. "Pressing the flesh" John called it, shaking hands and smiling. A lot. Carolyn's face felt broken. Not all the Oil of Olay in her medicine chest would ease or erase the smile lines of campaigning.

As the limousine moved slowly downtown toward its final destination, Carolyn listened to the loudspeakers attached to its roof urging passersby to vote for John Ollson on Primary Day. She regretted their intrusion as they were woefully inept in comparison to the in-person power of her husband. Carolyn had been stunned that morning listening to John as he addressed his possible constituency on both Ward and Roosevelt Islands and again at Eighty-sixth Street and Third Avenue. The man who just happened to be her husband was a low-key yet impassioned speaker with enormous charisma. Suddenly she had realized this was just the beginning, the first step on what might be a very long campaign trail leading to . . . She could not allow herself the luxury of completing her fantasy. First steps first.

At Seventy-second Street and Broadway, at the island across from the entrance into the IRT subway, the limousine stopped. John stepped out first, waving to the crowd assembled by his volunteers. Carolyn noted as she emerged from the car that those cheering John were mainly young, under thirty, and, according to his volunteers' studies, nonpolitical until recently. The stop lasted the planned ten minutes, during which no one would have guessed from the smile pasted on Carolyn's face that her right hand throbbed in pain each time someone new went to shake it.

Back in the limousine for the nine-block ride down Broadway to the planned site of the rally, Carolyn continued to wave out the window at people who undoubtedly hadn't the vaguest idea who the woman in the limousine was. As they approached Lincoln Center, Carolyn saw the weather was finally cooperating. What had been a gray morning was now about to become a shiny end-of-May afternoon.

When the limousine stopped at the pie-shaped island wedged between Broadway and Columbus Avenue at Sixty-third Street, the first place Carolyn saw was O'Neal's Baloon. She thought of the many times she and John had sneaked into the restaurant for hamburgers, and instantly felt hungry. Again she heard Margaret's voice warning her to: "Eat your words. You'll not only save calories but John a lot of embarrassment." Laughing to herself, Carolyn forgot her hunger.

A small podium had been set up near the statue, which Carolyn noted for the first time in all the years she had lived in New York was of Dante. A dirty Dante with a laurel wreath but Dante, nonetheless. It was a beautiful spot, thought Carolyn, even as she mindlessly shook hands with those assembled. Lincoln Center across the way, majestic and meaningful in what it offered the world; Fordham University just a block or so south; Juilliard, north; and on Broadway, restaurants and that Coward shoe store where she had bought JJ his first pair of "good shoes" for his prom. She wished JJ were there now, to hear his father address what was certainly the largest crowd that had yet assembled to hear him. He would be introduced by Marti while she would have nothing to do but look pleasant as she sat next to Margaret, if Margaret ever arrived.

There were eight wooden folding chairs before a makeshift rostrum from which John would speak. She wondered who the other chairs were for. As she was led to one at the center, she heard a roar from the assembled crowd. From a taxi, she saw this "thing" emerge—a "thing" in a red cape and a white sailor hat with a red ribbon flowing from it. Carolyn fought to keep her face impassive as Margaret curtsied to the crowd and cavorted for the cameras. Whatever anger Carolyn was feeling dissolved when she thought: if she wears this here, what will she ever do on Inauguration Day! Laughing at herself and at the lightness Margaret brought to the moment, she patted the chair next to her, designating to Margaret that this was where she was wanted.

Carolyn could feel the intentional pressure of Margaret's leg against hers as Marti was speaking. Because their chairs were just below and to the left of the rostrum, they could not see Marti but from the rapt look of attention on the faces of those before them, Carolyn and Margaret could tell that Marti was delivering her audience into the palm of John's hand. Carolyn heard her daughter introduce John as the next congressman from the Nineteenth District. She applauded as he rose from his seat next to her, started for the rostrum, stopped, turned toward Carolyn, and with a boyish smile, stooped to give her a noisy kiss. The spontaneous gesture drew more applause, such applause that it became deafening. Across Broadway and down Columbus Avenue, the applause was like thunder, ripping through the peaceful blue sky. Applause. Thunder. Screams.

Carolyn was trying to turn toward the rostrum, trying to understand why people were screaming as they ran. Why was Margaret preventing her from running, too. Let go of my wrists, she demanded as she freed herself momentarily from Margaret's grip. She looked. She saw.

No, I didn't! I didn't. I didn't. I didn't see that. That was not blood gushing from that man's head.

John! John!

Her screams were lost among the many others. As if paralyzed she stood, rooted, as the man who until that second had been her husband, slid slowly down from the rostrum over which he had been slumped to the ground.

More thunder burst from the ground and sky about her. As she fought to reach John, Margaret threw her to the ground and covered her body with her own until the gunfire that was raging above them had stopped.

And then the quiet. An awful deadly quiet, broken only by Margaret's command to Carolyn: not to look.

But she looked. She couldn't stop looking at a sight she would forget within the hour but would later always remember. There, on the pavement, reddened by blood, lay John, bloodied flesh where his face should have been. Next to him was the equally bloodied body of Marti Tiernan.

The look she gave Margaret was a command in itself. As Margaret fell off her body, Carolyn began to crawl toward her husband and daughter. What was louder, Margaret wondered from a shocked state, the wail of the police sirens or those of Carolyn. Which screeches were worse—the tires of the ambulances that ground to a halt, or Carolyn's?

She sat there holding what was left of John's head in her lap, as one arm played absentmindedly with Marti's blood-covered hair. She didn't fight the paramedics or the police. She let them gently lead her back to Margaret who opened her arms. The last thing Carolyn felt was a searing pain scorching through her body. Seconds later, police and medics were administering oxygen to her as she lay unconscious on the pavement, her head propped up by Margaret's red cape, folded now into a pillow.

*   *   *

Reese was pleased with herself. Her program was working. Here it was only a little after ten and she already had driven the children to school, done the marketing for the long holiday weekend, and was halfway through doing the week's laundry. At this rate, she would have the afternoon to herself. To play golf. Or go swimming. Drive to the San Diego Zoo or the art museum. See a movie. Anything but hang around the house feeling time hanging heavy on her shoulders. Reese was, as her children were fond of saying, getting it together. The tranquilizers helped but mainly she felt it was her new attitude that was making life better. No more making herself sick. That helped no one; not Thomas, not the children, and certainly not herself. Having cut back on vodka had cut back by half the weight she had gained.

Even the children had commented on the changes. No more did she give in to her "morning migraines." Once again, Reese was up early to make breakfast and chauffeur the children to school. Afternoons, when they returned, she was coherent—bubbly without the bubbly, as she put it. No more wine until dinner, she had decreed. Jog instead. Run in place. Deep knee bends. Those were the new rules, part of the self-help program she had embarked on just a month or so ago when brochures from Alcoholics Anonymous arrived anonymously in the mail. Yes, sir, getting it together, thought Reese as she opened the dryer door to see if the laundry was ready to be removed.

Her father had been of great help. Doctors do know best, Reese thought. He understood the strain she was under. Constantly. The Librium by day and the Dalmane by night really did relieve her anxiety as he had promised. She felt peaceful, quiet even, and the more quiet she felt, the less anxious the children seemed to be. Of course the nighttimes were still difficult. She was alone in bed and the house felt . . . vulnerable. Yes, that was it. Vulnerable. It needed a man around to make it and her and the family safe.

Coincidentally, she became aware that her favorite morning disc jockey was playing "Lean on Me." Reese laughed as she thought of the many times she had leaned on that disc jockey—without his knowing, of course—for strength. He was a voice, a someone that filled her house. He wished her good morning and a good day. Company. Male company.

She automatically stiffened when the announcer broke into the Bill Withers song. Whenever they "interrupt this pro-

691

gram to bring you a special news bulletin," it was about Vietnam. Still, she only half-listened. The news she was waiting for would not come over the radio, she was certain, but by telephone. Maybe even from the President himself. It took a second, maybe two, before she realized what she had just heard. As awareness set in, she fell against the dryer, pleading with herself not to fall. Not again. The children would think she was drunk if they found her on the floor. Again she heard the announcer: "We repeat: John Ollson and his daughter, actress/writer Marti Tiernan, were gunned down today by an assassin's bullets during a campaign rally in New York just minutes ago. First unconfirmed reports say both father and daughter were dead on arrival at Roosevelt Hospital. Stay tuned to this station for further details."

As she sat on the floor, huddled against the warmth of the dryer, Reese wondered how she had fallen to the floor without being aware of it. She also wondered why she could not get up, why her legs refused her weight, even though she had reduced it by seven pounds. Do what a baby does, said Reese to herself. Hold on to something and pull yourself up. She tried with the refrigerator handle and succeeded only in opening the Kelvinator door. Terrified by her weakness, she crawled about the kitchen floor until she reached the other side of the counter. There, by reaching up, stretching out, she was able to knock the Princess phone down from its shelf and into her trembling hands.

The numbers on the phone were suddenly hard to see and the specific number she wanted to reach, although she had known it for most of her life, darted in and out of her mind. She was crying as her fingers struggled with the dial. Her breath caught in her throat as she waited for the ringing telephone to be answered. When finally it was, in a very weak, childlike voice, Reese said, "Ma? Mama? It's me . . . Reesie. Mama, please, I want you to take me home."

Thomas had been asleep in his "private" room—but most definitely a room—at the "Riviera," when they burst through his door and ordered him to march to the Camp Unity area. There, in the light of a quarter moon, he stood at attention with other able-bodied prisoners until the Rabbit appeared. This was hardly his first interrupted sleep or the first midnight "raid," as the summonses to march or just stand were referred to. As he stood somewhat wobbly on legs he could only strengthen through secret isometric exercises, Thomas wondered if this little "get-together" was another in the recent string of retributions for the resumed bombing of North Vietnam. It seemed every time an American bomb fell, his captors were determined to fell another prisoner.

The Rabbit stood before them silently. When he began walking the line, staring into the faces of his captive audience as it stood as one at attention, a little smile played hide-and-seek on his face.

"I do not understand you Americans," he began suddenly. "Truly, you are a most difficult people to comprehend. You say one thing and do another. And you," he said, designating the men before him, "particularly you I do not understand. Soldiers. Fighting. But for what? For butchers? For murderers?"

Having heard this rhetoric many times over, Thomas was only half-listening. His mind had drifted to another moonlit night, also in May. Unhappily, it seemed more like a hundred years ago than thirteen. It was the night he was packing to leave M.I.T. and Boston forever. It was the night when he and Reese had made love, outdoors, near the Charles River, and she had been excited yet hesitant to be publicly passionate although no one was near.

"I cannot understand why any man would want to fight, die, for murderers," the Rabbit continued in tones that were meant to sound sincere and persuasive. "Your so-called American way not only murders the people but the peace," he said as he came to a full stop before Thomas.

"Do you not agree, Captain?" he asked. "Do you not agree your system breeds murder—the murder of people and of peace? . . . Captain . . . I asked you a question. Have you nothing to say? Ah, well, perhaps the shock of what has happened is too great for you to comprehend," said the Rabbit as he turned away.

Thomas's eyebrow twitched but a fraction and but for a second.

With his back still to Thomas, the Rabbit continued speaking. "You do have our deepest sympathy, Captain Ollson. It is so shocking . . . so terrible and so tragic." Suddenly he was facing Thomas. "You do know, of course, Captain, that an assassin shot and killed your peace-loving father in America. Just an hour or so ago actually. And oh, yes, I do believe the radio said your sister was also caught in the gunman's rage."

It was not true, thought Thomas. He knew the enemy used everything to make a man crack. But this wouldn't work. No. These were lies. Fabrications. Falsifications. Concoctions. They were! Despite the look of smug satisfaction on Rabbit's face, they had to be. This was not the way the book he was writing was meant to end. No!

As he stood enveloped in his thoughts and the night, Thomas faded back in time, to another night in another decade when a little boy turned to the big man by his side at the Christmas tree, looked at the trains, and asked, "Daddy, how go?" And Thomas remembered something he had forgotten. As best as Daddy could, Daddy had explained.

It was a small brunch for the eight top syndicated feature and television writers in America. They had been flown to Toronto by the educational network and had just viewed the two-hour documentary which would be aired in a little more than a week on varying days and times in America. JJ could tell from the myriad expressions on the faces of the five women and three men of the press that they had felt *Soldiers* and were still reacting to it. He wished Marti were here with him to read their faces.

The interruption was maddening. JJ had wanted talk first and brunch later. But the station head thought otherwise, believing a full stomach made for kinder reception. Impatiently, JJ watched the platters of stuffed chicken, cheese blintzes, potato knishes, and Nova Scotia salmon being laid on the linen-covered conference table by the men from Switzer's Deli City. As they left, JJ was annoyed to see Ron LaPointe enter, the smile on the station manager's face saying one thing while his entire manner said another. Apologizing for interrupting, LaPointe asked to see JJ privately for a moment. Busy with the food at hand, the writers granted "the moment."

Annoyed that the immediate reactions of the press were being allowed to dissipate, JJ angrily followed LaPointe from the conference room into the hallway, demanding as he did to be told what could be so urgent as to interrupt him at a time like this. When told, JJ spun about and slammed into the wall as if struck by bullets from the same .38 revolver that had gunned down his family.

* * *

694

It was crazy. Nuts. Just plain nuts. No, just *plane* nuts, Vinnie corrected. And I love every crazy, nutty thing about it.

As the plane raced down the runway, Vinnie was holding Este's hand. Up, up and away. Far away. A weekend, just four days. Four. Count them. And they were going to Rio. So what if they would spend a day going and a day returning. Big deal. It would be fun. And how often did Este have a whole weekend off. And not just a weekend but a four-day one. Yes, indeed. Memorial Day. He would remember it forever. He might even establish a memorial to Memorial Day. He, Vinnie Tiernan, off to Rio for a weekend. Impractical. Stupid, some might even say. But not Este. It was fun. Or fun-fun.

Looking at his watch as the seatbelt sign went off, Vinnie noted it was ten minutes past one. Amazing. They had actually gotten off on time. And that seldom happened at Miami International Airport. Vinnie saw Este looking at him and at the wristwatch.

"Okay. I'll take it off and I promise I won't look at it again for three days," he said. It was part of their deal. If they were to do this "crazy thing," they were to leave it all behind. School. The job. Everything. No newspapers. No radio. Just sun, sand, and sex. And food, Este had added. And maybe some dancing. They had earned the right to be totally alone and self-indulgent. Once again, he had scored all As in his courses except for chemistry where he had "survived" with a C minus.

"I'm going to pretend you're Fred and I'm Ginger," said Este.

"What the hell are you talking about?" Vinnie asked. "This isn't going to be one of your awful Polish jokes, is it?"

"Fred and Ginger, dummy. Astaire and Rogers. *Flying Down to Rio?* Get it?"

"You really want me to be Fred, eh?"

"Sure," said Este. "Why don't you do something daring, like the Continental, right here, twenty-eight thousand feet up."

"As a matter of fact I will," Vinnie said happily. "You wait right here. Don't move. I'll be back," he added as he moved toward the lavatory near the plane's cockpit. Under his arm was a little leather case. From the colors of the stripes running across one side, it was unmistakably Gucci. In it was a small scissors, an all-purpose double-edged razor, and shaving cream.

It was a huge turnout—a tribute from the people with whom John had worked in publishing, films, television, and politics—and yet, as she looked about, Carolyn had the distinct feeling no one was there. Not Thomas. Not Vinnie. Not JJ. Not Marti—no, certainly not Marti. And not John. Even she, Carolyn Tiernan Ollson, felt among the missing. With half of her gone, she wondered if she would always feel that way.

All about her were drawn, concerned, grief-stricken faces. Carolyn had no more grief. It had been taken from her by the drugs doctors had administered. It wasn't that she was unaware a coffin was about to be lowered into the ground, it just all seemed unimportant. Only his "remains" were being buried. Except they weren't. Not really. The real "remains" remained, to both please and comfort, twist and torture. The remains are the reminders. Of events that were and that would never again be and yet would always be. In her heart. In her mind. They could never be buried unless she chose to bury them.

She heard Evelyn sobbing at graveside. Nancy looked distraught; for the first time unable to cope with life. I should go to them, thought Carolyn. Only Margaret's arm, encircling her waist, prevented her from going toward her friends . . . John's friends.

The service began. The priest was eulogizing a man he only knew from books and newspapers and a weekly television show. It was not the man she had shared the past thirty-six years with, although it was a part, Carolyn thought as she half-listened. A huge white cloud passed over the mourners, interrupting the bright sunshine that lit the area like many of the stages she had played upon. This is Act Three, thought Carolyn. The final curtain. Only this time, the actor, the male lead, would not pick himself up and go home.

It is a lovely day, thought Carolyn as her eyes searched the sky. He is with his Maker, the priest declared. No, not yet, thought Carolyn. He is here. She could feel him next to her as certainly as she could feel Margaret; her body strong, supporting, except for those moments when a sob escaped. Poor Margaret. Dear Margaret, thought Carolyn. She and

John were so close. They had such a deep understanding of each other. Two peas in a pod.

The twins were standing just in front of her, holding hands tightly, fearing to let go. She reached out to touch Ali's hair, so much like her mother's only softer. Her grandmother's hand upon her head caused Ali to fall out of the character she had so much wanted to play and to become a little girl again; one who was crying uncontrollably, her head buried against her grandmother's breast. Margaret placed her hands on Mark's shoulders to steady him.

Ashes to ashes, dust to dust. Carolyn watched as the coffin was lowered slowly into the ground. The mourners drifted by it and toward her, bidding their respects to John and then her as they did. Let them go, Carolyn thought. Oh, please, God, let them go and let them go soon! I want to be alone with John. I want to say good-bye and tell him not to worry. Not about me. Or anyone. We'll be fine.

Slowly, after everyone had gone except Margaret, Carolyn approached John's grave . . . alone. In that second, she suddenly realized despite Margaret standing but feet away, despite the twins hovering together in the background, she would be alone as she never had been before. Perhaps that is why after so many years, the bed that morning had seemed so terribly big, and she had felt so lost in it. Would that be how she would feel in a world without John? she wondered. The renewed crying of her granddaughter demanded her attention. Without further thought, Carolyn turned away from the dead to minister to the living.

Time. They say it heals all wounds. Please, God, let it be true, prayed Margaret as she thought of Carolyn walking the nights away in what had once been two people's bedroom but was now just one's, and Marti, her dear Marti, who didn't walk at all but who lay there in the hospital bed, inert, noncomprehending, not of this world but not yet of the next.

Alive! Thank God for that, thought Margaret as her hand rested lightly on her niece's. Thank God for the little things—like a movement of the eyeball, of a finger, of a vein that suddenly twitched. All were evidence of life. Perhaps not much of a life but of life.

They had taken Marti directly to the operating room. There was very little pulse at first, very few signs of life. Except for the blood. Of that, there was plenty. Doctors fought with the wound and the blood that continued to gush from the shattered carotid artery in her neck. She waited with Carolyn outside the closed doors, only Carolyn couldn't wait. Not that she had anywhere to go but with John gone and Marti going, she could not hold still. They had sedated her, not just for her sake but for those who didn't want Carolyn around as a reminder of what had just happened. Evelyn and Nancy had materialized from nowhere and taken Carolyn home where they could monitor her much as Marti was being monitored once she was moved to Intensive Care. Hooked up to an EKG machine, Marti's every heartbeat showed up in dits and dots on an oscilloscope at the nurses' station while her spittle was sucked out by a machine attached to the tracheotomy tube in her throat.

She lived . . . moment to moment, although doctors couldn't say for how long. Margaret had remained at the hospital for what seemed like days rather than hours. Eventually, a team of doctors cautiously explained how the gunshot as it splattered and splayed the carotid artery had caused a loss of blood from the left side of the brain and that this loss of blood had caused a stroke to the brain's left hemisphere. . . .

"Oh, my God! Does that mean she'll be paralyzed?" she had interrupted frantically.

. . . and that the right side of the body would be adversely affected as would be the front part of the brain. *If*, and it was *if*, she lived.

A day later, as Marti continued to struggle for every moment of life, the doctors asked for permission to put her in a barbiturate coma. "It will relax her body by slowing down her metabolism. It's necessary to help her breathe through the tracheotomy and thus prevent further damage to the brain." Carolyn had been advised and permission was granted.

As she now sat by Marti's bed, waiting but not certain for what, Margaret was thinking of how quickly life can change through circumstance. A lone circumstance. A man's life had been blown away and with it went the lives, the marriage, of two people who had been as one. A young woman lay dead to the world as she lay alive in her bed; her two children forgotten although they did not forget her. The bullets had killed something in all of them. No matter how much time passed or how much medicine was administered, there would be no full recovery or forgetting for any of them. Even now, it seemed inconceivable, although the police guard at Marti's door made it very conceivable. Margaret had scoffed at what she thought was the needless protection. A conspiracy? Ridiculous. It was a single gunman, a lone maniac, now dead due to the two policemen who had emptied their service revolvers into the fleeing man's body.

One gun. One assassin. This is not JFK or RFK or Martin Luther King. But one gun in the hands of one child/maniac . . . twenty-four years old . . . white . . . five-feet-ten inches . . . one hundred fifty-eight pounds . . . blond hair . . . green eyes. From Iowa. A "good boy" . . . active in 4-H clubs. With a closet full of Nazi memorabilia and paraphernalia. Who was wearing a green beret when he was shot down. Who had been a born-again Christian before his studies with the Maharishi. Who had been mustered out of the army and Saigon when his drug abuse interfered with his logic and his ability to serve.

No one had claimed his body, his parents stating they were too ashamed. As much as Margaret hated the "good boy" from Iowa, she hated his parents even more for the shame they felt too late in life. She thought them to be the true perpetrators of the crime. She thought and she thought and it was the thoughts that sustained her. Thinking of Marti, thinking of Ali and Mark, of Carolyn, of anyone and anything other than her own feelings. The doctors had advised, for Carolyn's sake, a quick burial for John so that Carolyn could adjust to the everyday trauma she was confronted with in Marti. So Margaret had made all funeral arrangements and had ordered JJ *not* to attend. To think of his mother first and then himself. What would she do if he were arrested and sent to prison now? She simply couldn't sustain such a loss, Margaret had argued convincingly. The round-the-clock private nursing care had also been arranged by Margaret despite her being told there was a shortage of "good nurses." She bullied the woman in white into assigning her best "girls" to Marti's case. And when the twins wanted to go back to their own home, she had bullied them into remaining at Carolyn's. She read between the lines of their terror-stricken faces and insisted their mother would be all right. You know how newspapers exaggerate, she had argued. You've always known how they distort things . . . blow them out of proportion. Now . . . pack your things—yes, you may take your guitars but don't you dare play them when Grandma is around—and get thee to Central Park West.

It was Carolyn who remembered that John was wearing the gold cuff links when he was shot down but it was Margaret who bribed one of the attendants at the hospital to seek out the thief and offer him triple the street rate. The cuff links returned, she had arranged for their immediate shipment to John J. in Toronto because Carolyn felt he should have what had been dear to so many.

And the phone call. That strange phone call.

"Hello? Who? I'm sorry, but do I know a Dr. Tomlinson? Oh . . . I'm so sorry, doctor. It just didn't connect at first." She had listened and although she had wanted to scream "Suffer, bitch!" she knew that was not what Carolyn would want.

"Yes, I see, doctor. Hold on and I'll ask her."

"Carolyn, Reese's father is on the phone. He says she is quite upset and needs to talk to you."

That moment she would remember forever. Carolyn, barely able to walk, to do anything other than make it from hour to hour, comforting a daughter-in-law, the wife of a son who had been of little comfort to her.

As Margaret watched a nurse change the intravenous bottle that continuously fed nourishment to Marti, she thought of the tranquilizers that had been fed to Carolyn and how Carolyn had flushed them all down the toilet that morning. "I think it best for everyone but particularly me if I live my life rather than let it pass on by in some kind of haze. It's better to be in pain than out of touch."

Looking at Marti, Margaret agreed. How much better it would be if Marti were crying out in pain, feeling something rather than such prolonged nothing. Soon, the doctors promised, they would decrease the barbiturates and bring her out of the coma.

"And then what?" she asked. "What then?" she prodded when they did not answer. "How will she be?"

There were no answers; only educated guesses.

"If your niece pulls through, she will have difficulties. When your niece was brought in, Mrs. Carrington, we cleaned the area; tied off the blood vessels. In effect, we did everything. But you should know that because the front part of the brain has been traumatized, so to speak, Miss Tiernan will have extreme difficulty communicating. In short, she will not be able to speak or write because she will be unable to find words to express her needs. They will be lost to her. When she attempts to talk she will only be able to make guttural sounds. This will cause her to become frightened and frustrated. Depression is a natural progression. In fact, in these cases, it's one of our worst enemies. It claims more victims than the trauma itself."

It was Mike Greer who gave her further answers. He had flown in with Brooke Canaday as soon as he could make arrangements with his office. His concern was evident to anyone who could read a face. With his credentials, he was privy to the doctors' confidences. Gently he took Margaret aside and explained: "It is just too early to tell anything. If complications arise, it would be almost impossible for her to draw on inner strength to combat them. But, if there are no complications, and if the brain damage is as minimal as hoped—in other words, if the other blood vessels in the brain will compensate for the ones that have been damaged or destroyed—Marti could make it back. Maybe not all the way but enough. To read and write. A lot depends on . . . some would say God, and a lot depends on Marti. She could come through this in six months, a year, or . . ." Mike Greer's sentence remained unfinished. It hung there like an ax suspended on cotton thread.

Margaret simply said thank you, understanding Greer did not need more than that. When he left to pay his respects to Carolyn, she asked that he say nothing to her of the possible length of Marti's recuperation. Carolyn had more than enough to digest without adding more.

Margaret was amazed by her own ability to cope. At the same time, however, she was afraid. To the moment, she had been unable to cry. Was *that* happening to her again? Oh, yes, she had cried at John's funeral but she had not really cried. Not for Marti. Not for Carolyn. Not for herself. It was all bottled up, the experience pushed away. Perhaps when it was all over, when Carolyn was stronger, she could let down a bit. But by then, would it all be so far away that it and nothing could touch her?

Standing, Margaret looked at Marti lying on the bed. Her color *is* better. No matter what anyone says, it *is* better.

No, I'm not pushing anything away, thought Margaret. It is all right here under my nose. The bandaged neck, the purple-bruised face, the cracked lips. Marti . . . my Marti, she repeated to herself, wanting to scream, to pound the walls in frustration and to break the windows in unfocused rage. Lost in her reactions and her emotions, Margaret was unaware that someone had entered the room and was standing behind her, looking first at what now was Marti and then at her. She didn't see the tears, only the shadow the person's body cast on the bed. Terrified of still more danger, she turned to strike, if necessary, the unknown.

The face confronting her was filled with anguish that dredged up her own. Slowly, like sands slipping out with an ebbing wave, she felt all her resolve to remain strong dissolve. She looked and blinked and looked again. The flower, the red, red flower, the single red rose was extended to her. Oh, good God. To her! He was giving her his flowers as he gave her his tears.

"Vinnie!" she cried. "Vinnie!" she cried again as she collapsed against him. His arms closed about her. As she let go, she felt him hold on. To her. To them. Clinging together, they cried as they comforted each other. Sensing she did not belong, Estelle Hollis put down Vinnie's extra suitcase and quietly left the room.

It was not the sudden turbulence that rocked the jet but Este's gasp that had drawn Vinnie's attention from the mindless movie being shown in the first class cabin on the return flight from Rio. The newspaper she had been reading was half in her lap and half on the floor. When he moved to collect it, she pushed the part on her lap onto the floor away from him.

"No! It's best I tell you myself," she explained.

Even as she did, Vinnie, ashen-faced, rang for the stewardess. "Have you a flight book?" he asked, "something that gives us the connecting flights to New York?"

There were some difficulties at Miami customs. Without his beard, Vinnie did not resemble his passport photo, a fact which had either escaped or not interested Brazilian authorities. The customs inspector, arrogantly suspicious, was stymied when Vinnie asked, "Look, mac. Why would anyone who wasn't Vinnie Tiernan claim to be him?" The man, approximately Vinnie's age, looked at the once well-known face and replied nastily, "You got one helluva point there," and passed him through.

At no time had Este's decision to accompany Vinnie to New York been discussed. She just acted, not asked, making but one phone call to her employers to say she would be another few days before returning. At the National ticket counter, Este, who still related to the Vince Malloy she had known these many months and not to the Vinnie Tiernan the public thought they knew, saw why Vinnie had covered his famous face for so long a time. Despite the years that had passed since he had been in the limelight, he was the object of stares and whispers. Her own reaction to the unshaven and thus unmasked Vince Malloy had been different. What she saw, she did not believe, and when she finally did believe, it had no meaning. Vince was Vinnie and vice versa. The man did not change for her; only his name did. But the ticket agent, like the people on line waiting to book or reconfirm their flights, could barely contain her excitement. As soon as Vinnie was aboard flight 607 bound for La Guardia, she picked up the phone on her side of the counter and informed her public relations department of the presence of Vinnie Tiernan on their dinner flight into New York. They in turn contacted their New York counterparts who then notified the press who were there en masse when Vinnie's plane arrived and he came into the waiting area.

Despite his surprise, Vinnie handled the barrage into his privacy with ease, assisted by Este, whose public relations persona forestalled a circus. Recognizing that to run was a no-win situation, she put Vinnie before the television cameras where, when questioned, he responded with the truth. He had been away, out of the country, and had not heard of the tragedy until reading of it on the return flight from Brazil. He had not yet spoken with any member of his family as they had not known where to reach him.

At that point, Estelle Hollis put herself in the picture, acting the professional PR person she was, informing the press that Mr. Tiernan had nothing more to say at this time but that he would be available for future questions. And now if they would please give him some room, there was his family to see.

Although most complied with the request, they were nonetheless followed to Roosevelt Hospital, where after producing his identification, Vinnie was whisked up to Marti's room. It was the police guard positioned outside Marti's door that brought the full truth home to Vinnie. His mother's back—just her *back*—bent over the bed as she peered down at . . . oh, my God, it was Marti! . . . twisted at his insides. When he saw Marti's bruised, seemingly battered face, and the tubes and tapes leading into and out of her, he had the

703

distinct feeling, had this not been a hospital, and had he not seen signs in the street as the taxi pulled up before the red-brick building, reading "Quiet Hospital Zone," he would have screamed.

They went directly to Carolyn's home from the hospital and when she opened the door, the lid, so barely containing her grief, was blown off by the surprise of seeing him. He held her, much as he had just held his mother, and allowed her to feel once again the pain of loss. Although he wanted to see Ali and Mark, Carolyn discouraged him from waking them as sleep, she explained, was their only relief from a constant nightmare.

If either Carolyn or Margaret had questions or feelings about Este's sharing his room in his aunt's home, neither voiced them. Carolyn simply asked if a nightgown or robe was needed and Margaret, before joining Carolyn in her room and bed, impulsively first kissed Vinnie good-night and then as if sensing there was something about Este Hollis for which she should be grateful, hugged and kissed her too.

It was past midnight when they finally bedded down. Every part of Vinnie, inside and out, hurt either physically or emotionally. He had traveled from one part of the world into another; one he had not known in a very long time. Maybe even never. His mother . . . different. Was she? Or was it him. His aunt . . . different. So much smaller than he remembered. Aunt Carolynnie had been bigger than life, above its traumas. Not Carolyn. And John. It was inconceivable his Uncle John would not be at the breakfast table the following morning. It would be easier to accept the loss, the death, if he had seen the body or attended the funeral, Vinnie realized. At that second, as he drifted from consciousness to sleep, Vinnie thought of JJ and wondered how he could accept what he, too, could not see.

He was half in sleep and half out when he became aware first of the morning light drifting in through the partially opened Venetian blinds and then the child standing at the foot of his bed. He looked at her and smiled. She tried to smile back but couldn't. He patted the side of the bed and she sat down. He stroked her hair and touched her face. Such a lovely face, even with tears streaming down its smooth planes. She laid her head next to his and as he silently stroked her hair, smelling its youthful sweetness, she cried. He said nothing, realizing it was not words Ali wanted to

704

hear. She needed only to feel he was there, not blown away like others she had loved.

Mark's reaction was far different. When he walked into the kitchen and saw Vinnie, he went running to his room where he remained locked behind the bathroom door. In a sentence, Margaret cut to the core of the problem: "He doesn't cry."

Later that day, when Este was leaving for her late afternoon flight back to Miami, Vinnie asked Mark to come with him to the airport. "That way," Vinnie explained, "I'll have company on the way back." Mark was fearful, wanting Ali to come too, but Ali thought they should attend their music lessons, particularly if the rock group they had recently formed was to be ready to play parties by Christmas. Vinnie did not press and Mark did not go with him. When Vinnie returned in the early evening, he found Mark in what had once been JJ's room watching the beginnings of a twi-night doubleheader with the Mets from Shea Stadium.

Although he hated baseball, Vinnie collapsed into the canvas sling-back chair and asked, "Who's pitching?"

"Tom Seaver. He's my favorite," Mark said.

"Are we winning?" asked Vinnie.

"Since the score is tied nothing–nothing and since this is the Mets, I'd say yes, we are winning. Anytime the Mets aren't losing, they're winning. If you know what I mean."

There was a moment when Vinnie was lost, rotating between the present and Shea Stadium and the past, at the Olympic Auditorium. My God. JJ must have been just about Mark's age when he took on . . . what was her name . . . Little Poison? No . . . Little Iodine . . . at the Roller Derby. He wondered why the two events seemed one and the same. Because they were, he realized. Despite the proximity of their ages, he had always felt fatherly toward JJ. Which is what he now realized he had always felt in part toward Mark. He looked at the boy as if for the first time. They say it is difficult for anyone to see their likeness in another but in looking at his cousin, Vinnie saw himself at that age. Only now the fashion allowed for a full head of curls. But it was more than just the look of the boy, it was his droll humor and a naturalness, if not quite an ease, in presenting himself. So unlike Ali, who was extroverted and quick to act.

The game had progressed from the third to the fifth inning

when Vinnie suddenly said, "I suppose you're too old to sit in my lap like you used to."

Mark didn't answer but remained on the floor in front of the color TV set.

In the middle of the sixth, with the score still tied but now at two runs apiece, Mark inched his way onto Vinnie's lap. By the top of the seventh, he had relaxed from his upright position on Vinnie's knee to a reclining one in which his body slipped comfortably into the contours of the man he had always called uncle. His head was acting as a chin rest for Vinnie.

By the end of the seventh inning, Vinnie's arms were wrapped about Mark's middle. Lightly . . . lovingly. There were two outs in the bottom of the eighth when Mark started crying. When the game ended twenty minutes later and Tom Seaver stepped off the mound a winner, he was still crying and Vinnie was still holding on, not for but to a dear life. As with Ali, Vinnie said nothing, as there was nothing he could say. Certainly he couldn't bring back Grandpa or bring back his mother, at least not as she had once been. Nor could he guarantee that it could not, would not, happen again. So Vinnie said the only thing he could. "I'm here, Mark. I'm here," he kept repeating and they seemed to be the words Mark most wanted to hear.

They were the words everyone seemingly wanted to hear. Attorneys for both John and Marti besieged him for answers, as did John's and Marti's respective publishers. Although she busied herself as best she could with the classes she didn't have to but insisted on teaching, Carolyn could not bring herself to enter John's or Marti's world of business. Margaret also declined, pleading what everyone knew to be true—that she had no head for figures and finances. Vinnie didn't either but Nancy Blanchard helped him to attain one. Side by side they sifted through "estates" and "royalties" and "commissions." Subsidiary rights, too. Other responses and decisions Vinnie had to make on his own. After seven years he had resurfaced: a former child star, film star, and murderer. He was news and he was hounded for that news. As was Este. Reporters tracked her to Miami for the story they knew she had. As a seasoned professional who understood the tenacity of the press, Este decided if she were ever to have any peace, it would be best to tell her side of the story once and once only to the world's largest syndicator of news, the Associated

Press. To one of its stringers, she talked openly and affectionately about Vinnie, his work as a drug counselor at New Hope House, his studies at the University of Miami, and the life he had made for himself as Vincent Malloy. The reporter, as she interviewed around Este, speaking to those within New Hope House and those who had attended class with Vinnie, uncovered what amounted to a modern-day miracle . . . a true resurrection. She reported it that way.

With no stomach to see the press in any numbers, Vinnie chose to speak only with Barbara Walters on the "Today" show. Under her careful but expert questioning, he talked about not just the last seven years of his life when he had gone "under cover" but the years before. When she asked about the murder of Franklin Killerbrew, Vinnie replied that yes, he did remember—and yet he didn't. "It is as if I am watching another self through a frosted windowpane. I'm not exactly sure of what I see but I do see something." He refused to discuss any past feelings about his mother. That, he explained, not only belongs to the past but to my mother and me. No one else, he added emphatically to ward off any further questions. "My mother and I have talked it out, talked it through. Through *and* through. It is in the past now and it has no place in the present." Margaret, watching in her bedroom at the Lowell, had cried.

It was Walters's last question, almost a throwaway, that noticeably rocked Vinnie.

"Over the years, it has been reported how close you and your cousin were—how she helped nurse you back to health. How do you feel now that she is the helpless one?"

His mouth opened to speak but no words came forth. His hands made helpless gestures that in themselves said nothing yet everything. Finally, he stammered . . . "I . . . er . . . I guess . . . It's just . . . Well, it's hard for me to think of Marti as helpless. I know she is and yet I guess I don't feel that at all. Maybe I just haven't dealt with that yet."

Which was true; there had yet to be time for him to deal with anything other than the immediate realities. Later that day, as he sat in Marti's hospital room, watching her, he realized how totally helpless she was. Not partially; totally. Everything had to be done for her which seemed so . . . mean. Yes, that was the word: mean—particularly when one realized how Marti had prided herself on having learned to do everything for herself.

707

She opened her eyes at precisely that moment. Not just opened but saw through them. She was staring at him in confusion but recognition. She was not just alive but conscious! Panicked, not knowing what to do for her, he wanted to scream for a doctor, a nurse, anyone who would help record this moment. Her left hand slowly reached toward him. As he went to take it in his, she opened her mouth to speak.

He saw reflected in her eyes what she must have seen in his: terror. Terror and revulsion. From somewhere in her throat came sounds one makes when a tongue is cut out or a throat is slashed. Horrible, awful noises of stark terror. Her eyes were those of a trapped animal. She was screaming as she fought to break out of a cage which kept her as locked in as any with bars. Her guttural screams filled the room and leaked out under the door and into the corridor. As he stood, rooted into helplessness by his horror, nurses came running into the room, pushing him aside as they did.

In the hallway, he looked for someplace he could go or for someone to whom he could turn.

Ten minutes later, he stood at the entrance to the classroom where Margaret was teaching voice projection. The class was recessed instantly.

In Miami, as Vinnie watched a repeat broadcast of *Soldiers* on a UHF channel, he was struck anew by the articulateness of the script, its point of view and narration. The irony, of course, was that now one of its writers and narrators, Marti, had been rendered speechless, a writer without words, while the other, JJ, was floundering in his struggle to refine his voice.

As the program ended and a news bulletin gave the latest position of the season's first tropical storm, Vinnie thought about his visit to Toronto two weeks after the June 6 national airing of *Soldiers*. He had been disturbed to find JJ removed not only from his achievement—one for which predictions of an Emmy were rampant—but from himself. It had been obvious to Vinnie from the moment he stepped off the plane from New York and met JJ in the terminal, that his cousin was at arm's length from his emotions and determined to remain that way. Vinnie understood.

Initially, they acted more like acquaintances, careful not to trespass on forbidden territory, than like the friends they had been and were. They talked without really talking. Vinnie soon realized that JJ had few friends. It was as if JJ was reluctant to invest emotional energies in new relationships, aware that these new ties would be broken as soon as amnesty was granted, *if* it were granted. Although JJ's house was open to transient resisters in need, *he* was not. Whatever JJ was feeling or had felt was known only to himself.

To Vinnie, JJ seemed obsessed with the assassin. Over and over, from a strictly intellectual point of view, JJ would ask: "What kind of person assassinates?" In neat stacks in the study/bedroom, Vinnie found press clippings on John's murderer. It was as if JJ were trying to piece the various news clippings into one that would make sense of the whole. On those rare times when JJ did speak about Marti, it was of the past, as if his mind rebelled against any possibility that she might now be changed.

Vinnie ached for JJ. He had come to Toronto somehow knowing that JJ needed the physical presence of a family member. Yet, in the big house, they would lose one another. Frequently JJ would hide in his newly constructed top floor, made inviolate by a brick wall with a steel door, behind which JJ could live in a soundproof inner sanctum of gray felt walls and gray industrial carpeting.

One evening, as they sat in JJ's private quarters of heavy chrome and steel-supported tables and chairs, the coldness of the room, the silence that was hanging so heavily, triggered a reaction in Vinnie. An echo. But of what? Agitated, he sought comprehension. *What was it?*

The quiet. The Rosedale quiet. The John J. quiet. The *deadly* quiet. Like a morgue or a hospital. Like a person lying in one or the other.

Suddenly, the silence in the room was smashed by the sounds that were ricocheting in his head. Not sounds. Not even noises. A combination of the two for which they had yet to invent a word. And they came from Marti. *His* Marti. The horror enveloped Vinnie. All of it; from Carolyn and Margaret's grief to the twins' terror. All that had prevented him from feeling his loss . . . the damages done. To everybody! But mainly to Marti. There, in that soundproof room, he became overwhelmed by his emotions and his shame at having reacted so grossly to Marti's fumblings for speech. My God, how I must have hurt her—helped to lock her away again deep inside herself!

709

The tears he had not yet shed for his uncle, for Marti, burst free from his own private storage place. They flooded his body as they flooded the room, bringing JJ from his own world into Vinnie's. Helplessly, JJ stared at Vinnie. Then, despite the inhibitions and prohibitions with which both had been raised, they found their way into each other's arms. It didn't take long before the sounds wrenching free from JJ were as harsh and ugly to the ear as those that had come from Marti. And when they had finally subsided, a little voice, as though coming from a little boy, said, "Vinnie, I'm alone. I'm all alone."

Now, as Vinnie heard Este's key in the lock downstairs, he was thinking about John J.'s words, the only ones with which he couldn't identify. As he listened to JJ talk out what he had been holding in for too many weeks, he heard him say: "My father is gone and with him has gone a part of me. I'm not a boy anymore, Vinnie, and I'll never be a boy again. 'Cause you need a daddy to be a boy."

Este's arms wrapped about his chest as her head lay against his back. Despite the FOR SALE sign on the road in front of the house and the shipping company that already had two trunks filled with his things moving back toward New York, Vinnie understood he would never leave Este totally. She was a part of him and she had always known their friendship would survive long after their passion had gone. She had not only understood but had approved of his decision to move to New York. It was where he was needed and where, she now suspected, he belonged. Of the last Vinnie was not sure. Not at all sure. As he turned to face Este, he saw her eyes shining on him much the way the spotlight would the moment word was out that Vinnie Tiernan was back in town. No, he thought, he wasn't at all sure how he would like that happening again.

The house was empty. There was no one . . . nothing, and it wasn't about to come to life, as it usually did, when the twins returned from where they had been, because the twins were not returning. Except for occasional visits. Just as before. Before the . . . A blanket of panic covered Carolyn which instead of warming, chilled her. Suddenly she was keenly aware that the stillness of the house would not soon again be broken by the clatter and clutter of others. Frantic, she picked up the telephone to dial Margaret. No, she thought as she replaced the receiver on its hook, best to deal with the

inescapable fact that . . . *You are alone, Carolyn Ollson.*
Alone. And you damn well better deal with that fact here and
now because it is here and it is now. Just sit at this kitchen
table with just you, yourself, and your coffee. And remember.
You have a life. At the Company. With your family. In
essence, you are only physically alone.

The fear in her stomach, mixing poorly with the acid from
her coffee, informed Carolyn that her little talk with herself
was not succeeding. Quickly, despite the diet she had determined to begin that day, she dropped two pieces of wheat
bread into the toaster. The phone rang as she did. It was
Margaret.

Carolyn's first impulse was to reject Margaret's offer. If she
were to go it alone—and obviously she must—then she should
go it alone that day. But why? she asked herself. Why make
things more difficult than they need be? Yes, she told Margaret, do pick me up on the way to work. That would be nice

Where was I the last few weeks, Carolyn wondered as she
sat down with her coffee. Strange what the mind can do. For
weeks, the discussion, often bordering on battle, had raged.
What was best for Marti? The camps had been split; everyone
versus her. And the captain of their forces had been Vinnie;
his sergeants at arms, those doctors who agreed with his
reasoning. Margaret, too. Of course they had been right.
Dammit. Why did she know that now but not then? Why had
she acted as if it were Marti's best interests rather than her
own with which she had been concerned. If Marti had come
directly here, thought Carolyn, I would not be alone this day
or next and maybe never. Selfish, Ollson. That's you. Selfish,
she again admonished herself

This morning Carolyn was aware that she had not been
alone from the moment a stranger's bullets had destroyed a
life and the one she had known. When Margaret hadn't been
with her, the twins were. There was always someone to take
her mind off "things"—to take her away from the fact that she
was in one, very profound way, alone. Margaret had warned
her—had said, "You cannot make your children your life."
Now, at ten minutes past eight, Carolyn understood that
Margaret had seen what she herself had not.

John J. called frequently now; thank God for some blessings, thought Carolyn, who no longer was concerned who
might be tapping her telephone. Had the repertory company's funding not still been dependent on corporate funding,

nothing would have prevented her from visiting JJ. He needed her. She felt that just as she had felt Reese's need for her when she called weeks ago asking if she could visit with the children. Of course, Carolyn had replied. The child had moved her. She looked as pitiful as she had sounded on the telephone. As she had said to Margaret: Thomas was a prisoner of war but Reese was one of its casualties.

Carolyn was glad to be needed. It made her feel useful. John had needed her. Strong as he had been—strong and confident—he had needed her. Not to keep his house in order. Any maid could have done that. No. He had needed *her*, for whatever the reasons, just as she had needed him . . . for whatever the reasons.

She thought about him often. Too often, she assumed. He was everywhere in the house, which is how she wanted it to be. His den remained as it was the day he died. Only recently had she finally removed his clothes from their bedroom closet but she had been unable to do as Margaret had suggested: donate them to Goodwill or Catholic Charities. They were now in his den, which she wandered into almost daily. The constant reminders of John were comforting and not upsetting. They kept him alive. She had thought it so strange when Nancy suggested she move because there were too many reminders in this apartment. Start over. Begin afresh! she and Evelyn had advised. Wasn't that after all what Margaret had done? Regardless, it was not what she would do. This was her home, their home. And Marti's. Except, as she was made to realize, it was not Marti's. Marti had her own home and her own life and if she was to resume the latter, it would have to be as a woman and mother and not as the coddled daughter of Carolyn Tiernan Ollson.

Ever since that day when Marti "spoke," the staff at the hospital had worked with her around-the-clock. Passive and active physical therapy, it was called. Passive was when a therapist moved her right arm and leg, out and in, about and around. Loosen up those limbs, lady! Only "lady" wasn't having any of it at first, not unless forced. By mid-July, she had been coerced and pushed into "active" therapy, encouraged to move her once paralyzed and still affected limbs on her own. Move. Push. Stand. Use the walker. Use a crutch. But move, and move on your own! By the first of August, Marti had made remarkable strides, overcoming a good part of her physical handicap. Unfortunately, the determination

712

she evidenced to regain her motor abilities, the fight she waged to regain usage of the once paralyzed right side of her body, was totally missing in her attempts to relearn how to speak and write. Although repeatedly told by doctors that she could do both, she refused to cooperate with the speech therapists. Defiantly, she remained isolated from others, within her solitary confinement . . . within her silence. When pushed too hard or provoked, she threw things. Petulantly, like a child. Which is why Vinnie believed she was best off in her own home; taken from the coddling comforts of a hospital where all the patient's needs are tended to; much the same way a mother tends to the needs of an infant.

The doctors agreed. Put her in her own environment and make her cope; make her realize she has responsibilities—namely, children—who require communication. Ali and Mark could help Vinnie with Marti's speech lessons, they added.

"What the hell do you think I'm teaching at the Company?" Carolyn had exploded then. "Who better to teach my daughter than me?" she had demanded.

"Almost anyone," Vinnie had replied harshly. He had said nothing more but had stared at her from across the doctor's desk until she had looked away.

And so Vinnie had moved from Miami into the house in Chelsea. The children had returned to their home last evening and Marti would be joining them there today, as soon as she was formally released from the hospital. And no, it is best you *not* be there, Mrs. Ollson. She must do this as a woman and not as a child.

And the same is true of you, Carolyn Ollson, and of this day. You must face it as a grown-up. A woman. A widow.

It was the first time Carolyn had applied the word to herself. Don't you cry now! she demanded. Not now. Not when you've been so brave for so long. As the tears fell, Carolyn laughed in spite of herself. See? No one—not even your tear ducts—listens to you anymore, Ollson. Your days as a dictator are over.

Looking at the wheat toast lying there brown and death-like, Carolyn shook her head in disgust. Not today, she decided as she threw the pieces of bread into the garbage. No, this is a Sara Lee day if ever there was one. Nothing less than toasted pound cake will do. With Weight Watchers margarine. To hell with that, too. Make it grape jelly. Welch's. Gobs of it.

713

The house was still and although Reese had prepared herself
for it, saying over and over again that it would be still and
empty when the children returned to school after Labor Day,
she found she was still not prepared for the aloneness. And
she had practiced. When still at her parents' house, she had
urged them to picnic with the children, to leave her for a
day. They had and she had managed quite well. But then,
she knew they were coming back to their own home. She
didn't know, she suddenly realized, whether Thomas was
ever coming back to their own home. Still, thought Reese
cheerfully, it was nice to be home, to feel strong enough to
allow the children to continue their education with their
friends. In familiar surroundings.

It had been a lovely summer. A lovely rest. A lovely
respite. So much love and good food. Comfort, too. She
would listen to her father from now on. Now that she understood what the nerves could do to one, she would take the
Librium at the first signs of stress. After all, what was there
for her to be ashamed of? Her life was stressful. Far more
than most. As her father had said: difficult situations produce
anxiety. Wasn't hers a difficult situation? A husband, supposedly alive . . . somewhere. But if alive, how alive? Then, too,
wasn't this war an ongoing stress? Funny how it was now
termed an "unpopular war." She wasn't aware that any war
was or could be popular. She didn't think the World Almanac
had a category labeled: All-Time Favorite Wars.

What she had to do, Reese knew, was keep busy with
meaningful activities. Not just cooking and cleaning but activities outside the house. She would look for a job tomorrow.
Anything, provided it was part time and it allowed her to be
home when the children returned from school. Something to
occupy her time. Not a career. Oh, no. Lord knows she
didn't need that, not when being Thomas Ollson's wife and
the mother of his children was enough of a career for any one
woman.

Suppose he doesn't come back? a little internal voice suggested. *Panic*. Suppose he does come back but he is not the
same? *Panic*. Suppose we have nothing to say to each other?
Panic. Suppose he is seriously impaired in some way? *Panic*.
Suppose he finds me different, not what he remembered . . .
not what he wants now?

It had been months but Reese immediately recognized the

first signs of hyperventilation. Quickly, she walked to her bathroom where she removed the Librium bottle from the medicine chest. Without water, she threw two capsules down her throat. It was one more than what had been prescribed, but as Reese saw it, it was one for good measure and later, if needed, there would be another for good luck.

Squared off, facing one another, Vinnie's words fired up the blaze in Marti's eyes. "You're copping out, goddammit. Chicken-shitting it all the way! And it's a fucking bore, Marti. A real fucking bore. So you had a bum break. But you at least are alive. Your father wasn't so lucky. Or don't you remember that little fact?"

The hard, orange-colored ball in Marti's right hand, the one she squeezed repeatedly to develop her arm and hand muscles, was hurled at Vinnie's head. Missing, it bounced weakly off the wall where it came to rest at Vinnie's feet. Stooping, Vinnie picked it up. As he held it just beyond Marti's reach he said, "Why don't you try again? But first: repeat after me. This is a B-a-l-l. Watch my mouth. B-a-l-l."

Vinnie's mouth was making slow, exaggerated movements so that Marti could imitate. Only Marti wasn't. As usual, she was refusing. Annoyed, she had turned her back on Vinnie, the ball, and the never-ending attempts Vinnie made at her speech therapy. Why doesn't he give up, she wondered. Doesn't he realize she was not about to humiliate herself again. She knew what she sounded like. Oh, God, how could she forget! The sounds she had made in the hospital room continued to echo in her consciousness.

"Listen, shithead!" Vinnie yelled toward her turned back. "Halloween is in two days. If you're attending the party I'm giving for the kids as Helen Keller, that's your business. But it's been done, baby. And in case you forget, she learned to do what she could so why the fuck don't you? By the way, Pat Neal sends you her love," added Vinnie sarcastically.

During the moment of truce that suddenly was observed between the warriors, Vinnie sat on the loveseat that served as a divider between Marti's bedroom and the fireplace, around which the sitting room was focused. "I know what you're doing, Marti. Sure as shit I know. You're punishing the whole goddamn world for what happened. But Marti, it's October and the world has moved on even if you haven't. Guess what? They don't give a fuck what happened back in

715

May. It's yesterday's news. So who are you really punishing, Marti? Who?"

Marti put her hands over her ears. Vinnie, rising from the candy-striped sofa, stood before her, blocking her way when she tried to move past him. "I repeat: who?" he yelled into her face. As she stared at Vinnie with hatred, she saw not anger but tears in his eyes. She closed her own to blot him out. When she opened them again, he was still there. But she wouldn't speak. No, she couldn't do that to herself again. Not when she still couldn't remember the simplest of names for the simplest of objects. She could name them in her thoughts but not in words. And she had tried, although Vinnie didn't know that. In the privacy of her room, with the tape recorder turned on even after her lessons—if you could call her nonparticipation a lesson—she would hold up a book, a letter, a record album and try to name them. In her head she heard it quite accurately. But the tape revealed that what she heard and what she spoke were very different. And Vinnie's assurances were not assuring. Over and over he repeated the litany of the doctors: "The patient, with time and training, can recover the function of the left side of the brain. That is encouraged by relearning to use the muscles necessary to speak . . . to walk . . . all while blood flow is restored from the other blood vessels in the brain to the affected traumatized area." She heard it; heard it frequently, but she didn't believe it, even though through sheer determination and constant effort she had regained 90 percent usage of what had so recently been the paralyzed right side of her body.

The slamming of the downstairs front door took Vinnie from the room to investigate. Exhausted, Marti flopped onto her queen-sized bed, rumpling the Martha Washington bedspread Mrs. Yemen had taken great pains to smooth like icing on a cake. Knowing she would need her strength for the onslaught of the afternoon when Vinnie returned, Marti practiced her deep breathing exercises. Not only did they strengthen the muscles surrounding her rib cage, but the increased intake of oxygen energized her. Minutes later, she was on her feet, preparing for her midday stroll. Fearful of slipping, she avoided the scatter rugs that decorated the highly polished parquet floors.

Suck in your gut, she commanded. Come on, pull in those abdominal muscles. Now tighten your buns. Tighter. Feel

716

where those bun and abdomen muscles connect. Weld them together. And don't let go. Suck that gut and butt in! Now . . . rise up . . . raise your rib cage and lower your shoulders. Lift your neck. Ready now . . . walk.

Minutes later, she stopped before the floor-to-ceiling mirror that lined the wall opposite the fireplace. Her eyes searched for weak spots in her carriage. Finding none, she felt pleased. She no longer looked crippled. True, there was still a trace of a limp but only a trace and if she concentrated, on really good days, she could control even that. Suddenly, Marti saw something other than her posture in the mirror. She saw herself. She was thinner than she had been in years and that was becoming but her overall appearance was that of someone heavy . . . lumpy. Despite her standing erect. My God, it's the attitude! she realized.

"If you're playing Snow White in front of that mirror, just remember I'm not the wicked witch," said Margaret as she burst into the room carrying lunch on a tray. Marti noted with chagrin that there were two plates. Usually lunch was the one time of day when they let her be. Breakfast was a horror. She still remembered that first morning when Vinnie had dragged not only the covers off her but her off the bed to the breakfast table. He insisted she would eat breakfast and dinner with the twins. Like it or not, she did, listening to Ali and Mark chattering away, nodding yes or no to their questions, marking time—and hating it—until she could withdraw into her room and her world. She could not decide which was worse—her force-feeding at breakfast or at dinner. At the latter, Vinnie would invariably open the "discussion" with: "So, anything new at school today?" and the twins would take off, talk a blue streak. They called it "rapping." She called it annoying because they spoke to her as if she could and would respond. Obviously Vinnie's doing; his instructions to the twins.

"Mrs. Yemen, Lord love every inch of the Julia Child in her, has prepared eggs Florentine for our lunch," said Margaret brightly as she set down the tray. "Isn't that sweet? And so terribly elegant. Marvelous, isn't it, how just adding the ole 'Florentine' makes it seem like something other than what it is—plain old shirred eggs on spinach. And we all know how much dear Aunt Margaret loves spinach, don't we? Well, dear old Aunt Margaret will be a dear and not complain. Now come on, Marti. Be a good little girl and eat your spinach.

You do want to grow up to be big and strong just like Jane Fonda, don't you?"

When Marti laughed, Margaret, purposely not looking at her, added; "Fonda certainly does *speak* her mind. A bit shrill and strident perhaps," Margaret said as she pushed her spinach aside and scooped some egg onto her fork, "but effective nonetheless. I guess there is nothing like opening one's mouth and telling it like it is—as the kids would say today."

In response, Marti threw her fork halfway across the room.

"My darling! I didn't know you also felt that way about spinach," said Margaret, her tone still that of a parent addressing a child. As Marti tried to stand and walk away from the coffee table where lunch had been served, Margaret grabbed her arm and yanked her back down on the sofa.

"Listen, Marti. It's time we talked. Yes, you heard me correctly; that was 'we talked.' Now I have something to say and I'm going to say it. But only once. That I promise you. Don't make a face, Marti. Just listen. You might just learn something."

Now it was Margaret's turn to pick herself up off the sofa and pace as she spoke. "When I was your age, I fucked up with my son. You did hear that, Marti? Fucked up, I said. Just checking. I want to make sure there's nothing wrong with your hearing. My fuck-up was that I didn't communicate with my son and I should have. My excuse then was not knowing any better. In those days, you didn't really communicate with your children. You lectured or you punished or you spoke *at*—far different from *to*, as we now know—but you certainly did not communicate with them. And oh, my dearest child, Marti my love, I'd give anything to go back to then, to those years, to be able to talk to my boy, to hear who he is and what he has to say."

Margaret was standing at the windows, peering through the lacy white curtains into the street. "I mean . . ." she stammered . . . "Look at this man today, this man who was once my boy and who is always my son. Look at his strength . . . his caring. Where did it come from? Where did *he* come from? Were they both always there to be seen but not heard? Why didn't I listen? Or does it take talk to make one speak so that another may hear?"

Turning toward Marti, Margaret's manner was one almost of supplication. "You have the most wonderful children. The *most!*" repeated Margaret. "They are such beautiful little people. And they're reflections of you and of what you learned from our mistakes. Marti, Marti, darling," said Margaret as she sat next to her niece on the sofa, "don't miss out on them. More important: don't cheat them. They need you. Your being there is not enough. They need to hear you. To talk to and with you. They need a voice. They need to communicate. And in the way you have always communicated with them . . . honestly, without frills or fluff or fiction.

"Marti, I can't be in your place so I can't pretend I know how you feel," Margaret said as she rose. "But I can tell you how I feel. And I regret my mistakes with my child. Don't make the same. If you can't do it for yourself, do it for your kids. Marti, I'm begging: don't let the sparkle fade from those sparkling little people. Marti, you can regain your voice but I can never regain those years with my son."

There were no good-byes. No verbal or physical farewells. Just suddenly, Margaret was gone. Only the mountains of spinach piled on the side of her plate attested to the fact she had been there. That and the tears that fell from Marti's eyes down her face, onto her plate, making the already cold eggs that much colder. And wet.

On her feet abruptly, Marti moved toward the door slowly but with studied sureness. The same technique took her from the top to the main floor where she found Vinnie eating his lunch in the dinette. He watched confused as she walked to the refrigerator, opened the door and, as she sobbed, removed an apple, an orange, and a pear. She placed all three before Vinnie. When she had sat down opposite him, she nodded her head, signaling for him to begin.

Vinnie said nothing. He just took a second, during which time Marti saw his Adam's apple move up and down several times.

"Marti, watch my mouth. Watch the movements I make when I pronounce the word. The word, Marti, is the object. Marti, this is an orange. An o-r-a-n-g-e. Marti, reach across the table. Put your hands on my lips, my cheeks, my throat. Feel me as I say the word. Feel the muscles. O-r-a-n-g-e. Try it, Marti. Begin with the orange and we'll go from A to Z and before you know it, we'll have a fruit salad.

"O-r-a-n-g-e. Say it, Marti. No. Not right. Try again. O-r-a-n-g-e."

"I have but one thing to say about six-thirty in the morning," said Margaret as she squeezed herself and her full-length

719

mink coat into the front seat of the Country Squire station wagon next to Carolyn. "It's early. Very damn early."

"Well, you do know how they say the early bird catches the worm," Carolyn replied with uncharacteristic early morning cheerfulness.

"How'd you like a broken beak, birdbrain? Keep up that chipper chirping and I can practically guarantee you one," warned Margaret. "Hey! Anyone in this worm-catching group think to bring a thermos of coffee?"

"And doughnuts," said Ali as she handed the already sticky bag over the front seat.

"Mom, did you bring the maps?" Vinnie asked as he searched for signs that would take him from the East Side to the George Washington Bridge and then to the New York Thruway via New Jersey.

"Yes, indeed!" said Margaret as she reached into her satchellike handbag. "The red marker is the AAA's. That's the route they suggest," added Margaret as she reached over Carolyn to shove the map onto the steering wheel.

"Ma, I don't think this is quite the right moment for me to look at it," Vinnie said patiently. "Why don't you keep it on your lap and advise when and where we should turn."

"Her? Read a map?" said Carolyn, derision ringing in her every word. "Oh, you dreamer!"

"Now look, Ollson," Margaret protested, "if God had wanted me to read maps, He'd have made me a pirate."

The silence that greeted Margaret's remark prompted her to add: "Pirates . . . You know, treasures . . . maps to find them. Honestly. What a bunch of stiffs in this car."

"Yeah, that was real keen, Aunt Margaret. Boy, my sides hurt from laughing so hard," said Mark, his voice free of any intonation whatsoever. "We sure could have used you to warm up the audience when we played our gig."

"Oh, how nice!" said Carolyn delighted. "Nobody told me you played jigs. And here all this time I didn't think anybody danced to Irish music anymore."

More silence.

"Carolyn, that was gigs, not jigs," said Margaret. "Nobody does jigs anymore. Not even Maggie."

Again silence.

"Oh, God!" moaned Margaret. "To think I'd live to see the day when I'd be riding in a car full of people and none has

720

heard of or remembers Maggie and Jiggs. Life is cruel. Particularly at six-thirty in the morning."

"As they say, it's always darkest before the dawn," said Carolyn sweetly.

"Aaagh!" screamed Margaret.

"They're at it again," Ali said to Mark. "Honestly! How much you want to bet it's gross-city from here to Canada."

"Maybe they'll wear themselves out," Mark offered. "After all, it's a long trip and they are old."

"How would you like an *old*-fashioned knuckle sandwich?" asked Margaret as she whirled around to face Mark, knocking Carolyn's arm in the process and thus causing coffee to fly about the front seat the way the snow was flying about the car. "If your mother hasn't taught you any respect for your elders, I can."

"Whip it to him, Aunt Marg!" Ali said.

"Whip it what?" asked Margaret.

"Whip it to him," Ali repeated. "Some respect. Like Aretha done said."

"Aretha said that? Carolyn, did you hear? Aretha Rosenblum—you remember: she lived next door to Augie and Arthur—is going around talking about whips and respect. Well, to each his own and live and let live I always say."

As the laughter bounced about the car's interior, Carolyn, pensive, said, "I don't know what you're talking about. There was no Aretha Rosenblum living next door to Augie. There was a Greenberg. Or was it Greenbaum."

The laughter had turned to screams and Carolyn, oblivious to its derivation, said, "I honestly fail to see the humor in this. I distinctly remember now it was Greenhut. Sylvia Greenhut. A nice lady although she always struck me as being a bit humorless."

As the laughter now reached deafening proportions, Carolyn, choosing to ignore it, turned to Marti in the back seat and without thinking said: "Remember: If you need anything, speak right up."

To which Vinnie instantly replied, "If it's an apple, orange, or pear, rest assured, Aunt Carolynnie, she will do just that."

As everyone screamed anew at the humor, Marti reached to pat her mother's shoulder reassuringly. Carolyn, deciding everyone was "quite mad," threw her hands up in the air to dismiss everyone and everything from mind. As they all settled down and into their respective thoughts, Marti felt a comfortable silence fall as gently over the occupants as the snow. Her mind went to the twins' first-ever "gig," played at their school the day before Christmas recess. She had slipped into the gymnasium unrecognized in the same wig she had worn to see JJ and she had been stunned not only by the twins' excellence but by their energy. Theirs was a Tiernan talent but of a very different kind. It had shocked her at first to see Ali, still just shy of being a teenager, act seductively with her lyrics and her audience. Yet, Ali had not been offensive, although Marti could see where some other parents might not agree. And Mark had been perfect: a sort of George to Ali's Gracie even though it was not comedy but music they were selling. But that was it. They had been selling and their audience had been buying. Watching her progeny take charge and be in full command had been very emotional for Marti. Those children onstage—children she had borne and raised the best she could—were on their own and doing fine. And hadn't that been her intent all along!

Marti's next thought was of the Tiernans' private party— complete with pageant—for their own students. Marti doubted whether the rep company's rep would ever be the same. Carolyn had written, and as the director, had rehearsed, an original version of *The Story of Christmas*. In it, she, Margaret, and Nancy Blanchard portrayed the three wise men. At its opening and closing performance, there was a wide philosophic difference between what Carolyn had written and what was performed. Thinking about it, Marti laughed. The Three Wise Men had emerged as Groucho, Chico, and Harpo and the playlet as *A Night in Bethlehem*. Into this shambles, she had ridden on the back of a donkey led across stage by Vinnie who had wrecked whatever semblance of religious order might have been left by asking the wise men . . . "Do you know the way to San Jose?"

From there on, it was strictly improvisational theatre with enough sacrilege to cause Carolyn to bless herself several times onstage and off. The student assemblage had rewarded their efforts with standing ovations and numerous curtain calls, during one of which, Carolyn, as if hearing the word of the Lord, said, "We should go to JJ's for Christmas."

And there they were, driving to Canada, avoiding the airlines to avoid publicity and detection. For Marti's consideration, a foam mattress lay across the very back of the car, a down quilt and pillow upon it. All Marti had to do if she felt tired was, as Carolyn had said: "Speak up."

As she stared out the window, Marti was aware of the contrasts in her life to which she had been all too long oblivious. Outside, the sky was gray, threatening a winter rain that would turn the snow to sleet. The whirring of the wind, whipping past their car as it raced down the highway to whip another, sounded cold. But it was warm in the car and the warmth was not, Marti knew, solely the result of heaters in the front and back.

How glad I am that we are visiting JJ, thought Marti. It's going to be wonderful being all together again. And how strange, she realized, to already accept that "all together" means without Dad; how, unlike JJ or Thomas, he would never be coming home again. Funny about life, Marti thought; funny how you can feel so good and yet so bad, so full and yet so bereft, all at the same time. Would it be easier, she asked herself, if my father's death had come from natural causes? Would I miss him any less or be any more reconciled to the loss? Is anyone ever reconciled at any time to any kind of death?

Vinnie came to mind. She thought how he had refused to be reconciled to her self-imposed death; how he had fought for her life. Margaret, too, only Margaret was fighting against the death of her relationship with the twins. How right Margaret had been! How right Vinnie was! How right he had helped make her children! They laughed at her. Not just with her but *at* her. And it wasn't so awful. The sounds and the mistakes she made warranted laughter. It wasn't cruel. It was human. And it didn't embarrass but somehow released her. Particularly for, as the twins would say, the "right-on" times; those words and sentences that came out just right. Or almost. It wasn't easy. It would never be easy. But they had all made it easier.

Marti's head turned toward her thoughts. Looking at her children, she saw that both were plugged into their transistor radios, their fingers moving on imaginary guitars. It always amazed Marti how the twins didn't fight between themselves. That certainly hadn't been true of her and Thomas. They had always been at odds in one way or another.

The rush of feeling for Thomas surprised Marti as she didn't remember being particularly fond of Thomas at any age. Yet, as the car was speeding north, her feelings, if not her memories, were saying otherwise. Moments of past Christmases, of sneaking out of their bedroom and into the living room, looking for Santa or at least one of his elves, surfaced in her mind. And going off to school together that first day. It was strange, she decided; strange to be yearning for a brother who had ceased being a brother many years ago. Only he hadn't. He couldn't. Any more than she could stop being his sister. That was a marriage that could not be dissolved by decree or even desire. Particularly for twins. A part of her was missing, and that she hadn't noticed it before was also surprising.

As Marti thought about Thomas—we were the Tiernan Tots—Terrific Tiny Thespians—the past swirled about her as quickly and as quietly as the snow that continued to fall about the countryside. Within minutes, with her head resting on the window, Marti fell asleep.

"Aunt Margaret, I gotta go."

"What do you mean? You just went."

"That was Mark."

"Are you sure?" asked Margaret.

"Honestly! I think I'd know if I went and you're sure going to know if I don't."

"Charming," said Margaret as her eyes searched the highway ahead for a gas station or rest stop. "You have such a way with words. I can't imagine from whom in this family you get it."

"And I'm hungry," Mark said. "And don't tell me I just ate because that was Ali."

"I am not stopping this car again for food," said Margaret. "When Vinnie went to sleep in the back an hour ago, we were ninety-three miles from Buffalo and now we're ninety-four."

"She'll stop, darlings, don't worry," Carolyn said soothingly. "Your aunt always gets as funny as her driving and we all know how funny that is."

"How would you like to get out and walk," said Margaret, "on the one good leg you'll have left after I run you over."

Ali sighed. "Why don't the two of you grow up? Honestly!"

From the back seat, where her shoulder was supporting Vinnie's head, Marti was laughing. Good God, please, she implored, don't ever let them grow up. They'll lose half their charm and three-quarters of their strength if they do.

"You know, John and I once came up to these parts for Christmas."

A silence fell over the car.

"Yes, it was during the time . . . Margaret, you were living in Paris, I think. Or was it London? And JJ was at Cornell. Lord only remembers where the rest of you were. But anyway, it was to be our first Christmas alone and I was dreading it. The idea of that big apartment empty at the holidays was very upsetting to me. So John said, Why don't we go to Lake Placid for Christmas. Well, I thought I'd hate that too—you know, being in a strange place at Christmastime—but it was lovely. We took long walks in the snow and John—oh, God rest his soul!—he tried to teach me how to ski and when that failed he rented a snowmobile and we went zipping about the countryside. And Christmas Eve, well . . . he surprised me by renting a horse-drawn sleigh. I had never been in one but he, coming from Minnesota, had, and well, it was quite lovely. Quite."

No one spoke and the silence was moving from uncomfortable to a pall when Carolyn, realizing the reactions, said, "It really is all right to mention John. I prefer it actually to not. We can't tiptoe around the fact that he's not with us. We can't pretend what happened didn't. Yes, it's Christmas and that makes me miss John even more. But, my darlings," said Carolyn, her voice soft, her face even softer, "as painful as memories can be, that's how comforting they can also be. I cannot bring John back but I can keep him here with me through memories. I've had a lot of time to think about this. Without John, time is something I've had lots of. But . . . anyway . . . I had a wonderful marriage. I have a wonderful family. I think the best, as a matter of fact. A little weird perhaps but the best nonetheless. John is a part of each and every one of us and I don't think we should deny that for in doing so we deny him. So don't you think you are sparing me when you don't mention his name. I'm quite all right about it and I want you to be too. You see, what I've learned is: the only way to get over a loss, any kind of loss, is to admit you've lost it."

In the back seat of the car, Vinnie was awakened by the heaving of Marti's body as she cried. For her father and . . . Mike Greer.

* * *

"Only you could get us lost in Buffalo," screamed Carolyn.

"You were the one with the map. And the glasses you wouldn't wear, you vain old thing. If you had worn them, we wouldn't have missed the turnoff," Margaret yelled.

"There *was* no turnoff. How many times do I have to tell you: no turnoff."

"Oh, yes, there is! And I'm looking right at it."

"That's right. Blame it on me. We were to rim the city. Rim it; not go through it. Three times. Right onto the Peace Bridge and into Canada. But you managed to take us on a tour of beautiful burnt-down, downtown Buffalo."

"Actually, it was very educational," said Margaret philosophically. "The children got to see the remnants of the race riots. *Burn, Baby, Burn* now has meaning for them."

"The first time, yes," said Carolyn sharply.

"And the second time, they saw Mark Twain's house."

"Wonderful!" Carolyn said sarcastically.

"You didn't like Chippewa Street either, I suppose," said Margaret mockingly.

"The children don't need to see such goings-on. Particularly Christmas Eve."

"The children, as you refer to these dolls who continuously wet, were baked in the Big Apple. Buffalo has its Chippewa Street; we have Broadway and Forty-second. You know, I just thought of something . . . Chippewa. Do you think that's where the word *chippy* comes from?"

"Oh, shut up and find the crossing for the Falls."

"Talk to me that way again and you'll find yourself crossing the Falls in a barrel!" Margaret threatened.

"Would you please both be aware the bridge we are trying to find is called Peace. As in: Sleep in Heavenly. Honestly!" said Ali disgustedly.

"You know, Ali," Margaret said, "you have a real snotty manner sometimes. Honestly!"

"Well, Mother always said I was you all over again."

"I think with that you better let me drive, Mom," said Vinnie, rising up from the back where he had been half-listening, half-dozing.

"And to think I gave up a Wesley Wyckleson weekend for this," muttered Margaret as she stopped the car. As she got out, and Carolyn with her so that both could sit in the back while the twins had their turn up front, she added, "The man practically got down on his knees and begged me to stay.

Instead of insults, I would have been wined and dined. *Fêted* is what they call it, I do believe."

"Well, you got the F part right," grumbled Carolyn as she moved past Margaret to climb into the back seat next to Marti.

It was near seven when the station wagon pulled up before the brick house in Rosedale. There were no reindeer atop the house's roof or galloping through its front garden. Nor were lights strung through the many trees on the property. On the door was a simple wreath. As if he had been waiting, watching for their arrival, as soon as the car parked at the curb JJ was standing in his doorway. The ignition had not been turned off when Carolyn reached past Margaret, opened the door, crawled out, and was running up the walkway, calling and crying, laughing too, before falling into JJ's arms. Margaret, watching from the back seat, shook her head knowingly as her gloved hand brushed the tears from her cheeks.

"Come on, old lady, let's go see JJ," said Vinnie as he reached into the back for her. When she stood at the curb, Margaret looked from Carolyn and JJ to Vinnie. As if reading her mind, Vinnie took her in his arms, much as JJ had just taken Carolyn, and held her. For a second, they clung together. Then, with the twins already racing each other to the door and to JJ, they walked toward the man they both loved.

Marti was the last to leave the car. As the family returned for its luggage, JJ came down the walk to greet her, oblivious to the winter wind that ripped through the light sweater he was wearing. They didn't hug but stood for a second looking at each other until JJ took his ungloved hand and gently touched Marti's face.

"Hi," he said casually as he beamed at her.

Looking proudly at her brother, Marti replied . . . "Hoy."

"Shit, Marti!" said JJ as he saw her face fall. "You'd think after all this time you'd have something more to say than just the ole tired 'hoy.' Anyone can 'hoy.' Sailors when they see another ship say 'hoy' all the time. I mean even 'hoy vey' would have been more original."

Marti flung her arms about JJ. As they turned from the cold into the house, she said simply and easily, "I missed you."

Holding each other about the waist as they were, they could barely fit through the front door. But, they managed.

As he lay in bed, JJ took the tiny portable TV that had been propped on his stomach and placed it on the floor. Forgetting to push the off button, he heard the commentators who were still reacting to the momentous news continue their analyzing as JJ contemplated what it meant to him. From the floors below which he rented or donated to those resisters and dissenters in need, came the sounds of celebration; the first such sounds he had heard from this group since he had arrived in Canada. He understood their joy.

Yet, as he stretched out on his bed, his head cushioned by king-sized pillows, it was not the cease-fire in Vietnam that would take place Saturday, 7 P.M. Washington time, not the prisoners of war who would be returning, not the possible amnesty that might be granted to such as he, but the President, Richard Nixon, that filled JJ's thoughts. Over and over he kept seeing the face of the bearer of good tidings—his face and that of Lyndon B. Johnson. Over and over. Until they merged into one.

His own face turned toward his desk where the bound galleys of *Soldiers* waited for his editing attention, unmindful and uncaring of the moment and the news it had brought. The book had not been an enjoyable project. Still, it had made sense to document in print what he and Marti had done so artfully for television. Besides, JJ had reasoned, it will stand as a tribute to Marti. JJ's eyes drifted over the dozen or so folders that had captured and held his attention for months. They too were filled with faces. And facts. And fictions. But the faces were real and the acts each face had committed were also real.

Faces . . . Sirhan Sirhan . . . James Earl Ray . . . Lee Harvey Oswald . . . John Wilkes Booth . . . Brandon Copague Bettylwin. A strange name. A strange boy. A not-so-strange face. His father's murderer. Faces . . . Strange how at the moment when Nixon's and Johnson's faces became one, the idea that wanted to but couldn't take a definite shape or form crystallized in JJ's head. Finally, he knew what his next work would be: an investigation into the lives of assassins, those men who killed with forethought. He would search for the connective tissues between the men; the pyschological, first; the political to follow. He would root out the man from his environment, the one that had produced him. He would trace the Face from the womb to the moment of murder.

Only a moment but one whose effects were felt for year upon year. He would attempt to "visit" the man through his peers and his pressures. Through it all, perhaps he, John J. Ollson, would find what others had not: the slender thread that wove these men together even if they were separated by decades or centuries.

As he rose from the bed to once again look over his folders and files of facts and faces, JJ suddenly realized that America's so-called "longest war" was over. At the same time, he saw his own was just beginning and it was called: *The Face of an Assassin*.

Carolyn had rushed to seven o'clock mass but it had not helped. When the service ended, she was left with the same pervasive anxiety and it was as chilling as the winds that jetted down Central Park West and into the mainstream of Manhattan. As the taxi drove her to the repertory company, Carolyn realized that whereas the nation had much to celebrate this January 24, she did not yet know if she did. What meaning did it have if the war was not only over but with it, her son's life? The headline on the *New York Times* resting in her lap shouted:

VIETNAM ACCORD IS REACHED
CEASE-FIRE BEGINS SATURDAY
P.O.W.'S TO BE FREE IN 60 DAYS

It was the last sentence that mattered most to Carolyn. That she would have to wait four days and four nights until names of the surviving prisoners were released seemed an impossible task for any mother, wife, or concerned person. As she clutched her rosary, Carolyn prayed, repeating the same plea over and over: Let Thomas be alive, Lord. She was not asking. She was not saying "Thy will be done." Carolyn was demanding. And for her demands, she was not offering a bribe. She was making no bargains or promises. At one time in her silent prayers, she was shocked when she heard an inner self say: You owe me one, Lord. You owe me and a woman named Reese and the three children she has created in Your image with my son.

Reese was watching "The Mary Tyler Moore Show" in the downstairs den while the children, in their bedroom, gath-

729

ered around John Wayne on "Saturday Night at the Movies." It was their weekly treat and Reese never interfered with their choice unless it was a horror movie. Those were forbidden. Horror kept her children awake as it did her. Only theirs was often fake, fed by celluloid monsters and madness, while hers was real.

And she had been doing so well, she said as an apology to her own harsh inner voice. So very well. True, her work in the greeting card store was not difficult and most anyone could do it, but she did seem to have an almost uncanny talent for matching the person with the proper card. Which made it fun and rewarding. It was helping people to find words that said it—whatever "it" was—better than they could. And the job didn't interfere with Important Time, as she called the hours she was needed at home. With the children. That and they came first! But the job did take away the time that had been so heavy on her hands. Until this week. Until the declaration of a cease-fire that was happening at this very moment. Or close to it. As was the preparation of a list saying which prisoners were returning, in part or intact.

She had tried not to think about it all week and thus could think of nothing else. Not even the assortment of pills helped. But by tomorrow she would know whether or not Thomas was alive and whether or not she still had a life as Mrs. Thomas Ollson. The children reacted to her anxiety and their own. She repeatedly had to remind Karl to stand up straight and to walk as he had repeatedly demonstrated he could. Nor had she allowed Kristan to slip into her bed as she had tried on several consecutive nights. No! They all had to fight their way through this week like good little soldiers.

That she had been. Strong! Brave! She had set an example for the children and to the child within her, the one that was secretly terrified. Her mother called daily and, had her father not been suffering with an upper respiratory infection, they would have flown out to help her through the week.

How old was her father now? About Lou Grant's age? Older. Her father must be sixty-three or sixty-four. Too young to die, she decided. Her panic said otherwise. Her intellect said no one is ever too young to die. On the television screen, the doorbell interrupted the repartee between Rhoda and Phyllis, much to Mary's relief, which made the studio audience laugh but not Reese, particularly when she realized her own doorbell was ringing too. An odd hour for drop-in company. Or did a neighbor need help? Or was a neighbor about to offer help knowing something she did not?

When she opened the door, Reese's hand flew to cover her mouth. No screaming! Absolutely none! she commanded herself. The man in uniform standing on her doorstep saw the terror in her eyes and as he removed his hat, he looked at her with compassion.

"Mrs. Ollson? Mrs. Thomas Ollson?" he asked softly.

Reese nodded.

"I'm from the Air Force. Lieutenant Culver. I'm a Casualty Assistance Officer."

Was she the imminent casualty, Reese wondered as she stared at the face that was trying to be both impassive and caring at the same time?

"May I come in, Mrs. Ollson?" he asked.

Reese was shaking her head almost wildly. No, he could not come in. If she kept him out, she shut out the inevitable. If he could not speak, she could not hear. What you don't know can't hurt you, she said to herself as she closed the door, still shaking her head no.

"Mrs. Ollson, your husband is alive," she heard the voice say almost as the door closed. "He is one of the prisoners to be released."

Reese said nothing as she opened the door. Searching the man's face for deception, she saw none.

"It's true!" she screamed. "It's true!" she screamed again as she left Lieutenant Culver standing in the doorway. As she ran up the steps, two at a time, to the upstairs bedroom, Reese was screaming over and over, "It's true! It's true!" Karl was first to reach the stairway, followed by Kristan and Kelly. He stared at his mother's tear-dotted face and heard her say, "He's alive. Your father is alive!" before she collapsed at the top of the stairs.

Casualty Assistance Officer Lieutenant Christian Culver stood in the doorway watching as the children stooped to collect their mother. It was one of those sights Culver knew he would never forget, for never before had he witnessed such joy and pain intermingled; one beginning where the other left off before starting over again.

Lieutenant Colonel Matthew Strohl looked from the manila folder labeled *Ollson, Thomas* to the man bearing that name sitting to the left of his desk. Any resemblance between

731

persons living or dead is strictly coincidental, thought the doctor as he matched the man in the folder to the man looking passively at him. *Ollson, Thomas,* according to his medical records, was six-feet-one-inch tall and 176 pounds. This man was shorter by almost a full inch and forty-six pounds lighter. Yes, the eyes were blue. That remained the same. But the hair, described as blond, was now white.

Ollson, Thomas was one of the many who had been flown over the past six weeks by C-141 medical evacuation planes from the camps of Indochina to Clark Air Force Base just north of Manila. One of the many who looked gaunt, emaciated even, and yet, almost singularly undefeated. Strohl, as the supervising medical officer, had seen most of the returning POWs. *Ollson, Thomas* was not the first not to match his preincarceration photograph and the biography that accompanied it. Nor was he in any worse shape physically than his brethren. Most had amebic dysentery and even Ollson's spastic colon was not unique. Nor was his irregular heartbeat, which medicine and rest would correct. In fact, there was little that was unique about *Ollson, Thomas* on the surface. Except his father had been assassinated as nearly had his sister. But *Ollson, Thomas* did not speak of that. Actually, *Ollson, Thomas* spoke of very little. Except his wife. And his children. And that bothered Matthew Strohl.

There was much that had begun to bother Matthew Strohl. Although he had believed and still did believe in United States involvement in Vietnam, his military mind was now in constant battle with his medical self. Why were our best men returning mutilated in mind and body, although many, like Ollson, refused to acknowledge their wounds—physical or mental. Daily, Strohl was seeing the ravages of the war; men like Ollson who did their duty returning with partial usage of limbs or worse yet, partial limbs. So many had twisted arms and legs, the result of no care rather than poor care. Why hadn't the Vietnamese reset broken bones? Was it true, as he had been told, that their doctors didn't have the medical knowledge? How could that be? Or was it . . . had it been . . . simply an act of cruelty? So many now would have to undergo the agony of having the arm, or the leg, rebroken and reset. And with no guarantee of cure.

Ollson's leg was a mess although it had not been broken. It had been gored. By a rusty nail used to dig out the leeches that had caused the infection. Which caused still more infection and the nearly gimpy leg he now had. The leg could come back. With exercises and weights and corrective therapy that would be painful and take Lord only knew how much time.

Strohl's mind drifted to that moment when *Ollson, Thomas* had strode off that C-141 evac plane— Right! The man strode off the plane and delivered the kind of salute that one associated only with John Wayne or Audie Murphy. Only later did doctors see the pain and the limp that the pain caused. And they marveled. How does a man, particularly *this* man, *Ollson, Thomas*, undernourished, underweight, manage to resurrect himself because duty calls. Pride, thought Strohl. Goddamn pride. They can say it goes before a fall but those who say it haven't seen the *Ollsons, Thomas* of this world.

Throughout the interview, *Ollson, Thomas* had not maximized or minimized his ordeal but spoke about his many months in isolation almost dispassionately. Yes, he knew it had been a form of torture but it was preferable to the beatings which had intensified with the resumed bombings of North Vietnam and Cambodia. One you could escape through your mind; the other you could not. Or at least, he could not. But even the pain of physical torture was bearable when bombs were dropping in retaliation. Major Thomas Ollson had the utmost respect for President Nixon's knowledge of the Vietnamese mind. To get you got to give, and we finally gave it good. It could have been better but the President's hands had been tied. Still, Major Ollson repeated, he had the utmost respect for President Nixon's courage in the face of national condemnation. Great courage. And great wisdom, the Major had maintained.

Strohl did not disagree as it was not his mind that was in turmoil but his emotions. What was it about this Thomas Ollson that upset him? Why couldn't he remain *Ollson, Thomas*? Was it his total lack of self-pity? Thomas Ollson considered himself one of the fortunates. He avoided worry. And how? By writing an autobiographical novel. In his head. Day and night.

It was an incredible act of survival. But it, too, was not unique. Over the past weeks, Strohl had heard how some of the men survived by rethinking the Bible while others, those of other bents, dissected *The Magic Mountain*. They turned inward to turn off the horror of their immediate world. And he had also heard, perhaps never so succinctly and in its own

733

way eloquently as from *Ollson, Thomas*, of those men who could not turn to themselves for support and sustenance. They were the ones who took to their mats or beds if they were lucky enough to have them. They lay down and died. Slowly. They lay on their sides with their thumbs stuck in their mouths; their eyes fixed on some far-off place. Some called for their mamas. Yes, *Ollson, Thomas* admitted impassively, he could still hear their calls. And their cries. And their cryings. And no, doctor, said *Ollson, Thomas*, they weren't one and the same.

It was the twitch, unnoticeable unless one was trained to look for telltale signs of stress, that revealed that *Ollson, Thomas* was not saying all he felt, possibly because he refused to feel all he had seen. And could one blame him? thought Strohl. But the set of Ollson's straight back matched the set of his face. He was a soldier and he was making damn sure no one would forget it. How he must have irked the enemy! thought Strohl. This was one man they could beat to death and still never beat.

Lieutenant Colonel Strohl went through the checkpoints necessary to complete the dossier on *Ollson, Thomas*, who was seemingly undisturbed by the many questions that were asked of him and the many silences that followed. Strohl, despite misgivings, scrawled across the top of the folder: "No evidence of CCS—concentration camp syndrome." And there wasn't. *Ollson, Thomas* evinced no signs of mental anxiety, forgetfulness, loss of rationality, or emotional instability. He checked out. Perfectly. And who would understand if Strohl wrote as he wanted to across the dossier: "He is still standing at attention when he has been told 'At Ease.' "

Matthew Strohl looked across his desk at *Ollson, Thomas* and as if aware the doctor was trying to make some kind of contact with him, Thomas smiled. Strohl wanted to say something to *Ollson, Thomas* but didn't know what. He wanted to reach out and touch the man but he knew the gesture would be neither understood nor appreciated. *Ollson, Thomas*'s emotions were somewhere but definitely not with him at Clark Air Force Base. Perhaps like the luggage the airline loses and sends wherever you are two days later, Ollson's feelings would be sent from the Hanoi Hilton and its Las Vegas Strip some other day in time. Strohl hoped so. For *Ollson, Thomas*'s sake. His record showed he deserved that.

The interview over, Thomas Ollson rose. His handshake

was firm although his walk was not. But at the door, almost as an afterthought, he turned and in a voice surprisingly full of emotion he said to Lieutenant Colonel Matthew Strohl, "You have been of great help. Thank you. I *do* appreciate it."

It was the accent on "do" that stayed with Matthew Strohl for days afterward. Even as another C-141 lifted *Ollson, Thomas* and dozens like him into the sky toward Travis Air Force Base in Fairfield, California, the doctor was thinking of the major's parting words. *Ollson, Thomas* had seen and had felt. He had just opted not to speak of either. And he was thanking Strohl for not having forced him to open himself to things he wanted, for now, to lay to rest. And when Lieutenant Colonel Matthew Strohl thought about that, he found his medical and military minds were finally in agreement. Both immensely respected Thomas Ollson the man and *Ollson, Thomas* the statistic who would receive hero's honors.

Reese was first to see the C-141 as it dipped over the burnished hills that surrounded the Air Force base, its wings glistening in the first rays of the morning sun. For a moment, Reese felt rushing to her throat the nausea that had greeted her mornings ever since learning Thomas was alive. She swallowed hard, tasting vomit, as she commanded herself to breathe. In the early morning March chill, Reese shivered. As if to protect herself from the light wind and what was about to face her, she collected the children about her. The C-141 touched down on the far end of the runway.

Breathe, damn you, breathe! she commanded, demanding composure where very little was felt.

Besides the families waiting, there were military personnel to take the POWs in aeromedical evacuation buses and C-9 aerovac planes to hospitals throughout the area. Reese noted, as if it were of consequence when she knew it was not, that the Air Force blue of the waiting buses matched the now blue sky that seemed a painted-on backdrop by Disney, appropriate to the drama that was about to take place.

Much of Reese's panic diminished when she turned and looked into the passenger terminal. As she had hoped, there was her mother, her face turned toward her, the chin ever so slightly raised. As if she understood how Reese was feeling, Mrs. Tomlinson closed her eyes and nodded the very same way she had twenty-seven years ago when Reese had stood backstage, paralyzed with fright, the day of her first piano recital. It had been the simple nod that had prodded Reese into movement. Then and now. Suddenly she became aware of the woman standing next to her whose eyes were on the C-141 as it halted perhaps one hundred feet from where they stood. Her mother-in-law's hand, now firmly grasping her arm, was a statement without words for which Reese was grateful. Dear God, she silently prayed as the plane door opened, let it be all right.

Oh, God, let him be all right, prayed Carolyn as a red carpet followed by a rolling staircase was ceremoniously laid on the makeshift path leading to the rear of the plane where the door opened. Carolyn had taken Reese's arm without thought. It was a gesture noticed only by Margaret, who was waiting within the glass-walled interior of the terminal overlooking the runway. It made Margaret's throat tighten as she remembered all too well how it felt to see a son one had not seen in far too many years.

A little cry escaped from Carolyn's partially opened mouth as the plane's door opened and the first of the sixty to return came slowly down the stairs. From the sidelines where they had been established, the news media began their photographing, recording the moment for tomorrow's front pages on worldwide newspapers and that night's evening news.

Specifically, it was not explicable. Nor had Carolyn even considered beforehand the possibility of her bursting into tears. But that is what she did. As Kelly and Kristan turned to look at her, Reese took Carolyn's hand in her own.

What is it about the moment that so touches me? Carolyn asked as the second and then third man alit from the plane. Why Augie? And John . . . Franklin . . . all the people of my life . . . here, on the runway? Why? Why do I feel as if we are all finally coming together . . . all finally coming to rest . . . at home.

Thomas is home, thought Carolyn. My son has returned and his sister and her children wait for him in the terminal with his aunt. Whether or not he wants to see them, they are here . . . for him . . . for themselves. For all of us. Vinnie, too. Yes, even Vinnie, forgetting that moment in Bakersfield. So long ago. Another time; other people. Forgetting all but what had once been and would always be . . . Family.

It has been such a long trip, thought Carolyn, such a long

way for each person to have traveled here and by such circuitous routes. But, here we all are.

"Major Thomas Ollson!"

The name rang out and there was an audible buzz among the spectators as the celebrated war hero stood at the top of the steps. Framed by the rays of the morning sun, he was a commanding figure, made even more so than ever before by a face that was so strangely youthful and old at the same time. Slowly but with sureness, Major Thomas Ollson walked down the steps where he presented himself to his country with a salute to his flag and to the welcoming officer whose hand he then shook.

And then he turned toward the crowd, his eyes searching for a very particular someone. The smile that broke his face into separate parts when he found her made him look boyish and vulnerable. He moved toward her slowly but as she began to run so did he. As best he could. When he was in her arms, his hands moved up and across and down her back, her neck, her head, as if touch alone could assure him she was indeed the woman who in many ways had kept him alive. She clung to him, no longer being a brave little soldier but allowing the tears to fall on his shoulder, making his uniform damp and splotchy. His face was buried in her hair, the scent of which he had so tried to recall as he lay in Calcutta, when his eyes saw what he thought he remembered, but only vaguely.

Kelly was crying as Thomas approached. Frightened by the man she was told was her father but whom she did not know, she moved back behind Kristan. His gorgeous Kristan with the tears in her gold-flecked eyes. His arms opened and she ran into them. As he scooped her up, held her high above and looked at this miracle, he realized as did she at that precise moment that she was too old for such treatment. Neither cared.

From where he was standing, his mouth quivering, his every muscle fighting the urge to cry, Karl looked at his father. When he had his attention, he threw his shoulders back, straightened his spine into a perfect line, and walked stiffly toward him.

For a moment, Carolyn was standing alone, outside the immediate circle, watching a family reunite. Just as Margaret was about to rush to her, Thomas looked up from his children

737

and saw Carolyn standing there. The look on his face stopped Margaret from taking another step.

"Ma," said Thomas in half a voice, half a cry. "Ma," he repeated as he walked toward Carolyn.

In that fragmented split second, Carolyn tried but couldn't remember the last time her son had called her "Ma." Such a beautiful word. So simple. And yet so complicated. And then there was no time for further thinking. There was just this child she had once nursed, held to her bosom, who was now holding her to his. They clung together, rocking back and forth, kissing and crying. Thomas . . . crying! He was nodding at her as tears rimmed his eyelids. As if to say . . . I know. I know. I understand. She saw John all over again and then she saw . . .

Thomas stiffened. She followed his eyes as they stared through the glass into the terminal. She knew what he was seeing but she didn't know what he was feeling. What? Oh, God! What? He gently pushed her aside and then without hesitating half walked, half ran toward the beautiful young woman who was doing likewise as the glass doors closed softly behind her. She was laughing through her tears as she opened her arms at the same time he did. Laughing and crying as Marti said words that made no sense and words that did. They were holding each other when Margaret, sobbing uncontrollably, began stroking the sleeve of Thomas's uniform. Thomas looked directly into his aunt's eyes and then took one hand from Marti's back to cover the one that was massaging his sleeve, loving it as if it were the material and not the man that was precious to her.

Vinnie was standing off to the side near his mother when Thomas saw him. The men stared at each other until Thomas's hand reached out toward Vinnie in a handshake. Vinnie took the outstretched hand in his, squeezed it, and then touched it to his face and then to Thomas's. And then they were lost, surrounded by Ali and Mark and the Tomlinsons and Reese, moving in next to her husband, reclaiming what she had lost, with a new determination to discover if all they had once could be found again.

As Carolyn gave her silent thanks, watching what was once again her family, she felt Margaret's arm slip about her waist. As they stood side by side, a typical March wind blew an icy blast across the airfield. If Carolyn felt it—and her involuntary shivering said she did—she made no motion. But Margaret, without thinking, slipped out of her Blackgama mink. Carefully, she draped half the coat over Carolyn's shoulder and then, as they stood wedded together, she pulled the other half over her own.

As Walter Cronkite commented that night on his evening TV news: "If you ever wondered what becomes a legend most, look at this picture. It tells perhaps a far more complete and satisfying story than any in which these two famous actresses have ever appeared."

EPILOGUE

WEEKLY VARIETY
Wednesday, June 27, 1973

Tiernan Sisters (Carolyn and Margaret) sail on the *Da Vinci* Friday for three-week Caribbean cruise. Return to Gotham early Aug. for rehearsals on Broadway-bound *Mothers and Other Relics from the Dark Ages* to be directed by former film star Vinnie Tiernan, son of Meg T. Summer and fall session of the Tiernan Rep Co. to be under the joint direction of Marti Tiernan—mother, Carolyn, is joint founder—and Evelyn Randolph.

In Toronto, John J. Ollson, whose *Soldiers*, cowritten and produced with sister, Marti Tiernan, won an Emmy last month, announced his *Face of an Assassin* begins filming in Sioux, Iowa, where late John Ollson's assassin, Brandon Copague Bettylwin, was born.

Other Tiernan TV news: NBC announced plans to film a two-hour biopic on war hero Thomas Ollson, son of Carolyn Tiernan and the late John Ollson. Airdate of the biopic of the former child star, now a director of the Extraordinary Committee on Vietnam Veterans (Ollson is a Ronald Reagan appointee) newly established by the state of California, will coincide with the publication of the Trinity hardcover which chronicles Ollson's fight for life as a POW in Vietnam.

ABOUT THE AUTHORS

ALAN EBERT is the author of several nonfiction books and has written articles for many magazines, including *Ladies' Home Journal, Good Housekeeping, Essence,* and *Family Circle.*

JANICE ROTCHSTEIN, a former public relations executive, is the author of *The Money Diet* and has contributed to *Good Housekeeping, Mademoiselle,* and *Redbook.*

Traditions is their first collaboration. Their second is *The Long Way Home.*

SPECIAL
MONEY SAVING
OFFER

Now you can have an up-to-date listing of Bantam's hundreds of titles plus take advantage of our unique and exciting bonus book offer. A special offer which gives you the opportunity to purchase a Bantam book for only 50¢. Here's how!

By ordering any five books at the regular price per order, you can also choose any other single book listed (up to a $4.95 value) for just 50¢. Some restrictions do apply, but for further details why not send for Bantam's listing of titles today!

Just send us your name and address plus 50¢ to defray the postage and handling costs.